A Song in the Night

Men cry out under a load of oppression;
they plead for relief from the arm of the powerful.
But no one says, 'Where is God my Maker,
who gives songs in the night,
who teaches more to us
than to the beasts of the earth
and makes us wiser than the birds of the air?'

Job Chapter 35 vs 9–11 (NIV)

JULIE MARIA PEACE

Grosvenor House
Publishing Limited

This book is published by
Grosvenor House Publishing Ltd
28-30 High Street, Guildford, Surrey, GU1 3EL.
www.grosvenorhousepublishing.co.uk

A CIP record for this book
is available from the British Library

ISBN 978-1-908596-63-5

For Alan, precious fellow sojourner.
The journey is sweeter because I make it with you.
Together we have sung in the brightest of days
and in the darkest of nights,
always held close by the One who gives source to
the most beautiful song of all.
It is to Him that we owe everything and so
it is for Him that we tell this story.

Acknowledgements

I know that without the help and encouragement of a number of people, this book would still be sitting, half-finished, on my laptop.

My special thanks to Andrea Fereday, Eunice Marrow and Yvonne Taylor for giving me honest, much-needed feedback on my earlier draft. Your input was invaluable. Thanks also to good friends in South Yorkshire and Bridlington who encouraged me, supported me, read the manuscript, prayed for me and plain old chivvied me on. There are so many folk, I can't possibly mention everybody, but I'm grateful to every one of you. Thanks especially to Anne Hill, Rose Roberts, Sheelagh Steele, Tom and Doreen Shaw, Bill Caine, Shirley Page, Freda Gibbons, Anne Couper, Shirley Green, and last, but certainly not least, my little sis, Paula Rooke. What would I have done without you guys?

Special thanks to my Mum and Dad for all your love and generous support during this project. So much of what I value and appreciate in life today can be traced to you two. Between you, you've given your family a heritage rich in character, fun, colour and music. I feel greatly blessed to be your daughter.

Grateful thanks to my children, Aaron, Rebecca and Naomi, for making space in your lives for that pesky new member of our family – Mum's Book. Where would I have been without your patience and understanding? Every encouraging word, every hug, every little note (I've kept them all) were incredibly precious to me. I thank God for each one of you. You're my treasures.

Alan, my husband and best friend, your love is a constant revelation to me. We both know I never could have done this without you. Thank you for releasing me to spend so many hours researching and writing (your takeover of the domestic front was nothing short of incredible). You inspired me, uplifted me, and generally kept me sane during this whole venture. You made it possible. You're my hero.

Prologue

Ypres Salient
August 1917

The acrid scent of gunfire was drifting in on the night breeze, and the thud of distant shelling rattled the air at intervals. Still, for the moment at least, things along the trench were quiet. Eerily quiet, thought Sam. He shivered. The calm before the storm no doubt. He couldn't remember ever having felt so miserable in all his life as he did tonight. And hungry too. There had been no rations through yet. Blown sky-high before they got up to the line, by all accounts. He reached into his haversack and pulled out a small pocket knife and a stubby pencil. He had to do something to take his mind off his discomfort. With swift, deliberate strokes, he began to whittle at the wood until the lead stood out, proud and sharp.

"Doing a spot more writing, Sammy boy?" Boxer's cheerful voice seemed incongruous with the dismal setting.

Sam blew the pencil hard in an attempt to dislodge any stubborn shavings clinging to it. "Nope. I'm just making sure it's ready for when I need it next. Assuming I'll get to use it again." He opened his bag and quickly inserted the pencil between the pages of a leather-bound notebook. He felt strangely uneasy tonight. They'd got a big battle coming up in a few hours and they'd been told to try and grab an hour's sleep. How could a man sleep? His stomach was cramping with hunger and his joints were stiff from standing in the wet. Sweet dreams, he thought sardonically.

Boxer leaned over. "You alright, Sam?" There was concern in his tone now. "You're not yourself tonight, pal."

Inwardly, Sam had to concede that Boxer was right; somehow he wasn't himself tonight. All this time, he reasoned to himself, he'd coped quite stoically with his lot; the filth, the lice, the rotten food, no food at all, the utter bone-weariness of the whole thing. The unending, nerve-jangling thump-thump-thump of shells, the morning hate, the dead faces with their unseeing eyes, the unclaimed, uncherished scraps of humanity rotting in undignified heaps like surplus potatoes. Oh yes, thought Sam, a twinge of bitterness playing in his mind, up to now he'd taken it all in his stride. Yet, as a veteran Tommy with almost two years front line service under his belt, he felt embarrassed to admit that, suddenly, it was the weather that was getting to him. The last few weeks had seen more rain than he could ever remember. Torrential, unending downpours. As if having to fight out here hadn't been bad enough, now they were forced to continue the conflict knee deep, thigh deep, even waist deep at times – in mud. He hated it. It was adding insult to injury, and something inside him was at breaking point. Yet he knew deep down it wasn't the rain itself that bothered him. It was the ominous sense that the very earth was turning against them. The continuous artillery bombardments of the past months, combined with the torrential rainfall, had rendered the whole front a swamp. A joke in fact. Whoever was dishing out the tactical orders obviously hadn't been within miles of the place. The land was, in turn, devouring them and spewing them out of its mouth, and still these dreamers were coming up with their strategies.

In his mind's eye, Sam could see a boy. Small, slightly built – probably about seventeen, but with a baby face that made him look much younger. He'd slipped off a duckboard the day before. Most likely out of sheer fatigue; he'd just lost his footing and suddenly he was in the mud. Sam had seen it happen. He and a few of the lads had tried to form a chain to get him out. "Keep still!" they'd hollered. "Try not to struggle – we'll soon have you out of there."

The boy had been good. He'd done as he was told. Sam could still see the bright eyes, imploring, trusting. But they just hadn't been able to get a grip. Sam had wrestled like a desperate man, slithering on the slimy boards, almost falling in himself. The boy had stayed calm almost to the end. He'd done everything right – everything they'd told him to, like a good soldier should. Then, as the mud had begun to curl over his shoulders, he'd panicked. The realisation that his situation was hopeless had hit him long after it had hit his would-be rescuers. Sam could still hear the boy's screams as he'd thrown his head back to face the sky, frantically trying to gain a few more seconds. Just as the mud had seeped into his mouth, he'd uttered his final, wretched cry.

"Mother ...!"

Sam had seen men die. He'd seen friends die – good friends, shot to pieces in front of him. But something about this young lad felt like the last straw. He thought of the boy's mother. With all his heart, he hoped she'd never find out how her son had really died. 'Killed in Action' was the usual line, and Sam was glad of it. He certainly wasn't going to be the one to inform the poor woman that her beloved boy had perished in a curdling cesspool simply because his legs were too tired to hold him upright. Sam found himself thinking of his own mother. On the few rare occasions he'd managed to get home on leave, he'd noticed how she'd aged. Her once fine features were etched with lines now, her corn-coloured hair streaked with silver. The past two years had taken their toll. Oh, she never said anything of course; she always tried to be bright and cheery when her boy was home. But Sam could remember the morning towards the end of his last leave, when his younger sister had taken him aside. "Be careful, Sam," she'd begged. "Mamma's almost sick every day till the telegram boy's been past the house. You make sure you come back to us."

And then there was Emily. The girl he loved more than life itself. Not that she knew it yet. Strangely, she'd been a part of his existence for as long as he could remember. Old school pals, Emily's father and his own had kept in touch even when Sam's dad had moved villages to find work. Sam recalled the monthly get-togethers between the two families and smiled ruefully now as their memory washed over him. Those visits had been part of the fabric of his life. During his boyhood years, most of the occasions had been spent planning adventures with Emily's older brother, Jack. Emily, and Sam's little sister, Kitty, had amused themselves doing girl things. Funny. He'd never really noticed her back then. Then suddenly, almost imperceptibly, it had happened. He must have been about fifteen or so. One day, a gloriously hot summer's afternoon, as the two families had sat in the sprawling garden at Emily's home, he'd suddenly caught her looking at him. She had blushed and turned away with an awkward smile. Why had he never seen it before? When had her eyes become the colour of the sky and her chestnut hair grown so long that it fell to her waist? From that moment, he'd been smitten. How bittersweet those visits had become for him. He looked forward to each one with an intensity that almost made him ill. And when it was over, it was as if the sun had fallen out of the sky. Not that he'd ever dared breathe a word to her. It was an unspoken adoration he'd carried for years now. How could he know if she felt the same? He'd been trying to pluck up courage to say something when this wretched war had broken out. All of a sudden, it seemed that everyone's plans were on hold.

Dear, beautiful Emily. She'd seen more than her fair share of this conflict. Her coming out here as a nurse had only made him love her more. He was glad she was stationed in one of the Base Hospitals; some of the CCS girls had copped it pretty badly. Nowhere was completely safe, but there were places more safe than others. He didn't like to think of her exposed to all that misery; no woman should have to see the things that were going on. But she was a darling. He couldn't imagine being nursed by anyone better. Being shot to ribbons would be almost bearable if it meant having Emily around to tend his wounds ...

He brought himself up with a start. What on earth was he thinking of? He was angry at himself for allowing his imagination to run away with him. The thought of Emily looking down at his poor, mutilated body suddenly sickened him. He wanted to marry the girl, for pity's sake. He had to get a grip – shake off this gloom. It was sticking like the confounded mud.

Boxer's voice cut into his thoughts. "It wasn't your fault, Sam – the boy yesterday."

Sam shook his head miserably. Trust Boxer to get straight to the nub of the thing. "Such a waste." It was all he could think of to say. He picked a louse off his sleeve and cracked it against his thumbnail.

Sensing his friend's anger, Boxer sat quietly for a few moments. "We've been mates for a good while, Sam. We've seen a lot of things."

Sam looked down without replying. Suddenly, he'd seen too much.

Boxer waited a moment before continuing. "You know, Sam, everyone in this world's marching towards the front, soldier or not."

Sam straightened up. "What d'you mean by that?"

Boxer measured his words carefully. He'd seen men lose hope before. They did stupid things. He had to get through to Sam; he loved him like a brother. "We're all heading for the front, pal – from the minute we take our first breath. Some of us get taken out early on. Some of us are out on the field for the duration. But in the end, it gets us all. Even if we survive this, Sam, our day will come. Even if it's by some cosy fireside, with all of this just some dim and distant memory."

Sam stared at him. "For one mad minute, mate, I thought you were trying to cheer me up."

Boxer grinned. "Sam, over the months I've told you all I know. I wish we could have met in happier times. But if we had, I would have told you exactly the same things."

From far away, the monotonous boom of heavy gunfire echoed across the plains. It was difficult to gauge the distance, but it hardly mattered. Some poor souls somewhere were getting it. Everyone got their turn in this game. Suddenly, from out of the gloom, a nightingale began to sing. Sam looked around in surprise. He knew enough about birds to know that nightingales didn't usually sing at this time of year. Strange, misplaced creature. And yet, he found the sound oddly reassuring; a token that perhaps Nature still had some compassion for these poor, crippled sons of earth.

"Funny," he said into the air. "Wonder why Rosie's out tonight." Earlier in the year, 'Rosie' had been their pet name for the little Flanders 'rossignol' which had serenaded them through the short, warm nights of May and June. The melody continued

for some time, and Sam felt a more gentle sadness beginning to envelop him. A sense that, perhaps, this night would be his last.

He turned to Boxer. "Do you think she's singing our requiem?"

Boxer stared out across the blackness as Very lights lit up the distant sky. "Maybe. For some of us." His tone was thoughtful. "Or perhaps she's trying to show us that it's possible to sing in the darkness."

The two men watched as flares rose into the night like fireworks. It was almost beautiful. Boxer turned to face his friend. "That is, Sam, it's possible if we know the One who gives songs in the night."

Without warning, Sam found himself trying to stifle a sob. A silent sob, one that held all the fear and grief he suddenly realised he was carrying. His voice came out in a broken stammer. "With all that I am, I wish I had your faith, Boxer."

Boxer put a hand on his shoulder. "Then, my friend," he smiled through tear-filled eyes, "I will pray that, before the end, you shall have it."

Chapter 1

London
October14th 2005

And … hold.

Beth stood motionless, her breath clutched in her throat as the last plaintive note drifted high into the atmosphere.

Fly, little lark, fly …

She willed her trembling hands to be still, just a few seconds more. Her stomach lurched. That lousy nausea again.

Ignore it, Beth. Try not to think about it. Inwardly she gripped herself. *Not much longer now, girl –*

As the music faded into silence, a tingle of nervousness ran down her spine. Had she done it? The weakness in her limbs and the heady exhaustion told her that she'd certainly given it her best shot. She couldn't have done any more. She must wait. In just a few moments she would know. Her guts churned again, but she did not move. There'd be plenty of time for throwing up later.

In the balcony, Rosie Maconochie felt a strange sense of amusement. Like the rest of the audience in those closing moments, she found herself transfixed by the figure on the stage. The violinist was standing, eyes closed, fingers fused to her instrument, her cheek resting against it as though she and it were one. Her face seemed to shine with the serenity of a sleeping angel and, with her long fair hair, specially crimped for the evening, and flowing velvet gown, she looked for all the world like some melancholy pre-Raphaelite princess. Rosie had never seen her friend like this before. She looked almost ethereal.

Rosie smiled wryly to herself. Some makeover this was. In the last few weeks, Beth had looked anything but ethereal. Baggy shirts, faded jeans, her hair a wild mess scooped on top of her head. Practise, practise, practise. Rosie was sure the violin even went with her to the loo these days. Music had always been number one with Beth, but she'd taken it to a new level this time.

Rosie had hardly been able to get a coherent word out of her this past fortnight. "You're gonna need to get that thing surgically removed," she'd joked a couple of days before. Beth had just grinned. "You don't know what this concert means to me, Ros," was all the defence she'd managed. Well, the effort had paid off for sure. Ciaran had said they were in for something special and he'd been right. Tonight's had been a top class performance and now, centre stage, Beth looked perfect. Slight as she was, her presence seemed to fill the platform.

For a few seconds, an expectant stillness hung in the air almost defying anyone to break its tension. And then it broke. It was like a reaction to some invisible spark; a roar of rapturous applause exploding from the audience as people began to stand to their feet. The violinist opened her eyes and swept the auditorium with her gaze. She gave a slow, dignified bow and, as she straightened up, her face seemed to relax into an expression of relief. That was one of the endearing things about her, thought Rosie; she really did not know just how good she was.

Beth opened her eyes in semi-bewilderment. The response was more than she could have hoped for. Three years in first violins had never felt like this. Trying to quell the excitement mounting inside her, she turned to the orchestra. As they stood to take their bows, she glimpsed across at the strings section and scanned the faces, searching for Ciaran. For the briefest moment their eyes met, and the intensity of his look said everything. Beth smiled at him knowingly and turned to face the audience again. As the clapping continued, she gave several more bows towards the different areas of the hall. Another swirl of nausea made her catch her breath.

Oh no, not now. Not tonight of all nights. Take your time, Beth. Careful. Take the bend gently – no sudden movements.

She inhaled deeply and breathed out slowly, deliberately. This thing was beginning to tick her off. She'd been taking Stugeron all week. And ginger biscuits. They were supposed to help. She tried to keep smiling as her stomach seemed to turn over. How embarrassing would it be if she suddenly had to belt off stage? At least it had had the decency to wait till the end; any earlier could have been disastrous. It was a relief to her when, a few moments later, the nausea began to subside. Sweeping her hair back from her face, Beth looked out over the applauding crowd. They had loved it, and their reaction was intoxicating. Suddenly she knew she wanted to do this for the rest of her life.

People were starting to move now, and the whole auditorium buzzed with the hum of a thousand conversations. It felt like the well-fed aftermath of a good concert; the bustle of a multitude of coats being pulled on, bags being picked up, and feet shuffling distractedly towards exits as though their owners were reluctant to leave. But up in the balcony, certain occupants of two particular rows were sitting tight. Chattering excitedly among themselves, they seemed oblivious to the movement all around them. Beth's family had turned out in force. They had made the two hundred and fifty mile journey down from North Yorkshire; her parents, Ed and Cassie Simmons, and her two brothers, Ben and Josh, along with their wives and children.

Though Rosie was sitting amongst them, she felt decidedly separate from them. Their closeness, their humour, the combination of their eccentricities and empathies intrigued her. The banter between them all seemed to flow with the ease and rhythm of the ocean on a summer's day. She'd been around Beth's lot before, but tonight, for the first time, it hit her. That brother of hers had gone and got himself a real family. How on earth had he managed *that?* The irony almost made her smile; yet, for a moment, she wasn't sure how she felt about it.

A small voice cut into her thoughts. "What was that last song called, Rosie?" Nine-year-old Meg crinkled her face. Meg was the eldest daughter of Beth's brother, Josh.

Rosie leafed through the programme. "I'm pretty sure it was – hang on a sec while I check … ." She flicked the pages until she came to Beth's photo. The face was young and relaxed, and the large eyes shone mischievously. She skimmed the writing.

'Beth Maconochie has been with the Avanti Sinfonia since 2002, and tonight she will be giving her first performance as violin soloist with the orchestra.'

Rosie jumped another page. "Here it is. Yes, that's what I thought. That piece was called *'The Lark Ascending'* – written by a man called Ralph Vaughan Williams. I seem to think it's your Auntie Beth's favourite. Did you like it?"

Meg nodded, a dreamy expression on her face. Her younger sister, seven-year-old Tammy, sighed in admiration. It seemed she was equally smitten.

"Are we off then?" Ed Simmons' voice boomed cheerily in the atmosphere of the almost empty gallery. They wended their way out of the auditorium and onto the first floor landing of the concert hall. The broad corridor was still brimming with people making their way towards the staircase which led down to the foyer, and the warm air hung heavy with the intriguing mix of scents and perfumes that emanated from the well-dressed crowd. Large, ornate chandeliers illuminated the whole scene, sparkles of light glinting from a million drops of shimmering pink glass. Tammy slipped her small hand into her sister's. Rosie was amused to see Meg's arm jerk as the younger child made slight, springing steps on the plush, rose-coloured carpet. It was obvious the evening had been a real treat for the young girls. Rosie found herself wondering what it must be like for them being in the capital at night, going to a classical concert in an opulent hall. A lot different from Yorkshire, she was sure. She remembered the strangeness she herself had felt when she'd first moved to London. She'd thought back then she would never get used to it. Yet here she was, almost a native. You could get used to anything given time.

Outside in the cool October night air, the group met up with Beth and Ciaran. Hugs, kisses, and congratulations overflowed as they waited for taxis to take them to the train station. The area was full of Friday night revellers; theatres and concert halls spilled out their colourful crowds who quickly mingled with ambling restaurant diners and nocturnal tourists until the streets were a sway of good-natured merrymaking. Meg and Tammy observed it all with eyes large and bright. Once inside their taxi, they pressed their small faces against the windows and watched the lights of London flash by. Tom, Ben's teenage son, chattered amiably to the driver who nodded and mumbled as he negotiated his way towards their destination. When they arrived at Victoria, they all piled onto a train and spent the short journey making plans for their next few days together. Beth's family were treating themselves to a break in a hotel. "Not every day you come down to London," Ed had said. "We'll splash out a bit. See 'ow the other 'alf live."

As they all prepared to separate for the night, Cassie took Beth in her arms and hugged her. "I'm so proud of you, sweetheart. You were absolutely wonderful."

Beth's face glowed. But before she had chance to reply, Josh came up behind them and, linking his arm through his sister's, began to spin her round on the spot. Ben struck up a tune and, together with Ed and Tom, began to clap as though at some impromptu roadside ceilidh. The children jumped up and down on the pavement with delight, and Beth punched the air jubilantly as the spinning gathered pace. Rosie exchanged glances with Ciaran. He was watching the scene, his eyes filled with quiet pride. "They're all as mad as each other," he whispered to her. But Rosie knew he wouldn't have had it any other way.

"Whoa! You'll have to stop ..." Beth panted breathlessly after a couple of minutes. She was still laughing, but her voice came out in small gasps.

Josh steadied her. "You okay, sis? Getting too old for this kinda thing?"

Beth bent forward with her hands on her knees as she tried to catch her breath. She tilted her face up at him and grinned. "Some of us have been working very hard tonight – just in case you didn't notice."

Josh rubbed her shoulder affectionately. "We'll let you off then. Looks like you need to get your feet up."

It was late by the time Ciaran and Beth finally flopped onto the sofa of their Streatham home.

"Don't you wish we could do concerts in jeans?" Ciaran loosened his collar and sighed. There was always a slight hint of Irish in his voice when he was tired.

"Or combats?" Beth ventured. "Only I guess they wouldn't look quite so glam."

Ciaran took her small hands in his and tenderly kissed the tips of her fingers. "You were so beautiful tonight, Bethy. You played like an angel. At one bit I wanted to stand on my seat and shout – *Listen up, you lot! That girl's mine. My bride! Isn't she just gorgeous …?*"

Beth shook her head and grinned. "I'm very glad you resisted the temptation. Your Rosie would've thrown something at you." She looked down at her hands for a few moments, her expression becoming serious. "D'you think I did it justice? I mean, was it as good as you thought it would be?" Suddenly, away from all the applause and adulation, she knew she needed to hear it from him. What *he* thought meant more than all the compliments in the world.

Ciaran took her gently by the shoulders. Pulling her round to face him, he looked deep into her eyes. "Bethy, you were awesome. Absolutely out of this world. I have never been so proud in all my life as I was tonight. Really." He kissed her then for a long time until she knew. She was his treasure.

Some time after midnight, he got up to make a hot drink.

"Bring me a couple of paracetamol with mine," Beth called out.

"You got a headache?" Ciaran's voice could just be heard through the clinking of cups and the buzz of the kettle.

"Nah, not really." Beth flexed her arms and hands. "Just need to loosen up a bit. They might help me sleep." She tried not to think about the sickness, but it was there again, lingering somewhere in the pit of her stomach. She placed a hand against her belly. Was it her imagination or was it not quite so flat as it used to be? Her heart quickened as her stomach lurched again. *What kind of timing would that be? Just when things are taking off for me …*

A flash of guilt seized her. She shouldn't be thinking this way. Her mind went back to the morning she'd sat with her mother in a doctor's surgery, just a few weeks before her wedding to Ciaran.

Her periods had always been few and far between; one year she'd only had three. Dr Meluish had warned her gently that she might struggle to conceive. She'd cried that day, all her girlhood maternal aspirations cluttering her throat in great sobs. Now, as she remembered, she felt bad. She instinctively hugged herself and leaned forward on the sofa. There was no doubt about it; she'd definitely thickened up in the old waistband department. She hadn't said anything to Ciaran yet. No point in getting him in a lather – *or* getting his hopes up. Distractedly, she twirled a strand of hair around her finger. She couldn't imagine quite how he'd take it. They'd always hoped it would happen in the future, but it certainly wasn't something they'd reckoned on right now. *Now* of all times.

The thought of it scared her. She pulled herself up with a start. She was probably being premature. Perhaps it was all the junk food she'd been living on these last few weeks. Yes, that could account for it. Junk food and stress; a lethal combination for any girl. It was a desperate straw to cling to, but by the time Ciaran came in with the drinks, Beth had managed to push the subject neatly into a corner of her mind. This *was* her big night after all. She should be savouring the moment, not speculating as to whether her career might be about to take an unexpected nosedive. She forced a smile as Ciaran set the tray down.

I'll keep an eye on things. He doesn't need to know anything yet.

Rosie was feeling exhausted. She'd been into work extra early that morning and now it was catching up on her. After briefing her housemate, Mel, about the concert, she went off to her room. She had to be up early again tomorrow, sightseeing with Beth's family. *Beth's family – what a bunch.* She yawned. Without warning, a picture floated across her mind. A picture of a man and a woman, a young lad and a little girl, sitting on a seaside promenade, posing for a photo. The breeze was pulling at their hair and their faces were wide with smiles ...

For a moment, the memory held her motionless. A sudden knot gripped her stomach. The old pain, the one she thought had gone away. She shook herself and ran some water into the sink. Splashing her face, she blanked the picture from her head. *That's the trouble with burning the candle at both ends,* she chided herself. *Time you were asleep, girl.*

Going over to the window, she opened the curtains slightly so that she could see the moon from her bed. A shaft of pale light fell across the covers and, as she lay in the stillness, Rosie's mind went back to the image of Beth on the concert stage. As her eyes grew heavy, the lark sung its haunting, silvery melody and serenaded her to sleep.

The next few days were spent showing Beth's northern relatives the sights. It had been Beth's suggestion that Rosie try and get a few days off work to join them. They visited all the usual spots and, to Rosie's amusement, acted like complete tourists much of the time. She noticed that Ed and Beth's brother, Ben, kept making hasty pencil sketches of various scenes.

"Nobody's told them about the invention of the camera," Beth joked in a low voice. Rosie laughed, but secretly she admired the snatched drawings; there was something immediate and personal about them. Ed noticed her interest.

"Do you do any drawing yourself, Rosie?" They had stopped by the Jewel Tower and Ed was doing a quick outline of the Houses of Parliament.

Rosie shrugged. "I like doodling. Never done anything impressive. Well, only once perhaps."

"Oh, and what was that?" Ed squinted as he flicked his pencil across the page.

Rosie was dismissive. "Just something I did at secondary school."

Something from another time, another place, she thought wistfully. Something so far removed from her present life, it was tempting to wonder if it had ever really happened at all. She tried to focus her attention on Ed's sketchpad. But her eyes saw something altogether different.

An early summer morning in County Wicklow. Sitting on a hillside still damp with dew, gazing down into a steamy, golden valley. Ciaran pointing out insects to her and quietening her to listen to the sound of a blackbird.

The world had seemed brand new back then. To her childhood eyes, that valley had been the beginning and end of it. Many years later, after moving to England, she'd made a sketch of the memory. She'd turned it into a painting and shown it to the art teacher at school. To her embarrassment, it had been put on display for the rest of the year. Mr Retford had said she showed real talent, even talked about further education. At that time, her only ambition in life had been the thought of escaping to London. Now, as she watched Ed's deft pencil movements, she couldn't help wondering if she'd missed something along the way.

On the Thursday, Beth's family had to go back to Yorkshire. There were tearful scenes at the station as everyone exchanged hugs and promises to see each other soon. 'Don't leave it too long!' and 'Come up before Christmas!' they yelled as they piled onto the train.

Just before she boarded, Cassie took Rosie's arm and spoke into her ear. "That means you too, Rosie. You're very welcome to come and stay with us anytime you'd like to. You *remember* that."

"Thanks –" Rosie faltered, "I will." She felt oddly moved by the gesture. Though they didn't see each other often, Cassie always treated her with a maternal care which Rosie found strangely unfamiliar.

As the train began to pull away, tears streamed down Beth's face. As it snaked into the distance and the waving arms of her family grew smaller, she stood like a lost child, staring up the line. Ciaran slipped his arm around her. "Come on, princess," he whispered, kissing her hair. They all walked slowly up the platform towards the exit.

Beth dabbed her face with a tissue. "I never get used to the goodbyes," she said between sniffs, "no matter how many times we do it."

The following Saturday morning, Rosie went round to catch up with Beth. Ciaran was just on his way out. "See you, sis. Gotta go – late for a lesson." He ruffled her hair and dashed off.

"Gets no better for keeping, does he?" Rosie grinned as she took off her jacket.

Beth was looking through a magazine. "Honestly! Have you seen this?" She thrust the page in front of Rosie's face. They read the article together. It was a glowing piece. The columnist had reviewed Beth's violin performance in lush, poetic tones and ended with the enigmatic question, '*What next from the angelic Beth Maconochie?*'

"Who writes this rubbish?" snorted Beth, but Rosie could tell she was pleased. She went to make them both a coffee, leaving Beth still mulling over the review.

"So … what *does* somebody with your new iconic status do next?" Rosie placed the drinks on the table as she shot Beth a teasing half-smile.

"Very funny. I carry on doing my job. What else?"

Rosie took a slow mouthful of coffee. "Must be great doing a job you really love."

Beth shrugged. "Well, it's hard work and it doesn't pay that well; so yeah, I guess I must love it. But anyway, what about you? I thought you were happy working at the nursery."

Rosie was quiet for a moment. "It's okay. I mean, I'm not *unhappy*. But sometimes you wonder, don't you?"

"Wonder what?"

Rosie shook her head with a slight laugh. "Oh, I dunno. Sometimes you ask yourself, if I could do anything in the whole wide world, what would it be? Somehow I don't think I'd be working at the nursery, that's all."

"So what *would* you do?"

Rosie paused as she pondered the question. "To be honest, I've absolutely no idea."

Beth grinned. "I feel some real angst coming off you all of a sudden, Ros. Trying to find ourself are we …?"

Rosie felt a flush of embarrassment. She'd been too open. Straightening up, she forced another laugh. "Go on then, Mrs Maconochie. What would *you* do?"

"Oh, that's simple." Beth threw her head back with easy confidence. "I *know* what I'm going to do. I'm going to start working on my own compositions. It's a thing I've fancied doing for a while. I reckon it's a good way forward for me now that I've broken into solo. You watch, Ros. I'm gonna write something that'll take the world by storm. Tour all over performing it. Make enough money to come back home and write some more – and so on. I've been planning it all out this morning."

"That article's gone to your head, hasn't it?" Rosie smirked.

"Absolutely!" Beth beamed. "Well, at least I can dream, can't I?"

It was Tuesday evening. Rosie and her housemate, Mel, were in the middle of London, making their way, as quickly as Mel's stilettos would allow, towards a wine bar. Rosie glanced at her watch.

"You nervous?" Mel smiled tentatively.

"Nah –" Rosie lied. "Do I need to be?"

Mel shook her head. "No, Dan says he's a really nice guy. He's just been going through a bit of a hard time recently."

Rosie turned on her. "You never told me *that* bit. What's he looking for – a shrink? Oh boy, why did I ever let you talk me into this?"

Mel patted her arm consolingly. "Don't be daft, it'll be fine. It's only for a few hours. If you don't hit it off you don't have to see each other again. I just thought it might be a nice idea. You've been single for a while after all."

"Being single isn't a disease, Mel." Rosie's voice was gloomy. "Anyway, have you ever met *this – this* – what's his name again?"

Mel thought for a moment. "His name's Gavin. And no, I haven't met him."

Rosie rolled her eyes with a look of mock menace. "I'm warning you, sunshine. If he's got a face like a bear's backside, or I get the remotest hint that he's having therapy, I'm outta there."

Mel pretended to look hurt. "Is that all the thanks I get for trying to do you a favour?"

Rosie grimaced. *Favour? That's the thing about you, Mel. You and your endless quest for love. Does it ever occur to you that some girls are quite okay to be on their own from time to time?* "I'm just letting you know, that's all. In case you suddenly see me legging it out the door."

Mel nodded sympathetically. "Okay, I understand. But this could be your lucky night, Rosie. Didn't you ever watch *'Blind Date'* when you were younger? Some of them ended up getting married."

Rosie screwed up her face in disgust. *Yeah – and some of them nearly ended up in casualty with heart failure when the screen went back ...*

All of a sudden, she really *did* feel nervous. She hadn't been on a date for a while. Okay, so what if this guy was alright? What if he simply didn't like *her*? As the wine bar came into view, she tried to picture herself in the mirror back home. Slim, a good height; not too small, not too tall. Dark, wavy hair, very dark eyes. Ciaran always said it was the Celtic genes. All in all, passable. She thought about Mel. Blonde, blue-eyed, Barbie-doll figure Mel. A girl so stunningly naïve, Rosie was amazed she hadn't had her heart broken in a million pieces already. Mel, who believed that Prince Charming was lurking in every bar and bistro in the city. Rosie sighed. She'd never had much success on the dating front herself. Oh, there'd been a few guys – some of them really quite okay. But somehow she never seemed to click with them. Mel assured her she was gorgeous; even fixed her hair and helped her rustle up killer outfits whenever a new date was on the scene. But it didn't make much difference. 'Perhaps you need to loosen up a bit, Rosie,' Mel would say helpfully. 'Let them know you're enjoying their company.' That was the problem. Most of the time she wasn't. Most of the time she felt awkward, uneasy. It was okay for Mel. These days, *she* was so in love with the idea of getting hitched, her requirements were pretty basic. All she looked for in a guy was a cute face and a decent wallet. No brain required, all conversation kept to a minimum. Sooner or later Mr

Right was bound to come along. But for Rosie, the idea of settling down didn't have quite the same appeal. Her mind instinctively threw up an image of her mother. She tried to push the troubling thought out of her head. *That* was enough to put a girl off for life. Anyway, none of the men she'd dated so far had inspired her to want to spend a weekend with them, let alone a lifetime.

"Here we are!" Mel's excitable voice broke into her thoughts. "De Souza's Wine Bar. Haven't been here before. Looks a nice place." She shot Rosie an anxious smile as she opened the door. They stepped inside. As they scanned the room, Mel caught sight of her latest boyfriend, Dan, sitting at a table by a window. He was deep in conversation with another young man who had his back to them. At that moment, Dan looked up. He quickly said something to his friend and the two of them stood to their feet as the girls approached the table.

"Good evening, ladies!" Dan grinned broadly and popped a kiss on Mel's cheek. Mel huddled closer to him, a besotted smile spreading over her face. Dan turned to his friend. "Ladies, this is Gavin. Gavin, this is Mel. And *this* –" he gestured towards her as he spoke, "this is Rosie."

For a moment, Rosie was speechless. Her eyes tried to take in the vision standing before her. Gavin was a tall, muscle-bound hunk of suntanned perfection, his mid-brown hair streaked with blond, his teeth impossibly white as he stood smiling at her. Rosie instinctively held out a hand as she tried to collect herself. Gavin shook it, his grip more gentle than his biceps would have suggested.

Dan seemed pleased with the introductions. "Right girls, we'll go and get the drinks. What will you be having?"

Mel gave him her order, giggling as she did so.

"I'll have a tomato juice, please." Rosie felt mortified at the quiver she heard in her own voice. Dan and Gavin headed off towards the bar and the girls sat down.

Mel was almost beside herself. "Rosie! He's the most beautiful thing I've ever seen." She looked deeply impressed, and if Rosie hadn't been so taken aback herself, she would have found the whole thing highly amusing. As it was, she felt distinctly uncomfortable. This guy looked like he'd just stepped off a catwalk. Suddenly, everything in her told her she was way out of her depth.

"If I wasn't so crazy about my Dan, I'd snap your hand off for him," Mel drooled. "Did you smell that aftershave? He must get showered in it." A look of satisfaction spread across her features. "Well, Rosie, all that worrying for nothing, eh? I reckon you owe me."

Rosie smiled weakly. "Alright, so he's good-looking. He still might be a lousy creep. I haven't exactly had chance to get to know him yet."

Mel shook her head and gazed across at the bar. "No. I can tell by his eyes. You could swim in those eyes, Rosie."

Rosie didn't bother to argue. She needed to save her strength for the evening ahead. But one word summed up the way she was feeling right now. Inadequate.

Mel seemed to sense her struggle. "You look fabulous tonight, Rosie. You two'll make a beautiful couple. Move over Posh and Becks, that's what I say."

Rosie appreciated her effort and forced as warm a smile as she could manage. Just then, Dan and Gavin arrived back at the table.

"So, you don't drink then, Rosie?" Gavin's voice sounded smoothly curious as he handed her the tomato juice.

Rosie took a sip. "Not when I'm working next day."

"Ah right, I see." Gavin sat down and leaned back in his chair with controlled confidence. "And where's work?"

Rosie took another sip. What was wrong with her? *Get a grip, girl. This guy can't possibly be perfect.* She tried to convince herself but, looking at the Armani-clad Adonis, it was hard to believe he wasn't. "I work at the same day nursery as Mel – in Streatham."

"Ah ... *children.*" Gavin nodded slowly.

He made no further comment. For a moment, Rosie felt slightly disconcerted. *Ah children?* What was that supposed to mean? Maybe she should have lied and told him she was into cabbage farming. She looked at him directly. "And where's work for you?"

His face seemed to brighten. "I'm a fitness instructor, at the Apex Health Club. I do quite a bit of teaching around London too. Y'know, personal health and fitness regimes – that kind of thing. And in my spare time, I'm training up in computer programming. Fancy another string to my bow. But at the moment it's mostly the fitness scene." He picked up his glass and chinked it against hers with a grin. "I don't drink either. Orange juice. Much better for the waistline."

Rosie wasn't sure how to respond. Should she tell him a few anecdotes about physical activity sessions with the kids at the nursery? At this stage, she couldn't think of anything else they might have in common. Thankfully, at that moment, Dan broke in with a question for Gavin, and soon Dan's conversation had spread like an umbrella over the four of them. Rosie was relieved. Gavin wasn't nearly so intimidating when shared with friends. The rest of the evening passed pleasantly enough. From time to time, Rosie would catch Gavin looking at her. Each time their eyes met, he would smile; a cool, confident smile which she found slightly unnerving. Whatever hard times this guy had been going through, they certainly didn't show up on his face.

Later on, as they were saying their goodbyes, Gavin took her hand. "I'd like to see you again, Rosie." He paused for a moment as his eyes searched hers. "I can't make it till after the weekend. Away on a course, I'm afraid. But I should be home Sunday evening. I'd like to call you when I get back, if you're okay with that."

Rosie found herself struggling to meet his gaze. "Yeah, that'd be nice. I've enjoyed tonight." She wasn't entirely sure whether she meant it, but it seemed the right thing to say.

Gavin looked pleased. "Great! I'll be in touch then."

Feeling her cheeks beginning to warm, Rosie returned his smile. "I'll look forward to it."

Chapter 2

The following evening, just after eight, the phone rang.

"Hi Ros, it's me!" Beth's voice bubbled over the line. "Just ringing to see if you're doing anything this Saturday. It's just that Emmett's starting us on rehearsals next weekend for our Christmas concerts, so this is gonna be my last free Saturday for a while. Not got anything planned with Mel, have you?"

"Not very likely. She'll be off somewhere with her new bloke." *As for my new bloke, he'll be off somewhere finding out how to make himself more beautiful than ever.* "Why, have you got something in mind?"

"I rather fancied a drive into Kent. Ciaran says I can have the car. We could wind up at Whitstable for fish and chips later on if you like. Just thought it might be nice to get out into the country while the weather's still okay. What d'you think?"

Rosie thought it sounded great. She liked the idea of getting out of the city for a day. It appealed to her rustic roots.

"Brilliant! Shall I pick you up about nine o'clock? That should get us off to a decent start."

They agreed the time and said goodbye. Rosie came off the phone quietly uplifted at the prospect of a day out. No doubt Mel would be busy. Gavin certainly would be. But now she had something planned too. It was a nice feeling.

"Rosie's okay for Saturday," Beth confirmed to Ciaran as they went to bed that night.

"You're still planning to go into Kent?"

"Yeah, I think so. Unless you have any objections – and I know you wouldn't dare." Beth's voice was teasing, but she noticed that Ciaran looked thoughtful. "What's the matter? D'you need the car or something?"

Ciaran hesitated for a moment and stroked her hair. "You feeling alright, Bethy?"

Beth straightened up. "Why? What makes you ask that?"

"I noticed you threw most of your dinner away tonight. And I know it's not the first time."

Beth inwardly squirmed as she remembered the few mouthfuls of spaghetti carbonara she'd managed to swallow earlier that evening. So, Ciaran was onto her, was he?

"You been spying on me then?" She pinched him playfully, her heart quickening as she debated whether this was the right time to say something.

Ciaran laced his fingers through hers. "Just an observation, Bethy. It's my job to look after you, me being your personal minder and all that." He smiled, his dark eyes fixed on her. "You know, *Beth Maconochie – hottest thing on the classical music scene ...?*" He leaned forward and kissed her forehead.

Beth's thoughts began to race. How would he take it? He'd be pretty shocked, she knew that much. But then again – *would* he? A wave of panic went through her. What was so hard about telling him anyway? He wasn't the kind of guy to throw a wobbly when life didn't go quite according to plan. Looking into his face, she suddenly felt bad. Ciaran wasn't the problem. Deep down, she was pretty sure he'd be thrilled to become a dad, once he'd made the initial mental adjustments to the idea. No; Ciaran wasn't the problem at all. She lowered her head as the realisation lodged itself obstinately in her mind. The problem lay with her. Life was just beginning to pay off, and she wasn't ready for anything to interrupt that. The phone rang out shrilly, making her jump.

"*Who the ...?*" Ciaran paced across the bedroom and picked up the extension. "Oh hi, Matt. No, you're okay – we've only just come upstairs." *Pause.* "I'll just nip down and look in my diary. I think the number should be in there. Hang on." He shot Beth an apologetic glance. She smiled. *Take as long as you like for me. I wasn't enjoying the conversation anyway.* When Ciaran had gone downstairs, she settled under the duvet and closed her eyes. She had to sort this thing. She'd been feeling off it for weeks. Up to now she'd blamed the stress of practise, the rubbish food, the pressure of translation from first violins to solo. She still nursed a vague hope that it might be just that. But she had to face the possibility ...

Ciaran's gentle face floated across her thoughts. She hated not being honest with him. She made the decision; she would give it another fortnight. Try and put the whole thing out of her mind. Eat as well as she could; certainly be more crafty about slinging stuff away when Ciaran was around. And then, if her system still hadn't settled down by that time, she'd just have to face facts. She'd buy a test.

Miles away, in a little Blean village in Kent, it was almost eleven thirty. In the kitchen of the small cottage he shared with his wife, Thomas Frederick switched on the kettle for his bedtime cup of tea. He popped his head round the doorway of the sitting room. "You having one, Mary?"

But Mary had fallen asleep in the chair, her knitting needles poised mid-stitch in her plump, satin-skinned hands. He went over and tried to gently wake her.

"Come on, love. You need to be in bed," he said softly, easing her out of the chair. "I'll bring you up a cuppa."

Mary put the knitting away and padded sleepily across the room to the bottom of the stairs. Just as her foot touched the bottom step, she turned as though remembering something. "Forgot to tell you – a lady rang earlier, Tom. She left a message. I wrote it down on the pad. See you in a bit, love."

Thomas went over to the phone. As his eyes perused Mary's scribbled handwriting, a smile crept over his lips. *Interesting, very interesting*. Thoughtfully, he made his way back into the kitchen as the kettle clicked off. *So, she'll be dropping them off Saturday morning, eh*? Well, he'd look forward to that.

Saturday was bright and crisp. Beth drew up just after nine and Rosie climbed into the car.

"I told Ciaran I wanted to take you exploring." There was a glint of humour in Beth's eyes as she adjusted one of the side mirrors. "I'm pretty sure he thought *exploring* was a euphemism for shopping. I saw his face starting to go pale."

Rosie grinned as she snapped her seatbelt on. "Where are we going then?"

"I'd like to try and find an old church I visited years ago," Beth suggested as she pulled out onto the road. "A group of us from music college went there to do a special charity concert once. I was part of the string quartet. But that's quite a while back. To be honest, it's a bit of a blur. All I know is that the church was in some little village in the Blean Woods near Canterbury. Lovely place as I remember. Just fancied seeing if we could find it."

Rosie smiled to herself. The thought of the two of them propped up in a pew looking all angelic didn't sit easily in the imagination. "Is the vicar expecting us then?"

Beth laughed. "Let's hope he won't be there. I hear they're pretty choosy in that neck of the woods. He probably wouldn't let *you* anywhere near the place."

"Funny, aren't we?" Rosie bent over to flick on the CD player. *Enya* floated serenely into the airwaves like a soothing mist, and Beth began to sing along quietly. They chatted as they travelled; about the orchestra, the nursery, the delectable Gavin. Beth said she was dying to meet him. Rosie felt a twinge of guilt that she didn't feel more enthusiastic herself. They laughed as they went along. It was easy to put the world to rights on a day like this. The sky was seaside blue and the stunning scenery of the Kent countryside was bathed in rich, golden light.

After about an hour and a half, Beth pulled over to the side of the road. "Reckon we're nearly here, Ros." She spread a map over her knees and looked at it for a moment. "Here it is – Applemarket. I'd guess we're about ten minutes away. Told you we'd find it." She hummed with triumph as they meandered down sleepy country roads towards their destination. Ten minutes later, they pulled into the village of Applemarket. Beth found a small car park next to a cricket club and parked up. They decided to have a look around the place before lunch. As Beth was pulling on her jacket, something caught her eye. "Hey, isn't that the necklace Mum sent you for your twenty-first?"

Rosie instinctively reached for her neck. "Yeah. Thought I'd wear it, seeing as we're having a day out."

Beth peered closer. "It's beautiful, isn't it? Really unusual. She's got a good eye for things, Mum has." Hanging from the slender curb chain was a pendant in the form of a bird, finely worked in filigreed silver.

"It was really nice of her to send me a present. I wasn't expecting it." Rosie's mind went back to her birthday at the beginning of that month. Ciaran and Beth had spoiled her rotten; taken her out shopping, treated her to a slap-up meal. 'Not every day you're twenty-one,' Beth had said when she'd tried to protest. It had been the best birthday Rosie had ever had. Her own mother's card had arrived from Leicester the following day with a ten pound note and a short covering message. *'Couldn't think what to get you. Buy something nice.'* Rosie had used it to top up her phone. There'd been nothing from her father – for the fifth year running. 'It's my twenty-first, for crying out loud,' she'd grumbled to Ciaran. 'You'd think he'd remember this one at least.' Ciaran had responded with a stoical shake of the head. 'Forget it, Ros,' he'd said bluntly. 'He didn't send me one either. He might be dead for all we know.'

Beth's voice broke into her thoughts. "She thinks a lot about you, y'know."

Rosie felt momentarily disorientated. "Who? Who does?"

"My mum, you dope." Beth grinned. "She thinks a lot about you."

Trying to recover herself, Rosie concentrated on fastening up her jacket. "Yes. I can tell that she does."

Though fairly small and compact, the village of Applemarket was a gem to explore. There was an unspoiled rural charm about it, yet, at the same time, several quaint gift shops and tea houses peppered its neat little lanes, making the visitor feel immediately welcome. The two girls spent quite a while trekking round the different shops, looking at craftwork and trinkets, and sniffing at various scented delights. In one gift shop, Beth found a tall, apple-patterned coffee mug which she fancied as a souvenir for Ciaran.

"At least if he's going to OD on caffeine, he can do it in style now," she joked as the assistant gift-wrapped the present. On leaving the shop, they were about to return to the car when Beth suddenly spotted something. "Hey, Rosie – over there! There's a little second-hand bookshop. Come on, we've got to take a look!"

Rosie groaned, but she knew better than to argue. Beth had a passion for books. Ciaran had once remarked that Beth took in old books like some people take in stray cats.

From the outside, it was clear that the bookshop was well cared for. The window casings and door were painted in a clean magnolia, and the lettering in the sign above the shop was picked out in a strong brown, shadowed with gold. *'Good Quality Second-Hand Books – Prop. T.W. Frederick'* read the calligraphic letters. Beth was almost beside herself with excitement. "This looks a bit classy!" she grinned as the bell on the door tinkled to signal their entrance. The inside of the shop had a distinct smell; something like the archive section of a public library, but laced with the sweet, nostalgic scent of pipe tobacco. Beth scanned the shelves, not knowing where to start. Rosie stifled a smile as she observed her. Beth looked like a kid on Christmas morning. Rosie wasn't sure where to start herself. It wasn't really her kind of shop. Not that she didn't like books; it was just *old* books she wasn't crazy about. Still, there must be something in here that wasn't fusty and full of mildew. She set about trying to spot it.

Thomas Frederick was pleased. He'd had an hour sifting through a newly donated batch of stuff that had been delivered early that morning. It had come in three lots; two fair-sized boxes, both crammed with books, and a small, battered case which had clearly seen better days. He'd smiled when he'd seen the case. It reminded him of the one he'd used as a small boy in the war, when he'd been evacuated from London. For a few moments he'd toyed with the idea of taking it home as a souvenir, but he'd thought better of it. Poor Mary put up with enough of his junk, and the cottage really wasn't big enough. His attention had turned then to the boxes. To his delight, he'd found a number of first editions and some very nice volumes of poetry, all in pristine condition. They'd obviously belonged to someone very discerning. It was a pity the lady who'd dropped them off hadn't left any contact details. Having gone through the items, Thomas would have got in touch and positively insisted on sending her some payment; the books were certainly worth it. But she'd been in something of a hurry to get to another appointment. No sooner had Thomas managed to unload the boxes from her car, than she had sped on her way, declining to take so much as a penny from him. The books hadn't been her own, he was fairly sure. She'd brought them in as house clearance, only too glad to find a decent home for them. As far as Thomas could see, that was the end of it. In his heart, he thanked the mystery benefactress and wished her well.

Beth's arms were beginning to ache. It always happened when she came anywhere like this. Ciaran would no doubt roll his eyes and ask her where on earth she was going to put them all. It was always the same.

Rosie approached her softly. "Do you think you've found enough yet?" There was the merest hint of sarcasm in her whispered voice. "We've been here nearly forty-five minutes."

Beth gasped. "We *haven't*! Oh heck, I got carried away … ." She made her way to the counter, almost staggering from the weight of the books she'd amassed.

The old shopkeeper smiled, his grey eyes crinkling. "My my, you have been busy. I do hope you've come in a motor car."

"Oh yes," Beth bubbled, "and my friend here will help me carry everything to the car park, won't you, Rosie?" There was a flash of mischief in her eyes.

Rosie responded with a satirical smile. "Actually, I was rather thinking of trying to flag down someone with a wheelbarrow."

Beth paid for the books. As she was putting her purse back into her bag, she stopped. "You don't happen to have any sheet music, do you?"

The old man thought for a moment. "As a matter of fact, I do. I got some in only today, as part of a house clearance lot. I've been going through the stuff this morning. There were some smashing books. Hang on, I put the rest under here." He reached down and lifted the old case onto the counter. On one of its side panels was a worn, yellowed label that read '*MUSIC*'. He fumbled at the rusted catches. "It's a bit tricky to get into, I'm afraid." There was a sudden clicking sound and the lid snapped open. Beth's eyes lit up. The case was packed full with musical scores. Thomas Frederick thumbed wistfully through the top few. "I haven't bothered to go through them. I'm not a musician. Can't read a note, I'm sorry to say."

Beth leaned over and gazed thoughtfully at the case. "How much do you want for each piece?"

The old man beamed. "You can have the whole lot for nothing. I was only going to throw it away. Not much call for stuff like that these days. People tend to buy new. As I say, *I* can't do anything with it, 'cept use it to light my fire on a morning. Anyway, you've been by far my best customer this week. Take it with my blessing. And let me find you a box for all your other stuff."

Beth grinned. "Thanks, that's very kind of you."

Thomas smiled as the two young women struggled out of the shop with their loads. He watched them as they made their way down the lane, and then went back to his books. So far, it had been a very good day.

"I've just remembered a good place where we could have lunch," Beth announced enthusiastically. They found a bench by the side of a small stream and settled there to eat their picnic. Despite being late October, the air was warm, and the sky, a deep, reassuring blue. It seemed hard to believe that winter was just around the corner. Beth sighed contentedly. "Ah, this is the life! You enjoying yourself, Rosie?"

Rosie was on the verge of making a facetious comment about the length of time they'd spent in the bookshop, but she checked herself. Somehow Beth looked too happy.

After lunch, they took the picnic things back to the car. They could see the village church from the car park. It took them about five minutes to reach it. From the road, they entered through a small, wooden gate and walked up a narrow path which cut through the sprawling graveyard. Ancient-looking headstones, like silent sentinels, rose up out of the neatly cropped grass. By the south side of the church was a large yew tree, and nestled beneath it, a few stones which were so old and weather-beaten, Rosie found it impossible to decipher a single word chiselled upon them; just a series of intriguing marks that had once been letters, but now held their secrets in tight-lipped decay. How old *was* this place, she wondered? The outer walls of the church were pale grey flintstone, and slender lancet windows betrayed the building's medieval origins. As they arrived at the arched wooden door, Beth stopped. "Hope we can get in. These days some churches are kept locked when they're not in use. Wouldn't *that* be a pain?"

She pushed slightly and, to their relief, the door swung open. A combined smell of incense, furniture polish, and old hymnbooks wafted over them as they stepped inside. To their left as they entered the building, Rosie noticed a beautiful trailing flower display, and next to it a sign, printed in the form of illuminated manuscript. She read it out. "*Welcome to the Church of Saint Ethelbert.*" Her face broke into a grin. "*Ethelbert*, eh? That's one rockin' name."

"I seem to think the guy was pretty big round these parts at one time," Beth whispered knowingly, feigning an air of erudition.

Their eyes scanned the interior of the church. The stark white walls gave the place a light, airy feel, while the timber roof and wooden altar were striking in their simplicity. Simplicity seemed to be the key at Saint Ethelbert's. There were the inevitable features; a pulpit, a font, and a couple of memorials, but otherwise, ornamentation had been kept to a minimum. The only tokens of extravagance in the décor were a number of stunning flower displays placed in strategic locations throughout the church.

"I'm going to have a sit-down," Beth said quietly. "You have a look round if you want."

Rosie walked over to a large oak table on the back wall of the building. On it were a number of publications; a *'History of Saint Ethelbert's'*, a book on the life of Saint Augustine, several small pamphlets on subjects such as prayer, adversity and bereavement, and the Parish Magazine. She picked up the latter and began to look through it. It seemed to belong to another world; a 1950's world of bell-ringing, and homemade jam and pickles. Though it amused her, there was something strangely appealing about it. Even the advert for *'Good Quality Second-Hand Books – Prop. T. W. Frederick'*. The memory of the bookshop made her smile. There'd probably be a photo of Beth in the next edition of the Parish Magazine. At the back of the table was a rack of large postcards showing various scenes from the village of Applemarket and its surrounding countryside. There was one particular picture which caught her eye. It was a photograph of Saint Ethelbert's in winter. The sky in the scene was grey and dramatic, streaked with slashes of pale winter light, whilst the church, the graveyard, and the tops of the headstones were shrouded in snow. Rosie found it a striking image. All at once, her mind was seized with a powerful longing. It happened so fast, she was caught off guard. She felt a sudden sense of ancient identity; a strange thrill at the thought of the endless cycle of seasons that Saint Ethelbert's had weathered down the centuries. Yet, at the same time, she felt an almost painful yearning for something beyond that dark sky, as though its slits of light were enticing her to break through the cold winter veil and enter into them. As quickly as it had come, the intensity of the feeling disappeared, and Rosie stood there wondering what to make of it. She turned round and saw that Beth was sitting in a pew halfway down the church. She sidled in next to her, the aftershock of her strange experience still playing in her mind.

Beth turned and smiled. "It's weird, y'know. I've just been thinking; it's years since I was in a church."

"Same here." Rosie ran her hand over the smooth wood of the pew.

"I thought you Irish were supposed to be very devout. Your brother excepted of course." Beth's tone was inscrutable. Rosie couldn't tell if her remark was serious or tongue-in-cheek. She decided to give her the benefit of the doubt.

"I'm sure a lot of 'em are. But not me. When you're born into a family with a Protestant father and a Catholic mother, I guess you're born sitting on the fence. Fences aren't the most comfortable places to sit. Eventually you jump off and make a run for it."

Beth laughed. "Twice bitten, twice shy, then?"

"Yeah, I guess so." Rosie attempted a smile, but suddenly she didn't feel like laughing. Thoughts of her parents always affected her like a cold shower. In truth, she doubted that either of them had bequeathed her so much as a slither in the way of spiritual inclination. She tried to collect herself. "Anyway, what about you? I thought *your* parents were religious."

Beth nodded thoughtfully. "They are. *And* my brothers."

"So, infidel. What happened to you? Don't tell me you're the only one of your family that hasn't set foot in a church for years."

Beth shrugged. "I used to go all the time when I was young. Sunday school, children's camps – the lot."

"What happened? D'you get kicked out for bad behaviour?"

"Nah, nothing like that." Beth sat forward and gazed towards the front of the church. "I guess I just got too busy. In my early teenage years, I was working my butt off trying to get to music college. Once I got to music college, I was working my butt off to make sure I stayed there. Being away from my family, such a different environment – and then meeting your brother of course – I just seemed to carve out a totally new life for myself. Suppose you could say God was the casualty. There just didn't seem to be room for him."

Rosie was curious. "What did your mum and dad say to it all?"

Beth sighed. "Not a lot really. They never tried to pressurise me. I guess they were sad. I dunno, I try to avoid the subject these days. A bit of guilt, I suppose."

Rosie frowned. "You still believe in God?" She wasn't even sure why she was asking the question.

Beth was quiet for a moment. "Yeah. If I'm honest, I guess I do. What about you?"

Rosie looked down at her knees. "I dunno. I'm not sure what I think. And does it matter anyway? In the end, I'm not sure it makes a whole lot of difference."

They fell into silence, their words hanging open in the atmosphere between them. It was an uncomfortable topic of conversation for both of them, and neither knew quite how best to follow it. Rosie was trying to figure out a way of changing the subject when she suddenly perceived movement at the front of the church. Straining to see better, she caught sight of a white butterfly flitting around the flower display at the base of the altar. Glad for the distraction, she tapped Beth and pointed. They watched as the creature hovered around the gorgeous array, alighting from time to time on several of the blazing autumnal blooms. At one point, it left the display and ascended high into the roof space above them. For a while they lost sight of it, until it suddenly descended again and moved out towards the main body of the church, fluttering around as though in some delicate dance. Then, quite unexpectedly, it landed on Beth's arm.

"Wow, this little chap's a late one," she said softly, turning her head to get a better view. "I thought they'd all died off."

"Serves you right for coming out in a bright pink jacket," Rosie hissed. "Probably thinks you're a carnation."

The butterfly was in resting position. From time to time it flexed its wings, but it remained there for several minutes nevertheless.

"It seems to like you," Rosie smiled after a while. "It's in no hurry to leave. Are we still off to Whitstable in a bit?"

"Course we are," Beth affirmed, still in hushed tones. She turned her head to the side again. "See you, little friend." She blew softly. The butterfly flicked its wings a couple of times and then it was off, climbing higher and higher towards the roof until they saw it no more.

"Well, I reckon that's our cue to go." Beth stood up and stretched her limbs. "It's been nice seeing the old place again. If we get a move on, we can be in Whitstable in time for tea."

Rosie followed her down the aisle to the door of the church and they stepped outside into the afternoon sunshine. A flurry of russet leaves swirled across the path as they walked through the graveyard.

"Well, that's that," said Beth decisively. "Au revoir, Saint Ethelbert's."

They spoke very little on their way to Whitstable. Beth put on a CD of Vaughan Williams' *Fifth Symphony*, and the atmosphere in the car was almost meditative. Rosie thought about the postcard with the winter scene and found herself remembering the powerful emotion she had experienced in the church. What had all *that* been about? Yet somehow, she knew it was something she wouldn't forget in a while. They arrived in Whitstable at just after five.

"Is it fish and chips all round?" Rosie asked as Beth switched off the ignition.

Beth shook her head. "I'll just have a fishcake if they do them. I can still feel my lunch. We did eat pretty late, after all."

"Just a fishcake – are you kidding?" Rosie pulled a face. "Well, pardon me for being a greedy pig, but I'm going for the full deal."

They made their way to Harbour Street and bought some there. After they'd eaten, they decided to walk down to the harbour itself.

"I remember coming down here when I was about ten," Beth reminisced. "We came on holiday to Whitstable. Funny, I never thought I'd end up living so nearby."

When they got to the harbour, they walked down the South Quay. Already the sky was turning a deep red, dappled and streaked with gold, one of Whitstable's famous sunsets. They stood on the quay and looked out to sea. There was an almost surreal calm about the water. Faint ripples glowed pink in the evening light, and the air was filled with a stillness that was almost tangible.

"Who says there's no God?" said Beth thoughtfully as she gazed out towards the horizon. As if she had heard the seriousness in her own voice, she turned and winked at Rosie. They watched in silence as the sun dropped lower and lower into the west. Rosie found herself thinking that it was one of the most beautiful sights she had ever witnessed. As a little girl in Southern Ireland, she'd been surrounded by nature in all its magnificence, and her present situation near Streatham Common was not without its aesthetic high points. Yet there seemed something almost otherworldly about this evening in Whitstable. Standing on the simple harbour; watching as the sun, like a dying red giant, sank majestically beyond the horizon. It dropped to a thin rim on the edge of the sky as the wash of soft waves seemed to usher in the twilight. And then it was no more.

Beth looked at her watch. "Guess we should think about getting back, Ros." They strode back up the quay, a light breeze whispering through their hair and touching their lips with salt. "I've really enjoyed today." There was an air of satisfaction in Beth's voice. "Can't wait to look through my books. Hey, not to mention my case full of treasure!"

Rosie smiled to herself. *Old junk more like.* But she said nothing. When they got to the end of the quay, Beth suddenly stopped and looked back out to sea.

"We must remember that sunset, Rosie. It's the end of British Summer Time – the clocks go back tonight. From now on we have to get used to the dark." She pulled a spooky face and they both started laughing. Night was coming.

Chapter 3

It was Monday tea-time. Beth closed the front door and wearily peeled off her coat. She'd been out doing private tuition since just after lunch. One sweet, housebound old lady with a burning desire to play an ancient violin left to her by a neighbour; that had been a double session. And an hour-long lesson with a young boy who'd been off school three weeks with a broken leg. Neither pupil had been at their musical best that afternoon, and Beth's powers of encouragement had been stretched to the limit. Added to that, three sickly bus journeys, and suddenly she felt more exhausted than she could ever remember. She didn't feel particularly hungry, even though she'd only managed an iced finger since breakfast time. The vague queasiness she'd felt all day had taken the edge off her appetite again. At least Ciaran wouldn't be in to check up on her. He was going to be heavily involved in an inter-schools music marathon for the next fortnight, and she wasn't expecting him in until at least ten that night.

She made herself a coffee and went into the bedroom to change. Five minutes later, sitting cross-legged on the floor listening to Mendelssohn's *Violin Concerto in E Minor*, she felt like a student again. Her mind sank back into the memory of it all. The endless round of music college life with its early mornings and taut, demanding schedule. The battle as she'd set about beating her body into subjection. The aching arms, the strained fingers, the blistering weariness of working towards assessments. Even as a child, she'd always taken practise seriously. But this had felt like practise to the point of torture. One day she'd broken down, battered by self-doubt and wondering if she'd taken leave of her senses, ever imagining she could make this her career. Her tutor, Mr Kapowski, had instructed her to put away her violin for the day. 'Go for a walk,' he'd said. 'Ask yourself what you really want to do with your life. Do you *really want* to be a musician? You'll only make it, Beth, if you want it so bad that it hurts.'

Walking through the college grounds that December day, she'd thought long and hard about things. There was no doubt about it, being a music student was tough. And she missed her family desperately. Sometimes the urge to jump on a train and go home was almost more than she could bear. *And yet …*

Suddenly, her eyes had been drawn to a small sapling trembling in the cold air. Its branches were grey and skeletal, and the handful of leaves still clinging to it so brown and brittle, they looked as though the next gust of wind might rip them from their tenuous hold and send them flittering into oblivion. She'd known then. Without her music, she would simply shrivel up and die. It would be a slow death too. A lingering torment of *'if onlys'*, a creeping paralysis of disappointment and gnawing regret. Life might be hard, but mere existence would surely be unbearable.

She'd gone back into college, her mind made up. She would do it, even if she went crazy in the effort. And later that night, sitting in the common room, her hands cradling a steaming mug of hot chocolate, she'd had her first conversation with the gentle, dark-eyed Irishman who, less than three years later, was to become her husband.

She hugged herself as she remembered. That day had been a turning point, though at the time she could not have known it. It was hard to believe how far she'd come since.

As the CD continued to play, her gaze moved towards a pile of stuff under the window. Of course … her new books.

She'd had no time to look at them since Saturday. Shuffling across the floor, she reached into the cardboard box the bookshop man had given her. Her hand pulled out a small, beige-coloured volume; *The Poetical Works of John G. Whittier.* For a moment or two, she flicked through its gilt-edged pages, her eyes lingering on a few random sentences. Poetry was a strange animal. She had to be in the mood for it. She reached into the box for another book. *'The Little White Horse'* by Elizabeth Goudge. The title wrapped itself around her mind like a warm blanket. She'd read the book as a young girl and been totally entranced by it. Her childhood copy had long since disappeared, but seeing this old hardback version in the bookshop had been like stepping back in time. She'd known immediately she had to have it.

She spent the next hour or so sifting through the rest of the box. It was some time after eight when she straightened up and looked around. Books were spread haphazardly all over the floor, each one vying for her attention. She hardly knew which one to start reading first. Good thing Ciaran wasn't here. He'd say she was mad buying all this old rubbish. She grinned to herself. She'd have to select one book to read and find a home for the rest before the thing turned ugly.

It was then that her eyes fell upon the old case full of sheet music. She decided she might as well look through that too; she'd soon know if there was anything worth keeping. She pressed her small fingers against the catches which, at first, stubbornly refused to budge. Then, just as had happened in the bookshop, they suddenly flew open. Beth lifted out a pile of sheets and began to leaf through them. They were piano scores; a mixture of easy-listening music – some of them forties wartime songs – and popular classical pieces. There were even a few old hymns thrown in amongst them. She took out the rest of the scores and flipped through them. Nothing outstanding at first glance. But then, she reasoned to herself, she'd got them for nothing after all. She glanced back into the case to make sure she'd gone through everything. The bottom of the case was lined with a fusty, yellowed newspaper. On its top sheet, an archaic-looking advert caught her attention. A beaming, fifties cartoon lady smiled up from the page, the patter below her extolling the virtues of some kind of wondersoap Beth had never heard of. Finding the picture rather quaint, her curiosity was aroused. Surely there had to be a date on this thing. As she reached into the case to take the newspaper out, her thumb hit on something hard. Removing the newspaper, she realised it wasn't lining the bottom of the case at all. Rather, it was concealing a strange array of objects. An old tobacco pipe half-swaddled in a greyish-looking man's handkerchief. A wad of cigarette cards held together by a thin elastic band. A miniature Toby jug with laughing eyes and bright, grinning mouth. A small, shallow tin, tarnished and dull. And an old, dog-eared notebook. Beth picked up the cigarette cards and flicked through them. They were mostly famous cricketers of yesteryear. Her brother Josh was into cricket; he might like these. Looking next at the Toby jug's manic expression, she couldn't imagine anyone liking that. The pipe was nothing special either, but holding it to her nose for a moment, she could still pick up the faint, woody scent of tobacco. It made her think of her own late grandfather. She could still see him sitting in his chair, his stained fingers meticulously pushing and compressing a carefully constructed nest of pungent brown shreds, his lips working carefully to coax the thing to smoulder. The smell of it all had hung in his very being, and as a child she'd found it intoxicating. In those days, it had been a source of secret indignation with her to realise that little girls were not encouraged to smoke pipes themselves. She replaced the pipe and picked up the tin. It was a brassy colour, but dirty and rather dinted, not quite the length of a six inch ruler and about three inches wide. It was embossed with the profile of a lady's face, on either side of which were some rubbed inscriptions which appeared to be capital 'M's. Underneath the woman's face it read, *'Christmas 1914'*, and around the edge of the lid were the names of various countries. Beth eased the tin open. Crammed inside was a small New Testament. Bound in crazed black leather and inscribed with gold lettering, Beth could see that its dimensions marginally exceeded those of the tin which contained it. Its edges and corners had been bent and squeezed into its accommodation by someone determined to make it fit. She didn't attempt to remove it. It seemed quite happy in there, and besides, she'd grown up in a house full of Bibles and rarely had the slightest inclination to read one. She flipped the lid down and put the tin back in the case. Her eyes moved to the old notebook.

It too was leather bound, its battered cover a shabby, mottled brown. She lifted it out of the case and opened it. As she did, a folded piece of thin, yellowed paper fell to the floor. She picked it up and unfolded it. The paper was about A3 size, and she was surprised to see that it was filled with bars of music, written carefully out in pencil. At the top of the page it bore a title, *'Chant du Rossignol'*. Beth frowned as she hummed her way through the notes. It was just the bare bones of a tune, but whoever had written it had certainly understood the rudiments of music. After a few moments, she folded up the sheet and made a mental note to try it out sometime on the keyboard. She turned her attention back to the notebook. Flicking through it, she was amazed to see that it was almost completely full of writing. All but the last few pages at the back had been used. Though the book was obviously old – its pages browning with age and reeking of antiquity – the writing, though tiny, was in strong, dark pencil and still clearly legible. There were dates and strange place names. Beth frowned again. It appeared to be someone's diary. She moved back to the first page. On the inside of the front cover was what seemed to be some kind of dedication. Curious, she began to read.

To my dearest Emily –
Sweetest girl,
Gentlest soul,
My inspiration,
My reason to survive.
If I should perish,
Keep these pages
And know I died thinking of you.

Beth gave a low whistle. *Wow* – what was all this about? Her eyes flicked to the first diary entry on the facing page. It was dated July 24th 1916. Well, at least that had made the decision easy for her. The other books would have to wait. This one was first in line now. She went and made herself another coffee, came back, and curled up on the bed.

Franvillers (billets) July 24th 1916

I wonder, Emily – do you ever think of me, your old friend, Sam? I hardly dare to hope that you might. And yet I have to tell you, though more than a year has passed since I last saw you, there's not one hour goes by when I don't picture your face …

Sam chewed on the end of his pencil and closed his eyes. It was true. Emily's face was never far from his thoughts. What would she think of him if she knew? He'd never spoken his heart to her before; he'd never dared. But his time out here had taught him a lot. His teeth bit hard on the pencil. He'd made up his mind. If by some miracle he should make it through this war, he would do what he should have done ages ago. He would take his courage in both hands and ask her to be his bride.

The faint rumble of distant artillery rolled across the fields. There was no getting away from it, even behind the line. It had become an integral part of life. The dreary signature tune of their existence. Disagreeable it certainly was, but Sam had long since given up trying to remember what silence sounded like. He ran calloused fingers over the soft leather binding of his new notebook. Still so clean, unspoiled; a little touch of civilisation in this world of filth and noise. In truth, he'd had the book well over a month and had been carrying it around in his bag, still wrapped in its brown paper packaging. He hadn't known what to do with it at first. His mother had sent it over; for his beautiful poetry, she'd said in her letter. Dear Mother. Had she any idea where her boy had come to? Hardly a place to inspire the sort of bucolic offerings he'd penned in peacetime. Maybe he'd been an idealist back then – something of a romantic perhaps. Whatever the case, those lyrical days seemed an awful long time ago, and war had a way of changing a man. His poetry had a somewhat darker tone now. Somehow Sam doubted his mother would find it quite so beautiful.

Then suddenly it had occurred to him. He would use the book to write a journal. A record of these peculiar times. He would scribble down his thoughts and make believe he was sharing them with Emily. It would be like a letter. One that he would never send of course. Yet one that they might read together some day, when they were older and times were kinder. And if, heaven forbid, he should find himself among the fallen, at least she would know something of the lad who'd thought the world of her these many years. Of course, he'd have to be careful. It wouldn't do for anyone to know what he was up to. The officers weren't too keen on diaries and the like. Too much secret information should a chap be taken into enemy hands. Anything deemed sensitive material would no doubt be confiscated without a second thought. Still, it was worth a shot. This war had silenced too many already.

On the mattress next to him, Harry Burton was trying to snatch a bit of sleep. Harry and Sam had been thick as thieves from the time they'd met at a training base in Kent and gone on to find themselves in the same platoon. That had been over a year, and many weary travels ago. Now their company had just arrived in new territory. They'd been drafted in from Bethune to help support the depleted 11th Battalion stationed in the area of the Somme Valley. After suffering heavy losses in recent action at Contalmaison, the 11th were being rested for a couple of days.

"Rest ..." Harry yawned, stretching his arms till his joints clicked. "I remember rest. That was when you had Sundays off and you could go to sleep whenever you felt like it. You didn't have to worry about dodgin' shrapnel or some blinkin' sergeant barkin' orders at you."

Sam grinned. "What's up with you? At least we're still here, aren't we? Still here and in the pink, mate. That's more than can be said for a lot of our lads."

He became thoughtful. Everyone knew about the horrific slaughter of British troops that had been going on in the area for the last three weeks. This so-called Somme offensive had begun with a massive preliminary bombardment of the German lines. The gunners had been full of it. They were going to smash the enemy front line trenches to smithereens, cut to shreds the barbed wire in front of them, and let the infantry stroll over and capture the German lines. "It'll be a picnic for you lot by the time we've finished," they'd joked. "The Bosch'll come out of their 'oles beggin' for mercy!"

The initial bombardment had been planned to last for five days, but had been extended a further two because of bad weather. So terrific had the firing been, everyone had been confident that the follow-up attack would be a walkover. In the lead up to zero hour, infantry troops had been given the order that they were not to run, but to *walk* steadily towards the enemy front line. Word was going round that some had even been given footballs to kick through no man's land, just to keep themselves focused.

The big battle had begun just over three weeks ago, on the morning of July 1st. When the whistles had blown at 7.30 a.m., thousands of men had climbed the scaling ladders and gone over the top, believing the thing was as good as in the bag. They couldn't have been more wrong. The British artillery bombardment had made little more than a dent in the enemy defences. What was supposed to have been a walkover had in fact been a massacre. German machine-guns had mown down wave after wave of advancing infantrymen. Sam wasn't sure of the figures, but he knew it ran into thousands – and that just on the opening day. The slaughter had been going on every day since.

He turned over on his bed. It was a discomfiting thought to imagine that they might be next. Still, there was no point brooding on it all. It wasn't good for morale. He looked down the hut. The platoon had been reorganised since their arrival, and there were a number of new faces. Amongst a small group playing cards at the far end of the building were two lads who were identical twins. Sam gestured to Harry. "Reckon we'll have some larks with those two."

"Yeah," Harry nodded sleepily. "Thought I were seeing double at first."

Sam closed his eyes. At least they were still under Lieutenant Colton. Sam had a lot of time for him; decent chap, not afraid to muck in with the rest of them. His head began to swim as a regiment of faces marched through his mind. Company officer, Captain Brierley. Sergeant Jack Fogg, Foggy to his men. Poor old Corporal Wilkie wounded back at Souchez ...

Oh Emily, it doesn't do to get too attached in this game. We're back to the line tomorrow. Peake Wood – sounds glorious.

Beth rolled onto her back, her mind trying to digest the lines she had just read. *1916? Somme Valley?* That could only mean one thing. This guy had to be writing from the Western Front. It was almost unbelievable. She read on.

Becourt Wood July 29th 1916

After limited action at Peake Wood, we moved here and have been in close support these last days. Two caught out by a sniper, one rather badly, I'm afraid. It's not that we didn't warn him ...

Sam had already told the boy several times to keep his head down. That was the trouble with these young ones. Far too scared of missing something. Things had been pretty quiet for the last couple of hours, and the lad seemed to be getting restless.

"He's a right twit that one," Harry muttered, drawing on his cigarette. "You watch. Somebody's goin' to do for him if he's not careful."

The boy shinned up onto the fire step. "D'you think they've retreated? They're not making much noise." His voice came out as a loud, rasping whisper. Harry looked over at Sam and rolled his eyes. Some of these new lads were just plain stupid. Suddenly, the temptation was all too much for the boy. He bobbed his head above the parapet. *Bang!* A sniper's bullet whistled through the air. The boy fell backwards into the trench, landing heavily on top of Sam.

Harry was on the scene in a second. "Come on, you idiot –" He pulled the boy over onto his back. Slightly winded, Sam scrambled to his feet. He looked down at the lad who was screaming and holding the side of his head. Harry bent down to get a better look. "Keep still, will ya?" Knocking the boy's hand out of the way, he swore. "They've taken his ear off. We've got to get him seen to."

Sam could see that the whole of the boy's left ear had been blown away. An inch further over and he'd have been a goner for sure. "You're alright, mate," Sam tried to encourage him. "We'll get you to the dressing station." He pressed a piece of rag to the wound and they hauled the lad to his feet. They moved down the trench, dragging him, almost carrying him as he became weaker and weaker. It wasn't long before the rag was dripping with blood. It ran between Sam's fingers, down his wrist, soaking into his sleeve. The lad was near collapse. His war was over for sure.

Sam found himself thinking about Emily again. Poor girl. She was nursing out here somewhere. She must see this kind of thing all the time. He hated to think of her exposed to such awful sights, even though he knew she had the courage for it.

They stumbled round a bend into the next bay. The twins were there, counting out ammunition. They looked sympathetic as the injured boy staggered past them. Seeing their faces, Sam found himself remembering a funny incident from the day before.

The previous day, things in the sector had been fairly quiet since early morning. Just after noon, the men had been sitting around eating their midday meal. It had been the usual stuff; stew and army biscuits, *'iron rations'* as they were affectionately known in the ranks – no tooth was safe near them. Suddenly Twinny Two had arrived back from taking a message to Captain Brierley. Unfortunately for him, it was twenty minutes after everything had been dished out. Even more unfortunate was the fact that the cook on duty was a recent arrival to the company – Paddy O'Heany, a sour-tempered, vinegar-faced character who could make grown men squirm as though they were Oliver Twist asking for more. Paddy had glared at Twinny Two's apparent impertinence, adamant that he'd already fed him. Twinny Two had stood there, dish in hand, desperately trying to convince the antagonistic cook that he'd got him mixed up with his brother. Twinny One, meanwhile, had been doubled up with laughter in a dugout some yards down the line. He'd been just about to come clean when suddenly they'd heard the dreaded sound of a stray whizz-bang. Dishes had gone flying as everyone had dived for cover. Sam could remember the rush of adrenaline surging through his body as he lay sprawled across the ground. The confounded thing had come to rest in a small crater about five yards from where Paddy and Twinny Two had been arguing. For quite a few moments, everyone had lain there, frozen in their positions. But incredibly there'd been no explosion. The thing had been a dud. Sam smiled as he recalled Paddy scrambling to his feet. 'Don't you worry, lad,' he'd promised the Twinny. 'I'll make sure you get something.' He'd been so relieved to be in one piece, he couldn't do enough for him all of a sudden. Ironically, by this time, the remains of everyone else's food was strewn across the ground in the aftermath of the failed shell. There was one small consolation. At least the biscuits had managed to stay intact ...

As Harry's fond of saying, Emily, sometimes it takes a strong stomach to dine at the line. Someone suggested we tie fuses to the biscuits and use them instead of Mills' bombs. You have to keep your sense of humour, Em. You'd go quite mad if you didn't. Good job there are plenty of comics in our platoon. I hope for Paddy's sake that the incident has softened him a little. I can't see how he can continue to take his high-handed attitude with everybody and not end up with a stew pot on his head. Well, we'll see.

Don't know how the injured boy went on. I just hope he didn't bleed to death before they got him off the field. If he survives, they'll no doubt be sending him back to Blighty for good.

Talking of Blighty, I've heard nothing from home this week. Was rather hoping to, it being my birthday and everything.

Beth closed the book and sat up. She reached for the phone extension on her bedside table, her hand trembling with excitement.

"*Hello?*" On the other end, Rosie's voice sounded uptight, almost suspicious. She always answered the phone like that.

"Ros – it's me!" Beth could hardly contain herself.

"Oh, hi you." Rosie's tone relaxed. "To what do I owe this honour?"

"Ros, you'll never guess what I found in that case. Y'know, the one the old man gave me the other day ...?" Beth was trying not to race her words.

"Hmm, I wonder. A *bomb*?" Rosie found Beth hilarious sometimes.

Beth ignored her sarcasm. "It's a diary! Looks like it belonged to a soldier in the First World War. How incredible is *that*, eh?" She waited for a response, but was rewarded with an unintelligible mumble from the other end. Had Rosie heard her right? She tried to press the point again. "I'm pretty sure it's written from the Western Front. Y'know, Ros – the *trenches* – the First World War *trenches*! Museums and war buffs go crazy for this kind of thing."

A slight pause. "Worth a bob or two then?"

Beth tried to hide her exasperation. "I'm not thinking of *selling* it, Rosie. It's a fascinating document. Some people would give their right arm for something like this." Another pause. Beth couldn't help feeling a squeeze of disappointment. She'd hoped to find her friend slightly more enthusiastic about the whole thing. After all, Rosie had been there when the old man had given her the case.

Rosie's voice came on the line again. "Sounds great. I'll have to take a look next time I'm over."

Beth realised Rosie was trying her best. Obviously military memorabilia didn't tick any boxes for her. They spoke for a few minutes more and then said goodbye. Beth came off the phone slightly bemused. What did it take to get some people excited? Glancing at the clock, she decided to tidy away all the stuff she'd been looking at earlier. The place was a tip and Ciaran was due home any time. Looking down, she spotted the folded composition that had fallen out of the diary when she'd first opened it. She picked it up and went over to her violin case. Flicking it open, she slid the sheet behind her violin. It seemed as good a place as any to put it for now. As she closed the case, she suddenly heard the sound of the front door opening. There were footsteps on the stairs and a moment later, Ciaran stepped into the bedroom.

"Hello beautiful." He slipped his arm around her waist and kissed her. He looked tired.

"Shall I make you something to eat?" She smoothed back the unruly hair from his forehead.

He flung himself back on the bed with a sigh. "No, I'm okay. I grabbed a burger on the way home. But I'd love a cuppa tea, Bethy. Big one."

She kissed him and went downstairs. Minutes later when she returned with his drink, he was almost asleep. "Come on," she coaxed, "get ready for bed. You're shattered."

He responded with weary obedience, trudging into the bathroom in zombie fashion. Beth knelt down and began to tidy up the remainder of the books. There was no point telling him about the diary tonight. He had to be in Croydon by eight the next morning – she'd probably end up with an even less enthusiastic response from him than she'd had from Rosie.

As she stretched over to pull together some of the music sheets, a searing flash of pain shot down through her stomach. It was all she could do to stop herself from calling out. Holding herself, she got up from the floor and went over to the bed. She fell onto it and hunched over. There came a surge of nausea, and with it, a new, strange sensation. A deep burning which seemed to creep through her insides as though her guts were being punctured with red-hot needles. Groaning quietly, she willed Ciaran to hurry. She had to get to the bathroom, and fast. Just then, he came back into the room. To her relief, he seemed not to notice her discomfort. The last thing she needed right now was to start launching into explanations.

"I'm terrible tired tonight, Bethy," he muttered as he began to undress. "I'll be glad when this fortnight's over."

Beth smiled weakly and forced herself up from the bed. "I'll just go brush my teeth."

She limped to the bathroom, closed the door and leaned back against the wall. A second wave of nausea swept over her. She bent forward and gripped her knees, her forehead clammy with perspiration.

Is this supposed to happen? What if it's one of those ectopic things?

Suddenly, she felt like a little girl. Ignorant, frightened, out of control in her own body. She really didn't like this at all. A rush of vomit forced its way up her throat. She heaved violently. Times like this, she wished her mother lived just around the corner.

She was in the bathroom for some time. Eventually, when the sickness had subsided and the pain had reduced to a slight tenderness somewhere deep in her guts, she washed quickly and went back into the bedroom. Ciaran was already asleep, his breathing barely audible in the stillness. But Beth lay wide awake. As her eyes struggled to adjust to the darkness, a strange unease began to play in her mind. She didn't fancy any more episodes like that. Maybe it was time to bring the test forward.

Rosie looked at her watch and groaned. Ten to eleven. She felt edgy, and it was practically bedtime. She hated going to bed feeling like this. She tried to tell herself that it was because of the kids. They'd been pretty hyper all day. But she knew deep down it wasn't that. The house phone had gone five times that evening, and each time, her heartbeat had doubled in speed as she'd gone to answer it. Four of the calls had been for Mel, and Mel, true to form, had been out all night. The only call for Rosie had been from Beth, telling her about some dumb book she'd turned up.

Despite herself, Rosie had been rather hoping that Gavin would ring. Not that she was eating her heart out over him, even though he was drop-dead gorgeous. No, it was the waiting around that got to her. *Will he call – won't he call?* She'd been here too many times before. And it was almost a week since she'd last seen him. Maybe he'd been less than truthful with her. All this *'I'd like to see you again, Rosie – I'll call you when I get back'* rubbish. Maybe he'd been letting her down gently. Perhaps she wasn't his type. Not quite the image of perfection he'd been hoping for on his blind date.

She pulled herself up with a start. What was the matter with her? Poor guy probably only got back yesterday. But that was the worst thing about the dating game. The not knowing where you stood. Apparently it wasn't so bad once you got past the first bit. The bit where both partners are trying to play it ultracool and not look too eager. Once you managed to negotiate your way through that stage and pass onto the comfortably familiar bit, when either party could ring the other at any time and for no particular reason, things usually went okay. Or so she'd heard. Getting to the Mr and Mrs Comfortable phase was a bit out of Rosie's experience.

At that moment, a bleeping sound came from her handbag. Caught by surprise, she pulled out her mobile, her hands beginning to tremble slightly.

"Oh hi, Gavin. Yes, I'm fine. No, no I wasn't in bed. Tomorrow …? Yes, that should be okay. You'll pick me up at seven? Right – great. See you then."

She clicked off her phone and mentally kicked herself. *Well, that went swimmingly, didn't it? Couldn't you have played a little harder to get? What if he's got the notion you've been sitting around waiting for him to ring?* She kicked herself again. What was it about this guy?

She went to bed completely annoyed at herself. He was too confident was Gavin, that was his trouble. Too confident for his own good. She was going to have to take back some ground. Rosie Maconochie didn't jump for any guy.

Chapter 4

It was Tuesday evening and Rosie and Gavin were sitting at a restaurant table waiting to order. Mel had managed to persuade Rosie to wear a scarlet halterneck evening dress that had been hanging in her wardrobe for the past year. Rosie had bought it for a wedding do. It was the only occasion she'd ever worn it.

"You look fabulous!" Mel had gushed when Rosie had tried it on. "It's perfect with your hair colour. You look like a model!"

Rosie had felt less than happy about it. "Don't you think it's a bit much? I feel really overdressed – I mean, I'd hate him to think I was trying to impress him."

Mel had smiled at that. "I don't think you could outdress Gavin, Rosie. You might outdress everyone else in the place, but I don't think you could ever outdress *him*."

Somehow that observation had niggled Rosie, and she'd ended up wearing not only the dress, but also a flamboyant necklace of coloured gems that Mel had offered to lend her. Mel had pinned her hair up, done her nails, and now Rosie was sitting across from Gavin, aware that he was looking intently at her.

"You're looking lovely tonight, Rosie." Gavin's voice was smooth as butter.

Rosie merely smiled in reply. *If you think I'm gonna say the same about you, sunshine, you've another think coming.*

Gavin leaned slowly back in his chair, never taking his eyes off her. Feeling self-conscious, Rosie turned her head and stole a discreet glance around the room. Soft jazz music was playing, and there were candles and orchids on every table. The place was very tasteful – very Gavin.

"Not knowing too much about you, Rosie, I'd no idea what your eating preferences were," Gavin began. "I wasn't sure if you preferred to go for hot and spicy, or whether you were more of a sushi lady. So I decided to play it safe. I figured an English girl *had* to like English food. And as far as I know, this is one of the best places in London for English." He was still looking at her, a composed, perfect smile on his face.

Suddenly Rosie couldn't resist the temptation. "There's just one problem." She looked at him directly. For a split second, she saw a flash of consternation pass across his eyes.

He frowned, his mouth still set in its smile. *"Oh?"*

"I'm not English." For the first time since they'd met, Rosie knew she had the upper hand. She guessed it might not be for long, but it was a moment to savour. Gavin looked at her questioningly. Was it her imagination or was he feeling ever so slightly embarrassed? Served him right for jumping to conclusions. It was Rosie's turn to lean coolly back in her chair. "I'm Irish," she said simply.

Gavin shook his head, still smiling. "My apologies, Rosie. Your accent gave nothing away."

"I've lived in England most of my life," Rosie countered, her confidence beginning to grow slightly. "But I can assure you, I *am* one hundred per cent Irish."

Gavin began to nod, an expression of amusement on his face. "I see," he said at length. "So tell me – what do young *Irish* ladies like to eat?"

Rosie was quiet for a few moments. For someone so charming, there was something incredibly irritating about Gavin at times. Before she had time to think, a bizarre notion flashed through her mind. She suddenly found herself leaning forward and looking him straight in the eyes. "Ever heard of Jack and the Beanstalk?"

Gavin looked nonplussed.

Rosie took a deep breath. *Oh shoot. I've started so I'll finish.*

"*Fee, fi, fo, fum …*" she growled in a low voice that she hardly recognised as her own, "*I* smell the blood of an *Englishman. Be* he alive or *be* he dead, I'll *g-r-i-n-d* his bones to *make* my bread."

Gavin looked momentarily shocked. Not that Rosie perceived he'd taken the threat seriously. It was more, she suspected, that he'd never dated a girl who recited fairy stories at the dinner table. For Rosie herself, it was time for a horrible reality check. Where had all that come from? He probably thought she was completely bonkers now. Maybe this was the time to remind him that she worked with children. That while he spent *his* days doing grown-up things like pumping iron and Pilates, she spent *hers* knee deep in kids' books and elbow deep in play dough. Trying to regain her composure, she sat back, smoothed her dress over her knees, and said, as breezily as she could and in her best Irish accent, "With Guinness of course. A good meal always warrants a Guinness."

For a few seconds there was an awful silence. Gavin looked puzzled at first. Then a quizzical half-smile began to play around his mouth. After a few moments, he threw his head back and began to laugh quietly to himself. Rosie wasn't quite sure what to do next.

"Well, that's a new chat up line on me, Rosie," he said at last, straightening up in his chair. "You're not part of a paramilitary organisation, I trust?"

Rosie hoped that he couldn't tell how stupid she was suddenly feeling. "Be very afraid," she retorted, narrowing her eyes.

Gavin took her hands across the table and squeezed them gently. For the moment, his cool, confident expression had given way to one of bemusement. "Oh yes. I can tell I'm gonna have fun with you."

Rosie was relieved to see the look of good humour in his face. She felt herself beginning to relax. Poor old Gavin. Maybe he wasn't so bad after all. Perhaps he was just used to girls going totally gaga over him the minute they clapped eyes on him. Girls like Mel. But what was it Sadie at the nursery always said? *Treat 'em mean, keep 'em keen?* Obviously that didn't extend to threatening to eat a guy on one's second date, but there was a principle in there somewhere. All the same, Rosie noted to herself, for the rest of the evening she must at least try and zip her mouth until she was sure her brain was in gear. It would be a shame to lose a catch like Gavin over some silly culinary misunderstanding.

They met again the following evening. This time they went for a drink and spent the time talking about London, Leicester and Ireland. London was the only place Gavin had ever lived. He was proud of it too. "It must be strange for you living so far from home," he said suddenly.

Rosie was caught off guard. "Sorry?" she returned, genuinely not comprehending his meaning.

Gavin frowned. "You know – your being Irish and everything."

"Oh right." Rosie forced a smile. *Home?* Where was *home?* She'd spent far more of her life in England. Even though it was the land of her birth, Ireland was something of a childhood blur, punctuated by vivid, yet disconnected recollections of various places and happenings. She hardly looked on it as home. Leicester certainly wasn't either, even though she'd spent the biggest part of her existence there. No; if home was the place where one's nearest and dearest were to be found, then the only home she had now was London. With Ciaran and Beth. At this stage, however, she hardly wanted to explain to Gavin the complexities of her family life. She smiled as disarmingly as she could. "I'm like a tortoise," she announced, finishing her drink. "Everywhere I go, my home goes with me. My parents very nearly called me Michelle." It was an old joke, but Gavin clearly hadn't heard it before. He laughed loudly when it clicked.

Later that night as they pulled up outside Rosie's house, Gavin turned to her and took her hand. "I like you, Rosie." His expression was gentle, almost serious. "You're different. What my grandad always used to call *a feisty lass.*"

Rosie was a little surprised at his directness. "Is that supposed to be a compliment?"

Gavin's face broke into a helpless grin. "Oh dear – don't you like feisty?"

Rosie shrugged. "Feisty's fine by me."

"And it's fine by me." He leaned over and kissed her softly. Rosie found herself responding. Suddenly it was good to feel his arms around her, the brush of his face against hers, the smell of his skin. It was almost funny. Here she was kissing the most gorgeous guy in the world according to Mel – and he *liked* her. Could it be that life was beginning to look up at last?

Raindrops drummed on the roof and ran in rivulets down the windscreen. Gavin pulled her close to him, wrapping his jacket around her shoulders. "This is nice, isn't it, Rosie? Reminds me of caravan holidays when I was a kid."

Rosie glanced at him. "I can't imagine you in a caravan." Her own sole experience of a caravan holiday brought back memories of outside toilets and trips to the shower block. Gavin didn't seem the type.

"I used to love it," Gavin reminisced. "Me and my older brother ... you wouldn't believe the things we got up to. I'd probably hate it now, mind. Not so keen on roughing it these days."

Now there's a surprise, Rosie smiled to herself, but she huddled up closer to him and said nothing. They agreed to meet two days later on the Friday night.

"I won't be able to see you after that until next week," Gavin apologised. "I'm going away Saturday morning till Monday. Health and fitness convention. But I'll call you the minute I get back." He kissed her once more and they said goodbye. As she stepped out into the driving rain and hurried towards her house, Rosie couldn't help wishing she'd had the common sense to fish out her key before leaving the car. By the time she eventually got inside, she was pretty soaked. She went to her room and closed the door. Glimpsing herself in the full length mirror, she smiled. Her hair hung in damp, dark curls round her face and her clothes were spattered with rain. But her eyes were shining. The most beautiful guy in the world actually liked her.

Beth was ready for bed. She'd just been sick again and now she felt washed out and achy. This whole thing was really beginning to get to her. She remembered once reading an article about a woman who'd not been able to keep anything down but digestive biscuits for practically the whole nine months. The magazine had carried before and after photos of her. And a picture of her baby. An eight and a half pounder too. That being said, the woman had been a pretty buxom wench to start with. Plenty of fat reserves for little Junior. Beth pressed at her own ribs. They felt scrawny and pronounced. She might be gaining inches round her waist, but the rest of her seemed to be shrinking. It was depressing. That evening on her way home from rehearsals, she'd finally plucked up the courage to buy a pregnancy test. Now as she sat on the bed, she wrestled with the thought of using it. She looked at the clock. Just gone ten. She was expecting Ciaran in about eleven. That gave her an hour. Sixty minutes that could change everything. Should she do it now or wait until just before he got in? She knew these things didn't take long to work; she also knew they were highly accurate. It was like waiting to be hung. Her eyes fell on the diary. It was where she'd left it on the bedside table. Perhaps she could read a bit more of that. Do the test in half an hour or so. She climbed under the covers and opened it. There was nothing like a bit of procrastination when your future was hanging in the balance.

Pozieres (trenches) August 5th 1916

Just grabbing a few minutes to get this down before I get hauled off to do something else. What a time we're having of it, Em. We're in close support at the moment, bringing up bombs and ammunition to the line. There's been no let-up in the shelling and strafing the whole time we've been here …

Sam felt exhausted. They'd been lugging stuff around for hours now, in full kit and with their throats parched from lack of water. It was a wearying business. *Shreeee-bang!* They heard a shell come down further up the line. Horrible screams, then shouts of "*Stretcher! Stretcher!*" Some more poor wretches blown to shreds no doubt. This noise was terrible – enough to drive a man mad. But it was all they'd heard all day. It was beginning to make everyone nervy.

"Poor sods," Harry commented grimly as they picked their way back through the communication trench. "Wonder how many that one got." His voice gave way then and he began to cough. Within moments he was doubled over in a paroxysm of choking. Sam put a hand on his mate's shoulder. He was worried about him. Harry had been coughing and wheezing like an old engine for the last few days. Sam was sure he'd caught something nasty. "You need to get yourself off to the MO," he'd suggested. "See if you can be put on something lighter." But Harry, stubborn old mule that he was, wouldn't hear of it. "We have to stick together, don't we?" he'd protested between coughs. "How we ever goin' to clobber the Germans if everybody buzzes off the minute they get a sniffle?"

That was one of the good things about this war, Sam had to concede. Mates looking out for each other. His mind went back to the previous night. They'd lost a chap from the platoon, out on a working party. His mate had come back to the trench covered in his blood and crying like a baby. Said there wasn't enough left of him to give him a decent burial. Harry had nudged Sam. "You can bet the officer'll write to his widow and concoct some cock 'n bull story of his funeral service."

Sam knew he wasn't being cynical. It wouldn't do for the folks back home to know what really went on out here. But back home, they wouldn't understand the comradeship either. The way men stuck together, risked their own necks at times to help a friend. It was a thing peculiar to war.

Not that you didn't want to get out of it sometimes. The last couple of days had been atrocious. Sam certainly didn't envy the poor beggars who'd been right up front. The stretcher parties had been struggling to cope with the high casualties, and because a number of communication trenches had collapsed with the shelling, some stretcher bearers had found themselves having to transport their patients overland to the aid posts. Sam had seen fellows blown off stretchers before now ...

At times like this, you find yourself wondering when it's going to be your turn. A sorry kind of fatalism, but one has to be realistic. I suppose the best a man can hope for is a nice, neat wound that's bad enough to get you sent home, but not that bad that it maims you. Oh dear, Em, it feels rather grim to be thinking like this. But I have to say, if it's all the same to the Germans, I'd rather like to keep my arms and legs, thank you very much. Lieutenant's approaching – back to work.

Behencourt (billets) August 8th 1916

I write with a sad heart, Em. Harry's war is over.

Heavy attacks were launched yesterday on Torr Trench. Several killed and many wounded, though none from our unit. Last evening, after dark, a few of us from the platoon were out on a working party doing repairs ...

No one liked being on working parties. It was a dangerous job; you were just too obvious to the enemy. There was one thing worse than being in a trench, and that was being up in front of one, on the perilous edge of no man's land. And then, as if being stuck out in full view of the whole world wasn't bad enough, if a bullet or two *did* happen to come over, you were supposed to stand stock still and pretend to be a tree, if your nerves could hold out. That way, the enemy might think he'd been mistaken and lose interest.

Tonight the group had been given the task of shoring up the trench and re-laying the barbed wire in front of it. They were working as quietly as possible, not easy when one's hands were being ripped to pieces. A sudden Very flare lit up the sky. Harry swore. "If I'd wanted my picture takin', I'd have worn my best clothes," he hissed.

"*Freeze!*" came the sergeant's order. The group froze, their hearts pounding as a clatter of machine gunfire sounded through the night. A shell exploded close by and someone cried out.

"They've spotted us – get down!" the sergeant yelled.

Everyone hit the ground. There were a couple of big shell holes in the area they'd been working, and each man had the same idea – to crawl over to the nearest one and get hidden. Shells came in useful for some things.

But Sam soon realised Harry was missing. They'd been standing near to each other when the firing had kicked off. This hole had been by far the closest to their position, and Harry wasn't in it. For quite a few minutes, the machine guns raked the ground relentlessly. Sam kept his head down, willing them to stop. Was Harry the one who'd cried out? It was more than likely. Sam felt sick. He dreaded to think what he might find.

When the firing had eased off a bit, he stuck his head out of the hole and looked around. He spotted Harry's crumpled form lying some twenty yards to the left of them. *Time to find out what I'm really made of …*

With his heart thudding uncontrollably, Sam scrambled out of the hole. His mind began to play tricks as he imagined the whole German line with their guns trained on him. Muffled voices sounded in the darkness. "He's gonna get 'is ruddy head blown off," someone muttered. "Yeah, but it's 'is best mate," came the reply. Sam was fairly sure it was the Twinnies.

He suddenly realised that someone had crawled out of the hole behind him. The two of them slithered along on their stomachs through the blackness, Sam hoping beyond hope that they wouldn't draw enemy fire. Harry was moaning faintly when they reached him, his right leg blasted to ribbons. Sam looked around. It was no use waiting for a stretcher. There wasn't a bearer in sight, and Harry was in a bad way. Trying not to think about the vision of mangled pulp in front of him, he slid his hands carefully under Harry's legs and signalled to the other fellow to grab him under the arms. They had to get him to an aid post, and fast.

Sam was glad for the other chap's help. He recognised him, though they'd never spoken more than a few words to each other. He was big, strongly built – and Sam was glad of it. Harry was a dead weight. Sam realised now he could never have managed him on his own.

Another spatter of machine gunfire. They'd been spotted. Sam's heart pounded fiercely as the air began to bristle. Surely it was only a matter of time – seconds even – before they went down. "I don't think I'd do this for anybody else, mate," he muttered under his breath. "This is practically suicide …"

There was a saying among the men; *if a bullet's got your number on it, there's nothing you can do about it.* Fatalism. It was the only way to cope with the inhuman demands of trench life. But somehow it seemed the Germans were struggling to find *their* numbers tonight. They were certainly wasting an awful lot of ammo trying. Minutes later, as he helped lower Harry into the trench, Sam could hardly believe that nothing had hit them. It was almost as if they'd been invisible.

Harry was barely conscious by the time they reached the aid post. The MO, a kindly man who looked to be in his late forties, patted the back of his hand. "You've got yourself a Blighty there, lad," he said gently. But Sam could see the sadness in his eyes.

"Will he make it?" It was a question he hardly dare ask.

The MO shrugged, an incredible tiredness etched on his face. "We'll get working on him straightaway – see if we can get him moved tonight. We'll do our best ..."

I was choked, Em. We've been together in this thing from the start, Harry and me. I can't imagine it without him around. You're not just mates out here, you're more like brothers. As we were leaving, H. rallied slightly and whispered, 'Thanks pal.'

It cut me up saying goodbye. With all my heart I hope he does make it.

What a waste. Beth put a bookmark in the diary and laid it on top of the duvet. *What a terrible waste of young lives.* She thought about Ciaran. Twenty-six years old; he would have been called up for sure. It was hard to imagine a beautiful, gifted man like Ciaran being sent away to war. How did they cope with it, the women who were left behind? The girlfriends, the wives – her hands instinctively went to her stomach – *those with child.* What a horrible thing, to have the one you love torn away from you. To be left with just memories; at best, a tiny face with features so achingly familiar. She sat up in bed, rocking gently backwards and forwards, trying to quell the mixed emotions that were mounting within her. The bathroom was beckoning. Everything inside her began to churn. She felt scared, guilty, confused. She had to get this thing over with.

A sudden noise at the front door made her jump. Her eyes shot to the clock. *Ten twenty-five?* It couldn't be ...

But it was. She heard a few sounds from downstairs in the kitchen. A couple of minutes later, Ciaran bounded up the stairs and came into the bedroom.

"You're early." Beth's heart had quickened. This wasn't quite how she'd planned it.

Ciaran grinned. "We got away quicker than I thought." He sat on the bed and loosened his tie. "Glad we did. My brain's ready for exploding, Bethy. I was on keyboard all afternoon, then accompanying on piano all evening. I've got a shorter day tomorrow though. Violin taster session – starts at twelve thirty. Then first round of the choir competition at half four. We're hoping to be done by eight, once we've got everything tidied away. Half eight at the latest."

"That's good," Beth commented absently. She'd hardly taken in a word he'd said. What was she supposed to do now? Did he have any idea how psyched up she'd got herself?

Ciaran's chatter interrupted her thoughts. "Hey, you'll never guess who was there today with some of his singing pupils."

Beth looked blank.

"Dave Marchant ... y'know, the guy who dropped out of my year. The one who was dating the American girl."

Suddenly Beth did remember. She tried to appear interested, her mind struggling to tear itself away from the lure of the bathroom.

"They got married, y'know," Ciaran continued. He shook his head. "Poor guy. They've not been wed five years and she's expecting their third child anytime now."

Inwardly Beth recoiled. "Why poor guy?"

Ciaran ran his fingers through his hair. "Bethy, he looks terrible. He's real overweight now and he's got this permanently stressed-out look on his face. To see him, you'd think he was in his forties. He'll be working till he's seventy-five, the way they're going. They're gonna end up with their own football team."

Beth swallowed hard. "Didn't make you feel broody then?" She tried to make light of it, but her heart was pounding.

Ciaran shook his head again. "Can't say it did, Bethy. Poor old Dave's not a very good advert for family life." He stood up then, stretched and went over to the door. "Anyway, we've plenty of time for all that. We're still young. Who wants to be forty in their twenties?"

He winked at her and disappeared into the bathroom. Beth looked down at her hands. They were trembling. She felt sick, but she knew this time the sickness wasn't physical. This was turning into a nightmare. She lay down and stared up at the ceiling, hot tears pricking her eyes. Surely Ciaran didn't really feel that way. So what if Dave Marchant *was* a lousy example of fatherhood? Surely there were plenty of young dads around who seemed happy enough. She thought about Mrs Marchant. Had her American dream exploded in the midst of an endless round of sleepless nights and dirty nappies? Beth shivered as she tried to imagine a baby in their own domestic scene. It wasn't easy. Economically, Ciaran was the main breadwinner. The orchestra aside, he was involved in numerous strands of work. Private tuition, peripatetic tuition, funded projects like the music marathon, even the odd private gig – the avenues were many and varied. For Beth herself, the focus was narrower. Apart from a few private lessons a week, the orchestra had her full attention. Since the time Emmett Mallory had first pointed out her potential for solo, she'd given up all her peripatetic work and devoted the extra time to rehearsals and private practice. Ciaran had insisted she give the thing her best shot. "Live your dream, Bethy," he'd said. "I'm gonna help you live it." Ciaran had high hopes for her. So had Emmett Mallory. "I guess we won't have you long," he'd joked. "Once you get noticed, someone'll come along with bigger bucks than I've got. Remember me when you're a star."

Where would a baby fit into the equation? She closed her eyes against the tears. There simply wasn't room.

Ciaran came back in then. He set the alarm and climbed into bed. "Love you, Bethy." His voice was a soft whisper as he reached for her.

Beth froze as his fingers began to caress her neck. Without thinking, she reached for the diary again. "I think I might read for a while. I've felt a bit off it tonight." She hoped he wouldn't notice her damp eyes or pick up on her misery.

He looked momentarily hurt, but smiled then and stroked her cheek. "I haven't been looking after you, have I?"

Hearing the kindness in his voice, Beth hated herself for her dishonesty. "I'll feel better in the morning. Probably just tired."

"You *will* feel better in the morning." Ciaran's voice was gentle, reassuring. "Because I'll be at home to spend it with you. I don't have to go in till just before lunch; that should give us a good couple of hours together." He kissed her then turned over. "Night, sweetheart."

"Night ... ." Beth turned over to face the bedside lamp. She opened the diary and forced her eyes onto the page.

Fletre (billets) August 14th 1916

Yesterday I got chance for a good conversation with the other chap – my fellow rescuer. He's Pte. Philip Bocking, known to most, it seems, as Boxer. I thanked him for helping me get H. back the other day. Said he was more than happy to do it. Apparently he lost his best pal at Givenchy in February of this year. He's a tall, robust-looking chap, with a healthy, outdoor sort of face and very bright eyes. He's a Yorkshireman, he tells me, though I'm not sure I could have guessed it from his accent. Seems he's a bit of a religious type too – mentioned God a couple of times as we talked and told me he was praying for Harry, which I thought was rather decent of him. Some of the lads give him stick about it, but he takes it in good part. Very cheerful– pleasant company, I'd say. It's a funny thing, Em. I can't say I ever think of praying myself. I'm not sure how I'd go about it. I suppose one has to believe in God for a start off. I'm a bit ambivalent even on that point. Sometimes I do, sometimes I don't. And as for the afterlife, well, I'm not sure what to think. A lot of the lads here are very matter-of-fact about things. We see so much death around, they're really quite stoical. 'Once they put you in the ground, that's an end of it,' they say. 'Unless the next shell blows you out again!' Funny how you find yourself laughing at things like that. But it seems a sorry state of affairs to me, if this is all there is.

I wish I knew how you felt about it all, Em. I think I could believe in anything with you at my side.

Beth hadn't expected it. Tonight the diary had been no more than a distraction tactic; something to throw Ciaran off scent. Yet, as she lay in the stillness listening to his breathing, her mind wrestled with a multitude of thoughts. *Pray?* How long was it since she'd done that? It seemed like forever. Her mind went back to the conversation she'd had with Rosie in the church at Applemarket.

Did she still believe in God? Yes; she did. She might ignore him. Even try to pretend he wasn't there. But deep down, she wasn't so deluded as to think that her feeble philosophical whims determined whether or not he existed. It seemed to her that he *was* there – quite independently of *her* belief or acknowledgement, and totally without her permission. It was a frightening thought, especially now. Praying was pretty much out of the question. What could she possibly say?

Dear Lord, please don't let me be pregnant. I've got a career to think about, we can't afford childcare, and my husband doesn't want to turn into Dave Marchant. Forget everything I ever said about babies when I was younger – this is NOT a good time, Amen.

Beth turned over and buried her face in the pillow. She'd spent all her adult life blanking God out. She wouldn't have the nerve to start being awkward with him now.

Chapter 5

The following evening, Rosie was looking through some paperwork when a sharp knock at the bedroom door made her jump. Ciaran walked in and hugged her briefly. "Hiya, Ros. Mel just let me in." He looked tired as he flung himself down into the armchair. "Not interrupting you, am I?"

Rosie picked up the remote and flicked off the TV. "Nah. I'm just going through some of this stuff for work. What brings you here, Kitch?"

Ciaran ran his fingers through his dark curls. For him it was a familiar gesture, but she couldn't help noticing a trace of agitation in his movements.

"I need a favour, Rosie."

Rosie smiled tauntingly. "I'll have to *charge* you."

Ciaran's face relaxed then and he sat forward in his chair. "Can you spare an hour tomorrow lunchtime? I know it's a bit short notice –"

Rosie nodded. "Can as a matter of fact. I've got a whole afternoon. I wouldn't normally on a Friday, but we've got a big inspection coming up soon at work. The boss needs a couple of us to go in Saturday morning to do a bit of sorting out. Guess whose name was first out of the hat." She grimaced, then shrugged. "At least I get tomorrow afternoon off. I finish at twelve."

"Oh, that's great!" Ciaran gave a smile of relief.

"Not for me it isn't. I hate working Saturdays." Rosie tried to look disgruntled. "Anyway why – what're you after?"

Ciaran looked down and began to pick distractedly at a piece of loose thread in the lining of his jacket. "It's Beth." He sighed heavily. "Normally I meet up with her on Fridays and take her out for lunch. Y'know, for a pizza or something. But I can't tomorrow. She's got rehearsals in the middle o' London and I'm in Croydon again all day." He paused and pulled thoughtfully at the thread. "I wouldn't usually worry, Ros, but I think there's something up. She's not herself at all. I've been so busy working on this music marathon thing, I haven't been able to spend much time with her.

But this morning I had a free slot; I didn't have to go in till practically lunchtime. We had nearly three hours together, Ros. But she was – well – *distant*. Something's wrong, and she's not telling me."

Rosie's eyes widened slightly. "*Go* on ..."

He shook his head. "That's all I know. Oh, and the fact that she's chucking her dinner away sometimes. Like she of all people needs to lose weight."

Rosie frowned. "That's weird."

"Yeah." Ciaran leaned forward and looked at her directly. "You couldn't meet up with her, could you, Ros? For lunch I mean. She might talk to you, woman to woman and all that."

Rosie eyed her brother curiously. He seemed unusually vulnerable tonight. "Course I will. You set it up with her and let me know when and where."

Ciaran fumbled in his wallet and pulled out a twenty pound note. "Here, take this. Should go some way towards it. It's all I've got on me at the moment."

She tried to refuse but he insisted. They talked for a little while, about work, the weather and being tired. It seemed to Rosie something like the old days. She hadn't realised how busy they'd become, how rarely they got a chance these days to spend time together. Ciaran's visit had been quite unexpected, yet when he eventually got up to leave, she realised how much she'd enjoyed it.

"Thanks, Ros – I owe you." He gave her a peck on the cheek.

Rosie grinned. "No worries. The twenty should cover it fine."

The following day, the two girls met in Trafalgar Square. Rosie arrived slightly late to see Beth already waiting, sitting on the steps of Nelson's Column like Shakespeare's *patience on a monument*. Her blonde hair was piled casually on top of her head, and her Indian cotton skirt flowed down to her feet, its hem undulating gently in the breeze. Her gaze was fixed on something far away, if anywhere at all, and she sat, perfectly poised, striking in her own neat, diminutive way. And yet her face was sad.

"Beth!" Rosie called out, knowing she hadn't spotted her.

Beth seemed to wake up from a dream. She smiled and stood hastily to her feet, but Rosie observed that the smile never reached her eyes.

"You okay then?" Rosie tried to play it cool. She didn't want Beth thinking she was on some kind of errand of mercy. Nevertheless, she couldn't help noticing the pallor of Beth's face and the dark circles under her eyes.

They wandered up past St Martin-in-the-Fields and Beth suddenly started to reminisce. "I remember the first time I played there. I really thought I'd arrived ..."

Rosie let her talk. She seemed in reflective mood, at least for a few moments. Then she fell quiet again.

"You got anywhere to go this afternoon?" Rosie ventured.

Beth shrugged. "No, I'm finished for today."

They made their way to St James's Park and spent some time by the lake. While they were there, two middle-aged men in dated pinstripes ambled down to the water's edge. They were having a loud, animated conversation, and though it was difficult to make out their exact words, Rosie sussed that it was some kind of political discussion. Suddenly, as if by magic, one of the men produced a small, white bag and, dipping his hand into it, began to toss tiny pieces of bread to the birds on the lake. The other man immediately followed suit. And still they continued in their dispute. When the bread was finished, they screwed up their bags in perfect synchronisation and went on their way, still arguing. Rosie found herself strangely affected by the scene. Its incongruity seemed to her both amusing and poignant. Perhaps it was the glimpse of a hidden fragility in the two serious, world-weary men. Did their hearts long to know – at least for the duration of their dinner hour – something of the joy of being boys again, she wondered? A feeling of immense sadness swept over her. The sight of these two busy souls caught between the relentless grind of their daily existence and an intrinsic desire for simple, childish happiness, filled her with a sudden sense of gaping futility.

She pulled herself up with a start. This was no time for existential musings; she was supposed to be sorting Beth out. She turned to her and grinned, ready to make some acerbic comment about the two duck-feeding combatants. But Beth didn't seem to have noticed them. She was in a world of her own.

Rosie looked at her watch. "Ready for lunch? If we set off now, we can be at *Mama Bellini's* before two."

They got up and meandered their way out of St James's Park, a cool, sharp breeze making their faces tingle.

"Been nice coming in here," Beth said simply. "It's a while since I last came."

Rosie nodded quietly in agreement, but she couldn't shake off the unsettling feeling that the visit had been some kind of gentle harbinger. It clung to her like a vapour, grey and vague, out of place in the autumn sunshine. They walked on in silence and soon found themselves in a familiar side street, outside *'Mama Bellini's Pizzeria'*.

The pizza house was a riot of chatter, bustle, and garlic. As was the custom there, Rosie and Beth stood just inside the door as they waited for a seat. In the very rare moments when everyone fell quiet at the same time, Italian music could be heard playing in the background. One could almost taste the atmosphere at *Mama's*. After a few minutes, they were guided to a window table by a young fair-haired lad who was barely as tall as Beth and looked very new. He gave them menus, smiled shyly, and left them to make their choices.

"Doesn't look old enough to be working, does he?" Rosie grinned.

"Be careful making comments like that." Beth tried to smile as she opened her menu. "It's a sign of age."

Rosie noticed that her friend's hands were trembling slightly. She forced her eyes back to her own menu. Ciaran had been right; Beth certainly wasn't herself today. After a few moments, she made her selection. "I'm going for the Calzone Quattro Formaggi. What about you?"

Beth said she just fancied garlic bread.

"You're sure that's not too adventurous? Wouldn't you fancy something a bit more plain?" Rosie's tone was facetious but not unkind. Just then, the timid waiter returned for their orders. He took them and scurried off to the kitchen.

"What's up, not hungry?" Rosie spread a napkin carefully over her knees as she spoke. She was fast running out of small talk. Conversation was bordering on torturous today.

Beth shrugged. "Guess not."

Silence again – and that same far away expression. Inwardly Rosie sighed. Why had she ever agreed to this? It was clear Beth didn't want to be here. She was just debating whether or not to ask her straight out what was up, when Mama Bellini herself came over to the table.

"*Allo laidees!*" Her accent was rich and musical, her manner warm. "*And 'ow are you today? I 'aven't seen you for a while.*" She chatted with them for several minutes, the girls smiling and nodding at appropriate junctures. Mama Bellini had a remarkable gift for making each customer feel like a long lost friend. When their pizzas arrived, she wished them '*Buon appetito!*' and went over to another table.

"I'm ready for this." Rosie took a mouthful of Calzone. But she didn't mean the pizza. *Ready for a break from trying to make chitchat with someone who clearly wishes they were a million miles away, more like.* She felt like she'd spent the last ninety minutes trying to plait water. All the natural ebullience that usually went along with Beth seemed to have evaporated into thin air. As she chewed absently on her food, Rosie glanced across the restaurant. The young fair-haired waiter was taking orders from an elegant couple at table seven. The woman looked to be mid-twenties; platinum white hair, ice-blue eyes – very Scandinavian. Her partner was probably around the same age, Rosie guessed. But all she could see of him was the back of his head. A mop of dark, soft curls which suddenly made her think of Ciaran. The hair was slightly longer, slightly lighter, and certainly less unruly than her brother's, but the similarity was sufficient to remind her of her failed mission. Irritated, she jabbed at the Calzone. She knew Ciaran was counting on her to do the whole woman to woman bit – get to the bottom of Beth's woes and bring her home to him all counselled, smiley, and together again. He'd even given her twenty quid to finance the operation. Somehow, the idea of letting him down made Rosie feel more awful than she could quite understand. *But,* she reasoned gloomily, *how was I to know when I agreed to this whole thing that Beth had gone in for a stupid personality transplant?*

She was jerked out of her thoughts as she suddenly caught sight of Beth's face. "Beth? Are you okay?"

Beth didn't answer. She was leaning over the table, holding herself so tightly that Rosie could see her knuckles whitening.

"Beth – *talk* to me! What the heck's wrong?" Rosie was alarmed by the urgency she heard in her own voice. Beth tried to look up. Her skin was ashen, her facial muscles contorting with every movement. Rosie jumped out of her seat and crouched down beside her. "C'mon Beth – please talk to me. Tell me what you're feeling."

She began to do a quick mental round-up of her first aid signs and symptoms. *For crying out loud, girl, don't go and have a heart attack on me.* She reached over and took hold of Beth's wrist. For a few seconds, Beth let her. Then she muttered something and sank her forehead onto the table. She was breathing fast now and despite the noise in the restaurant, Rosie could tell that she was moaning slightly. Mama Bellini suddenly appeared at the table again. "*Ees something wrong – your friend ees ill, no?*" She looked worried.

Rosie wasn't sure what they were dealing with. "She sounds like she needs to be sick. Could you help me get her to a toilet?"

Mama thought for a moment. "*You take one arm and I take the other,*" she instructed. "*We go to the staffroom. Eet will be more comfortable for 'er.*"

Rosie bent down close to Beth's ear. "Do you think you can make it to the staffroom if we help you? It'll be better there – you won't have an audience."

Together they gently eased Beth out of her chair and began to manoeuvre her towards a couple of steps situated at the end of the restaurant. As they drew near to them, the young fair-haired waiter suddenly came hurtling out of the kitchen. When he saw Beth being hauled helplessly along, he stopped in his tracks and stared, a look of shock registering on his face. He glanced over at Rosie questioningly. She felt almost sorry for him. Poor kid. He'd probably only been working there two minutes, and here was this strange woman – from one of *his* tables – looking like she was being carried off to die.

"I told her she should have had the Calzone," Rosie quipped in a low voice as she passed him. He smiled falteringly, almost gratefully.

There was one young woman in the staffroom. As they entered, she was drying her hands ready to go back on duty. Mama signalled to her and began to chatter rapidly in Italian. From the accompanying gestures and the compliant nods of the young woman, Rosie guessed that Mama was giving her the low-down on Beth's plight. Mama then turned to them and apologised that she needed to go back downstairs for a few minutes, but promised she would get back as soon as possible. She eased Beth over to a bright, floral sofa. Beth slumped gratefully into its cushions.

"*Anna weel look after you!*" Mama called as she swept out of the room.

Rosie sat down beside Beth and took her hand. "How do you feel now?"

Beth seemed slightly out of breath. She squeezed Rosie's fingers weakly. "*My – stomach – it's like – a knife.*"

She looked ghastly, and Rosie sensed from the rhythm of her breathing that she was still feeling nauseous. "D'you need to be sick, Beth?"

Beth screwed up her face and nodded. Anna obligingly led the way and within a couple of minutes, Beth was leaning over the toilet, panting. "*Ros – could you – hold my hair?*" Her voice came out in tiny, whispered gasps. Rosie quickly bunched up the unruly pale tresses and held on as tightly as she could. As she did so, a split second memory assailed her.

She must have been about five at the time. Yes, she couldn't have been any older. They were on holiday and she'd had mussels.

Boy, had she been ill. Throwing up all night long, feeling like a limp rag doll. But her mother had been an angel. Sitting patiently holding her hair, cooing soothingly in her soft Irish lilt; it all came back so clearly. That was the only time Rosie could remember her doing that ...

Beth's sudden retching whipped her back to the present. She tightened her grip on the hair and tried to concentrate on the ceiling as the vomit hit the water. Certain things made her squeamish, and sick was one of them. It was an occasional aspect of her childcare work, but one she tried hard to avoid. Beth heaved continually for several minutes, while Rosie stared hard at a health and hygiene poster on the cubicle wall. It was hardly a distraction. Each time Beth vomited, she made an effort to say something encouraging, secretly hoping that she wouldn't throw up herself. Eventually Beth sank back against her heels, exhausted.

"Think you've finished?" Rosie ventured.

"I – I – think so." Beth's voice was shaky.

Rosie stood behind her and helped her to her feet. "Come on, let's get you back to that sofa." She helped her to the settee and laid her down with a towel under her face. She put a hand to her friend's forehead. The skin felt clammy and strange.

Beth stirred. "Ros," she faltered, as though the effort of talking was all too much, "I – don't think – we flushed the loo."

Rosie slipped back to the toilet to rectify the matter. Going into the cubicle again, she noticed that the toilet bowl was full of an insipid looking liquid. In fact, there was very little solid matter in there at all; except for the presence of something that looked almost like coffee granules. A noise behind her made her turn round. Mama Bellini smiled kindly.

"*Ow ees the little lady? She seems more comfortable, no?*"

Rosie shrugged. "I hope so. She's been pretty off it all day."

Mama glanced down into the toilet. Stepping out of the cubicle, she stroked her chin thoughtfully. After a few moments she made a suggestion. They should call an ambulance and get Beth properly checked out. Rosie wasn't sure. It seemed a bit drastic. But as she remembered the ghastly look on Beth's face half an hour earlier, she found herself being persuaded by the idea.

As Mama phoned the emergency services, Rosie watched her gloomily. She knew she had to call Ciaran. It went onto voicemail after a few rings. He was probably right in the middle of something. She decided to try again rather than leave a message. This time, he picked up.

"Sorry Ros, didn't get to it in time. What's up?"

She tried to play the situation down, but the sight of Beth hunched into a ball on the settee and the intermittent sound of her whimpering softly, didn't make it easy. On the other end, Ciaran sounded frantic. As he promised to get there as soon as he could, Rosie promised to keep him posted with any developments. Miserably, she flipped her phone shut and sighed. She'd heard the panic in his voice; he'd probably try and sprout wings. What a day this had been.

The ambulance arrived quite quickly, parking round the back of the restaurant where there was an outer door which connected directly to the staff quarters. Two paramedics – a tall rake of a man and a young, dark-haired woman – came into the staffroom and gently examined Beth. They asked several questions and Rosie told them all she knew.

"We need to get her seen by a doctor." The female paramedic spoke kindly. She seemed to exude an air of calm authority far beyond her years. Rosie found herself wondering if the woman could be much older than herself.

It was obvious Beth couldn't walk very far and a trolley was brought in. She briefly opened her eyes as they wheeled her out, but Rosie could see that she was utterly exhausted. She squeezed Beth's hand and smiled as reassuringly as she could. "See you up there. Ciaran won't be long."

Within a couple of minutes the ambulance was gone. The sun was still shining and the afternoon still young. Everything looked just as it had a couple of hours ago. Rosie shivered. So why did everything feel different all of a sudden?

Ciaran gave an agitated sigh. They'd been here three hours at least now. Why didn't someone come and tell them what was going on? Rosie glanced at him sympathetically but said nothing. She'd slipped out of the hospital about an hour earlier to ring Gavin. He was supposed to be picking her up at seven thirty.

"Really sorry, I don't think I'm gonna be able to make it tonight. My sister-in-law's been taken into hospital. We're up there now. My brother's pretty shaken – I really need to stay with him."

"Oh right. That's a shame. I'd booked us in to a film at nine."

Rosie had tried to think fast. "It's possible we might be out by that time. I could always ring you if I am ..."

Gavin had dissuaded her. "No, don't stress yourself. I can still go myself. I'll see if I can get one of my mates to come along. It's not a problem."

Well, thanks for your understanding. "Er right, okay then. See you when I see you."

"Yeah, I'll give you a ring. Hope everything goes alright. Bye Rosie."

It had been a strangely cold phone call. Just when things between them had seemed to be looking up. She'd tried to bury her disquiet as she'd walked back into the hospital. Her brother didn't need any more hassle.

Ciaran shook his head disconsolately. "I *hate* that smell," he grumbled to no one in particular. He began to wring his hands, then became conscious of it and stopped. He let out another sigh. This was not a side of her brother Rosie was used to.

"I knew there was something up, Ros."

There was such a pathos in his voice that Rosie put a hand on his shoulder. For a few moments neither of them spoke. At length, Ciaran shook himself with a slight, embarrassed laugh. "D'you remember when we first came over from Ireland, Ros?"

Rosie frowned. "Vaguely. I was only a little kid."

Ciaran gazed down the corridor. "I hated England at first, y'know. Seemed so ugly. And everybody talked so weird."

Rosie laughed. "We talk just like them now."

"That was one of the first survival lessons we learnt." Ciaran looked thoughtful. "Do you remember Mum's cousin – the one we came to live with?"

Rosie screwed up her face. "Not very well. Was she called Bridie or something?"

Ciaran nodded.

"Didn't she move pretty sharpish after we arrived? Where did she go?"

Ciaran sat back in his chair. "She moved to Saudi. Nursing. Mum once told me about it when I asked her if she'd gone because of us. Apparently it paid better than the NHS. After she left, Mum carried on renting the house for a couple o' years."

Rosie grimaced. "Yeah, until she shacked up with Mickey you mean ..." She hadn't intended to sound harsh, but even she had heard the bitterness in her own voice. That name almost stuck in her throat.

Ciaran looked surprised. "You remember *that* bit then?"

How could she forget? The dank winter day they'd moved in; the coldness of the house with its foul-smelling rooms. Oh yes. She remembered it well. She tried to make light of it. "Like it was yesterday."

Ciaran smiled and then went quiet as though deep in thought. After a while he turned to her, his eyes troubled. "You didn't mind that I got married, did you, Ros?" He paused as though he wanted to get his words just right. "I mean, I know I'd promised to find you somewhere to come to once you were old enough to leave home. You didn't mind sharing it with Beth – *did* you?"

"What goes on in that mind o' yours, Kitch?" Rosie stared at him quizzically. What on earth had prompted him to ask a question like that? But looking at him, she could see that he was entirely serious. She thought hard for several moments. It was something she'd never even asked herself. She pictured herself as a sixteen-year old again, arriving in London for the first time. Moving in with her brother and his young wife. Feeling cared for, *really* cared for ... for the first time in a very, very long while. The memory of those days was warm and clear. The period she'd spent in their Streatham home had truly been the happiest of her life.

"Beth's the best thing that ever happened to you, Kitch. I'm gonna hate myself for saying something as naff as this – but you two were made for each other." She rubbed the back of his hand and forced a grin. "Anyway don't forget, I got a new sister out of this deal."

A grateful smile crept over Ciaran's face. "Thanks, Ros. I needed to hear that today."

A doctor suddenly appeared on the corridor and began to make his way towards them. Ciaran jumped to his feet, his jaw stiffening.

"Mr Maconochie ...? I'm Doctor Stafford." The doctor extended a hand and Ciaran shook it nervously.

"This is Rosie, my sister. How's my wife?"

Dr Stafford invited them to sit down again. "We need to keep her in to run some tests. There are several possible causes of the problem, but it's impossible to diagnose accurately without further investigation. She's actually very weak. She informs me that she hasn't been eating well for the last couple of months. I'm pretty sure she's anaemic. We've done some blood tests and we need to wait for the results from those. We're going to put her on a drip for the time being – build her up a bit."

Ciaran glanced at Rosie then shook his head. "I could kick myself. I should have tackled her about the eating business earlier. Made her get help."

Dr Stafford smiled sympathetically. "You'll be able to go up and see her in a few minutes. She's been taken to Ward 7a; Whitstable Ward."

Whitstable Ward ...? Rosie was faintly amused by the coincidence. She hoped the irony would not be lost on Beth. Okay, so maybe her sense of humour *had* been a bit lacking today. Rosie smiled to herself. *Wait till she wakes up tomorrow, she'll find it hilarious. A couple of free nights at a Whitstable health farm.*

Ciaran's voice interrupted her thoughts. "*Blood?* Are you sure?" His face had paled.

Dr Stafford nodded. "Yes. She was sick as soon as she arrived here. And there *was* a fair amount of blood present."

Rosie's heart quickened as she tried to work out what was going on.

"Beth obviously didn't realise what it was," Dr Stafford continued. "It's altered blood, you see. Looks more like coffee grounds." He looked at them kindly, his expression warm and reassuring. "There are a number of conditions which can cause haematemesis. Our priority is to stabilise her and identify the root of the problem as quickly as possible. Don't worry, she's in good hands. We'll look after her." He proceeded to give a few more details of the various procedures Beth would undergo next. Rosie and Ciaran exchanged glances. No wonder Beth hadn't been herself – she was vomiting blood. How long had *that* been going on?

The next morning was a drag. The impending inspection had put Rosie's supervisor in the worst of moods, and it seemed that neither Rosie nor her colleague, Ellie, could do anything right. After biting her tongue for what felt like the millionth time since arriving at work, Rosie looked at her watch irritably. Only another half an hour, then home sweet home. She hadn't been in the mood for working. Her mind had been on Beth most of the time. She'd tried ringing the hospital in her break but they hadn't been very forthcoming. "*Spent a comfortable night*," was all they would say. It had been on the tip of Rosie's tongue to ask what brand of pillows they used, but she'd resisted the temptation. Being facetious would get her nowhere. Perhaps Ciaran had managed to glean more information. Half past twelve crawled slowly round and she left at last. It felt like the longest shift she'd ever done.

She'd only been home about quarter of an hour when there was a knock at the front door. She went to answer it and was surprised to see Ciaran standing there.

"Hi. Thought I'd call by and see if you were back." He looked pale. "Wondered if you fancied a walk on the Common. I've got sandwiches if you haven't eaten – *chicken tikka* … ." He rattled a little bag in front of her and gave a hopeful smile. Rosie hadn't the heart to disappoint him. Besides, maybe a walk would do her good; clear her mind a bit.

"Give me five minutes."

There were quite a few people out walking. Though the sky was bright, there was a definite coldness in the air, as though the last ragged vestiges of mellow autumn had conceded defeat and gone home.

"Winter seems to have come all of a sudden," Ciaran shivered, pulling up the collar of his coat. They ate the sandwiches as they walked, their bare fingers stiffening in the wind chill. "Seemed weird without Beth last night." His voice was tinged with melancholy. "It's the first time we've spent a night apart since we got married. It's funny how you get used to someone just *being* there."

Rosie nodded but said nothing. She wasn't sure what she could say.

Ciaran continued. "I've been in touch with Ed and Cassie. They were on about coming straight down here, but I said they might as well hang fire – wait until we know a bit more. They look after Meg and Tammy some days after school. It seemed daft messing everything up till we find out what's wrong. I mean, I'm guessing she'll be out of there soon. Might be nice if they come and see her once she gets home again. Just seems an awful long way to come for a couple of hours' hospital visiting."

"Did they sound upset about her?"

"Well, it was Cassie I spoke to. Obviously she was very concerned, but she's a steady sort of a woman. She told me to try not to worry. Said they'd be praying for us – and something about getting Beth on a prayer list. Not sure what all that was about. But it was good to talk to her."

Rosie nodded quietly as a question began to form in her mind. "Don't suppose you've spoken to Mum?" Her words sounded small, and suddenly, stupid.

Ciaran shook his head. "Not much point in that is there, Ros? Can't imagine *her* belting down here to do her Florence Nightingale bit, can you?" With a weak smile, he threw his arm around her shoulders as if in a gesture of solidarity. "No, little sis. It's just you and me as usual, I'm afraid. 'Cept that we've got Beth's family now, eh?"

By this time they had reached the Rookery, a formal landscaped garden area adjoining Streatham Common. Ciaran spotted the café. "Cup o' tea, Ros? I could murder one myself." They went inside and sat down by the window. Ciaran closed his eyes as he warmed his hands on his mug. "I'm glad it's Saturday. I couldn't cope with any school kids today. I hardly slept a wink last night."

"So, what's the situation with her? Are we any nearer finding out what's what?"

Ciaran shrugged. "Looks like it'll be Monday before they get cracking on the tests. Unless she takes a turn for the worse. Y'know, if she starts vomiting again or anything like that. I spoke to her on the phone this morning and she said they're gonna do a barium meal, and possibly put a camera down into her stomach. Routine procedure from what she tells me." His face was strained. "I can't believe it, Ros. Vomiting *blood*. I should have known there was something wrong. I should have made her get herself seen to."

Rosie felt for him. "Don't blame yourself, Kitch. You weren't to know. Anyway she's in the best place now – they'll sort her out. What time are you going to see her?"

Ciaran looked at his watch. "Visiting's three till eight. Guess I'd better get going soon."

Rosie gave a knowing smile. "And wild horses wouldn't drag you away before eight, would they?"

"You think I'm getting soppy in my old age, don't you?" Ciaran grinned sheepishly. "But I'm missing her so bad already, Ros. I daren't think how long they'll keep her in there. Still, so long as they get to the bottom of things, that's all that matters, isn't it?"

They left the café and made their way to the Rookery's 'White Garden'. Everything there was white by design, from the benches to the flowers in its borders. Not that there were many flowers left in bloom, Rosie observed. Even this place seemed curiously subdued today.

Ciaran was thoughtful as they walked around. "Beth loves it here, y'know, Ros." He kicked distractedly at a stone. "She always calls it 'Mary's Garden'. Something about it once being a favourite place of Queen Mary."

Rosie suddenly found herself remembering the white butterfly in the old church at Applemarket. It wouldn't have been out of place here. A blast of wind made them shiver. They decided it was time to leave.

"By the way, are *you* planning to visit, Ros?"

"I'll come up now with you, if you're alright with that. Don't worry, I'll just stay an hour. Give you two lovebirds plenty of time on your own."

Ciaran smiled appreciatively. "I'm not expecting anyone else to visit at the moment. I rang Emmett to put him in the picture, so it should be all round the orchestra by now. But I asked him to pass it on that she wouldn't be up to seeing anyone till after the weekend. To be honest, Ros, looking at her yesterday, I think it'd wear her out. I reckon she could do with a couple o' days complete rest before she starts dealing with visitors."

Rosie's mind went back to the night before. She pictured the small, white face slumped against the starched hospital pillow. Beth had barely managed to open her eyes before they'd left. *Couple o' days?* Rosie couldn't help thinking it was going to take a bit longer than that to get Beth socialising again.

Chapter 6

There were six beds in Room 3, Whitstable Ward. Only four of them were occupied but, unfortunately for Beth, both beds near the window had already been taken. Hers was a middle one and despite her usually easygoing disposition, she felt oddly hemmed in. The other women on the ward were nice enough – all older than her and, seemingly, hospital veterans. Listening to them chattering away like old friends, Beth found herself wondering if that was one of the strange quirks of being trapped in an institutionalised regime. You only had to be there a day or two and you were fully in the swing; comrades and fellow sufferers, knowing the ropes, ready to pass on your vast wealth of experience to the next poor rookie. These women were on first name terms with the morning news vendor, felt comfortable enough to tell the young Spanish orderly that he'd 'missed a bit', had nicknames for the nurses, opinions on the doctors, slated the food, and generally seemed to thoroughly enjoy being there. How long, Beth wondered, before she became a seasoned veteran herself? She glanced over at the clock. Two forty-five. Another quarter of an hour until visiting. She closed her eyes.

So, she wasn't pregnant after all. She felt almost silly about the whole thing now. She'd mentioned it to one of the nurses on the early observations round. "When did you have your last period?" the nurse had asked matter-of-factly. Beth had had to go into explanations then. "Can't actually remember. Probably about three months ago, but that doesn't mean anything in my case." Obligingly they'd tested her. Negative. Beth's relief at the result was tempered by a new concern. If she wasn't pregnant, what on earth *was* the problem? The conversation she'd had with Dr Stafford earlier that morning came back to her. *Any personal or family history of this kind of thing?* What kind of thing was he meaning? *Stomach problems, nausea, reflux – anything like that.* The questions sounded familiar. She was sure he'd asked her the same stuff the night before, only she'd felt too ill to respond properly. *Family history?* No, not that she was aware of. *Personal history?* Actually, yes. She'd almost forgotten. There had been something, just after she'd turned eighteen. Discomfort, a burning sensation after eating – in the end they'd detected Helicobacter Pylori infection in her stomach. The treatment had been pretty lousy, she remembered, but there'd been no recurrence. Dr Stafford had seemed interested in this disclosure. "Some people have a predisposition to such things," was all he'd said. His face had brightened. "Well, at least you've had an endoscopy before. It shouldn't be such an ordeal for you when we decide to do one."

Beth had winced at that. He had to be joking. Knowing what was coming made it worse. She found herself thinking about the pregnancy test back home in her drawer, well hidden under a pile of underwear. She'd never got round to using it. Funny – a few days ago, getting a negative showing would have been the best news she could have imagined. Now she felt oddly detached about it all. In the last few hours, a strange exhaustion had wrapped itself around her, making the whole situation seem almost surreal. She suddenly felt terribly tired, more tired than she'd ever felt in her life. Perhaps it was the drugs they were giving her. Random snippets of conversation flitted through her head. Her mind went to the tests that had been mentioned. It was all a bit daunting. She felt too weary to do anything at the moment, least of all be brave while a bunch of total strangers did nasty things to her. Still, she tried to console herself, at least they wouldn't be doing much before Monday. She might as well make the most of the respite.

The first visitors began to trickle onto the ward. Ciaran and Rosie came in, their faces flushed from the cold outside. Ciaran was by the bed in an instant. He cupped Beth's face in his hands. "How's my princess?"

"I've felt better," Beth smiled, touching his cheek. She turned to Rosie. "Sorry about yesterday, Ros. Hope I didn't scare you."

Rosie grinned. "Nah, I'm alright. It's Mama Bellini you should worry about. She's sacked all the staff and boarded the shop up."

The conversation was gentle and undemanding. Beth was glad to see them both. It was easier to feel a bit more cheerful now that the strong medication had taken the edge off her pain. Ciaran kept stroking her hair as though he hadn't seen her in days.

"John and Cheryl rang to ask how you were." He rubbed the back of her hand gently, then turned to Rosie with a wry smile. "That's cello and oboe to you, Ros."

Rosie pulled a face at him. He always did this to her, ever since the day she'd admitted she found it easier to identify the members of the orchestra by their instruments rather than their names. It was true. She could picture them quite readily dressed in their blacks and seated in their orchestral sections.

"Oh *and* Nika ..." Ciaran remembered. "She wants to visit as soon as you feel up to it."

Rosie had no difficulty recalling Nika. At the previous year's orchestra Christmas party, the flame-haired Russian soprano had spent half the evening trying to initiate a group of them into the delights of her native language. And not quietly either. Nika's natural effervescence, coupled with several glasses of dubious plonk, had made her an exceptionally raucous teacher. '*Zdravstvuite!*' was about the only word Rosie had come away with, and she'd never dared use it since. Nika had been far too inebriated to be reliable. The word could have meant anything.

As the clock came round to four, Rosie got up to leave. "I'll be getting off now. Let you have some time with lover boy." She turned and gave Ciaran a wink.

Beth took her hand and squeezed it. "Thanks for coming, Ros. Look after him for me, won't you?"

"Don't worry, I will. By the way, enjoy your stay in sunny Whitstable."

Beth grinned weakly. "Guess I timed it right. Reckon if I'd got here a couple of days earlier, I'd have been down the corridor – Peckham Ward."

Rosie grabbed a takeaway on the way home. She couldn't be bothered cooking; all she wanted to do tonight was chill. When she arrived back, Mel was straightening her hair ready to go out.

"How's Beth?"

Rosie shrugged. "Well, she *looks* better. I mean, she couldn't really look worse than she did yesterday. But they don't know anything yet; they have to do a lot of tests. At the moment they're just making her comfortable, I guess. Anyway, where are you off to – anywhere nice?"

Mel's face lit up. "Dan's taking me to see Miss Saigon. Birthday treat!"

"It's not your birthday," Rosie frowned.

"Not *mine* ... it's Dan's. But he insists on paying, *and* he's booked us in for a meal afterwards. What a babe, eh? I think he's crazy about me."

Rosie shook her head with a smile. Maybe Gavin could learn a thing or two from him.

A little while later, she was halfway through a chapter of the novel she'd been reading when the phone rang. She glanced at her watch. It was just gone nine.

"Hi Ros, it's me."

"Hi you. Just got back?"

Ciaran launched into a convoluted explanation of how his train had been delayed, how he'd mislaid his keys, how he'd accidentally tripped the burglar alarm ...

"Honestly, Rosie, this is so not me. I don't know what's happening today."

Rosie couldn't help smiling. "Face it, Kitch, you're hopeless without her. Like a phone without a SIM card. Absolutely useless."

"Thanks, Ros. You sure know how to build a guy up. How did you think she looked this afternoon?"

Beth had looked a lot better, Rosie tried to reassure him. A whole lot better.

She wasn't just *saying* that, was she?

No, Rosie insisted; Beth had looked a hundred per cent better than she had the day before. Honestly.

Ciaran drank in her comments gratefully, repeating them back several times during the course of their conversation. He seemed like a man dying of thirst trying to eke out a teaspoon of water.

By the time she came off the phone, Rosie's head was buzzing. This was unfamiliar territory. Ciaran had always been so strong, self-assured. Now she'd found the chink in his armour. Beth.

It was Wednesday morning and Beth was feeling woozy. Remembering the experience of her first endoscopy, she'd opted for a sedative. Now here she was lying on her side, a tube wedged down her throat, with the room swimming and swaying like a cork on the high seas. She was aware of a vague choking sensation, but it felt strangely like it was happening to someone else. Every time the pipe moved, she burped, but the medication had taken care of her dignity. She closed her eyes and tried to think about something else. There were low voices all around but she couldn't pick up what they were saying. Their words were a jumble of hushed syllables, occasionally punctuated by a direct address to her. *"You okay, Beth?" "Not be too long now, Beth." "Not hurting you, is it, Beth?"* Trying to respond, she gurgled and spluttered. It was more trouble than it was worth. At one point, she became aware of Dr Stafford's presence in the room. He hadn't been there at the beginning, had he? It was too much effort to think about it. All she wanted to do was get this lousy tube out and go to sleep.

The following day, Rosie finished work at half past two and went straight through to the hospital. She hadn't visited the day before. According to Ciaran, Beth had been a bit ropey after her endoscopy, so she'd decided to give it a miss. She arrived bang on three o'clock and Beth's face lit up as she walked in.

"How's it going then?" Rosie gave her a quick hug. Touchy-feely wasn't her thing as a rule, but Beth's being ill in bed made it somehow easier.

Beth screwed up her face. "I'm cheesed off of being stuck in here. I'm beginning to show signs of cabin fever, I reckon."

Rosie grinned. "Hang on a minute." She turned round and spotted one of the nurses just finishing her observations round.

"Could I possibly abduct this patient for half an hour? I won't take her any further than the restaurant, I promise."

The nurse agreed, and after getting Beth fixed up with a wheelchair, the two set off.

"Sweet freedom ..." Beth exhaled with relief as they wended their way down the corridor. "Why didn't we think of this before?"

"You weren't in any fit state, Mrs M."

They went up a couple of floors in the lift and found the restaurant. Rosie rummaged for her purse. "You having anything?"

"No, I'm not bothered, Ros. You just get what you want."

They sat over by the window and Beth looked out longingly. The restaurant was on the fifth floor of the hospital and commanded an expansive view of the surrounding area.

"I've only been in here six days and it feels like six weeks." She sighed heavily. "I can't tell you how good it feels to get off the ward."

Rosie eyed her satirically. "You must be a desperate woman. You've come out in your purple bunny PJ's. Let's hope you're not being stalked by anybody from the music press. Get that headline – ***The Angelic Beth Maconochie, Jammin' in her Jimjams ... .***" They both laughed. "So how was it yesterday? Did they find anything out?"

Beth shrugged. "When I had the barium meal on Monday, they said there was something they needed to look further into. Didn't say what. I'm thinking it's an ulcer or something like that. Anyway, they took a biopsy yesterday when they put the camera down, and now we have to wait for the results. I'm stuck here until they find out what's what."

"Poor you." Rosie smiled. She couldn't help noticing how frail Beth suddenly looked. Still, at least her colour was much better. And she was sitting up talking instead of lying down groaning. There must have been some improvement. "You'd better hurry up and get yourself home. That brother o' mine's acting like he's one sandwich short of a picnic."

Outside, an ambulance was heading up the main road towards the hospital, its sirens blaring. It sped into the entrance to the grounds and disappeared from view. Beth became thoughtful. "D'you ever wonder who's in there, Ros?"

Rosie wasn't sure she understood the question. "*Huh?* In where?"

"In an ambulance – y'know, when they go speeding past with their sirens going. Don't you ever ask yourself who could be in there ... *why* they're in there?"

Rosie frowned. "No. I can't say it's a thing that occupies my mind if I'm honest."

Beth was quiet for a few moments. Her eyes had a strange, troubled expression. "For all we know, Ros, someone could have been gasping their last breath in there. Fighting for their last few seconds. And here we are, just sitting in a restaurant having a coffee, watching life go by – while some poor beggar's being sucked out of this old world forever. It seems almost indecent." Her voice trailed away.

Rosie sat back in her chair, a faintly amused expression on her face. "Have they *put* you on something, Beth?"

Beth caught the irony in her tone and coloured slightly. "Sorry, Ros. I sound a right misery, don't I? I've been thinking about a lot of bizarre things while I've been stuck in here."

Rosie felt a flash of guilt. After all, Beth *was* the one who was ill. She was entitled to a little morbid reflection if she wanted. "Perhaps it wasn't anything quite so drastic," she said, her voice softening. "Maybe they'd just eaten a dodgy pizza at Mama Bellini's."

Beth smiled gently. "Yeah, I guess so. By the way, while we're on the subject of drastic dramas, I wanted to ask you a favour."

Rosie grimaced. "So long as it doesn't involve me feeding you grapes or changing your bedpan."

Beth gave a slight laugh and shook her head. "No, nothing like that, Ros." She hesitated. "You know the diary I told you about, the one I found in that old case?"

Rosie thought for a moment. "Yeah, go on."

"Well, the other day I asked Ciaran to bring it up to the hospital for me. I wanted to carry on reading it. There's been a bit of a problem though." Beth's face creased into a frown. "Tuesday,

I got the diary out to have a look at it, and Velna – one of the women across from me on the ward – started asking me what it was. I made the mistake of telling her it was an old diary I'd picked up from a second-hand bookshop. 'Oh,' says she. 'What period?' 'First World War,' says I, like an idiot. Her eyes lit up, Ros. I'm telling you, her eyes lit up like I'd just told her I'd got the Venus de Milo stuffed under my bed. Turns out her son's a military historian. Really keen apparently. Got a house full of stuff – books, paintings, weapons, the lot. She asked me if I'd be interested in selling it. 'Let him have a look at it,' she says. 'He'll give you a good price if he thinks it's worth it.' "

"That's great!" Rosie broke in. "Maybe you'll be able to afford to get away for a few days convalescence when you get out of here. Get that brother o' mine out of my hair."

"No, Ros, it's not great at all," Beth burst out in exasperation. "I don't *want* to sell it. I haven't even read it yet. Besides, you don't *sell* something like that. It's not as if you can go down to Tesco and get another. Things like that are one-offs; they don't come along very often." She leaned back in her wheelchair. "Anyway, this morning Velna informed me that her son would be coming to see her at eleven. Apparently he'd managed to get permission for a morning visit because he's working afternoons all this week, and he's about the only visitor she gets. At five to eleven I just got under my covers and pretended to be asleep. I was stuck like that for nearly an hour. It wasn't funny."

Rosie smiled wryly. "You little sneak!"

Beth's expression was a mixture of guilt and frustration. "I know, I feel bad about it, Ros. But I'm just rubbish at saying no to people. Besides, the diary's old and fragile. I don't like the thought of everybody's sweaty hands all over it. It needs handling with care."

"Right. So where do I come in?" Rosie eyed her friend with amused curiosity.

Beth breathed out slowly before announcing her plan. "Well. For starters you can take the diary home. That way, if Velna brings the subject up, I can quite truthfully say that I haven't got it with me any more."

Rosie nodded. "I think I can just about manage that. But why don't you just give it to Ciaran when he comes later?"

Beth countered with a reluctant half-smile. "Well, Ros, that's where the favour comes in ..."

Rosie raised her eyebrows enquiringly.

"Rosie, you know how brilliant you are at typing?"

Rosie nodded dismissively. "Yeah, yeah, fastest fingers in the West. Flattery will get you nowhere, Mrs M. Where's all this leading?"

"Well, Velna's interest got me thinking," Beth continued. "It would be really good to get the thing typed up. Bang it into the computer, store it on a memory stick – y'know, so that we've got a permanent version. I mean, who knows? One day I might feel like handing it over to a museum or something. Somewhere it'll be looked after properly. Frankly, I'm amazed it's lasted as well as it has."

"So you want me to do the honours then? Type it up?" Rosie frowned, unsure as to whether she should greet the prospect with excitement or dread.

"*Would* you, Ros?" Beth's face was suddenly a picture of childlike supplication. "I was thinking you could print the entries off as you went along. That way we'd have a hard copy. Perhaps we could set it all out in a little folder. Then other people could read it without me having to hand over the diary itself. I mean, it's the kind of thing you want to show folk – my brothers for a start, they'd be well impressed. But I'm a bit scared of lending it out. It could get damaged being passed around to all and sundry ... ." Her voice tailed off then as though she was starting to lose confidence in the persuasiveness of her request. Looking down, she began to trace invisible patterns on the table in front of her. After a moment or two, she lifted her head and gave a hopeful grin. "At least you could run a copy off for me so I can keep reading it while I'm in here. What d'you say, Rosie?"

Rosie shrugged resignedly. "How can I refuse? I couldn't live with myself if Velna ransacked your locker in the middle of the night." *Besides, it's not like I've loads of other stuff to do. My phone hasn't exactly been going mad these last few days.* She suddenly found herself thinking of Gavin, and as she did, her stomach turned over. She hadn't heard a thing from him since Friday when she'd called from the hospital. What was the deal with him? Had she unwittingly committed the ultimate crime in his eyes – cancelling a date with Mr *'How Dare You? I'm The Most Fanciable Guy This Side Of Pluto'*? Well, she certainly wasn't going to ring *him*. If his ego couldn't make allowances for people being rushed to hospital and spoiling his neat, little designer plans, he'd just have to take his beautiful self elsewhere.

She suddenly realised Beth was looking at her, grinning. "Thanks, Ros, you're a star! I'll give it to you when we go back down to the ward. I'll slip it in with some washing, then Velna won't suspect a thing."

"That should do it the power of good," Rosie remarked dourly. "Surviving the trenches, only to be suffocated by a mound of dirty knickers. Shouldn't think there'll be many folk queuing up to get their mitts on it once this news gets out."

Beth punched her playfully. "Don't be daft. I'll wrap it in something first. But we need to use a bit of subtlety, don't we?"

Rosie smiled. *You missed your way, Beth. You could have been a dab hand at organising prison breaks.*

It was just after five when Rosie got home. She made herself a coffee and flicked through the mail. Nothing for her. Obviously Gavin hadn't mastered the art of letter writing either. She looked down at the carrier Beth had given her. It wasn't really a bag of dirty washing at all; just a couple of token nightshirts, not a pair of smalls in sight. A couple of neatly folded nightshirts, wrapped around something concealed in a Waterstone's bag. Beth was an expert at subterfuge. Rosie sank back into a chair and positioned the bag on her knee. *Well, here goes. My mission, should I choose to accept it ...*

She reached inside and pulled the diary out. The first sight of it made her shudder. Something about its appearance unsettled her.

Its battered leather cover was blotched in various places with dark, suspicious stains that made her think of ancient blood, and it seemed to give off a stale, musty smell which she found slightly disturbing. For a few moments she stared at it. Why on earth had she let herself be roped into this? She took a long, slow mouthful of coffee and sat back in her chair.

She hated to admit it, even to herself, but she'd never been able to stomach stuff like this. She remembered the grotesque, old gas mask Lydia Martin had once brought into class. That thing had given her nightmares for weeks. Another incident, even further back in her memory, started to surface in her mind. The time she and Ciaran had been parcelled off to their great-aunt's, shortly after their parents had separated. That house had been like a museum. No – a mausoleum. Aunt Mariah had suffered from a strange, pathological sentimentality which had led her to cram her home with bizarre and ancient keepsakes, plundered from the houses of deceased relatives and kept as memorials to them. Rosie had hated that place. Its ghastly memory stood like a tombstone amongst all her childhood recollections. The two weeks they'd spent there had been hideous. She wondered if the experience still haunted Ciaran; it wasn't a thing that could be easily erased from the mind. She looked down at the old diary again. This wasn't going to be easy. Beth's wonderful treasure left her cold. Still, she'd given her word.

After a bite to eat, she settled down at her computer and propped the diary open. What was it Beth had said? Something about getting up to entry number six – *August 22nd 1916* – whatever that all meant. Rosie looked down at the dedication on the inside of the front cover. At first glance, she was surprised at the size of the writing. It was tiny. She'd no doubt be wearing jam jar glasses by the time she finished typing this thing up. Still, the dedication was cute. Just the sort of stuff she'd expect from Gavin. Not.

She began to type. Owing to the smallness of the letters and the difficulty of deciphering some of the words, it took her over an hour to get through the first five entries and bring Beth up to speed. By the time she arrived at the sixth entry, her eyes felt tired and she decided to have a break. As she lay on her bed and looked up at the ceiling, she found her mind drifting back to long forgotten history lessons. And to Mr Lowry, a long forgotten history teacher.

It was all coming back to her. He'd had a passion for the First World War; two of his great-uncles had fought in it. The flower of a generation cut down, he was fond of saying. Lions led by donkeys, wasn't it? She remembered he used to recall a story told to him by his grandmother, of the parade of proud, young lads in her town who'd so eagerly joined up to fight. Only a dozen of them had returned, and two of them so horribly mutilated, their families had hidden them away. *"Just think,"* he used to say, *"young lads, not much older than you lot, going off on their big adventure. Coming home, mere stumps of men – if indeed they came home at all."* Old Mr Lowry; he'd certainly had a way with words. He'd have loved to have got his hands on a diary like this. Rosie found herself trying to picture Sam. Blue eyes, she imagined; yes, definitely blue eyes. And light hair. A similar height to herself – not too tall, not too small. Expressive too, at least on paper. Certainly in touch with his feelings. When was the last time she'd come across a guy so emotionally clued up? Gavin hadn't even got off the starting block. She imagined the parade of proud, young lads in Mr Lowry's tale and mentally inserted Sam in the line-up. Had *he* survived, she wondered? Had he come home? For Emily's sake, she hoped he had.

It was almost an hour later when Rosie awoke to the sound of her mobile ringing. She was momentarily disorientated. She hadn't even realised she'd dropped off. She hurriedly tried to collect herself before answering it.

"Hi Rosie. How you doing?" Gavin's voice was as smooth and composed as ever.

"I'm fine. And you?" Rosie's response was decidedly more clipped. *So he thinks he can just ring up, turn on the charm and expect me to come running, does he?* She was picturing Gavin's self-assured smile as she spoke. It made her feel irritated.

To his credit, Gavin picked up the iciness in her tone and tried to assuage it. "Sorry I haven't been in touch till now. A couple of things came up. You know how it is –"

Rosie wanted to scream at him down the phone, '*No, I don't!*' But she kept her annoyance in check. "I was rather thinking you might at least have rung to see how Beth was, seeing as that was the last thing we talked about the other day."

There was a pause at the other end, then the sound of shuffling. "I don't actually *know* Beth, Rosie," Gavin said at last, sounding genuinely confused.

Rosie wasn't about to let him get away with that one. "You know *me*, you know that she's *my* sister-in-law, and you know that I broke off our date to be with her in the hospital. I would have thought that might have been enough reason to ring."

The second the words were out, she wished she hadn't been so open; that she hadn't let him know how much his failure to make contact had niggled her. But there it was, the whole unadorned truth lingering accusingly on the airwaves, waiting for him to concoct some reply. It wasn't long before he did.

"I'm sorry, Rosie. Hands up – you're quite right. I should have shown more concern." An almost nervous laugh. "I think it's a man thing. Can you forgive me ...? *Please?*"

Rosie was still guarded, but she didn't want to sound petulant. She mumbled something in the affirmative, unsure where to take the conversation next. Thankfully, Gavin came to her rescue.

"Tell you what – how's about I take you out Saturday to make it up to you?" His voice was deliberately contrite. "By the way, how *is* Beth?"

Rosie couldn't help smiling to herself. There was nothing quite so satisfying as listening to a guy like Gavin trying to crawl his way back into favour. She gave him the few brief details on Beth that she had, then agreed to let him take her out. When she came off the phone a couple of minutes later, her mind was throbbing. Any triumph she might have felt was offset by a strange sense of embarrassment which taunted her brain like a pointing finger. Why had she let him see that she cared anyway? She should have been cool about it. After all, Gavin was just a guy. And let's face it, the world was full of those.

Le Bizet (Flanders) August 22nd 1916

We're all having a bit of a rest at the moment, which is nice. We've been deloused; that's a rest in itself, though we know it won't be long before we're chatty again. I can't say how many times I've run a candle over the seams of my clothes, Em. It's a kind of miserable vengeance, I suppose, hearing those confounded little eggs fizzling in the flame ...

Sam sighed with satisfaction. For the moment – lice-free, in clean clothes, and with access to something that resembled a real bed – he felt like a king. He'd never properly appreciated such basic living conditions in peacetime. Now he saw them as luxuries, and made a mental note never to take them for granted again.

Life had seemed something like normal since they'd arrived at the rest billets two days previously. Getting a good wash was one factor. Football was another. They'd managed to get a couple of lively matches with some of the boys from 'D' Company. Sam couldn't help grinning as he remembered the day before. They'd been well into a game, when suddenly one of the lads from 'D' Company had gone down with a great howl. Sam had recognised him straightaway; Big Malc, a real joker if ever there was one.

'*What's up, you got a Blighty, Malc?*' his team-mates had started on at him, assuming he was acting the goat. '*Get up, yer great lummock – they'll be sendin' us back to the line before we get this game finished.*'

Sam and his pals had roared with laughter as they'd listened to the banter going on between the opposite team and their resident comedian. After a couple of minutes, however, it had become clear that the injury was no joke. The ill-fated Malc had, in fact, twisted his ankle rather badly. It had quickly begun to swell and, by the time help had arrived, was approaching the size of the football itself. The poor chap had been mortified. Not the most heroic thing to happen to a soldier. His mates had ribbed him mercilessly as he'd been carted off, threatening to get him court martialled for self-inflicted injury. Sam doubted Malc would live this down in a hurry.

At times like this, one could almost forget there was a war on. They were all just lads mucking in together. Since Harry's departure, Sam had found himself palling around with Boxer much of the time. They had some interesting chats. Sam couldn't always go along with everything Boxer said, but all in all, he found him a sincere and decent fellow.

"What would you like to do when we get out of this?" Sam leaned back on his elbow and gazed across the camp. They were enjoying a quiet quarter of an hour between dinner and drill.

Boxer looked up from the letter he was writing. "I want to be a minister – like my brother."

"Your brother's a minister? I didn't know that." Sam frowned. "Does that mean he hasn't joined up then?"

Boxer grinned. "Oh, he's out here alright. He's a padre in a different sector. He was wounded at one bit, early last year. He went out under fire to rescue an officer who'd been shot. He managed to get him back to the trench, but not before he took a shrapnel hit himself. Nearly lost an eye. He was sent home of course. But it wasn't long before he talked them into letting him back out here."

Sam was intrigued. "He *wanted* to come back? Is the fellow mad?"

Boxer laughed. "No. He just loves his work. He says there's no other like it. That's why I want to follow in his footsteps. Meanwhile, I keep my eyes open for the little things I can do now. The good book talks about us being faithful in small things."

Sam shook his head, smiling. "Sorry mate, you've really lost me."

Boxer leaned forward, his eyes suddenly bright with purpose. "Well, it's like this, Sam. You know that new chap who's just been put in our unit? Most of his platoon was wiped out recently at Albert. Jimmy his name is –"

Sam pictured the lad. Very quiet, hardly said a word, went about with a windy expression on his face most of the time, which, Sam had to concede, was probably not surprising if he'd seen most of his mates blown to pieces around him. He nodded. "Yeah, I know the one you mean."

"Well," Boxer continued, "I had quite a talk with him the other day. Turns out he has no living relative in the whole world. Can you imagine that, Sam? Back home he works for a baker. That's the nearest thing he has to family. When he joined up, he palled up with a young Scottish lad called Eddie. I think he was probably the first real friend Jimmy had ever had. A few weeks ago at Albert, he saw Eddie ripped clean in two by a chunk of shell. It's really affected him, Sam. He could hardly bring himself to talk about it all. He was almost in tears." Boxer paused, a look of concern lining his face. "I'm a bit worried about him, Sam. Fancy having no one in the world to care if you live or die. I wonder how he can fight. The whole thing must be an absolute nonsense to him. I've decided to keep a close eye on him – try and make sure he doesn't lose his nerve. I wouldn't want him to go absent. There's not much mercy for chaps that run away. How's about you help me, Sam? We could watch out for him together ..."

I've agreed with Boxer to look out for Jimmy. It seems the least we can do. I can't think what it must be like to be so alone, Em. No wonder he looks unhappy all the time. We have to make sure he doesn't get cold feet. Some fellows have already been shot for desertion. I'd hate to see that in our platoon.

Rosie sat back from her computer. It was almost midnight and she had work tomorrow. She needed to get some sleep. A few minutes later she lay in bed, her eyes closed, her mind drifting ...

In a creaky, dimly lit classroom, Mr Lowry was about to tell another of his stories. Outside, the winter sky was darkening, and the stripped elms in the school grounds shuddered in the biting wind. Last period was always a difficult time to stay awake. He told them the tale of Matthew Peakefleet, a pit lad from a small village in the North of England. Barely sixteen when an underground explosion killed eight men, including his dad. Matthew had been on the other shift.

'Couldn't bring himself to go back down after that.' Mr Lowry always knew how to pause for effect.

Decided to enlist in Kitchener's New Army, even though he was under age. Anything had to be better than working in the mine. The experience might broaden his horizons for the future, and after all, everyone knew the war wouldn't last long. Twelve months later, reality had set in for Pte. Peakefleet, the slaughter at the battle of Loos the last straw. He was a broken lad. Ran away. Couldn't stand any more of it. Captured and court martialled for desertion. His plea of defence – '*My mind is shattered, I cannot carry on*' – ignored. He'd found no mercy. Shot at dawn the following day, three months after his seventeenth birthday.

Lying in the stillness, Rosie remembered. Even as a fifteen-year-old the story had sickened her. Especially as a fifteen-year-old. She'd known back then what it was to be trapped, to dream of nothing but escape, to live with her head in the future.

She thought then about Jimmy, completely alone in the world, fighting for King and country when he hadn't a soul to call his own. It wasn't hard to imagine life without parents. She didn't find that hard at all. But life without anyone? *Without Ciaran and Beth?* She couldn't do that. She yawned and pulled the duvet round her face. No, that didn't bear thinking about. Everybody needed someone.

Chapter 7

Saturday arrived. At twelve thirty sharp, Rosie heard Gavin's car draw up outside the house. Taking a last, fleeting look in the mirror, she opened the front door and stepped outside. In the brief time it took her to lock up, Gavin got out of his car and slipped round to the passenger side to wait for her. When Rosie turned round, she was surprised to see him standing there, and even more surprised to see what he was holding in his hands.

"For you." A boyish awkwardness seemed to tinge his words as he held out a huge bouquet of flowers towards her. Rosie was slightly taken aback, but tried to hide it as she reached out and took the flowers from him. Exotic-looking lilies mingled with tight-furled rose blossoms and bold gerbera blooms to create a riot of fiery colour, the whole spray being delicately tempered with stems of gypsophila and soft, feathery fern.

"Do you like them?" Gavin asked expectantly, as if any woman in her right mind could say no. Far from trying to decide whether or not she liked them, Rosie was busy trying to work out just why Gavin had brought them. This was no ordinary bunch of flowers; it must have cost him an arm and a leg. Gavin seemed to perceive her dilemma. "To say sorry." He smiled disarmingly. "For last week. I should have made contact – you were right to be upset."

Rosie felt herself colouring and pretended to look down at the flowers. "That's okay. Guess I've been a bit stressed with everything going on." She hesitated. "D'you mind if I take them in and put them in some water?"

"Not at all. I'll wait out here for you."

Rosie found a large ceramic vase and ran some water into it. As she trimmed the bases of the flower stems, she tried to harness her thoughts. *This guy could charm his way out of a straitjacket.* One by one, she thrust the blooms haphazardly into the vase. She could arrange them properly later. A smile crept over her face as she imagined Mel's reaction when she saw them. Her eyes would probably pop out on stalks. *'Oh Rosie,'* she would say, *'it must be love! I'd better start saving up for a hat.'* It would be a shame to disillusion her, Rosie decided. She didn't have to know that Gavin was just trying to make up for being such an insensitive creep. When all the flowers were in the water, Rosie carried the vase into the lounge and set it on the coffee table. *Prepare to be impressed, Melanie,* she thought as she locked the front door for the second time.

"It seems funny seeing you in daylight," Gavin commented later as they were eating dessert after a lunch of panini and salad.

Rosie frowned. "Why – did you expect me to look different? Did you think I morphed at nightfall or something?"

It was Gavin's turn to be puzzled.

"You know," Rosie continued, "like Fiona on '*Shrek*' ... only the other way round. Did you think I turned into an ogre at daybreak and morphed back at sunset?"

Gavin's eyes twinkled with amusement. "Haven't seen '*Shrek*', I'm afraid, so I haven't had the privilege of meeting your friend Fiona. And the only time the word *ogre* occurred to me was when you got upset with me the other day. But if I remember rightly, that was well after sunset."

"Ha ha, very funny." Rosie tried to suppress a smile.

Gavin sat back and looked at her admiringly. "I'm sitting here thinking how you look just as good in natural light, Rosie." He surveyed her with an air of satisfaction. "Some girls don't, you know. They look great when the lights are low, like when you're out clubbing. Then you meet up with them in Starbucks a couple of days later and you wonder if it's the same girl. It can be a bit embarrassing. You find yourself wondering how you can make your exit as painlessly as possible." For a moment he grinned. Then his voice softened. "But you – you're the real thing."

Rosie smiled, not knowing quite how she was supposed to respond.

"I guess all that sounds awful, Rosie." Gavin seemed suddenly awkward. "But hasn't anything like that ever happened to you? You know, you get off with someone, meet up next day, and come away convinced you need specs? What I'm trying to say is … *you're* no disappointment."

"So I pass then?" Rosie couldn't help laughing now. She knew there'd been a compliment in there somewhere. But had she really wanted to know that Gavin went about selecting suitable partners by standing them in full daylight and checking them for blemishes? No, not really. *Perhaps that's why he's brought me out in the middle of the day,* she thought with some amusement. *To check if I'm ready to ascend to the next stage in his elaborate filtering process.* She found herself almost wishing she'd woken up with a faceful of zits that morning. That would have served him right. Still, she had to admit that his candid admission had been cute – if slightly clumsy.

"Anyway, Rosie," Gavin's voice interrupted her thoughts, "I've been going to ask you. What do you normally do at Christmas?"

Rosie was caught completely off-guard. "Christmas …?" *Did I miss something? What has Christmas to do with anything?*

"Yeah. I remember you saying that you never really went back to Leicester these days, and that you hadn't been back to Ireland in ages. I just wondered what you did at Christmas, that's all."

Rosie thought about it for a few moments. "Well, since I've been living in London, I spend it with Ciaran and Beth. Mel's never around. She goes to her mother's. So I spend Christmas Day over at my brother's. On Boxing Day a lot of their orchestra get together for a party and we go along to that. After that, Ciaran and Beth always go up to her parents for New Year. By that time, I'm practically due back at work so I stay down here." She shrugged. "That's about it."

Gavin nodded slowly but said nothing.

Rosie frowned. "Why do you ask?"

Gavin leaned back in his chair. As he did so, the waitress came to the table with their coffee. Gavin smiled up at her and Rosie couldn't help noticing the effect he had on the young girl. She returned his smile and left the table hurriedly, her face reddening as she went. Rosie watched her thoughtfully. *Another one bites the dust …*

Gavin focused his gaze back on Rosie. "You remember the health and fitness convention I went to last weekend?"

Rosie nodded.

"Well, I met a guy there who's recently bought a country hotel somewhere in Wiltshire – a little place called Salmoncoates. He's been having some refurbishment done and it's not due to open officially while February. But he's going to open it over the Christmas period for family and friends. Just something he fancied doing as a one-off I think. Not something he'll be able to do again once the place is up and running."

Rosie frowned again. She couldn't help wondering where all this was leading.

Gavin cleared his throat. "The thing is, he invited me along too."

Rosie narrowed her eyes. "I thought it was just family and friends."

Gavin leaned forward, his face brightening. "Well, Rosie, apparently this place has a fantastic fitness suite. When we got talking, he told me he was really keen to get someone in to manage that side of things. He thought I might be ideal. So he asked me if I fancied going over for a few days once I finish work for the Christmas break. It sounds like a brilliant opportunity. I really fancy looking into it."

"Go for it," Rosie said as enthusiastically as she could. Despite herself, she couldn't help feeling a twinge of disappointment. Was this the bit where he tried to let her down gently – tell her in a roundabout way that he wasn't going to be around for much longer, but not until he'd made sure she had somewhere to go for Christmas dinner? Was *that* what the flowers were all about?

"He said I could bring a friend."

Rosie realised Gavin was looking at her intently. Her heart gave a sudden lurch. *Bring a friend?* Surely he wasn't meaning …

"You mean *me?*"

Gavin laughed gently. "Well, we *are* friends, aren't we? I thought you'd be a nice friend to ask along – if you could bear to spend that long with me." There was that boyishness again, as though he was finding the subject awkward to broach.

Rosie hardly knew what to say. This was the last thing she'd been expecting. A rush of questions flooded her mind. Wasn't all this a bit sudden? Just how friendly was he wanting to get? She realised her discomfort must be evident but felt powerless to hide it. Gavin was still looking at her, his eyes searching her face for a reaction.

"Can I think about it?" she asked quietly after a few moments. "I'm not sure what Ciaran and Beth have got planned. I'll have to talk to them." It wasn't true of course. She had no intention of mentioning it to either of them. But as a stalling tactic, it was the best thing she could come up with.

Gavin smiled. "Sure. Take all the time you need." He leaned over the table and took her hands in his. "Don't look so worried, Rosie. I think we'd have a great time."

Trying to pull herself together, Rosie returned his smile. "I'm not worried. I just can't give you an answer right now."

Gavin nodded. "I understand. You have a think about things and let me know when you've made up your mind. Okay?"

During the rest of their time together, the subject wasn't mentioned again. But, for Rosie at least, it hung over their conversation like a shadow. Later on, as they sat in the car outside Rosie's home, Gavin turned to her. He ran his finger along her cheekbone, his touch as gentle as a butterfly.

"Thanks for this afternoon, Rosie."

Rosie looked down at her knees. "Thank *you* ... *you* insisted on paying for everything." She heard something in her own voice that sounded scarily like meekness.

Gavin tilted her chin towards him. "You're worth it." He moved his face towards hers and kissed her softly. "Like I tried to tell you earlier, Rosie, you're a beautiful girl."

There was a warmth in his eyes that Rosie had not seen before. For a brief moment she found herself wondering if this could be the real Gavin at last. There'd been slight hints on previous occasions. Sporadic outbursts of genuine niceness which had suggested the existence of a Gavin quite unlike the Mr Body Beautiful that the rest of the world perceived.

As their lips met again, Rosie's heart began to pound. At first it felt like passion. But suddenly she realised; something deep inside her was coming unglued. He'd asked her to go away with him. Was this the moment she'd been dreading all her life?

It was Monday evening. Beth glanced at the ward clock as the last of the visitors drifted past the door on their way out. Eight twenty. Well, she reflected, that was it for another day. All that remained now was bedtime drinks in an hour or so and then big lights out. *Oh boy, I really need to get out of here – it's like being at Enid Blyton boarding school. I'm actually getting excited about my Horlicks.*

Apart from Beth, there was no one in the ward except a thin Scottish woman called Sandra. Everyone else seemed to have disappeared in a hurry. Sandra climbed out of bed and pulled a pale, satin dressing gown around her skinny frame. "I'm off outside for a ciggie. You comin' to watch the telly in a minute, Beth?"

"What's on?"

Sandra shrugged. "Dunno, but it must be somethin' good. Everyone else shot off straight after visitin'."

Beth shook her head. "I'll give it a miss."

"Okay. See you later." Picking up her cigarettes and lighter, Sandra went off for her smoke. Beth watched her leave, then looked around at the roomful of empty beds. Reaching onto her bedside table, she took the envelope Rosie had just brought her. A couple more entries. Time for a little light reading.

Le Bizet (Flanders) August 23rd 1916

Well, here we are, Em; our last day of rest for a while. We move back to the front tomorrow. Things have been so pleasant here these last few days, I'll be rather sad to leave. This morning a few of the lads were having a moan about going back. I think some of them have had enough. They'd just like to go home now and forget the whole thing. Earlier I was saying to Boxer and Jimmy that this war seems to me a sorry kind of business ...

Even out here behind the lines, the ground could get boggy. The continuous movement of men, drilling and training, gave the land little chance to recover itself.

Boxer was scraping mud off his boots with a fragment of shell. It was a small piece he carried everywhere, ideal for the job. "A sorry kind of business, you say. Is that what you think, Sam?"

Sam sighed. He'd been thinking about Emily again. "Yeah, it seems so to me."

Jimmy nodded quietly in agreement. His sallow skin and the dark circles under his eyes belied his handsome features.

Boxer carried on scraping, not lifting his head. "You wish you weren't here then?"

Sam laughed as he exchanged a look with Jimmy. "Don't we all? But no, it's not that." He paused for a few moments as he tried to put his thoughts into words. "I know we're serving our country, and it's right that we're out here. To be honest, I'm proud to be a part of it – wouldn't want anyone shoving a white feather in *my* lapel. But I was listening to some of the lads earlier, especially those with wives and little ones. It seems quite awful to think that the army has more claim on them than their own kith and kin." Sam thought of the men he'd helped to bury. Cold meat, names on telegrams. You had to look at it like that or you'd never be able to get on with the job. But to each man's family, that man was the only one in this whole war that mattered. Sam suddenly hoped he hadn't been insensitive to Jimmy. After all, should the worst happen to *him*, who would mourn him? He didn't even have anyone to send a telegram to.

Sam looked down at his hands. Even after four days on rest, they were calloused and ingrained with dirt. He scanned the field. Somewhere in the distance a sergeant was bellowing orders to his men. He shrugged. "I suppose it hit me just how much our lives are not our own anymore."

Boxer nodded thoughtfully. "You're right, Sam. It is a sorry business." He straightened up and put the shell fragment back in his haversack. "But can I tell you both what I think is even worse?"

There was something about his tone which made Sam look up. Jimmy fixed his dark eyes on Boxer. Boxer was gazing into the sky, a strange, inscrutable expression on his face.

"For me, the sorriest part about it all is that a man die without ever having discovered why he was born in the first place. That he spend his whole life chasing the wind, and never understand why he was put here. That's the real tragedy."

Sam stared at him. What on earth did he mean by that? He and Jimmy exchanged glances again, but neither of them spoke. For a few moments Boxer continued looking into the sky. Then he dropped his head and smiled broadly at them both.

"I'm confident, though, that this will not be the case with you two."

Puzzled, Sam felt a sudden urge to question his friend further. At that moment, however, a familiar voice broke into his thoughts ...

Before I got chance to say another word, Em, our platoon sergeant called us up for kit inspection. We're moving on in the morning; who knows what's waiting for us? It's night-time now, and I'm just lying here thinking about what Boxer said. There's a lot more time to think when you're on rest. I suppose that's why they try to keep us busy. I don't know how Jimmy feels about it, but the whole thing bothers me. Have I discovered why I was born, or am I just chasing the wind, whatever that means? I'd never even thought about it until now. What's worse, we're going back to the line tomorrow. Suddenly, Em, I really don't want to go.

Station Redoubt August 27th 1916

I am sickened today. Three of our lads were gassed earlier. One, Tommy Shipham, died almost straightaway. Poor fellow couldn't breathe at all. He had a weak chest to start with – I don't know how he ever ended up out here. He went fairly quickly. I think his lungs just disintegrated, but it must have been a horrible way to go. The other two – Ernie Tennant and Tim Pocklington (Pocket to us) – were fairly gasping for breath and clawing at their throats and eyes ...

This was their third day in the Armentieres sector and, all in all, things had been pretty hot. So far, however, Sam's platoon had got off fairly lightly; a couple of gashes, quickly patched up at the aid post, and other than that, not much to write home about. It was nearly three o'clock in the afternoon and 'B' Company was enjoying a lull in the firing.

"Get any post, Pocket?" Twinny One's voice sounded down the trench.

Tim Pocklington grinned as he made a fist at him. "You know I didn't."

"D'you reckon she's forgotten it's yer birthday?" Twinny One wasn't about to stop ribbing him. "I thought you two were devoted to each other."

There were hoots of laughter from some of the others. Tim shook his head in mock disgust. "In case you hadn't noticed, idiot, there's a war on. The post isn't quite so reliable as it used to be."

"Excuses, excuses," Twinny One guffawed. "I bet she's run off with the postman –"

Tim was about to make some caustic reply when the platoon sergeant appeared on the scene. "Come on, lads. I need a couple of volunteers to bring some supplies up from reserve. You Shipham, Pocklington – come with me." That was the neat thing about volunteering in the army. You didn't get a say in it. As if having second thoughts, the sergeant turned round again. "And you can come as well, Tennant. The more the merrier, eh?" He signalled to an older man who was leaning against the back wall of the trench. The four of them set off, turned into the next bay and disappeared from view.

"Wish I'd gone with 'em," Twinny One remarked gloomily. "I hate sitting around waiting for the Bosch to kick off."

For a good forty minutes things were quiet, only the sound of birdsong and the occasional shot breaking the monotony. Men talked or played cards. It looked like it was going to be a long afternoon.

A sudden, distant shout jolted the stillness. "They've sent one over – it's coming this way, boys!" The sound of cursing. A moment's confusion as raised voices resounded down the trench. Then the noise everyone dreaded. The gas rattle. There was a furious scramble as men pulled on respirators, their trembling fingers working as quickly as nerves would allow. In the split second before he managed to cover his face, Sam almost thought he glimpsed the noxious yellow cloud drifting towards them on its venomous breeze. Then the sky turned misty green, and all the world seemed suddenly a strange and surreal place. He inhaled, his heart pounding madly as he did so. Everyone knew what gas did to you. *Please let this thing be working …*

Difficult to breathe through and uncomfortable though it was, Sam knew immediately that the respirator was intact. He looked round to see Jimmy securing his mask. Good, he'd managed okay too. Now it was just a matter of waiting for orders. Either the Germans would attempt a trench raid, or they'd released the gas cylinder just to remind the Tommies that they were still there. A rather unpleasant way of relieving their afternoon boredom.

A muffled order came down the line; help was needed further up. Sam felt a prod from behind. It was Boxer. Kitted up in respirator, it was impossible for him to speak, but Boxer pointed along the line towards a section where the wind had carried the gas to its thickest concentration. Sam nodded. Within no time at all, a small group of men was wending its way clumsily through the front line trench. When they arrived at the worst affected area, they could see that the trench was in chaos. Most men had managed to pull on protective masks, one or two had even urinated on rags and were holding them to their faces, but others were in the throes of agony. Sam saw to his horror that Tommy Shipham, Ernie Tennant, and Tim Pocklington were among the victims. Tommy Shipham was lying in the bottom of the trench, his streaming eyes livid with terror, his body jerking with pain. "*Help me – Sam – help …*" he gurgled, his lungs seeming to corrode with every breath. Sam felt sickeningly helpless as he looked down. A yellow liquid was beginning to ooze from Tommy's mouth, and his hands were clenched into desperate, trembling fists. Sam knew he'd had it. Kneeling down by the injured soldier, he placed his hand on the writhing chest, trying hard not to recoil at the sight of the tortured convulsions. It was almost a relief when, after a few minutes, Tommy's body gave a final spasm and Sam realised it was all over.

"*Biddy! Biddy!*" Sam heard a mournful cry and then a violent fit of coughing. He spun round to see Tim Pocklington rubbing desperately at his eyes. "I'm blinded – God help me – I'm blinded – *Biddy!*"

Everyone in the platoon knew that Biddy was Pocket's beloved sweetheart. Boxer put an arm around the injured man's shoulder and began to guide him up the trench. A steady stream of walking wounded and goggled helpers was now making its way towards the aid post. Sam and Jimmy took hold of Ernie and began to help him along too. Coughing and choking, the distressed man pressed repeatedly at his eyes, as though by doing so he might make himself see again. He became more and more heavy as the three of them proceeded awkwardly through the trench. Sam was afraid the older man might collapse. He felt sadder than he could ever remember ...

It was a terrible thing to watch, Em. Somehow, I'm struggling to understand how human beings can come up with such devilish inventions. There is nothing glorious about being gassed, and there's nothing heroic about gassing somebody. It seems to me a poor way of fighting a war. Nothing can prepare you for this, Emily. To see one's fellow men suffer as terribly as we did today and be so helpless in the face of it – that can turn a soul to despair.

Beth put the letter down and lay back against the pillow. Well, this wasn't exactly bedtime reading, was it? She closed her eyes. The idea of being gassed made her feel claustrophobic. She could remember once being held under the water by a vindictive schoolmate during a class swimming lesson. She'd honestly thought she was going to die. Her lungs had burned for air and she'd very nearly given in and inhaled. How long she'd been under, she had no idea. Probably not very long at all. But it had been long enough. Time had seemed to stand still. She was sure it was the closest to death she'd ever come. Perhaps that was how it felt to be gassed. Gasping for air that wasn't there. Panicking as your whole life flashed before you like some jerky home video. The thought made her shudder. It was like something out of a horror movie. No wonder Boxer philosophised like he did. These guys must have walked through hell every day. It was a wonder any of them managed to stay sane.

A sudden noise made her open her eyes. Dr Stafford had walked onto the ward and was coming towards her bed. "Hello, Beth. All alone?"

Quickly trying to recover herself, Beth sat up. "Yeah, for now at least. They're all in the TV room."

Dr Stafford smiled gently and sat down on the chair beside her. "I'm going off duty in quarter of an hour, Beth, but I just wanted to let you know that we're hoping to get some results through in a couple of days."

Beth nodded. "Glad to hear it. Any idea what we're expecting?"

Dr Stafford sat forward, his voice soft and low. "Well, Beth, there are one or two possibilities. That's what I wanted to talk to you about."

Dan took a long, slow drink from his bottle of mineral water. "Ah, that's good. Just what I need after a pasting like that." He had just completed a gruelling gym session with Gavin, and now the two of them were chilling out in the upstairs café.

"Good workout tonight." Gavin pulled off his sweatbands and tossed them into his bag. Dan noticed the expression of satisfaction on his face. He'd seen it all evening.

"You're looking pleased with yourself."

"Am I?" Gavin seemed momentarily taken aback. "What makes you say that?"

"I dunno." Dan eyed him curiously. "But you've got that look that says *I know something that you don't.*"

For a few moments Gavin was thoughtful. Then he grinned. "Okay, Danny boy. You've got me sussed." He tapped his nose conspiratorially. "I popped the question the other day."

Dan's face furrowed into a frown. "You did *what?*"

"I popped the question. I asked Rosie if she'd like to go away with me for Christmas."

Dan looked slightly confused. "*That* was the question?"

"Yeah." Gavin was still grinning. "I'm still waiting for her to get back to me on it."

Dan shook his head with a wry smile. "You had me going there, mate. Thought you'd gone and got yourself hitched."

"What kinda guy do you take me for?" Gavin laughed. "No – it's just that Rosie hasn't got much in the way of family by the sounds of things. Thought I might sweep her off her feet. Give her a Christmas to remember."

"You don't waste time, Gav, I'll give you that."

Gavin smiled quizzically. "How d'you mean?"

"Y'know, getting all cosy with Rosie. You've only known her – what is it – a month? Do I take it you're over Kate then?"

Gavin lowered his eyes. Dan immediately felt bad. "Sorry, mate. That came out all wrong ..."

"It's okay." Gavin wasn't smiling any more. He took a slow, deliberate swig of water and sighed heavily. "You know, Dan, you don't get over a girl like Kate in a hurry. I'm still finding it hard to believe we're through." He ran his hand slowly across the surface of the table. "I found out she was back in town last week so I asked if we could meet up for old times' sake. Saw her twice. I guess I'm still hoping there might be a chance."

"So what's with Rosie?" Dan spoke quietly. "How serious is *that?*"

Gavin's face lightened. "She's a great girl. Not the type I'd normally go for – but quite a looker. And a bit fiery. I like that in a woman." He shrugged his shoulders. "I can't sit around waiting to see if Kate will change her mind, can I? I have to get on with life. And Rosie suits me fine at the moment."

Dan exhaled slowly. "Gav ... don't hurt her, will you?"

"Hurt her? I don't follow."

"She's Mel's friend, remember." Dan's face was serious. "And you seem to be moving in pretty fast to say you're still carrying something for Kate. I'd hate to see Rosie get hurt."

Gavin shook his head. "You don't have to worry about Rosie, mate. She's a tough nut that one. That's one girl that can give as good as she gets." He took another swig of water and grinned. "It's me you should be worrying about, if anybody."

It had been a long day for Dr Michael Romily. He felt tense as he stretched out on the soft leather sofa of his spacious walk-through lounge. Reaching for the remote, he flicked on a CD. A track from Vivaldi's *'Four Seasons'* immediately filled the room with measured baroque poise. He loosened his tie and rubbed his neck slowly as the music melted over him. *Ah, if only all of life could be so impeccably scored.*

Sarah came into the room and sat on the arm of the settee. Michael's wife of twenty-seven years, she understood his silences just as well as his conversation.

"Tiring day, darling?" She stroked his hair gently. Michael looked up at her and reached for her hand. Words weren't necessary right now. They could talk later, when he'd relaxed a bit.

"Dinner will be ready in ten minutes." Sarah stood to her feet. He kissed her hand and she swept with quiet elegance into the kitchen. Michael closed his eyes and tried to lose himself in the music. How appropriate; the track playing was '*Winter*'. Michael recalled the squally, wet evening that had met him as he'd stepped out into the hospital car park just over an hour ago. November already. Time seemed to have flown this year, and what a year it had been ...

He remonstrated with himself. He mustn't start thinking about work. He must relax and let his mind clear. Focusing on the music, he began to hum along. Vivaldi was good for the sanity, Michael reasoned; there was something vital and enduring about his work. His eyes were drawn to the new Heather Emmerson painting hanging on the far wall by the bookcase. They'd spotted it at an exhibition for up and coming young artists at the beginning of October. Michael had loved it on sight. A delicate seashore watercolour, it was simple, yet powerfully evocative. A painting he could lose himself in. At the time, Sarah had not seemed to share his enthusiasm. A couple of weeks later, the reason had emerged. Recognising the opportunity to surprise him with a perfect gift, she had kept her own delight in check and feigned indifference. A fortnight after the exhibition, on the occasion of their twenty-seventh wedding anniversary, Sarah had presented him with a beautiful hand decorated cake – and the painting. Michael smiled as he remembered. Sarah understood him so well. She shared his love of music, she understood his love of art. In fact, during the course of their years together, they had grown to appreciate much of life as an art form – sometimes beautiful and gracious, sometimes garish and shocking. But art nevertheless; a constantly evolving, widening, mutating creative entity that swept every soul alive along with it. Michael hadn't worked out the philosophical premise behind it, but he managed to see art in most things these days. Even in his own job. Maybe it kept him from going crazy. Maybe Leonardo da Vinci had had the same approach, cutting up cadavers for the sheer thrill of seeing how everything was put together. Michael looked across at the Emmerson painting again, and then down at his own strong, slender hands. Art was sometimes little more than a gentle means of escape. But in some cases, one man's art might be another man's salvation.

Chapter 8

It was a couple of days later and Rosie had invited Ciaran round for supper. He'd been to visit Beth and now, at quarter to nine, they were tucking into lasagne and focaccia.

"This is good, Ros." He was eating as though he hadn't seen food for a week. "We'll get ya married off yet. Anyone who makes a mean lasagne like this deserves to be wed, I reckon."

"Oh, ha ha." Rosie gave him a withering look, but the grin he tried to return somehow made her feel sad. There was a strange vulnerability about him these days. He seemed incomplete without Beth. She hit him playfully. "Be quiet or I'll tell you what I put in it."

Ciaran tore off a piece of bread. It was a slow, preoccupied gesture, and the sudden pensive look that passed across his face didn't go unnoticed by Rosie. "Well, Ros – we should get somewhere tomorrow. Dr Stafford wants to see Beth about the test results." He looked down at the table and started to doodle with the end of his fork. "It's a week since they put that camera thing down. I can't understand why everything takes so long."

"Suppose they have to be absolutely sure they know what they're dealing with," Rosie offered. "She certainly looks a lot better than she did a fortnight ago. They must have been doing something right. Are we still assuming it's an ulcer?"

Ciaran shrugged. "Well, that's what *I'm* thinking. Seems to match up as far as I can see – that or some kind of inflammation. Beth hasn't talked about it much this last couple o' days. She's probably fed up of waiting and guesswork. Anyway, tomorrow we'll know where we are and they should be able to start her on some proper treatment. I'm going in about two thirty. She wanted me to be there."

Rosie dug out a comedy DVD and they watched it for an hour or so. Ciaran seemed vaguely entertained but Rosie could tell his mind was elsewhere. At last, he looked at his watch and stood up. "I'd best be going, Ros, or neither of us'll get up in the morning. Thanks for supper."

Rosie gave him a brief hug. "You're welcome. By the way, I won't be able to get in to see Beth tomorrow. We've got a parents' open evening and I'm working straight through. Give me a ring when you get home – let me know how things went."

"Yeah, I will." Ciaran gave her a kiss on the cheek and, with a wave, disappeared into the night.

Alec Stafford looked at his watch. Two twenty-seven. They'd be here at any time. He went over to the window and closed it against the draught. Seconds later, there was a knock on his door.

"Beth Maconochie to see you, Doctor."

Alec smiled and welcomed Beth and Ciaran into his office. "Please, have a seat." He gestured warmly and watched as the young couple sat down. The husband looked expectant, the young woman, quietly prepared. Inwardly Alec sighed. Time for his professional head.

"Well, Beth – we have the results back from your tests so I'm going to talk you through them." He cleared his throat and straightened the pile of papers on his desk. He knew he was stalling. Some parts of the job never grew any easier.

"Right. Well, the barium meal that you were given last Monday indicated some blockage in the upper gastro-intestinal tract. Obviously this made it necessary to investigate further, which is why we did the gastroscopy on the Wednesday."

He swallowed hard. This was always the bit he hated.

"When you were first admitted and I palpated your abdomen, Beth, I suspected a mass. The endoscopic examination confirmed a growth in the stomach. As you know, we took a tissue sample and … ." He paused. "I'm sorry to say the news is not as we'd hoped, Beth. I'm afraid the biopsy shows that you have cancer."

There was a slight gasp, and then, silence. For several moments no one made a sound, then Ciaran's voice came out in a low, stuttering whisper. "No. No, it *can't* be –"

He glanced across at Beth as though somehow, one word from her would alter everything. Beth was staring straight ahead, her features impassive, her expression inscrutable. Ciaran turned to Dr Stafford. "Couldn't there be some mistake? I mean, she's only just been taken ill."

Alec Stafford shook his head. "Very often with stomach cancer there are no visible symptoms until the disease has been present for some time." He spoke gently, a wash of sympathy flowing over him for the young man who sat now with a look of pained incredulity on his face. He turned to Beth. Her face was giving nothing away as she stared towards the window. Alec knew he needed to take this carefully. "I'm sorry, Beth. It's always a shock." He paused. Beth's blue eyes seemed to him like the ocean before a storm. Still, unknown deeps, hiding a maelstrom of thoughts and questions he could only guess at. He'd seen this before. He leaned forward, elbows on the desk, both hands supporting his chin. "Is there anything you'd like to ask me? Anything at all? Take your time."

For a while, there was not even a flicker of response. At last, Beth lowered her gaze to meet his. "Am I going to die, Dr Stafford?"

It was a clinical question. Simple and straight and devoid of emotion. Out of the corner of his eye, Alec saw the young husband drop his head. He straightened in his chair.

"I don't want you to look at cancer as a death sentence, Beth. Many, many people recover and go on to lead full lives – many say fuller for having gone through the experience. Hard to believe, I know, when you've just received news like this. But it's worth holding on to." He paused for a moment. The histology report had not been encouraging. They were dealing with a high-grade and the thing hadn't even been staged yet. It was impossible to give an accurate prognosis, but Alec had been in this business long enough to know they needed to get things moving. "The biopsy suggests that the tumour is quite aggressive, Beth. We really need to find out if it has spread from the primary site before we can offer you treatment options. I'm referring you on to our Senior Oncologist, Michael Romily. I've spoken to him already and he's happy to meet with you tomorrow if you would like to do that."

Beth glanced at Ciaran. He gave a slight, anxious nod as a man grasping for a lifeline. She smiled weakly. "Yes. Yes, I *would* like that."

Alec was pleased. "I sense you're a strong lady, Beth. And that's good. That's half of it. We must try to look at this as a skirmish along the way – by no means the end of the story."

Attempting to impart hope to someone who'd just received such a body blow was not the easiest thing in the world, thought Alec as he measured his voice and carefully chose his words. But it was part of the job and a part he took very seriously. He looked at her warmly. "Michael really is an expert in this area of medicine. One of the best in the country. If I were in your position, I'd ask for him personally."

But you're not me, are you? Beth tried to look grateful. *You're you and I'm me. And apparently, I'm the one with cancer.*

In the time that followed, Ciaran put forward several questions and Alec did his best to answer them. Beth said little. Only the preoccupied expression in her eyes gave any indication as to what she might be thinking. When eventually the interview came to an end, Alec Stafford shook hands with the young couple. It was time to pass the patient on and he was almost sorry. They thanked him for all his care over the past fortnight, and he wished them all the best for the future. Ciaran paused in the doorway. "You must find your job real hard at times."

Alec frowned slightly. "Yes. Yes, it can be."

Ciaran hesitated for a moment. "You just gave me the worst news of my life. But I doubt it could have been done better ... thank you." His voice trailed off and with a brief smile, he took the handles of Beth's wheelchair and set off down the corridor. Alec Stafford shook his head sadly as he closed the door of his office. Sometimes his job felt like the hardest in the world.

There was a knock at the front door. It was a rapid, agitated knock which made Rosie jump. "Okay, okay, I'm coming," she muttered under her breath as she went to answer it. Mel had probably forgotten her key. It was Ciaran.

"Hey – come in, Kitch. I wasn't expecting you to call. I thought you were going to ring later."

He followed her into the kitchen.

"Have you eaten?" Rosie made them both coffee and started to rummage in one of the cupboards.

Ciaran shook his head. "I'm okay, Ros. I'm not bothered about anything." He ran his hand distractedly through his hair. "Could we talk in your room?"

Something in his tone unnerved Rosie. "Sure. Course we can."

They went into her room and she closed the door. Ciaran flung himself into the armchair and sat, head thrown back, staring upwards at the ceiling. Rosie said nothing. Suddenly she felt scared. Outside in the night, the muffled sound of an emergency siren echoed in a distant street. At last, Ciaran leaned forward and picked up his coffee.

"It's cancer," he said simply.

Rosie bit her lip. A tingle of horror crawled through her being as the word injected itself clinically into her mind. Images of Beth began to loom in her head. A chaotic jumble like a speeded-up video. *Ward 7a – Mama's staffroom – Nelson's Column – the concert …*

A splash of scalding coffee stung her fingers, bringing her back to reality. She put the mug on the table and tried to get her thoughts together. "Where? Where *is* it? I mean, how *bad?*" It was all coming out wrong. But then, how could anything sound right?

"Stomach." Ciaran's voice was flat. "They dunno if it's spread anywhere else yet. She has to see the specialist tomorrow. More tests by the sounds of it. They'll go from there."

"How's she taken it?" Rosie tried to imagine Beth. Bright, fun-loving Beth. Irrepressible, inquisitive Beth. If anyone could beat this thing, it was her.

Ciaran shuffled in his seat. "Y'know, it's funny, Ros." He paused, a frown shadowing his face. "She didn't seem exactly surprised. It was like she already knew. She was real quiet for the first couple of hours, like she was trying to get her head round it. But she didn't get upset or anything. It unnerved me a bit. I kept expecting her to cry or –" He swallowed hard. "But there was nothing like that. By the time I left she was talking positive. Said it was like her setting out to master the *'Rach 3'* on piano. Not something she'd ever thought of trying before, but she'd sure give it her best shot. I think she was doing it for me as much as anything. She must have known how sick I felt."

They fell into silence again. It was a heavy, hopeless silence that Rosie felt desperate to break, but wasn't sure how to. In the end it was Ciaran who spoke. "I feel responsible. I knew something wasn't right, Ros. We had a do about it a few weeks ago, but she threw me off scent. Said she'd been working too hard." He shook his head and swore. "If only I'd made her get checked out then." He sat back in the chair and stared up at the ceiling again.

"You can't blame yourself, Kitch. If it's any consolation, I never noticed anything. I thought she might be a bit run down, but nothing like this ever entered my head. How were any of us to know any different?" Rosie tried to sound sincere, but inwardly she was mad at herself for not having spotted any of the signs.

Ciaran sighed heavily. "You can tell now though, can't you? She looks pitiful, poor little thing." He swore again. There was heartbroken anger in his voice and Rosie felt her own throat tightening. Outside, the familiar drone of night-time traffic hummed through the airwaves like some meditation soundtrack. Rosie stared at the window with its drawn back curtains. How dare the world just carry on as though nothing had happened? It was almost obscene.

"D'you know what gets to me most, Ros?" Ciaran looked at her bitterly. "Leaving her. That's what really gets to me. Leaving her there on her own. No one to talk to if she gets upset in the night. If it hits her – if it suddenly hits her – no one to comfort her. It cuts me up." His voice trailed away and he buried his face in his hands.

Rosie felt a sense of helplessness. "I'm sure they must be geared up for that kind of thing. Trained counsellors, special nurses ..."

Ciaran straightened. "Not in the middle o' the night. Besides, she hasn't been moved to the *cancer* section yet." He spat the word like a curse. "She's on the bog standard aches and pains ward. No special nothing there, Ros." The same anger. He buried his face again and Rosie went quiet. She walked over to the window and gently pulled the curtains shut. It was an act of respect. An attempt to hide the tears of a shattered man, to shut out the unseeing, uncaring world and tell it to mind its own lousy business. This was no time for onlookers.

It was some time before Ciaran sat up. He looked shaken and gave a slight, embarrassed laugh. "Sorry, Ros. Haven't felt like that since I came to London, when I left you behind."

Rosie frowned. "How d'you mean?"

Ciaran gazed down at the floor. "Y'know, when I left you there in Leicester. It nigh on killed me doing that. I very nearly came back."

Rosie stared at him. His eyes glistened moist and the dark lashes were still damp. It was the first time she'd seen her brother cry in a long, long while. "Why didn't you?"

Ciaran shook his head. "Your letters for one thing. Full o' London this and London that. You'd set your heart on it. I just wanted to make it all come true for you. You were only a kid."

Rosie bit the inside of her cheek. *How ironic.* Back then, she'd have been quite happy to move to a shed in the next village, let alone London. Anywhere to get away from home. But she hadn't wanted to mess things up for Ciaran, not after he got the scholarship for music college. And London had sounded an enticing place to escape to. Even if she had had to wait five years to join him.

Ciaran gave a wistful smile. "You were a sad little thing back then, Ros."

"Weren't *you?*" Rosie scowled as an unexpected surge of agitation swept over her. "I mean, come on. It was hell on earth living with those two sometimes."

"I guess I just channelled my energy into getting us out. Seeing if we could make something of our lives." Ciaran gazed into the middle distance as though he could see it all taking place again. "And we did it, Ros, didn't we? We got out in the end … even if I did cry myself to sleep over you for weeks."

Rosie was moved. "I never knew that."

He shrugged sadly. "I never told you."

Ward 7a was quiet, but then it *was* 1.30 in the morning. Beth couldn't sleep. She lay on her back, arms by her sides, sandwiched between the stiff, white sheets. Low voices from the nursing station drifted down the corridor. The occasional burst of light laughter. A buzzer sounded. Efficient footsteps off to investigate. At least she wasn't the only one awake. She breathed out slowly.

The thought came to her again. It had been hovering all night. She laid a trembling hand on her stomach. There was an alien inside her; something sinister, something that didn't belong. To think she'd imagined she was pregnant. For weeks she'd been trying to get used to the idea of having another human being living inside. But instead – *this*. This entity. Greedy, unwanted, feeding insolently off her. Trying to starve her. She shuddered. Under her hand, her abdomen felt hard. A wave of claustrophobia swept over her and, for a moment, a strange, desperate urge to disembowel herself with her own hands. How long had it been squatting there with its foul, mutant tentacles? How long had it been hiding?

You can try to run away but you can never get away from yourself. You're stuck inside, Beth, stuck inside … there's no escape …

Footsteps down the corridor broke the moment of terror. Beth moved her hand sharply. This thing was messing with her head. She tried to rationalise. After all, she'd been half expecting it, hadn't she? Alec Stafford had hinted at the possibility a couple of days ago. Not that she'd mentioned anything to Ciaran then. It was the first time she'd kept anything from him. Her mind flicked to the pregnancy test. Well, perhaps not *quite* the first time. A sudden sense of guilt gripped her. What had been happening? She'd never believed in having secrets from each other, yet there seemed to have been so many recently.

Dear, beautiful Ciaran. Her mind pictured the strong face, the dark, grave eyes, the unruly hair. And the tears. Not that he'd let them fall. But she'd seen them all the same that afternoon; somewhere behind the encouraging words and fighting talk, she'd seen them. Surely ignorance was bliss, even if it had only lasted a short while for him.

Dear God, please look after him. I love him so much, please don't let this hurt him.

It was a spontaneous moment. Her eyes filled up and she closed them, forcing the warm tears to spill down her cheeks and into her hair. She hadn't prayed in such a long time. For a few minutes she lay in the stillness. No thunderbolt of chastisement. No sense of divine indignation. Just a quietness at first, and after a few moments, a sweet, gentle peace which seemed to enfold her like warm liquid. The words of an old song came back to her, a song that she hadn't sung since her childhood.

What a friend we have in Jesus, all our sins and griefs to bear.
What a privilege to carry everything to God in prayer.
O what peace we often forfeit, o what needless pain we bear,
All because we do not carry everything to God in prayer.

Suddenly she was back in Saint Edwin's. Eight or nine years old, gripping her mother's hand and gazing round as the congregation sang the hymn with great conviction. The rousing swell of the music, the comforting smell of beeswax candles and polished wood, the motley family of unmatched, colourful characters all offering their worship, the solid sense of being part of a much bigger picture. It came back to her now as though it had happened only the Sunday before. She turned over onto her side, overcome by a sudden, bittersweet longing. What she would give to go back to those innocent, untroubled days. As if in response to her heart cry, a soft voice seemed to whisper,

You are still my little one. And I've been waiting for you ... .

Michael Romily was restless. He'd made the stupid mistake of falling asleep on the sofa earlier in the evening, and now here he was in the small hours, wide awake and fidgety with not an ounce of slumber in him. He turned over to Sarah. Her breathing was almost silent, but the rhythmic rise and dip of her shoulder told Michael she was firmly in dreamland. Conceding defeat, he gently swivelled out of bed and padded downstairs. His eye caught the accusing face of the mahogany grandfather clock in the hall. *Two fifteen.* He wasn't going to let it get to him. That was the worst thing one could do. Making himself some hot milk, he went into the lounge. He realised something was niggling his mind. At first it was a vague, grey disorderliness, the sort of cloudy-headed feeling one might expect after the kind of stressful day he'd been through. But as he pondered on what the problem might be, it narrowed into a specific; something he'd meant to check out, a question he'd meant to answer ...

Of course. It came to him in a moment. He went over to a cabinet by the Hi-Fi system and clicked open the door. His fingers leafed systematically through a wedge of glossy publications: *Country Living, House and Garden, The Lady.* He frowned to himself. Surely it was still here; Sarah couldn't have thrown it away. His confidence in her was suddenly rewarded as his hand fell upon an item sandwiched between the rest. A magazine they'd only just started taking – *The Maestro.* He quickly flicked through the pages. Yes, here it was. He skimmed the words and smiled wryly. Well, this guy had certainly rated her.

'A tiny figure with an almost luminescent fragility, whose slender arms and small white hands moved with such lyrical intuitiveness, she succeeded in producing a performance of quite ferocious tenderness ...'

He skimmed again. *Blah blah blah –*

'For my money, only one question remains. What next from the angelic Beth Maconochie?'

Michael sat back in his chair. The spelling was certainly the same. He remembered the girl from the concert. *Could it possibly be?* London was a big place – there could be dozens of Beth Maconochies out there. Still, it wasn't a common name. He breathed out slowly, thoughtfully. Well, he'd know soon enough. She was on his clinic list for tomorrow. A humorous image forced its way into his mind. *If she turns out to be six foot four with the body of a beached whale, I'll know alright. Absolutely no connection whatsoever.*

Of course it *was* her. The moment she walked in and he shook one of the *'small white hands'*, he knew it. She looked even more slight now than he remembered, and to his trained eye, the drawn anaemic face was a sure giveaway. The decline had been rapid.

"Mrs Beth Maconochie, I believe you're a musician."

Her eyes lit up. "Yes, yes I am! And my husband too."

Michael shook hands with Ciaran and gestured them both to sit down. He felt almost pleased with himself. This was proving to be an excellent icebreaker.

"I saw you perform at the Laureate Hall a few weeks ago. Most, most impressive. I bought tickets as an anniversary treat for my wife, and I must say, we were not disappointed. Absolutely marvellous."

Beth's pale face suddenly glowed. In a few well-chosen words, Michael Romily had given her a point of reference. A reminder of who she was. Somewhere outside the crazy chain of events that was overtaking her, there was normal life and music and dreams. Whatever happened, she had to hold onto that.

Later that afternoon, Michael Romily managed to find a quiet space just long enough to have a cup of coffee. It had been a tiring day and it wasn't over yet.

He thought about Danny Rossington, the nine-year-old boy he'd bumped into earlier on the ward. Michael had been treating Danny's father for the last five months. The prognosis was not good. He doubted Ben Rossington would last much beyond February. One of the nurses had been chatting with Danny's mother. "And what will you be wanting for Christmas?" she'd asked the young boy, just to bring him into the conversation. Danny had replied in a quiet, hopeful voice. "My dad. I want my dad back home – better." That had shut the nurse up, Michael recalled; and it had left *him* standing there like some impotent Santa Clause, frustrated that he couldn't grant the boy's wish. Cancer had been his life's work for the last twenty-two years. He both hated it and respected it. In his war against the disease, Ben Rossington was one battle he looked like losing. And Michael hated losing.

He allowed his mind to flag up his schedule for the next few days. Tomorrow Angus Baldwin was coming in for review. Mattie Lennon was due to be discharged; that was always a pleasant task. Various other names swirled round his head. Courageous people he'd come to think a great deal of. It had been a heavy few weeks; some cases were tough going. That was the thing with cancer, he reflected. No matter how many victories he managed to win, there was always another battle to be fought, another trusting hopeful looking to him to deliver them from the enemy's clutches. Not until this formidable foe had been wiped off the face of the planet could people like him claim total triumph. Something told him his job was secure for a good while yet.

He found himself thinking about his new patient. Such a gifted young woman. But then in this game, what did that matter? Talent, money, education, pedigree – all the things that society coveted were paper swords in the face of this opponent. Cancer was no respecter of persons. In Beth Maconochie's case, even the statistics went against her. Twenty-four years old with stomach cancer – that certainly wasn't the norm. His own daughter Carmen was the same age. A Cambridge graduate with a brilliant scientific mind, she was also beautiful. Beautiful, tanned and healthy, nothing like the pallid girl he'd spoken with earlier.

He filed some notes into a cabinet. *Let's hope there's no extensive metastasis.* He shut the drawer with a clunk. *Local invasion at the very worst.*

It was the first time Rosie had seen Beth since the diagnosis. They sat in the hospital restaurant as they had just over a week ago, but this time Rosie felt strangely awkward. They'd already exchanged superficial pleasantries on the ward, but now there was a strained quiet between them. It was Beth who spoke first.

"It's okay, Ros. I'm not going to dissolve into tears or anything freaky."

Rosie shuffled uncomfortably. "Sorry. It's just ..." She paused, unsure what to say next. "How *are* you – in yourself, I mean?"

Beth gazed out of the window, a troubled half-smile on her face. "To be honest, Ros, I feel a bit of a schizo at the moment. I mean, in a weird way it's almost a relief. I've felt off it for ages, but you just ignore it, don't you? Pretend it's not there, hope it'll go away." She toyed with the idea of admitting that she'd bought a pregnancy test, but decided against it. It hardly mattered now. "Three weeks ago I guess it all came to a head."

"Three weeks ago? Why, what happened?" Rosie frowned.

"I had a real bad do at home. Felt like someone was strangulating my insides. Suppose that's the first time I got really scared. Things went pretty pear-shaped after that. Four days later I ended up in here. Still, as I said, at least now I know what we're dealing with. In some crazy way, it's a relief to have it out in the open." She gave a small, ironic laugh and stared down at her hands. They looked sinewy and fragile, and seemed ill-fitting on one so young. She exhaled slowly. "From time to time I'll get these strange surges of mad elation, like my adrenaline's psyching up for a fight. And then at other times, it all seems unreal, like I'm in some film or stupid hospital soap. Then I think I can make anything happen. Y'know, change the script, walk off set, and everything'll be back to normal. But then it hits me. In no time at all I'm as low as I think it's possible to get. It's all so scary.

Overwhelming. I feel just too small. I think, *Why me?* Then I think, *Why not?* All my fight goes out the window and it feels like everything's over for me." She shook her head and laughed weakly again. "No kidding, Ros, it's exhausting. I can move through all these moods within an hour. It's like having some kind of weird multiple personality disorder."

They sat in silence for several moments. Rosie could certainly identify with one thing. It did all feel unreal. Okay, so Beth did look very thin and not particularly well. But that could be put down to anything, surely. A tummy bug or a bad dose of flu. Not cancer. That seemed almost unthinkable.

"So what happens next?"

Beth sighed and rolled her eyes. "Well, I'll be moving to B1 – that's the cancer wing. I think they're sending me up there in a couple of days if they can find a bed. This week they'll be doing more tests. Ultrasound scan, blood monitoring, full body scan. It's almost certain they'll do surgery at some point, but not till they've got a better picture of how things are."

"D'you have any idea when you'll be home?" Rosie realised she was thinking about Ciaran. She could only guess how tough he was finding it.

"Apparently I'm not up to it yet. Besides, Dr Romily says things will move a lot faster while ever I'm in here. It would only be for a little break anyway, y'know, before they whip me back in for surgery. Whether they decide to schedule that before or after Christmas will depend on what they find in the test results. Everything's a bit up in the air really."

"Well, at least you've got their attention. I'm sure they'll do everything they possibly can to sort you out." Rosie tried to sound positive.

Beth grimaced. "I can think of better ways to get noticed."

Their conversation drifted onto other things. At first, Rosie had been nervous about making any comment that might remotely smack of humour. She knew it was out of some distorted sense of respect; it seemed almost irreverent to pepper her talk with the usual wisecracks, Beth being in this condition and everything. For that reason, she'd found herself saying little and listening far more than was usual for her. But Beth was not so easily dampened. In the middle of recounting a long, unsavoury bedpan tale, she suddenly began to snort with laughter, and Rosie realised to her relief that Beth's irrepressible spirit had not been broken yet. By the end of their time together, they were laughing as they always had. Rosie was pleased. A barrier had been broken down. *The Big C* had been dragged out into the open. The unmentionable had been mentioned. And they were still friends.

"My parents are travelling down in a couple of days." Beth's face seemed to light up at the thought of it. "It'll save on Mum's mobile bill at least. I've lost count of the times she's called me this past fortnight. It'll have cost her a fortune."

A cold, empty shadow shivered through Rosie's mind then. *I don't begrudge you that, Beth. But I'd be lying if I said I didn't envy you.*

Chapter 9

Beth glanced up at the ward clock. The familiar squeak of the meals trolley as it trundled back down the corridor signalled the end of yet another lunchtime. Hospital routine was so unvarying and predictable, she found herself forgetting what day it was sometimes. Not today though. Today was Tuesday, and Beth had made a request. Now she sat by her bed waiting expectantly. At about quarter past one, a young woman came onto the ward. She looked about sixteen or seventeen and was tall and heavily set. She had, Beth noticed, the body of a large woman, but the chubby face of an adolescent girl. Her mousy hair was taken up into a ponytail and she wore no makeup at all. It was clear that the young woman had made no attempt to pretty herself up in any way. Even her clothes were dowdy and practical.

"Beth Maconochie ...?" She plodded purposefully over to the bed.

Beth nodded, pleasantly surprised at the confident tone of her visitor.

"I'm Laura, your hospital volunteer. I've come to collect you."

They went out onto the corridor and towards the lifts.

"It's the chapel you want, isn't it?" Laura pressed the lift button with a pudgy finger. "We'll soon have you down there. It gets boring when you've been in here a bit, doesn't it?" She spoke with a command that seemed at odds with her played down appearance.

Beth began to warm to her. "How long have you been working here, Laura?"

The lift arrived then and Laura skilfully manoeuvred the wheelchair into position with well-practised ease. She pressed for the ground floor. "Since I did my GCSEs in the summer. I'm doing a course at college at the moment but I try to get in here for a few hours a week when I'm free." The doors opened and she spun Beth out onto the corridor.

"What are you hoping to do in the end?"

"I want to go into some kind of care work – probably with the elderly. Or I might even end up working here. Care work of some sort."

"I think you'd be very good at it," Beth said thoughtfully. "You certainly know how to handle this thing. I feel very safe with you. There's a lot to be said for that when you can't get about on your own so well."

"Thanks."

Beth smiled as she detected the first hint of bashfulness in Laura's voice. They had reached the chapel by now. Laura pushed open one of the semi-glazed outer doors. "Did you want me to stay with you or would you rather I came back in a while?"

Beth straightened. The thought of Laura *staying* had never occurred to her. She spoke gently, not wanting to appear ungrateful. "Would it be okay if you came back – say, in twenty minutes, half an hour?"

Laura grinned cheerfully. "No probs. I'll nip down to the coffee shop and get a drink. If you get into any difficulties there's a cord here at the back. Someone will be with you in no time."

The door gently swung shut and Beth found herself alone. She looked around. The inside of the chapel was lit from the ceiling by small, chrome downlights. They were dimmed to a mellow softness as warm as candle glow, yet over the simple beech altar shone a single spotlight which illuminated the front of the sanctuary as though it were a ray from heaven. On either side of the altar, tall, waxy-leaved plants climbed from raffia tubs, their shiny, dark foliage stunning against the pale wood of the table. But it was the area behind the altar that most caught Beth's attention. On the facing wall, looking out over the whole chapel, hung a richly coloured mural depicting the crucified Christ. Dressed in a simple robe, his crowned head fell forward so that his face could not be seen, but inscribed in a semicircular sweep above his bent neck were the words: –

I AM WITH YOU ALWAYS

Beth stared at the painting. It was at once both simple and profound. Simple and raw and honest, with a gentle, uncomplicated piety. Yet profound enough to satisfy the deepest, most searching question of a child.

I am with you always.

Did that mean he was still with *her?* She looked at the outstretched arms. Had it been *his* voice she had heard the other day?

You are still my little one. And I've been waiting for you.

She felt a stab of guilt. Was it right – decent even – to come looking for God when she'd spent the whole of her adult life ignoring his existence? Harsh, accusing thoughts began to prick her mind. Why should God take her back now? She'd shown she wasn't interested, hadn't she? She was only running to him because she needed something, because she was scared. A rat leaving a sinking ship.

Outside in the grounds, an ambulance siren began to wail. Its discordant cry seemed to fill the airwaves for a few moments, then it thinned to a sad plaint as it disappeared down the road.

Never send to know for whom the bell tolls ...

Beth clasped her stomach and rocked forward in her chair. *Oh God, I'm sorry. So, so sorry. I acted like you weren't there. You gave me so much and I acted like you weren't there –*

A great sob engulfed her then and she began to cry. She wept for herself, for her sick body and her confused, terrified mind; she wept for Ciaran and the sadness she saw in his eyes; she wept for the childhood she had lost and now longed for. And she wept for the God she had once known. As she hugged herself through the thin satin dressing gown, her fingers could trace the outline of every rib. Skin and bone. Only a month ago she'd been flying high, her dreams just beginning. Now she was reduced to this.

Could God ever take her back like this? It seemed a pathetic offering. Tears dripped onto the back of her sleeve as her heart gave way to raw grief. *Oh God, look at the state I'm in. I've got nothing to bring you.* Another broken sob. *I'm so scared – this thing is far too big for me. Please. Do you still have room for me?*

For a few moments she remained with her head bowed, staring at the carpet through her tears. Had he heard her? The place was heavy with stillness. She waited. The silence seemed to draw near to her. Nearer and nearer. Soft, almost tangible. And with it, memories of words from long ago, washing over her now like gentle waves on a sleepy shore.

Just as I am, without one plea
But that thy blood was shed for me
And that thou bidst me come to thee
Oh Lamb of God, I come,
I come.

From outside the chapel window came the faint sound of birdsong; the dreamy, desolate cry of a mistle thrush. Beth knew it immediately. As a girl she'd grown up with the sound. From one of the ancient trees in the garden at Oak Lodge had come the song of a mistle thrush ever since she could remember. Just before Christmas it would start. As the weather turned cold and the days shortened, its sound would ring out from the top of the oak. Singing all through the icy blasts and shivering gales of winter, welcoming in the soft, green warmth of spring, pouring out its song well into the hot and balmy days of summer. Every year, right up to her leaving home.

She lifted her head and looked at the painting again.

I AM WITH YOU ALWAYS

In that small moment, she suddenly saw it with different eyes. The roughness of the robe, the majesty of the crown. The surrender of the crucified king, the great humility of God. The Creator dying for his creation. Willing to take in the whosoever. She had known it all her life and yet she had forgotten. Now she was like one waking from a dream. As the mistle thrush sang outside the window, Beth let herself remember. And gradually, the storm which had been raging in her heart began to give way to a peace she hadn't felt since she was a little child.

Rosie kicked off her shoes and flopped onto the bed. She had a couple of free hours before Gavin was due to pick her up at eight. Flicking open her laptop, she found her page in the diary. As the computer was booting up she thought about Gavin. She'd seen him twice since he'd made his Christmas proposition, and thankfully he hadn't mentioned it either time. She hadn't seen him since Beth's diagnosis. He'd been away over the weekend again but had rung on the Sunday evening to arrange tonight's date. Rosie had broken the news to him.

"*Cancer?*" He had sounded genuinely shocked. "I'm real sorry to hear that, Rosie. That's awful news to get."

"Yeah. My brother's pretty devastated." Rosie hadn't been able to get Ciaran's distraught face out of her mind since Friday night. "But she'll come through, I'm sure she will."

Gavin had said some encouraging stuff then about one of his aunties – how she'd pulled through when she'd only been given a twenty per cent chance of survival. He had been sweet and Rosie had found herself warming to him again. Locked away somewhere in there was a nice guy. He just managed to hide it well at times.

Bailleul (Billets) September 4th 1916

A thousand apologies, Emily, for the miserable wretch I was last time. Poor girl, you've probably seen just as many gassed men as I have. Forgive me for my unhappy thoughts.

Well, we've moved down here and at the moment we are billeted in this lively little place and having a rather pleasant time of it. Jimmy has an admirer! We came across a small shop yesterday where he found a nice postcard to send to Mrs Egley, the baker's wife back home. The shopkeeper's daughter seemed quite taken with him. She was all shy smiles and coy looks. You could get a cup of tea in there, which we did, and it was the girl who served us. Boxer and I tried to be discreet of course while she attempted to strike up conversation with Jimmy. I didn't realise his French was coming on so well. There was no shutting him up once he got going! I don't think I've ever heard him speak so much in English, let alone French. Nothing can come of it of course – we'll be leaving here in a day or so. But it's done wonders for Jimmy's morale. He seems a different lad. She was only seventeen, but then, he's only nineteen. They would have made a handsome couple, but we cannot always choose our paths, can we? War can be cruel on the heart. I speak as one who knows.

Bailleul (Billets) September 8th 1916

Some of the boys were in a spot of bother this morning. Several of them were at an estaminet last night, and a couple of them came back dead drunk. The officers don't mind us having a drink, but these lads were rather beyond that. We're due to move on tomorrow and they look like it will take them a week to recover ...

The two lads were in a sorry state. They'd been given a very stout warning and there'd been talk of some kind of punishment. It seemed, however, that Captain Brierley was being lenient on account of their young age. Sam couldn't help feeling sorry for them. They claimed to be nineteen, but it clearly wasn't the case. They'd no doubt lied about their ages to join up. Some kids did that. Obviously thought the whole thing was some great big wheeze and only found out the truth when it was too late. That was the trouble. There was no going back once you were out here. The two boys were probably just finding that out. Perhaps drink was their way of making the best of a bad job.

Boxer seemed rather subdued about the whole business. Sam wondered if he disapproved of what had happened. After all, he *was* religious. Maybe he didn't like that kind of thing.

"You're quiet, mate." It was just after four in the afternoon and they were cleaning rifles.

Boxer forced a smile. "Sorry, Sam. Suppose I'm not much company today." He fell into silence again as he worked.

"Something up?" Sam pressed. It wasn't like Boxer to be so uncommunicative. He was usually such a sanguine and cheery type.

Boxer whistled a sigh. "I'm feeling very unsettled, pal. Can't stop thinking about those two boys. Y'know, Sam, the Bible talks about being overcome with drunkenness and the cares of this life, so that day comes upon you unexpectedly."

Sam frowned. "*What* day?"

Boxer looked straight at his friend. "If you knew you were going to die tomorrow, how would you spend tonight?"

Sam took a moment to consider the question. He was almost afraid his answer might disappoint Boxer. In truth, he'd never really thought about it, simply because since being out here, a steady stoicism had overtaken him. One got so used to the dead. It was strangely numbing. He shrugged his shoulders. "I dunno. I could *easily* die tomorrow. Any one of us could. But I can't see how that would affect how I spend tonight. What difference would it make?" He threw a glance over at Jimmy who was within earshot of the conversation, but Jimmy just lowered his eyes and continued working on his rifle.

Boxer smiled sadly. "The fool has said in his heart that there is no God. That's what the good book tells us. Y'know, Sam, if there's no God, it really doesn't matter how you spend tonight." He hesitated for a moment. "But if there *is* a God, wouldn't it make sense to try and get to know him before you have to stand before him?"

Sam said nothing. *Was* there a God? He had no idea. Did that make him a fool? Well, from what Boxer had said, perhaps it did. Half a fool at least. He wasn't offended at his friend's bluntness, but somehow Boxer's words made him uneasy. Life had never before demanded that he examine such eternal issues. Yet suddenly it seemed the issues were examining him.

"I tried talking to the lads for a few minutes this morning," Boxer said quietly, "but they were upset and feeling too rotten to pay much attention. I'll bet they'd never touched drink till they got out here, poor bairns."

Sam felt depressed. They were all going back to the line in a couple of days. It was anybody's guess as to who would make it through the next few weeks ...

Oh, Em. Suppose Boxer's right with all his funny ideas? Where does that leave me? All I know is that I saw no trace of judgement in his face when he talked about the two drunken boys. He just seemed immensely sad for them, and I am left chewing on the thought that we're all being led like lambs to the slaughter and any day could be our last.

Contalmaison (Support Trenches) September 22nd 1916

Dearest Em. It has been almost impossible to grab a moment to write these last two weeks. We've been in various spots, all of them lively, and I don't think I've ever felt so dead tired in my entire life. This whole area is in ruins now; roads torn up, buildings pulverised by shellfire, a choky sense of desolation about the place. One wonders if the French will ever forgive us.

We were badly shelled near Martinpuich the other day. Sad to say we lost a handful of men, including one of the young lads who got drunk. His mate, Wilf, was quite beside himself ...

It was late morning but the sky was dark with the weight of smoke hanging in the air. The enemy had kept up a continuous barrage since dawn 'stand to', and now nerves were getting frayed. Sam's company was two hundred yards behind the line, moving through a small wood which had been almost decimated by the firing.

"Hey, look at this –" The young subaltern went over to a splintered tree where two dead Germans were laid out, their bare feet pale and wet in the drizzle. "Somebody's gone off with their boots. I wouldn't mind some new ones myself. See who can bag me a pair in my size!" He flashed a cheery grin at the men behind him. They continued to make their way through the wood and it wasn't long before they stumbled upon an abandoned German pillbox.

"Check it out," came the order. "See if there's anything in there we can use."

It wasn't uncommon to come across weapons, ammunition, even bits of foodstuff in such places, but that usually depended on why the occupants had vacated the post in the first place. Two of the men went over to take a closer look.

"Dead Bosch in here, sir," one of them called out. "Nothing much else."

At that moment there was a deafening explosion. A long range shell had come over, landing some twenty yards from the back of the pillbox. The point of impact was a tall deciduous tree, one of the few still hitherto intact. It split with the blast, cracking with a noise like a thunderbolt. A volley of shrapnel ricocheted from the trunk and hissed through the air. Sam saw the subaltern go down, the top of his head sheared off by a slither of burning steel. He wouldn't be needing new boots now, Sam thought, sickened. Within seconds the air was filled with screams as men all around fell from hideous wounds. A second shell came over, landing slightly further away than the first. The scene was turmoil.

"Sam! Over here!"

Sam spun round in the direction of Boxer's voice. Boxer was trying to restrain one of the boys who'd got drunk a week previously. As Sam reached them, he could see that the boy's mate had taken a bad hit. Most of his insides were on the ground next to him.

"Come on, Wilf, he's gone, mate. You can't do anything for him now." Boxer was trying to shout above the noise of everything else that was going on. Wilf was wild-eyed, shaking the dead lad, bawling at him to get up. It was a pitiful sight. Sam closed the dead boy's eyes and joined Boxer in trying to pull Wilf off. But grief had made the boy mad and lent him an uncommon strength. Lieutenant Colton came over. He bellowed at the distraught boy, who was by this time almost hysterical. The shock of the lieutenant's voice seemed to bring Wilf to his senses, and as the officer yanked him to his feet, the lad began to sob like a baby.

"That's *enough!*" ordered the lieutenant. "It could be any of us next. This is war, lad. And war doesn't care who your best friend happens to be." His voice was firm, but Sam could tell that he was finding it hard to rebuke the boy. After a few minutes, satisfied that Wilf was sufficiently calmed, the lieutenant turned on his heel and left them. Sam and Boxer looked at each other, neither of them sure quite what to do next. Wilf was rocking on the ground now, oblivious to everything around him.

Jimmy came over and looked down at the dead boy. He shook his head sadly and gestured towards Wilf. "I pity the first German he comes across after this," he muttered in a low voice. "He'll be like a maniac."

A short while later Sam and Jimmy got the job of sorting out the burial. Boxer read from his Bible and spoke a few words. It was all quite moving. Certainly, reflected Sam, a better send-off than a lot of poor beggars got out here. Wilf was heartbroken, and Sam couldn't help noticing that Boxer seemed pretty cut up about the whole thing too. What was it the lieutenant had said? *This is war, lad ...*

Well, that was a few days ago, Em. It's afternoon now as I write, and for the moment quieter. The three of us (Boxer, Jimmy and I) have been watching the birds overhead. We're quite fascinated by them. It's hard to believe that they're here at all, what with all the noise and smoke and shrivelled trees. There they are, soaring free, high above no man's land. I can't help but envy them. Why do they stay around here, I wonder? There are surely more pleasant skies to roam. I remember at Bethune back in early summer, we even had a nightingale. Every night she would sing as though she were in the middle of some lovely scented garden. Harry and I nicknamed her Rosie (short for 'rossignol'). A small attempt to introduce some feminine grace into our rather ugly male surroundings.

For a moment Rosie was faintly amused. *Rosie short for rossignol* – that was a new one on her. Her mind went to Beth. How could she tackle stuff like this in her state? Surely it was enough to push her over the edge. She tried to imagine being in Beth's position. *If it was me, I'd be going down the pretend-it's-not-happening route. Celebrity gossip mags, brainless hair and fashion glossies … even sudoku if I got really desperate. Not this hardcore realism stuff. Anything but that.*

But then, she thought, wasn't that just the same as the two boys in Sam's diary? Pretend it's not happening. Try and blot it out with a few jars. One of them was dead within a fortnight.

If you knew you were going to die tomorrow, how would you spend tonight?

Rosie smiled gloomily to herself. Panic, big time. Surely that's what *anyone* would do – unless they were religious like Boxer. And Rosie wasn't religious.

The fool has said in his heart that there is no God. She had just typed the words and now they came back to her. *Guess that makes me a fool.*

But supposing, just supposing people like Boxer were right. Rosie's thoughts flicked back to the little church in Applemarket and the conversation she'd had there with Beth. Hadn't Beth said back then that she still believed in God, even though she'd admitted she'd gotten too busy for him? Had the cancer changed that? Had that flickering faith been snuffed out by the unfairness of everything that had come upon her? It wasn't something Rosie felt she could ask her. It was all too personal, too intimate.

But somehow, all of a sudden, it mattered.

A couple of hours later as they sat in De Souza's, Gavin seemed full of sympathy for Beth's plight. "What will happen now, Rosie? Will she need an operation?"

Rosie shrugged. "Dunno yet. They've started another whole load of tests on her to see if it's spread anywhere else. Apparently they can't really begin treatment until they find out what stage it's at – whatever that means."

Gavin nodded thoughtfully. "The waiting around must be terrible … when it's your own health that's at stake. How's she handling it all?"

"Very well, considering." Rosie had been impressed at Beth's resilience. "I've seen her a couple of times since she found out. All in all she seems quite strong. Her parents have travelled down today from Yorkshire."

Gavin straightened in his chair. "Oh? How long will they be staying?"

"I'm not sure," Rosie began. "I think they're leaving it flexible. Guess they could stay as long as she needs them to. Her mother doesn't go out to work, and since her dad retired, he's been a local artist. I suppose he can choose if and when he wants to paint. I don't get the impression they're too tied. Apart from sometimes looking after grandchildren that is."

Gavin looked decidedly interested in this disclosure. "They might stay down here for Christmas. After all, we're getting towards the end of November already. It's not long now. That would be nice for her. *And* your brother."

"I hadn't thought about it," said Rosie, suddenly quiet.

Gavin reached across the table and took her hands gently in his. Rosie felt limp. She almost knew what was coming.

"Have you thought about what I asked you, about coming away with me?"

His hazel eyes looked intently into hers. She wanted to look away; there was something so searching about him tonight. But she found she couldn't. As Mel had expressed only a few weeks ago in this very place, he really *was* the most beautiful guy she'd ever come across. It was easy to detach herself from that fact when Gavin was acting like an insensitive moron. But when he allowed his humanity to come through – when he was kind and thoughtful, and interested in the things that mattered to her – Rosie was undone. Any woman would be. Her thoughts raced. She'd be out of her mind to say no. How many girls would give their right arm for an offer like he'd made her?

Gavin pressed her fingers to his lips for a moment. "I *have* to go myself, Rosie; I've given the guy my word now." His voice was huskily soft. "But I really would like you to come with me. It would mean a lot ..."

Before she knew what was happening, Rosie found herself nodding. "Assuming everything's okay with Beth, I guess I'll have to say yes."

There. The words were out. Too late to go back now.

Gavin looked delighted. "Oh Rosie, that's fantastic. I'm sure we'll have a great time." His eyes were shining as he squeezed her hands. "Don't look so worried. I'll take care of you."

I'm sure you will, thought Rosie. *Maybe that's what I'm worried about.*

The fingers on the ward clock flicked to eleven thirty-five, but Beth was wide awake. This was to be her last night on Whitstable. Tomorrow she would move to B1 – the cancer wing. It was a scary thought. She'd seen her parents briefly that evening at visiting time. They'd arrived in London just before seven and headed straight for the hospital before going back to Streatham with Ciaran. It had been so good to see them. Her mother had filled up as soon as she'd set eyes on her.

"What's up?" Beth had done her best to joke. "Do I look that bad?"

Cassie had quickly wiped away the tears and taken her daughter in her arms. "No, darling. I'm just so happy to be down here. It's been awful not being able to see you."

Ed had been quiet. He had spent much of the time just looking at Beth, as though struggling to comprehend that his little girl could possibly be as ill as they'd been told.

Beth had squeezed his hand reassuringly. "Don't worry, Dad. I'll be okay. They're looking after me."

Ed had just smiled, a perplexed look in his eyes. It had made Beth feel sad.

Now as she lay in bed, her mind swirled with images and questions. She'd had an ultrasound the previous day, and a battery of blood tests. There was an additional scan they wanted to do, and some other, unpronounceable procedure. She'd been warned it would take a few days before any results were available. Her heart quickened as she thought about it. This all felt too unreal to be true. Yet she knew it was – and it was happening to her.

In the bed opposite, Velna was snoring. *She* could afford to sleep soundly, thought Beth flatly. She was due to go home within the next couple of days, all patched up, sorted, ready to get back into life. Not that Beth begrudged her that. Velna had been particularly sweet with her since the diagnosis. Quite motherly in fact.

"I'll come back and see you when I've got myself together," she'd promised brightly. "A few days at home and I should feel up to it."

Beth had smiled politely, but with a certain degree of scepticism. Velna couldn't wait to get out. It was hardly likely she'd be coming back to visit once she'd managed to escape. Still, Beth had appreciated the thought.

She sighed and turned over. *Oh God, I'm scared. What are they going to do to me? What are they going to find? Why is it me, God? Why?*

Chapter 10

Michael Romily took a long, slow mouthful of coffee and looked down at his desk again. The results were worse than even he had feared. Inoperable high-grade adenocarcinoma, extensive lymph node involvement, metastatic disease in pancreas, multiple liver tumours. The girl was on borrowed time. He cast his mind back to the concert. She must have had symptoms back then. How on earth had she managed it? Yet understanding these things as he did, he knew that she would have pushed herself regardless. The human spirit could be very resilient. What a tragedy. He'd not even had a shot at helping her beat it. The thing was practically over before it began. He drummed his fingers on the desk in frustration. If only she'd presented earlier.

He knew Sarah would cry when he told her. This would be one anniversary neither of them would forget in a hurry. He allowed himself the morbid luxury of brooding on it for a few minutes more, then shook himself. He needed to see her. Give her the score, talk about the choice of treatment. He would run things by another senior colleague first – just to make sure. But deep down, he knew. Palliation was the only option now. To the fighter in Michael Romily, palliation was like a white flag.

Beth sat in her chair staring out of the window. She was now in a quiet, four-bedded room in B1, on the top floor of the hospital. The wing looked out over miles and miles of surrounding landscape. As far as the eye could see stretched a jumbled tableau of variation. Smart, grey office buildings, clean-bricked housing developments, a power station which belched steam into the atmosphere and made the pale sky hang heavy with cloud; thin, snaking roads with cars that looked like Dinky toys, an equally toylike train chugging along a barely visible railway track, and in the distance, sprawling somnolently towards the horizon, acres of fallow farmland. Beth hardly saw any of it.

"Beth – your mum to see you." The voice of the young nurse broke Beth's reverie. She wheeled slowly round and smiled weakly as her mother came towards her.

"Hello, darling. Your dad gave me your message." Cassie put her arms gently round her daughter and kissed her cheek. She felt frail enough to break. "I was just having a quick shower when you rang."

Beth nodded slowly. "You didn't mind coming, did you?"

Cassie laughed. "Course not, silly girl. That's why we're down here. We were coming after lunch anyway. I didn't realise we *could* visit mornings."

Beth lowered her head. "Strictly speaking you can't. But I asked them if I could ring you. Can we go somewhere – the coffee shop or someplace like that? I just need to get away from here for a while."

Cassie looked at her, concerned. "Come on. Let's take you for a drink."

The coffee shop was fairly full when they arrived there. Beth shook her head. "I don't fancy that. Wonder if there's anywhere quieter." Then she remembered. On her trip to the chapel the previous week, she had passed something on the main corridor. At the time it had only momentarily caught her attention, and being in the middle of conversation with Laura, she hadn't bothered to ask about it. Now as her mother wheeled her towards the same spot, Beth's eyes scanned the corridor wall. Yes, there it was. She quickly made indication to Cassie and within moments they had stopped by a small sign. *'The Conservatory'* it read, an arrow directing the visitor to a set of double doors immediately to the sign's right. Passing through the doors, they made their way along a narrower corridor which suddenly opened up into an annexe. It was in the design of an old-fashioned glasshouse, light and spacious and airy with a high, glass-panelled ceiling. There were plants and climbing vines and a couple of benches in verdigrised wrought iron.

"This is rather lovely," Cassie smiled as she pushed Beth over to one of the benches. The conservatory looked out over a small garden. It was neatly maintained but colourless in its winter garb. Only the evergreen shrubs showed any sign of life as they shivered out in the late November air. Beth hugged herself and stared down at her feet in their pale blue slippers. She hadn't worn shoes for weeks.

"Well, what's all this about then?" Cassie ventured at last, stroking her daughter's arm gently.

Beth closed her eyes and bit her lip. She didn't want to say it. She didn't want to hear herself speaking the words. While ever she kept the thing quiet, it was suspended, arrested. So long as she told no one, so long as no one knew, it had to stand still and wait. Wait for her permission to continue. Her hands pressed into the hard mass under her nightie. It was waiting for nobody.

"Mum ... I don't think I'm gonna make it." Her voice tumbled out, half panicking, half sobbing. It was the voice of a little girl to her mother.

Cassie frowned and looked at her intently. "*Course* you are. Don't talk like that, sweetheart. Of course you're going to make it."

Beth began to shake her head in distress. "You don't understand, Mum. It's all too late."

A look of confusion shadowed Cassie's face. "What do you mean? What are you saying, Beth?"

Beth dug her fingers into the arms of the wheelchair and tried to pull herself together. "I saw Michael Romily this morning for my results. I didn't tell you I was seeing him. I didn't tell any of you."

Cassie was suddenly nervous. "Go *on* ..."

Beth covered her face with trembling hands. For a moment she was unable to continue. Then she spoke in a low, small voice. "It's spread, Mum. They found it too late. It's incurable. I only have a few months at the most."

Cassie stared blankly at her, her mind at first uncomprehending. Then Beth's words began to penetrate like ice-cold needles. She took one of the small, fragile hands in her own. "Oh Beth. *Beth* ... ." Her voice was a broken whisper. "Oh God, no. No, please –"

Beth began to sob uncontrollably. "It's my fault, all my fault. I knew there was something wrong. It's all my fault." She flopped forward, her whole body convulsed with anguish. Cassie caught her and cradled her, and the two of them wept together.

"You should have had someone with you. Why on earth didn't you say anything?" The thought of Beth receiving the news on her own tore into Cassie's heart.

"I just thought – I thought it might be easier," Beth stammered between sobs. "I don't even know what I was expecting to hear. I think perhaps –" She was struggling to articulate. "I – I guess I imagined they'd be able to do something to make it better."

Cassie held onto her, her own hot tears stinging her eyes. Suddenly Beth was a little child again. Somewhere in a rambling North Yorkshire garden she cried out, and Cassie was beside her in an instant. Grazed knees and dirty hands; whatever the problem, somehow Cassie had always been able to make it better. Now as she watched her daughter's distress, a terrifying realisation broke upon her mind. This time, she was completely helpless.

Rosie had been on a course all day. She was fast coming to the conclusion that the more courses she went on, the less she found herself wanting to do the job. Now it was six o'clock and she'd only just arrived home. The course tutor had been passionate about her subject. Not one of these *let's-see-if-we-can-finish-early* types. Oh no. She'd rattled on ad nauseam and overshot the estimated finishing time by forty minutes. It had put Rosie in a lousy mood. She really had to start thinking about a career move. For a few minutes she toyed with the idea of visiting Beth, but eventually decided against it. Ciaran would go straight from work, and Beth's parents were down in London so they'd no doubt be visiting. No, she'd give it a miss tonight. She went to her room to check something out. One of the girls from work was throwing a makeup party. Rosie had promised to look on her planner to see if she was free. It had been a stalling tactic. She hated things like that. But it seemed only decent to check anyway and come up with an excuse later. Perhaps she could wangle a date with Gavin for that night.

Mel came in shortly afterwards. She was seeing Dan later that evening and wanted to have a long soak. "How's it going with Gavin?" she asked as the bath was running.

Rosie was deliberately noncommittal. "Good. We're getting on fine." She didn't mention Christmas. That would make Mel unbearable.

"You seeing him tonight?" Mel called out from the bathroom.

"No, we've not arranged anything. Besides, when I've had a bite to eat I want to get a bit more of Beth's diary typed up."

"Oh, that old thing!" There was a giggle from the bathroom.

Yes, thought Rosie, *that old thing. But I don't suppose you can get your dizzy little head round something like that, can you?*

Lozenge Wood October 1st 1916

Here we are, Em, bivouacked in this delightful sounding place. Due to move on again tomorrow. Tired, tired, tired. Been doing all the usual stuff, lugging around ammo and supplies, shoring up trenches etc., but quite a few of us are suffering from heavy colds, and the temptation to dream of home comforts is overwhelming at times. Watching Wilf mourning his pal, I find myself thinking of Harry. I've heard nothing about him. I've no idea if he's living or dead. But somehow I think I coped better than Wilf is doing ...

Wilf was in an awful state these days. He hardly seemed to know where he was. Losing his friend had made him nervy and agitated, nothing like the excitable youngster he'd been at first. His big adventure had blown up in his face.

It wasn't as if he was the first one to lose a mate. The only way to not lose friends out here was to not have friends in the first place. No; losing mates was a part of life. You just had to accept it and get on with things. But, Sam reflected, everyone was different. Some men, usually the more sensitive types, seemed to find things harder to handle than others. But a man couldn't very well change his nature, could he?

You met every kind of chap out here. The officers were in a class of their own of course. But even then, there were good officers and there were brutes. Fortunately Sam had only come across a couple of the latter. Most of the officers were decent fellows who didn't expect their subordinates to do anything they weren't prepared to do themselves. Sam hadn't crossed paths with any of the funk wallahs that other lads talked about.

As for the ordinary men in the ranks, they were a real mixed bunch. There were the young hotheads who wanted to blow the Hun into the sky and who took the most terrible risks at times. Then there were the older, quieter men who spent their spare moments writing letters home or gazing at photographs of their wives and children. And of course, there were the comedians who somehow managed to turn everything into a joke. Sam smiled to himself. The humour could get a bit black out here. He'd met hopeful men and cynical men, sensitive men and hard men, generous men and selfish men. But whatever kind of a man one happened to be, Sam had come to the conclusion that it all came down to one thing in this game. You were either alive or you were dead. Simple as that ...

At the end of the day, Em, we're just the PBI; the 'poor bloody infantry' as they call us. Whether we happen to be a builder or a baker, a poet or an errand boy, there's no difference between us. We all bleed the same, our flesh is the same soft flesh. Not one of us can catch a lump of shrapnel and not be ripped to pieces – and that doesn't matter whether you're a Tommy or a German. You'll have seen enough of that to know what I mean, Em. Pardon my misery today!

Better go, officer's shouting up ahead. Don't want field punishment for writing seditious material, do I?

A banging at the front door startled Rosie. When she opened it, Ciaran practically fell inside. His hair was damp and dishevelled and his coat spattered with raindrops.

"Didn't realise it was raining." Rosie held the door ajar and looked out into the night. On closing it, she turned round to see Ciaran slumped against the wall in the passageway. The sudden sight of his drawn, grey face alarmed her.

"*Kitch?* What's the matter? You look terrible ..."

Ciaran said nothing. His head had dropped forward, and for a few moments Rosie was unable to see his expression. She noticed, however, that he seemed to grind his fingers into the grooved Artex, his agitated movements causing his knuckles to whiten. Suddenly, without warning, he gave a low, strange moan which began quietly but became gradually louder and, to Rosie's ears, more terrifying.

Panic gripped her. She took him by the shoulder and started to shake him. Her heart was thumping wildly. "Kitch! Come on! What on earth's up with you?"

The moan became a howl, like that of a wounded animal, and Rosie felt an instinctive pull to get him to safety – whatever that might mean. She was relieved to find that he offered no resistance as she began to propel him towards her room. When she had managed to get him into a chair, she stood back watching him. Seemingly unaware of her presence, he made anguished rocking movements, gripping his wet coat around him as he continued to wail. Rosie had never seen anything quite like it. At first, everything inside her longed to storm in and put an end to his torment. Yet the longer she watched him, the more she wanted to get out of the room. She had to collect her thoughts, brace herself. Something was badly wrong and shortly he would tell her. But right away, she needed caffeine.

She went back to the room five minutes later to find Ciaran hunched forward with his hands covering his face. He was whimpering softly like a small child, and the sound of it caused Rosie's throat to tighten into a lump.

"Coffee for you, Kitch." She spoke gently, afraid of adding to his distress.

At last he looked up. His eyes were swollen and his face puffy and blotched. He glanced at her hopelessly as fresh tears began to spill down his cheeks. "She's dying, Ros."

Rosie's heart lurched. "What d'you mean?"

"They can't treat her. It's too far gone." A sob caught him then. He shook his head repeatedly as though it tortured him to say it. "They told her this morning. They can't operate – just make her comfortable – give her stuff for pain – sickness – *until* –" He stammered the words, all the time twisting his hands and rocking gently in his chair.

Rosie sat in horrified silence. This did not compute. Where was the girl who planned to take the world by storm with her wonderful music? People like Beth didn't die. They were too full of life, too alive to die. Rosie breathed out slowly. There must be some way of changing this. They couldn't just sit back and let it happen. Surely there was something they could do. But as she looked at the wild grief in her brother's eyes and saw the desolation in his countenance, she felt sick. Ciaran had always been her hero, but it seemed that even he couldn't sort this one out.

His face contorted in distress. "I'm losing her, Ros. My beautiful Bethy. I'm losing her forever … ." His voice trailed off into an inaudible whisper.

Rosie swallowed hard. Her throat felt like it was packed with marbles.

It was just after eleven o'clock. Ed Simmons lay on the bed staring up at the ceiling. Cassie sat by the window, hunched over in a small rattan chair, her face expressionless. They were staying in the spare room at Beth and Ciaran's home, but neither of them was ready for sleep. Cassie hadn't even closed the curtains. Somehow the familiar sound of passing cars punctuating the night stillness was a welcome distraction from the gathering storm in her head. Outside, the cold winter air had left a sprinkling of frost on the pavements and the road glistened silver under the street lamps. Cassie shivered.

"Can't believe it," Ed mumbled for the hundredth time since that afternoon. "I can't believe it."

Cassie didn't reply. She'd had the job of breaking the news to her husband on her return from the hospital. Beth had asked that they let Ciaran visit on his own that evening so that she could break the news to him. Cassie got up from her chair and walked over to the bed. She lay down next to Ed and reached for his hand. "I hope that boy's alright."

"Wonder where he's got to," Ed said quietly. "It's late enough."

"He'll have gone round to Rosie's I should think. Poor thing." Cassie's eyes filled up. This was pain she'd never known before.

"How come they haven't picked up on it before now, d'you suppose?" Ed's face was a picture of misery and bewilderment.

Cassie shrugged sadly. "She's kept quiet about things. Today she admitted to me that she's been vomiting for a while. She went to a pharmacy some weeks back and got something for nausea and stomach upset." Cassie remembered Beth's distraught face that afternoon as she'd related the chain of events. It went through her. "She didn't pick up on the blood thing. I don't think she realised what it was. She'd even started to imagine she was pregnant, bless her." Cassie swallowed. "With the concert almost upon her, she put all her concentration on that. She was hoping the symptoms might clear up once the pressure was off."

Ed turned over onto his side. "I always thought our Beth had more sense. I mean, what can be more important than your health, Cass?"

Cassie touched his face gently. "She'd no idea it was anything like this, love. At twenty-four you think you're going to live forever. Don't you remember?"

Ed's eyes misted. "It's not right, Cass. Here I am an old man; she's just a little girl. None of it's right. I wish it was me."

Cassie rubbed the back of his hand. "Don't, Ed. Don't talk like that." But deep down inside, she had found herself wishing she could swap places with her daughter from the moment Beth had broken the news to her. "We must look to God now. Either he gives us a miracle *or* –" Her voice faltered. "Or he gives us strength to bear the pain. One or the other."

Ed nodded slowly. "Whatever happens, Cass, we must pray that she's ready."

Beth was rummaging in one of the drawers of her bedside cabinet. It was hard to rummage quietly at two o'clock in the morning, but the singsong snoring of the woman in the next bed assured her that she wasn't being too disruptive. There must be one in here. There *had* to be. Still, she hadn't noticed one when she'd put her stuff in just days earlier. A wave of frustration swept over her. And then a sense of panic. She was going to die. How could a person live with that thought and stay sane? She flopped back onto the bed, tears pricking her eyes. At that moment, soft footsteps padded across the room and Beth saw the figure of a young nurse standing by her bedside.

"Are you alright, Beth?" The voice was gentle, half-whispered. "Were you looking for something?"

For a few seconds Beth hesitated. She didn't recognise the nurse; the night staff had just changed rota. Should she tell her? For a brief moment, embarrassment silenced her. Then she shook herself. It wasn't like she had anything to lose now. "I was looking to see if there was one of those Gideon Bible things. I thought they normally had them in hospitals."

The nurse arched her eyebrows. "I'm afraid we don't have any on this wing at the moment. They were all removed during recent refurbishment. Nobody's got round to putting them back yet."

Beth closed her eyes as she tried to swallow the new wave of panic that was threatening to choke her. She felt trapped and hopeless. They didn't even have a Bible, for crying out loud. What sort of lousy place was this? A sickening sense of despair swirled round her head and she began to cry.

The nurse bent down and took her hand. "Beth, I have a Bible you can read if you want to. If you ask me, I'm allowed to get it for you." She gave a little smile. "Hospital rules, y'know."

Beth looked at her, her face wet with tears. "*Really?* You have one with you?"

The young nurse nodded. "I never go anywhere without it. But I have others at home, so you can keep it as long as you need."

Beth pulled a tissue from her sleeve and began to dab her face. "Are you into God then? Hope you don't mind me asking ... it's kinda important to me right now. I could do with talking to someone."

The young nurse smiled again. "We're quiet at the moment. Would you like to go into the sitting room and have a chat? I can make us a cuppa."

The nurse was called Belinda. It turned out she had worked on the unit for two years, hailed originally from Chingford, and had been a Christian since her late teens. Beth asked her if she found her job depressing. Belinda said it was very hard at times but immensely rewarding. Beth couldn't imagine what possible reward there was to be found in watching people die, but she kept this opinion to herself.

After the initial introductions were out of the way, Beth found herself wondering how to get the conversation rolling. As Belinda sat across from her, her expression gentle and unhurried, she decided to get straight to the point. "This morning I was told I only have months to live. I don't know what to do with that." She pushed her long hair behind her ears in thinly disguised agitation. "I'm twenty-four years old. I just can't get my head round it."

Belinda looked at her sympathetically but said nothing. The young ones often got angry; it was best to let them vent it before trying to counsel them.

"I had such dreams. I was on the point of really making something of my life. I'm *twenty-four*, for crying out loud." Beth shook her head, a look of desperation in her eyes. "Why? Why would God let this happen to me? Is he mad at me? Is it some kind of punishment?" She shuddered then, as though afraid of the answer. "I know I've let him down. But I'm sorry. Really sorry. I wish I could turn the clock back. Do all the things I should have done – undo some of the things I did do." She buried her face in her hands and began to cry again.

Belinda came to her side and began to stroke her shoulder. For the moment there were no words to be said. The girl was crumpled with grief, and though Belinda's mind teemed with a thousand things she wanted to say, she knew she had to let Beth weep. Some time later, when the raw emotion had subsided and Beth, dazed with exhaustion, was slumped back in her chair, Belinda looked at her intently.

"God loves you, Beth. Your illness isn't a punishment." Her dark eyes searched Beth's face. "I don't pretend to have all the answers, but one thing I know for sure. The Lord loves you very, very much."

Beth shook her head again and looked down at the table. "I don't want to die, Belinda. I don't want to. I want someone to tell me it's all a dream – a *nightmare.*" She was shaking now and her lips trembled as she spoke. "How would you feel if it was *you?*"

It was a direct question, but there was no malice in it. No accusation of injustice or hint of resentment. Just a pleading enquiry from a girl who was scared to death.

Belinda thought for a moment. "I can't say, Beth. I honestly don't know."

Beth shuddered. "I feel trapped inside my own body. I want to be someone else, somewhere else – anywhere but here … ." She gave a sob. "But I can't, can I? I'm me. I'm stuck in me." Her voice thinned to a thread. "Please help me, Belinda. *Please.*"

Belinda closed her eyes. The sight of this young woman so desperate to live cut into her like a knife. She breathed a silent prayer before continuing. "A long time ago, Beth, I had a little brother. He was ten years younger than me. My mother once told me he was her 'lovely surprise'." She smiled gently. "I thought the world of him, we all did. But you know, Beth, he was born with a congenital immunodeficiency disease. From the start, we knew that without a miracle we weren't going to keep him long. I found that terribly hard to deal with." Belinda lowered her eyes. "I remember my parents used to pray for him every day. Sometimes I'd catch my mum crying when she thought no one was around. All his short life she knew what was coming. She was preparing herself for it. He was only seven when he died."

Beth wiped her face with the back of her sleeve. "I'm sorry to hear that."

Belinda smiled again. "That little boy was so special, Beth. He loved Jesus with all his heart. Somehow he seemed to know he wouldn't be staying around. But it didn't upset him. He talked about heaven all the time, like he couldn't wait to go there. I learnt something so precious from him. That there's very little we can hold onto in this world. Not even life itself. From the moment Jamie was born, we knew he'd only been lent to us. We had to change our outlook on a lot of things – the whole family did. Make the most of every moment, not knowing how long we had. And *I* had to start searching for a deeper meaning to all this *'life'* stuff. My parents had banged on at me for years about getting right with God, but well, you know what stroppy teenagers are like. I had to find it for myself."

Beth nodded slowly. "Yeah. At that age I was pretty stroppy too."

Belinda sat back in her chair. "In the end, I did get it. I figured, why spend your life trying to cling onto this old world when you're only gonna lose it anyway in the end? That's when I started getting into God I guess. Somehow, losing Jamie took the fear of death away for me. I knew exactly where he'd gone. That's when I felt God calling me to do this."

Beth frowned. "Do what?"

"Work with cancer patients. When I began my nurse training, I knew this was where I wanted to end up. You know, Beth, many people find that cancer's a wakeup call. They have to make changes. Everything begins to take on a new perspective. For those like yourself who find themselves terminally ill, the perspective is even sharper. People who are facing death usually have questions. I don't have all the answers, but I *can* pray that they will ask the *right* questions – the ones that really matter."

It was several moments before either of them spoke again. Beth sat with her eyes closed, her thin hands stretched flat on the table in front of her. Eventually she lifted her head and looked straight at Belinda. "So what *are* the questions that matter, the ones I should be asking?"

Belinda looked towards the window. *Please Lord, help me out here. Help me get this right.* Her face broke into a smile. "I was hoping you'd ask me that, Beth."

Rosie felt too keyed up to go to bed. Ciaran hadn't left until past midnight, about half an hour after Mel had texted to say she wouldn't be coming in. Since then, Rosie's head had been milling with questions that seemed to have no answers. She'd made up her mind not to go into work tomorrow. How could she work, how could she do anything? Beth was dying. It was too much to take in. As she mooched about the living room wondering what to do with herself, Sam's words suddenly came back to bite her.

It all comes down to one thing in this game. You're either alive or you're dead. Simple as that ...

How could anybody be so laid back about it? Was it possible, Rosie wondered, to be so surrounded by loss that one no longer felt it? Her mind went back to her schooldays. She could see the boys in her class playing football on the top field. She tried to imagine them in army uniforms. Surely it would have been like that; whole classfuls of boys, not two minutes out of school, answering the call of duty. She found it hard to think of lads like Blondie Savage or Shane 'Six-Pack' Robertson coming under orders. They'd have probably been shot within a week of joining up. Still, most of the guys in her class hadn't been so bad. Just big kids really. They'd have loved a bit of war – make a change from computer games at least. A whole nation of lads queuing up to get a taste of the action; a whole heap of them on a one way ticket. It was like Beth times multitudes.

A dark sense of futility swept over her then. What was it all about anyway? A few years trying to get by in a world that didn't seem to know why it was there either. Just a miserable little ball spinning around in space. No explanation for its existence; its cities swarming with the living, its dust heavy with the debris of the dead. None of it made any sense when you really looked at it. It was all so stupidly pointless.

What was it Boxer had said? The sorriest thing in the world was that a man die without ever having discovered why he was born in the first place, or something to that effect. Rosie sighed ruefully. It wasn't something she'd ever given much thought to. She'd always been far too busy dodging the clouts and swipes that life had aimed at her; philosophising about her own existence had never been a luxury she could afford. But now it seemed the question had caught up with her.

So ... why was I born in the first place?

She allowed herself to brood on it for a few moments, but no answer came. Only a vague, shadowy emptiness, and a sudden sense of being terribly alone. Beth was dying. The best friend she'd ever had. There was no explanation for something like that. Why should she expect anything else to make sense?

Losing mates is a part of life. You just have to accept it and get on with things.

Chapter 11

Rosie had woken with a terrific headache. She'd hardly slept at all and now she was trying to distract her mind with a bit of aimless housework. She'd rung Mel early that morning to put her in the picture.

"Oh, you poor thing!" Mel had gushed. "I'll bring you in something nice to cheer you up. Vienna slice, chocolate fudge cake – something yummy like that."

Rosie had tried to protest but Mel had insisted. It was vital, she had counselled, to comfort eat. The body had to keep strong when all around was going pear-shaped. Rosie hadn't bothered to argue. *It's me that'll be going pear-shaped by the time you've finished feeding me up, Melanie.* Still, Mel meant well. In her own dopey, mindless way.

Around dinnertime Rosie's mobile bleeped. She was slightly surprised at the caller ID. Gavin didn't usually ring in the middle of the day.

"Hi Rosie!" His voice was bright at the other end. "I'm just calling to let you know that we're booked in. And this morning Mike e-mailed me some photos of our room. It's got a fantastic view over the golf course, right down to the lake. Can't wait to get over there – won't be long now!"

Rosie's heart quickened. *Our room?* No doubt what *he'd* got in mind then. She made no reply.

"You okay, Rosie? Kids playing you up or something?"

"I haven't gone in this morning," Rosie said flatly. "I didn't feel up to it."

"Are you ill?" Gavin jumped in before she had time to finish her explanation.

"No, not me. It's Beth. They can't treat her. We found out yesterday she only has a few months to live."

For a couple of moments there was silence at the other end of the phone.

"Rosie, I'm so sorry. That's just awful." Gavin's voice was suddenly quiet. "Listen, I'm coming round. I can take an hour off work – they'll understand. I'll be there shortly. Is that okay?"

It wasn't a response Rosie would have expected, but then, Gavin seemed full of surprises these days. She mumbled affirmatively and clicked off her phone. She was badly in need of some TLC today. Perhaps Gavin would surprise her again.

Mel arrived home first, brandishing a box of cream buns. It was her half day and she seemed intent on spending the rest of the afternoon waiting on Rosie's every whim. When the doorbell rang half an hour later, Mel looked puzzled. "Wonder who *that* can be ..."

Rosie didn't bother to enlighten her as Mel hurried towards the front door. She'd find out soon enough, and there was just something so entertaining about this girl when sprung upon by a desirable male. Mel's voice sounded squeaky and excitable from the hallway. Seconds later, she hurried back into the living room with Gavin in tow.

"Look who's here, Rosie – and just look what he's brought for you!"

Even Gavin looked slightly embarrassed as Mel presented him like some trying-too-hard, adolescent suitor. He smiled knowingly at Rosie and held out a bunch of flowers, just as large as the one he'd given her before. There was a Thorntons' bag hanging from his wrist. He reached inside it and pulled out a box of chocolates. "You need to spoil yourself," he said kindly. "You've had a nasty shock."

"That's just what I was telling her earlier," said Mel triumphantly. "And now she's got two of us here to look after her. We'll have her feeling brighter in no time, won't we?" She beamed at them both. "Cup of tea, anyone?"

Rosie and Gavin exchanged glances. Rosie couldn't help smiling as she saw a twinkle of amusement in Gavin's eye. Mel was the most attentive gooseberry anyone could wish for.

Le Sars October 5th 1916

Early this morning a group of us stumbled across a couple of Bosch taking shelter in some old ruins. Actually, it was Wilf and I that discovered them. I didn't think we'd have any trouble taking them prisoner; the young lad went sheet white when he saw us and seemed ready to do anything I told him to. But suddenly the older chap lost his head and made a rush for us ...

There was a light drizzle in the air as the group trudged wearily along the broken road. They'd been on an overnight working party and were off to locate the rest of their company. A steady, rhythmic thud sounded out as tired feet tramped the shattered *pavé*. The last few weeks had tested even the fittest man. Exhaustion was a constant companion these days. It marched alongside, its boots heavy and cumbersome, its voice like an agitated lullaby.

Fatigued as they were, the men kept up a cheerful banter as they walked. There was always someone ready to dig out a joke from somewhere. Several yards in front of the others, Sam and a very subdued Wilf were leading the way. For the last ten minutes Sam had been trying to draw Wilf into conversation. He'd met with little success. Wilf was distant and withdrawn. He moved along with his head down, and it seemed all he could do to mumble a reply to Sam's comments.

"Look at that." Sam pointed as they approached a group of ruined farm buildings just up ahead. "Poor beggars won't be coming back to much here." The buildings had been badly shelled. Large chunks of masonry had fallen into the road, and the roofless structures which remained bore the familiar pockmarks of repeated shrapnel hits. No doubt the farm's civilian occupants had fled months ago, probably right at the start of the conflict. Where were they now, Sam wondered sadly? And could they possibly imagine the state of their beloved family home?

Suddenly something caught his eye. A gap in the front wall of the ruined structure afforded an eyelet of view into the interior of the main farmhouse. It appeared as though one of the downstairs window frames had concertinaed in on itself leaving a tall, narrow opening, rather like a lancet window in a church. It was through this gap that Sam perceived movement. He signalled behind him to the others to stop. His heartbeat quickened. It could be Tommies of course. Possibly officers who'd set up quarters in there. They were pretty adept at that kind of thing. Bringing in chairs and gramophones and the like, and transforming forsaken hovels into relative palaces. He waited a few moments. The rest of the group had come to a halt some yards down the road. None of them made a sound now, and the sudden silence felt decidedly eerie. Sam had the distinct feeling they were being watched. It couldn't be Tommies. They'd have come out by now and declared themselves; unless they were deserters ...

Another slight flicker of movement. Sam tried to think fast. He couldn't help feeling that if there were armed Germans in there, they definitely had the advantage. As his eyes scanned the building, he located several more gaps in the walls. No shortage of lookout positions or sniping posts for anyone hiding inside. They could let rip at any moment. Sam felt a shudder of fear go right through him. He and Wilf were the most obvious targets. It was like standing in a shooting gallery.

However, as the moments passed without any action, Sam felt emboldened to investigate further. Surely if it was anyone who meant trouble they'd have kicked off by now. He beckoned to Wilf, and the two of them made their way towards the far end of the farmhouse to see if it would give them a better view of the building's interior. It did. Most of the gable end had collapsed, and all that remained of it was the bottom three feet of its outer wall and a pile of smashed stonework. But the state of the edifice was not the thing that held their interest now. Inside, pressed up against the back wall of the house, Sam could see two figures. He recognised the uniforms. Germans.

"They don't look armed to me," he said to Wilf in a low voice. "You cover me. I'm going to have a look." He readied his rifle and moved nearer. At times like this it would be good to know a bit more of the lingo.

"Soldat! Soldat!" he shouted to the two men. Not terribly impressive, but at least he'd got their attention – and he would shoot if he had to. Even from his position outside, Sam could see that the two Germans were very different in appearance. One was an older man, grizzled and thickset. The other was little more than a boy, slim and almost delicate by comparison to his fellow. He blanched as Sam called out to them. Sam signalled to them to come out, raising his hands above his head in a gesture of surrender to indicate what he wanted them to do. The two Germans began to pick their way out of the ruins as quickly as they could, though Sam could see that it was no easy task for them to keep their hands up whilst stumbling over the shattered stonework.

"Kamerad – Kamerad! No shoot ..." the young boy appealed pathetically as his feet slipped and slid over the wet masonry.

Sam couldn't help feeling sorry for him. He and Wilf exchanged glances. "Don't worry, mate," he called out. "No shoot if you behave yourself."

Soon the two Germans had come out onto the open road. They stood, hands above their heads, blinking the drizzle out of their eyes as Sam and Wilf covered them with their guns.

"Nice one, Sam," said Twinny Two, striding towards him with a grin. "You bagged a couple o' Bosch. Our boys are checkin' out the rest of the buildings."

A few minutes later there came a shout. "All clear down here. Nothing doing."

The rest of the group began to make their way towards them. Well, thought Sam, it had all made for a bit of excitement. Livened up the morning at least.

He hardly knew what happened then. One moment he was calmly standing guard over his prisoners, and the next, the older German was lunging at him wildly.

"What the ...?" Sam was almost knocked over by the sudden burst. The younger boy seemed to panic and flung himself to the older man's side, yanking Sam's arm as he did so. A couple of rifle cracks rang out through the chilly morning air. The older man was the first to hit the ground. The bullet had gone in at the temple,

killing him outright. Seconds later, his comrade staggered backwards and fell heavily, hitting his head as he landed.

Sam recovered himself quickly and bent down over the young German. The boy lay looking up at him, his lips moving slightly as though he was trying to speak. Sam bent nearer. He could feel the boy's breath on his skin.

"*Wasser – bitte –*" The words were barely audible.

Sam slid his arm under the boy's neck and lifted his head into a more comfortable position. It was obvious he was going. "Water, Wilf, find some water!" There was an urgency in Sam's voice. But Wilf was frozen to the spot, a strange look of horror on his face. Sam glanced around desperately. The others had practically reached them by now and Sam could see Jimmy still holding his Lee Enfield in firing position.

Jimmy approached the scene and shook his head. "I was sure the old fella was about to try and kill you, Sam. It was just instinct. I couldn't take any chances." He looked down at the young German, an expression of pity in his eyes. "I'd have gone for the boy's head but I'd have probably hit you." He knelt down and took the boy's hand. "*Es tut mir leid, Kamerad.*" His accent was broken and faltering but the lad seemed to pick up on the sincerity of his apology. He fixed his gaze on Jimmy and lay staring up at him. The others in the group maintained a respectful distance as the boy's life dimmed to a close. A few moments later, his eyes swivelled, rolled back in their sockets and he was gone ...

Poor lad, Emily. I think he just happened to be with the wrong person at the wrong time. We could have taken him prisoner if the other fellow hadn't lunged at us. Jimmy just made a snap decision to save Wilf and me, but I know it's upset him. It's far easier to talk about pasting the enemy when you can't see the whites of their eyes or hear them spluttering their last breath.

St Riquier October 15th 1916

Wilf shot himself today. I saw it coming, Em. That lad was past himself – he wasn't fit to be out here. Nobody's talking about it much; it's almost like everyone's trying to pretend nothing's happened. I overheard one of the officers referring to him as a 'bloody coward'. But he wasn't a coward, Em. His nerves were wrecked. Losing his mate knocked him badly and I just don't think he could cope with the loss. I saw it when Jimmy shot the German boy. Wilf just stood there with a look of terror in his eyes, almost as though he was reliving it all. It's a rotten tragedy. Neither Wilf nor his mate were old enough to join up. They both lied about their ages just to get out here. Thought it would be an adventure I suppose. But once you're here, you're under orders, no matter how old you are. You can't run away if things get a bit hot. They'd just shoot you. You have absolutely no say in anything. A man feels terribly expendable out here, Emily.

It's knocked Jimmy, that's for sure. I sense that in some way he feels partly responsible for Wilf's death. He thinks that his shooting the German boy was the last straw, the thing that pushed Wilf over the edge. Personally, Em, I think it's in danger of pushing Jimmy over the edge too. He doesn't say much, but I know he's struggling to forget the business. He told me that the boy's face haunts him. I tried to buck him up. I said we could all feel bad about some of the things we've had to do out here, but that's war – that's what we're here for. It didn't help. When you see the enemy close up, you realise they're not the villains they're made out to be. Not all of them anyway. That young lad certainly wasn't. He was just a frightened boy like Wilf, and now they're both dead.

Rosie chewed on her lip. Why was she even reading this stuff? At a time like this she must be crazy. Could she possibly have managed to find anything more depressing?

Yet deep down, she knew why she'd done it. Nearly three hours of Mel's overbearing attention had left her feeling empty and almost self-indulgent. She'd come to her room just to escape. Poor Beth was the one with cancer, yet Rosie felt like all the sympathy had been lavished on *her*. Even Gavin had been impossibly kind. He'd promised, in tender, loving tones, to take extra special care of her. He was going to make sure she had the most memorable Christmas ever. *Christmas?* She'd hardly given it a thought. And yet Gavin seemed to view their forthcoming Christmas holiday as the panacea for all ills, the remedy for all misery – even the imminent death of her best friend.

That was why she'd read the diary today. As some kind of distorted reality check. In a weird way, typing up the entries had managed to assuage some of the guilt that was trying to fix itself onto her. Away from all the distraction tactics and emotional analgesia, the diary had plunged her straight back into raw, real life – where horrible things do happen, and no number of cream buns or fancy holidays can soften the blow. Closing Sam's notebook, Rosie stared out of the window and thought fleetingly of all the young guys who'd had the dubious distinction of being around in 1914. There'd been nothing to soften it for them as their one shot at living had been ripped from their hopeful hearts. Forced into a situation like something out of hell itself and completely unable to escape from it. Run away, and they stuck you up against a post and shot you. Stay, and you were more than likely to get your brains blown out. Take your pick.

She leaned back in her chair. It wasn't surprising Wilf had shot himself. How could a person keep going when there was no hope? In her mind's eye she tried to picture him. But she saw only Beth.

She closed down her laptop. This stuff was enough to put years on you. Looking at her watch she saw that it was five twenty-five. She needed to get ready. She was going to visit Beth, but everything inside seemed to scream at her to stay at home. What did you say to someone who was dying? *How are you doing? Are you feeling better?* It was all so pointless. Rosie was suddenly overwhelmed with fear. Her legs felt like lead. She simply didn't want to go.

Almost a week had gone by since Beth had received her prognosis. Now it was late Monday afternoon and she and Ciaran were sitting in the hospital chapel. Beth had suggested it. They had wanted to be alone together, and during visiting hours she felt it was the one place they were unlikely to be disturbed.

Ciaran stared at a spot on the wall. He had cried so much, the skin of his face was taut and sore. And yet his eyes were filling again. He turned to look at Beth. She seemed so shrunken, and in such a short time. How could he let her go? The idea of life without her was unthinkable. Yet how could he stop her? She was fading away before his very eyes. His mind replayed the moment she'd broken the news to him. In one tiny second of tragic revelation, his life had imploded. It didn't seem real.

Beth smiled at him gently. "I love you."

The tears spilled over then. Reaching for her hand, he held it against his cheek.

"I'm sorry. So sorry to hurt you like this." Beth's voice was choked. "I don't want to leave you. If I could change anything – if there was anything I could do to stay ..."

Ciaran shook his head and put a finger to her lips. "Shush. Don't. It's not your fault, princess. It's no one's fault." They held each other and cried. Ciaran buried his face in her hair. It smelt of hospitals. The odour of medication seemed to ooze from every pore of her being. This place got inside you.

After some time, Beth twined her fingers through his. "Ciaran, there's something I want to ask you."

Ciaran straightened. "What is it?"

Beth was hesitant. "I'd really like to spend Christmas at Oak Lodge. The three of us could go up there – you, me and Rosie. I'm sure Mum and Dad wouldn't mind." In that moment there was such an earnest pleading in her face, it gave her the look of one very young; a schoolgirl begging a favour from a reluctant parent. Her eyes searched his for a response. "I'd so love to. I really would."

Ciaran looked away, afraid of being drawn in to the notion. The thought filled him with dread. He'd got her for precious little enough time as it was; he hardly wanted to jeopardise that. "It's an awful long way, Bethy. And what about your medication? It sounds a lovely idea, but there's the practical side of things – I just can't think how we'd get round it."

Beth looked as though she might burst into tears. "Ciaran, this would mean so much to me. It's going to be my last Christmas, after all."

Ciaran dropped his head. The blunt finality of her words made him want to be sick.

Beth composed herself and began her next round of reasoning. "I mentioned the thought to Michael Romily. He said they could arrange for district nurse cover up there, y'know, to sort out my syringe drivers and stuff. I'm sure we could do it. Michael seemed perfectly okay about it. They can't do an awful lot for me down here anyway. *Please* ... think about it at least."

In the end Ciaran agreed to talk to Ed and Cassie. If they were up for it, then they would go. Beth was confident there'd be no problem there.

The next day at visiting, Beth put the proposition to Rosie. "You'll love it up there, Ros, and Mum'll spoil you rotten. It'll be a real family Christmas."

Whatever one of those is, thought Rosie. Gavin's face stuck itself obstinately in her mind's eye. A family Christmas certainly wasn't on *his* agenda. "Are you fit to travel?" Rosie couldn't help feeling sceptical. "It must be a few hours' journey."

Beth nodded. "It's a fair way, but Mum and Dad are going to stay down here until I get clearance from the hospital to leave. We can drive up with them. Theirs is an MPV so there's plenty of room for me to recline if I need to. But I feel okay. I'm sure I'll be fine."

Rosie couldn't help noticing how surprisingly calm she looked. Ill and a little wasted maybe, but somehow bright-eyed and relaxed. She momentarily imagined being in Beth's shoes. Twenty-four and on her way out. *I'd be tearing my hair out,* she thought to herself. *Tearing my hair out and in a state of permanent sedation.*

Beth's voice brought her back to reality. "I wish I could take you exploring, Ros. There are some fantastic walks in the area." Her eyes grew wistful. "I should be able to get out a bit though. Even if it's just for quarter of an hour. Oh, Ros, I can't wait to get back up there."

"I hope it isn't all going to be too much for you, Mrs M. I haven't seen you walk more than a few yards in weeks." Realising the negative tone of her words, Rosie suddenly felt bad.

Beth grinned. "I still have a pair of legs, y'know. That chair hasn't been soldered onto my backside. You're just like your brother – a natterer. I'll be great. Stop worrying." She gave a small sigh then, as though even the prospect of activity made her feel tired. She sank back against her pillow. "Anyway, if you take your laptop up there, we can work on some diary entries and start making up a folder. That should keep me out of trouble."

Rosie shook her head. "You must be mad. Can't you think of anything more cheerful to read? I mean, come on, it's a bit heavy going."

For a few moments Beth seemed to consider this. "I suppose it is. But I can't leave it half-read. Not now. I want to know what happens ... I can't just leave the poor guy in no man's land." Whether the pun was intended, Rosie wasn't sure, but Beth broke into a giggle. "I hope you appreciate the privilege of helping to preserve this historical masterpiece, Rosie. Anybody would think you weren't enjoying it." There was something of the old mischievous sparkle in her eyes.

Rosie shrugged. "No, it's quite interesting. I just don't want you depressing yourself, that's all."

Beth smiled. "I'd like to try and finish it if I can, Ros. Besides, I'm not feeling half so scared as I was the other day. Something happened to me. I'm still trying to work some stuff out, but things seem a bit clearer now." There was a pause. "I'll tell you all about it when I've got my head round it."

Rosie hadn't a clue what she was talking about. She nodded absently. "I'll look forward to it."

"You're going up to *Yorkshire?*" Gavin sounded faintly incredulous. Rosie could detect a twinge of thinly concealed annoyance in his tone. "I thought we had all this arranged, Rosie."

"I know, I'm sorry. I didn't plan for Beth to get sick." Rosie spoke in as calm a voice as she could muster. She wasn't sure whether to feel guilty or indignant. Gavin wasn't even trying to be understanding.

"You knew she was sick when you agreed to come," Gavin persisted irritably.

"I didn't know it would be her dying wish to spend her last Christmas up in Yorkshire with all her family. What did you expect me to say? Sorry, no can do. I'd rather spend it with a bloke I've only known a month and a half." Rosie was fighting to hide her anger. This guy really needed to get over himself. For a few moments there was an uncomfortable silence.

"I'm sorry, Rosie. You're right." Gavin's tone suddenly softened. "I guess I'd have done the same in your position. Look, I need to go. The boss is giving me the eye. We'll have to arrange to meet up so I can give you your present. I'll call you. See you later."

Yeah, like never. Rosie clicked off her phone and threw it onto the bed. *I have a present for you too, Gavin – and I've got a few good ideas where I'd like to shove it right now.*

Some time later when she'd calmed down, she tried to analyse the conversation in her mind. Obviously Gavin was disappointed. He'd been looking forward to the trip; he'd made no secret of that. But surely her own change of plan wasn't unreasonable in the circumstances. If he cared about her, he ought to understand that.

She looked at herself in the mirror. Her face seemed sallow and sad, her eyes somehow darker than usual.

Can't say I'm disappointed myself.

She only muttered the words under her breath, but suddenly their veracity echoed loudly in her head. In truth, she'd been dreading going away with Gavin. She really wasn't ready for anything like that. She'd only agreed for want of a good reason to refuse. Deep down, she'd known that to say no would have been to say goodbye. And somehow, in a shallow, cosmetic way, she'd got used to having Gavin around. Now it was anyone's guess as to whether he'd want to see her again. She'd just have to wait for a call.

As it turned out, Gavin *did* ring – a couple of days before Rosie was due to travel up to Yorkshire. He apologised for not having been in touch, said that the health club had been extremely busy with last minute bookings, and asked if he could call round later for an hour with her Christmas present. Rosie had agreed. The 'hour' was pleasant enough. Gavin's irritation with her seemed to have evaporated and he was his usual charming self, but Rosie couldn't shake off the feeling that they'd lost most of the ground that had been gained over the last few weeks.

"We'll have to get together when you get back," Gavin said lightly as they exchanged gifts. "Pick up where we left off."

They kissed before they said goodbye, but Rosie was left with the feeling that the whole thing had been like an unconvincing piece of theatre. A play without passion; an insipid Act I with no promise of a second half.

It was the week before Christmas when they were able to travel up to Yorkshire. Arrangements had been made for Beth's healthcare, Ciaran had managed to cancel some of his peripatetic engagements, and Rosie had negotiated some extra holidays from the nursery. They had three whole weeks before they must return to London, Beth's condition permitting. The journey went better than any of them had expected. Beth slept for a lot of the time, only waking up when they were about ten miles outside her home village of Ridderch Standen. When she realised where they were, her face lit up. She gazed out at the passing scenery, her eyes gleaming with relief and quiet excitement. "Thank God," she muttered under her breath, "we're almost there. I did it."

Twenty minutes later, the car turned into the drive at Oak Lodge. As they rolled towards the old stone house, Beth pressed her face to the window, drinking in the familiar sight of the rambling garden in its winter starkness.

Ciaran squeezed her hand. "You happy?" he whispered.

She leaned her head on his shoulder. "Very, very happy."

As if on cue, the front door opened and Beth's brother Ben came out to greet them. "I've got a good fire going and the kettle's just boiled." He hugged Beth gently. "Come on, little sis. It's great to have you home."

So, this is Oak Lodge. Standing in the spacious hallway with her suitcases, Rosie tried to look around discreetly. It was a welcoming place with a bohemian, slightly dishevelled feel. The fittings and décor were tasteful, and the bits of furniture she could see were quality – possibly antique, Rosie suspected. But it was the little touches that stood out. A fringed scarf draped round a picture; a bunch of dried flowers hung by a ribbon from a banister; a series of children's paintings displayed on a wall, framed and labelled as though in some mini art gallery. A faint smell of pine seemed to drift in from an adjoining room, accompanied by the distant sound of logs splitting and crackling in the fire. There were photographs, sepia as well as modern, affectionately arranged in a long, wall-mounted cabinet, unusual ornaments which drew the eye and made one think of country craft fairs – and books. Books in a bookcase, books on shelves, even books piled haphazardly on a window sill. And that was only the view from the hallway. Rosie smiled to herself. Well, that explained Beth's fetish for the things. She unfastened her coat and prepared to await further directions. This was going to be home for the next three weeks.

Ben appeared then and began to pick up her luggage. "Where's Rosie going, Mum?" he called into the next room.

Cassie bustled past, a pile of bed linen already in her arms. She turned to Rosie. "I'm going to put you in the boys' old room if that's alright, love. It looks over the garden and you'll have plenty of space in there. I'll just take these sheets up and then we'll all have a cup of tea before I start making the beds."

Rosie picked up a couple of small bags and followed Ben and Cassie upstairs. Ben made his way to a room at the far end of the landing. He opened the door and took Rosie's luggage inside.

"This is our old turf," he grinned. "You might find a few dints in the skirting board, but don't tell Mum."

Rosie thanked him for bringing her stuff up.

"No problem. Good to have you with us, Rosie." He turned and went back downstairs. Rosie looked around. There was nothing to suggest that two boys had ever slept in that room. It was clean and airy and the décor decidedly neutral – no sign of Power Rangers or Spiderman on the walls. Rosie suspected she'd be hard-pressed to find any dints in the skirting board either. She made her way to the window. This would be a nice view to wake up to in the morning.

She had just started to unpack when Ed's voice sounded up the stairs. "Want a cuppa, Rosie?"

She went down and joined the others huddled round the fire in the living room. Beth looked pale and seemed slightly trembly, but she was smiling as she listened to the gentle conversation of her family. Ciaran was quiet as he sat beside her, his expression serious. Rosie felt a stab of sympathy for him. What was going through his mind? How could he enjoy any of this, knowing it would all be snatched away from him so soon? It made her feel terribly sad.

Some time later, when Cassie got up and said she was going to sort out the bedrooms, Rosie suddenly heard herself offering to help. The sound of her own voice volunteering almost shocked her. Not that she had any objections to helping out; but the moment the words left her lips, she was filled with a sudden, overpowering sense of inadequacy. What on earth would she talk about while they were doing it? What if she made beds in a totally different way to Cassie? What if Cassie thought she was a complete idiot? She pulled herself up with a start. What was wrong with her? They were only making *beds*. What was so hard about that?

Cassie's voice broke into her turmoil. "That would be lovely, Rosie. Shouldn't take us long."

They began in Rosie's room. Cassie opened up a white sheet and handed two corners to her. As they tossed it into the air and let it fall back to the bed, a light scent of lavender wafted over them.

"It's lovely to have you all here for Christmas, Rosie." Cassie smiled as she tucked a corner under the mattress. Rosie nodded as she did the same. She wasn't sure how to reply. Should she make some sympathetic comment like, *"It's a shame it's not in different circumstances"*, or something similar? Deciding against it, she concentrated hard, determined to make the best bed of her life. As they put the last smoothing touches to the job, Cassie thanked her. "You're very neat, Rosie. You've obviously done this before. Your mum must have taught you well."

Rosie was bitten by the irony. This was the first time she'd ever made a bed with anyone's mother, let alone her own. She smiled guardedly. A few minutes later as they were making up a bed for Beth and Ciaran in another room, Rosie looked across at Cassie's hands. They were mother's hands; strong, hardworking, ribbed with thick, blue veins and sinewy tendons which seemed to flex with every movement of her chores. Yet tender, kind hands, which Rosie sensed instinctively could bring comfort to a total stranger. She felt gently impressed by Cassie. She hadn't seen one ounce of petulance or irritation in her, no charge of cosmic injustice that *her* daughter should be dying while the daughters of other women were allowed to live. Just a flow of caring goodwill which seemed to fragrance the atmosphere around her.

When the bed was finished, Cassie walked over to the window and gazed out. "Come here, Rosie. I'll show you our church."

The room was situated on a back corner of the house and looked out over the surrounding farmland. The ground lay desolate under the winter sky, its dark, frozen ridges, impenetrable and lifeless. The only reminder of more clement days was a scattering of bare, scrubby bushes which bordered the fields. Life had visited there once. In the distance, half-hidden by a clump of tall, stripped trees, was the church. The only part of it clearly visible was its dark spire which seemed to climb into the icy sky. Rosie was suddenly reminded of the church at Applemarket and the peculiar longing which had gripped her there. What a happy day that had been.

Cassie touched her arm lightly. "This was Beth's bedroom when she lived at home. She always loved looking out of this window when she was a little girl." She smiled sadly as though remembering. "After she got married we put a double bed in here. We thought it would be handy if anyone came to stay. But we still call it Beth's room. It'll always be Beth's room."

As she spoke, Rosie heard a slight falter in her voice. A rush of compassion for Cassie overwhelmed her. If only she could do something to ease her pain. Put comforting arms around her maybe; offer empathy and understanding. But as she glanced at this brave woman staring misty-eyed over the fields, Rosie felt a sense of frustration at her own impotence. Her limbs seemed locked with embarrassment, her tongue, tied with inexperience. The moment passed, and in no time at all, Cassie's face was bright again. But Rosie was left with a gnawing sense of emptiness that did not leave her for the rest of the evening.

Chapter 12

"On Thursday morning we'll be having a little get-together in the church hall, Rosie." Cassie looked across at her warmly. "Cuppa tea, mince pie, that sort of thing. It's something we do every year around Christmas. Do you fancy coming along?"

Rosie glanced over at Beth. Beth grinned. "Go on, Ros, it's not to be missed. Go for the mince pies if nothing else. Nobody makes mince pies like Nora Weldrake." She sniggered to herself, and Rosie wasn't sure whether to interpret her amusement as an encouragement or a warning. Beth straightened her face and tried to look serious. "Now as for Betty Flavel's fruit cake – desperate women would kill for that recipe, wouldn't they, Mum?" She shook her head in mock gloom. "Many a fella's had his head turned by Betty's fruit cake."

Cassie raised her eyes with a wry smile. "You're a storyteller, Beth, I'll say that for you. Anyway, what d'you say, Rosie? Beth and Ciaran are coming." Her grey eyes twinkled encouragingly.

Rosie felt herself relax. At least she wouldn't be the only outsider then.

Beth winked at her. "She'd love to, wouldn't you, Ros? She's really into that sort of thing."

Rosie shot her a withering look. *If we were at home, Beth Maconochie, I'd tip the rubbish bin all over your head.* She smiled at Cassie. "In that case, yes. Count me in."

Some time later Rosie went up to her room. It was Tuesday afternoon and only two o'clock, but the sky was dark and heavy and everyone expected snow. She took Sam's diary from a drawer and went over to sit by the window.

Erie Camp October 19th 1916

Well, Emily, another change for us. Yesterday we moved up to Belgium by train. Arrived in the town of Poperinghe and are encamped here until we move on to Ypres in the next couple of days. I hardly dare imagine what state Ypres will be in now. It was in a pretty bad way last time we were there, and it's bound to have had a pounding since. 'Wipers' we call it – every soldier worth his pay should be posted over here at least once, I reckon.

Today we saw a group of men coming back from the line. They were a sobering sight, Em. I can honestly say I've never seen men look so dead tired. Their faces were haggard and their uniforms caked with sludge. To be truthful, none of us are particularly clean out here – that goes without saying. We all see our fair share of mud, no matter where on the front they shove us. But these men were filthy, Em, absolutely filthy. Matted hair and hollow eyes. Quite awful. I remember the last time we were here, Corporal Phinn told us that this whole area was a natural bog once. The Belgians constructed an extensive drainage system so that they could turn it into farmland. A bit of heavy rain tends to make the place waterlogged at the best of times, but because the shelling has smashed so many of the drainage ditches, the place can easily turn into a swamp. I suppose that accounts for the appearance of the poor beggars coming off the front line. Still, no doubt we'll soon look like that too. No room for vanity here, I'm afraid.

Zillebeke October 22nd 1916

Got our first glimpse of Ypres yesterday, Em. It's hard to imagine the beautiful city it apparently once was. The heavy guns have done one heck of a job and parts of the place are completely pulverised. The Cloth Hall and Cathedral of St Martin are looking more miserable than ever. Broken ruins, heaps of rubble, and lumps of masonry everywhere – all sense of history confined to the dust, I'm sorry to say.

A sad little thing comes to mind. Yesterday, at dusk, we left the city by the Menin Gate to begin our journey out here to Zillebeke. After about half a mile we passed an overturned provisions wagon and a horse that had been slit from end to end by shrapnel. Poor creature, its entrails were all over the road. Its driver was kneeling there with his arms around the beast's neck and his rifle on the ground next to him. He seemed completely distraught. He'd obviously shot the animal to put it out of its suffering, and looking at him, I think he would have been only too glad for someone to do the same for him.

It's awful for the animals, Em. They're forced to go through all of this because of us, but how can the poor things understand what's really going on? They're particularly distressed by the noise. There are times you see sheer terror in a horse's eyes as it rears up and tries to break loose. For the men that work with them it's an upsetting business. And in a gas attack most of the animals have no protection at all. At least we can get a mask on if we're quick enough. They just have to retch and choke. Still, in the end I don't suppose there's much difference between us. Suffering is suffering, and I've seen more than one mutilated man begging his mates to shoot him like a dumb creature.

We're losing light now, nearly time for 'stand to'. Wonder if we'll have a lively time of it tonight. Oh Emily, how I wish I could see you.

Rosie reached into the pocket of her jeans and pulled out a packet of M&M's. She opened it slowly as her eyes looked out over the garden. A phrase was running through her mind. *They Shoot Horses Don't They?* Was it a film? A book perhaps? She couldn't be sure where she'd heard it. Nevertheless, it planted a strange notion in her head. Would Beth want someone to shoot her? It seemed a bizarre idea, but then, who could know what sort of misery lay ahead of Beth before the end? Would she suffer horribly – would she want to be put out of her agony like the dumb animal in Sam's diary? Rosie shuddered and tried to push the disturbing thoughts away. A flurry of snowflakes swirled outside the window.

I'm dreaming of a white Christmas ...

The words slid incongruously into her mind.

Just like the ones I used to know.

Ah yes – *Christmas.* It was almost upon them. She found herself remembering the conversation where she'd broken the news to Gavin that she'd be spending Christmas in Yorkshire. Her announcement certainly hadn't filled *him* with festive cheer. Still, credit to him, he'd managed to recover pretty quickly. She wondered what he was doing now. He might have rung at least; just to keep in touch, see if she'd arrived safely. Well, one thing was sure. She certainly wasn't going to ring him. He'd have to make the running if he was still interested. She was tired of trying to work him out.

She pressed her face against the window and looked out over the garden. In the middle of the frosted lawn was an old-fashioned, wrought iron lamppost that looked like it had come straight from C.S. Lewis's *Narnia.* She watched mesmerised as the snowflakes danced in its light. What *was* it, she wondered, about this time of year, and snow, and lamplight? Somehow they seemed to kindle in her an aching for days long gone – some elusive golden time, somewhere way, way back. She tried to think about past Christmases, but struggled to find anything in the way of festive nostalgia to pull out of her memory. Christmas Day back home had always been like an episode from *Eastenders.* Mickey stoned out of his head, only the occasional belch reminding them all of his disgusting presence. Her mother, stressed up and teary-eyed, moaning about the lousy dinner she'd subjected them to. Ciaran and Rosie had usually spent the afternoon upstairs out of the way, playing board games or reading. It could have been any old day. Christmas had always been the biggest non-event of the year, not even worth the slight twinges of hopeful anticipation that had always managed to sneak their way into her heart. No, she certainly didn't ache for days gone by. Yet here they were again, those strange, deep longings. They seemed to reach out to memories that weren't even there, and the sweetness of it all made her sad with a sadness that was almost unbearable. She threw a couple of M&M's into her mouth and breathed out slowly. *Just like the ones I used to know?* She chomped cynically on the sweets. *I don't think so.*

How ironic, she mused, that this year she should find herself here; amongst this most robust and well-adjusted of families, staying in this most cosy and welcoming of homes, about to celebrate Christmas in the most traditional and wholesome of ways, whilst all the time, Beth was dying. In almost every sense this was going to be Christmas like it ought to be. Christmas as it always was in books or schmaltzy films. Except that now, every second of every day, Beth's cancer, like some huge Sword of Damocles, was hanging ominously over them all, ready to slice each heart asunder the moment it fell.

Rosie bit her lip till it hurt. This was so unfair. For the first time in all her years, things had been starting to come together. She was trying hard to move on; slowly, tentatively building a new world for herself. And in that world, Beth was her best friend, the first person outside of Ciaran she'd ever got close to. Life without her now was simply unimaginable.

As the horrible prospect formed in her mind, Rosie's hands tightened into fists. *Why do things have to turn out like this? Why? Why …?*

Without warning, a surge of heartbroken anger welled up inside her. *What's wrong with me? Why does stuff just seem to follow me around?*

It was a peculiarly selfish moment, but she hardly cared. As tears threatened to spill, she buried her face in her hands. *Isn't it time I got a break? Hasn't life been lousy enough so far?*

She steeled her jaw and blinked hard, determined to hold back the wave of grief that was threatening to engulf her. She felt afraid to give in to it, afraid of where it might take her. But she was quite unable to stem the unexpected wash of guilt that suddenly broke over her head. It was the same guilt she'd felt the day Mel had brought her the cream cakes and Gavin had taken an hour out of work to visit her. Here she was again, thinking it was all about her. This thing was far bigger than that.

She forced her mind to think of Ciaran. How would *he* carry on? Beth was everything to him; his dream, his princess. Even in his beloved music he was joined to her. Their music was their backdrop, the signature tune for their intertwined lives. What had he said once? *She's the only person I don't mind playing second fiddle to.* He'd meant it as a joke, a playful remark, but he'd meant it all the same. From the moment he'd met Beth, his personal ambitions had taken a back seat. She'd become his whole world.

And then there was Beth's family. So brave now, but after Christmas – what? When all the celebrations were over and the trimmings taken down, what then? Rosie remembered Cassie's face the day they'd stood together in Beth's bedroom. She'd seen then what Beth meant to her family. Losing her would be like having a limb ripped off.

They Shoot Horses Don't They? Rosie stared grimly down the garden. Suddenly the lamplight didn't look quite so magical. As her eyes rested on the frozen trees creaking in the wind, a cold depression began to seep into her mind.

Anyone have a gun?

"Ciaran and me are going down to Tom Bennett's to pick up some logs," Ed announced as they walked into the kitchen. "Should think we'll be back about half five. He usually has plenty to tell me when I go down."

Cassie nodded. "Well, dinner'll be ready about six. Don't worry if you get stuck there. It's stew – it'll keep."

Ciaran moved round to the back of Beth's chair. "Will you be okay?" he whispered, rubbing her cheek softly.

She squeezed his hand. "You go. I'll be fine. It'll give me chance to have a chat with Mum."

"See you in a bit then, princess." He kissed her gently and the two men left.

Cassie flicked the kettle on. "You go into the living room, love, it'll be warmer for you in there. I'll bring the drinks in when they're ready."

Beth sat in the armchair closest to the fire. She leaned back and closed her eyes. One of the logs was singing in the heat, and for a few moments she focused on the sound in an attempt to still her mind.

Lord, I'm going to die.

The thought had crept in again. Her heartbeat quickened and she instinctively clasped her hands to her stomach. But then she remembered. It wasn't just her stomach now, was it? It was taking over the whole of her insides. Little by little, this thing was eating her alive. She tried to fix on the log song again.

Lord, I'm scared. Soon I won't be here any more. All of this will just carry on ... but I won't be here. I won't be part of any of it.

She stared into the fire. As she watched the familiar sight of flames flickering and playing amongst the pine, an overwhelming sensation began to fill her. She loved this fire. This room. This house. She loved being out in the open air. Getting wet in the rain. Listening to the birds. And the wind. And music. Playing her violin – wild as a storm, soft as a whisper. Losing herself in its song; mistress of it and yet under its spell. Crescendo, decrescendo ... rising and cascading in the glorious sounds that had taken her years to perfect. Each melody a birth, each cadenza a droplet distilled from the sum of all she had ever known, and been, and loved. It hit her with force. She loved being alive.

Oh God, I don't want to die. I want to stay here. I want to be with you, Lord – but does it have to be so soon? I feel I hardly know you. And there's so much here I don't want to leave just yet. Please ... please don't let me die.

Sudden panic gripped her. She felt her skin crawl as her mind began to wrestle with a dreadful notion. The ugliness of death. The unnatural wrenching of spirit from body. Surely God had never intended that for his precious ones? Surely death was an enemy?

She tried to harness her chaotic thoughts. Belinda had shown her some Bible verses about all this, she remembered. Fumbling in her bag, she pulled out the small Bible that Belinda had given her.

Somewhere there should be a list of scriptures they'd discussed. She leafed through the pages until her trembling fingers fell upon a piece of paper inserted in the Bible. The telephone rang. Her mother's voice sounded in the hallway.

"Oh hello, Janie. How are things with you?"

Janie Fellows – good. She always talks for ages. That should give me a bit of extra time.

She scanned through the list of Bible verses. Romans 5: 12 –

Therefore, just as sin entered the world through one man, and death through sin, and in this way death came to all men, because all sinned –

She scanned again. Hebrews 2: 14-15 –

Since the children have flesh and blood, he too shared in their humanity so that by his death he might destroy him who holds the power of death – that is, the devil – and free those who all their lives were held in slavery by their fear of death.

For a moment she found herself wishing Belinda was there to help her out. She turned to the book of John. Ah yes, here was a familiar one. She remembered it from her Sunday school days; the story of Lazarus.

Jesus said to her, 'I am the resurrection and the life. He who believes in me will live, even though he dies; and whoever lives and believes in me will never die.'

She closed her eyes. She'd won a prize once for memorizing that verse. But now it meant more than the chance to impress her Sunday school teacher. Her whole eternal destiny was riding on this one.

Cassie came into the room with a tray. Beth was slightly startled. She'd been so absorbed in her cogitations, she hadn't noticed the end of the telephone conversation. She stuffed the Bible behind her cushion.

"Sorry about that, love. Janie always picks her times, bless her." Cassie set the tray down and took a mug of tea over to Beth.

She noticed the discomfited expression on her daughter's face and frowned. "Are you alright, sweetheart?"

Beth faked a smile. "Yeah. Yeah, I'm fine. Just a bit tired."

Cassie picked up her own tea and sat down, her eyes filled with concern. "Not hurting anywhere, are you?"

"No, not at all." Beth spoke as reassuringly as she could. "Since I've been on the meds, the pain and sickness are a lot better." It was a truthful answer. The morphine tablets had taken care of the gripping stomach pains, and since she'd been fitted with the cyclizine syringe driver, even the relentless nausea that had plagued her for months had subsided. It was almost tempting to imagine that she was recovering. These days, the most prominent physical symptom was a nagging sense of exhaustion. But without the more obvious signs of a medical condition, it would have been easy to attribute the fatigue to some other, less sinister cause. The truth that the cancer was now devouring her silently and painlessly was somehow harder to grasp than the illusion.

She gave a dismissive laugh. "I suppose the thing that really reminds me I'm ill is when I look in the mirror. I look awful. Like I badly need a makeover."

Cassie wasn't having any of it. "You don't look awful, sweetheart. You've never looked awful."

There's time yet, thought Beth, not really wanting to think about it.

Cassie took a long, slow drink from her mug. "Ciaran's finding it hard, isn't he?"

Beth looked down sadly. "He's really struggling. I know he's trying to be brave for my sake but ..." Her voice tailed off. She couldn't imagine how he was going to cope. She remembered the day she'd told him her condition was terminal. The news had devastated him. He'd hardly smiled since. "To be honest, Mum, I'm finding it all a bit tricky. Having to come to terms with everything ... plus trying to keep my chin up in front of Ciaran. Even Dad. I don't think either of them could handle it if I got upset." She forced another little laugh. "It's not so hard with you. I already lost it in front of you at the hospital, so I know you're not gonna fall apart."

Inwardly Cassie winced, but she didn't let it show. "No pressure then, eh?"

Beth smiled. "Sorry, Mum. But you've always been strong. And I've never been more glad of it than I am now." She stared into the fire again. "It's an awful thing to be told you only have a few months left. Everything seems to become terribly real all of a sudden."

Cassie frowned gently. "What do you mean, love?"

Beth watched as a flame curled round a log and thinned into a smoky spire as it disappeared up the chimney. What *did* she mean? It was hard to explain to someone who wasn't experiencing this same heightened sense of reality. She shook her head. "I dunno. It's as if I've just woken up from a dream. I'm noticing things – things that were always there I guess. Only now I see them. I suddenly see everything as it really is. Bright and full of life. Wonderful somehow. All the things I've taken for granted – they seem so precious, so very, very precious ... now that I know I'll be leaving them soon." Her voice broke then and it was a few moments before she could speak again. "Can you understand, Mum? Can you understand what I'm saying? Everything seems so beautiful all of a sudden. So desperately beautiful." She cast a longing glance around the room. "And I so desperately, desperately want to stay here."

Cassie clenched her jaws together. Beth needed her to be strong; she'd just said so. But as hot tears pricked mercilessly at her eyes, Cassie knew she was in the darkest trial of her life.

Oh God, how can I be strong? I feel like my heart is crumbling to pieces. Help my baby, Lord. Please help my baby.

For a little while neither of them spoke. Apart from the hum and crackle of the fire, the room was still. The clock chimed on the hour and then all was quiet again. Both women were lost in their thoughts. At last, Beth sat forward in her chair.

"Mum ... can I tell you something?"

Cassie straightened and looked at her.

"I want to be buried up here. At Saint Edwin's."

Cassie fought to hide her shock. Even though she'd been planning to ask Beth about her final wishes, her daughter's blunt request came as a surprise. "Really? Not in London?"

Beth shook her head. "I don't belong in London, Mum. I never did. It got me where I wanted to go – musically anyway. But it's not home. I want to come home."

Cassie frowned as she considered the implications. "Have you told Ciaran about this?"

Beth shook her head again. "No, I haven't brought it up yet. I know we really need to start thinking about all this practical stuff, but he's hurting so much already. And there's something so final in talking about where you want to be buried. I'll have to pick my moment to tell him. But I wanted to bounce it off you first."

Cassie nodded slowly. "Do you think he'll object?"

Beth leaned back in her chair. "No. No, I can't imagine he will. He's no more attached to London than I am. It's where we live, where we work. But we're both so busy all the time. Tutoring, practising, teaching, rehearsing. Always racing here, racing there; it would hardly matter where we were really. Ciaran could get Peri work anywhere. We're only in London for the Avanti. Take that away and the place has no soul. Not for me anyway."

Cassie gazed through the window. *Oh God. She talks about soul. What about her own soul?* She held her tongue, afraid to broach that subject, yet desperate to do so.

Beth ran her fingers thoughtfully through her hair and looked across at her mother. "Well, what d'you think? Do you think it's a possibility? You don't have any objections yourself, do you? Having me up here full-time, I mean?" She smiled awkwardly.

Cassie's eyes filled with tears. "Oh Beth. *Beth* … ."

Beth shuffled in her chair. Perhaps this was the right time to say something. "It's not some kind of insurance policy, my wanting to be buried at St Ed's." She paused, suddenly embarrassed. *Well, Beth – time to admit that they've been right all along.* "I know I haven't been near the place in years. I haven't let you talk God stuff to me in years." She cleared her throat. "I've been hard as nails towards all that. I know I've been running from him."

Cassie stared at her.

Beth leaned forward and focused her gaze on the fire. "I'm still working things out, Mum. There's a lot I don't understand. But I wanted you to know, I've made my peace with God."

Cassie swallowed hard. She looked expectantly at Beth, willing her to elaborate.

Scrutinising the expression on her mother's face, Beth felt encouraged to continue. "I guess I started to feel something just after I first got diagnosed. It kinda puts things in perspective getting news like that. But when I realised I wasn't going to get better, that really clinched it for me. I met a Christian nurse on the ward and she talked me through a lot of things." A wistful smile came as she remembered Belinda. "I wish I had more time, Mum. There's such a lot I don't know. Sometimes I feel a real peace, and other times I'm frantic at the thought of leaving all of this – all of you. But one thing's sorted. Whatever happens to me now, I know where I'm going. I just wanted you to know that."

Cassie left her chair and came over to embrace her daughter. There were no words to express the joy she felt in that moment. But her heart overflowed with gratitude as tears spilled down her cheeks.

My God, I've prayed all these years for her. Thank you, thank you for your faithfulness.

Rosie was in slightly better humour as she went up to bed that night. The evening meal had been convivial enough and afterwards, as the wind rattled the rafters and the fire sang in the hearth, the family had played board games together. Beth had joined in with such gusto, it had been easy to pretend that everything was okay.

"Typed up any more entries for me?" she'd asked in a low voice as they were in the middle of a bout of Scrabble.

"Slave driver," Rosie had hissed.

Beth had pulled a face then. "If it's all the same to you," she'd teased with a growl, "I *would* like to get it finished before I'm obliged to make my exit."

Later, as they'd made their way upstairs for bed, Rosie had turned to Beth. "Do you want the diary back? I mean, is there any point me hanging on to it now you're out of hospital?"

Beth had looked thoughtful. "Hold on to it for now, Ros. I really appreciate what you're doing with it. It helps a lot." Leaning against the banister she'd sighed, and Rosie had seen the weariness in her eyes. "To be honest, I don't know if I'd have patience deciphering the writing now. It's so tiny, and I get so tired, Ros. Your typed up A4's are just right for me. That is, if you don't mind doing it."

Rosie had grinned then. "Frankly I'd rather eat my own toenails. But for you, dear sister-in-law, I'm prepared to suffer."

Now in the quiet of her room, Rosie picked up the diary and opened it again.

Zillebeke October 24th 1916

We had an unexpected visitor earlier today, Em. A certain Reverend Nathanael Bocking – Boxer's brother! His battalion is currently stationed at Hooge not far from here. Apparently he got wind of the news that we were in the area and decided to pay us a call. He's very like Boxer to look at, except that he's not so ruggedly built and he wears spectacles. Seems a jolly nice fellow; talked with several of the men and spent a good quarter of an hour or so chatting with Jimmy. I suspect Boxer had something to do with that. He's still concerned about him. His decision to watch out for him is something he takes very seriously. Anyway, Jimmy seemed much brighter after the conversation so the good Reverend must have said something to buck him up.

I have a lot of respect for the padres, Emily. They really put themselves out to help us men. You'll see them assisting with the wounded or giving out hot drinks, always as cheerful as you like. Often they're right there in the thick of things, even when it's lively, offering to say a prayer with you or just talking in that special, calming way they have. Somehow I think everybody feels comforted when there's a chaplain around, even if they won't admit to it. I know I do. Some of the chaps are a bit cheeky and pretend they've no time for all that religious stuff. But I tell you,

Em, when we've got a big one coming up, they're usually the first at the church services. As for me, I'm still struggling to know what I think about it all. The more I listen to Boxer, the more I wonder if he might be right. I never gave any of it much thought when I was younger, but since I've been out here, I find myself half-hoping that there's more to things than I'd previously imagined. Sometimes I look at the lads around me, especially the really young, fresh-faced ones. I think of their mothers back home; feeding them, clothing them, watching over them with pride for all those years, only to have them ordered out here to get blown to bits. What sense can you make of that, Em? Surely there must be more to it all, don't you think? If not, then it seems to me that life is nothing more than a huge tragedy.

Rosie flicked off the lamp and lay in the darkness. Well, that pretty much equated with *her* view of things at the moment. She certainly hadn't been able to come up with a more positive interpretation of life over the last few weeks. Not, she chided herself, that she should even be giving brain space to this kind of musing. She was pretty sure Mel never did. Or Ellie. Or any of them down at the nursery come to that. No, from what she'd managed to pick up in staffroom conversation, most of them seemed to lead a fairly vacuous existence. Pubbing, clubbing, snogging and shopping. What was more, they appeared quite content to do so. She'd never heard one of them agonising over the meaning of life. And why should they? They were young, they had their dreams, and even if their aspirations never went much beyond who they were going to pull at their next weekend pub crawl, what did it matter so long as they were happy? *That's more than I am,* thought Rosie, as though she had just realised it for the first time. Her mind turned to Beth. *She* was young. *She* had dreams. But it seemed that Life hadn't stopped to consider that. It was marching on regardless, and soon Beth would be gone. Just an empty space where she used to be. A string of broken hearts. And a boatload of questions.

Chapter 13

Beth looked around the church hall. It was years since she'd been in here. There was a definite freshness about the paintwork and one or two of the old fixtures had been replaced, but apart from that, everything was just the same as she remembered. Interspersed amongst the familiar faces, however, were quite a few new ones that she didn't recognise, and she suddenly realised how long she had been away. She leaned over to her mother. "I see Betty Flavel really *is* still here. How old is she exactly? She was ancient when I was a kid."

Several of the old faithfuls came over to say hello. For their sakes Beth did her best to look bright and cheerful. At least they'd had the guts not to ignore her, even if a couple of them had become a little tongue-tied after the first few words. She couldn't help feeling for them in their awkwardness.

Her mother nudged her gently. "There's Tim, look – over there. I bet he's hardly changed since you were here, has he?" She pointed discreetly across the room to a man who appeared to be in animated conversation with two young children. Beth recognised him immediately. It was a good eight years since she'd last seen him, but despite a few silver flashes in his hair and a slight thinning in his face, he looked very much the same.

She could remember the stir Tim Fitzpatrick had caused when he'd first arrived at Saint Edwin's all those years ago. She'd been about eight at the time. Even at that age, she was already a seasoned churchgoer. Church had always been a great place to be, socially at least. She thought of the countless 'aunties' and 'uncles' she'd managed to collect during her childhood years, and of all the kids she'd regularly sparred with in the weekly Sunday school quizzes. They'd been good days.

Then suddenly, along had come this strange, excitable guy wanting to change the world – starting with Saint Edwin's. It hadn't taken long to upset the applecart. Several stalwarts had disappeared from the scene pretty soon after his arrival. She'd only been a kid back then and hadn't really understood what was going on. Except that she'd soon noticed some of her friends were no longer around either. Explanations had been vague at the time. It was only later, as she'd got into her teenage years, that she'd twigged. Things had gotten just too hot for some folk. Tim Fitzpatrick didn't exactly swing from the chandeliers singing *'I've seen the light'*, but he wasn't like any vicar Saint Edwin's had known before. He talked about God with such a sense of reality and challenge that pretty soon it became impossible for anyone to sit on the fence. Either you made up your mind to follow his lead, or you left for new, less radical pastures. A few hopefuls had stuck around hoping things would go back to the way they'd been before, but eventually they'd tumbled to the fact that change was here to stay. Ed and Cassie Simmons had been among those who'd been stirred by the charismatic young preacher. Suddenly their lives had been turned around by the things that were happening in the hitherto staid parish of Saint Edwin's. At first, Beth had been in the thick of things too. Even Sunday school had buzzed with a new excitement. In her young heart she'd felt the pull, the same pull that her parents and countless others were experiencing. They'd been happy days. Back then, God was in His heaven and all was right with the world.

Until she'd become a teenager.

Beth smiled sadly to herself. To think it had taken cancer to bring her back to her senses. And now here was Tim Fitzpatrick making his way over to say hello. Ah well, she ought to try and look enthusiastic. She had a favour to ask of him.

Rosie was feeling slightly out of place. Sitting at a table with a cup of tea in one hand and a slice of the famous Flavel fruit cake in the other, she was beginning to feel like she'd joined the Women's Institute. She turned to Ciaran and made a wisecrack to that effect, in the hope of drawing him into conversation. But he just smiled absently and said nothing. Rosie gave up. It was the third attempt she'd made; he obviously wasn't in the mood for chitchat. Just then, a tall, slim man who looked to be in his early forties came over to the table. Cassie made the introductions.

"Tim – this is Ciaran, Beth's husband ... and this is his sister, Rosie. We're all going to be spending Christmas together."

She flashed a reassuring smile in Rosie's direction. "Rosie, Ciaran – this is Tim, our minister."

Rosie didn't think he looked much like a minister. He was dressed very casually in jeans and a sweater, and he had soft, brown eyes which twinkled when he grinned. No, he looked way too happy to be a vicar.

"Great to have you with us." Tim shook both their hands warmly and apologised that he was rather busy. "I'm afraid I can't stay and chat at the moment. In a few minutes our children's choir will be giving us a carol recital, so I have to go and make sure everything's ready. But I'll catch you both later." He checked his watch. "Better be going. Enjoy the show … and look out for the angels!"

It was Tim who introduced the choir. They trooped out onto the small stage and lined up in three rows, their nervous faces expectantly searching the audience before them. The 'angels' were on the front row. The very youngest of the group, they were dressed all in white and wore tinsel halos. Rosie couldn't help smiling to herself. They reminded her so much of the kids back at the nursery. Children were the same the world over. The choir began by singing *'Silent Night'*. The older members carried the song well. Their voices were surprisingly strong and melodic, and it was obvious they'd sung in public before. Though the 'angels' gave little in the way of vocal contribution, their facial expressions and unselfconscious fidgeting more than made up for their lack of participation in the singing. Rosie's attention was particularly captured by one little girl who was standing right at the far end of the front row. She had very dark hair and eyes, and a genuinely cherubic face with shiny pink cheeks which dimpled every time she smiled. And smile she did. It was as if she'd spent the last month practising. One minute she'd be turning around and pulling faces at her fellow choristers, as though totally oblivious of the audience's presence. The next, she would give the widest, most winning smile imaginable, as though she had suddenly remembered why she was there. Rosie couldn't take her eyes off the child. It had been worth coming just to watch this hilarious display.

The next carol had a slightly Caribbean feel to it. The 'angels' didn't seem very sure of this one either. They moved their little mouths from time to time, as if trying to find a familiar word, but on the whole, most of the song was spent twiddling with halos or having a scratch. The dark-haired cherub seemed more in tune with this particular number. She made no attempt to sing, but swayed happily from side to side, clapping her chubby hands to the rhythm of the music. When the song finished and the audience began their applause, the little girl gave several rapid, ostentatious bows in the various directions of the hall. Rosie wanted to laugh. This kid was an absolute scream.

Tim came back onto the stage and announced that the choir would be finishing with a rendition of *'Away in a Manger'*. As the pianist played the introduction, a change seemed to come over the 'angels'. Suddenly their small faces became gripped with concentration as they waited for their first note. As the song began, Rosie watched her little friend. The child's expression had become deadly serious, and now she sung every word with great feeling. Her head was tilted back and her large, dark eyes gazed into the air as though she really could see angels. The little girl did not miss one syllable of the carol. As it went on, she became more and more impassioned, so that towards the end of it, her tinsel halo had slipped over one ear with the efforts of her delivery. Never had Rosie seen such a simple childhood song offered up with more earnestness.

Quite unexpectedly, a powerful wave of emotion washed over her. As she watched the child, she realised that her own throat was beginning to tighten. She swallowed hard and tried to pull herself together. This was *'Away in a Manger'*, for crying out loud. Everybody did *'Away in a Manger'* at Christmas – what was the big deal? Yet she couldn't remember the last time she'd sung it herself, or where, or with whom. And suddenly, she felt terribly suffocated.

As the song drew to a close, she knew she had to get out. When Tim Fitzpatrick climbed onto the stage once more and asked if he might share a few words, she seized her chance.

Quietly, she took her coat from the back of her chair and softly nudged Ciaran. "I'm just going outside for a breather," she whispered. "See you in a bit."

The hall was situated a few paces from the south side of the church itself. Now as Rosie ventured out into the cold December air, she found herself with a choice of two paths, both of which led into the sprawling graveyard. She veered left, hardly thinking where she wanted to go, and soon found that the path had ended and she was walking amongst the headstones. The ground beneath her feet was brittle with frost. It crunched as she made her way along it with agitated steps.

What the heck was all that about? I must be going crazy or something. Filling up over a Christmas carol ... man, I'm really losing the plot now.

She walked a little faster, trying to shake off the disquiet that was gripping her. *Maybe I should have stayed in London. At least I'd still be sane.*

But she knew deep down that *that* had never been an option. She couldn't have refused Beth this last Christmas. Her stomach churned. *Beth's last Christmas* – what a hideous thought. She swore under her breath. Everything was so wrong. So very wrong.

She didn't see what she slipped on. But one minute she was striding along, and the next, she was flat on her back. She fell so heavily that for quite a few moments she lay on the frozen ground, hardly daring to move. *Great. Now I go and break every bone in my body.*

But she felt too shaken up to be angry. There was a slight throbbing in her ankle and the bottom of her back hurt. Trying not to wince, she drew her legs slowly up into bent position. *Well, that's positive I suppose. At least they still move – I haven't gone and paralysed myself.*

Some rooks flew overhead, cawing loudly as they circled in the overcast sky. Rosie waited for a few moments before attempting to move again. Her head was teeming with gruesome facts she suddenly wished she didn't know. Why was there never a first aider about when you needed one? She gently rolled onto her right side and propped herself up on her elbow. *So far so good.*

Looking around, she realised she was completely surrounded by gravestones. They were in varying shapes and sizes, and appeared to be arranged in no particular pattern at all. There was certainly nothing of the modern linear cemetery about this place. Some of the stones looked very old, and some, much more recent, but they seemed to sit together quite easily in their haphazard setting. The most arresting feature in view, however, stood only about three yards from where Rosie lay. It was a marble monument, about nine feet in height and in the shape of a cross. Rosie's eyes went to the words chiselled on its frontage.

TO THE GLORY OF GOD

AND

IN HONOURED MEMORY

OF

THE FALLEN OF OUR VILLAGE

There followed a list of names. Rosie pushed herself up into sitting position, wincing lightly as she did. *They must be used to folk tripping up round these parts,* she thought darkly. *They've even gone and shoved up a memorial to them.*

She rubbed her ankle, wondering if she dare try standing on it. Deciding to give it a go, she was just about to test it out when she suddenly heard the faint sound of footsteps crunching along the ground. *Now what – a haunted graveyard? Can today possibly get any worse?*

"Are you okay over there?"

A voice seemed to shout from somewhere behind her. She turned round to see an approaching figure. From a distance it was hard to know whether the person was male or female. Whoever it was, they were dressed in dark trousers and what appeared to be a scruffy duffle coat with the hood pulled up. Inwardly Rosie groaned. *Oh wonderful. It's either an overgrown Paddington Bear or some weirdo with really dodgy fashion sense.*

A few seconds later the mystery person was standing beside her. "Are you alright? You went with a right bang there." The enquirer pushed back the duffle coat hood with a soily hand, and Rosie could see that he was a young man who looked to be in his mid-twenties.

She tried to straighten up. "I was going for the backflip. Didn't quite make it."

The young man smiled and crouched down beside her. "Have you hurt anything – I mean, can you stand up?"

Rosie rubbed her ankle again. "I think I'll be okay. Just feel a bit shaken that's all."

The young man looked concerned. "D'you think someone should take a look at you, make sure you haven't broken anything?"

Rosie shook her head. "No, no I'm sure I'll be fine." She smiled in an effort to reassure him. *Apart from feeling a complete jerk, that is. Why is there always someone watching when you go and do something stupid?*

The young man extended a hand to her. For a second, Rosie wasn't sure whether she was supposed to shake it or grab it to pull herself up. Either way, she wasn't too keen. It was filthy. The guy looked like he hadn't seen a bath in weeks. Thankfully at that point he glanced down at his hand and, realising its grimy state, hurriedly withdrew it.

"Sorry about that. I'm forgetting myself." He looked slightly embarrassed and grinned. "Anyway, I'm Jonathon. And *you* are ...?"

"Rosie."

Jonathon nodded. "Well, I'm very sorry, Rosie – about your fall. I have to say I feel partly responsible."

Rosie frowned. "Why? It wasn't your fault." *Not unless you're some psycho that goes around laying tripwire to leg up unsuspecting victims.*

Jonathon ran a filthy hand through his tousled hair. "Well, not directly maybe. But I'm a bit behind schedule with everything.

I'd planned to get in first thing this morning and have all this cleared by lunchtime. But my car started playing up – I didn't get here until after ten. I've been ringing round trying to get someone to have a look at it. You know how hard it is just before Christmas, everywhere's booked up solid ..."

Rosie looked blank. What on earth was this guy on about?

Jonathon gazed around the churchyard with a gloomy expression. "Wow, there's far more to go at than I realised. This is gonna take me a good two days by the looks of things." He seemed to be thinking out loud.

Rosie suddenly clicked. "Are you the *gardener* or something?"

Jonathon shook his head. "Not exactly. Our regular guy broke his leg back in the summer and he's been having a lot of trouble with it. Things have got a bit overgrown here. I offered to help out – y'know, spruce the place up for Christmas. Unfortunately for you, I hadn't got round to this bit yet." He grinned as though something had just occurred to him. "Hey, you didn't think I normally went round dressed like this, did you?"

Now it was Rosie's turn to smile. "Well, I did wonder ..." *That's a relief. At least this guy's not as barmy as he looks.*

Jonathon slapped his dirty hands together several times as if to try and get rid of some of the filth. "Eric – that's the gardener – he told me to make sure I wore my oldest clothes, and I'm glad I did. I've been tidying up some of the graves round the back there. Y'know, the really ancient ones that nobody ever visits. It's a never-ending task once you start. I was just raking leaves when I saw you fall." He looked down at the ground where Rosie was still sitting. "I reckon that's what you slipped on. *Leaves*. They can be pretty nasty when there's been a frost."

Rosie shivered as she suddenly realised how cold she was.

Jonathon frowned. "Look, there's a bench over there. Do you think you can make it?" He pointed to a wooden seat a few yards from them. "We really ought to get you off this cold ground before you catch something."

Rosie managed to get to her feet, and with quiet encouragement from Jonathon she made it to the bench. Her back felt sore and her ankle slightly sprained, but she was sure it was nothing that a hot bath wouldn't sort out. As they sat on the seat, their breath steaming in the frosty air, Jonathon turned to her, a curious expression on his face. "You're not from round here, are you, Rosie? We don't get many strangers in Ridderch Standen."

Strangers – that's nice. First he leaves stuff all over the place for me to break my neck on, then he insults me. She smiled. "No, I'm from London."

"That's a London accent?" Jonathon looked puzzled.

"Not entirely." *Oh boy. Where do I begin?* "I'm actually Irish. But we moved to England when I was a little girl. Leicester actually. When I was sixteen I moved to London – been there ever since." *Why on earth am I telling you all this? I hardly know you.*

Jonathon nodded. "I see. So what brings you here?"

Rosie dug her hands into her pockets as she gazed across the churchyard. *Do I tell him that my sister-in-law's got terminal cancer and one of her dying wishes is for us all to be together up here for Christmas?*

She decided to simplify. If he was gardening for the place, he must be part of the church. *Therefore –*

"Do you know Ed and Cassie Simmons?"

Jonathon smiled. "Oh yes. I've known them years."

Good. This should be straightforward then. "Well, my brother's married to their daughter."

Jonathon's eyes widened slightly. "You mean *Beth?*"

Rosie nodded. "We're all spending Christmas together."

"Ah right, I understand." He seemed to hesitate for a moment. "How *is* Beth? I was terribly shocked when I heard about her illness. I know her two brothers very well. How's she coping with it all?"

Rosie shrugged. "Well, she's on plenty of medication to help control her symptoms, so I guess that bit's okay for the time being. As for all the rest of it – I have to say she's doing brilliantly, considering." It didn't seem much of an answer but Rosie wasn't sure how to elaborate further. Somehow, trying to speak on Beth's behalf felt a little awkward.

Jonathon smiled sadly. "Bless her. I was at school with her, y'know. Really nice girl. Very talented too. She was in the school orchestra." He looked genuinely upset.

Rosie didn't know what to say. She looked down at her knees, wishing she could think of something to make the moment less uncomfortable. She rubbed her gloved hands together as if to warm them. "Guess I'd better go and let you get on with your work. I've taken up enough of your time already."

Jonathon lifted his head, and for a moment they looked at each other. It was only for the shortest time and then he turned away. But in those few seconds she couldn't help noticing the deep blue of his eyes, and the kindness in them.

He gave a slight cough. "I think I might come down to this bit and make a start. The leaves are pretty bad down here. Are you sure you're gonna be okay?"

Grateful for the change of subject, Rosie assured him she would be.

Jonathon rubbed his hands together purposefully. "I'll go get my rake then." He pointed to the marble monument. "See the memorial there. We have an old guy in the church whose dad died in the Great War. Don't think he ever got to meet him, mind. He was just a baby at the time. But he brings a wreath every Christmas – folks say he's never missed a year. I'd hate him to fall like you did. I don't think he could take it."

Rosie gave a little laugh. "Suppose that was my good deed for the day then, eh – alerting you to the hazard?"

"That's one way of looking at it," Jonathon grinned.

Rosie suddenly frowned. "Is it a *First* World War memorial, did you say? I didn't take much notice while I was down there."

Jonathon stood up. "Come and have a look. There are two panels. One for each of the world wars."

Rosie stood to her feet and began to follow him. She walked slowly at first, testing every footstep. It was a relief to her to find that she could get along quite well. When she got to the monument, Jonathon was gazing up at it intently.

"Here, Rosie, this is the First World War side. There are far more names on this one."

Rosie counted. Twenty-seven names to be precise. She scanned some of them. *Pte. Walter Birkinshaw. Sapper Harold Ellis. Pte. James Henry Link. 2nd Lt. Albert Spears –*

Jonathon's voice interrupted her. "*Pte. William Rowney.* That's him – y'know, the old guy's dad I was telling you about." He pointed to the name on the monument. "He was a gunner apparently."

Rosie nodded slowly. "Sad, isn't it?" she found herself saying. "So many men from such a small village." She was thinking about Wilf, and his mate, and the German boy. *Multiplied by millions. Every village in Britain must have one of these. And Europe. And beyond.*

"Are you interested in history then, Rosie?" Jonathon ventured.

Rosie was quiet for a moment. *Not as a rule. Usually avoid it like the plague. But since I came across Sam and his buddies ...*

She rubbed her arms against the cold. "I guess you could say I'm developing an interest. The thing is, Beth recently came across something in an old bookshop. A First World War diary – written by a soldier out on the Western Front. She found it by accident really. It's quite detailed. Gives a pretty good picture of what things were like out there."

Jonathon's eyes widened. "Wow, Rosie, I wouldn't mind taking a look at that. Do you think she'd let me see it?"

As she heard the boyish eagerness in his voice, Rosie felt a sudden, inexplicable pride at being temporary custodian of Sam's grimy notebook. "Actually, *I* have it at the moment. Beth gave it to me while she was in hospital, for safekeeping. I've been typing up the entries and passing them on to her. Beth really wanted to get it all printed up so that we'd have a permanent copy. Y'know, with the diary being so old and everything. I'm only part way through; it'll take me a while yet to finish."

Jonathon looked truly impressed. "You've got a treasure there, Rosie. That kinda thing's like gold dust. Some people would snap your hand off for something like that."

Rosie smiled to herself. He was beginning to sound like Beth.

Jonathon took a step towards the monument. "See *this* guy ..." Proudly, he ran his finger under one of the names. "He was my great, great –" He hesitated a moment. "I think there might be another great in there somewhere – anyway, uncle. I believe he was only in his mid-twenties when he died. About my age, I guess."

Oh boy, thought Rosie as she moved closer to take a look. *I've really got him going. Now he's starting to sound like Mr Lowry.*

She peered at the name. *Pte. Philip Matthew Bocking.* She frowned. *Private Philip Matthew ...?*

"Rosie! *Rosie!*"

Her thoughts were interrupted by a voice calling out from somewhere at the top of the churchyard. She spun round to see Ciaran waving to her. She turned to Jonathon. "It's my brother. I bet he thought I'd got lost." She waved back. "I'd better go. They're probably all waiting for me."

A momentary look of disappointment passed over Jonathon's face. Then he quickly smiled. "Yes – you'd better go. It's been nice meeting you, Rosie. Might see you again perhaps, before you go back ..."

Rosie wasn't sure if it was a question or a statement. She hesitated for a second, then returned his smile. "Yeah, perhaps. Thanks for your help and everything. Bye."

Feeling slightly self-conscious, she thrust her hands into her pockets and began to make her way towards Ciaran. When she reached him, Ciaran had a quizzical expression on his face.

"You okay, Ros? I wondered where you'd got to."

"Yeah." Rosie kept her head down. *Why am I colouring up? This is so not like me.* "Just took a bit of a tumble, that's all. I'm okay though. Didn't break anything."

Ciaran nodded thoughtfully. "So who's the guy?"

Rosie could see that he was trying to stifle a smile. She hadn't seen him smile in ages. She tried to play it cool. "He's the stand-in gardener. He came to my rescue when I fell over and nearly ruptured myself."

Ciaran grinned. "Ouch!"

To Rosie's relief he didn't mention Jonathon again. They joined the others and went back to Oak Lodge for lunch. Later that afternoon, Rosie helped Cassie with some food shopping.

"Only three more days to Christmas, Rosie," Cassie puffed as they loaded bags into the car. "Are you all ready for it?"

"Just about," Rosie answered tentatively.

It was true. She'd got all her presents, except one. Beth's. She was really struggling with Beth's. *What would be appropriate? What would I want if I only had months to live?* She sighed. This had to be the most difficult gift she'd ever had to buy. *Whatever I decide to go for, I've only a couple of days to get it sorted. I need to give it some serious thought.*

She knew Ciaran was planning to go shopping in Northallerton the following day. She'd just have to cadge a lift with him and hope for some inspiration.

That night in bed, she picked up Sam's diary again. As she read the words, she couldn't help picturing the dirty young man in the churchyard with his deep blue eyes and unkempt hair.

Poperinghe Billets October 26th 1916

Glad to be out of Zillebeke. We weren't there too long, but things were getting pretty lively just before we were relieved. Right at the last minute we lost a man from our platoon – a chap called O'Grady. I'll be honest, Em, I didn't much care for him. He was a sour-tempered fellow with a rather coarse way about him. Still, it's never pleasant to see a man go west, no matter how much you might dislike him. You could say he was unlucky. As the relief troops were coming down, a bit of shrapnel came over into the trench and got him in the chest. He screamed out at first, then began to make the most horrible gurgling sound. When I saw the blood coming out of his mouth, I knew it was bad. But imagine our shock when he suddenly clawed his way up onto the firestep and started trying to shout obscenities at the enemy. A sniper got him straight through the throat and he fell back in on top of us. For a few moments we stood staring down at him as he lay there with his eyes wide open and a look of awful rage still on his face. After a couple of minutes, Boxer closed O'Grady's eyes and turned to me. Then in the quietest voice he said, "Make sure you don't die like that, Sam."

I knew what he was getting at, Em. Boxer's a great fellow, but I must confess, sometimes he unnerves me. He has a way of saying things which can really put the wind up a chap. He hasn't mentioned O'Grady again, and I have to say, I'm glad.

Feeling tired and still a little sore from her fall, Rosie switched off the lamp. She needed to be up early next morning to set off shopping with Ciaran. As she curled up for sleep, her mind went back over the events of the day. She thought about Jonathon and smiled. It made her cringe slightly to think he'd actually seen her go flying. *Ah well,* she consoled herself. *At least he'll have given the place a good going-over because of it. The old man should be safe enough when he goes to lay his wreath.*

Her eyes grew heavy and she started to drift off. A few moments later, however, she came round with a jolt. Of course! *That* was where she'd seen the name before …

Private Philip Matthew Bocking.

Boxer.

Chapter 14

It was late on Christmas Eve and Saint Edwin's was packed. The atmosphere buzzed with the sound of chatter and muted excitement. Rosie looked down at her watch. Ten fifty-four; another six minutes to go. She turned to Ciaran at her side. He was staring straight ahead, his face a picture of grim sobriety. She guessed he was feeling as uncomfortable as she was. *Fancy us two sitting together in a church,* she mused. It seemed an awful long time since they had.

Beth had been determined to come tonight, even though she'd had to spend the afternoon in bed just to build up the strength. This was part of her Christmas, she'd insisted. An old family tradition – something she'd never missed when she was living at home. 'You'll come too, won't you, Ros?' she'd entreated. 'I'm sure you'd enjoy it.' Rosie hadn't had the heart to refuse. And so here they all were, sitting, waiting. *It isn't like I've never set foot in a church before,* Rosie told herself as her heart thumped nervously. *How hard can it be?*

At precisely eleven o'clock, Tim Fitzpatrick walked to the front of the church and greeted the congregation. He announced that the service was to begin with a selection of carols. Rosie was determined to steel herself this time. She didn't want a repetition of the '*Away in a Manger*' episode. As the organ began to belt out the music, she kept her eyes fixed on her song sheet and mimed along to the words as convincingly as she could. It would be far too embarrassing to let Ciaran hear her actually *singing*, she reasoned to herself. Nevertheless, she was amazed at the volume of song coming from the rest of the congregation, and slightly disconcerted at the enthusiasm of certain folk in the rows in front of her. She tried to think about something else. All her Christmas presents were wrapped, she'd washed her hair – she'd even found time to put on some nail polish. *Why is the guy two rows ahead waving his hands about in the air?*

She'd settled on a lava lamp for Beth. Apparently they were very therapeutic, or so the man in the shop had said. *Why are all these people jumping up and down to a Christmas carol?* Come to think of it, *was* it a Christmas carol? It wasn't one *she'd* ever heard before.

She tried to get her mind back onto lava lamps. She'd nearly gone for a hippopotamus filled with wheat and lavender – the kind you put in the microwave to warm up. Beth felt the cold these days. *Oh boy, now they look like they're gonna do a Mexican wave.*

Rosie tried to sneak a glance at Ciaran. It looked like he was miming too. If he'd noticed the strange characters in front, he certainly wasn't letting on. She forced her eyes back to the song sheet and tried to concentrate. Thankfully, it wasn't long before Tim Fitzpatrick came to the rescue. He asked everyone to take their seats and then made a couple of announcements.

"Tomorrow morning – Christmas Day – we'll be meeting here at ten o'clock. Just for an hour. Everyone's welcome ... if you can tear yourself away from all your presents! It's good to share the day with the Lord."

Rosie grimaced to herself. *Think I'll give that one a miss. Some of this lot must spend half their lives sat in church.*

The service went on. Rosie was surprised to hear some Bible readings which she vaguely recognised from years ago. She remembered sitting like this in a Catholic church in Wicklow, and in later times, another one in Leicester. Every Christmas Eve their mother had taken them along to midnight Mass. It was their only church visit in the year. "Father Christmas won't come if you don't go to Mass," she'd warned gravely. And so they'd complied. One Christmas Eve, it had occurred to Rosie to ask why he came to all the other kids at school who never ventured near a church. Her mother had brushed the question aside with a cursory reply. "It's different for Catholics," she'd said. And it had been different again once Mickey had come onto the scene. One year, he'd come into church straight from the pub and joined them on the back row, halfway through the service. Rosie shuddered as she remembered. She'd been sitting at the end, and they'd all had to move up to squeeze him in. How she'd hated it. So close to him.

Smelling the drink on his breath, and that horrible odour, so sickeningly familiar. Had her mother ever realised? Had she ever suspected, even slightly? Rosie's mouth tightened into a thin line as she thought about it. No. She couldn't have. She might have been dysfunctional at times, but she wasn't cruel. She was just blinded.

'The people walking in darkness have seen a great light;
on those living in the land of the shadow of death
a light has dawned ...'

Tim's voice sounded out over the hushed church as he began his sermon. Rosie felt frustrated at herself. Was she ever going to get over this? Up till recently, she'd almost imagined it was all behind her. Something that belonged to another time, another place; something better left well alone. But over the last few weeks it seemed to have been raising its head more and more often, jumping out at her from the shadows when she least expected it. It was pain. Pain that came from deeper than her very guts. Pain that, despite all her best efforts to pretend otherwise, seemed just as alive as it had ever been. Suddenly, Rosie thought bitterly, it was pain behaving badly.

She tried to focus on Tim's words from the front, but a dark sense of foreboding had seeped into her mind. She spent the rest of the service feeling woolly-headed and distant. Even Ciaran sitting next to her now, the one person to whom she'd clung, the one person whose promises had held her little girl world together, had never known about *that*. Her hands tightened into fists as she tried to bury the memories. She really had to get herself sorted on this one. But just how was another matter.

She found herself standing for the final hymn, and then the service was finished. People began to turn round, shaking hands and exchanging festive greetings. Rosie smiled weakly at Ciaran. "That was fun, wasn't it?" she commented gloomily. Ciaran smiled weakly in return.

"Hey, you two –" Beth broke in, "shall we go down and look at the nativity?" Her face was expectant as she gestured towards something at the front of the church. Ciaran stood up to follow her and the three of them began to wend their way down an aisle. The large nativity scene was situated in an alcove to the left of the altar and was lit up by a soft spotlight and two tall candles, one on either side of the display. As they neared it, Beth turned to Rosie. "Atmospheric, isn't it? I used to love it when I was a little girl."

They hadn't quite made it to the front when Beth was spotted by an elderly couple leaving their seats. Recognising her from times past, they stopped to greet her. Rosie, who had been walking a couple of steps in front, hadn't realised that Beth and Ciaran were no longer behind her. It was with a flash of consternation, therefore, that she suddenly found herself at the nativity scene – alone. Turning round, she caught sight of the little group in conversation. She decided against going back to join them. Nothing in her felt like talking tonight, especially to total strangers. She turned back to the nativity display and tried to focus her mind on the scene in front of her. It made her think of religious Christmas cards, the sort her mother used to insist on sending. And school nativity plays. Funny how she'd almost forgotten about those. The annual 'let's-see-how-many-kids-we-can-squash-onto-a-stage' fest. This sudden childhood recollection made her smile, and for a moment or two her mind was brightened by the memory of it. The good old school nativity play; it had surely been something of a highlight in the academic year. Even now she could still recall the buzz of anticipation that had simmered amongst the would-be thespians as the deputy head had called auditions. Each little girl nursing her own secret longing to be Mary, each little heart hopeful that *maybe this year …* (could Mrs Pemberley possibly have realised just how many fragile dreams were hanging on her final decision?) Oh, the dubious solace of being cast as a shepherd. An angel had always been the preferred alternative, Rosie remembered. She could only speak for the girls, of course. She had no idea if being cast as Joseph had ever meant anything like as much to the boys. Suddenly it all seemed an awful long time ago. She hadn't seen a nativity play in years and years. *But then,* she thought ruefully, *if my experience in the childcare business is anything to go by, most places these days are probably far too busy minding their PC p's and q's to stage anything like that.* Things, it seemed, had moved on. Still, it was nice to have unearthed one aspect of Christmas Past that had managed to bring a smile to her face.

She became aware of a CD playing in the background. The sound drifted out from speakers fixed high on various pillars around the building, giving the impression that the whole roof space was filled with the strains of angelic song. Rosie tried to identify the familiar carol that was playing. Ah yes. *Oh Little Town of Bethlehem*. That had always been a favourite at Saint Joseph's ...

She stared at the pot figures in front of her. Had any of this stuff ever really happened – the whole *'born in a stable'* thing? And even if it had, what difference did it make? A little baby, a few animals. What was there to get so excited about?

How silently, how silently
The wondrous gift is given,
And God imparts to human hearts
The blessings of His heaven.
No ear may hear His coming
But in this world of sin,
Where meek souls will receive Him still,
The dear Christ enters in ...

As the words floated mellifluously through the airwaves, Rosie's eyes fixed on the infant laid on his bed of straw. It was a nice story, whatever sense it might or might not make. Better than the storylines in the *Eastenders'* Christmas special anyway. The next carol began to play. As she stood there, Rosie felt her mind beginning to clear slightly. Somehow, standing in front of this ancient scene, listening to music which seemed to echo from another sphere, she felt safe. Wrapped up from the world outside, hidden from its demands and its scrutiny. She could understand why Beth had wanted to come.

"*Rosie!*"

A familiar voice made her spin round. She was surprised to see that it was Jonathon. But apart from the deep blue eyes and the laughing smile, nothing about his appearance tonight was familiar at all. He was dressed in a dark suit and cobalt-coloured tie. His fair hair, which had looked so tousled and unkempt in the churchyard, was now combed and parted to the side and looked lighter than Rosie remembered. To her horror, she felt her cheeks colouring.

"Hey, it's great to see you," Jonathon enthused. "We were just about to leave when I spotted you. I had to come over and say hello."

Rosie suddenly felt desperately tongue-tied. He'd caught her totally unprepared. She smiled and tried to think of something sensible to say. "It's been lovely tonight," was about all she could manage.

Jonathon nodded warmly. "Yes it has, hasn't it?" Hesitating for a moment, he jingled his car keys thoughtfully. "Will you be here in the morning, Rosie?"

A reply was on her lips before she had time to think about it. "I'm hoping to be ..."

She felt herself reddening even more. *What? Where did that come from? Since when did I go to church on Christmas Day?*

Jonathon gave a broad smile. "Oh that's great! I'll be able to have a chat with you tomorrow then. We normally have a cup of tea after the Christmas morning service. It's just that I'm in a bit of a hurry now. I'm taking Albert home – you know, Albert Rowney, the old guy I was telling you about the other day. It's way past his bedtime, bless him."

Rosie attempted to think of a clever reply, but no words came. Somehow Jonathon fazed her. His manner was so open, his eyes so kind, that suddenly it was difficult to come up with the usual witticisms and sparring banter. He even made her blush.

"Well, see you in the morning then, Rosie. Hope you get lots of presents!" Jonathon flicked his car keys up into the palm of his hand and, with another smile, set off back down the aisle.

Rosie hurriedly turned back to the nativity scene. She felt flustered, yet strangely happy at the same time. Well, at least tomorrow she'd be able to tell him about Boxer. A troubling thought came to her. What if none of the family were going to church in the morning? She could hardly turn up on her own, could she?

She needn't have worried. That night back at Oak Lodge, Cassie stopped her in the hallway. "Don't feel you have to, Rosie, but I just wondered if you fancied going along to Saint Edwin's in the morning. Ed and I are going. I think Ciaran and Beth are gonna give it a miss – she's a bit tired. But you're very welcome to come with us if you want. Entirely up to you, love."

Rosie didn't want to sound too eager. "Erm, okay then. I will. Thanks."

Cassie seemed delighted. "It doesn't go on too late. We'll have plenty of time for Christmas dinner. We're going to have a lovely day, Rosie." She suddenly leaned forward and kissed Rosie on the cheek. "We're so glad to have you with us, love. Makes it all the more special."

Rosie smiled awkwardly. Tonight had been full of surprises.

Shortly afterwards, she was in her room about to get ready for bed when there was a knock on her door. It was Beth. She came in and sat by the window. "Did you enjoy it tonight then, Ros?" She looked pale and washed out, and Rosie wondered that she hadn't gone straight to bed.

"Yeah. It reminded me of days gone by." Rosie forced a grin. *In more ways than you could imagine,* she thought sadly. *But I won't bore you with the gruesome details.*

Beth nodded. "I see you've met Jonathon Kirkbride." There was a twinkle in her eyes. "I was crazy about him at one bit, y'know. Back in my schooldays, I mean. Most of the girls in our class were too. *Until* –" She broke off and began to laugh softly to herself.

Rosie stiffened slightly. "I met him the other day in the churchyard. I had a bit of a fall and he came to check that I was okay, that's all." *Most of the girls in your class were too, until what exactly?* She cleared her throat and tried to smile nonchalantly. "So what's the joke, Mrs M? What's so funny about him?"

Beth frowned. "Oh … it's not Jonathon that's funny. I'm just thinking it's funny the way things turn out sometimes. We all fancied him like mad and then he suddenly went and turned all religious. Just seems ironic really." For a moment her expression was thoughtful. Then she shook herself. "Anyway, I left for music college not too long after that." She grinned disarmingly. "How was I to know my heart would be stolen by a gorgeous, wild Irishman?"

Rosie still didn't see what was so amusing, but she didn't press further. She rolled her eyes in mock disgust. "Don't talk about my brother like that. It's disturbing."

Momentarily, she toyed with the idea of mentioning to Beth the business about Boxer, but decided against it. All of a sudden, she felt reluctant to let Beth know that she was planning to see Jonathon in the morning. Maybe it was best to keep her cards close to her chest for the time being. Check the thing out with Jonathon first. See if there was any possibility of a link. After all, she reasoned to herself, there seemed little point in getting Beth's hopes up if the whole thing was going to come to a disappointing dead end.

When Beth had gone off to bed, Rosie did another check on the diary. She leafed through the earlier entries until she came to the one that cited Boxer's name. Could it really be the same guy? Realistically, what would be the chances of that? Still, as she thought about sharing the news with Jonathon, a shudder of excitement went through her. Suddenly, she could hardly wait for morning.

Tim Fitzpatrick was true to his word. The Christmas morning service ended at five past eleven. Rosie was in benevolent mood as she walked across to the church hall with Ed and Cassie. She felt she could forgive Tim the extra five minutes.

The hall was filling up quickly when they arrived. Victor Hely-Hutchinson's *'Carol Symphony'* was playing in the background as they queued up at the serving hatch for drinks. Rosie felt as though she'd stepped back in time.

Cassie turned to her. "Did you enjoy it, love?"

Rosie nodded. "Yes, I did." Looking at Cassie's gentle face, she felt she wanted to say something positive. "I don't normally go to church. It takes a bit of getting used to. But this morning was nice."

Cassie smiled. "Good, I'm glad. By the way, Rosie, you're looking very pretty today. That jumper's gorgeous – it really makes your dark hair stand out."

Rosie felt herself flushing. She instinctively looked down at the cream-coloured top and smoothed it straight. It was one that Mel had helped her choose; a flattering long-line style with a cowl neck, in the softest angora. *Bet it makes my bright pink face stand out too,* she thought, feeling suddenly self-conscious. Just then, out of the corner of her eye, she saw the back door swing open. Jonathon stepped inside and glanced around the hall. Rosie willed her face to cool down, but to no avail. Within seconds he had joined them.

"Hi everybody! Happy Christmas!" He kissed Cassie's cheek and shook Ed warmly by the hand. Extending a hand to Rosie, Jonathon grinned at Ed and Cassie. "I met this young lady the other day. I'm afraid she came a cropper in the churchyard. I reckon that new gardener needs sacking; she could have broken her neck." He turned his eyes to Rosie and she saw the twinkle in them. "Thankfully she's agreed not to sue."

Rosie was relieved. That had explained things anyway. Once they'd all been served, the group moved to a corner of the hall. Rosie was just wondering how to broach the subject of the diary when a couple came over to talk to Ed and Cassie, enquiring about Beth. Rosie swallowed hard and seized her chance.

"I've brought something to show you."

Jonathon seemed curious. "You *have?*" He looked around. Nearby there were two empty chairs by a small table. They went over and sat down.

Rosie opened her handbag and pulled out the diary. "You remember me telling you about this the other day?"

Jonathon nodded and stared at the old notebook, a look of fascination spreading across his features.

"Well," Rosie continued, "the other night I remembered something. I was just dropping off to sleep when it suddenly came to me. Here ... it's in one of the entries." She opened the diary and carefully passed it to him.

Jonathon took the book from her hands with a gentleness that Rosie found oddly touching. For a few moments he gazed down at it, letting it rest on his palms as though it was some precious treasure. Then Rosie heard his voice softly muttering the words.

Fletre (billets) August 14th 1916

Yesterday I got chance for a good conversation with the other chap – my fellow rescuer. He's Pte Philip Bocking, known to most, it seems, as Boxer ...

Jonathon glanced up at her, his eyes wide. "Philip Bocking?" He read on. "*A Yorkshireman ... a bit of a religious type too ...* . Oh wow, Rosie, I can hardly believe it. This is amazing." He shook his head incredulously.

Rosie felt quietly pleased. "Do you think it could be him?"

Jonathon looked up from the page. "Well, it's not a very common name, is it – *Bocking?* Wonder if he's got an army record somewhere. Are there no more clues to his identity?"

Rosie thought for a moment. "Hang on. You know this uncle – er *great* uncle, or whatever he was. Did he have any brothers? *This* guy did. He was a chaplain – name of Nathanael." She turned the pages gently until she found the entry about Boxer's brother.

Jonathon read it and frowned. "Well, obviously there was my great, great granddad, but I don't think he fought. I've a feeling there *was* another brother, but I can't be sure." His face suddenly broke into a smile. "I know someone who could tell us though. My great grandmother, Maisie." He looked intently at Rosie, his blue eyes filling with excitement. "Rosie – how do you fancy coming to meet her?"

Rosie spent the rest of Christmas day at Oak Lodge. Beth's two brothers and their families came over for dinner and stayed until late in the evening. The day was filled with games and songs, memories and tales. At one point, Cassie even played a few ballads on the piano. There were calls for Ciaran to accompany her on the violin, which he eventually did. Rosie felt a rush of pride as she watched him. How brave he seemed to her. How brave and how sad.

"You'd make a smashing fiddle player!" Josh enthused as the music came to an end. "I know an Irish band that's after someone like you. I reckon they'd snap you up."

Ciaran shook his head with a smile and began to put his instrument back into its case. Suddenly, Josh's daughter, Meg, made a new request. "Auntie Beth, won't *you* have a go?"

Rosie saw Ciaran and Beth exchange glances. Beth hesitated for a moment, then gestured to Ciaran to pass her the violin. Cassie gently began to play again, and after a few bars Beth joined her. A hush fell over the room. One by one, the family members closed their eyes and listened. Rosie stared into the fire. Her mind went back to the Laureate Hall and the concert. How different things had been just a couple of months ago. The whole family had been riding high that night. She looked furtively round the room. *Poor things. How could they have known back then? This is the last Christmas they'll ever do this.*

When Beth had finished, everyone applauded and made a fuss of her. Rosie caught her eye and Beth winked with a knowing smile. Rosie noticed that she was trembling, as though the effort of playing had exhausted her. But she humoured her family, smiling and pretending to bow, just as she had two months earlier. Rosie couldn't help but be impressed at her fortitude.

That night, realising it was going to be impossible to keep secret her forthcoming trip to see Maisie, Rosie decided to tell Beth about her discovery on the war memorial.

Beth was intrigued. "I wonder if it's him. Wouldn't that be fantastic, Ros?"

Rosie shuffled in her chair. "Well, apparently Jonathon has a great grandmother still living. He seems pretty sure she'll know the name of Philip's brother if he had one. She lives in a retirement home in a village called – *Aylesthwaite*, I think it was."

Beth nodded. "Yes, Aylesthwaite. It's not far from here."

Rosie hesitated. "He's asked me if I'd like to go and meet her."

"Whoa, listen at you!" Beth smirked. "It's normally mum and dad who get the first inspection. He must be keen if he's dragging you off to meet great granny …!"

Rosie aimed a pretend swipe at her. "Will you cut it out? This is research. Just research, *okay?*"

Beth stifled a smile. "Makes a change from etchings, I guess."

Rosie gave her a withering look. "It's a good job you're ill. I'd slug you if you weren't." Though the comment was only made in jest, she wondered for one awful moment if she'd gone too far.

Beth's face, however, was calm and relaxed. "I'm only winding you up, Ros. You go. I can't wait to see what you come up with. When are you going?"

Rosie's voice softened. "Jonathon mentioned Wednesday."

"Great. Well, we'll wait with bated breath then, eh? Night, Ros." She patted Rosie's arm and went out of the room. Thankfully, Rosie never saw the look of amusement on her face as she walked along the landing.

Wednesday morning came. It took less than fifteen minutes to get to the village of Aylesthwaite. As he drove, Jonathon explained that his great grandmother was ninety-one and had lived in the home for six months. "Mum asked her to come and live with us, but she wouldn't. Said she didn't want to be a burden to anybody." He laughed softly to himself. "She's a right character, Rosie. I think you'll like her."

"Do your parents go to Saint Edwin's?" Rosie wondered if she'd bumped into them without realising.

"They *did*. They moved from Ridderch Standen last year, across to Northallerton for my dad's job." Jonathon pulled up at traffic lights and turned to her. "So you could say I was booted out at the same time. I wanted to stay over here so I had to find my own place quick. But I've forgiven them."

Rosie smiled. "Do you see much of them now?"

"Oh yeah." Jonathon set off again. "I went over for Christmas dinner and stayed till last night. They don't get away from me that easily!"

The retirement home was a clean-looking, stone fronted building with a large sign which read:

ANGELGATE HOUSE – RETIREMENT HOME FOR THE ELDERLY

Jonathon pulled into the car park and switched off the engine. "Well, Rosie – let's go see how the old girl's doing this morning. She'll be wondering what's up. We only visited her on Christmas day."

Maisie Wallace was a tiny, white-haired bundle of mischief. For all her diminutive size, her voice was the sound of roasted gravel. She greeted each of them with a pronounced kiss on the cheek, holding them still as she did so by gripping their shoulders with bony, deceptively strong fingers. Rosie was quite taken aback. She'd never been kissed on first meeting before, and never with such unexpected force. This granny didn't know her own strength. Maisie gestured them to sit down.

"So, you're Jonny's friend are you, m'dear?" She peered at Rosie through jam jar thick lenses. "I can't rightly see what you look like. I 'av a bit of trouble with me eyes. That's why they sent me in 'ere, y'know. They said I couldn't look after meself, on account of me eyes bein' a bit foggy. 'Onestly! I'm as safe as 'ouses. Don't know what they're talkin' about, Jonny."

Jonathon looked across at Rosie and winked. "Mum said you could come and live with us – don't you remember, Grandma?" His voice was slightly raised, and Rosie guessed that as well as having a bit of trouble with her eyes, Maisie probably had a bit of trouble with her ears as well.

The old lady sighed theatrically. "Well, that's just it, Jonny. Just as I was thinkin' about takin' her up on the offer, they went and moved, didn't they? They can't expect an old girl like me to up sticks and move all that way, now can they?"

Jonathon shook his head, smiling. Rosie suspected this wasn't the first time they'd had this conversation. He leaned forward in his chair. "Grandma, we've come to ask you about something."

Maisie frowned. "Not after me money are you, Jonny boy? I don't 'av a lot, y'know."

"No, nothing like that," he assured her patiently. "We wondered if you could tell us anything about your uncle Philip. Remember? The one who died in the Great War."

"Ah ... uncle Philip." Maisie stroked her chin thoughtfully. "Now wait a minute while I get me thinkin' cap on. Yes, he was me dad's brother. A wee bit older than me dad he was. I never met him tho'. He was at war when I was born. Died when I was only two or three, I think." She sighed again. "Terrible thing, y'know. All those young men gettin' killed like that. My dad never went to war." She looked over in Rosie's direction. "He was a cripple, me dad was. Fell downstairs when he was just a littl'un. Broke both his legs – they never mended right. Handsome man he was too. My mother always said she was glad of 'is being crippled cos it meant he couldn't join up. Dad used to tell us that none of the recruitin' officers would give 'im a second look." She shook her head sadly. "That upset 'im, that did. He couldn't understand it. A God-fearin' man, me dad was. Just wantin' to do 'is bit for king and country. Mum would tell us how he'd look at her many a time and say – 'Polly, I can't see why they won't 'av *me* cos o' me legs, when half the fellas they take come back wi' no legs anyway.' Aye, that's what he used to say, bless 'im."

Rosie had to suppress a smile. The old lady's face was entirely serious.

Jonathon broke in. "Do you know which regiment Philip served in?"

Maisie shook her head. "I'm afraid I don't, Jonny. All I know is, he died about 1917.

At Ypres if I'm not mistaken."

Rosie's ears pricked up. *Ypres* ... wasn't that where they were now in the diary?

Jonathon shot her a glance. She sensed a slight nervousness in his eyes, as though he was afraid to ask his next question. This one would determine the truth.

"Grandma, did your dad have any *other* brothers who served in the conflict?"

As she looked across at Jonathon's wistful expression, Rosie became conscious of her own heart beating harder. Suddenly, she desperately wanted Philip to be Boxer.

Maisie screwed up her face for a few seconds, with the look of one dredging through the hinterlands of memory. Then she relaxed as though all had become clear. "There *was* another lad as I think about it. He was the oldest of the lot of 'em, I believe. Yes. Yes, I remember now. He survived the war – became a vicar, y'know."

Rosie and Jonathon exchanged glances.

The old lady continued. "I *do* remember 'im as I come to think about it. He lived quite a distance away from us, but I *did* meet 'im several times. When the Second World War broke out, he went overseas as an army chaplain. Somethin' he'd done in the First War, I seem to think."

Jonathon shot Rosie another look. "What was his name, Grandma? Can you remember his name?" He was talking fast now.

Maisie straightened in her chair, a slight look of indignation on her face. "*Course* I remember 'is name. Do you take me for a silly old duffer, Jonny?" She gave a triumphant smile. "He was called uncle Nat. Well, that's what *I* called 'im anyway. It was years before I could get me tongue round Nathanael."

Chapter 15

"Wow, Rosie, would you believe that? What are the chances, eh?" Jonathon shook his head in disbelief as he started the ignition. "I mean, you couldn't make it up, could you?"

Rosie felt pleased. She could hardly wait to get back and tell Beth. It would be like a second Christmas present.

"Well, I guess this needs some further looking into." Jonathon was mumbling thoughtfully as they rolled out of the car park. "There must be ways of finding out more about him. I'll give Lauren a ring. She'll know where to look."

Rosie frowned slightly. *Lauren?* Was she supposed to know who he was talking about?

Jonathon caught her puzzled expression. "Sorry, Rosie. I was thinking aloud. Lauren's my girlfriend – she's at Durham doing a Ph.D. She's a bit of a local historian on the side though. She'd probably know where to get some further info on Boxer."

"Oh right, I see." Rosie felt an inexplicable tinge of disappointment. Somehow she hadn't been expecting that. The revelation made her feel suddenly awkward. She tried to show interest. "Is she from round here?"

Jonathon shook his head. "No. She's from Cornwall. She's there at the moment actually, spending Christmas with her family. I'm planning to go down and join them on Friday for New Year. A quick break before work starts up again."

"Where's work then?" Rosie interjected, glad for the diversion.

"I'm a teacher. Primary school."

Rosie was genuinely surprised. She'd never imagined Jonathon doing anything like that. Perhaps it was the memory of her first encounter with him that had thrown her off the scent. Something to do with the duffle coat and scruffy hair.

Jonathon accelerated gently as they pulled onto a country lane. "Lauren's wanting to become a lecturer. Bit of one-upmanship, I reckon." He grinned.

Realising that she hadn't managed to change the subject, Rosie reluctantly rejoined the flow of his conversation. "Do you get to see her often?"

Jonathon shook his head again. "It's an e-mail and phone romance, I'm afraid. We're both pretty busy. It's hard to take time out to travel at the moment. But she only has another few months in Durham. We're hoping things will change after that."

Rosie nodded. Well, it all sounded pretty serious anyway. No mention of wedding bells, but she knew how to read between the lines. She couldn't help envying them. She couldn't help envying anyone who had positive plans for the next year. She tried not to think about Beth, but she knew that Beth's departure was the only sure thing looming up in her own near future. As for Gavin – it was hard to hold out much hope on that one.

"Could I ask you a tremendous favour, Rosie?" Jonathon's voice jolted her from her thoughts. "You know as you type up the diary entries for Beth, would it be possible to e-mail a copy through to me? I'd so love to read it."

Rosie shrugged. "Can't see any problem with that. I'd better check it with Beth first. The diary's hers after all. But I wouldn't think she'd object."

"Great!" Jonathon's face lit up. "When we get back to Oak Lodge, I'll give you my e-mail address. Then if she agrees, you're all set up."

Yeah, thought Rosie absently. *Super.*

"*Well?* Is it him?" Beth was waiting in the hallway when Rosie arrived back. She looked very pale, but curiosity had animated her countenance with a certain glow.

"Looks very much like it is." Rosie couldn't help grinning. "Right down to his Right Reverend brother. Jonathon's pretty chuffed about it."

Beth's face broke into a smile. "Ooh, that's brilliant! I could see us getting on the telly with a story like this." There was a sudden catch in her throat and she began to cough. Rosie could see her whole frame shake with the effort.

"Come on, you – you're getting overexcited." She led Beth into the living room and sat her in a chair by the fire. After a couple of minutes and a few sips of water, the coughing died down. Beth lay back in her chair.

"He's nice Jonathon, isn't he?" She spoke into the air.

Rosie wasn't sure if it was a trick question. She decided to play safe. "Yeah. He thinks his girlfriend might be able to help us find some stuff on Boxer. She's into history apparently."

Beth looked disappointed. "He's *attached?* That's a shame."

"Shame for who?" Rosie's eyes narrowed.

"Well – I thought perhaps …" Beth's voice tailed off and she smiled sheepishly.

"If you're meaning me, forget it. I'm attached too, remember." Rosie tried to sound convincing. She felt about as attached as a loose awning in a force ten gale.

Beth sighed. "Ah well. Should have realised he'd be spoken for. The good 'uns always get snapped up."

Despite her best efforts not to be, Rosie was curious. "Did you ever go out with him? When you were at school, I mean."

Beth shook her head. "No. But it certainly wasn't for lack of wanting to. I remembered him from primary school. He grew up round here as a kid, but then his family moved away for a few years 'cause of his dad's job. They came back when Jonathon was about fifteen. That's when he joined our class. We girls didn't know what had hit us." She laughed as she remembered. "I confess I had him lined up for myself. But then, I suspect, so did every other female in my form. He did go out a couple of times with one girl – Loretta Hurst I think her name was. The rest of us just sat tight, hoping he'd do the rounds – y'know, so we'd all get a turn. Then suddenly he just changed." Beth's face became serious. "Started getting really into God. Started going to *my* church. To be honest, Ros, I found it all a bit much. Specially on Friday afternoons when he'd shout *'See you Sunday, Beth!'* at the top of his voice." She rolled her eyes at the memory.

Rosie couldn't help smiling. "So he started to lose his appeal then?"

"Yeah, I'm afraid so. At that time I was pretty switched off spiritually. Y'know – the whole rebellious teenager thing. So it wasn't long before I went off Jonathon too. I didn't fancy going out with somebody who was starting to sound like Tim the vicar." They both laughed. After a few moments, Beth became quiet. Her eyes seemed to glaze as she stared into the fire. "He said something to me once, Ros. It seemed a strange thing to say at the time."

Rosie waited for her to continue.

"I remember going to Saint Edwin's the Sunday before I left for music college. I went more for Mum's sake than anything. When the service was finished, people started coming up to me, wishing me all the best, offering me bits of advice – that kinda thing. Then, just as I was about to leave, up came Jonathon. He wished me well and we made a bit of small talk. Then he came out with the funniest thing. He looked me straight in the eyes and said, '*Whatever happens, don't forget who you are, Beth.*' Just like that. Then he turned and went. I've never forgotten it."

Rosie tried to picture the scene. A disconcerted teenage Beth struggling to hold onto her cool as Jonathon's blue eyes bored into her soul. It wasn't hard to imagine. Those eyes could leave a girl in pieces.

"I guess I was a bit narked at first. I thought it was his roundabout way of telling me not to get above my station – y'know, if I ever made it big or anything. Remember your humble beginnings and all that. It niggled me if I'm honest, Ros." She stared into the fire again and the room became silent.

As they sat in the quietness, Rosie became aware of the steady ticking of the clock. Every moment registered by a tiny note ... then gone. Forever gone. Life ticking away, so quietly yet so surely. And for Beth, so quickly. Rosie wondered how she could stand the sound of it.

Beth shuffled in her chair. "It's funny, Ros. After I first got diagnosed, I found myself thinking about his words more and more. '*Whatever happens, don't forget who you are, Beth.*' Suddenly I realised I'd done exactly that."

"How d'you mean?"

"You remember that day in the church at Applemarket? When you asked me if I still believed in God?"

Rosie nodded.

"I guess that was the first time I'd faced the question in years."

Catching sight of Beth's troubled expression, Rosie shifted awkwardly in her seat. She wasn't sure where this was leading, but she had a feeling confessions were on the way. Conversations like this usually made her uneasy.

Beth twisted a strand of hair distractedly round a finger. "I never told you, Ros, but I had a dream a few nights after that."

Rosie straightened. "Dreams now, eh? This gets better." She tried to sound light-hearted about it, but a sudden nervousness had gripped her.

"I dreamt I was on a beach," Beth began slowly, ignoring her sarcasm. "It was a lovely beach. Not one I could identify in real life, but in the dream it was somehow familiar. You know what dreams are like."

Rosie nodded but said nothing.

"The place was perfect. Blue sky, not a cloud in sight. Sea like a millpond. There were people all around, swimming or playing in the sand. But I wasn't taking too much notice of them to be honest. I was just lying there soaking up the sun. It was all too gorgeous to do anything but enjoy." She went quiet for a moment and Rosie noticed a shadow pass across her face. "Get this, Ros. There I was, perfectly happy in my own little world. Sun on my skin, sea lapping in the background ..."

"Buckets of sangria –" Rosie quipped, keen to lighten up the conversation.

But for once, Beth seemed in no mood for levity. "Skip the sangria on this occasion," she retorted flatly. She twirled a tendril of hair round her finger again. "Suddenly, Ros, without any warning, I heard someone shout out. The voice was loud, agitated – a man's I think. It hardly matters. Before I even managed to open my eyes, other voices started up. Within seconds people were shouting, screaming. Within seconds – literally. It all happened so fast, it took me a moment or two to get my brain in gear." Her face furrowed as she played the memory back. "Then sheer panic set in. At that point I jerked upright to see what the heck was going on. That's when I saw it."

"Saw what?"

Beth shuddered slightly. "Stuff coming in from the sea."

"*Stuff?*" Rosie frowned. "*What* stuff?"

Beth was shaking her head slightly. "Don't know what it was exactly. It was like fog, I guess. But it seemed to be rolling in from the horizon like a huge wall. You just knew that when it hit that beach, everything was going to disappear into it. You could feel it even before it got there. So cold, so terribly cold."

Rosie shivered despite herself. "So what happened then?"

Beth had closed her eyes now. Her face grew taut as she continued to relate the strange dream. "I realised that people were starting to run. Running off the beach they were, yelling as they went. But me – I couldn't move. It was like I was riveted to the spot. And all the time, I could see this thing getting nearer and nearer. I was so terrified, I couldn't even scream."

Rosie could detect the distress in her friend's voice. She wanted to get this dream thing over and done with, yet somehow, she was reluctant to break Beth's flow.

"I knew the exact moment the thing hit. One minute, there was blue sky above me ... the next, everything was plunged into a chilling greyness. I just stood there, paralysed. I couldn't even see my own feet, the fog was so dense. It felt like it was going to suffocate me. And silent! I've never known a silence like it. All the shouting had disappeared and I realised everyone else had managed to escape. I sensed I must be totally alone on that beach now. But for me there seemed no way out. Somehow, I knew that I was the one the fog had come for. It was horrible, Ros, it really was."

Rosie needed no convincing. She was finding Beth's story pretty unnerving. She forced a grin. "I hope you're going to tell me you woke up at that point."

"No, not quite." Beth gave a weak smile. "I seemed to stand there for a few minutes, waiting. Waiting for something to happen. I knew something had to happen; I just wasn't sure what. Then slowly, in the midst of the fog, I began to make out the shape of a figure. It was standing about fifteen yards from me. Just a black figure at first – I had no idea who, or what, it was. Then I saw the figure look upwards and point. I looked up. But I could see nothing. Just thick grey. The figure pointed upwards again, this time with more agitation. Still I could see nothing. I heard muffled shouts coming through the fog, as though this person was trying to tell me something. And then I realised. The figure was my mother. I called out to her, but the moment I did, she was gone. And then I woke up."

Rosie was relieved. "Weird," she commented as breezily as she could. "Totally weird."

Beth shrugged. "The weirdest thing about it all happened when I did wake up. Jonathon's words were running through my mind – *'Don't forget who you are, Beth, don't forget who you are, Beth …'* – like an old record that had got stuck. That was the weirdest bit. I lay in bed for ages trying to put the whole thing together. It was only when I got diagnosed that any of it began to make sense to me."

Rosie frowned. "Well, I'm sure glad *you* managed to figure it out. I can't say it makes one iota of sense to me."

"Don't you see, Ros?" There was a fire in Beth's eyes now. "When I found out I was ill, my mind seemed to go back to some automatic default setting. I started praying again, just as I had when I was a child. At first I felt bad – like I was only using God because my life was all screwed up. But then I realised. It was exactly as Jonathon had said. I *had* forgotten who I was … but suddenly I was remembering. The fog had come to swallow me up. But suddenly, it was as if I could see more clearly than I'd ever seen. D'you understand, Ros?"

Rosie shook her head. "At the risk of looking completely thick, I have to say I haven't a clue what you're talking about."

Beth suppressed a sigh. "Ros, I …"

The muffled hum of approaching voices sounded outside the door. Rosie was almost relieved. As the door swung open to reveal the speakers, Beth turned to her with an anxious smile. "We'll have to continue this some other time."

Rosie pretended to smile back. *Not if I can help it.*

It was the following Thursday. New Year's Day had come and gone, hardly observed by the Simmons' family. For all its highs, the old year had signed off with such dreadful tidings, it was hard to welcome in the new, knowing it was about to reap the harvest of its predecessor. The week had passed gently, a startling contrast from the frenetic pace of city life. Yet already, their stay in Yorkshire was almost at an end. In two days' time they would travel back down to London. Beth had an appointment to see Michael Romily first thing Monday morning. Still, sitting in the drowsy-warm living room at Oak Lodge, listening to the steady rhythm of the clock and the hum of the afternoon fire, all that seemed a million miles away.

"I could stay here forever," Beth sighed, nestling her head against Ciaran's chest. "Isn't this just the most beautiful place on earth?"

Ciaran looked over at Rosie, his eyes dark and sad. It hurt her to see him like this.

"I'm so glad we came up," Beth continued, without a trace of melancholy. "It's been the best Christmas ever." She snuggled up closer to Ciaran and closed her eyes.

How can she say that? Rosie couldn't help wondering if the cancer had affected Beth's judgement. Yet glancing over at the pale, drawn face basking in the glow of the firelight, she could see an expression of genuine satisfaction. She looked away and the room fell into quietness again.

Moments later, however, the stillness was broken by a sharp, rasping cough. Beth jerked upright and put her hand to her mouth as her body seemed to go into spasm. Ciaran held her shoulders gently. "Come on, princess, you're okay." He pulled a couple of tissues from a box and pressed them into her hand. Beth held them to her mouth, wiping her lips after each bout of coughing. The attack lasted several minutes. When at last it died down, she collapsed back on the sofa.

"Whew – where did all that come from?" Though Beth's voice was little more than a croak, Rosie saw the shadow of a grin on her face. She was trying to play it down, but Ciaran looked worried.

"Do you need a rest, Bethy ? D'you fancy a lie-down upstairs?"

Beth seemed to think it over for a couple of moments. "Yeah. Perhaps that wouldn't be a bad idea. Give me chance to get my breath back."

Ciaran was on his feet in an instant. He carefully pulled Beth up from the sofa and shot Rosie a glance. "See you later, Ros."

Beth gave a wink and a wave as she left the room. "Afternoon siestas, eh ...?" Her voice was hoarse. "How very continental."

Rosie found herself alone with her thoughts. So. What to do with herself for the rest of the afternoon. She'd already pulled most of her stuff together into suitcases, so packing wasn't really an option. Ed and Cassie had gone into Ridderch Standen just after lunch, so there wasn't even anyone around to talk to. There seemed nothing for it but a spot more transcribing.

As her laptop was loading, Rosie looked around the room which had been hers for the last three weeks. As her eyes took in the expanse of light and space, she felt a strange sadness. There was something about the high ceiling and the view from the large sash-windows which gave her a sense of freedom. She pictured her bedroom back in Streatham. It suddenly seemed poky by comparison, and Rosie couldn't help wondering how she would adapt to it again. In the short time she'd been here at Oak Lodge, she had grown used to the stillness and tranquillity of the place. Even when the house was filled with family, it seemed to retain an atmosphere of calm and serenity. It would be hard to readjust to the bustle of London.

Opening the diary, she leafed through its musty pages until she found her place. She'd already e-mailed Jonathon the first eighteen entries, but there'd been no reply. She knew he was in Cornwall; perhaps he hadn't even taken his laptop with him. Ah well, she reminded herself as she screwed up her eyes and tried to focus on the tiny writing, she wasn't doing this for him. She was doing it for Beth.

Poperinghe Billets October 28th 1916

Well, Em – I'm still here, in one piece and in the pink. We had an inspection yesterday by Lieutenant General Plumer. What about that, eh? He seemed happy enough with things, and it gave us a bit of a lift to know that we hadn't been forgotten by the big fellows. Sometimes you can't help wondering if the brass hats at the top have any idea what it's like to be out here following their orders. Still, he seemed an alright sort of a chap, so I guess they must know what they're doing.

As I write, Em, I'm sitting in a topping little hideaway if ever there was one. It was Boxer's brother who put us onto it ...

"Well, I must say, I'm very glad we found this place." Boxer spoke in hushed tones as he pulled a book down from its shelf. He sank into a chair and began to flick through the pages like a man who hadn't seen a book in years. This particular afternoon found Boxer, Sam and Jimmy in the library of a large, welcoming house on the Rue de l'Hôpital in the centre of Poperinghe. Outside, the sky was bleary, and the roll of artillery fire could still be faintly heard from the front line some distance away. But for the three friends, and two other soldiers huddled intently over their books, this small reading room felt like a shelter in a storm.

Anyone who'd been on the Salient more than a fortnight had heard of the place. Talbot House, or Toc H as the Tommies preferred to call it, had been set up in the December of the previous year by two British padres, The Rev. Neville Talbot and the Rev. Philip Clayton. It was a club where any soldier was made to feel welcome, where friendship and goodwill was prized above status or background. Toc H was said to be about the only place an ordinary private could socialise with his officer cousin on equal terms. *'All rank abandon, ye who enter here'*, read a sign in the house. It pretty much summed up the ethos of the place, as did another notice in the hallway. A hand, with a pointing finger extended towards the door, illustrated the point –

TO PESSIMISTS – WAY OUT

On first entering the building, the three friends had spotted a few familiar faces from 'B' and 'D' companies, but none from their own platoon. The rest of their boys had gone elsewhere. Sam was sure the local estaminets would be doing a thriving business, as no doubt would other, less reputable establishments. The Tommies certainly worked hard for their pay; nobody could begrudge them a penny. It was just unfortunate the way some of them went about spending it.

It had been a recommendation from Nathanael Bocking that had prompted today's visit to Toc H. "If you find yourself in Pop, you must call in," Nathanael had enthused to Boxer when they'd last seen each other at Zillebeke. "You'll get to meet Tubby Clayton – now there's a marvellous fellow! You'll like him a great deal … remember me to him."

True enough, they'd come across 'Tubby' almost the moment they'd stepped into the house. A short, bespectacled man with a genial face and friendly manner, he had greeted them warmly and briefed them about the facilities available. "Gets a little lively round here," he'd smiled wisely. "If your ears need a bit of a rest, try the library – or the chapel."

The three of them being avid readers, the library had naturally been their first port of call. Now Sam's eyes searched the shelves. He pulled down a thick tome by Dickens and opened it. Inside the front cover someone had stamped the words, *'Do not scrounge'*. It made him smile. Tubby had explained to them that soldiers were requested to leave a cap badge in exchange for the loan of a book. With that kind of lending arrangement, Sam couldn't imagine scrounging being much of a problem.

They spent a couple of hours in the library. Despite an occasional din coming from beyond the door, the atmosphere in the room was peaceful and comforting. Sitting there in civilised quietude, it was tempting to try and forget the slaughter that was going on just a short distance away. Sam wondered if there could be any greater contrast than between this gentle haven and the shell-battered, vermin-ridden trenches they'd grown so used to. And to think they'd be back there so soon.

"Hey, you two," Boxer ventured in a loud whisper. "Fancy a look at the chapel before we go?"

They left the library and proceeded to jostle their way past other soldiers who were standing around in small groups, chatting. Talbot House certainly seemed full today. Soon the three friends were climbing the steep staircase to its loft, and a few moments later, found themselves in what Tubby had affectionately referred to as the 'Upper Room'. He'd advised them against walking on the middle part of the floor. "I'm afraid it's a bit temperamental underfoot ..." he'd warned. "Not quite safe you might say. But you'll be perfectly alright if you stick to the seats round the sides."

Making their way towards the front of the small chapel, Boxer and Jimmy sat down on a wooden bench. Sam found a seat near the back and looked around. Everything about the place felt makeshift and homely, yet Sam couldn't help sensing that there was something sacred in its simplicity. As his weary mind began to drink in the stillness, a hush seemed to come over his whole being. Even the library hadn't felt like this. He saw Boxer lower his head, and after a few moments, Jimmy did likewise. Were they praying? It seemed to Sam that they must be. What else could a man do in a silence like this? It invited one to pray. It almost expected it ...

How does one begin a journey towards God, Em? In the midst of this awful darkness in which we find ourselves, it seems hard to focus on anything good. And yet I cannot bear to think that there is nothing more than our present hell. This house has made me wonder. Though its façade is as pockmarked as any of the buildings round here, I've sensed something within its walls which, I think, can only be the fragrance of heaven. Whatever it is, I don't want to forget it. I will carry its memory with me, even into the face of death.

As Rosie typed the last few words, there was a light tap at her door. "Come in," she called out as she pressed the save icon. It was Cassie.

"There's a visitor for you downstairs, love. He wanted to see Beth and Ciaran too, but I've just put my head round their door and they're both fast asleep."

"Who is it?" Rosie whispered, her face gathering into a frown.

Cassie leaned forward and lowered her voice. "It's Jonathon."

"Hi Rosie – hope you don't mind me calling in." Jonathon rose from his seat as she entered the living room.

"Not at all. I didn't know you were back."

"I'm only *just* back. I arrived last night." Jonathon gave a broad grin as he flicked his blond hair away from his eyes. "I nipped into Ridderch Standen early this afternoon and bumped into Ed and Cassie near the post office. They told me you're all back off to London on Saturday. I wanted to come and say bye."

At that moment, Cassie brought in a tray of tea and fruit cake. "Thought you might like a bit of refreshment." Smiling gently, she left the room again, closing the door quietly behind her.

"Lovely lady, Cassie," Jonathon commented thoughtfully as he reached for a plate.

"Yes, she is. I'm going to miss her." Rosie had grown very fond of the older woman over the last few weeks. "Still, they'll be staying in London for a few days when they take us back down, so it's not goodbye just yet."

The clock chimed the hour just then, and inwardly Rosie sighed. That sound was something else she would miss. *And* the scent of pine that seemed to hang in the air, the morning birdsong outside her window, the glitter of frost on the garden lawn, the fragrance of lavender on her sheets ... in fact, she realised sadly, pretty much everything about this place. Suddenly she didn't want to go home.

"Anyway, Rosie," Jonathon's voice broke in, "thanks so much for the e-mails. I only hooked up my laptop this morning – I didn't realise you'd sent them. I read them all in one sitting though. Absolutely brilliant! I'm really made up about it!" There was a boyish excitement in his face which Rosie found amusing.

"Did you mention anything to Lauren?"

Jonathon shook his head. "There didn't seem to be an opportunity to be honest, Rosie. We were visiting here, there and everywhere. I never realised she had so many relatives. I hardly got to see her on her own." He took a sip of tea and smiled. "It's nice to be back up here actually. I think it'll take me at least a week to recover. I enjoy my peace and quiet too much – must be getting old."

It was Rosie's turn to smile. "Here's you, glad to be home in the land of the peaceful, and there's us, heading straight back to the craziest place on earth."

"Looking forward to it?" Jonathon looked across at her, his blue eyes suddenly serious.

Rosie shrugged. Somehow it was hard to lie to someone with eyes like that. "Guess I've got used to the quiet too."

A look of sympathy passed over Jonathon's face. "You ought to come up here more often, Rosie. Have a break once in a while."

Rosie said nothing. That was hardly likely, was it? Once Beth had gone, what possible pretext could she have for visiting a place like this? It was then that the realisation hit her. This had been a complete one-off. A glimpse into another world. A world so far removed from her own that it had made her own seem temporarily unreal. Yet come next week, Oak Lodge, Saint Edwin's, and Ridderch Standen would all be a million miles away. Nothing but a lovely memory, their doors forever closed to her. She forced a smile. "Yeah, perhaps. Meanwhile, I'll keep banging in the e-mails for you."

The journey back to London was nothing like the one they'd made up to Yorkshire. Beth's cough had worsened considerably over the last couple of days, and it soon became evident that she was running a temperature. It made travelling difficult for her. She felt nauseous and miserable and they were forced to make several stops. It was a great relief to everyone when, at just after eight in the evening, they arrived back in Streatham. Beth looked wretched.

"I'm not happy about her at all," Cassie confided to Ciaran when they'd got Beth settled in bed.

"Me neither." Ciaran ran his fingers through his hair in agitation. "She begged me not to send for a doctor – she's terrified she'll end up back in hospital. But we've got the nurse calling in later to sort her syringe drivers. To be honest, when she sees her she may well insist."

Cassie nodded slowly. "What time are you expecting her?"

Ciaran shrugged. "Could be any time up to midnight. When I first arranged it, we were looking at about seven, but I'd no idea it would take us so long to get back. When I rung up to reschedule they said they'd have to put us in at the end of the list. They apologised, but there's not a lot they can do about it I suppose."

Cassie smiled sadly. "Well, at least she might get a couple of hours' sleep before they come and start messing about with her again."

Rosie made them all a cup of tea while Ciaran checked the answering machine. There were various messages from friends and well-wishers, mainly people from the orchestra. Even Emmett Mallory had called to pass on his love and to ask if he could pay them a visit once they got back to London.

"Don't think so, Emmett mate," Ciaran said into the air. He was pale, and Rosie couldn't help noticing that his face had a drawn, emaciated look. He seemed unable to sit still, busying himself with whatever he could – ferrying suitcases upstairs, skimming through post, making several trips to check on Beth. Rosie wanted to grab him and throw him into a chair, but somehow, she couldn't be sure how he would react. Suddenly she felt there was a part of her brother she didn't know.

When it got to ten o'clock, Rosie stood up to leave.

"You off, love?" Cassie came over to help her on with her coat, a faint whisper of her scent trailing in the atmosphere around her. In the last few weeks it was a smell Rosie had come to cherish.

"I don't want to leave it too late. Mel will keep me up half the night talking anyway. If I go now, I might just get to bed by midnight."

"Oh I see." Cassie's eyes twinkled with understanding. "Bit of a chatterbox, is she?"

Rosie smiled. "Well, let's just say we have a lot of catching up to do." She kissed Cassie and Ciaran, said goodnight to Ed and went over to the door. "Give me a ring if there are any developments with Beth. I'll see you all tomorrow."

"Sure we can't give you a lift home?" Cassie offered.

Rosie shook her head. "No, I'll be fine. It's only a couple of streets away and I could use a walk. I'll leave my suitcases here till morning. I've got everything I need."

By the following morning, Beth's condition had deteriorated further. Ignoring her protests, Ciaran called for a doctor. The young locum who attended was not about to take any chances, and insisted that Beth be admitted to hospital immediately. Beth was beside herself. It was a very distraught Ciaran who rang to put Rosie in the picture.

"I'm just about to run her up there now, Ros. She's real upset with me, but what am I supposed to do? She looks absolutely shocking."

"Is Cassie there?" Rosie knew that if there was anybody who could calm Beth down, it was Cassie.

"Yeah, she's with her now. Look – if you want to come up to the hospital later, Ros, feel free. I'll be up there all day anyway. I feel like asking them to find me a bed."

Rosie's heart was heavy as she put the phone down. She felt desperately sorry for Beth. After her best Christmas ever, here she was, going straight back into hospital. As Rosie launched into the washing up, a wave of helpless anger engulfed her. Beyond the kitchen window, the sky was a sheet of pale, dismal grey. Not a bird in sight; not even so much as the outline of a cloud. Streatham had never looked more ugly to her. She tried not to think about Yorkshire as she banged and clattered her way through her chores. That would be like rubbing salt into a wound. But it was hard to ignore the sudden sense of darkness that was swirling around in her head.

When she'd finished cleaning up, she decided to check her e-mails. There were five messages – three spam, one from the nursery, and one, surprisingly, from Jonathon.

Hi Rosie –
Hope the journey went well and Beth managed okay. How's London? Not too crazy, I trust. I bet we seem like a load of country bumpkins now you're back down there. Still, I meant what I said. I think you should visit us once in a while – to recharge your batteries and all that. Looking forward to the next instalment of the diary!
Luv
Jonathon.

Rosie stared at the screen for some time. It was like a message from another world. A warmer, gentler world that suddenly seemed so far away. Everything in her longed to be back there. Only a few weeks ago, she hadn't even known such a place existed; London had been the sole arena of her life and she'd been quite happy with that. Yet now, having returned, London seemed strange to her. Empty somehow. Even having Ed and Cassie down here didn't make things feel right. They were out of place. Everything was out of place. She recalled Ciaran's face from the evening before. Never had she seen him so fraught, so unhappy. Life was falling apart for all of them and there was no way of stopping it.

Zillebeke November 4th 1916

Well, Em – here we are in the thick of things again. Got here a couple of days ago and relieved 10th Northumberland Fusiliers. Our time in Poperinghe was quite marvellous. I, for one, look forward to going back there. It's hard to believe one could find such a place as Talbot House in the middle of all this chaos. I could have cheerfully stayed there. Still, I suppose we have to get back to the real world. We don't fight well when our minds are elsewhere.

Anyway, I received great news today. Harry is home in Scarborough. His leg was amputated just below the hip, and by the sounds of things, he's had a pretty rough time recovering these last few months. But he assures me that he's fit and well now and has even found a little job as a cobbler's assistant. He joked about it in his letter. 'At least I'll be able to custom-make me own shoes. No point me payin' out for a pair when I've only got one foot, is there?' He thanked me for saving his life and asked me to pass on his regards to the fellow who helped me. I told Boxer and he was greatly encouraged. I must confess, Em, I really didn't think Harry would make it. He was in such an awful way when we left him. As you can imagine, his letter bucked me up no end. It seems a lifetime ago since it all happened, and yet here I am, still plodding on. Looking back, it's a miracle any of us have survived this long.

Zillebeke November 6th 1916

This evening, Em, we're near Clonmel Copse and the temperature is beginning to drop quite steeply. There have been a couple of casualties from our company since we got back here – a young officer and his batman. Both killed outright, so they wouldn't have suffered. Still, it's a shame, and a stark reminder of our precarious hold on life. For the last hour the Twinnies have been playing 'shoot the rat'. Not the most pleasant game in the world, but it passes the time, and there's the consolation of knowing there's one less rat to crawl over your face when you're trying to grab a bit of sleep. We hate the things. As big as cats some of them – better fed than any living creature on the whole front. That's the most troubling aspect of it, Em. We all know they feed off the dead. I've been told they go for the eyes and the liver first. After that, I don't suppose they're fussy. They can strip a body clean in no time. It's a hideous notion to think that any one of us could be their next meal. That's why we enjoy taking a pop at them. Not that we're supposed to waste ammo on the wretched beasts. And the stench of them when they start to rot is quite unbearable. When you're stuck in a trench with a decaying rat carcass just beyond the parapet, it's enough to turn your stomach. Those creatures are twice dead – dead inside and out. I reckon that of all the things we're forced to put up with here, I loathe the rats the most. Though everything else is miserable, uncomfortable, even painful sometimes, I suppose one can expect that in war. But rats are an insult, Em. Just a greedy, bloated reminder that even in death we have no dignity here. I think of the few hours we spent in Toc H and find myself wondering which is the reality. That, or this. I'm sure I don't know anything anymore.

Rosie filed the two entries, then went into e-mail.

Hi Jonathon.
Lousy journey to be honest. Beth's back in hospital – chest infection I think. Let you know more details when I find out. London's not feeling my favourite place at the moment. You country bumpkins don't know you're born(!) Here are some more bits for you. They pretty much sum up how I'm feeling at the moment.
Rosie.

She attached the latest entries, pressed send, and groaned. Not the most uplifting e-mail she'd ever come up with. She printed off the last two diary segments and inserted them in their folder. Did she honestly want to give any more of these to Beth? Some of them were so horrendously depressing. Come to think of it, Beth hadn't asked for any recently. Perhaps she'd come to her senses and decided it was all too much for her. In any other circumstances, Rosie would gladly have put the whole diary thing to bed, at least for a while; taken Beth on one side, made out the writing was becoming illegible, even pretended there were pages missing or something. Yet suddenly, here on the scene was Jonathon, brimming with enthusiasm, hinting for the next instalment like a kid hinting for a new toy. And even though she was finding Sam's journal tough going at the moment, Rosie knew deep down that her e-mails to Jonathon were her only link with anything that resembled sanity. Her only escape from the gloom that was gathering all around her.

Chapter 16

"Come on, princess, have a drink." Ciaran gently pushed Beth's hair back from her face as he tried to urge her to swallow some fluid. Beth closed her eyes and turned her head away from him, her countenance the very picture of dejection. It was Wednesday, three days after her impromptu readmission to hospital. She'd been put on a strong course of antibiotic treatment, but though her physical condition was beginning to improve slightly, her general state was not encouraging. She'd hardly spoken a word in the last three days. Every so often she would turn onto her side, tears streaming unchecked into her hair; it was the only indication of what was going on inside her. For Ciaran, the situation was becoming intolerable.

Later on that evening, he managed to get a few minutes with Michael Romily. "I don't know what's wrong with her all of a sudden. Is she supposed to be like this? I mean, has she taken a turn for the worse or what? The more I watch her, the more I'm convinced she's going downhill fast. Is this what we're to expect from now on?"

Michael Romily frowned. "To be honest, Ciaran, at the moment we've only picked up evidence of a chest infection. I had suspected we might find some secondary hot spots in the lungs, but there was no sign of anything like that. And the infection *is* beginning to respond to the treatment we're giving her." He rubbed his chin thoughtfully. "I'm pretty sure that the thing we're dealing with here is depression. It's quite common in patients with terminal illness. We need to get her some counselling if she'll agree to it. It's important; her psychological health can have a significant bearing on the progress of her cancer. The more positive she remains, the more chance she'll have of delaying the inevitable outcome of the disease." He looked at the young husband gently. "Put bluntly, Ciaran, the fighters usually last longer."

Ciaran scowled. "I don't know that I could fight in her situation. I should think it's difficult to remain positive, knowing what's coming."

"I should imagine it is." Michael felt for the young man. He could hear the bitterness in his voice and it saddened him. "We must give her every chance. I'll talk to her about counselling in the morning. I think that has to be the next step."

Ciaran nodded, a look of helpless resignation registering on his face. Michael put a hand on his shoulder. "We're here to support you both as much as we can."

On Wednesday night, Rosie popped round to see Ciaran. She hadn't visited Beth since Monday; she found Beth's present state difficult to cope with.

"Come in, love." Cassie hugged her warmly as she stepped into the hallway. "Ciaran's not in, I'm afraid. As soon as we all got back from the hospital, he went off for a walk on his own. Said he needed to clear his mind."

"Beth no better?"

Cassie shook her head. "Not really. She did talk a little bit tonight, but then she just seems to go quiet. Within no time she's filling up again. It's quite upsetting to watch."

Which is precisely the reason, thought Rosie, *that I haven't been to visit her these last two days.* "Has she said anything to you about what's up?"

Cassie shrugged her shoulders. "She just keeps saying that she doesn't want to *be* there. That's all I've managed to get out of her." There was a sadness in her eyes that Rosie hadn't seen before. "Your brother's finding it hard. He almost broke down on our way home."

Rosie's throat tightened. She felt again a surge of that same helpless anger that had been dogging her ever since they'd returned to London. "I'd better be getting back then." Her voice faltered as she spoke, and suddenly she knew she had to get out.

"Why don't you stay and have a cuppa with us, love?" Cassie urged gently.

Rosie shook her head as a wave of anxiety began to grip her. Whatever this thing was, she didn't like it. "No, I'd better not.

I only called to say hello anyway. It's getting late. Soon be my bedtime."

Cassie nodded. "Well, if you're sure –"

"Yeah, I'm fine … ." As if to try and convince her, Rosie leaned forward and patted Cassie's shoulders hastily. It was an awkward gesture; a gauche attempt at a hug. But suddenly, the urge to leave was almost overpowering. As she stepped out into the night and heard the door shut behind her with a clunk, Rosie began to shake. A sound escaped her lips; somewhere between a gasp and a sob. What was happening to her? As she thought about Ciaran, her eyes burned with tears. What had happened to their London dream? It was fast turning into a nightmare.

The last thing she was expecting as she arrived back at the house was visitors. As she wearily shut the front door, she heard Mel's voice squeaking from the kitchen.

"Yoo-hoo! Is that you, Rosie?"

Rosie scowled. Who did she *think* it was – Kylie Minogue? Honestly, Mel could be so dim at times. Rosie heard the sound of footsteps scurrying towards the passageway, then Mel appeared looking slightly pink. "We have someone to see us, Rosie!" She spoke deliberately loudly, winking in a much exaggerated way.

"Who is it?" Rosie hissed under her breath. Mel bent towards her and whispered that Gavin had called round with Dan on the off chance of seeing her. Rosie's heart sank. She'd been too preoccupied to notice any give-away cars out in the street. This day was going from bad to worse.

"You only just caught them," Mel continued in a whisper which seemed to rasp like a rusty saw. "They were about to leave."

Rosie mentally kicked herself. She should have stayed for that cup of tea after all. When Mel had turned to go back into the living room, Rosie straightened her hair and tried to set her face into an expression of nonchalance.

"Hi Rosie." Gavin stood to his feet as she entered the room. It reminded her of the first time she'd met him in the wine bar. "Long time no see."

Long time no hear either, Rosie thought dourly, but she said nothing. She smiled as inscrutably as she could and sat in a chair by the table.

"Did you have a good Christmas?" Gavin seemed suddenly rather uncomfortable.

Rosie nodded slowly. "Very good, thanks. Just wish it could have lasted a little longer. And you?"

Gavin was temporarily distracted by Dan's sudden departure into the kitchen.

No doubt in response to Mel's beckoning, thought Rosie as she stifled a groan. *Trust Mel. She's probably trying to give us some time to ourselves – like I want it.*

Gavin shuffled awkwardly in his chair. "Yeah, it was okay. Would have been better if you'd been there though."

For a moment Rosie wondered if this last comment had been meant as a dig, but glancing across at Gavin, she saw that his face was gentle. She dismissed the suspicion. "What about the job? Did you get it?"

Gavin lowered his head. "No. I decided against it. There were a few things I wasn't happy about. Not to worry though – something else will turn up. How's Beth?"

It was Rosie's turn to lower her head. "Not good at all." She explained briefly about Beth's sudden deterioration during the past week. "My brother's finding it really tough."

Gavin looked sympathetic. "I'm sorry to hear that, Rosie." He paused for a few moments, a tentative expression shadowing his face. "Look, I don't know if you feel up to it, but Dan got himself a bit of a promotion a couple of days ago and he's wanting to celebrate. Wondered if we'd like to make up a foursome with him and Mel – go out for a meal or something. I understand if you're not bothered. But you never know, Rosie, it might do you good."

Rosie shook her head. "I'm not much in the mood for celebrating. I'd put a damper on things."

"I'm sure you wouldn't." Gavin's voice was gently insistent. "Think about it at least."

"No. No, I couldn't. I'm completely miserable at the moment." Rosie gave an apologetic half-smile. "I'd only spoil it for everyone. But thanks for asking."

Later on when the boys had gone, Mel was aghast to hear that Rosie had turned the invitation down. "You said *no?* You do know this whole thing was a set-up, Rosie? It was all Gavin's idea. He wanted to find an excuse to take you out again." Mel flushed slightly as she suddenly realised she'd said too much.

Rosie was momentarily confused. "So Dan *hasn't* got promotion?"

"Oh yeah, course he did. But he'd have been just as happy celebrating in front of the telly with a few cans. The meal idea was Gavin's. I don't know quite what's gone on between you two recently, Rosie, but whatever it is, Gavin's certainly trying to kiss and make up. He still seems pretty into you as far as I can see."

Rosie was quiet. Somehow her brain was struggling to process this latest information. Over the Christmas period, she'd just about resigned herself to the idea that Gavin was history, and yet here he was, back large as life, cooking up crazy pretexts for taking her out again. None of it made any sense. But then, none of the rest of her life did either.

"Come on, Rosie," Mel begged, "give him another chance. You need cheering up."

Rosie would have found her hangdog expression irritating if it hadn't been so pathetic. "I – I dunno. I'll think about it." She wanted to kick herself the moment the words were out, but Mel seemed suitably appeased.

"If you do decide to change your mind, we're thinking about Friday."

Two days later when Ciaran arrived at the hospital straight from a teaching stint, he passed Michael Romily on the corridor of B1.

"Ciaran ... just the man I wanted to see. Can you spare five minutes before you go in to see her?"

Ciaran frowned nervously. "Sure. Is everything okay?"

The consultant led him into an interview room and the two of them sat down. "I've spoken with Abby Whittaker, the counsellor who saw Beth this morning." Michael glanced quickly at his watch. "I think she should still be in the hospital, Ciaran, and I know she wants to talk to you. If I can get hold of her now, would you let her put you in the picture about some of the things they discussed?" His hand was already on the phone.

Ciaran shrugged. "Yeah, course."

Abby Whittaker was a slight, dark-haired woman in her late thirties. She spoke in a soft, lilting accent and her eyes were animated with well-practised empathy. When formal introductions were out of the way, she leaned forward in her seat and began to speak with a comforting familiarity.

"Beth has given me permission to share with you the things we talked about this morning." She smiled almost apologetically. "I know that all sounds rather official, you being her husband and everything, but we have to do things this way these days."

Ciaran nodded. "I understand."

Abby looked down at a small notebook on her knee and scribbled a couple of jottings. Then she looked directly at Ciaran. "You and Beth aren't from round here, are you?"

Ciaran shook his head. "We both moved to London when we were younger to go to music college."

Abby smiled. "Yes, so Beth was telling me." Her face became serious. "I'm afraid she's very unhappy, Ciaran. It took a while before she would admit it to me, but she really doesn't want to be here."

Ciaran's frown deepened. "You mean in hospital?"

Abby shook her head. "No. I mean in London. It does happen sometimes. Everyone responds differently in a situation like Beth's. Some people want to fulfil lifelong ambitions – go on cruises, visit Disneyland, even climb mountains if they're able. Some people spend their last months fundraising for research. It's their way of kicking back against the disease that's killing them. Others, like Beth, find they have an innate wish to go back to a particular place. It's often the place where they were born or raised. Somewhere they associate with happiness. It's a kind of security thing. It seems to help them face the end." She paused. "Beth kept telling me this morning what a wonderful Christmas you've all just spent. She said she'd never been so happy. Whenever she talks about her home in Yorkshire, she seems bright, almost hopeful. From the sound of it, the problem really started when she got back down here. Obviously her contracting the chest infection hasn't helped her general state, but I do think the sudden decline in her condition can be more accurately attributed to emotional causes rather than physiological ones."

Ciaran exchanged glances with Michael Romily. He turned to Abby in consternation. "What are you saying exactly?"

Abby was scribbling again. "I don't know how direct Beth will be with you, Ciaran. When we were talking this morning, there was a real reluctance on her part to tell you how she felt. She didn't want to put you under pressure."

"Pressure to *what?*" Ciaran looked slightly confused.

Abby's clear gaze met his troubled eyes. "Deep down, Beth wants to go back up to Yorkshire – to her family home."

"*Yorkshire?* What – *now?*" Ciaran ran a hand through his hair in frustration. "Is that even possible? I don't know a thing about the health care up there. Surely she's better off down here – with someone like Michael looking after things?"

Michael shot a glance at Abby then leaned forward in his chair. "If Beth had presented earlier, Ciaran, I might have been able to do more. As it is, I'm afraid my expertise is no more valuable now than the next man's. We caught it too late. That's the simple truth. I wish with all my heart I could tell you otherwise."

Ciaran dropped his head dejectedly. "I don't honestly know what to say. I wasn't expecting anything like this."

Abby gave a sympathetic smile. "I suppose it's a bit of a bombshell for you, isn't it? As I say, she was very reluctant to mention anything. But in Beth's condition it's inadvisable for her to keep quiet about issues like this, even at the risk of sounding selfish. I think that's her main fear."

Ciaran frowned. “I don’t understand.”

“Well, there’s your job situation to think about for one thing. And your home. Beth doesn’t want to put you in danger of losing everything.”

Ciaran scowled. “I’m losing everything anyway. Who gives a damn about the house or the job …?” His voice trailed away.

Michael Romily looked thoughtful. “You have to weigh all the pros and cons, Ciaran. There’s no problem transferring her to another health authority. I can’t say that Beth will live any longer if you decide to make the move. But quality of life is a definite factor to take into consideration.”

Ciaran stared down at the floor. “How long, Mr Romily?” His tone was blunt. “Being honest, how long do you think she has?”

Michael Romily squared his jaw. “Given the aggressive nature of Beth’s disease, and the fact that it’s in her liver and pancreas – I think four months max.”

Ciaran swallowed hard. “That’s with everything on her side?”

Michael nodded. “Yes. I’m afraid so.”

Ciaran swore under his breath. After a few moments he looked up, his eyes damp. “I’ll talk to her parents.”

Rosie felt strangely distant as she sat in the lounge of *Le Papillon Rouge*. They weren’t due to eat for another half hour, and Dan and Gavin had gone to get some drinks. Though the lounge was a swirl of chatter, the acoustics of the room were such that each conversation seemed trapped in its own private bubble – tastefully muted in volume, and largely indecipherable to anyone sitting more than a couple of feet from whoever happened to be doing the talking. Rosie felt that she could quite easily have been absorbed into the fancy flock wallpaper without anyone noticing. The idea was almost appealing. Even Mel’s excitable comments floated somewhere above her head. Rosie was in a complete world of her own.

Meanwhile over at the bar, Gavin was in victorious mood. “I’ll get all the drinks in tonight, mate.”

Dan frowned. "What – all night? Your ship come in or something?"

"I owe you, don't I?" Gavin was grinning. "I don't think Rosie would have come out with me this evening without you two being around."

Dan's frown deepened. "Dunno if I like what I'm hearing."

Gavin slapped his shoulder playfully. "Hey man, don't get in a lather about it. We just didn't leave each other on the best of terms at Christmas, that's all. Things didn't work out as planned."

"But you still like her?"

Gavin winked. "Let's just say Rosie intrigues me."

"Intrigues you, eh?" Dan shook his head. "I've never got to grips with your take on women, Gav."

Gavin laughed. "I like a challenge. And Rosie's certainly that. She's pretty smart – and she doesn't throw herself at me. I'm not used to that, mate. But I like it. Brings out the conqueror in me."

Dan raised his eyebrows. "*Conqueror?* Are you for real?"

Gavin shrugged. "Give me a break, Dan. I'll bet you've done *your* fair share of conquering with Mel over there."

It was a distasteful comment to make, and Dan felt the sting of it. For a split second he contemplated countering the attack with a mouthful of his own. But he decided against it. Obviously Gavin's testosterone levels were running high and impairing his sensitivity. For the sake of friendship, he swallowed his annoyance and spoke in a quiet, measured voice. "I really like Mel, Gav. I don't look on her as a conquest. I never have."

Gavin looked away as Dan's meek reply brought him up with a start. "Sorry, mate. I wasn't meaning anything. I like Rosie too. Really I do."

It was nearly midnight when Rosie and Mel got home. Mel was giggly and flustered; Rosie wasn't sure if it was the result of too many glasses of Chardonnay or just an overexposure to male company. Whatever it was, she was clearly in talkative mood. Rosie made her excuses and went off to bed. "Catch up with you in the morning," she called out as she went into her room. "Think I'm just getting the mother of all headaches."

It wasn't true, but Rosie knew it probably soon would be if she stayed around for one of Mel's girly gossip sessions. She slid the lock on her bedroom door as an extra precaution, then threw herself onto the bed. How had she ever ended up sharing a house with somebody like Mel? They were so different – polar opposites in many respects. She felt a twinge of guilt. Poor old Mel meant well. She was just so irritating at times. And at the moment, she was more than Rosie could cope with.

Rosie thought back over the evening. Gavin had been super attentive. He'd laughed loudly at her jokes – which, in view of the fact that she hadn't actually made any, had been quite an achievement. It had come as something of a revelation to Rosie to discover how amusing she managed to be without even trying. The downside of this remarkable gift had been Mel's insistence on trying to outlaugh Gavin every time Rosie inadvertently dropped a wisecrack. The bizarre carry-on had had all the appearance of flirting. Rosie hoped for Dan's sake that it had not been so. Throughout the evening, Dan had seemed quiet; smiling and affable enough, but quiet all the same. Rosie couldn't help feeling that Mel needed to be careful. Perhaps joint dates were not the best idea if she wanted her relationship with Dan to last. As Rosie's mind played over the last few hours, a faint breath of Gavin's aftershave floated across her face. She put her nose to her sleeve. Great – she even smelt like him now. But then it was hardly surprising; he did go a bit mad with the stuff. She remembered his kiss at the end of the evening. It had been a relatively restrained affair, nothing like as passionate as some of the clinches he'd had her in during the period leading up to Christmas. Obviously he was playing it cool. That suited her just fine. She wasn't sure how she felt about the whole thing anymore. In the early weeks of her relationship with Gavin, something in her had hoped, deep down, that he would be genuine, sincere – as sound on the inside as he was gorgeous on the outside. It was easy to find him attractive. It was also easy to enjoy the attention he generated. Rosie had got almost used to being the object of envious glances from other females whenever Gavin took her out. It was strangely affirming. If truth were told, she'd even secretly revelled in Mel's fascination with the beautiful man. Even if Rosie hardly ever knew where she herself stood with him, at least she stood nearer to him than Mel did. Yet therein lay the crux of the problem. The never knowing where she stood with him. Gavin was slippery. One minute things would seem to be going well, the next, everything would be up in the air and infuriatingly uncertain. Several times over the last few weeks, her hopes had been built up, only to be dashed by periods of unexplained silence or crass insensitivity on his part. Rosie knew she would never be able to open her heart to someone on such part-time terms. She swallowed hard. Then again, how did she know if she'd ever be able to open her heart on *any* terms? She never had before. Her stomach gave an unexplained lurch and she turned over onto her side. Before she could stop it, her mind threw up a memory of the day she'd met Jonathon in the churchyard at Saint Edwin's. Caked in dirt, his piercing blue eyes laughing out from beneath his tousled fringe, there had been a warmth in his smile she'd never encountered in a guy before. She tried to imagine Gavin clearing leaves so that an old man wouldn't fall and break his neck. The picture didn't come easily. She remembered Jonathon's last e-mail. *I think you should visit us once in a while – to recharge your batteries and all that.*

She exhaled slowly with a weariness that seemed to come from her bones. *Life's not that simple, Jonathon. Not my life anyway.* A sudden sense of despair swept over her and she sat bolt upright as panic threatened to grip her again. *Man, I'm losing it. I'm cracking up ... I must be.*

She instinctively reached for her laptop. She had to e-mail Jonathon. Just to make contact. If she couldn't visit, at least she could do that. No. What was she thinking of? He'd think she was desperate. He might even think she was coming onto him. *Hang on a minute ... .* She quickly scrambled for the diary and found her page. Surely this was a reasonable excuse for getting in touch? Her hands were trembling as she tried to prop the book open. *Come on, girl, get a grip.*

Tuileries November17th 1916

I think perhaps I will not write very much this evening, Emily. We're back on the front line and the Bosch are giving us a merry time, but tonight I feel oddly detached from the whole business. I'm strangely weak; ill I fear. Hardly surprising when we stand for hours in these temperatures, knee-deep in water at times. I must try to keep going, Em, but I'm not sure how much longer my legs will hold me upright. My mind keeps drifting. Memories assail me, memories of our beloved England. How I wish we could all be back there. I find myself thinking of that day we left the village for the training barracks. Could it really have been only eighteen months ago? I have seen so much since then ...

"You alright, Sam?" Boxer was counting out Mills' bombs as he shot his mate a look of concern.

Sam sighed heavily and pushed his notebook back into his bag. "I dunno. I'm not sure how I feel." Except for a bone-gnawing weariness that was steadily creeping through his whole body, and a throat so dry it felt like he'd spent the last week in a desert. His head was hurting too, and his skin was hot to touch. It certainly wasn't on account of the warm weather.

"You ought to see the MO, Sam," interjected Jimmy. "You look pretty rough to me."

"How can you tell in this light?" Sam tried to laugh, but it seemed to make him ache all over. "I don't think any of us look like oil paintings when it's nearly pitch black."

"Maybe not." Jimmy's voice was low as he drew on his cigarette. "But the rest of us aren't hobbling about like old women."

Seeing a wry smile pass over Boxer's face, Sam tried to straighten up. He was beginning to feel terrible.

"Egg and brandy!" Twinny Two's voice hissed through the darkness.

"Eh?" someone else retorted sharply.

"Raw egg and brandy. Best medicine when you're nursing a cold."

Twinny One started to snigger. "You remember that time we tried it at home with that bottle of Dad's?"

"Oh yeah ... and me hand slipped," Twinny Two recalled. "Got a right whippin' for that, didn't we?"

The two brothers began to chortle like naughty schoolboys. Sam ran his hand over his forehead. What wouldn't he do for a drop of brandy right now? A sniper's bullet whistled through the blackness, followed a split second later by an agonised scream from the latrine just ahead.

"Poor beggar, whoever he is," Jimmy growled, stubbing out his cigarette. It was a fact of life; relieving oneself could be a very risky business. A clatter of gunfire came from behind them and echoed across no man's land.

"Looks like our lads are returning the favour," Boxer said grimly.

But Sam hardly cared. By now he was feeling so awful that he would have gladly lain down in the trench and let someone shoot him. A new volley of fire opened up between the two sides. Flares lit up the sky as a burst of machine gunfire raked the ground.

"Not a good time to go to the lav," Twinny One winked at Sam. "Otherwise it'll take more than eggs and ruddy brandy to bring you round."

Sam hardly knew what happened next. He had just forced a grin in reply when there was a sudden explosion a few yards ahead of their position. The parapet itself took most of the shrapnel, but the impact of the shell's blast blew in the front wall of the trench with remarkable force. Sam groaned as a mountain of sodden soil buried him. The last thing he knew was the taste of earth in his mouth and then, blackness.

****

"His temperature's still rising, Doctor." The young nurse lays another strip of wet fabric on the patient's forehead.

The doctor places a hand on the sick man's burning cheek and frowns. "The next few hours will be crucial. It's clear this man was ill before he ever took a hit. His injuries are fairly superficial."

He glances around the gloomy ward, his face furrowing as he surveys its other pitiful occupants. "Do your best for him, Nurse Parker. This is one that could be saved – unlike some of these other poor wretches."

This was the day Sam had been waiting for. Today he would leave everything he had ever known and start out on a journey to somewhere he'd never been before, somewhere he'd never even dreamed of going. Going abroad was for the rich, for those with means. Yet here he was, little old Sam, off on the adventure of a lifetime. Of course there were things he didn't want to leave behind. His family for one. And Emily. Still, it wouldn't be for long. And then what stories he would have to tell. There were eight of them leaving from the village. They would walk into the next two hamlets, meet up with the other new recruits, and then travel together by rail to the training barracks in London.

"He's burning up, Sister ..."

The older nurse shakes her head sadly. "I think we're going to lose this one, Nurse Parker. Influenza is difficult to fight when the body is already weakened. He won't be the first we've lost to it." She strides down the ward and disappears out of a side door.

"Come on, Sam!" The young nurse checks his pulse again. "Come on – fight it! Think of all those back home who love you. Don't die, Sam. Dear God, touch this man. Spare his life, I pray."

The village band was on fine form today. They marched respectfully behind the little group of recruits, their instruments sounding glorious in the warm sunshine. It seemed that the entire village had turned out for the occasion. Fathers saluted proudly as the procession passed by, whilst mothers waved handkerchiefs and fought back tears. Little children clutched flags as they gazed admiringly at these brave young men who were off to defend their country, and village maidens twirled ribbons and smiled coyly, hoping to catch the eye of their favourite recruit. Of course, Sam only had eyes for Emily. He hadn't seen her yet, but he was sure he would. Somewhere along the route, he knew she would be there. He caught sight of his own mother and father standing with a group outside the village church. They looked quietly proud, though Sam knew his mother well enough to know that this would be the hardest day of her life. Nobody was saying anything, but everyone was aware of the casualty lists coming back from the front. Sam heard a voice shouting to him from the crowd. His younger sister, Kitty, was blowing kisses to him in her unabashed, childlike way. For a moment, a lump came to his throat.

They walked out of the village and along dusty country roads towards the next settlement. The band still followed, and by now, several villagers had tagged onto the procession. They passed hedgerows, streams, and fields that stretched out as far as the eye could see.

"Look at that!" A young man at Sam's side pointed into the sky. Hovering high in the pure blue was a skylark. The young man stopped and turned to the bandmaster. "Sir, could we lads listen to yon lark a moment? Perhaps in weeks to come it'll remind us of what we're fighting for."

The bandmaster signalled to the players and they quickly fell silent. All that could be heard was a rich, chirruping song that seemed to fill the whole countryside as the bird soared higher into the sky. For several moments everyone stood still, mesmerised by the creature, each person lost in their own thoughts. By the time the lark eventually made its plunge to earth, a sense of contemplation had come over the whole gathering.

It was then that Sam saw Emily. She was standing by the roadside with a little group of folk from her own village, and her eyes were fixed on him. As the procession began again, Sam moved over to the edge of the road, an urgency gripping his heart. He stepped aside and looked into her eyes. "I'm so glad to see you before I go, Emily."

Emily laid a hand gently on his arm. "I'm coming out myself soon, Sam."

Sam frowned. How he wished these few moments could last forever. "I don't understand."

"As a nurse. I've applied and I've been accepted."

Sam nodded slowly. "Be careful, Emily." It was all he dared say, though his heart ached to say so much more.

"And you, Sam."

Sam could see that the procession had left him behind. His mind was torn. Should he declare his feelings? It was hardly the place. For a few seconds he stood staring at her, his heart racing, his mouth unable to speak. Then the moment passed. He gave a brief smile. "Goodbye, Emily. See you when we both get home."

As Emily smiled gently back at him, Sam turned and began to walk briskly towards his friends. He had to make sure he got home now.

"I think he might have turned the corner, Doctor. Would you be able to take a look at him?" The young nurse runs the back of her hand over Sam's forehead. The raging fever has abated at last and the skin is cool.

The doctor seems pleasantly surprised. "Well done, Nurse. I was beginning to think we'd lost this one. I daresay it'll be a good few weeks before he's fit to go back out though."

The young nurse inwardly sighs. What a shame to be sent back out at all, having just come through the fight of his life. What a senseless war.

Sam opened his eyes. Where was he? For a few moments he blinked as he tried to remember. He ran his hands along the sheets. *Sheets?* He was in a proper bed!

"Hello, Sam. How are you feeling?" The young nurse smiled down at him. She was plump and not pretty at all. Yet to Sam in that moment, she was one of the loveliest sights he'd ever seen.

"I'm *alive …!*"

"Yes, Sam, by the skin of your teeth you are." She grinned at him. "You came pretty close. But God was smiling down on you."

Sam closed his eyes again and tried to breathe deeply. His chest felt tight and sore. "Am I wounded?"

"No, not badly. You've been very sick with influenza. You were buried in a shell blast but your friends managed to get you out before you suffocated."

Good old Boxer, thought Sam gratefully. *Good old Jimmy – and the Twinnies.* "What happens now?"

"Doctor Ross will see you in a little while and explain everything to you ..."

Carlesands January 11th 1917

... That's how I came to be here, Em, back home on extended leave. I've been ill for about eight weeks (spent Christmas in hospital, can you believe?) Doctor Ross said it was a miracle I pulled through. My chest was in a terrible way and I've lost so much weight, my poor mother nearly fainted when she first saw me. She's been busy trying to fatten me up before they send me back out again. One of the nurses who looked after me – Milly Parker her name was – told me she prayed for me every day I was in the hospital. It seems that someone up there was looking out for me. Happily, I'm well on the road to recovery now.

Sitting here in the comfort of my home, it's hard to believe the slaughter that's going on just over the water. I think of my pals out there – and you, Emily, brave girl. I find I can't bring myself to talk to folk here about what's going on. Somehow I don't think they would believe it. They would imagine our tales to be foolish bravado, or exaggerated nonsense. Sitting here by my fireside, I can almost pretend it to be so myself. But we know the truth, Em, don't we? Whatever happens in the end, we'll both know what really went on out there. There's just one thing I regret. That day on the roadside, how I wish I'd told you how I felt. Having come so close to death, I now realise, more than I ever did, just how much you mean to me. You were in my every dream, my every restless thought ... .

Rosie filed the entries and went onto e-mail.

Hi Jonathon –
Just a bit more for you. Hope everything's okay up there. Must confess, I'm still struggling to settle back into things down here.

Yorkshire has a lot to answer for. Was it Samuel Johnson who said 'When a man is tired of London, he is tired of Life'? I wonder if he was out of his mind.

Bye for now
Rosie

She sent the e-mail and closed her laptop. A solitary tear splashed onto its lid.

Out of his mind? Even if he wasn't, I'm pretty sure I soon will be.

Chapter 17

"You're *what?*" Rosie didn't want to believe what she was hearing.

"Please, Ros. Make this easy for me." Ciaran hung his head miserably and Rosie bit her lip.

"When did all this come about?" She forced her voice to be calm.

"We spoke last night. It was Michael Romily and some counsellor woman who primed me about it just before I went in to see her. She broke down when I mentioned it on the ward. I think she feels bad uprooting me and everything. But I'm past caring about anything like that." Ciaran stared blankly out of Rosie's bedroom window.

Rosie's hands were trembling. *Left down here without Ciaran and Beth?* The thought made her feel sick to the pit of her stomach. "What about the house? Where will you live afterwards?" *Afterwards?* Flinching at her own insensitivity, she wanted to pull the words straight back into her mouth.

But Ciaran seemed not to have noticed the inference. "I saw Ed and Cassie this morning. They've offered to keep the house on for me – rent and everything. I'll have to give up all my teaching for the moment. Guess the money will dry up pretty quick."

Rosie frowned. "And the orchestra?"

Ciaran shrugged. "I'm sure Emmett will save my place if I want it."

"If you *want* it?" A shiver of alarm went through Rosie. "You can't give up on your music, Kitch. Beth would never want that."

Ciaran hung his head again. "The music's fast going out of my life, Ros. Beth's a far better musician than I'll ever be, and look at her. She can barely play for five minutes now without getting exhausted."

Rosie was at a loss as to what to say. The whole room seemed suddenly swathed in an atmosphere of despondency. It was claustrophobic, yet she knew it must be so much worse for him. "When will you go?"

"I dunno. I might get a chance to talk to someone this afternoon. I suppose they'll have to get this infection thing sorted out first before she can travel. After that, I guess the sooner the better. If I only had four months left I'd want to make every minute count."

Rosie nodded quietly, her jaws set tight. In that moment, she knew she'd have done anything to be going with them.

Gavin was genuinely surprised to hear the news. It was Mel who spilt the beans when she went to meet Dan straight from the gym.

"Poor old Rosie, down here all on her own. She was pretty upset when she told me about it."

Gavin was thoughtful. "I never did get to meet her brother and his wife. What sort of guy is he?"

"Oh, he's really nice," said Mel breezily, omitting to mention the fact that she'd never had more than the most fleeting of conversations with him. "Quiet, serious – y'know, the musical sort."

"A bit like Robbie Williams, eh?" Dan teased, putting his arm around her shoulder.

Mel frowned, uncomprehending.

"Well *he's* a musical sort."

For a moment Mel's expression was blank. Then she burst into giggles. "Have you heard him, Gavin? He's sending me up."

But Gavin was lost in his own world. Mel had given him food for thought.

Later that evening he called Rosie. "Hi, how's things?"

Rosie was deliberately noncommittal. "Fine. And you?"

Gavin decided to come straight to the point. "I hear Beth and your brother are moving up to Yorkshire."

Rosie was slightly taken aback. "Good news travels fast, eh? I only found out a few hours ago myself. Guess I have Mel to thank for telling you."

"You weren't planning to keep it a secret from me, were you?" Gavin pretended to sound hurt. "I would have thought this was the time to have friends around you."

Rosie mumbled something to placate him and Gavin seemed satisfied.

"How's about I pick you up tomorrow and we go and visit Beth at the hospital?"

"*Tomorrow?* Tomorrow's Sunday," Rosie spluttered, as though the day made any difference. This was all rather sudden. Since when had Gavin been bothered about wanting to visit Beth? She found herself trying desperately to think of a good reason to turn down his magnanimous offer. "Aren't you doing anything else?" *Like washing your hair perhaps, or dyeing your eyebrows.*

But Gavin wasn't about to be put off. "I haven't had chance to meet them yet. I just thought it might be a nice thing to do before they go."

Rosie's mind was reeling. "Look, Gavin – I know what visiting times mean to Beth. I think it might be awkward if you were there for any length of time. After all, you *are* a total stranger. I don't like the idea of her sitting there feeling self-conscious while we all try to make small talk around her bed."

"Point taken." Gavin's voice was clipped.

Inwardly Rosie groaned. "Okay. How's about this? We go to the hospital together. I go in and have half an hour with her while you go for a coffee in the restaurant. Then you come up to the ward. Just for five minutes or so, to give me chance to introduce you." Rosie paused. "Then we go home." *Take it or leave it, sunshine. That's as much as I'm bending on this one.*

Gavin perked up at this idea. After making brief arrangements, Rosie managed to extricate herself from the phone call. But she couldn't help feeling strangely irritated. Setting up her laptop, she sat drumming her fingers as it was loading. She hardly wanted to admit it, even to herself, but she was hoping beyond hope that there would be a reply from Jonathon. There was.

Hi Rosie –
Don't like to hear you sounding so fed up. I saw Maisie earlier – she was asking about you. I think she's quite taken to you.
Sounds like old Sam went through the mill in our last instalment, doesn't it? Can't wait to find out what happens next.
Try to keep smiling
Luv Jonathon.

As Rosie stared at the words, memories of her time in Ridderch Standen flooded her mind again. For a few brief moments, she could almost forget the oppression that was pushing in on her. Life had seemed so much slower up there – calmed to a nice, digestible pace. The sky had been open too. Open, vast and majestic – not like the dark, sullen sky that looked down on London. She tried to remonstrate with herself. She was being ridiculous. London was a great place; plenty of people thought so. She'd thought so herself only a few weeks ago. But, she now realised miserably, nowhere was a great place when your heart was somewhere else.

Carlesands January 15th 1917

Well, Emily, here I am just enjoying the last few days of my leave. I've finally been declared fit to return to the front, and though I never thought I'd say it, I'm almost glad. Somehow, leave is a difficult business. Small snatches of cosy normality do not sit easily with those who've been living in hell. It's been rather hard fitting in at home. Lovely to see everyone of course – that goes without saying. But the war has done something to me. My eyes have witnessed things my own father could never conceive in his worst nightmares. Set against the backdrop of ordinary civvy life, our experiences seem almost unbelievably grotesque. Only in the trenches themselves do our stories fit comfortably. I fear that those of us who survive this thing will carry our memories, for the most part unspoken, to the grave.

A rather unpleasant experience yesterday, Em. Kitty wanted to go to the big town, so I accompanied her. She was looking in a shop window and I was standing a few paces back. Suddenly a young lady approached me, a strange expression on her face. To be polite, I smiled and removed my cap. Then she stepped right up to me, stared hard at me and said, 'To think such a brave fellow as yourself is here gazing in shop windows when my own poor brother is buried with most of his pals at Beaumont-Hamel.' Of course, I was in my civilian clothes, and she could hardly have known that I'd just been shipped home from Ypres having been within a hair's breadth of death myself. Before I had a chance to explain, she turned on her heel and walked away almost in tears. I've never had anyone give me a white feather like some chaps have, but honestly, Em, she might as well have done it. I don't think Kitty saw any of the business, but I know I was quiet on the way home. It left a rather unpleasant taste in my mouth.

I have to say, I'm very much looking forward to seeing my mates again. I hope they're all in the pink. I'm being posted back to my old unit which is good news. After an episode like this, a fellow can be sent anywhere.

I called to see your family the other day, Emily. Your brother is recovering well from his wounds, though I don't think he'll be seeing any more action in this conflict. Your parents are terribly proud of you even though they miss you dreadfully. They're not alone in that.

It will be good to be near you again, Em. Even though we're stationed so far from each other, I know I'll be closer to you on that side of the channel than on this. For my sake, you must stay safe. This war cannot last forever.

Attaching the diary entry, Rosie typed a quick message to Jonathon.

Hi Jonathon –

Life gets better and better. My brother has just broken the news that he and Beth are moving up to Oak Lodge. Beth wants to spend her last few months back there. Understandable I know, but I'm pretty miserable about it all. Guess I'm being selfish, but I'm gonna miss them like crazy. Keep an eye on them for me. You know how to get hold of me if you feel there's anything I should know.

Bye for now
Rosie.

PS Tell Maisie I said hello.

The next day on the ward, Rosie felt nervous. In keeping with their arrangement, Gavin had brought her to the hospital then gone off to the restaurant for a drink. Rosie had already forewarned Ciaran and Beth that he'd be putting in a brief appearance at some point. Beth seemed in better spirits today, and Rosie could only deduce that the thought of her impending return to Yorkshire had gone a long way towards bucking her up.

Beth seemed to view the prospect of Gavin's visit with some amusement. "Wants to meet me before I pop my clogs, does he?"

Rosie smiled but said nothing. Beth was much easier company when her sense of humour was up and running.

"You will come and visit us some weekends, won't you, Ros?" Beth looked at her directly.

It was an invitation Rosie had been secretly hoping for. "Yeah, course I will. If it's okay with your mum and dad."

Beth's face broke into a smile. "Oh, there'll be no problem there."

Just before five, they heard footsteps in the corridor outside followed by a light tap at the cubicle door. It opened to reveal Gavin. It could have been an awkward moment, but Ciaran rose to the occasion. Extending a hand to Gavin, he introduced himself then gestured towards the bed. "This is my wife … Beth."

Gavin shook Ciaran's hand enthusiastically, then turned to Beth with a gentle smile. "Hello, it's great to meet you. Rosie's talked a lot about you both."

"All good, I hope?" A sparkle of the old mirth lit up Beth's pale face.

"Oh yes," Gavin assured her in a voice that Rosie was convinced could have charmed the birds off the trees. "All good."

Gavin drew up a chair and seemed surprisingly at ease as he quickly fell into conversation with Ciaran and Beth. After telling them a little about his own job and background, he suddenly turned the discussion round to the topic of classical music. Even though Rosie suspected he was virtually clueless on the subject, his apparent avid interest proved an instant hit with the two musicians. As the moments went by, Rosie could hardly believe what she was hearing. Since when had *he* known the first thing about Max Bruch or Tchaikovsky? *What was that – he likes Khachaturian? Is he having a laugh? I'm surprised he can even pronounce his name.* This was getting scary; Gavin was beginning to sound almost intelligent. He must have spent the whole morning trying to memorize *The A-Z of Classical Composers* specially for the occasion. *Gotta hand it to you, Gav,* she conceded grudgingly, *you're good. Boy, you are good.* After twenty minutes, he was well into his swing and showing no signs of wanting to leave. Rosie was beginning to feel restless. This was supposed to have been a five minute visit and it was starting to look like they'd be here until throwing out time. Besides, she thought cynically, how could they be sure Gavin's aftershave wasn't interacting with Beth's medication? She tried shuffling in her chair, hoping he would take the hint. Then she made a couple of attempts to look at her watch when she was sure his eyes were focused in her direction. Eventually, she gave up the subtle approach and began to pull on her coat. "Guess we ought to be getting off now, huh…?"

Gavin glanced down at his own watch with a look of surprise. "Is it that time already?" He stood to his feet, zipped up his jacket, and smiled down at Beth. "It's been great meeting you …" He put his hand out towards Ciaran. "And you, sir."

As the two men shook hands, Rosie said goodbye to Beth and moved towards the door. Stepping out into the corridor, she didn't see Gavin lean towards her brother with an air of confidentiality. "Don't worry about your sister when you go up to Yorkshire. I'll be looking after her."

Ciaran smiled gratefully. "Thanks, Gavin. I really appreciate that."

On their way back to the car park, Gavin was unusually quiet. Rosie wondered if she'd upset him by her attempts to get him out of Beth's room. "You okay?" she asked lightly in an effort to bump start some sort of conversation.

He mumbled something in reply, but the wind seemed to snatch his words and scatter them into the night air.

Rosie decided to wait until they were in the car before trying to pursue the matter further. "Something up then?" she ventured a couple of minutes later as she clipped on her seatbelt.

Gavin breathed out slowly as he stared hard at the windscreen. For a few moments he was silent. "Brings it home to you, doesn't it?"

Rosie frowned. "What does?"

"Seeing them together. She's so young. And your brother – he's a nice guy. A really nice guy." He was still staring straight ahead. "I know you've talked about them before, Rosie. But actually meeting them ... it's different. Makes you realise the situation." He swore under his breath. "I'll be honest, Rosie, it's upset me. It really has."

It was the last thing Rosie had been expecting. She wasn't sure what to say, and was half afraid Gavin might suddenly burst into tears. She felt a flash of guilt about her earlier cynicism. So what if he'd been brushing up on his Beethoven? He'd obviously just wanted to make a good impression. Kind of sweet really. Tentatively she reached for his hand. "Now you know why I haven't been the life and soul of the party in recent days."

"Yeah." Gavin nodded quietly. "Actually, from what I've just seen, I think you're all doing amazingly well."

Rosie found this vindication strangely uplifting. "And now you understand why I wanted to spend Christmas with them?"

Gavin turned to her, a remorseful expression in his eyes. "I'm sorry, Rosie. I was a selfish pig. Forgive me?"

Rosie smiled. "Just one thing. How did you do all that in there?"

"All what?"

"All the classical music stuff. Gotta say, I came painfully close to being impressed."

"Ah, *that.*" There was a twinkle in Gavin's eye. "That's down to good old Granddad Pennington. He was a classical music buff. Always had it on in the house when we visited. Whenever Khachaturian's *Masquerade* waltz came on the radio, he'd grab my grandma and twirl her round the living room at high speed. Me and Bellamy used to do impressions of them – till we got to an age when it became embarrassing. We had a pretty neat routine for Borodin's *Polovtsian Dances* too." He grinned. "Not really my scene nowadays, but some things you never forget. Hey, maybe I could teach you a few nifty moves, Rosie."

Gracious in defeat, Rosie shook her head with a laugh. *You've managed to melt me yet again, Gavin. How many more times am I going to let you do that?*

And later that evening on the phone to Ciaran, it seemed Gavin had managed to melt him too. "He's a good bloke, Ros." Ciaran's tone was one of approval. "I reckon you've done well for yourself there."

Before she went to bed that night, Rosie checked her e-mails. There was a reply from Jonathon.

Hi Rosie –
I feel for you right now. I know what it's like being left on your own. When my folks moved, it took a bit of getting used to. Guess it was easier for me tho'. Ridderch Standen's a pretty small place – everyone knows everyone. I suppose London's a different ball game. Still, if I can be of any help – an electronic shoulder to cry on and all that – you know I'm here. And besides, now you really will have to pay us a visit. I'll tell Cassie to start getting your room ready.

Luv Jonathon

Rosie smiled to herself as she got ready for bed. All in all, today had turned out to be a much better day. Her confidence in Gavin had been renewed – yet again. She had seen another, rather surprising side to him. Ciaran had been positive about him too. That had to be good. But if all else should fail, there had also been two very important offers. One – the invitation to visit Ridderch Standen again. And two – Jonathon's promise of help if she should need it. She hoped she would not. But it was nice to know the option was there.

During the next few days, Beth's condition improved considerably. Michael Romily was pleased. "I think we've pretty much knocked the chest infection on the head, Ciaran. It's obvious that a more positive mental attitude goes a long way towards combating this kind of thing."

"How soon can we think about going up to Yorkshire?"

Michael considered the matter for a moment. "You start things moving from your end – employment, house, packing – whatever else needs to be done. And I'll start contacting the appropriate bodies concerning her health care. If she stays stable, it shouldn't be too long."

Gavin had been the perfect gentleman since his visit to the hospital. He had been in touch with Rosie every day, if not in person, then by phone. On the Thursday, Rosie decided to call and see Beth on her way home from the nursery.

Beth was beaming as Rosie entered the room. "What d'you think of my flowers then?" She gestured towards a huge bouquet on her bedside cabinet.

Rosie grinned. "Has that brother o' mine come into some money?"

Beth shook her head mischievously. "They're not from your brother. They're from your boyfriend …!"

"*Gavin?*" Rosie was incredulous.

"Yep! He had them delivered. How sweet is that? *And* they're silk – he must have known we're not allowed real ones on this section."

Rosie shook her head in amazement. "Didn't realise he was so clued up."

Beth seemed to find the whole thing rather entertaining. "Shame I'll not be around to see you two get wed."

Rosie tried to ignore the remark. She wasn't sure if it was Beth's allusion to her own forthcoming demise or the thought of being married to Gavin that niggled her. Perhaps it was a combination of the two. "Well," she quipped dismissively, "at least Gavin can rest assured that the small fortune he shelled out managed to put a smile on that sweet little face of yours."

"She liked them then?" Gavin asked later that evening as they sat in De Souza's.

"She loved them."

"I'm glad." Gavin gave a smile of relief. "I wasn't sure if she'd think they were a bit over the top."

"No. They made her day."

Gavin looked at her gently. "I'm still trying to work out how to make *your* day, Rosie."

Rosie hadn't been expecting the comment. She laughed disarmingly. "Am I that hard to please?"

Gavin didn't take his eyes off her. "I'm serious, Rosie. I'm still trying to work out what makes you tick. But don't worry, I don't give up easily."

Who said I was worrying? Rosie's smile was fixed. *What's he trying to make out – that I'm some kind of weirdo or something?* "Hey, it's not rocket science. A couple o' verses of '*Wheels on the Bus*' and a McDonald's Happy Meal – I'm happy as a sandboy."

Gavin was still looking at her intently. She felt suddenly self-conscious. "Guess you're gonna tell me it's time I had a career change, eh?"

Gavin reached over and took her hand. He pressed her fingers to his mouth and kissed them softly. "Rosie Maconochie ... what am I going to do with you?"

She was sure this wasn't the first time he'd asked her the question. But sitting here this evening, basking in the soft, amber light, jazz music playing unobtrusively somewhere in the background, Rosie read an affection in Gavin's eyes that warmed her. He'd seemed a different man over the last week, and something in her badly wanted to trust him. This suddenly felt like the bit in films where the guy takes the girl in his arms and tells her for the first time that he loves her. Rosie wasn't quite ready for anything like that, but neither did she want the whole thing to slip back into the casual, unpredictable pattern of the last few months. She looked into Gavin's eyes, willing herself to hold his gaze. She knew this was no longer the time for flippancy or slick comebacks, yet somehow all other words failed her. She would just have to speak with her eyes and hope he understood. *Understood what?* She wasn't even sure she understood herself.

Zillebeke January 22nd 1917

Well, Em, I've arrived back here and feel like I've never been away. The lads were very happy to see me, and I have to say my heart was warmed to see them. One of the Twinnies and a couple of other lads from our platoon are currently out of action – in hospital, being treated for the same thing as me, would you believe? It's been a bit of an outbreak by the sounds of things.

At the moment, it's colder here than I can describe. Everything seems to be freezing around us – kit, clothes, everything turning stiff with ice. Even our drinking water is solid in no time. Unpleasant as the temperatures may be, this weather does have its advantages. The ground has actually frozen too, which brings a welcome relief from our having to stand for hours in waterlogged trenches or wade through miles of sinking mud when we're lugging around supplies. I'd forgotten how tiring life out here could be.

Since I got back, I've noticed Jimmy seems to have a different look about him. He still has that thin hollowness about his face, but then he's a slim lad to start with and we're all half-starved anyway. No – it's the scared, haunted look that's gone. He seems calm somehow, very much changed from the timid lad that joined our platoon only a few months ago. I reckon it's something to do with Boxer's influence. Boxer's as calm a man as you're likely to come across; never seems to get anxious, no matter how close the shells are landing. I've rather missed him these last few weeks. In fact, I have to admit, Em, I've even missed his 'sermons'. I keep thinking about what Nurse Parker said at the hospital. She told me God had been smiling down on me. I reckon she and Boxer would have made a good pair.

It was almost midnight as Rosie tapped in the last few words. She filed the instalment and quickly e-mailed Jonathon.

Hi Jonathon –
Another episode for you. Your Uncle Boxer seems to come out positively glowing in this one.
I think you can expect to see Beth and my brother in the very near future. Beth should be released from hospital soon and then, as far as I can see, it'll be all systems go.
It looks like I may be coming up to Ridderch Standen soon after all. Beth has asked me to visit whenever I can, so if it's okay with her parents, I'll no doubt be taking her up on the offer.
I may not get chance to e-mail much in the next few days. I'll be spending as much time as possible over at my brother's. So if you don't hear from me, don't think I'm ignoring you
See you soon
Rosie.

Sleep seemed to evade her as she lay in bed. She was glad there was only one more day at work before the weekend. Her brain felt in need of some serious sorting out. Part of her wanted, more than anything, to follow Beth and Ciaran up to Oak Lodge. Yet after this evening, another part of her wanted to stay around Gavin to see if he really *had* metamorphosed into the nice guy she'd always suspected was lurking in there somewhere.

But then there was another part. A part of her that was suddenly scared. What if he genuinely *had* changed? What if he wanted to get serious now? Surely that presented as many problems as it solved. Quite objectively, Gavin was gorgeous. Deep down, Rosie knew he'd be able to get pretty much any girl he wanted. She'd hardly dared ask herself the question before, but now as she tossed and turned in the darkness, she realised it was troubling her. *Why* was he sticking around? After the fiasco at Christmas, why had he not given up and gone elsewhere? What made him keep coming back to her, even when she herself had given up on the whole thing more than once? She'd seen the hunger in his eyes many times – and felt the heat in his touch. So far, she knew she'd disappointed him. Now she had to face the issue. Someone like Gavin wasn't going to stay around forever without something more. She put her face into her pillow. Was she really ready for anything like that?

As soon as the question began to wrap itself around her head, Rosie knew she'd made a mistake. This was not the time of day to start playing with thoughts like these. But it was too late. Her brain had flipped into automatic search, and now a disjointed succession of images began to throw itself up on the screen of her mind. Panicking, she sat bolt upright, trying frantically to blot out the intrusion. But somehow she couldn't find the off-switch. With every passing second, the bombardment became more brazen and more rapid. Suddenly, somewhere deep inside herself, she could hear the sound of movement outside her room, the slow creak of the door, the lumbering pad of approaching feet, the rasp of hot, beery breath ...

"*No!*" she tried to scream into the darkness. But the word came out as an inaudible whimper, just as it always had. Trying desperately to choke in the tears, she sank back against the bed and buried her face in the pillow once more. In no time at all, she was sobbing as though her heart would break.

Please, Ciaran. Please don't leave me on my own again.

On the following Tuesday evening, Rosie called round to see Beth at home. Beth had left hospital earlier that morning and was now trying to get some of her stuff ready for the big move. Cassie was helping her sort things out, but the whole operation seemed to be taking forever.

"I can't bear to leave anything," Beth muttered, a look of faint exasperation on her face. "Knowing that I won't be coming back, I mean."

Rosie was silent as she stood watching her. She couldn't imagine being Beth; going through a lifetime of possessions and trying to decide which ones to keep for the end.

Cassie spoke softly. "If it makes you happier, love, just take everything up with you. We'll find room in the car, and then at least you won't be getting upset about anything you've left behind."

"Will that mean there'll only be room for Ciaran to take a pair of boxers and his toothbrush?" Beth was trying to smile, but

Rosie was sad to see how painfully thin she looked, and how sunken her cheeks were. Somehow it had been less obvious in the hospital. You expected to see sick people there. But here in her own home, Beth's emaciated appearance seemed so at odds with that of the bubbly, energetic girl who'd lived here until so recently, it was hard to believe they were one and the same person.

Beth lay back in her chair and sighed, as though the effort of trying to pack was all too much. "I've told Rosie she must visit us, Mum. That's okay with you, isn't it?"

Cassie smiled and put an arm around Rosie's shoulder. "I've told you before, Rosie – you're welcome to come and stay any time you want."

Though Cassie's offer of hospitality found an instant resting place in her heart, Rosie felt herself stiffening. Yet again, the older woman's affectionate manner had managed to inflict upon her a strange sense of awkwardness. "Thanks," she mumbled tentatively. "I'd like that." Trying hard to make herself relax, she forced as much of a smile as she could manage. *I'd like that more than you could possibly, possibly know.*

"Y'know what, Ros?" Beth broke in. Her voice was quiet and wistful. "I'm really gonna miss you."

Rosie tried to think of something to reply, but her mind only reeled with thoughts she would never have dared speak out. *How do you think we feel, Beth? Long after you've ceased to miss any of us, we'll still be missing you. For years. For some of us, perhaps a lifetime.*

During the next few days, Beth and Ciaran were inundated with visitors from the orchestra. Ciaran had been in touch with Emmett Mallory to explain the situation, and suddenly it seemed that everyone wanted to pay their last regards before Beth moved out of the area. Emmett had been the first to call. It had clearly been a difficult and emotional experience for him.

"I'm so sorry to see you go," he'd said awkwardly, as though Beth had simply decided to change allegiance and join some other, more lucrative outfit. "I had my eye on you from the very start. A violinist like you, Beth, only comes along once in a blue moon. And you know I've always had a soft spot for you." His eyes had begun to mist then, and Beth had found herself trying to comfort him. She had enormous affection for this middle-aged, tousle-haired man who had worked so tirelessly to win public support for the Avanti Sinfonia.

Nika had visited too. She'd been uncharacteristically subdued. Death, it seemed, was not a subject that lent itself easily to vibrant conversation. There had been several others – John and Cheryl, Phil 'Fishface' Rowan, Matt and Sissy, Clem, Tom and Aled, and a host of others. Beth was beginning to be exhausted by the constant round of callers, and Ciaran was worried that she might not be fit to travel when the big day came.

The day before they left, Beth received a visit from a timid, silver-haired lady from second violins.

"Martha! What a lovely surprise ..."

It was indeed a surprise. Martha was one of the least loquacious members of the whole orchestra, and Beth had hardly managed a handful of decent conversations with her during the entire time she'd been with the Avanti. It seemed the older lady found it far easier to express herself through her violin than through her words. Over a cup of tea, however, Martha finally found the courage to bare her soul.

"I've been praying for you ever since I found out about your illness, Beth." She shuffled awkwardly. "I don't know how you feel about things like this, but I – I just want you to know ..." She hesitated as though her shyness were threatening to silence her.

Beth sat forward, her eyes wide with anticipation. "Yes! Go *on*, Martha."

Martha cleared her throat and continued a little more confidently. "I just want you to know that the Lord has a beautiful place ready for each of us – if only we're ready to meet him." Her face became locked in an uneasy frown as she tried to work out how to elaborate on this statement.

But Beth's face was shining. "Martha, I talk with him every day. I do – *really!* If any good has come out of this whole thing, it's that I've come back to the Lord."

In the half-hour that ensued, Beth went on to explain about her childhood, her parents' faith, and her own experiences since her diagnosis. Martha was almost beside herself with joy as she listened to Beth's account, and by the time she got up to leave, the two women were hugging each other like old friends.

"Thank you for praying for me, Martha. You couldn't have done anything better."

Martha smiled as her eyes misted with tears. "You'll continue to be in my prayers every day, Beth. And even if we don't see each other again this side of eternity, I can rest now ... knowing I'll see you again in heaven one day."

Chapter 18

The big move was fixed for the following Monday. Early on the morning of that day, Ed and Ciaran began the job of loading up the MPV. Rosie had managed to get time off work to be with them all. To her surprise, so had Gavin. He rang her just after nine.

"Rosie, I'd really like to be with you guys today. I called my boss a few minutes ago and explained the situation. He was really good about it. Said they'd get someone to cover." He paused as he waited for her reply.

Rosie's mind went into overdrive. What was going on with him? First flowers for Beth, and now this. For someone who'd at first struggled to show even the remotest sliver of concern for Beth's predicament, Gavin was suddenly turning into the most attentive well-wisher anyone could hope for.

"Yeah, okay. I'm sure it'll be fine." She wished she could have sounded more enthusiastic, but she couldn't help finding Gavin's increasing cosiness slightly disconcerting. Especially now that the day had come. Ciaran really was leaving her again.

She waited for Gavin to pick her up, then they drove round to her brother's home. When they arrived at the house they could see boxes and cases strewn across the pavement. Gavin parked up in front of Ed's vehicle and switched off the engine. He turned to her gently. "You okay, Rosie?"

Rosie sighed heavily. It was happening. Beth was leaving, never to return here again – all her life packed up in the back of an MPV. "No," she said quietly. "Would you expect me to be?"

"No. Don't suppose I would." Gavin took her hand in his own and for a few moments they sat like that, neither of them speaking. Finally he tilted her face towards him and spoke softly. "You'd better go in and see Beth. I'll stay out here. These two look like they could use some help."

When Rosie went into the house, Beth was sitting in an easy chair going through some post that had just arrived. Her face lit up when she saw Rosie. "As from tomorrow it'll be – *Not Known At This Address* – eh, Ros?"

"Don't worry. I'll make sure it's all sent on to you. Specially those in the nice brown envelopes."

Beth grinned. "I'm gonna miss your cynicism, kiddo, I really am."

Rosie avoided her gaze, pretending to busy herself in taking off her coat. *If you did but know it, Beth, my cynicism's about the only thing holding me together today.* "Where's your mum anyway?"

"She's upstairs doing a bit of cleaning. She wants to leave the place looking nice. You know what mums are like."

Not really, if I'm honest, Rosie thought miserably. "I'll go up and say hello. Won't be long."

She walked slowly up the stairs. Everything felt strange, sad, and somehow final, as though even the house knew what was happening. She found Cassie cleaning the bath. The older woman had not heard her approach and was singing quietly to herself as she worked. Rosie gave a slight cough to signal her presence.

Cassie spun round. "Hello, love!" She instinctively popped a kiss on Rosie's cheek. "Didn't realise you were here."

"Anything I can do to help?"

Cassie shook her head. "No. You go down and talk to Beth. You two need to spend as much time together as you can."

"Okay. Thanks." Rosie tried to smile, but smiling seemed terribly hard today. She made her way back downstairs and sat on the sofa across from Beth.

"I hope they manage to get all our stuff in," Beth said into the air.

Rosie didn't comment. The spectacle of luggage strewn all over the pavement was still fresh in her mind; it hadn't been a promising sight.

Beth cast her eyes wistfully about the room. "We've had some good times here, haven't we, Ros?"

Rosie nodded. "Don't worry about this place. I'll keep an eye on it – make sure no squatters get in or anything like that."

"And you'll keep an eye on your brother too – afterwards I mean?" Beth looked at her directly. "He's going to need it I think."

Rosie felt a lump come to her throat. "Course I will. He's always looked after me. 'Bout time I returned the favour."

They sat quietly for several minutes, each lost in their own thoughts. On any other day the silence might have been awkward, but today nothing was normal, and there seemed no point in pretending it was.

It was Rosie who eventually spoke first. "I've been meaning to ask you ... what d'you want to do about the diary? Do you want it back so you can take it up to Yorkshire with you?" She'd taken the precaution of bringing it along with her in case Beth should agree to this idea. In her heart of hearts, Rosie hoped she wouldn't. "Or do you want me to just e-mail the entries on to you – let you have it back when it's all finished?"

"Hmm – the diary." Beth frowned. "I haven't looked at it for a while, have I?" She seemed to think it over for a few moments. "Are you still typing it up for Jonathon?"

Rosie nodded. "Yeah. He's really into it."

"Okay, tell you what. You keep typing up the stuff for Jon and continue saving it all on file. E-mail on to me everything I've missed so far. That way, I can make up my mind whether or not to read it. It's been a bit hard to face recently with everything that's been going on."

Rosie smiled to herself. *So you've come to your senses at last, have you?*

"As for you, Ros ..." Beth was looking at her, a sudden twinkle in her eye, "I'm going to make you its official guardian. That's like an owner – only I won't say owner, 'cause one day you might want to put it in some museum or something. It'll be easier to part with if you're its guardian."

Rosie frowned. "You're *giving* it to me?"

"Yeah. Are you okay with that?"

"Well, yeah," Rosie shrugged, "course I am. I wasn't expecting it, that's all. I thought it was one of your prized possessions."

"Can't take it where I'm going, can I? And I want it to go to a good home. I think it'll be a long time before Ciaran can read anything like that. But you, Ros, you've been doing a brilliant job of looking after it for weeks now. I reckon you're the ideal person to inherit it." She grinned for a moment, then assumed an expression of mock solemnity. "I, Beth Maconochie, being of sound mind and judgement, do hereby grant full custody of the diary to you, Rosie Maconochie, to do with as you think fit." She gave a theatrical sweep of the room with her eyes. "Let all here present witness that this is my living will."

Rosie smiled wryly. "Wow, Mrs M. The sense of occasion overwhelms me. I don't have to make a speech or anything, do I?" But deep down inside, she was touched by Beth's gesture. Even if Beth found it hard to handle now, the diary had meant the world to her when she'd first discovered it. Somehow Rosie felt strangely honoured. Her face became serious. "Thanks," she said gruffly. "I appreciate that. I'll look after it."

"And remember," Beth winked knowingly, "don't let Velna within ten miles of it."

The subject of the diary had broken open the way for more relaxed communication between them. As they talked, Rosie became increasingly conscious of how much she would miss Beth's bright and easy conversation. Of course it would be in stages. First, Beth would move up to Yorkshire. Out of sight – but at least they'd be able to talk on the phone. It would be like a practice run. Then, at some unknown point in the not too distant future, would come the real thing. The goodbye forever. The real stone-cold separation. As Rosie looked across at Beth, the horrible thought hit her like a punch to the guts. She shuddered. It was too impossible to contemplate.

"Don't suppose you're gonna miss it down here then?" she ventured, fighting to push the prospect to the back of her mind.

Beth exhaled slowly. "No. But that's not because I don't like it here." Her eyes were thoughtful. "I've been very happy in London, Ros. This is where I began to see my dreams come true. If none of this had happened, I'd be staying here without a doubt."

"Or jet-setting all over the globe with the music press hot on your heels ..." Rosie interjected.

"Yeah, or that." Beth laughed, but her face soon became pensive again. "Funny how your priorities change when you find you have cancer. All the dreams and ambitions – they just seem to melt into nothing. It's like you wake up and realise that none of it matters any more. In the final analysis, there are far more important things to sort out. Know what I mean, Ros?"

Rosie wasn't altogether sure that she did. "I think if it was me, I'd be angry. I don't know that *I* could lay the dreams down without a fight – not if I saw everybody around me still getting on with theirs." She hadn't meant to be so blunt, but Beth seemed undisturbed at her comments.

"Fight, eh? I think I've been fighting for years if I'm honest."

Rosie frowned. "How d'you mean?"

Beth leaned back in her chair and closed her eyes. "When I was a kid everything was simple, Ros. Life seemed so gentle, so well-ordered. You know how it is when you're young."

Rosie bit her lip hard. *Gentle? Well-ordered?* Had they grown up on the same planet? She was glad Beth's eyes were closed. At least she wouldn't have seen her squirm.

Beth's finger traced a pattern on the arm of her chair. "Y'know, I never struggled to trust God back then. It was second nature to me. Whatever I did, wherever I went, I knew he was there watching out for me. Guess I thought it would always be that way."

Rosie felt slightly uncomfortable. It seemed like another deep philosophical discussion was on the way. She remembered the last one – Beth's weird dream. *Please don't say we're going there again.*

Unaware of her discomfort, Beth continued. "Suddenly – and I'm not quite sure when it started – I began to kick against everything I knew. My music became more and more important to me. Soon it was all that mattered. God went out the window. Guess I stopped trusting him, Ros ... perhaps I was afraid deep down that he'd try and take my dreams from me."

"*Hasn't* he?" Rosie's tone was cold.

Beth opened her eyes and looked over towards the window. "D'you know, I don't see it like that, Ros. I reckon I've done pretty well for myself in recent years. But if I'm honest, I always sensed there was an empty place somewhere inside me. I've had a stab at my precious dreams. But they couldn't give me what I really needed. Deep down, I knew I'd have to make my way back to God one day, no matter how long I tried to stall. I guess facing up to my own mortality has made it easier. Burned away my excuses. Stopped me putting it off any longer. I'm actually grateful for that." She turned and looked directly at Rosie. "If you were to ask me today which I'd rather give up – the peace I now have, or the success I could have had, I'd give up the success in a moment. You can't take success with you when you leave this earth. But peace – the peace of God – I wouldn't trade that for anything."

Rosie was quiet. So it all came down to the God business again. It was almost like listening to Boxer. "I'm happy for you," she said simply. "Not sure I understand it much. But if it makes things easier for you, that's great."

Beth looked across at her, a gentle fire in her eyes. "Ros, it's so much more than that. It's not just something to make me go to sleep without a fight. I wish I'd lived my whole life knowing what I know now. In the light of eternity, even concerts and rave reviews lose their importance."

Rosie shrugged. "I guess they must." She paused for a moment. "It means a lot to you to die in Yorkshire, doesn't it?"

Beth nodded. "Yeah, it does. When we went up at Christmas, I knew I'd come home. Not just physically. It was a spiritual thing too. I don't understand it ... I'm just a baby in all this spiritual stuff. But somehow I knew I'd come back to my roots. It felt incredibly safe there."

Rosie smiled. "It *was* pretty lousy when we came back down here after New Year, wasn't it?"

Beth's eyes lit up. "You felt it too, Ros? I honestly thought I was only gonna last a fortnight. When Ciaran talked to me about us moving back up to Yorkshire, I just wept. It was everything I could have wanted." She fell quiet for a moment. "I'm not looking forward to dying, Rosie. I've never done it before – and I don't know if I'll be any good at it. But I'm sure being at home will make it a whole lot easier. The Lord knows I'm a bit of a coward. I reckon I'm gonna need everything on my side for this one."

At that moment Ciaran came in from outside, his face flushed with cold. "Bang us the kettle on, Ros," he called out as he scooped up a pile of coats from the table. Shortly afterwards, the three men came in and sank into chairs, their task, it seemed, successfully completed. Cassie came downstairs to join them, and plans were soon being discussed for the departure. Rosie looked over at Gavin. He was listening quietly, his eyes bright from the fresh air, his hair slightly tousled by the breeze. Despite herself, Rosie couldn't help noticing that it made him look more gorgeous than ever.

It felt horrible to be on the outside of the conversation; to have no part in the arrangements – to know that this time, she wasn't going. The general consensus of opinion was that they set off as soon as the district nurse had been to check on Beth.

"What will you do about lunch?" Rosie asked as nonchalantly as she could, though she was secretly desperate for some delay.

"We can always grab something on the way up there. It's best we get off as soon as possible." Ciaran's reply was detached and functional. Everything in Rosie wanted to scream at them to wait – to go after lunch, after tea, tomorrow, never. But she made sure nothing in her countenance gave anything away. As they finalised the arrangements, she smiled and went quietly into the kitchen to wash up the cups. It was like waiting to be executed.

The house was locked up, the car loaded, and now Beth was sitting in the back seat by the window. Rosie leaned in through the open door to say goodbye. Beth grabbed her hand. "You promise you'll come up and see me, Ros? I don't want to think this is goodbye quite yet." Her eyes were brimming with tears.

Rosie felt her own eyes burning. "Course I will. But I'll be ringing you too – don't forget that."

Beth smiled gratefully as the tears spilled down her cheeks. After hugging her briefly, Rosie closed the car door and said goodbye to Ed and Cassie. Out of the corner of her eye she caught sight of Gavin. He was standing a few yards up the pavement, maintaining a respectful distance from the family. But Rosie was suddenly glad that he was there.

After doing a last minute check in the boot, Ciaran strode over to her. He handed her the keys to the house. "Well, Ros – look after yourself. You'll be okay, won't you?"

Rosie assured him she would be.

"We're only at the other end of the phone. And you'll be coming up to visit, won't you?"

Again Rosie reassured him.

"And Gavin – he's promised to look after you as well." Ciaran sounded like a man clutching at every possible straw.

Rosie felt sorry for him. She knew him well enough to imagine how hard he was finding all of this. "Stop stressing, Kitch, I'll be fine. You go. I'll see you all soon enough."

Ciaran's face crumpled. He pulled her towards himself and hugged her. "I'm sorry it's all turned out like this, Ros. I hate leaving you here – I feel torn in two. But I have to take Bethy home. You understand that, don't you?"

"Course I do, Kitch ... she has to be your priority. Enjoy every minute with her. Don't let anything spoil it."

Kissing her forehead, Ciaran turned and walked to the other side of the car. Within moments the engine was purring, and then they were off. Rosie summoned all her courage and began to wave. She felt Gavin's arm slip around her shoulder and realised that he was waving too. They stood there for what seemed an age, until the car was well out of sight.

Rosie felt numb. A wave of loneliness swept over her as she turned and looked at the house. Her fingers closed around the keys in her pocket. Only a couple of hours ago the house had been full of people and noise. Now it stood empty and stark.

"You okay?" Gavin brushed his lips across her hair.

Rosie tried to speak but the words stuck in her throat. Somehow Gavin's tenderness was the last straw. To her horror, she felt herself begin to shake. Within seconds her whole frame was racked with sobs. Gavin had the sense not to say anything. He pulled her close to himself and held her as she tried desperately to stop the tears. Rosie wanted the ground to open up. It was bad enough that she'd just had to wave goodbye to her dying best friend and her brother. But for Gavin to see her in *this* state ...

It was almost a relief when the slate sky began to spit drops of cold, biting rain. "Come on," Gavin said softly. "Don't want you catching anything." Putting an arm around her, he walked her to his car and gently helped her inside. There they sat in silence, listening to the raindrops pelting the roof and smacking on the windscreen. Rosie felt exhausted with emotion and more embarrassed than she could have described in that moment. When she felt she could trust herself to speak, she tucked her damp hair behind her ears and turned to Gavin with an awkward smile. "Sorry about that. Had a feeling I might lose it today. Just glad I managed to hold off till they were on their way."

Gavin stroked her cheek gently. "Hey, don't apologise." His voice was soft and reassuring. "I was getting pretty choked up myself."

Rosie was grateful for his diplomatic response. She turned her head and stared out of the window. The downpour was beginning to ease slightly now, and she suddenly felt her eyes drawn to a small, straggly sparrow perched on a railing outside. Despite the rain, it seemed intent on foraging from a branch that was overhanging from a neighbouring garden. It hardly seemed to notice how wet it was getting. She found herself wondering if sparrows minded the rain. Did they have the capacity to sense adversity? Or were they programmed to just get on with living, whatever the conditions? *How simple life must be for them,* she thought almost enviously. *How simple and how painless.*

Gavin squeezed her hand gently. "Feeling any better?"

Rosie hesitated for a moment. She wasn't quite sure how she was feeling. Stupid for one thing. Scared too. And heartbroken ...

Beth's face came to mind just then; Beth's pale face pressed against the car window as they'd set off. Those sad eyes drinking in their last glimpses of everything she was leaving behind. That had to be one of the most heartbreaking sights Rosie had ever witnessed. Afraid that she might cry again, she leaned forward and cupped her face in her hands. "Today's been tough," she said simply. "Beth's like a sister to me. I can't imagine what it'll be like when she's gone." Her jaw tightened as the prospect raised its head again. "It seems unreal to think that in a few months she won't be around anymore. Anywhere. Nowhere to be found – as if she'd never existed. I don't know how I'm gonna feel when it happens. It's kinda scary." Rosie bit her lip. Why was she offloading all this stuff onto him?

But her memory was quick to supply an answer to that one. *Maybe it has something to do with the fact that you've just bawled like an idiot in front of him for the last twenty minutes. Now you're just being courteous in offering him an explanation for the whole ridiculous performance.*

"Don't think about it." Gavin stroked the back of her hand. "You'll face it when you come to it. But don't try to face it before it happens. You'll find the strength when the time comes – I'm sure you will."

Rosie forced a smile. "Anybody ever tell you you'd make a great counsellor?"

Gavin laughed. "No ... but I *do* make a great cappuccino. How d'you fancy coming back to mine? Let me spoil you a bit."

Rosie stayed at Gavin's for the rest of the afternoon. They had a bite to eat, watched a film, and looked at some of Gavin's old childhood photos.

"I can't believe this is you!" Despite the upset of earlier, Rosie had managed to collect herself and was now finding Gavin's photo album highly amusing. There was something extremely gratifying about seeing the boy beautiful in all his humble beginnings. "I mean, come *on,*" she sniggered, pointing to one particular shot. "What was going on with your hair in this one? And who's the muppet standing next to you?"

"That *muppet* –" Gavin began, doing his best to keep a straight face, "happens to be my brother. His name's Bellamy."

That was almost too much for Rosie. "*Bellamy ...?* You're joking right?"

"And what's so funny?" Gavin tried to sound offended.

"*Bellamy Pennington?* Are you for real? Who picked the names in your house?"

There was a glint in Gavin's eye. "It's family tradition. My dad's Bellamy, and my granddad, and his dad before him. My mum wanted to claim a bit of ground for her side of the family, so I was named after her brother – my uncle Gav. I reckon it's bone idleness on my dad's side. They can't be bothered to come up with anything fresh."

"Like *Horace* perhaps ...?" Rosie snorted and promptly went into hysterics.

Gavin shook his head, but he was secretly glad to see Rosie's mood so much changed. It gave him a sense of achievement to think that their afternoon together had produced this result. Only a few hours ago she'd been inconsolable. Now she was laughing as though she hadn't a care in the world. He rather wished Ciaran could have been there to see it.

Later on when he took her home, Gavin held her close to him for a long time. "Don't worry about getting upset today, Rosie. If ever you need to sound off, I'm here for you." His kiss was gentle and unhurried, and she was surprised at how comfortable she felt in his arms.

"Thanks for everything. I'm glad you were around today." Her cheek was resting against the front of his shoulder and she could feel the steady rhythm of his heartbeat. They stayed like that for a few minutes more, then he kissed her again and let her go. As Rosie let herself in through the front door, her head was doing somersaults. What a weird day this had been. Her emotions had been all over the place, from one bizarre extreme to the other. Rainbow moods her mother used to call them; tears and laughter, like rain and sunshine, all in the space of half an hour. Yet strangely, she realised she no longer felt anywhere near as embarrassed as she had earlier. Gavin had taken it all in his stride and shown a tenderness which she'd badly needed today. Would it last? She hardly knew. But now, more than ever before, she found herself hoping it would. What was it he'd said? *If ever you need to sound off, I'm here for you.* She chewed the phrase over in her mind ... *I'm here for you.* They were pretty big words.

Suddenly she really wanted them to be true. Now, with Ciaran so far away, she felt terribly vulnerable. It would be good to think there was someone else there for her. Could Gavin step up to the mark this time?

Late that night, she found an e-mail from Jonathon waiting on her computer.

Hi Rosie –

Thought I'd drop you a line and see how you are. I bumped into Josh Simmons last night and he told me that Beth and your brother would be travelling up today, so I've been thinking about you. Hope the wrench isn't proving too painful. Things like that are never easy, are they?
Enjoyed the last diary entry. Uncle Philip sounds a cool sorta guy, don't you think? (Well, I must have inherited it from somewhere – lol ...!) Looking forward to further offerings.
I'm hoping to pop round to see your family soon – I'll just give them a couple of days to settle in. Are you planning a visit in the near future? We'll have to book some nice weather for when you come, eh?
Luv Jonathon

Rosie smiled to herself as her fingers hovered over the keyboard. It was nice of him to make contact today. She thought for a few moments before beginning her reply.

Hi Jonathon –

Thanks for your e-mail. Nice to know someone was thinking about me. Well yes – I was a bit upset when they first set off, but I managed to come round eventually ...

She paused. *A bit upset? That's a laugh – you were bawling your eyes out. Streatham was nearly put on flood alert.*

The other bit was true; she *had* come round eventually. Should she mention Gavin? After all, he'd been pretty key in the unfolding of today's events. No, she decided. Jonathon didn't need to know about all that.

I'll be coming up there as soon as I can. Beth's pretty insistent about it. Haven't got any dates yet – I need to look into it when I get back to work tomorrow. I'll let you know when I'm likely to appear.

There's still plenty more of the diary to go at. Sorry you've had to wait, but here at last are 'further offerings'. Enjoy.

Rosie.

Zillebeke January 30th 1917

It's still bitterly cold out here, Em. I can barely feel my hands and feet. Sometimes I find myself thinking that if the Bosch don't get us, the weather will. It seems even the dead are touched by it. They lie there, their blank eyes staring up at us, their mouths frozen into hopeless grimaces. I wonder who's the most to be pitied. And to think that two and a half years ago they said it would all be over by Christmas. Would we have joined up so eagerly if we'd known? I think not.

Boxer's been missing for a couple of days. We were out on a night working party when he took a shrapnel hit in the top of his leg. He didn't make much of it, but the lieutenant told him to get it checked out. He went to the aid post and hasn't reappeared since, so heaven knows where they've sent him. It feels strange without him around. I hadn't realised how reassuring his presence was until now. Jimmy seems calm enough about it. I happened to mention today that I was a bit concerned about the business. "Hope he'll be coming back to us," I said. Jimmy just nodded. "He'll be back," he assured me. "God's looking after him." I had to smile, Em. It was like listening to Boxer himself. Still, I have to admit, it did make me feel better in a funny kind of way. Never thought Jimmy could have such a comforting effect on me. This war really does seem to be making a man out of him.

Well, it's dark now and here we are, manning our bit of the trench and trying not to freeze to death in the process. It's hard to describe the tedium of our trench life, Em. We spend long hours hanging around, just waiting. Waiting in case the enemy should decide to kick off. It's a bizarre situation if you stop to think about it. The only thing likely to break our boredom is a skirmish – and that could mean losing a limb or worse. What's the best option, eh? To be sitting here in a frozen dugout, every inch of our bodies seizing up with cold and inactivity, or being caught in the middle of a bombardment, hearts thumping out of our chests as the shells rain down on us? Not much of a choice, is it? Ah well, Emily, I won't write any more tonight. I might lose my fingers to frostbite if I don't get them in my pockets soon.

Zillebeke February 4th 1917

I killed a man today, Em. In stone-cold blood, I killed him. Of course he's not the first I've done for since I've been out here. Grenades, Mills' bombs, rifle bullets – we don't send them over for fun. But this was different. I was different ...

The German bombardment had been going on for what felt like hours. It had been a long, testing day. For those in the allied front line, it was a case of sitting tight until the firing eased up. Then it would be full alert. The Bosch usually tried a trench raid after a pounding like this.

"Glad we're not up front for this one." Twinny One dragged on his cigarette and breathed smoke into the frozen air. Their unit was positioned in the support lanes a short distance behind the front line. "Bet it's been a blood bath up there. They haven't stopped all afternoon." He cursed and stamped his feet against the cold.

Sam sighed. Why couldn't they all just go home? Surely everybody had had enough by now. Why drag the thing out any longer? Sometimes, the temptation to turn round and walk away from everything was almost overwhelming. It was an idea which seemed to present itself most strongly when the weather was particularly cold, or particularly wet, or when they all felt particularly hungry because the rations hadn't come down. Extreme conditions always addled the brain more than normal – made it hard to think straight.

Walking away was a stupid idea of course. Totally impossible. If any man was foolhardy enough to try a stunt like that, he was signing his own death warrant. The army didn't have room for deserters and cowards. But for Sam at this moment in time, cowardice didn't come into it. He was, quite simply, fed up.

Darkness fell, and with it, the temperature. Sam tried to think of things to take his mind off the cold. He thought about Boxer and Twinny Two in hospital somewhere. He thought about home with its warm, welcoming fire, and the family singing songs around the piano. And he thought about Emily. He pictured her standing by the roadside that day, waving to the new troops as they'd set off from their villages. How beautiful she'd looked. His mind had sealed that vision like a photograph. One that he looked at a thousand times a day, one that kept him focused when everything else seemed hopeless.

"Sam!" Jimmy's voice hissed through the blackness. "*Stand to*, mate. What's up – you dropping off or something?"

Sam hadn't heard the order. Neither had he realised that the German guns had fallen quiet for the first time in hours.

Twinny One sniggered. "It's alright, Sam. We're not expecting any action this far down. You go back to sleep, pal."

Ignoring his sarcasm, Sam readied his rifle. He felt embarrassed. He'd been in a world of his own. Somehow, since his sickness, he seemed to be finding life out here twice as exhausting as before.

Twinny One's gruff laughter rippled through the trench as he shared a joke with the man next to him. "Hope they come over to say hello. This beauty'll give 'em a tickle they won't forget!" Defiantly, he ran his finger over the topside of his rifle blade.

Sam shuddered as he fixed bayonet. Sometimes he heard a callousness amongst the men which scared him. It was one thing to be forced to kill one's fellow human beings. But to actually relish the idea – to gloat and boast and make distasteful jokes about it, surely that bordered on barbarism. Sam hated bayoneting. He'd hated it ever since he'd been in training camp. It was something he found hard to bring himself to do. Whenever he'd been picked to go out on trench raiding parties, he'd always been selected for bomb throwing. There was something detached about that. Like shooting. But bayoneting, that was personal. Your brute metal strength against another's soft flesh. If the war were to continue for another twenty years, Sam doubted he could ever get used to bayoneting.

The time dragged slowly as the night air became colder and colder. Apart from the occasional thunder of heavy artillery much further up the line, all was quiet. Men stamped their feet and blew on their hands. It felt as if the very blood had frozen in their veins.

It had reached about two in the morning when Sam heard movement. The sound of light scuffling seemed to be getting nearer and nearer. Rats probably, coming straight from a big feed if the earlier bombardment was anything to go by. He certainly wasn't going to stick his head out to check.

Next to him, Jimmy frowned. "You hear what I hear?" His voice had dropped to a whisper.

Sam nodded. Two men at the side of them seemed to be dozing. They were standing with their backs against the trench wall, heads lolling forward and eyes closed. It was an easy thing to do. Sam had dropped asleep on route marches before now. How much easier tonight when the air was cold enough to stultify your brain. Sam and Jimmy stood stock-still as they tried to focus on the direction of the approaching sound. A sudden, agonised scream pierced the darkness, and then the noise of grappling. An enemy trench raid.

Sam and Jimmy readied their rifles, their hearts pounding. There was a lot of shouting now, some of it in German. Foul words and dull, ugly thuds seemed to fill the trench. In the dark it was hard to make out what was happening. A voice rang out. "Take *'im* – he's the one with the bombs – don't shoot the bag whatever you do!" A single shot followed by a groan. "There – got ya! Nice of you to call, Kamerad."

There was more scuffling, and then a man broke free into Sam's view. He was large and heavily set, and almost fell towards Sam in his bid to escape being taken. For a split second, his wild eyes rolled in confusion as he tried to work out his next move. He glanced at Sam, then turned his attention to one of the men who had been dozing only minutes previously. Sam shouted out to the Tommy but it was too late. His reactions were groggy and slow, and Sam could see it was about to cost him his life. The German thrust his bayonet clumsily into the other's chest. Twinny One's voice screamed down the trench. "Take 'im, Sam! I got my 'ands full up this end."

Sam felt panic rising in his throat. The young Tommy was still impaled on the German's gun, his face crumpling with the realisation that it was all over for him now. For a moment his gaze met Sam's, and the look in his dying eyes hurt like nothing Sam could ever remember. The German's teeth were clenched with effort as he tried to wrench the weapon free.

In that small second, Sam felt a surge of furious hatred he'd never known before. As the German turned to face him, Sam rammed his own bayonet full force up into the man's diaphragm. He pulled out quickly and thrust in again. The German's harsh expression seemed to melt into a look of surprise. He staggered forward putting his hand out to steady himself and, in doing so, caught hold of Sam's arm. For a moment they stood there, eyes locked, each searching the other's face. Then, with a gurgle of blood oozing from his mouth, the German soldier fell heavily into the bottom of the frozen trench …

For some reason the thing has really troubled me, Em. Just before he fell, when we were standing face to face, I realised he reminded me of someone. Then it came to me. You remember Mr Trippett who owned the post office in the village? He was his double. Fred Trippett, with his wife and four children. This man could have been his twin. When I looked through his pockets, I found a photograph of a lady and three little ones. I feel like a savage. I keep thinking of the telegram going home to his family – 'You'll never see your beloved husband and father again because some butcher of a Tommy made sure of it.'

The thing that really scared me, Em, was the rage I felt when I did it. Usually I feel some sense of remorse when we find ourselves in confrontation. Some kind of common humanity. I almost want to apologise for what I'm doing. But today, something in me had snapped. For an awful moment I felt real hate. I could have stabbed him over and over again. It wasn't till I looked into his eyes that I came to my senses. Something had made my brain mad, Em. Perhaps the cold, or the dead Tommy – I don't know. I wish I understood. But one thing I do know; I don't like what this war is doing to me.

It all happened in the early hours of this morning, and though I've tried to grab a bit of sleep since then, my mind won't stop tormenting me. Jimmy told me he felt the same when he shot the German boy at Le Sars. That was ages ago, but it seems that certain ones stick in your mind. Jimmy said Boxer had told him something that had really helped him. That Jesus will forgive us for anything, no matter how awful, so long as we're truly sorry and willing to accept his forgiveness. Well, Em – Jesus might forgive me, but I don't know how long it will take before I can forgive myself.

Chapter 19

In the days that followed, Rosie did her best to adjust to life without Ciaran and Beth around. She spoke to them most days on the phone or texted Beth with funny snippets from the nursery. It wasn't the same as being able to see them whenever she wanted, but it was contact. She continued to e-mail Jonathon too, assuring him that she was coping well on her own, and updating him with instalments from the diary. The diary seemed hard going at the moment. Rosie could sense the oppression of Sam's situation with every page she turned. As the Flanders' winter continued in its icy bitterness, Sam seemed haunted by guilt at the momentary hatred he'd felt for the German soldier. His preoccupation with the matter seemed to fill his writings. Rosie made a flippant comment about it in one of her e-mails to Jonathon.

He needs to get over it, don't you think? What are soldiers supposed to do anyway? I always thought that sort of thing was part of the job. I don't know why he's making such a deal out of it. He'd have been better staying home and knitting socks for the troops.

Jonathon's response had been enigmatic.

I think he's having a reality check. Guess there comes a time in all our lives when we're suddenly confronted with ourselves. Haven't you ever had one of those scary moments?

Rosie was vaguely baffled.

Scary moments? Not sure I'm with you. Please be good enough to explain ...!

Jonathon had promptly obliged.

You know – when you come face to face with your own demons. Might be when you see something about yourself that you didn't realise was there. Could be anything. In a case like Sam's, might be something that scares you – makes you wonder what you're actually capable of, given the wrong set of circumstances. But it could be anything. Shall we call it 'a moment of personal revelation'?

Rosie felt slightly ill at ease after reading Jonathon's reply. The whole banter had started with a couple of throwaway comments. From her angle, only half serious comments at that. But Jonathon's message had been unexpectedly sober in tone; *'a moment of personal revelation'* he'd called it. She'd had more than her fair share of those recently. She'd come close to feeling she was starting to lose the plot. Surely that was more personal revelation than anyone would want. For the time being, though, she'd managed to pull things round. She was coping – and she wasn't about to let anybody start psychobabbling their way through *her* scary moments. Her face was set with determination as she quickly punched a message into her laptop.

Hey, mister 'electronic shoulder to cry on' – don't go getting all serious on me! You're supposed to be cheering me up, remember? The last thing I need right now is to discover that deep down inside, I'm some weirdo wannabe axe-murderer. I really think that would be the last straw.

PS – I'm hoping to try and get up for a weekend visit on Friday 24th Feb, so go easy on me or I might just change my mind ...!

Miles away in Ridderch Standen, Jonathon smiled to himself as he typed his reply. He assured her he hadn't meant to upset her and that in future, he would try his best to keep his philosophical opinions to himself. He was thoughtful as he clicked on the send icon. *Poor Rosie. Something tells me I've touched a raw nerve with you.*

"You cold?" Gavin's arm was around Rosie's shoulder as they made their way back to his car. His breath was visible in the freezing night air and the pavements glinted with frost under the full moon. They'd been to see a film and now he was taking her home. Rosie shivered slightly in reply to his question and he pulled her closer to him. She nestled into his hold. It felt solid and warm, and she realised that over the last couple of weeks she'd been finding Gavin's presence increasingly strengthening. He'd certainly gone out of his way to soften the blow of Beth and Ciaran's departure. Phone calls every day, flowers, meals out, and now a film. She really couldn't have asked for more. Gavin was giving her TLC by the bucket load, and Rosie was beginning to enjoy it.

They reached the car and Gavin opened the passenger side for her. "Give me a minute. I'll have to de-ice the windscreen." As she climbed in, he gently pushed her long coat clear of the door and kissed her softly before closing her in. Rosie hugged herself against the cold as she sat listening to him scraping at the window. She felt strangely happy tonight. Her mind went back to their evening at the cinema. It had been a nice film. Nothing embarrassingly raunchy, but a heart-warming romantic comedy with a real feel-good ending. It had been Gavin's choice.

"You do know it's supposed to be a chick flick, don't you?" she'd asked when he'd first broached the idea.

"What's up – don't you like chick flicks?"

Rosie couldn't tell if he was teasing her. "Hey, I'm not fussy. I work with kids, remember. I get excited watching the Tweenies. I was thinking about you."

Gavin had smiled then – that gorgeous, winsome smile that Rosie had noticed made other women drool. "Rosie, *I'm* thinking about *you*. I read the reviews and I think you'd enjoy it. I reckon a bit of daft escapism would do you good – it'd do us both good in fact. I have to be careful this time of year. My seasonal affective disorder starts playing me up."

For a moment she'd glanced at him questioningly. *Seasonal affective disorder?* He was the picture of healthy, suntanned perfection – looked like he spent every weekend on the Côte d'Azur. He had to be kidding her. As their eyes had met, she'd realised he was.

"Come on, Rosie. Let's give it a whirl. If you don't enjoy it, I'll get you a Fireman Sam box set to make up."

She *had* enjoyed it. They had held hands throughout, and from time to time, Gavin had leaned over and kissed her cheek gently. Rosie had felt herself melting. At long last, it was starting to feel like a relationship.

Now as she sat in the car thinking about it all, her stomach began to flutter. It was an unfamiliar feeling; one that thrilled and terrified her at the same time. Was she falling in love? She wasn't sure. She'd never fallen in love before. One thing she did know – she was letting her guard down. Was there any going back?

When they pulled up outside her house, Gavin turned to her and ran a finger gently down her cheek. "Rosie, there's going to be a big party at the Mappin Hotel to celebrate the opening of a new Apex Health Club. Should be a pretty glitzy do. I'd really like to take you. Show you off."

Rosie could detect a slight hesitancy in his voice. She looked at him in surprise. "Show me off?"

Gavin read her glance and squeezed her shoulder affectionately. "Hey, I meant that in the nicest possible way. What guy wouldn't want to show off his girl – especially when his girl happens to be someone like you?"

It could have sounded smarmy, and a few weeks previously Rosie would have read it that way. But tonight, as their eyes met in the half-light of the car's interior, Rosie saw a candour and sincerity in Gavin's expression that made her heart turn over. So – she was *his girl.* He'd stated it quite plainly. And what was more, he wanted to show her off. Someone like Gavin wanting to show *her* off? It seemed the wrong way round. And yet his eyes told her he was serious.

"Will you come, Rosie?" His voice was huskily soft as he twirled a tendril of her hair between his fingers.

"When is it?"

"A week tomorrow. Saturday the twenty-fifth, I believe."

Rosie's heart sank. *The twenty-fifth ...?*

Gavin noticed the consternation in her face. "What's wrong? Got something planned?"

Rosie wasn't sure what to say. "It's just that I was intending to go up to Yorkshire on the twenty-fourth. I've already booked the Monday off to give me a bit more time."

A flash of disappointment crossed Gavin's face. He tried to hide it, but Rosie had noticed. She felt bad. "I'm really sorry, Gavin."

"That's okay. My fault. I should've asked you earlier." He made an attempt at a smile.

Inwardly Rosie groaned. She appreciated the generosity of his reaction, but she couldn't help wondering if the thing would cast yet another shadow between them.

That night as she lay in bed, sleep did not come easily. Just when things had been going so well between them. It felt almost like a rerun of the Christmas situation, except this time, Gavin had been much more gracious in his response. As she thought about him, she couldn't shake off the fear that she may have hurt him. He'd been a tower of strength to her in recent days; everything any woman could want from a guy. Sensitive to her emotions, checking on her every day, spoiling her rotten, and generally making her feel the most cherished girl in the universe. And now she was letting him down again. This party obviously meant something to him, and he had wanted her there. Surely she could give him that much. Suddenly she knew what she had to do. She would try to rearrange at work for the following weekend. Beth would understand. And Ciaran. After all, Gavin had managed to win *them* over the first time they'd set eyes on him.

"Wow, Rosie!" Gavin's eyes drank in the vision standing in the doorway. "Wow ... look at you. You look amazing!"

Rosie felt flattered, if slightly embarrassed. Thankfully, Mel wasn't long in coming to her rescue. "Isn't she gorgeous?" she gushed as she followed Rosie into the living room. "I knew as soon as we spotted it she'd look fabulous in it."

The dress was in cobalt-blue satin, its bodice fitting Rosie's slim figure like a glove, its skirt falling from her hip-line in generous folds. The thin satin straps were studded with diamanté and she wore a necklace and drop earrings to match. Mel had completed the look for her by fixing her hair in an elegant pleat, then pulling out a few wispy tresses to frame her face. Even Rosie had been surprised when she'd seen herself in the mirror. Now as she stood before Gavin's admiring gaze, she could feel her cheeks warming. "Not too much, is it?" She grinned nervously. "I didn't want to go over the top, but you did say it was going to be a posh do."

"You're perfect," Gavin said simply. "Absolutely perfect." He didn't seem to be able to take his eyes off her.

"Come on then, you two! You need to get going or you're gonna be late." Mel carefully placed a faux fur wrap around Rosie's shoulders. It was one of her own and she'd insisted Rosie wear it for the evening. "Hang on a minute … ." She disappeared for a moment and came back clutching a bottle of perfume.

"Oh no –" Rosie groaned, "not more of that. They'll know I'm there ten minutes before I arrive. You've practically marinated me in the stuff already." She turned to Gavin and rolled her eyes. "It's not like I haven't got any of my own."

Mel ignored her objections. "This is Dior. I always use it for special occasions. Posh parties need posh perfume." She sprayed Rosie generously then stood back with a satisfied smile. "Off you go! Have a fantastic time."

"I'm so glad you decided to come, Rosie." Gavin extended his hand to help her out of the car. "I'm gonna be the proudest guy there."

Rosie took his arm and smiled. There was no doubt about it. Gavin's affirmations had a powerful effect on her. In his black dinner suit and crisp, white shirt, he looked quite simply stunning. Like a Versace model. And yet *he* was going to be proud of *her*. That was some compliment.

They walked up the hotel steps and into the foyer. "Hey, Gavin!" A tall man who appeared to be in his mid-fifties strode over to them. His dark hair was shot through with wisps of silver and his lean face was tanned and animated. "Great to see you!"

Rosie sensed that the man was looking at her with some kind of approval. She willed her cheeks not to flush.

Gavin introduced him. "Rosie – this is Paul Warrington, Managing Director of Apex Health Clubs. Paul – this is my girlfriend, Rosie Maconochie."

Rosie's heart quickened slightly as she shook hands with the older man. *Girlfriend?* It was the first time she'd heard Gavin use the term in public, but it sounded good. Paul greeted her warmly and gestured towards a large room on their right. "We're in there, Gavin, if you want to make your way through. They're serving sherry and canapés at the moment. Have a good evening, both of you."

As they made their way towards the function room, Gavin's arm was around Rosie's waist, his touch gentle and protective.

"So – you're on first name terms with the MD? Pretty impressive." Rosie was smiling. Secretly, she wouldn't have been surprised if Gavin had been on first name terms with the Queen.

Gavin played it down. "You mean Paul? He's a decent guy. He was actually on the interview panel when I went for the job. Glad I didn't realise who he was at the time. But he's remembered me ever since. Nice bloke – and he's loaded."

The party was just warming up as they walked into the function room. One of the first things to hit Rosie was the heady mixture of aftershave and perfume which hung in the air like a luxurious intoxicant. She thought of Mel and smiled. It appeared her Dior had competition. Gavin found a table for two and they sat down. He took her hand. "Shall I get you a drink yet, or do you want to wait till the sherry makes its way down here?"

Rosie thought about it. She wasn't working tomorrow. Perhaps a sherry would help her relax. Gavin went off to get himself an orange juice. While he was away, Rosie cast an eye around the place. The room was large and spacious, one side of it lined with long buffet tables draped in starched, white cloths and adorned with sprays of carnations in slender, fluted vases. Huge crystal chandeliers hung from the high ceilings, though for the moment, the lighting had been dimmed, and only the soft, seductive glow of mounted wall lamps afforded any illumination to the gathering. At the far end of the room, a stage had been set up with instruments and sound equipment. *A band as well,* she thought to herself; it seemed no expense had been spared. She could see two young waitresses moving amongst the guests with trays of sherry. People momentarily broke off conversations to help themselves, or graciously turned down the offer with a dismissive gesture and a smile. Rosie couldn't help noticing that it wasn't your average get-together. Everyone looked toned and well turned out. Even the older guests had a youthfulness about them, helped, no doubt, by their perfect tans and trim physiques. *So these are the kind of circles Gavin moves in,* she mused wistfully. *No wonder he always looks so fabulous – it goes with the territory. These people must spend half their lives in the gym.* Thank heavens she'd been blessed with a naturally slim figure. Hopefully none of Gavin's colleagues would ever guess that *her* idea of a workout was a brisk walk to the sandwich shop in her lunch hour.

At that moment Gavin came back.

"Do you work with all these people?"

Gavin looked around the room. "No. A lot of them are from the other branches. The chain has five clubs at the moment. Tonight they're launching the sixth. But I do know quite a lot of the people who are here – I've done stints at three of the other clubs before." He looked across at her. "Thanks for coming, Rosie. You don't know what it means to me." For a moment their eyes locked, and Rosie's heart seemed to skip a beat. It was a sensation that was becoming increasingly familiar to her these days. The waitress arrived at their table just then, and Rosie took a glass of sherry. As she sipped it, the liquid slid down her throat like warm gold. She was aware of Gavin's eyes still on her, and for the first time in her life she suddenly felt beautiful. She pretended to be oblivious to his gaze. Instead, in her mind's eye, she remembered her own reflection as she'd stood in front of the full-length mirror shortly before Gavin had arrived to pick her up. *Could this really be me,* she'd wondered almost incredulously?

Even to her own eyes she'd looked like a princess, and now, here tonight, she felt like one. Gavin was her prince and everything felt right.

At just after eight thirty, the lights went up and the food was brought out. Gavin wanted to mingle as they ate and Rosie dutifully obliged, hoping beyond hope that she wouldn't drop anything down her front or end up with spinach between her teeth. Eating took over an hour, and during that time Rosie lost count of the number of people Gavin introduced to her. Thankfully he did most of the talking and Rosie's contribution to their conversations consisted of little more than a nod and a smile. She did not mind.

After the food came a few speeches, for the most part entertaining and well-timed. The manager and team of the new health club were presented to the assembly and were greeted with heartfelt clapping and cheering. Rosie had never seen so many beautiful people packed onto one stage. For a moment, she toyed with the idea of taking out membership. When the speeches were over, the band came up onto the stage and began their first number.

"D'you like dancing?" Gavin whispered into her ear.

Rosie gave a light shrug. She'd never danced to jazz music before. "Not sure I know how to. It's not like being down the local rave joint, is it?"

Gavin smiled. "We'll wait till the slower numbers. Then just stick close to me."

Rosie found herself looking forward to it.

For the rest of the evening they sat, fingers entwined, watching the other guests as they danced or generally stood about posing. Gavin made occasional snide comments about various individuals and Rosie laughed. She felt comfortable with him tonight. A few glasses of wine on top of a more than generous glug of sherry had gone quite a way towards helping her loosen up. She was happier than she could remember. When the music slowed down, Gavin pulled her up onto the dance floor and held her close as they swayed to its sultry rhythms. Rosie's head was spinning with a strange sense of elation. If this was falling in love, she liked it – she liked it a lot. After a few numbers, Gavin bent down and kissed her hair. "Fancy coming back to mine for a coffee? I think this thing'll be wrapping up soon by the looks of it."

"Yeah, okay," Rosie said dreamily. "Pity. I was just starting to get the hang of it."

"Not at all." Gavin put his arm gently round her waist as he escorted her back to their table. "You're a natural mover, Rosie. I could tell the minute we got up on the floor."

Rosie took a long, last look around the room. It had been a wonderful evening; one she wanted to remember. The band was still playing, the dancers still dancing, and in the soft jazz haze, everyone suddenly seemed to look more beautiful than ever. Stealing a momentary glance at Gavin, Rosie picked up her handbag and wrap. She sighed happily to herself. To think she was girlfriend to the most beautiful of the lot of them.

Gavin, meanwhile, had started to wave to various people around the hall to indicate that they were leaving. Paul Warrington came over with his wife to say goodbye. "Thanks for coming, Gavin – *and Rosie*." He shook hands with Gavin and kissed Rosie lightly on the cheek. "You look after this boy, won't you? He's going to go far."

Rosie glowed. If the Managing Director saw them as a serious item, things really must be looking up.

"So – we're going back to mine for a while?" Gavin checked as they stepped out into the cold night air. The sudden change in temperature made Rosie shiver. As they walked through the quietness of the car park, she was aware of the sudden change in atmosphere too. Behind them lay the heady ambience of the Mappin. She could still hear faint strains of music as the band continued to play. But out here, there was just the two of them – and she felt strangely floaty.

"Yeah. I mustn't stay too late though. I need my beauty sleep."

Gavin halted and tilted her face towards him. "I beg to differ there, Rosie. I've never seen you looking so beautiful as you do tonight." He kissed her then. It was a slow, gentle kiss and Rosie found herself melting into his arms with a sense of helplessness.

It was long after midnight when they arrived at Gavin's flat. Gavin flicked on the lights and strode across the walk-through lounge into the kitchen area. "Coffee okay?" he called to her as he filled the coffee maker. "I can do black, white, latté, or cappuccino."

Rosie stifled a yawn. She was beginning to wish she hadn't drunk quite so much. *Black, eh? Normally can't stand the stuff but I could do with coming round a bit.*

She was about to go with the first option when Gavin interjected. "It's all decaff by the way, but you'll never tell the difference."

I will if I try sobering up with it, she thought as she lay back on the settee and closed her eyes. *Why does he have to be such a health freak?* She decided on a latté. It would have been so easy to fall asleep just then. She'd drunk more tonight than she'd done in a long while, and her body didn't seem to be taking kindly to it. She forced herself to sit up.

"D'you want anything to eat?" Gavin's voice called out again.

His back was to her as he moved about the kitchen and rummaged in cupboards. Rosie could hear the crinkle of packaging as he pulled something out and tossed it with a light thud onto the work surface. *Probably lentils,* she thought to herself. She'd seen now the type of people Gavin mixed with; paragons of healthy virtue, every one. They certainly hadn't gotten to look that way by stuffing their faces with sausage and chips. Even the party food had been noticeably salubrious – not a pork pie in sight.

"No, I'm okay," she called back lightly. "I already ate plenty."

She cast a surreptitious glance around the flat. It wasn't the first time she'd been here, but tonight, somehow, certain details seemed to stand out to her. Over by the window, a column of black and white cityscape photographic mounts. Scattered tastefully around the room, various examples of abstract wall art in bold, arresting colours. The ceiling mounted light plates with their spotlight heads throwing a bright glare over everything in sight. And all this set against the stark, brilliant white of the walls. The effect of the décor was ultra modern, and very masculine. *A real bachelor pad,* thought Rosie with drowsy amusement. She yawned again. Despite its sterile appearance, the flat was surprisingly warm. Rosie pulled the wrap from her shoulders and lay back once more. The leather settee was suddenly cold against her bare back and arms. She gave a slight shiver.

"Here we are." Gavin came through with a tray and laid it on the glass coffee table. "I brought you a couple of biscuits in case you changed your mind."

Biscuits? Rosie smiled wryly behind closed eyes. *After tonight, I'm surprised any of you lot would let so much as a drip of hydrogenated fat over your thresholds.* She opened her eyes and sat up. The sudden glare of the spotlights made her frown as she reached out and took her coffee between her hands. Gavin noticed.

"It *is* a bit bright in here, isn't it? Hang on ..." He went over to a chrome floor lamp by the back wall and switched it on. Then he turned off the ceiling spotlights. The place was instantly transformed. "That better?"

Rosie nodded and took a sip of her coffee. Gavin smiled and went over to a sound system in the corner. "A bit of music too, eh?" He flipped through a few CDs and made a selection. "Can't go wrong with a compilation album," he said, almost to himself. He came back to the settee and flopping heavily into it, loosened his bow-tie and unfastened his collar. "It's been a good evening, hasn't it, Rosie?" He sighed contentedly and reached out to her, bringing his hand gently to rest on her thigh.

Rosie smiled in agreement, but felt suddenly disconcerted at Gavin's closeness. It wasn't as if he'd never touched her leg before. It was something he always did these days, especially when they were out; an alternative to holding hands when they were sitting together having a drink. But she usually wore jeans or trousers on dates, and somehow tonight, the warmth of Gavin's hand through the flimsy satin of her evening dress made her feel slightly vulnerable. She couldn't help wondering if it would have been better for her to have gone straight home. She felt terribly sleepy, and the alcohol had dulled her ability to think clearly. She took another mouthful of coffee, willing herself to stay alert, but realising with every passing moment that she was losing the battle. She put her coffee on the table and leaned back into the settee with a sigh. It was all too much effort. Gavin reached for her hand. She offered no resistance and he moved closer to her.

"How's Beth doing?"

The question threw her. It was the last thing she'd been expecting him to say.

"She seems okay. Happy to be home at least. It's hard to know without seeing her. I'll be able to tell you better after next weekend."

Gavin nodded. "I think about her a lot, y'know. And your brother."

Rosie felt a sudden pang of guilt as the realisation hit her. She'd gone a whole evening without giving either of them so much as a thought. The night had been so perfect – she'd felt so happy. Beth's illness had slipped out of her mind. How could she have *done* that? How could she have been so busy enjoying herself that she could forget something like that? She felt strangely ashamed.

Gavin noticed her discomfort and frowned. "What's up, Rosie? Did I say something?"

Rosie shook her head, but she couldn't hide the feeling that had gripped her. She slid her hand away from his.

"Rosie, tell me – please, what did I say?"

To her horror, Rosie found herself beginning to fill up. She swallowed hard, determined this time not to let the tears fall. "I had such a good time tonight," she faltered. "It's just hit me. I almost forgot about them – Beth and Ciaran, I mean. They went right out of my head." She swallowed again and swore under her breath.

Gavin sat up straight and looked at her directly. "Rosie, you mustn't feel bad about that. You needed a night out. You've been carrying this situation for ages." He stroked her cheek softly.

"You needed to forget about it for a while. There's only so much a person can take without going crazy. Don't go beating yourself up over it."

There was something oddly releasing about his words, and for a few moments Rosie looked into his eyes. Then she dropped her head and stared down at her knees, embarrassed at her own candour.

Gavin took her hand again. "Hey – come on, pretty girl." His voice was soft as a whisper. "That's what I'm here for. To look after you. I told your brother I would." He leaned towards her and softly kissed her forehead. "I *have* looked after you, haven't I, Rosie?"

She looked up slightly and nodded.

He reached out and began to tenderly caress the back of her neck. "That's good ..." His voice was huskily low. "Because I want to look after you, Rosie. I want to look after you in every way I can." Gently, he reached his hands into her hair and unpinned it so that it fell over her shoulders. Rosie was taken by surprise. She opened her mouth to say something, but Gavin lifted a finger and pressed it to her lips. "Sshh. Don't talk, Rosie." There was a fire in his eyes that made her heart quicken. Ironic. The track just starting to play was Seal's *'Kiss from a Rose'*. Had he timed it, she wondered?

Suddenly she was in his arms, her resistance melting in the heat of his hold like a candle surrendering to a flame. She could feel his hunger as he kissed her, and realised with a sense of helplessness that she was hungry too. Her mind swirled with a thousand thoughts and feelings, and all the time, the scent of Gavin's skin, so close, so warm, intoxicated her.

"*Oh, Rosie* –" Gavin muttered almost inaudibly, "I've waited so long." His breath was hot on her neck as the strength of his body forced her back against the sofa. She tried to think. Was there any turning back now? Did she even want to?

"*Gavin, I* –" She tried to speak, but her words seemed to disappear in the waves of passion engulfing them both. She felt Gavin's hand move to the zip at the back of her bodice. He slid his fingers gently under the diamanté-studded straps of her dress and eased it from her shoulders. For a few moments, she lay exposed to his gaze. Then something in her head exploded.

"Gavin – *no* –" Her voice sounded pitifully weak, even to her own ears. Gavin's lips came down hard on her own, his hands pinning her back into a position of forced helplessness. Rosie felt panic rising in her throat. She pulled her head away from his kiss. "No! *No, please* –"

Gavin started to kiss her neck again. "Come on, Rosie. You know you want to. We both want to ..."

Rosie's mind went into overdrive. Suddenly she knew very clearly that she didn't want to. Whatever she may have felt a few minutes earlier hardly mattered. Now all she wanted to do was get out. She tried to move, but he held her fast. Gavin's arms were strong; taut, hard, pump-iron muscle. She knew she didn't have a chance of breaking free from his grip. She felt sick at the realisation. Here she was again, after all these years, helpless before a man. A plaything, a prisoner. Completely at his mercy.

In that moment, a sense of rage welled up in her. Gathering every ounce of her strength, she pushed Gavin off her and sat up, pulling the satin bodice around her and folding her arms across her chest to preserve what little dignity she could.

"*What the ...?*" Gavin's face was a mixture of anger and confusion. "What are you playing at, Rosie?"

"I want to go home."

"*Home?* Why?" Gavin's eyes were dark with frustration.

"I just want to go home."

Gavin shook his head incredulously. "I can't believe this." He sighed heavily and put his face in his hands. Rosie seized the chance to slip her arms back through the straps of her dress. It made her feel slightly more in control. She stood shakily to her feet and pulled Mel's wrap around her shoulders. Gavin glanced up at her and she couldn't help noticing something like hurt in his eyes.

"Why did you lead me on like that?"

Rosie swallowed. "I didn't."

"Yes, you did. Coming back to my place, sitting there with your come-to-bed eyes while I was making the coffee. Don't think

I didn't see you." He looked down again. "There's a name for girls like that, Rosie."

Rosie wanted to hit him. Hard. But she kept quiet. She wasn't out of his flat yet and she knew things could still turn ugly. "I'm sorry … I drank too much. I wasn't making any sort of eyes at you."

"Whatever." Gavin ran his fingers through his hair in agitation. For a few moments neither of them spoke. Then Gavin stood to his feet. "Come on. I'll run you home."

Rosie shook her head. "It's okay. Just get me a number for a taxi. That'll be fine."

"Don't be stupid, Rosie." Gavin's voice was irritable. "I took you to the party – I want to make sure you get home. At least allow me that."

The journey back was tense. Neither of them said a word. When they arrived at the house, Gavin turned to her. "I'm not sure where we go from here, Rosie. I'm confused. I thought we had a great evening – but then it went and turned out like this. I don't know how we follow it." He paused and looked out of the window. "Maybe we need a break to think things over … though I can't help feeling –" He stopped as though he had thought better of it.

Rosie was curious despite herself. "You can't help feeling *what?*"

Gavin shook his head. "It doesn't matter."

"Yes, it does," Rosie persisted, suddenly nervous. "Tell me."

Gavin breathed out slowly. "I was going to say …" His voice was low now. "I can't help feeling the problem's in you, Rosie. Maybe you need to give it some thought."

She looked at him hard until tears pricked her eyes, then she opened the car door. "Thank you for everything, Gavin. And for seeing me home."

She stepped out into the cold night air and walked towards her front door. She heard Gavin's car speed away down the street and held her breath until it turned the corner. As she fumbled in her bag for her keys, hot tears dripped onto her shaking fingers. Once inside her room, she sobbed as though she would never stop.

Chapter 20

Houtkerque March 18th 1917

Dearest Em – we're encamped here and, for the time being at least, having a break from the fireworks. All rather pleasant, I have to say. I'm happy to report that Boxer has at last returned to the ranks. He seems in good health and has lost that gaunt look that marks the rest of us. It's easy to spot a man who's spent a bit of time away from the front. He looks properly fed for one thing ...

Boxer had been in a military hospital in Etaples. In conversation with Sam and Jimmy, he explained that the medics had managed to get the shrapnel out of his leg quite nicely. At first reckoning, the whole thing had promised to be a fairly straightforward affair. That was until infection had set in. Sam was hardly surprised by that. The ground in the salient was literally rotten. It had been one of the first things he'd noticed when they'd arrived in the area. The horrible, sickly sweet smell of putrefaction – its stench could turn a man's stomach. It didn't do to think about the composition of the noxious sludge, but it seemed that there were probably as many men and mules buried *in* it as there were walking around on top of it. *That*, thought Sam darkly, had been one of the good things about the winter cold snap. In its frozen state, the solid earth had made a far better job of concealing its gruesome contents. Even the malignant odour had weakened somewhat. Obviously, as Boxer's infected wound had proven, the bacteria were still present in the icebound earth – just not as noticeably.

"They had me splinted up, with tubes here and drains there and all manner of paraphernalia," Boxer grinned. "But I kept thinking about the trip home they'd promised me when I was sorted out."

Sam found himself remembering his own recent trip home. It seemed like a lifetime ago.

According to the doctor, Boxer had been lucky to keep his leg. The whole hospital was full of men with wounds that had gone the wrong way. Boxer had come across a young Scotsman from the Black Watch who'd been admitted a few days earlier with a light wound very similar to his own, and in the same part of the leg too. Infection had set in and the man had undergone the same treatment as Boxer, but without success. Sadly, the wound had become gangrenous and the medical staff had had no option but to amputate at the top of the thigh. The day before Boxer had left for England, this soldier had shown him a letter which had just arrived from his sweetheart back home. She was writing to tell him that she'd met someone else and wanted to break off their engagement.

"Poor fellow was inconsolable. Said this woman was his reason for living, the only thing that had kept him going. Now that she'd given her heart to another, he said he could see no point in carrying on. It upset me a great deal, I can tell you." Boxer's face was lined with sadness as he remembered the thing. "I tried to talk some comfort to him, but he just kept staring down at his wretched stump and wishing himself dead. I've never seen a man so full of despair ..."

I've found myself wondering how I would be if I lost my hope of you, Emily. The more this war goes on, the more I realise I'm losing touch with all that is good and beautiful. Even my own heart seems a dark and frightening place to me now. How could I bear to lose you too? How do I know that you're not already promised to another? Oh Emily – that's too terrible a thought to contemplate. I will not think of it any more. A man needs hope to survive.

Houtkerque March 25th 1917

I think my spirits are a little more restored today. Rest and good company must be doing the trick, I tell myself. I reckon we've all just become weary during these last months. Continuous action is a terrible burden on the nerves. I daresay we were all ready for a break. Twinny Two knows how to time things ...

Twinny Two had only been back a couple of days, but he seemed energetic enough and was back to his usual clowning self.

"Bet you've forgot what the front looks like, 'aven't yer?" one of the lads ribbed him. "Was you tryin' to stay 'ome till the Bosch ran outta bullets?"

Twinny Two gave him a clout. "Leave off, sarky. I've been ill, I 'ave."

The other lad winked at the others. "What was the diagnosis then? *Terminal frigiped?*"

Twinny Two took it all in good part. "Listen – for your information, I was very sick. I 'ad a priest come in at one bit, wantin' to gimme the last rites. I opened one eye, I did, and told him – 'I've got a mate who can do that sorta thing. Only *he* don't wait till you're nearly snuffin' it before he starts preachin' at yer.' I told 'im good and proper."

Everybody laughed and looked round at Boxer.

Boxer gave a wry smile. "About time you started listening then, isn't it?" He aimed a swipe at Twinny Two and they ended up in a heap on the ground, wrestling like two idiots. It all made for wonderful entertainment.

It was good to be able to relax. Of course, there was still plenty to do; there was no such thing as complete rest out here. But at least, being this far behind the line, the men were not living on their nerves in the same way. They could go to sleep at night and expect to wake up in the morning. When in the line, that was something none of them took for granted any more.

It was late afternoon and Sam, Boxer and Jimmy were sitting in an estaminet eating soup and chips. A woman's voice crackled out from a gramophone in the corner. Sam could barely make out a word. He found spoken French hard enough to decipher – sung French was simply unintelligible. Still, it made for pleasant listening. It was music and that was enough.

"Reckon my stomach's shrunk. At one time I could have cleared that lot no trouble." Jimmy pushed his almost empty plate forward on the table and leaned his back against the wall. He looked around. Most of the wooden benches were occupied by soldiers, many of them eating or drinking, some of them trying out their language skills on pretty local maidens who had chanced to drop by. Jimmy smiled thoughtfully. "Wonder if we'll miss all this *après la guerre.*"

"Suppose that depends on how much longer *la guerre* lasts. Any wild guesses as to how long that might be?" Sam tossed the question out idly.

Jimmy shrugged. "Well, we've gone way past Christmas, that's for sure. I reckon it'll go on for the duration." They all laughed. Jimmy's was a typical Tommy reply; stoic resignation in the face of an unrelentingly awful situation. And in reality, there was no other answer. The war would last as long as it lasted and *they* were there for the duration, however lengthy that might be. Either that, or until their number was up. It was something one had to accept – or die trying. Shrill laughter broke out further up the room.

"Looks like old Ned's getting a bit fresh with the *mam'selles* again." Jimmy fired a carefully aimed chip in the direction of the amorous soldier. It hit him smack on the ear and Ned spun round, a perturbed expression on his cratered face.

"Hey! Who's lobbin' chips at me?"

But Jimmy was like lightening. By the time Ned had turned to face his direction, Jimmy was chatting intently with Sam and Boxer, seemingly oblivious of any untoward occurrence. A young, rather tipsy brunette soon managed to take Ned's mind off his injury and the incident was quickly forgotten.

Boxer grinned. "Thought you were gonna get your features rearranged then, mate."

Jimmy shook his head. "Some of these chaps need more than a chip chuckin' at them. Honestly, they must be crawling with all sorts." His face hardened into an expression of indignation. "Just look at that girl – she's hardly more than a child. But I know for a fact that Ned's in every brothel he can find. It's not right. If she finds herself doing him any favours she'll end up with more than she bargained for."

Sam looked over at the young woman who now sat with Ned's arm draped clumsily around her shoulders. It was true; she was indeed very young. He couldn't help noticing that she almost had a look of his younger sister, Kitty. It made him feel at once disgusted and strangely sad. It seemed this war had taken victims from every sphere of life.

"I was talking to one of the padres the other day," Boxer interjected in a low voice. "He told me he was trying to get something done about a particular spot just outside Pop. An estaminet – about six women working the place, a couple of them old enough to be grandmothers to some of the lads out here, by the sounds of things. He said all the boys coming out of there are rotten with pox. This padre was quite put out about it all. He'd talked with several of these lads and it seemed the syphilis was about the last straw for many of them."

"I don't understand it," Sam said into the air. "It's not like they'd ever do this kind of thing back home. Surely some of them have wives or sweethearts. What are they playing at?"

"I think this war has made them mad." Boxer's tone was suddenly heavy. "And the women too. Seems with all the killing, people are just living for the moment. Life's been reduced to little more than animal instinct. It's tragic." His voice tailed off as he stared over at the noisy rabble seated at the top end of the room. There was a shadow in his countenance, Sam noticed. But studying his friend, he could see that the expression in Boxer's eyes was one of sadness and compassion. After a few moments Boxer stood decisively to his feet. "Come on, lads. Let's go and fill our lungs with God's fresh air …"

The world is becoming a place I hardly recognise, Em. All the values I held dear, all the virtues and standards that were so much part of life back home – they seem so out of place here in this landscape of war. I wonder, sweet Emily, if you've found the same. Can we ever go back to things as they were? Can we, who have seen so much and changed so much, ever go back to life as we knew it before? Or has it all been ruined for us?

Rosie quickly tapped in a message for Jonathon. She'd been so absorbed with Gavin over the last few days, it had only just occurred to her that she'd not been in touch. She hadn't even told him about the change of date for her visit.

Hi Jonathon –
Sorry I didn't make it at the weekend. Been very busy recently and completely forgot to let you know I'd rescheduled my journey for this coming weekend instead. Should be travelling up Friday evening.
See you then
Rosie.

It wasn't until later that night that Rosie received Jonathon's reply.

Gutted Rosie – I won't be there! I've arranged to go over to Durham to some ridiculously posh do with Lauren. It's something I can't get out of – you know what these things are like. I even have to wear a tux ... lol! We'll have to try and arrange things better for your next visit. Have a good one anyway and laugh as you think about me dressed up like the dog's dinner.
Luv Jonathon.

Rosie shut down her laptop and closed the lid with a resentful click. Life was really starting to tick her off.

"You okay?" Ciaran brought Beth's wheelchair to a gentle halt next to a wooden bench on the village green.

"Perfect. This has to be one of my favourite places on earth." Seeing him frown, Beth smiled. "Down in London, whenever I thought of Ridderch Standen, this is one of the first views that came to mind. This and the church. Not that there *is* much else in Ridderch Standen."

Ciaran gave a little laugh and sat down on the bench. "Blink and you'll miss it, eh?"

"Small and charming," corrected Beth. She sighed contentedly. "No, we've got everything we need round here – for a simple life at least." She winked at him. "Guess I'm still a village girl at heart."

Ciaran twined his fingers around hers. "I don't know how you ever managed to settle in the city."

"Not sure I ever did really. I think I was just too busy to notice." A cool breeze rippled across the green. Beth shivered and leaning forward, began to rub her leg through her blanket.

Ciaran looked concerned. "You cold, Bethy?"

"No, no – I'm okay. It's warm enough for this time of year. My leg's a bit sore today, that's all. A bit stiff." She squeezed his hand reassuringly and leaned back in her wheelchair. For a few minutes they sat quietly, watching village life go by; an old man shuffling along, newspaper tucked precariously under one arm, a small black and white dog pattering submissively behind him; a corpulent, rosy-cheeked young mother half pulling, half cajoling an uncooperative child towards the row of neat, bright-fronted shops situated a stone's throw from the church. Beth turned to Ciaran and grinned. "It's always looked like this, y'know. I was just remembering the Sunday school parades when I was young. Sunday afternoon – all the shops would be shut of course. But Mr and Mrs Turpin from the Post Office, they'd have a little stall set up here on the green with sweets and bottles of pop for sale. We'd all come parading past – trying to turn our eyes away and walk nicely like we'd been told to. On the way back, though, we'd be waiting for the signal. We'd get as far as that lamppost over there, then the leader would give us the okay. After that it was every kid for himself. We descended on that stall like we hadn't seen sweets in six months. The Turpins made a right killing."

"Sounds like they knew how to corner the market," Ciaran remarked dryly.

"Well, they cornered me anyhow." Beth gave a low chuckle. "Sherbet dabs, flying saucers, black jacks. I've always been a sucker for a ten pence mix."

She blinked as she remembered. Somehow it seemed like only yesterday. And yet so much had happened since those happy times. She swallowed hard. How she loved this place.

"I want you to marry again, Ciaran – when I'm gone." Her voice was slow, deliberate.

Ciaran's shock was almost tangible. "*What?* What are you talking about, Beth?" His face was a mixture of hurt and indignation. "Where did *that* come from?" He cursed softly under his breath and Beth lowered her head.

"I'm sorry." She fidgeted with her gloves for a moment or two. "I know it's hard – but we have to talk about it some time. I'm scared to bring anything up for fear of upsetting you. But we don't have that long, Ciaran. If not now, when?"

"Please, Bethy –" It was Ciaran's turn to lower his head. "This hurts like hell."

Beth shuffled nearer to him. "I know ... I know." Her voice was little more than a cracked whisper. "Do you think *I* want to leave *you?*" She pressed his hand to her cheek as she tried to hold back the tears. "You're the only man I've ever loved – the only man I *will* ever love. But that's why I want to release you. To be happy again ... one day."

Ciaran was shaking his head incredulously. "How can you say that? How can you talk about me being happy again, Beth? Do you know what all this is doing to me?" He bit his lip guiltily as though he suddenly felt he'd said too much.

Beth cradled his hand in her own. "I'm sorry. So sorry. I wish I didn't have to put you through this."

"Don't –" Ciaran interrupted, his face a wash of anguish. "Don't apologise. It's not your fault, Bethy. I'm just being selfish, not wanting to think about things. But it hurts so much ... imagining life without you here." His voice broke then and, pulling free from Beth's grip, he ran both hands through his hair in a gesture of hopelessness. Beth said nothing. She tugged the blanket tighter round her legs as another breath of cold air blew across them. The sky was a thin, water-colour blue and the mid afternoon sunshine spoke all the promise of an early spring preview. Along the village's bare, soily verges, small spikes of green had been teased out of hiding by the unseasonably mild daytime temperatures. The irony was not lost on Ciaran. Slowly his eyes took in the view from the bench where they were sitting. To the right of them, rising up from the road at the bottom end of the village and hedged in by its ancient stone wall, Saint Edwin's Church. Immediately across from the green, the Post Office and the handful of small shops that made up the commercial hub of Ridderch Standen. After that, at the so-called 'top end', a row of tiny, white cottages and the village inn. And beyond them, as though Ridderch Standen had been a temporary interruption in some vast natural plan, the landscape opened up once more into acres of rolling countryside. As far as the eye could see, signs of life were starting to appear amidst the debris of the winter's decay. Fresh green amongst the sullied brown. Hope after despair.

Ciaran kicked the ground. "It's all wrong," he muttered. "All so wrong."

"What is?" Beth spoke gently. At least she'd managed to get him talking.

Ciaran gave a laboured sigh and stared towards the top end of the village. "When we first met – at college – I thought all my birthdays had come at once." He swallowed. "I know it sounds lame, but it's true. I could hardly believe you'd given me a second glance."

"Doesn't sound lame at all. I felt the same way about you." Beth rubbed his arm fondly.

Ciaran shot her a weak smile. "Honestly, Bethy, the night you said you'd marry me, I cried when I got on my own. In fact –" He stopped abruptly and hung his head.

"In fact *what?*" Beth coaxed gently.

"Doesn't matter."

"Yes it does. Tell me what you were going to say – *please.*"

Ciaran straightened. For a few moments he didn't respond. He hugged himself against the breeze, rocking slightly backwards and forwards as if trying to decide whether he should speak. Finally, he turned and looked her straight in the eyes. "I was going to say that I prayed. For the first time since I was a kid, I prayed. I just got on my knees and thanked God for giving you to me."

Beth was shocked. She hadn't expected an admission like that. "I didn't think you were into God."

"I wasn't." Ciaran's voice was suddenly cold. "I just thought that perhaps at long last my life was about to change. It seemed right to say thank you."

Beth eyed him questioningly. "What d'you mean – *change?*"

Ciaran lowered his head. "I've mentioned things before, Bethy. Me and Rosie, we didn't exactly have a charmed life back home. We were desperate to get away – both of us were. Getting to college was my big break. But meeting you ... well, that was something else altogether. Something I'd never expected in a million years. The most beautiful girl in the place. And she wanted me." His eyes brimmed with tears as he spoke and Beth's heart turned over as she looked at him. She threw up a silent prayer for wisdom. His whole body language exuded a sense of bleak, dark despair.

"Do you think there's such a place as heaven, Ciaran?" she asked softly, almost afraid to hear his answer.

Ciaran gave a slight shudder then, and Beth wasn't sure if it was the coolness of the breeze or her question that was to blame. "Shall I tell you what I *do* think, Bethy?" His expression hardened as he fought to contain his emotion. "When we got married, I knew I wanted to spend the rest of my life with you. I wanted to look after you, protect you, help make all your dreams come true. I wanted to make you the happiest woman in the world. I wanted you to have my kids – I wanted to grow old with you. I wanted you to be so glad you said yes to me."

"Ciaran, I *am* ..." Beth's eyes pleaded with him. "The years we've been together have been the best of my life."

Ciaran shook his head. "But I haven't managed to protect you, Beth, have I? Or given you children – or grown old with you. There were so many plans I wanted to make with you, so many things we could have shared, places we could have gone together. And now, it's never gonna happen." A sigh escaped his lips and he gazed down towards the church. "I look round and see other people – other couples – walking together, talking together. I just feel so helpless, so angry ... so desperate it makes me want to scream. The one person I love more than anyone else in the whole world is leaving me. And *she* doesn't want to – and *I* don't want her to. But there's absolutely nothing we can do about it. We just have to sit by and watch it happen. While all the rest of the world just carries on and doesn't give one toss about us, we have to go through every day knowing it's one day less together. One day nearer to the time when we're pulled apart – when I'll never be able to touch you again. When it's all over. Finished. Forever." His eyes glittered. "You ask me if I believe in heaven, Beth. No. I don't. I don't believe in anything any more. My entire experience of life so far convinces me that the whole thing's a pointless exercise. I hope I'm wrong, Beth. For your sake, I hope I'm wrong. For you, I wish it could be real. Because if anyone deserves a better future, it's you. But don't ask *me* if I believe in heaven … ." There was a catch in his throat and he looked away.

Beth felt sick. She pulled the blanket tightly around her legs. "Perhaps we should be getting back."

Ciaran turned to her. For a moment their eyes locked. She could see the pain in his – his dark lashes glistening with tears, his cheeks unashamedly wet. She had never seen him look so beautiful, or so broken.

"I love you, Ciaran. With all my heart and all my soul, I love you."

He leaned over and took her in his arms, and they wept together.

Oh God … please help us. This is harder than we can bear. She smoothed his hair and buried her face against his neck. *Please help him, Lord. Please show him what you've shown me. I can't tell him anything right now – he needs to hear it from you.*

It was Saturday morning and Rosie was sitting in the living room at Oak Lodge with Beth and Ciaran. She'd arrived the previous night after a journey fraught with delays. By the time she'd finally reached the house, Beth had already gone to bed, and after a hot drink with Ed, Cassie and Ciaran, Rosie had done the same. It had felt good to fall into bed and lie there listening to the silence as she breathed in the lavender scent of the sheets. It had felt like coming home.

Now as she sat in front of the fire, it seemed that hardly any time had elapsed since her last visit. And yet, Rosie observed, Beth's appearance had altered even in that short time. Her skin was slightly yellowed now, and the circles under her eyes were darker. She looked somehow older than her years, yet there was still a childlike brightness in her face.

"Missed you, Ros. It hasn't felt right without you around." Beth grinned. "Too quiet."

"Funny." Rosie pulled a face at her.

"How was the party anyway? Worth cancelling your trip up here, was it?"

She was only kidding and Rosie knew it. But she couldn't help feeling a twinge of guilt at Beth's question. She tried hard not to let it show. "It served its purpose," she answered vaguely.

Beth frowned. "*Meaning ...?*"

"Meaning it helped me see that Gavin really *is* the scumbag I always suspected he was."

Ciaran gave a low whistle and rolled his eyes at Beth.

Rosie felt herself flushing. She'd said too much. "Sorry," she muttered lamely. "Wrong time to vent."

Beth was eyeing her with some amusement. "What's up? Did he come on naughty with you – or blow you out for someone else?"

Ciaran gave a slight cough and hastily stood to his feet. "I'm gonna make a drink. Anybody want one?"

"We've only just had one," Beth said teasingly.

"Well, I'm thirsty." Ciaran strode out of the room and closed the door with a gentle click.

Beth smiled. "I think we embarrassed your brother."

"Correction – *you* embarrassed my brother." Rosie tried to give her a reproving look.

"Whatever. Anyway, come on – spill it. What happened?"

Rosie felt awkward. She shrugged as nonchalantly as she could, but she knew there was no way she was going to get out of this. "Let's just say he wanted to take the relationship to a new level."

"And you were happy staying at the level you were?"

"Something like that." *That's it. Keep the answers vague and evasive.*

"Did he get nasty about it?"

Honestly! What is this – twenty questions? "Let's just say he wasn't thrilled." *Why am I telling you this stuff? Come to think of it, why did I open my big trap in the first place?*

"Shame, Ros. I thought we'd got you fixed up there." Beth sounded genuinely disappointed. "Would have been nice to have met your future other half – y'know, while I'm still around." She seemed to think the matter over for a moment or two, then shrugged resignedly. "Still, any guy that really cared about you wouldn't try to pressure you into doing something you didn't want to. Guess you're better off without that kind." There was an air of finality about her tone which puzzled Rosie. She'd expected at least a little more resistance at the news of her breakup with the delectable Gavin.

"Hang on, I thought you liked him. I thought you both liked him."

"We did like him. He seemed an okay sort of guy. Like I said, I thought you were nicely fixed up there. All the same –" Beth stopped mid-sentence as though trying to picture Gavin in her mind.

"All the same *what?*" Rosie's eyes narrowed.

"Well, I'm not exactly surprised, Ros. I should have seen it coming, I guess."

"What d'you mean – *you should have seen it coming?*" Rosie felt suddenly irritated.

"Oh, I dunno. It's just that Gavin doesn't strike me as the kind of bloke that's used to taking no for an answer – I mean, where women are concerned. Fellas that look like Gavin tend to get their own way. Good on you, girl, for standing up to him."

Rosie felt slightly disconcerted. Beth was talking as though she'd been a fly on Gavin's designer wall.

"A bit of bruised ego won't do him any harm," Beth continued matter-of-factly. "Might even learn from it. Bet you were something of a shock for him, Ros. The woman who refused to fall at his feet and adore."

"Is that dubious distinction supposed to make me feel good?"

"Hey, don't knock it." Beth smiled wisely. "Perhaps he needed pushing off his perch. Any guy with Gavin's looks can always use a humility top-up. What could be more annoying than a bloke who's convinced he's irresistible?" A shadow crossed her face in that moment and she leaned forward and rubbed at her leg.

Rosie frowned. "What's up – you in pain?"

"Nah. It's just this leg. It's been a bit stiff these last couple of days." Beth flexed the muscle a few times. "I might mention it to the nurse when she calls. Maybe they can up my pain relief. Still, a stiff leg's the least of my worries, eh?" She grinned disarmingly. "Anyway, what were we saying before I so rudely interrupted myself?"

"You were talking about my irresistible ex." Rosie shot her a sarcastic smirk, but she couldn't help wondering if she should mention the leg to Ciaran.

"Ah yes ... the gorgeous Gavin." Beth nodded to herself. "Well, this is what I think when it comes to guys, Ros. If you have to sleep with him to keep him, you might as well wave him bye-bye."

"You sound like my mother," Rosie snorted humourlessly. Not that her mother had ever lived by her own advice. Life might have been a lot simpler for all of them if she had.

Beth shrugged. "I probably sound like everybody's mother. But let's face it, a girl shouldn't feel obligated to give herself away to every Tom, Dick and Harry that comes along. Just 'cause most people these days do the premarital rounds without batting an eyelid doesn't mean it's the best way of going about things."

"Now you sound like Sister Aloysius who used to teach us French," Rosie mumbled disdainfully. She'd always got on well with the venerable sister, but listening to a nun giving dating advice had never quite cut it for her.

Beth seemed undeterred by this comparison. "Hey, I'm serious, Ros. Look around you. Folk everywhere searching for that special someone. Every new partner that comes on the scene is suddenly *The One.*" Air-quoting this last phrase, she spoke the words with mock drama. "That is, until things fall apart. Then it's straight back out to find somebody else. Heartbreak to heartbreak ... like a rollercoaster with its brakes jammed. C'mon, does anybody really want to live like that?" She shook her head as though needing no answer. "But I guess we've been programmed to think that's the only way to go, eh?" She looked directly at Rosie. "I'm proud of you, Ros. It takes guts to say no. In this day and age anyhow."

Rosie didn't answer. She was too busy remembering Gavin's thinly veiled insult from the other evening. *There's a name for girls like that, Rosie ...*

They sat in silence for several moments as the fire murmured in the grate. A sudden, loud crackle from one of the logs made them both jump.

"Well, anyway –" said Beth, clapping her hands gently on her knees, "that's what I think about it all. Don't let anybody put you down for sticking to your principles, Ros. No one has the right to muscle in and pressure you into doing something you don't want to."

Rosie was loathe to admit that principles really hadn't come into it. As for the last bit, Beth's advice was just a little too late. About fifteen years late to be precise. She tried to stuff the subject to the back of her thoughts.

Unfortunately Beth seemed to be on a roll. "You save yourself, Ros. Somewhere out there is the right guy for you. And he'll be worth waiting for."

Rosie was annoyed to feel herself reddening. "Thanks, Mummy dearest. So nice of you to give me the motherly low-down on how to behave myself with boys."

Beth grinned. "Take it from me, hun. You're worth more than you realise. Wait for Mr Right and it'll be sweet music all the way." She winked provocatively. "Know what I mean?"

"Oh *please* –" Rosie burst indignantly, "I'm twenty-one not twelve." She wanted to add – *And just what makes you think I'm such a novice in these things anyway?* – but decided against it.

There were certain matters best left under wraps, and this was one of them. Better to keep quiet and be misunderstood than to open a can of worms and have the truth come wriggling out. "Let's just change the subject, can we?"

Doing her best to look apologetic, Beth smiled innocently. "Actually, talking of sweet music –"

"Which we *weren't*," Rosie scowled.

"Well, we are now. I meant to tell you about something, Ros."

Rosie's eyes narrowed in suspicion. "Hang on. Has it got anything to do with men?"

"No!" Beth laughed. "Well, only one man. Your brother."

"Go on."

Beth took a deep breath and her face became serious. "You remember the day I came across the diary?"

Rosie nodded. How could she forget? Beth had been almost delirious with delight when she'd rung to tell her about it.

"Well," Beth continued, "I don't know if I mentioned it at the time, but there was something else with it. A piece of music. Just a basic little tune scribbled on manuscript paper. But I reckon it was Sam who wrote it. There was a title and it was in the same handwriting as the diary. *Chant du Rossignol*, he'd called it."

"*Rossignol?*" Rosie repeated. "That's nightingale, isn't it?"

"Yeah – and *Chant* is song. *Chant du Rossignol* –" Beth tapped her head with a knowing smile. "My lightening-fast mind tells me that must mean *Song of the Nightingale*."

Rosie was thoughtful for a moment. "Or Rosie's Song."

"Hmm?" Beth frowned.

"*Rosie's Song*. Remember earlier in the diary? Sam said they nicknamed the nightingale Rosie – short for *rossignol*. It kinda stuck in my mind, me having the same name and everything."

Beth's eyes lit up. "Hey, Ros – you're right! How cool is that? *Rosie's Song* ..." She seemed to mull the idea over in her thoughts for a moment. Then her face broke into a grin. "You could be on to something there, y'know. It's like that *'Annie's Song'*. Mum used to have it on an old tape." She immediately burst into a raucous impersonation of John Denver.

Rosie covered her ears. "Okay, okay. Don't kill the thing. Go on, carry on telling me about Sam's tune."

Beth stopped singing and was quiet for a few seconds. "The thing is, Ros, I've been working on it in secret. You know, trying to develop it – fleshing it out a bit. I've started adding some orchestration to it. Don't know how far I'll get with that. Don't know how long I've got, do I? But I'll keep at it anyway. It's a simple little tune, but there's something beautiful about it, Ros." She paused and looked down at her hands. "I had this idea, see. I wanted to give it to Ciaran as a gift … something to remember me by."

Rosie felt her throat tighten. "I don't think he's likely to forget you. You've no worries there."

Beth smiled. "No, I know that. But I just thought a piece of music would be perfect. I know I've nicked the basic idea from Sam, but I don't have a lot of time to play with. I'm sure old Sam would forgive me if he knew my circumstances."

Rosie nodded slowly. "I'm sure he would."

"I keep having a little practice when Ciaran goes out with Dad. I don't want him to know about it just yet. I don't think I'll get it all finished, but I'll do as much as I can for as long as I can, then I'll give it to him." She looked down at her hands again and shrugged. "I never managed to give him babies, Ros. I just thought this might be the next best thing."

Rosie felt choked. She swallowed hard. "You always said you were gonna compose. I never doubted you would for a minute."

"Y'know, Ros?" Beth turned and looked at her. "If I could have picked anyone in the whole world to be my sister, I would have picked you."

For a moment Rosie was tempted to come back with a facetious comment. But looking at her friend's face, she could see that she was entirely serious.

Chapter 21

Rosie had only been back at work two days, but after her weekend up in Yorkshire it felt more like a month. She'd just finished a particularly lousy session at the nursery. It seemed to happen every once in a while; some sort of weird, agitating group dynamic that made the kids fractious and stroppy, and left the poor, frazzled staff wound up to the hilt. At six o'clock she pulled on her coat and stepped, exhausted, outside into the open. A blast of cold evening air tore at her hair and she shivered.

"Hello, Rosie." A familiar voice made her spin round. It was Dan.

"Oh ... hi." She tried to act cool, but being caught so off guard made it frustratingly difficult.

Dan smiled disarmingly. "I was hoping I might catch you. Mel said you were finishing at six, so I left her at the hairdresser's and had a walk down here."

Rosie's mind reeled. *He's come here on purpose?* "Look, if this is about Gavin ..." Her face felt hot. *If he thinks he can just send Dan round to do his dirty work –*

Dan interrupted her speculations. "Rosie, how's about we go for a coffee somewhere? It's a bit nippy out here and I really wanted to talk to you."

Rosie's eyes widened slightly. Dan grinned. "Don't worry, Mel's fine about it. She trusts me."

Who said anything about Mel? It's me that's not fine about it. But curiosity was fast getting the better of her.

Dan gave a reassuring smile. "Cratchett's looked quiet as I came past, if you're okay with that."

Rosie tried hard to look disinterested. In truth, she was suddenly intrigued.

They ordered drinks in Cratchett's and found a table by the window. Dan took off his jacket and hung it over the back of his chair.

Obviously means business. Wonder if I'm supposed to do the same. Rosie stared down into her coffee, her mind doing somersaults. *Wish he'd get on with it and let me know what this is all about.*

Dan slowly stirred around in his cup, a preoccupied expression on his face. At last he spoke. "I think I owe you an apology, Rosie."

Rosie straightened. "*Apology?* How come?"

Dan didn't look up. He continued stirring his coffee as though somehow it might give him inspiration. "I know you and Gav have broken up."

"Good news travels fast," Rosie said acidly. *Wonder how much else you know. Is Gavin low enough to have filled you in with all the gory details …?*

"To be honest, Rosie, I'm kinda glad you have."

Rosie frowned in surprise.

Dan placed his spoon carefully on the table and looked directly at her. "Guess I'm laying my friendship on the line here, Rosie. But I feel I need to be honest with you about one or two things."

Rosie's heart quickened. This was beginning to sound ominous.

"The reason I said I owed you an apology," Dan began, still looking at her intently, "is because it was my idea to fix up the whole blind date thing right at the start."

Rosie smiled awkwardly. "I think I can just about forgive you for that."

Dan shook his head. "No. Looking back, it was a really bad idea. Gav was in a pretty poor way at the time, and well – Mel had talked about you a few times. I just thought it might cheer him up."

"*Didn't* it?" Rosie tried to sound light-hearted about it.

Dan breathed out slowly. "Rosie, has Gavin ever mentioned to you anyone called Kate?"

Rosie swallowed. She wasn't sure she wanted to hear this. "No. No, he hasn't."

Dan nodded sadly. "I thought not. When you first met Gavin, he'd just come out of a long-term relationship with her. They'd been seeing each other for nearly eighteen months. The whole thing was pretty serious."

Rosie felt a stab of hurt. She steeled herself, determined not to let Dan see any reaction.

"A couple of months before you first met Gav, he'd bought Kate an engagement ring. For a surprise. She accepted at first. Then a few days later, completely out of the blue, she told him it was all over. No real explanation. She just said she wasn't ready for marriage. The following week she got a job transfer and moved away. Gavin was blown apart by it all. Really devastated. I'd never seen him so low. The blind date thing – it was really an attempt on my part to stop him going into depression."

"He didn't strike *me* as being very depressed," Rosie retorted, her eyes narrowing.

"He's a smooth operator, Rosie. Even I was surprised how quickly he managed to pull round once you were on the scene."

Rosie took a sip of coffee, her mind swimming with confusion. She wasn't quite sure where this conversation was going. "Okay. So what are you saying?"

"What I'm *trying* to say is –" Dan took a long, deep breath. "You're better off without him, Rosie. I'm not suggesting he will, but if he tries to start things up between you two again, I think I'd tell him where to get off. I've watched him do it to you before. Being absolutely blunt with you, I know for a fact that Gavin's met up with Kate while he's been seeing you – she's been in town more than once over the last few weeks." He paused and lowered his head. "If you want my advice, don't even think about getting back with him."

"I've no intention of doing," Rosie snapped coldly. But inside she felt sick. How could she ever have imagined that Gavin was serious about her when all the time he'd been seeing this Kate woman behind her back? And to think she'd come so close to sleeping with him. She felt like kicking herself. She realised Dan was looking at her sympathetically.

"I'm sorry, Rosie." His voice was completely sincere. "Gavin's not a bad guy. But I haven't liked the way he's been acting recently – not towards you anyway. I put it down to his breakup with Kate. He's not thinking right. I know he's my best mate, but I wouldn't wish him on any girl at the moment. Not till he gets himself sorted. The blind date thing seemed like a good idea at the time, but I wish I'd never come up with it, Rosie. I think you deserve better."

Rosie looked down into her coffee again. Why did she suddenly feel like crying? Surely Dan's advice was only confirmation of something she'd already decided. Was it the air of finality about it all? Perhaps – partly. But deep down, she knew that what hurt most was the revelation that Gavin had been using her. That all the time she'd imagined things were developing between them, Gavin's affections had been elsewhere. She'd been a fill-in, a substitute. No wonder it had felt like such hard work.

"Thanks, Dan." She picked up her bag and rose from her seat. She knew it was time to leave, before she started getting teary. "I appreciate your being honest. No hard feelings about the blind date. I'll just put it down to experience."

Dan stood to his feet and extended a hand. "Bye, Rosie. See you around, no doubt."

Rosie smiled weakly and shook his hand before heading for the door. If Mel didn't realise what a decent guy she'd got, she needed her head examining.

That evening, back in her room, Rosie was filled with a sense of dull, aching emptiness. Mel was still out with Dan and the house was depressingly quiet. She toyed with the idea of ringing Beth, just for the sake of having contact with someone. But she couldn't think of anything cheerful to say, and it didn't seem right to offload her misery onto someone whose situation was even more dire than her own. As for Ciaran, she couldn't even picture him now without wanting to cry. She certainly didn't want to add to *his* bucket load of troubles.

It struck her then that she had never felt so isolated in her whole life. So utterly, completely alone in the world. No one to turn to, no one to listen, no one to make her feel that she mattered. At least Gavin had done that – even if he had been lying through his teeth half the time.

A sudden coldness passed over her and she began to shiver. Falling onto her bed, she curled up in foetal position and hugged herself in an effort to keep warm. But it was not a natural coldness. It was an iciness that seemed to grip her entire being like a vice. A cascade of black thoughts poured into her head. *What point is there in anything? Nothing ever goes right anyway. Life is just one long test of endurance, punctuated from time to time with extra special misery. Maybe Beth's one of the lucky ones after all – at least she's getting out of it early …*

She hated herself the second the thought hit. An image of Beth came into her mind; Beth with her yellow skin and limp hair, her wasted body and sunken eyes. Beth, who such a short time ago had been radiant and full of bright hopes.

Rosie pressed her face into the pillow. *One of the lucky ones? What am I thinking?* But somehow, logic did not come easily tonight. Only despair, and a suffocating darkness that seemed to wrap itself around her like a shroud. She gave way to the tears that were burning her eyes, and cried until she could cry no more. At last, totally exhausted, she fell into a dreamless sleep.

It was ten twenty-three when she suddenly awoke. At first she was completely disorientated. It took a few moments before she could even work out what day it was. The sound of Mel banging about in the living room pricked her memory.

Cratchett's … the conversation with Dan …

She swore under her breath. How long had she been asleep? Glancing at the clock, she swore again. She was wide awake now and she had to work tomorrow. It was anyone's guess as to what time she'd be able to get back to sleep tonight. She climbed off the bed and smoothed her clothes. Maybe a hot drink would help.

"You okay, Rosie?" Mel looked concerned as Rosie made her way to the kitchen. "You look like you might be coming down with something."

Rosie glanced into the kitchen mirror and inwardly groaned. Why hadn't she checked her face *before* coming out of her room? Her eyes were puffy and swollen and her cheeks blotched with pink. "I think it's hay fever," she said unconvincingly.

"Hay fever? At this time? I would've thought it was a bit early." Mel seemed genuinely confused.

For want of a better argument, Rosie decided to press the point. "There was a bit of early tree blossom out in Yorkshire. My eyes have been itching like crazy."

This explanation seemed to satisfy Mel. Relieved, Rosie warmed some milk up in the microwave. A few minutes later, back in the safety of her room, she sat by the window and looked out into the street. A cat was preening itself under a lamppost. Rosie watched it for a while, something inside her longing to reach out and touch its fur, to find comfort in its living, breathing body. After several minutes, the creature gave a sudden, elegant stretch and stole off into the blackness.

If I can be of any help – an electronic shoulder to cry on and all that, you know I'm here ...

The thought jerked her back to reality. *Jonathon. Of course.* She hurriedly set up her laptop and pulled the diary out of her drawer. She'd throw in a couple of entries for good measure. She had to play it casual; she didn't want him knowing he was practically the only human being on earth she had access to right now.

Tuileries (Support Trenches) April 15th 1917

There's a sense in the air that something's going to happen soon, Emily. It's common knowledge that mining operations have been going on in this area for months now. Jimmy and I recently got talking with some miners from the North East who've been brought over here to work in tunnelling teams alongside the Royal Engineers. They told us they've been laying tunnels to various points deep beneath the Messines Ridge – and packing them with explosives. According to these chaps, our boys are about to blow the whole ridge into the sky any day now! We've not heard anything official about it all yet, mind. But I have to say, those fellows certainly seemed to know what they were talking about. I can't help hoping they're right, Em. I'd love to see that ridge go up. But you'd have to be in our position to understand why I say that. Let me try and give you the picture.

The ground we hold at the moment along the Ypres sector is a wedge of land that juts out into the ground held by the enemy – if you can try to imagine it. Instead of two armies ranged against each other in straight lines, our front line bulges forward into the Boschs' territory so that they almost surround us. That means they can fire on us from three sides at any one time if they feel like it. Not only that, but they hold the ridge of high ground to the south of Ypres which looks right down on our position – that's the Messines Ridge I was talking about. Geographically, they've got a real advantage over us. They're able to watch practically every move we make. We're easy targets really. Don't get me wrong, Em – we put up a pretty stiff fight, and our gunners give them a merry time of it, that's a fact. But while ever the Germans hold that ridge of high ground, we're vulnerable. I find it a thing of amazement that we haven't all been picked off already. Every day one manages to survive here is a little miracle. Meanwhile, we carry on with our orders, hoping that someone, somewhere amongst the brass hats is going to come up with a bright idea to break the stalemate we're in.

Life here in the trenches goes on as normal. Now the freezing weather's behind us, the ground is quickly becoming churned up again. It's an exhausting business; tramping in full kit, bringing up supplies, hauling telephone wire and ammo – working parties, carrying parties, every kind of party you can imagine – while the mud sticks to your boots and everything seems to weigh twice as much as it should. (It reminds me of that day our two families visited the sea many years ago. Do you remember it, Emily – when we tried to race along the soft sand and we kept falling over because our feet were so heavy? That's rather how it feels. Alas, our present situation is not so picturesque as that was, nor so peaceful.)

Yes, I have to say, Em, the idea of seeing the Bosch blown off their perch is an attractive one. After all, you can understand that we're getting a little weary now. Any encouragement would be welcome. Sometimes it feels as if this war will go on forever. Who would have thought that men could witness the things that we have seen and not go mad? And yet, my dear, brave Emily, you have seen things too. Things no woman should ever have to look upon. Oh my dearest, how I long to see your face again – I can't bear to think that I might not live to look upon it one last time at least.

Zillebeke (Front Line Trenches) April 24th 1917

Death comes ever closer, Emily. Yesterday I felt its breath and wondered if it had come for me …

It had been a lively day. Since early that morning, the British gunners had fired numerous barrages towards the enemy lines, and the German guns had responded generously in kind. Now as darkness fell, things had eased off considerably. Sam's company found itself once again in Zillebeke, this time manning the trenches on the front line. The men in his platoon were killing time.

"You lot, take it in turns to try and get some kip while it's quiet," the platoon sergeant instructed. "I'll be down later if anything kicks off."

A young lad's voice sounded in the darkness. "Anything planned for tonight, sir?"

The sergeant ran a grimy hand over his face. "I'm gonna have a word with the officer in a bit. I'll probably be back later for some volunteers." He moved off down the trench and disappeared into another bay.

"Volunteers, *my* –" Twinny One spat out a vulgarity. "Anybody else gettin' fed up of this game?" He lobbed an empty tin over the parapet in frustration. A sniper's bullet whistled through the black night in reply. "*Dodge the Shell*, followed by *Dodge the Sniper*, followed by …"

"Followed by *Dodge the Firin' Squad* if you don't put a sock in it," his brother grinned. "What's up with you tonight? You're like a bear with a sore head."

"He would have been if yonder tin *had* been his head!" someone joked.

Twinny One came out with another string of unsavoury comments. "Don't tell me I'm the only one here who isn't havin' a whale of a time." He cursed again. "My foot's killin' me. I swear my toes are workin' loose."

Sam had noticed that Twinny One had been limping for the last couple of weeks. Come to think of it, Sam reflected, the disgruntled Twinny had been moaning about his foot for the last couple of *months*. Probably trench foot. Not that he was likely to get much sympathy from any of the lads. After all, everyone was in the same boat. No one could avoid standing around in the waterlogged trenches; it was just part of the job. So what if *your* boots happened to let the mud seep through and your feet swelled up and became so painful you felt like wrenching them off? That was your hard luck. You certainly couldn't bunk off over something like that. There was a war to be won – feet or no feet.

As the night wore on, a drowsiness descended on that section of the trench. Some of the men dozed, some smoked, some chatted in low voices. Apart from the occasional distant shell, the guns had fallen quiet. It seemed that both sides were ready for a rest. Boxer had been sitting by a small oil lamp reading his Bible. Now he put it back in his haversack and stared down at the ground, his expression grave.

"I have a bad feeling about tonight, Sam."

Sam's heart lurched. He knew Boxer well enough to know that he wasn't in the habit of spreading gloom. If Boxer had a bad feeling about something, there was probably good reason for it. "Reckon we've all had it then – think they're gonna try and spring another trench raid on us or something?" Sam tried to laugh, but Boxer's words had disturbed him.

Boxer shrugged his shoulders. "Dunno, Sam. I dunno." He squatted down into the bottom of the trench. "I'm gonna try and pray a while."

Sam nodded and reached into his bag for his diary. Maybe he should write something more for Emily – it would be a distraction at least. A terrific burst of fire suddenly broke overhead. It made him jump. He sighed resignedly and put the diary away. He'd write later. He wasn't really in the mood just now. Boxer's presentiment had made him nervous.

"Game o' cards, Sam?" Twinny One hissed in the darkness. "Might take me mind off me ruddy feet."

"Yeah – why not?"

Moving over to a pile of sandbags where an oil lamp was casting its soft, yellow glow, they began their game. From further down the trench came the sound of muffled guffaws as some of the lads talked and joked, trying to wile away the time. The card game had been going for almost twenty minutes when Twinny One looked up.

"You got a girl, Sam?"

The question took Sam slightly by surprise. For a moment he wrestled with the idea of disclosing his feelings about Emily, but somehow he hardly wanted to bring her into the trench. Some of the boys might get smutty about things if they found out. He'd heard their coarse remarks about other girls. He couldn't bear the thought of anyone tarnishing his Emily.

"No, not really."

"*No, not really*, eh? Sam, you old rascal! That mean you've got several in mind?" Twinny One winked at Sam and laid his handful of cards on a sandbag. Fishing in his pocket, he pulled out a small photograph. "*I've* got a girl. Here she is –" He handed the photograph to Sam. A young woman smiled up from the worn print, dark curls framing the delicate features of her face. Twinny One's eyes were shining with pride. "She's called Tilly. We'd been walkin' out together four months before I came out here. We plan to marry when all this is over. I asked her in one of my letters and she wrote back straightaway to say yes."

There was a tenderness in his voice which Sam had not heard before. He smiled as he handed the photograph back. "She's lovely. You're a lucky fellow."

Neither had noticed Twinny Two moving towards them. He suddenly grabbed his brother in a headlock from behind and ruffled his hair violently. "Is he gettin' all soppy on you, Sam? Showin' you his little Tilly, is he?" He plonked down beside them with a grin.

Twinny One shook his head in disgust and put the photograph back in his pocket. "You're only jealous."

"Too true." Twinny Two threw an arm around his brother's shoulder. "I've already told you what I'm gonna do tho'. On yer wedding morning I'm gonna lock you up in a cupboard and go marry the lass meself. See how long it takes before she notices. Mind you – it'll be too late by then!" He threw his head back and laughed raucously.

Sam looked from one to the other. With their identical pale red hair and green eyes, it was hard to tell them apart. A small childhood scar on Twinny Two's left cheekbone did make the distinguishing process slightly easier.

Twinny One rolled his eyes at Sam. "Just let 'im try it –" He gave Twinny Two a hefty shove so that he fell headlong onto the trench floor. "She'd be able to tell the difference with her eyes shut, matey. Somethin' to do with that distinctive smell that follows you around."

"Keep it down, you two," the sergeant's voice hissed as he approached them. "Save your energy for later – you never know when you're gonna need it." He signalled to the other soldiers in the bay to gather round. "The RE's need a carrying party. I want about ten of you." He randomly counted off ten heads and gestured them to follow his lead. Finding himself among the number, Sam turned and caught Boxer's eye. Boxer patted his shoulder. "Go on, mate," he said in a low voice. "I'll be praying for you."

Sam soon found himself at the back of a line of shadowy figures. The sergeant quickly gave orders to the group, then signalled them to advance behind him. It was in everyone's interest to draw as little attention as possible to their movement. As quietly as they could, the men began to pick their way along the communication lane, artfully manoeuvring over duckboards which slipped and sucked beneath their feet. For this part of the journey, they had moved from behind trench cover and were completely reliant upon the darkness to shield them from the enemy's view. Indeed, the night *was* very dark, the moon for the most part obscured by thick cloud. From time to time it would make a brief appearance, illuminating the shattered landscape with eerie, silver light. Then just as quickly, it would slip coyly back behind its cover, and tired eye muscles were forced once more to stretch and strain in the blackness. Several yards up ahead, Sam could just make out the hobbling outline of Twinny One. Poor chap; he was probably struggling to put one foot in front of the other.

They had gone about three quarters of a mile when a huge explosion sounded not far from their position. The sergeant signalled them to stop and the group froze to an immediate halt. For a few moments they stood rigid in the darkness. Sam's heart pounded as he remembered Boxer's warning. Every nerve in his body seemed to tighten as Very lights suddenly rose into the air, brightening the sky for miles around. It felt like they were on stage, with all the German army as the audience.

There came a second explosion. Sam heard something whizz past his ear. Eight yards in front, Twinny One jerked violently and smacked onto the duckboard. Another whistle and there were screams from further up the line. Sam rushed towards his friend and bent down. For a moment or two he could barely make anything out, but as more flares climbed into the sky, he could see quite clearly.

Twinny One was groaning gently. "Get someone to have a look at me feet, pal –" he rasped. "They're bad today."

Sam swallowed in horror as he looked down. Twinny One *had* no feet. He had no legs at all. A piece of shrapnel had torn them both off and flung them some several yards to the right of the duckboard where the soldier was lying. All that remained was a mass of bloody pulp which was fast colouring the ground underneath him. Sam could see that his friend was losing consciousness. He put his hand into the Twinny's tunic pocket and pulled out the photograph of Tilly. He pressed it into the dying man's hand and bent down to his ear.

"Here, mate," he said gently, his voice cracking. "Your lovely girl. Kiss her goodnight before you go." He moved the Twinny's hand towards his face so that the photograph was touching his lips. Twinny One murmured something and then he was gone. Sam began to shake. Death had come too close this time ...

It was hours before we were able to retrieve his body, Em. I hadn't been able to get him back on my own, so we had to wait till nightfall again to go back along the duckboard. We didn't want to leave his body out there, him being a mate and everything, so we sneaked out under cover of darkness. Incredibly he was still there. Often they disappear into the mud without a trace. His brother was mad with grief, coming along behind us holding one of his tattered legs of all things. We buried him in a little copse and had a makeshift service for him. I plan to write to Tilly and tell her how her brave boy died. I find the whole thing heartbreaking, Em. Only hours before, his mind was full of happy plans for the future. Thank heavens his Tilly never saw him in his final moments. We've lost six men from our unit and the platoon sergeant has been badly wounded. I can hardly believe I managed to come through unscathed myself. I actually heard the thing that killed Twinny One – it very nearly got me first. Maybe I have Boxer's prayers to thank for my being spared.

Rosie sat back from her computer. This was one entry she hoped Beth wouldn't read. Perhaps she should accidentally-on-purpose forget to e-mail it through to her …

She decided to think about that later. The most pressing thing at the moment was an e-mail to Jonathon. Suddenly she wasn't sure what to write to him. She didn't want to come across as desperate – even though desperate was exactly the way she'd been starting to feel recently. She tapped her fingers on the keyboard, willing the words to come.

Hi Jonathon,
Not the happiest of entries today. In fact, be warned – it's positively depressing. Still, I suppose it's quite fitting. I'm not the happiest of senders at the moment; I think 'positively depressed' just about sums me up. Life down here without Beth and Ciaran really sucks. London itself isn't to blame. It's just the whole 'being down here on my own' thing I don't like …

She chewed on her lip. Was that too open? Was she telling him too much? She drummed her fingers on the keyboard again. Why was she telling him any of this anyway …? Oh yes, she remembered grimly. Because right now, he was the only person in the whole wide world she could spill her guts to. She sighed in resignation. She would just have to swallow her pride and risk looking like a head case. At least Jonathon seemed the kind of guy that could handle it. She decided to try and inject a bit of humour into the thing before he got the idea she was about to run amok with a couple of razor blades and a bottle of paracetamol.

Guess I'm just in the middle of one of those 'moments of personal revelation' you were on about. I'll get over it. Meanwhile, I'll get back to my pity party. Didn't invite anyone else – they're so much more miserable when you're on your own …!

(PS. Hope the 'electronic shoulder to cry on' offer still stands or else I'm gonna feel a right dork …)

Hoping to be more cheerful next time
Rosie

By now it was almost midnight and Rosie was still wide awake. Leaving her laptop on, she went back to the kitchen. There was no sign of Mel. No doubt she'd gone to bed. After making another drink, Rosie decided to check her mailbox again before shutting down for the night. To her surprise there was a new message.

Hi Rosie,
That was a good bit of timing. I've been working online all night – just about to shut down when your e-mail came through. Haven't had chance to read the entries yet 'cos it's way past my bedtime and I have to be up early for work, but I'll read them ASAP. Thanks for 'em!
Meanwhile, I just wanted to tell you something. Even tho' you feel all alone at this time, there's someone out there who longs for you to get to know him. The Bible calls him 'a friend who sticks closer than a brother.' Rosie, has anyone ever told you about Jesus? Get back to me –
Luv Jonathon.

Rosie stared at the screen. Just what was she supposed to say to *that?* She realised her hands were trembling slightly. Part of her wanted to reply, but no reply seemed to come. Only Beth's words resurfacing in her memory – *'I didn't fancy going out with someone who was starting to sound like Tim the vicar … .'* Rosie frowned and bit the inside of her cheek. *Tim the vicar?* Jonathon was sounding more like his Uncle Boxer. She ran her eyes over the message again.

A friend who sticks closer than a brother …

She'd never had a friend like that. For most of her life, her brother had been the only friend she'd had. Until Beth came along.

Without warning, a sob forced itself into her throat and with it, a sense of thick, suffocating hopelessness. It felt as though her whole world was being sucked into a vacuum, its structure snapping and breaking like a matchstick house in a twister.

Has anyone ever told you about Jesus?

The tears began to flow now, hot and copious. Jonathon's question seemed to burn a hole in her mind. She couldn't answer him right now. Her heart felt like it was breaking. She quickly logged off and crawled into bed. How much longer could she go on like this?

The rest of the week was hard to get through. She couldn't bring herself to reply to Jonathon, and he hadn't pushed the issue any further. It seemed to her that they had reached an electronic impasse. On the Friday evening as she made her way home from work, Rosie called off at a shop to make a special purchase.

It was night-time – when Mel had gone out with Dan, and Rosie knew she had the house to herself – when she finally opened the smart, green Brompton's carrier bag and pulled out a new A3 sketch pad and a pack of pencils. She placed the pad on the living room table and closed her eyes. The idea had come to her the previous evening, just after she'd struggled with something that had felt dangerously close to a full-blown panic attack. A scene had drifted across her mind; a gentle, pastoral scene – one that she could quite happily have lost herself in. It had only lasted a moment, but later, when the panic had subsided and she'd felt slightly more in control, she'd realised that the brief impression had planted a seed. She hadn't really sketched in years. But now, if only to save her sanity, she was prepared to give it a go.

She opened the sketch pad and pulled a pencil out of the pack. Placing the nib against the blank white of the page, she looked around the room for inspiration. Aesthetically speaking, there didn't seem much to go at. Nothing that leapt out at her anyway. Then she remembered a cyclamen plant on the kitchen window sill. She brought it in and set it in front of her. Taking a deep breath, she made her first mark on the virgin page.

She sketched the plant for some time, recalling hints from her old art teacher about shading and perspective. It was all coming back to her – and surprisingly easily. When she was satisfied with her drawing, she put her pencil down and sat back to look at it. *Not bad, though I do say so myself.* The exercise had been pleasantly therapeutic. Setting her mind to think of another subject, she decided to try sketching something from memory. Her first attempt was the nursery garden. After all, she saw it often enough; it was a scene she knew like the back of her hand. But as her pencil went back and forth across the page, she realised that it had been some time since she'd seen the garden in its full splendour. The sketch of it in its winter garb made a disappointing offering. Her second attempt was a view from Streatham Common. This had become one of her favourite places since she'd been in London. Yet now as she sought to depict the setting on paper, she couldn't stop her memory from throwing up images of the day she'd walked there with Ciaran, just after Beth had first been taken into hospital. They'd known nothing of the severity of Beth's condition back then, but somehow the atmosphere on the Common that day had held a portent of the news that was coming. After twenty minutes of trying to make the sketch, she scrapped it and ripped the page out of the book. The memories were too depressing.

After a while, the idea came to her to draw Oak Lodge. She closed her eyes and tried to see it in her imagination. She was surprised to find that the picture came quite clearly. The old, stone house with its big, rambling garden and tall trees – her hand moved deftly over the page as she warmed to her subject – the wrought iron bench and old-fashioned lamppost ...

With each pencil stroke came an increasing sense of peace. She understood why it had meant so much for Beth to go back there. Maybe Beth was right – maybe it *was* the best place on earth. She'd been working on the sketch for nearly an hour when Mel rung to say that she wouldn't be coming in. Rosie was secretly pleased. She settled down to finish the picture. Perhaps she could give it to Beth when it was complete.

She worked well into the night, altering, perfecting. When at last she put her pencil down, she felt exhausted but strangely thrilled at her achievement. It was just after two o'clock when she crawled into bed. At least it was Saturday. She didn't have to get up till dinnertime if she didn't feel like it. Surrendering to her weariness, she sank her head into the pillow. As she hugged the duvet around her, images of Oak Lodge floated dreamily through her mind. Drifting into sleep, she could almost smell the scent of lavender.

She awoke hours later to the sound of her mobile ringing. Disorientated, she reached for the alarm clock. *Ten thirty-four ...?* It was ages since she'd stayed in bed so late. She sat up and quickly tried to gather herself. Her phone was still ringing, but the incoming mobile number was not one she recognised. She picked up.

"Hello?"

"Hello, *Rosie?*"

"Yes –"

"It's Cassie." Her voice sounded oddly different. "I – I'm just ringing to let you know, love. Beth died an hour ago."

Chapter 22

Rosie stiffened, her mind refusing to believe what her ears were telling her. She swung her legs out from under the duvet and jerked to her feet, her heart pounding in her chest.

"Rosie – are you still there?" Cassie's voice sounded broken down the phone.

Rosie's breath came in short gasps as she began to pace across the room. "Yes. Yes, I'm here." She felt sick. "*How …?* I mean, I thought we had longer."

"We all did, love."

Rosie could tell from Cassie's tone that she was fresh from weeping. Rosie felt too stunned to weep herself. "I – I can't believe it. I only saw her the other day. How can it have happened so fast?"

"We're not really sure," Cassie said quietly. "The doctor's just left. He suspects it could have been a clot – Beth's been complaining for a few days about pains in her leg. Maybe her whole body was starting to wind down and we just didn't realise it …" Her words petered out into an inaudible blur. For a few moments there was silence between them. Then Cassie spoke softly. "It's been so sudden, we're all in a bit of shock up here. I just wanted to let you know, love."

Rosie mumbled her thanks, but somehow the whole thing felt like a terrible dream. She almost expected to wake up and find herself back in bed. She leaned against the wall to steady herself. "When can I come up there?"

"You come as soon as you want, Rosie love." There was a quiver in Cassie's voice now. "And stay as long as you want. You're family."

Rosie said goodbye and slumped heavily onto the bed. This could not be happening. She wrapped her arms around herself, digging her fingernails into her ribs until her knuckles whitened. But the pain did not waken her from the nightmare.

Beth was dead. As the realisation hit her, Rosie began to tremble. Everything in her wanted to get back into bed and pretend none of it was real. But it *was* real. Horribly, hideously real. She felt a sudden urge to vomit. Pulling a dressing-gown around her shoulders, she dashed into the bathroom and bent over the toilet. Her insides turned over as she started to retch. But there was nothing in her stomach. Nothing but a ball of paralysing panic that threatened to consume her with every breath she took. When it became clear to her that she would get no relief from trying to be sick, she sat down shakily on the edge of the bath and tried desperately to think. For an awful moment she felt completely void of identity, as though her mind had been smashed by a huge hammer and its pieces tossed brutally into the atmosphere around her. It was impossible to pull any coherent thoughts together. All that seemed to remain of her brain was a deep, black hole; a gaping abyss of nothingness into which Rosie felt herself being helplessly sucked. Panicking, she jumped to her feet and moved towards the mirror. For a few seconds she did not know the face reflecting back at her. But looking into those eyes, she saw something she recognised all too well. For a while now it had been stalking her; at first from a respectful distance, but slowly and insidiously growing bolder in its pursuit. She had smelt it, felt it, and tried her best to shake it off. But now as Rosie stood staring into the mirror, she saw it staring back at her. Dark and menacing behind her own eyes. Fear. Cold, black fear.

Forcing herself to look away, she tried to think again. She knew she couldn't go on like this. She had to do something, and fast. Less than an hour later, hair scraped into a rough ponytail and wearing no make-up at all, Rosie found herself walking into the nursery.

The supervisor was surprised to see her. "Hey!" she called hopefully, waving a wet paintbrush at her. "Come to join us, have you?" She and her decorator boyfriend had already spent the last two Saturday mornings doing some much-needed paintwork on the inside of the building. After apologising for her lack of availability, Rosie mumbled some half-hearted compliment about the colour of the walls, then explained the real reason for her visit. The supervisor was sympathetic but unable to bend the rules. In terms of compassionate leave, sisters-in-law were not considered close family.

"She's about the only family I have!" Rosie urged, another wave of panic rising in her throat.

The supervisor frowned. "Sorry, Rosie. If I do it for you, I have to do it for everyone. I'm sure you can see that."

Rosie was struggling to see anything.

"How long will you need?"

Rosie hung her head miserably. *How does forever sound?* "At least two weeks I should think." It was a random suggestion. In truth, she didn't think that half long enough. From where she was standing, six months would have been too short a time. She simply wanted to get away – as far away as possible – before she went totally out of her mind.

"Two weeks?" The supervisor shook her head. "That's quite a block, Rosie. I thought you were only looking at the standard three days. Have you any holidays left?"

Rosie said that she had, but not enough to cover a fortnight, not until the new holiday period anyway.

The supervisor smiled uncomfortably. "If you can take the rest of the time in unpaid leave, you're welcome to go."

Thanks, thought Rosie darkly. *That's real big of you.*

She left the nursery a few minutes later and headed home. There were things she needed to do; travel arrangements, packing – explaining to Mel. Mel was in the kitchen when she got back.

"Beth died this morning," Rosie said flatly. "I'm going up to Yorkshire as soon as I can get myself sorted."

Mel's face crumpled. She looked as though she might cry. "Oh, Rosie! I'm so sorry." She made as if to come towards her, but Rosie pretended not to notice and hurried off to her room. Somehow she felt that a hug might be the last straw.

She travelled to Ridderch Standen on the Monday afternoon. It was a fretful journey. Her whole being seemed to alternate between moments of calm and bouts of utter panic. During the latter, her heart raced and her breathing became rapid and self-conscious. She found herself willing the train to go faster.

Ed and Cassie were at the station to meet her. As Cassie embraced her, Rosie realised that never in her life had she been more in need of human touch. In Cassie's arms she felt young and vulnerable, like a small child. Yet today, she sensed Cassie's vulnerability too. She was surprised to see there was no sign of Ciaran. As the car pulled out onto the open road, she asked Cassie about him.

Cassie's eyes filled up. "He's taken it very hard, Rosie. He was going to come and meet you, but he fell asleep a couple of hours ago and I didn't feel it was right to wake him. He's barely slept a wink since it happened. I thought you'd understand."

Rosie nodded slowly. Her heart longed to see her brother, yet something in her felt apprehensive. She hardly knew what to expect. In one small moment everything had changed. Beth had meant the world to him. How would he be, now that his world had fallen away? It was hard to imagine. Ciaran without Beth seemed like a beach without the ocean.

When they arrived at Oak Lodge, Ciaran was waiting in the hallway. As Rosie came through the door, he fell into her arms and buried his head in her shoulder. His grief was so uninhibited, so out of character, that Rosie felt herself welling up.

"Thanks for coming, Ros," he managed between sobs.

She tightened her grip on him. "Hey, Kitch. Where else would I wanna be?"

Even Oak Lodge seemed strange without Beth. Rosie was desperately relieved to have made it up there. She didn't like to imagine what could have become of her had she stayed much longer on her own in London. Yet even here in this haven of tranquillity, she could sense that something was missing. Beth's brothers were frequent visitors to the house in the days following their sister's death. With them came their wives, and out of school hours, their children. How strange, thought Rosie, that a family could be so large, yet rendered so incomplete by the absence of just one small member. She almost expected the door to open and Beth to come bouncing in, her laughter irrepressible as ever, as if the whole thing had been one huge joke. It was only when she looked around at the other members of the household that Rosie knew the truth. Their red-rimmed eyes and pale, grief-stricken faces said it all. Beth was never coming back.

Over the next few days the house was fraught with activity. One of the early visitors was Mr Aston, the village undertaker, who called round to discuss details of the funeral. Tim the vicar called too, to offer the family pastoral comfort and talk through their wishes regarding the service. He sat in the living room with Ed, Cassie and Ciaran while Rosie made them all a drink. When she came in with the tea tray, Cassie invited her to join them. As the discussions progressed, Ciaran admitted that he felt totally out of his depth in the whole matter. He was quite happy, he said, to leave the planning of the service to Ed, Cassie and Tim. The only thing he had strong feelings about was the music.

"I don't really know any hymns," he said quietly. "I'll have to leave that to you guys. But I'd be grateful if we could bring her into church to Vaughan Williams' *'Lark Ascending'*. It meant a lot to her." There was a moment's pause. "And I want her to go out to Ravel's *'Pavane Pour Une Infante Défunte'* ..." He broke off and looked down, his face haunted and pallid. "Because that's what she meant to me."

Rosie wanted to ask for a translation. But no one else said a word, and the catch she'd heard in Ciaran's voice made her stifle her curiosity. Tim left about twenty minutes later, and almost immediately afterwards, Ciaran disappeared to his room. The whole ordeal seemed to have exhausted him.

As well as several other visitors to the house, there were also countless phone calls. One of them was from Jonathon. Rosie was in her room when Cassie came upstairs to ask if she wanted to have a quick word with him. "He'd no idea you'd travelled up here till I just mentioned it," Cassie said, looking slightly puzzled.

Rosie tried to think quickly. In a strange way she was missing her contact with Jonathon. Yet as she remembered the last e-mail he'd sent her, she felt a hesitancy about speaking to him. His question came back to her. *Has anyone ever told you about Jesus?* Even just thinking about it, she felt the same claustrophobic awkwardness that she'd experienced when she'd first looked at his words on the screen.

"Would you mind if I don't come down just now?" she mumbled apologetically to Cassie. "I don't feel up to talking to anyone at the moment. Perhaps I could ring him later."

"Okay, love – I'll tell him that." Cassie left and went back downstairs. But Rosie knew it was one phone call she wouldn't be making.

The funeral was fixed for Friday afternoon. On the Wednesday evening, Mr Aston rang to say that members of the family were welcome to visit the chapel of rest from ten o'clock the following morning. For the rest of the night, a gloomy anticipation settled over the house as everyone became lost in their own thoughts. It seemed an ironic and bitter blow to lose Beth so quickly and suddenly when her time had been so short anyway.

The next day, Ciaran went down early to the chapel. He returned an hour later, ashen-faced and silent. Ed and Cassie visited just before lunch. Rosie was busy making sandwiches for everyone when they returned. Ed disappeared straight upstairs, but Cassie came into the kitchen.

"Would you like to go and see her, Rosie?" she asked gently. It was obvious that she'd been crying.

Rosie had never seen anyone dead before. Memories of her time spent at Aunt Mariah's funereal home came flooding back. "I'm not sure how I'd handle it if I'm honest."

Cassie put an arm around her shoulder. "There's nothing to be afraid of, love. She just looks like she's asleep. But it's up to you. It has to be your choice."

Later that afternoon, Rosie made the journey with a heavy heart. It was more out of a sense of loyalty to Beth than any kind of desire to look at her. When they arrived at the chapel of rest, Mrs Aston showed them towards a little side room. Cassie reached out and took Rosie's trembling hand as they stepped inside. Rosie's heart was pounding as she found herself submitting to Cassie's lead. For a few seconds she averted her eyes, everything in her recoiling from the sight she knew was coming.

"There now ..." Cassie's voice was soft and reassuring. "Look. She's just sleeping, Rosie."

Rosie forced her eyes towards the coffin. Her heart lurched as she saw Beth. She lay, dressed in the crimson velvet gown she'd worn for the concert only a few months earlier. Her blonde hair had been carefully combed and positioned to look as though it was flowing over her shoulders. The yellowness had gone from her face. Instead, her skin was pale and her lips, which were set in a slight smile, had the faintest tint of colour. Her thin hands were joined across her stomach as though she were enjoying an afternoon nap. With some consternation, Rosie imagined she could see Beth's chest rising and falling. It was a surreal experience.

"You know, love – this isn't Beth any more." Cassie's low whisper broke into Rosie's consciousness. "It's just her old house really. They've made her all beautiful so that we can look at her one last time. And that's hard isn't it?" There was a slight catch in her voice. "The thought that this is the last time we'll see her on this earth. But in reality, Beth's with the Lord now. She doesn't need this old body any longer. He's going to give her a new one."

Rosie could tell they weren't cheap words. Tears were streaming down Cassie's face as she spoke. But Rosie knew Cassie believed every syllable of what she was saying. She stared down at Beth. It all seemed so unreal, so horribly unreal. How could someone so alive as Beth lie there, so still, so dead? She willed herself to wake up from the nightmare. *Surely it must be a nightmare?*

But as she listened to the silence, broken only by the faint sound of birdsong coming from the sunlit afternoon outside, Rosie knew that death was in this place. No matter how long she gazed down at her, Beth lay there unmoving, her face like cold alabaster.

After what seemed like an age, Cassie put a hand on Rosie's arm. "Ready to go, love?"

Rosie nodded. She gave a last glance at the lifeless form, unable to bring herself to touch the marble hands. "Bye Beth ... gonna miss you."

As they stepped outside into the sunshine, she couldn't hold back the tears.

When they arrived back at Oak Lodge, Rosie was slightly shocked to see Jonathon's car on the drive outside.

"Looks like we have a visitor," Cassie remarked thoughtfully as she switched off the engine. "Perhaps I'll ask him if he wants to stay for dinner."

Rosie wasn't sure how she felt about that idea. Seeing Beth had already disturbed her; she didn't know if she could cope with Jonathon going all other-worldly on her. But she said nothing to Cassie. She didn't feel it was her place.

Jonathon's greeting was low-key and Rosie felt grateful for it. It stemmed any awkwardness there could have been between them. Cassie fixed a quick meal and by six thirty they were all sitting round to eat. The conversation was subdued and Rosie noticed that Ciaran hardly made any impression on his food. As soon as dinner was over he excused himself and went up to his room. Rosie offered to wash up. She was slightly disconcerted when Jonathon followed her into the kitchen and armed himself with a tea towel.

"Thought you could use a little help." He smiled disarmingly but his eyes seemed to search her face. "How you coping anyway?"

Rosie shrugged as she filled the bowl with water. Somehow Jonathon always managed to draw her out of herself. She gave a light, embarrassed laugh. "You know I went to see Beth earlier? Well, I'd be lying if I said it hadn't spooked me a bit." Plunging some dishes into the water, she started to wash up. "Stupid I know, but it's the first time I've actually seen anyone – well – *dead*."

Jonathon nodded slowly. "I noticed your hands were shaking when we were at dinner."

"You *did?*" Rosie was shocked. She'd tried hard to conceal her nervousness, but it seemed that nothing escaped Jonathon's attention.

"Don't worry about it, Rosie. You've been having things rough recently. You're allowed to shake as much as you want. *Here* –" He pointed to his shoulder. "For you to cry on."

Rosie smiled sheepishly. This was a guy who obviously wasn't one to take the huff easily.

"So …" Jonathon didn't look at her as he carefully dried a large, ceramic serving dish. "Had any more moments of personal revelation since we last had contact?" His tone was sincere, without the slightest hint of mockery.

Rosie swallowed hard. Should she tell him how she'd been feeling recently, or would that just make him go all weird on her again? Her mind flicked back to the image of Beth lying in the chapel of rest. It made her shudder. She decided to risk it. Treading carefully of course, but she'd risk it all the same. After all, there weren't exactly crowds of folk queuing up to play agony aunt to her at the moment. Tentatively, she began to tell him of the loneliness she'd felt since Beth and Ciaran had moved up to Yorkshire, and of the sense of isolation that London seemed to inflict upon her these days. She even found herself mentioning her breakup with Gavin. Not, she insisted, that it had ever been a particularly meaningful relationship. But at the moment, every negative turn of events was bound to add to her unhappiness – *wasn't it?*

Jonathon listened quietly as he dried up, only interjecting from time to time in order to ask a question or clarify a point. For the most part Rosie did the talking, unburdening herself with a measure of conscious restraint and more than a smattering of black humour. When she had described her miseries as much as her pride would allow, she stopped washing up and stared at the window.

"As if all that wasn't bad enough, I've just been to see my best friend laid out in a funeral parlour. Feels like I'm part of some awful horror movie." She forced a laugh. "Now it's dark, I'm wondering if I'm gonna be able to sleep tonight. Best keep a light on, I guess …"

Jonathon looked at her sympathetically. For a few moments he didn't speak. Then he leaned back against one of the cupboards. "Rosie – look at me a minute."

Rosie was slightly taken aback. His blue eyes seemed to pierce right to her very core.

"I know I probably upset you with my last e-mail, when I asked you if anyone had ever talked to you about Jesus."

Rosie hung her head awkwardly. She'd been hoping this wouldn't come up.

"Hey, don't worry." Jonathon gave a wry smile. "It's not the first time I've been electronically blanked." His expression became serious. "Rosie, speaking as your shoulder to cry on, I can't offer you anything else. In the end, Jesus is all I've got."

Rosie's face creased into a frown. What on earth was he talking about? Yet as his eyes searched her own, she could see in them a compassion that she found hard to counter.

"I say he's all I've got – but believe me, Rosie, when you have *him*, you have everything you'll ever need. I think perhaps you ought to hear that right now."

Unable to say anything in reply, Rosie looked away. Jonathon moved over to the radiator and hung the tea towel there to dry. "Hope you don't think I'm trying to come on heavy here, Rosie, but I've been worried about you. I know you're really going through it at the moment, but I also know that Jesus specialises in desperate situations." He smiled gently. "I'm going to get off home in a minute, but I'd really like to tell you more some time. Have a think about it, eh? Whatever you decide, let's stay friends. Okay?"

Rosie nodded. Her mind was spinning. It was hard to deny; Jonathon Kirkbride was one of the warmest, kindest people she'd ever come across. For all his funny ideas, he seemed a genuinely sound guy. A far cry from the Gavins of this world, she thought bitterly.

Lying in bed two hours later, she tried to focus her thoughts. It wasn't easy. Somehow, alone in her room tonight, a strange horror seemed to be closing in on her. Outside, a wind had sprung up and it rattled the windows and made the trees creak eerily. Rosie pulled the duvet right up to her face. Even with the bedside lamp still on, her imagination was working overtime. Images of Beth crowded her mind. Every noise made her jumpy; she shivered, but not from cold. Several times, just as she was on the point of falling asleep, some spectral vision seemed to pass before her dozing eyes, jerking her back to wakefulness. She could almost picture Beth standing behind the closed bedroom door, dressed in her velvet gown, her dead, unseeing eyes staring right through her.

As the night went on Rosie became exhausted. One o'clock, two o'clock ... there seemed no release from the torment. She found herself frantically longing for morning to come. A solitary tear fell onto her pillow.

When you have him, you have everything you'll ever need.

In that moment, Jonathon's words seemed to swirl like ticker-tape around the frightening pictures in her mind. A sudden gust of wind blew against the window with force, howling like a banshee as it continued on its way. Rosie felt sick with fear. Gripping the duvet, she closed her eyes.

Jesus, I don't even know if you're really there –

The words came out in a low, desperate voice.

But Jonathon says you're everything I'll ever need.

She paused a moment, the storm in her head trying to drown out her tentative supplication.

What I need now is sleep – a great sob cluttered her throat – *before I go completely out of my mind ...*

The last thing she remembered was whispering thank you.

The time of the funeral had arrived. Oak Lodge was crammed with people, many of whom were family members Rosie had never seen before. Their conversations were low and hushed. Even the children were subdued. As Cassie busied herself making pots of tea, Rosie went up to Ciaran's room and knocked softly on the door. His voice was barely audible as he summoned her to enter. He was sitting on the bed trying to fasten his tie.

"You okay, Kitch?" Even as she spoke, Rosie's heart turned over at the sight of him. His face was gaunt and lined. Sitting there, so crushed and desolate, he seemed much older than his years, and yet he looked as helpless as a small boy. She knelt down on the floor to help him. His eyes filled with fresh tears which fell and bounced onto his suit trousers. *'My Princess ...'* was all he could mutter. Fighting to contain her own emotion, Rosie bit her lip hard.

The cars arrived at 1.45. A silence fell over everyone as the hearse came into view. An arrangement in white flowers ran along the side of the coffin. It read quite simply: *'BETHY'*. Rosie was standing on the path next to Ciaran. She heard him stifle a sob, and fearing that he might lose it altogether, she slipped her arm gently around his waist. Trembling, he reached for her other hand and gripped it tightly. Moments later, they made their way to one of the black limousines waiting in the road. The time had come for Beth to make her final journey from the home she'd loved so much.

Even going at a slow, dignified speed, the journey to the church took less than five minutes. Without releasing her grip on Ciaran's hand, Rosie looked out of the window as they travelled. It was a beautiful spring day. Even in the car she could feel the warmth of the sun's rays concentrated through the glass. Several villagers stopped and respectfully bowed their heads as the procession passed by. When they arrived at the church, Rosie turned to Ciaran. His face was set in a stare, as though he were trying to summon up all his courage for this last, most difficult act of love towards Beth. As they stepped out of the car, Tim the vicar was waiting to greet them. Rosie hardly noticed any of the other people standing outside the church; her whole concentration was on her brother. She willed him to hold himself together. If he broke down now, she was pretty sure she would too.

Cassie leaned over and whispered in her ear. "You go in first with Ciaran, Rosie. We'll follow on behind you."

Rosie was slightly surprised. She thought fleetingly of her battle to get compassionate leave at work. What was it the supervisor had said – sisters-in-law were not considered close family? Her going in first hardly seemed correct etiquette.

As if knowing her thoughts, Cassie squeezed her shoulder gently. "Beth looked on you as a sister, Rosie. And besides, your brother needs you today."

Slipping her arm through Ciaran's, Rosie smiled gratefully.

As the pallbearers made their way to the door, Tim took his position behind the coffin. Suddenly, the floaty, mellifluous strains of *'The Lark Ascending'* could be heard coming from inside the church. Rosie fixed her eyes straight forward as they walked into the building. She could almost feel Ciaran's legs going from under him. Somehow they managed to get to the front row and sit down; Cassie and Ed to Rosie's right, and after that, Beth's brothers and their families filtering in behind. Rosie stared at the wooden box in front of her. It didn't compute. The familiar music seemed to taunt her mind as she found herself recalling the night of the concert at the Laureate Hall. What had gone wrong? How on earth could something so triumphant have turned into something so tragic? As she listened to the poignant melody, her thoughts wandered to the many happy times she'd shared with Beth. It choked her to think that there would never be any more. But if *she* felt that way, she couldn't imagine how Ciaran must be feeling right now.

After several minutes, the music faded out and Tim took his place at the front of the church. When he had welcomed everyone and extended his deepest sympathies to the family, he prayed for a few moments and then invited the congregation to sing a hymn. It was one with which Rosie was vaguely familiar – *'Amazing Grace'*. She mouthed the words on the order of service sheet, but all the time she was conscious of Ciaran. He seemed to be staring straight ahead, the sheet clutched in his hand quite redundant. When the hymn was over, Tim asked everyone to sit down. Rosie noticed he was holding an envelope.

"Over the last few weeks," Tim began, his eyes looking across the congregation, "I had several conversations with Beth. On one particular afternoon, after having spent a most pleasant hour or so chatting together, she gave me something which she requested I read out at her funeral. And so, with your permission, I would like in these next few moments to bring you all –" He looked down and read from the envelope. "*A Final Word From Beth.*"

There was an air of expectancy as Tim tore the envelope open.

My Precious Family and Friends,

Well, if you're listening to this, it can only mean one thing; the time has come for us to say our goodbyes. I have not looked forward to this moment if I'm honest. My life has been blessed with so many beautiful people, it's hard to think of our being separated from each other. And yet I guess that's the way things have to be, at least for now. I thank God for every one of you. Each of you has helped mould my journey into what it has been. And what a brilliant time I've had! My life may have been short, but it has certainly been an adventure, made all the more so by my encounters with you fantastic folk. What stars you are!

Perhaps if you'd asked me a few months ago what had been the highlight of my life, I would have said it was the night I played solo violin with the Avanti Sinfonia – when we performed Vaughan Williams' 'Lark Ascending' at the Laureate Hall in central London. For me, it was the fulfilment of a childhood dream; something I had longed for and worked very hard to see. I had hoped that night would mark the real take-off of my musical career. Alas, that was not to be the case. Unbeknown to me, things were about to take an unexpected turn. Within a month of the concert I was to discover I had cancer.

What fear that word can strike into the heart. What devastation it can bring upon a life. I would be lying if I told you that I received the news calmly. No, not at all. I must be honest and confess that at first, I came close to sinking. Trying to make sense of my life, trying to make sense of my impending death – none of it made any sense at all. The situation seemed quite hopeless.

And yet talking to you today, I can tell you that I did find hope. In the midst of everything that came upon me following the night of my 'greatest triumph' back in October, I began to experience something more precious than I could ever have dreamed of. In the fear and heartbreak of my illness and diagnosis, I suddenly found myself crying out to the God of my childhood. He'd been so real to me once, back in the simplicity of my younger days. Jesus, the friend of little children, the Good Shepherd searching for his lost sheep, the loving Father watching and waiting for his prodigal son. I'd known all the stories back then, and a whole heap of songs too. Yet somewhere along the way I'd become an adult – self-sufficient, proud and successful. It had been so easy to persuade myself I'd outgrown my need of him. Somehow, along with all my teddies, dolls and dressing up clothes, I'd left God far behind. Beth was a big girl now, carving out her own path in the world.

But there are times on our earthly journey when we find ourselves facing situations that are far beyond even the strongest, most unshakeable amongst us. When we sense, as if for the first time, our own fragility and transience. When we're hit by the shocking realisation that we are not, and never were, masters of our own destiny. How terrifying it was to find myself in that dark hour. In all my life I'd never been in such an awful place. Yet as my shattered world began to fall apart, it was to God that I turned, albeit a little nervously at first. How would he respond after all my years of silence? Would he turn his back on me as I had turned my back on him? My prayer was not sophisticated or rehearsed; it was simply the broken sob of a hurting child. Imagine my joy and relief to discover that he had been waiting for me all along. No sooner had the pitiful cry left my lips than he reached down and scooped me into his loving arms. At my most wretched, I sensed his forgiveness and grace – at my most terrified, I felt his peace. And what an incredible peace it was! How could I have lived so long without his presence?

I have to admit something to you. One morning recently, I confided to him that I was afraid to die. Not so much of death itself, you understand, but rather the act of dying. Not exactly something one can practise for, is it? That very night I had a dream. In it, the Lord came to me and sat on the end of my bed. I remember the look of tremendous love in those eyes. "Don't be afraid, Beth," he said. "When the time comes, I'll send my angels to carry you home to me." The next morning, the fear had completely gone. Now, as you listen to this letter, I will have seen those very angels face to face. But even more precious than that, I will be looking into his.

And so for now, lovely people, I will say goodbye. As I leave this world, be sure to know I carry you all in my heart. Whatever you do, don't be unhappy for me. Jesus said, 'I am the resurrection and the life. He who believes in me will live, even though he dies; and whoever lives and believes in me will never die.'

Dear precious ones, I BELIEVE! In the words of the song – 'I'm gonna live forever!'

Love You and God Bless – Beth xxx

A profound hush had fallen over the church. Ciaran's arm was touching against Rosie's and she could sense that his whole body was trembling. His grief seemed almost tangible now. Rosie hardly heard any of the short message that Tim delivered following his reading of the letter. Her mind was stinging with memories; *the old church at Applemarket, the evening on Whitstable pier, Beth's dream of the fog* – it all fitted in. Yet listening to Beth's final thoughts had been almost too painful to bear, and Rosie had a sudden, terrible urge to run out of the place before she completely lost control. She forced her brain to think of mundane things; shopping at Sainsbury's, cleaning the nursery toilets, grilling nachos on a Saturday night ... anything that might pull her mind away from the awful reality of what was happening and stem the surge of grief that was about to engulf her. It was with some relief that she realised Tim had finished talking. Now it was time for the final hymn. She steeled herself to hold on. Surely they had to be nearing the end now. The singing was strong and, Rosie sensed, almost triumphant. When it was over, Tim asked the congregation to remain standing for the final prayers. There was a simplicity in the way he prayed; a gentle, sincere empathy. Rosie was sure she could hear his voice breaking slightly as he spoke.

"Could I ask you all to take your seats for a moment?" Tim requested. "Before we carry Beth's body to its final resting place, I would like us all to spend a few private moments remembering her life and thanking God for our precious memories of her."

As the congregation sat down, strains of music began to drift through the still church. It was music Rosie had never heard before; music of such melancholic dignity that she felt it could almost have been composed for the occasion itself. She reached for the order of service leaflet and stared down at the photograph of Beth on the front. It was the same photo that had appeared on the programme the night of the concert. Rosie felt a stab of pain. Trying to distract herself, she opened the leaflet and fixed her gaze on the words swimming in front of her.

Maurice Ravel – Pavane Pour Une Infante Défunte
(Pavane For A Dead Princess)

As her eyes fell upon the title of the piece that was playing, her heart quickened. Ciaran's words came sharply back to her – the day he'd picked the music for the funeral.

"... Because that's what she meant to me."

She had no idea how long the piece went on. Suddenly her whole consciousness was fixed on the trembling form of her brother beside her. He could no longer hide his distress. He made little sound, but hugging himself, rocked gently backwards and forwards in his seat. Swallowing her own tears, Rosie put an arm around his shoulders and prayed for the ordeal to end. After a few minutes the pallbearers walked quietly towards the coffin. Tim gave a little nod to the front row and they stood to their feet for Beth's final procession. Rosie quickly slipped her arm through Ciaran's. As they began to make their way slowly down the aisle, she hardly saw the faces of the congregation. The melancholy of the music had hurt her at a depth she could barely identify. It seemed to speak of something beautiful, now gone; something deeply loved, now lost forever.

The fresh air hit her like a slap as they stepped outside. She breathed deeply, still trying to steady Ciaran who was now sobbing without restraint. It was only a few yards from the church to the freshly dug plot. As they made their way there, Rosie's mind went back to the day she'd met Jonathon in this very place. Up until now this churchyard had carried pleasant memories for her. Surely after today she would never be able to think of it in the same way again.

She held onto Ciaran for most of the committal; except at the end, when Josh's young daughter, Meg, handed out white roses from a box to all those standing around the graveside. Rosie took one and clutched it for a few moments. So. It was all over. Beth was gone, and this was goodbye. She tossed the bloom miserably onto the coffin below, then moved aside to let others come nearer. It was only then that she looked up and saw just how many people had come to say their farewells. There was the crowd of family members she'd seen at the house earlier, there was Emmett Mallory and a number of familiar faces from the orchestra, and there were countless others that Rosie had never before set eyes on. As Tim concluded the burial, everyone stood around in respectful silence. After a few minutes, the crowd started to drift off towards the church hall.

Ciaran stood looking down into the grave, his face contorted in an expression of helpless grief. Cassie gently touched Rosie's arm. "Look – over there, Rosie love." She gestured towards two figures standing some way off. "You go. We'll stay with your brother."

At first, Rosie did not comprehend her meaning. She squinted her eyes against the afternoon sunlight and tried to focus. No. It couldn't be ...

Slowly she began to walk across the graveyard to where the couple was standing. As she approached them, she could make them out quite clearly. The woman was middle-aged and thin, her raven hair tinted with silver. She was dressed in black and her make-up had smudged under her eyes. The man at her side looked much older than her, though Rosie knew he was not. He was balding and overweight, and seemed to stand at a strange angle as though in some kind of discomfort. The sight of him turned Rosie's stomach.

"Hello, Rosie." The woman tentatively reached out her arms.

Rosie hesitated for a moment. "Hello, Mum."

Rosie allowed her mother to embrace her. She could not, however, bring herself to even look at the man standing with her. *How dare he come here? How dare he show his face on a day like this?* For a moment, she wanted to be angry at her mother for bringing him. But as she struggled to contain the maelstrom of emotion that was kicking off inside her, Rosie finally understood something. The very fact that her mother had brought Mickey here today only served to confirm what Rosie had suspected all along. Her mother had never known, never guessed, never had so much as the slightest inkling as to what had been going on.

"We're not going to stay for the tea, Rosie." Her mother's face seemed to her so sad and empty. "Mick's gout's real bad at the moment and it's a long way home for him. We just wanted to come and pay our respects." The sound of her soft Irish lilt made Rosie feel like crying. Somehow it seemed to throw up every memory of her life that she wanted to forget.

"Aren't you going to talk to Ciaran before you go?" Rosie urged. *Surely she hasn't made the journey all this way to go home without saying a word to him?*

Her mother shook her head. "No, Rosie. Poor lad's too cut up to talk today. Some other time, eh?"

"Yeah, I guess." *Like never, more like.* Rosie stiffened. She couldn't break down now – not in front of *him.*

Her mother kissed her cheek sorrowfully. "Bye then, Rosie. See you again sometime, love."

Rosie watched as they turned and began to walk away. Mickey was hobbling painfully and for a brief moment, despite herself, she felt something akin to pity for him. His strength was broken at last, but strangely, she could not find it in her heart to gloat. As she observed the wretched pathos of his appearance, it seemed to her that he was reaping a miserable harvest. She continued watching until they turned out of the gate and disappeared from view. So that was it. Her mother's token gesture of sympathy. Biting her lip, Rosie turned towards the church hall.

A few moments later, she found herself sitting on a table with some of Beth's relatives. There was an exchange of empathetic smiles, a few kind but meaningless words, and then Rosie stared down at the floor. She had no desire for any conversation now. She'd always known today was going to be an ordeal. Indeed, the image of Beth being lowered into the ground had sickened her to the core. That in itself was enough to send her spiralling into depression. But nothing could have prepared her for the shock of seeing Mickey again. As she pictured his face, a vice-like pain gripped her stomach. She could almost smell him in the atmosphere around her.

A soft touch on her shoulder jolted her from her ruminations. It was Jonathon. He was helping serve the tables with tea and coffee.

"Hi, Rosie." He bent down towards her ear and spoke in a low voice. "I thought you were incredibly brave in there. How you feeling now?"

"I'm okay," she lied, trying to force a smile. But seeing the concern in those blue eyes, she knew she hadn't fooled him. Hastily she looked down at the floor again. *Jonathon, I can't tell you the half of it. Just when I was thinking things couldn't get any worse ...*

Inside she felt utterly fragmented. All things considered, today had probably been the worst day of her entire life.

Chapter 23

In the days that followed, Rosie felt as though she was trapped in a dream. The mood in the house was strange; a mixture of collective anticlimax coupled with a feeling of numb unreality. Beth's loss seemed to permeate the very fabric of the building. The light, airy rooms with their lofty ceilings and sense of space seemed somehow smaller and more confined. The clock sounded dull and tired as though chiming the hours was suddenly too much effort. And the fire barely sang in the hearth. Rosie saw little of Ciaran. He came down for meals but hardly touched his food, only taking his place at the table for the briefest time before disappearing again. On one occasion, she noticed him leave the house through the back door shortly after dinner. He was dressed up warmly as though going off for a walk. Rosie suspected he was on his way to the churchyard. For all she knew, that was probably where he spent most of his time at the moment. But she was reluctant to ask him outright. One day during the week, Ed took him over to Tom Bennett's to pick up logs and fresh eggs. They made a subdued pair as they set off. And, it seemed, even Tom Bennett's company did not induce them to stay and chat. They were back within the hour, their faces sober and unrefreshed.

Rosie understood. Since the funeral, she herself had been finding conversation increasingly difficult. She made small talk with Cassie and tried to help her out with the cooking and cleaning. But she was always relieved when she found herself alone again. Deep down, she was afraid to engage with anyone at the moment. Since her encounter with Mickey, her mind felt raw. Losing Beth had been horrible enough – *but seeing Mickey too ...?* A huge emotional scab had been knocked off and the wound was fresh as ever. All it would take was the wrong word at the wrong time, and Rosie knew it. It made her feel terribly vulnerable.

Jonathon called twice during the next few days. On both occasions he was only able to stay about an hour – a particularly heavy workload, he explained with genuine disappointment.

Rosie was secretly glad. Not that she didn't enjoy his company. She was fast coming to the realisation that she enjoyed being with Jonathon more than she did most other people. But she also realised that Jonathon had an unnerving way of seeing right inside her, and just now that was the last thing she wanted.

"You're quiet," he observed on the Thursday evening.

Rosie knew he was eyeing her with concern. She shrugged and tried to smile, but Jonathon wasn't taken in by it.

"You don't want to go back on Saturday, do you?" He spoke so gently that Rosie wanted to burst into tears. He was right; she didn't want to. It was bad enough trying to deal with everything while she was here, in the safety of Oak Lodge. But the thought of being all alone in Streatham again ... that was a prospect that hardly bore thinking about.

"No, don't suppose I do." She made the admission simply. There seemed no point in pretending.

Jonathon nodded slowly. There was little he could say, but somehow she sensed that he knew how much she was hurting. The rest of their conversation was subdued and soon it was time for him to leave.

"Wish I could stay longer, Rosie. I really do." There seemed to be a reluctance in his voice, as though he wanted to say more. For a moment they stood looking at each other awkwardly. Then Jonathon shook his head with a sigh. "Come here, you."

He took a step forward and opened his arms towards her. Before she had time to think, Rosie found herself in his embrace. But it was unlike any embrace she'd had from a man before. It was full of warmth, yet without that blistering heat that always seemed to taint these things; full of love, yet completely pure. It was a brother's embrace, yet somehow more. And it left Rosie speechless.

"You make sure you e-mail," he said kindly but firmly. "Don't go quiet on me again, or I might just find out where you live and come down and sort you out."

Rosie mumbled something in reply, but inside, her mind was teeming. Why did she feel as limp as an invertebrate all of a sudden? And why was her heart thudding so uncontrollably?

Jonathon's cheek was pressed against hers and she could smell the scent of his skin. For a split second, her mind went back to Gavin and his overpowering designer aftershave. How different was Jonathon; lighter somehow, fresher. And so much less threatening.

After what seemed like an age, Jonathon pulled away and held her at arms' length. Gripping her shoulders gently, he fixed her with his blue gaze. "I'm going to be praying hard for you, Rosie ..." He stopped for a moment, looking for her reaction. "Dunno if you're happy with that, but I'll be praying anyway."

Rosie lowered her eyes. "You're welcome to pray if you want," she muttered in a small, resigned voice. "Guess I'm gonna need all the help I can get."

If she had looked up in that moment, she would have seen a flash of pure joy cross Jonathon's face. But Rosie was far too busy trying to calm the tsunami that was raging in her head.

It was Friday afternoon and Rosie was in the middle of packing for her return home. Her heart had never been less in a thing than it was today. There was a knock at her bedroom door. It was Cassie.

"Just came to see how you were getting on, love."

Rosie swallowed a sigh as she sat down on the edge of the bed. "I'm more or less done. Just a few last minute bits to go in tomorrow morning."

"What time do you leave?"

"My train's at 12.05. Should get my connection at Northallerton about 1.15."

Cassie nodded. "We're going to miss having you around, Rosie."

Rosie knew she meant it. Cassie wasn't the kind of woman to play around with worthless words. Yet somehow, her very sincerity cut Rosie to the quick.

"Looking forward to getting back?" Cassie asked gently.

For a moment Rosie was tempted to lie. *Oh yeah, really am. Never more so.* She decided to go for the honest approach. "Not really."

Cassie gazed out of the window. "I can't help feeling it might be some time before your brother's able to face going back down to London. I think he needs to feel close to Beth at the moment. He visits her grave several times a day. Part of his grieving process, I guess." She hugged her arms across her chest as though remembering her own grief. "He hasn't said anything to me, Rosie, but I'm thinking he'll want to stay here for a while yet."

Rosie winced. Cassie's words hardly came as a revelation, yet hearing them spoken out loud did not make comforting listening. For an awful moment she thought she might burst into tears. Steeling her jaw, she pretended to check for something in her case, but soon realised there was a limit as to how long she could continue the charade. Seeing Cassie still staring out of the window, Rosie slumped back against the headboard and the room fell into silence.

It was several minutes before Cassie turned to her. "Are you happy in London, Rosie?"

Rosie was slightly taken aback. Something in Cassie's tone told her that the older woman knew perfectly well that she wasn't. She shook her head, unable to meet Cassie's gaze.

"I didn't think so. Is there anything keeping you there, love? I mean, your job – or friends perhaps?"

Rosie's lips tightened to a thin line. *Job? Friends? As if.* She shrugged as nonchalantly as she could manage. "Guess I'm there because that's where Ciaran and Beth were. Ciaran always said I could come and join him in London when I was old enough to leave home. That's how I ended up in Streatham." She shifted awkwardly. "Don't get me wrong, I've always liked it down there. We've had some good times. But things are different now – with Beth gone and everything." Wanting to be sensitive to Cassie, she tried to smile. "The job's served me well. I've got some useful qualifications out of it ... and it pays the bills. As for friends, I don't get a lot of time for them. After a day with the kids, bed's my best friend." It was a feeble attempt at light-heartedness. Rosie was loathe to mention the fact that Ciaran and Beth had always been her closest friends; that she'd never felt the need or inclination to search for friendship anywhere else. *There. That's my life summed up in a few, uninspiring sentences.* Suddenly it all sounded more pointless than ever.

Cassie looked thoughtful. "I thought that might be the case." There was a pause. Then she looked directly at Rosie. "How would you feel about moving up here for a while – so you can be with your brother?"

Rosie was shocked. "*Here?* Ridderch Standen?"

Cassie smiled. "I meant *here* – Oak Lodge. This is your room; you can stay as long as you want. Ed and I talked about it the other day. We'd be thrilled to have you if you wanted to come."

Rosie wasn't sure she was hearing properly. "Are you saying to give up my job – my house – and *live* here?" Could Cassie really be meaning that? The thought of it seemed too good to be true.

There was an earnestness in Cassie's eyes. "Only if you want to, love. There's no pressure at all. I just wanted to let you know the invitation's there. Take as long as you like to think about it."

Rosie didn't need to think about it. If Cassie had offered her a million pounds on a plate, it wouldn't have looked as attractive as the offer she was making right now. But there were practicalities to consider.

"I'd need to find a job up here."

"I'm sure you'd find something, love. There are always things in the local paper for people with childcare qualifications. Seems to be one of the most popular areas of employment these days." She put a hand on Rosie's shoulder. "The most important thing at the moment is that you decide whether or not you want to be up here. We can fill in the details later."

Rosie looked at her suitcase, her eyes suddenly brimming with tears. Until this moment, she hadn't permitted herself to think about life beyond the weekend. The prospect of going back to London on her own had been too grim, too terrifying to contemplate. It was something she had pushed from her consciousness, steel-barring her mind against the waves of panic that seemed to be ever present these days. Now, as she allowed herself to remember the awful day Cassie had rung with the news of Beth's death, she shuddered. That day she'd felt fear of a different colour. A fear that the whole terrible thing would send her reeling over the edge. She still didn't know how she'd managed to make the journey up to Yorkshire; the memory of it was little more than a blur in her head. And yet somehow she'd done it. Could she ever have made it if she'd known that *Mickey* would show up at the funeral? Never in her wildest nightmares had she anticipated anything like that. Face to face with him again after all this time, after five years of trying so hard to forget and move on. And now, could she really have gone back to London with that scene in the churchyard so fresh in her mind?

It was only now that Cassie had offered her a refuge from the storm that she was able to look the situation full in the face. Images of Mickey swirled unchecked through her head as Rosie allowed her mind to grasp the reality of Cassie's proposition. Her repulsion was mixed with an almost incredulous sense of relief. There might be a few demons trying to raise their ugly heads again, but at least she wouldn't be on her own. She would be here – with Ciaran, and Cassie and Ed. As if to reassure herself that this whole moment wasn't a dream, she dug her fingers into the duvet. It sank, soft and cool beneath her touch. This was her bed, her room, for as long as she needed. Cassie had said so, and that was good enough.

As tears spilled down her cheeks, she reached out towards the older woman. "Thank you … so much. You don't know what this means to me. I can hardly believe it."

Cassie held her close and smoothed her hair softly. "It's our pleasure, Rosie. You just go down tomorrow and tidy up your affairs, then you can get yourself back up here as soon as possible."

Rosie felt her mind sink into the comforting balm of Cassie's words. She had never seen this coming. But she was overwhelmed with gratitude that it had.

Thank you, Jesus.

She didn't even try to stop the thought that instinctively rose up inside her. She was pretty sure he must have had something to do with it all.

Mel filled up when she broke the news on her return. "Oh Rosie, I'm going to miss you so much!" There was a childlike candour in her tone, and when she rushed towards Rosie to hug her, Rosie did not resist. Somehow, she didn't feel half so uncomfortable embracing Mel now she knew she'd be leaving.

"I'll keep up the rent payments till you find someone else to share the house," Rosie assured her.

Mel hesitated. "There's no need, Rosie. Dan and I have already talked about moving in together somewhere. But I didn't want to mention it just yet – with Beth and everything. We decided to wait until you were over things."

Rosie was touched. She'd underestimated Mel. This girl was a genuine friend, yet she'd always been too busy getting annoyed at her to realise it. Spontaneously, Rosie hugged her again. "Thanks, that was good of you. Both of you."

For the next hour they chatted about anything and everything. Rosie found herself thinking it was the best conversation she'd ever had with Mel. She knew that that was mostly down to her own frame of mind. Mel hadn't changed. She was just as ditsy and naïve as ever. But, Rosie realised, as if for the first time, she was also as big-hearted as ever too; generous, thoughtful, and utterly guileless. A real gem.

"What will you do with all your furniture?" Mel's face scrunched into a frown.

"I'm going to store it at Ciaran's for now. He'll have to come back down here at some point – when he's ready to face it. My stuff can stay at his till then. I'll just take up my clothes and a few personal bits."

Mel's face lit up. "We'll help you move things, Dan and me. It'll be done in no time."

Rosie smiled at her gratefully.

Monday morning felt different to any other day Rosie could remember. Rehearsing her speech, she strode purposefully into work.

The supervisor made it easy for her. “Well, I’m not entirely surprised to be losing you, Rosie,” she said, not unkindly. “Though I have to say, we’ll miss you. You’ve been a good member of the team.”

“Does that mean you’ll give me decent references?” Rosie laughed, relieved that the worst bit was over.

The supervisor nodded. “So long as you can work me this week with no major mishaps, I’ll think about it.”

“You’re happy with just a week’s notice?” Rosie wanted to be clear.

“Yeah, that’s fine. Some of the girls have been asking about extra time recently.” The supervisor grinned. “I’ll work their sweet little butts off. They’ll be begging me to set someone else on by the time I’ve finished.”

In her dinner hour, Rosie contacted an employment agency in Northallerton. The idea had come to her the previous day. Although Cassie had said that there were always plenty of jobs going in the childcare sector, Rosie didn’t like the thought of hanging around penniless waiting to go through the whole interview thing. Posts being advertised now would most likely have their starting date some three or four months down the line. That was a long time to be without an income. The agency idea had come as a flash of inspiration. That way, she could at least be earning while she was on the lookout for something else.

The woman who answered her call spoke with a rich, northern accent. She took Rosie’s details and arranged an interview with her for Wednesday of the following week. Rosie tried to sound calm as the woman at the other end of the line tapped the information into her computer. But inside, her heart was racing. *Wednesday?* Could she honestly have everything sorted by then? It struck her then that she really was leaving London behind. For how long she had no idea. Maybe forever – maybe not. It all depended on what Ciaran did. But at least for now she was going far, far away … another twist in a tale that seemed to be getting more surreal by the minute.

By the time she went back on afternoon duty, her head was in a spin. Everything was happening so fast. Indeed, it was hard to believe it was happening at all. She must try to keep a clear mind; there was so much to sort out and so little time to do it in. And in the meantime, there were children to look after.

Toronto Camp May 10th 1917

Well, Emily, still here and in the pink as they say. We go into reserve in a couple of days – never a dull moment. Twinny Two's not too good. The other evening he asked us to help him write to his parents about his brother's death. Poor fellow's hands were shaking so much he could hardly put two words together on the paper. He must have started again a dozen times; kept tearing the letter up, saying it wasn't coming across right. I don't know what he's hoping to get 'across'. The chap's dead – I'm not sure how you can fancy that up to make it sound better. Besides, the army will have sent official notification and that'll have been blunt enough. Look how hardened I've become, Em. I ought to be ashamed of myself.

Things are beginning to filter through about the mines I was telling you about. Sounds like it's true after all. One of these fine days we're going to be giving the Bosch a firework display they're not expecting. Mind you, Em, I'd be surprised if they're not suspicious. There's been a lot more activity in our area recently – extra munitions, machinery, heavy artillery – all arriving and being manoeuvred into position with a sense of urgency. I've noticed there's been quite a bit of troop movement as well. A lot of new men seem to have been drafted in, so one can only suppose it's for a follow-up offensive. No doubt we'll find ourselves right in the middle of it; they'll probably need all the numbers they can get. Times like this I rather wish I wasn't in the infantry. It's hard to get excited about a big fight when you know you're bound to be the first into the fray. Still, mustn't be glum. We've lasted this long, haven't we?

Toronto Camp May 11th 1917

We heard our first nightingale today. My thoughts went back to last year when we used to listen to the nightingales in quiet intervals between the shelling. Well, here I am again, Em. A year on and still here. The little bird's song has cheered me enormously. In keeping with tradition, I will call her Rosie.

Railway Dugouts May 13th 1917

We're in reserve now and things are fairly quiet. You wouldn't think it to look at Twinny Two though. The poor chap's in an awful state, I'm sorry to say. I think it must be very hard to lose a twin. It must be like losing part of oneself. He went missing for more than an hour yesterday. We were worried he'd got cold feet and run off. Jimmy and I eventually found him scrunched up in a big shell hole, sitting in two feet of water. He was absolutely soaked to the skin but seemed completely unaware of it. He seemed completely unaware of anything come to that. He was just rocking backwards and forwards, his head and hands shaking uncontrollably. We were trying to persuade him to come out when a shell broke quite some way up the line. It wasn't even near us, but Twinny Two started yelping like an animal and covering his ears. It was horrible to watch, Em; the terror in his eyes is something I'll never forget. To see a mate reduced to that is an awful thing. I couldn't help remembering what happened to Wilf after his pal died. I think the same thoughts were running through Jimmy's mind too. We soon realised we weren't going to get very far with Twinny without him getting completely hysterical. We were just debating what to do when one of the officers, Captain Banks, came by and asked us what was amiss. He'd seen us talking down into the hole and thought we might have bagged ourselves a German prisoner. We explained the situation to him as best we could. He took one look at Twinny Two and said we needed to get him out as quickly as possible. I'll be honest, Em, I was a bit nervous at first. Not all the officers are sympathetic with chaps that lose their nerve. Some would just as soon like to see them shot for cowardice. But Banks turned out to be a decent fellow. He helped us drag Twinny out of the hole and told us to get him to a dressing station immediately. He sent a note for the MO explaining that Twinny Two had just buried his brother and needed time to recover his wits. And that was that. We managed to get poor Twinny to field ambulance and left him there. He was still rocking and shaking as we came away. I don't think he even knew who we were.

Battersea Farm June 1st 1917

Well, Em, it's a good thing Twinny Two's still out of the way. A couple of days ago, our boys began the most intense barrage I've seen yet. The guns haven't stopped since – on either side – though I like to think we're giving them a hotter time than they're giving us. We've found out that the mines are due to go up in the next few days. We're still in reserve at the moment, but our battalion's going to be involved in the battle immediately after the bang, so we'll be getting our orders nearer the time. Meanwhile our good old gunners are pounding away at the enemy lines – keeping them busy, I suppose, while the finishing touches are put to our devious little plan. At least if our boys can weaken some of their front line positions, we've a better chance of coming out of this thing in one piece. Oh, to be in the infantry!

Even today some shells have dropped uncomfortably close to us. I thought one had our numbers on it. It would seem a shame to die in reserve, Em. If I have to go at all, I'd rather go in action, in the heat of battle as it were. Perhaps I'm trying to be a hero. But then, I don't suppose a dead hero is much use to anyone.

Rosie closed the diary and put it in her drawer. She was thoughtful as she settled back at her laptop. She felt a strange excitement about writing the next bit. Remembering the feeling of Jonathon's arms around her, her heart quickened. She quickly bit back the memory. Jonathon was attached after all; he'd made that quite clear. And yet, from everything he'd said and all the concern he'd shown her in recent weeks, Rosie was more than sure he'd be happy to hear her news.

Hi Jonathon –

An unexpected turn of events. Ridderch Standen is about to get a new resident – yours truly. Cassie suggested I move up to Oak Lodge for a while because she doesn't envisage Ciaran coming back down to London any time soon. Having thought it over, it seemed like a good idea. There's nothing keeping me down here now after all. Guess I'm ready for a change. So … I've given in my notice, am in the process of moving some of my gear over to my brother's house for storage, and I should be travelling up to Yorkshire next Monday if all goes to plan. Need a job fast. Failing all else, I might find myself distributing Yellow Pages or something like that. Thought you'd like to know anyway.

Bye for now
Rosie.

It was the following day when Jonathon opened the e-mail. He read it slowly, and then read it again. So. She was coming up to Yorkshire. He stared at the screen for some time, turning the thing over in his mind.

Lord … oh, Lord.

He dropped his head and began to pray silently. It was several minutes before he finally closed down his computer and stood up from his desk. Deep in thought, he went downstairs to make himself a strong coffee.

"*Hello?*" Headteacher Bev Carradine glanced at the wall clock in her office. *Eight thirty-five …?* Reception usually fielded calls until after nine, especially on Mondays.

The voice at the other end of the line sounded flustered. "Sorry, Bev. We've got Lydia Vardy's husband on the phone. He insists on talking to you. Sounds in a bit of a tizzy."

"Okay, Janet. Put him through." Bev frowned as the receptionist made the transfer. Lydia Vardy – Helen Walker's intrepid NTA. What had she gone and done now?

"Hello, Mrs Carradine?"

"Yes, speaking."

"It's Mark Vardy here. I'm afraid Lyd's had a bit of an accident over the weekend."

Bev took a sharp breath. *Accident? Weekend ...?* That could only mean one thing. The charity parachute jump. Before she had chance to ask, Mark started to explain.

"She landed real badly." He hesitated for a moment, then gave a slightly awkward laugh. "Mind you, the paramedics said it could have been a lot worse. Said they were surprised they weren't scraping her up off the grass."

Bev winced. "She's injured then?" She almost dreaded the answer.

"Fractured femur, fractured wrist, two broken ribs, and she lost a tooth. The tooth's upset her more than anything. She's still in hospital. She's going to be out of action for a while."

Bev rolled her eyes incredulously. That girl certainly knew how to do a thing.

Mark's voice sounded down the phone again. "There's one good thing," he quipped brightly. "People have been promising to double her sponsor money since it happened. So it's not all bad news."

Bev stifled a sigh. *Well, that's brilliant, Mark. Tell her from me that the minute she gets her casts off, she can do another jump to raise money for the school – to pay the whacking great agency fees we're going to have to fork out to get another NTA. Tell her I will personally push her out of the plane ...*

"Tell her we're all thinking about her, Mark. Helen and I will come and visit her when she's out of hospital. We'll get some flowers for her and a card from the children. That should cheer her up a bit. You keep us posted. Let us know when she gets home."

A few moments later the conversation ended. Bev walked gloomily over to the window, a twinge of guilt playing in her thoughts. She didn't want to feel cross at Lydia. Obviously she was relieved that the accident hadn't ended in tragedy as it so easily could have done. But the timing of it was awful. Helen Walker's class simply couldn't function without a full-time NTA.

Not with twenty-four Year Three children to be kept in check. And especially not now that the class had a new, rather troubled arrival. Bev walked back to her desk and picked up the phone again. She needed to bounce the thing off Helen first, but in her own opinion, they had to get someone in – and fast.

Rosie looked round her room. She was hit by the realisation that this was probably the last time she would stand here. It was completely empty, a mere shell, not the slightest hint as to whose life it had contained, or whose comings and goings it had witnessed over the last few years. It seemed small and pathetic in its emptiness, and Rosie felt a pang of sadness as her mind went back to the day she'd first moved in here. She'd been excited back then. An intoxicating sense of independence had gripped her as Ciaran and Beth had helped move her stuff in. For the first time in her life she was going to be mistress of her own affairs. No one to fuss if she came in late or didn't eat right; no one to programme her life out. There was, of course, the small matter of her housemate to consider, but she'd been sure they'd be able to come to some agreement on matters of personal space and privacy. Ciaran and Beth weren't going to be far away either; there was always a safety net if things didn't work out for her. But things had gone fine. She and Mel had quickly learned to exist side by side without too much friction. Mel had her life and Rosie had her own. A smooth, well-ordered set-up that had suited both of them quite perfectly. For a long time, everything had cruised along with no problem. Until Beth had got sick. That had changed the whole picture. Rosie found herself remembering the day Ciaran had first broken the news that Beth had cancer. It had been in this very room. And the day, not too long afterwards, when he'd told her the prognosis. Beth was dying. Funny – that had been here too, as had the day when Cassie had rung to say that Beth had passed away. Rosie could remember that phone call vividly, and she could still recall the fear and disbelief that had gripped her mind like a vice as she'd struggled to take in the news. It was a terror that hadn't really left her since. Now, with Beth gone and Ciaran so far away, this place no longer represented independence and freedom. It felt more like a prison, swirling with ghosts and dark forebodings. As she closed the bedroom door for the last time, Rosie knew that she would not miss this house. It had seen too much.

Her cases were in the hallway, packed and ready to go, and all her furniture had been put into storage. All, that was, except for her almost-new flat screen TV. She'd given that to Mel.

"You can't do that, Rosie! I thought it was your pride and joy," Mel had protested. But Rosie had insisted. Somehow, she'd wanted to give Mel something to say thanks. Mel and Dan had been absolute stars that week. Dan had borrowed a van from a friend, and the two of them had worked tirelessly, helping Rosie transfer all her stuff over to Ciaran's place. They'd left her a mattress on the floor for her last night at the house, but now, even that had gone. Having both taken an afternoon's leave to see Rosie off at the station, Mel and Dan sat quietly in the living room waiting for her to say the word.

"Think that's just about it." Rosie slowly pulled on her jacket as she came into the room. "Guess we'd better be getting off."

The journey to the station was strangely subdued. Even though Mel had made her promise to stay in touch, Rosie knew deep down that their relationship was coming to its end. There was little to keep them together. Their lives had crossed for a few, brief years, and now they were going their separate ways. There seemed little point in pretending that it was deep friendship that had bonded them. It had been convenience; a mutually advantageous arrangement that, for the most part, had worked well. But as Dan's car wended its way towards King's Cross, Rosie couldn't help feeling that in her dealings with Mel, she had wasted her cynicism on someone worthy of sentiments far more noble.

At the station, the three of them stood on the platform waiting for the train to arrive.

"You make sure you get someone to help you with all this lot," Dan said firmly but kindly. "You'll give yourself a hernia if you try and do it yourself. You did say Beth's dad was coming to meet you at the other end, didn't you?"

Rosie nodded. "I'll be fine, don't worry. I'll look round for a porter when I get to York."

Mel's face lit up. "Look out for a hunky one – and flutter your eyelashes like mad. That's the way to do it!"

Rosie shook her head with a smile. Coming from Mel, it seemed an appropriate piece of advice to part on.

A few moments later the train rolled in. Dan loaded up the luggage while the two girls said their goodbyes. Mel's eyes were brimming with tears as they hugged each other. "Hope everything works out for you, Rosie. You deserve a nice life – really you do."

The sincerity of her tone brought a lump to Rosie's throat. She smiled awkwardly. "And I hope everything works out well for you and Dan. You two are good together."

She couldn't help feeling that Mel was a more deserving candidate for happiness than *she* would ever be. But minutes later, as the train began to slowly pull away, Rosie found herself thinking about her friend's words. She stared out of the window at the passing landscape. As the train gradually picked up speed, she suddenly had a surreal sense that London was releasing her into a new, unknown chapter; surrendering her, as a child come of age, into the hands of some force far greater than herself. It was a scary feeling, and yet somehow exciting. She couldn't help hoping that Mel was right. If ever Rosie had been ready for a slice of nice life, it was now.

Chapter 24

Mendinghem June 11th 1917

At present I'm in No. 46 Casualty Clearing Station. I've been here three days apparently, though I didn't fully regain consciousness until yesterday. Funny, Em – one of the first faces I saw was Jimmy's. He was in here with a bit of a shoulder wound, but he's gone back to join our lot now. Don't know when they're going to let me back. I've spent today trying to piece together the early hours of Thursday morning.

As I recall, we spent most of Wednesday near Zillebeke, not far from Battersea Farm. A lively day, shells flying over thick and fast (from both sides, I might add, though I think our boys definitely gave them a worse deal of it). As dusk fell, our unit set off for the line with our officer, Captain Mackie, and our new platoon sergeant, Albert Bandy. We made it to the assembly trench in plenty of time, with, as far as I know, no losses …

The day had been long and noisy. The heavy bombardment had continued relentlessly, and with the increased sense of activity throughout the whole area and the preoccupied expressions on the faces of the officers and those in the know, there was a decided feeling of apprehension amongst the men. Sergeant Bandy looked over his platoon grimly. Some of these lads seemed so young. He had a boy at home not much younger. Thank God he was only fifteen. This war had to be finished by the time he was old enough to join up. He checked his watch. Three hours to go.

In the next bay, Sam had just made himself something that only vaguely resembled a cup of tea. He'd long since got used to the acrid taste that seemed to accompany all things edible at the front. He glanced over at Boxer. Boxer was writing a letter, quietly humming something Sam recognised as a hymn. A couple of yards away, Jimmy was dozing against a sandbag. A wave of gentle laughter sounded out as the shells fell quiet for a brief moment.

All through the trench men were trying to rest up before the battle ahead, even though the big guns were still going at it as they had been for days. Sam shook his head with a wry smile. All hell breaking loose around them; zero hour looming closer and closer. Yet men could still sleep and laugh and sing. The resilience of the human spirit. He found himself thinking about Twinny Two. That was what happened when a man's spirit broke. The thought of his friend made him suddenly sad and he closed his eyes. Perhaps that was why the army had little sympathy for such casualties of war. If every soldier went down like that, the thing would be over.

Sergeant Bandy's voice interrupted his thoughts. "Listen up, lads!" He gestured for everyone to gather round. "Right. Zero hour's fixed for 3.10 – so I want you all to double-check your equipment and make sure you're ready. If everything goes off as planned, you won't 'alf have somethin' to tell your grandkids about."

Someone made a bawdy comment and a ripple of laughter went through the trench. The sergeant chose to ignore the remark. "We go over in the third wave, so we sit tight till we get the signal. You all got that?" Satisfied that everyone knew what they were doing, Sergeant Bandy moved off to the next bay to continue his briefing.

Sam tried to focus his mind on the sergeant's instructions. He thought of the times he'd gone over the top before. Funny really, there weren't too many. It all depended on where you happened to be placed at any one time. If your unit found itself posted to the front line right in the middle of a major offensive, then going over the top was part and parcel of the thing. But most of the time, life in the trenches was just plain, hard work. Nerve-jangling and fraught with danger to be sure – death was always on the lookout for victims. But very often, it was danger with the element of surprise. The stray shell, the sneaky sniper, the poison gas that seemed to appear from nowhere. Going over the top was different. A man had to steel his nerves and switch off his brain to walk into the jaws of almost certain destruction.

For the next hour or so, the strafing continued, hot and heavy. But sometime after 2.00 a.m., for the first time in days, the home guns fell suddenly quiet. It wasn't long before the Germans stopped firing too.

"Bet they're glad for a break," Sam grinned to Boxer. The two of them looked up into the June sky. It was clear, with a bright, full moon, one of those early summer nights when the darkness never fully takes hold. It would have been beautiful in any other circumstances.

Jimmy came over to them and slouched against the trench wall. "Wish we could just get on with it." Irritably, he flicked a louse from his hand and trod it into the ground. "I hate this waiting. 'Specially when you don't know what's on the way."

Sam smiled sympathetically. He knew what Jimmy was trying to say. Before a battle like this, you had no idea what was 'on the way'. You just followed orders and hoped you'd come out at the end of it all. And tonight, there was no denying the feeling in the air. Something big was about to happen. How big was anyone's guess. It certainly wasn't for the likes of them to know the picture in advance. The officers might have all the details, but for the ordinary chap in the trench it was a case of being filled in with the necessary information and no more.

A gale of low guffaws rang through the night air. No doubt some of the boys were telling their dirty stories again. They usually did that when they were nervous. A kind of defiant bravado perhaps. Sam wasn't sure. He'd never had eyes for anyone but Emily.

Boxer clapped a hand on Jimmy's shoulder. "Don't fret, pal. You belong to Jesus now, remember? Nothing's on the way that he doesn't know about already. He won't leave you, Jimmy. He's got you right in the palm of his hand."

For a moment Jimmy seemed to think about his words. Then his face relaxed into a broad smile. He nodded and extended a hand towards Boxer. As Sam watched his two friends exchange their rough handshake, he felt strangely on the outside. So; Jimmy belonged to Jesus too, did he? Whatever that meant. But with just an hour to go before the action, it hardly seemed the right time to start asking for explanations.

"Listen at that!" A low whisper from Boxer cut into the darkness. Sam listened. Nightingales. Singing their hearts out. The whole front deathly quiet, not a shot to be heard – and nightingales were singing. It was a peculiarly beautiful sound.

"Thank God our madness hasn't driven them away," Jimmy murmured quietly.

Boxer looked up at the stars with a satisfied smile. "He's letting us know he's still with us. All creation praises him. It will always be that way."

At 3.00 a.m., men for the first wave began to scramble out of the assembly trenches into position. At 3.05, Sergeant Bandy reappeared in Sam's bay with Captain Mackie. "Everything alright here?" It was a statement rather than a question. The sergeant swept the trench with a glance. "Don't forget, lads – keep your wits about you and wait for the signal. We'll make short work of 'em this time."

Sam saw the officer glance at his watch, his expression taut and inscrutable. It made Sam feel nervous and excited at the same time. Jimmy was right; the waiting was the hardest bit.

Three minutes to go.

As the nightingales continued to sing, Sam closed his eyes and tried to think about home. Home ... and Emily.

Captain Mackie checked his watch again. One minute.

Sam's heart was thudding now. The tension in the trench was palpable. Thirty seconds. Twenty. Ten. Zero ...

A tremendous rumbling began to shudder through the ground beneath them. Some of the men exchanged glances. Sam turned and caught sight of the officer. The expression on his face had changed, and now it bore a smug, almost boyish glee, like that of a child about to spring a major practical joke.

Suddenly, a deafening explosion shook all the earth around them. The noise was so terrible that, for an awful moment, Sam wondered if someone had detonated the whole world. There was momentary panic as several of the men were flung backwards by the force.

"That's Hill 60 gone up," Sam overheard Captain Mackie say to the sergeant. Gingerly, Sam lifted his head above the parapet and looked out. What he saw shocked him. The notorious Hill 60 had been blown into the sky, and out as far as the eye could see were flames. Flames everywhere. The whole Messines-Wytschaete Ridge seemed to be on fire. A flash of pity went through him for the Germans positioned in that seemingly invincible stronghold. Surely none of them would get out of that inferno alive. Another huge explosion sounded somewhere far away to his right, compounding the already deafening noise. All around, billows of black smoke and smouldering debris choked the atmosphere. Feeling his throat beginning to burn, Sam rubbed his eyes then stared at the blazing landscape. In all his time at the front he had never witnessed anything like it.

A sudden burst of spontaneous cheering erupted in the trench as the realisation dawned that the first stage of the operation had gone well. Captain Mackie grinned encouragingly. "So far, so good. Looks like we really caught them out there. But it's not over yet. We still have a job to do."

A terrific roar broke out from the heavy guns behind them, signalling the start of a massive artillery bombardment. It was a strangely comforting sound. Sam thought about the infantry going over in the first wave and wished them well. The sky was darker now and thick with the aftermath of the explosions. But there seemed to be little return fire from the enemy. The element of surprise was obviously paying off.

Sergeant Bandy's voice sounded through the trench. "Right, listen up. Our guns are gonna be poundin' the lines the whole time. Just before we go over, our boys will send in a creeper and we follow in behind that. You go over when you hear the whistles – nice and steady, open formation. Remember, don't rush it or you'll end up on the end of our fire."

That was the thing about creeping barrages. You had to make sure you stayed in the right position at all times. The artillery would start up a barrage, the shells initially dropping quite close to the home lines. The infantry would then come up out of the trenches and follow in behind the artillery cover. The tactic required the artillery to advance the range of its shells by degrees, whilst all the time shielding the infantrymen heading towards the enemy line. It was a precise art. If a shell fell short, it could end up killing the very troops it was supposed to protect. Get it wrong, and for the infantry it was like being fired on by both sides. Knowing that the gunners were covering you as you scrambled out into no man's land was supposed to be a kind of reassurance – some big, powerful brother figure looking out to make sure you got home safely. But there were times when it went horribly wrong.

A few moments later the rum rations came down the line and each soldier eagerly took his due. There wasn't enough to inebriate a man. Just sufficient to numb his common sense and allow him to walk into a hail of fire without thinking too much about it. Several minutes passed as a subdued apprehension fell over the trench.

"Fix bayonets!" The order sounded down the line. The men obeyed as quickly as trembling fingers would allow. For some of them, this was the biggest action they'd seen since arriving at the front. But even for the most battle-hardened soldiers who'd been out here since early in the conflict, moments like this never really got any easier. Sam was well into his second year out here; right now, his heart was thudding in his chest.

"All the best, you two. I've prayed for you both." Boxer turned quickly to Sam and Jimmy and clapped a hand on each man's shoulder.

The whistles sounded. A furious scrambling as men climbed from their trenches to begin the advance. The air was acrid with shellfire and Sam was struggling to see who was ahead of him. *Nice and steady – don't rush it.* Sergeant Bandy's words echoed in his brain. He pressed on, the blood pulsing through his head as the sound of gunfire screamed in his ears. It was hard to know the direction the shells were coming from. Were they firing back?

When he saw Captain Mackie stumble a few yards in front of him, his question was answered. A sniper's bullet straight through the neck. Sam ran over to him but could see straightaway that the captain was beyond help. His eyes were still open and he fixed Sam with a bemused stare.

"Anything I can do for you, sir?" Sam ventured, raising the officer's head gently.

The captain's face contorted as he tried to swallow. He moved his lips with great effort. "Hoorah for England," he whispered. "Go to it, Tommy …"

That's all I can recall, Em. Something must have hit me soon afterwards because the next thing I remember was waking up in the CCS with a terrific headache and a shrapnel gash on the top of my scalp. The MO says it's only surface or I wouldn't have made it. So far, I've not heard how our platoon went on in the operation. I've no idea if we lost anyone else. The only one I can speak for is Jimmy.

It seems that about nineteen mines went up almost simultaneously – a great success they're calling it. News has got back here that a lot of the Irish lads at Spanbroekmolen went up with the mine. Not sure how accurate that is, but it's a darn shame if it's true. I'll be glad to get back to the line and find out what's what, but the MO hasn't given me clearance yet. Well, Emily – this has been rather a long account. The relative comfort of the CCS leaves me more time than I know what to do with. Oh my dearest, how I long for happier days.

It was Tuesday afternoon. Up in Yorkshire the sky lay heavy with cloud. Rosie had arrived the previous evening, unpacking and settling into her room as though she'd never been away. She'd seen little of Ciaran. He'd come downstairs briefly the night before to say hello, but had disappeared again soon afterwards. Cassie had tried to assuage Rosie's concerns. "He'll be alright, love. He just needs time. We're all dealing with it in different ways."

Rosie hadn't seen him at all that morning. She'd spent most of it with Cassie. Now she'd come up to her room and was sitting on her bed, poised to e-mail Jonathon. She felt slightly disappointed that he hadn't replied to her last message. Perhaps the news of her move hadn't gone down as well as she'd hoped. Or perhaps there'd been a glitch in the system and the thing had never arrived. She decided to give him the benefit of the doubt.

Hi Jonathon –
Don't know if you got my last e-mail. Just to explain if not – I'm now officially living in Ridderch Standen until further notice. All Cassie's idea! If you get in touch I'll explain everything. Just one entry this time. It took a bit of typing up.
Bye for now
Rosie

She closed down and clicked the laptop shut. The ball was firmly in his court now; it was up to him to make the next move. The last thing she wanted to appear was pushy.

She decided to try looking in on Ciaran. After knocking on his door and receiving no response, she gently creaked it open. Ciaran was sitting by the window, his back to her. Closing the door behind her, she padded quietly over to him.

"Hi, Kitch." Her voice was as gentle as she could make it. He gave no reply, but continued to stare out of the window as though she wasn't there. Moving closer to him, she put a hand on his shoulder. "Missed you." She waited. Still no reply. Not even the slightest flicker of acknowledgement. Rosie felt utterly helpless as she looked at him. She knew there was nothing she could say to take away her brother's pain, nothing she could do to bring Beth back and make him smile again. She'd had barely one decent conversation with him since Beth had gone, and now it seemed he wouldn't even look at her. Indeed, suddenly it seemed that hardly anyone was thrilled to welcome her arrival in Yorkshire. Cassie was enthusiastic of course; it had been her suggestion after all. But Ed had been terribly quiet, spending most of his time ensconced in the huge shed he used as his painting studio. The benefit of the doubt she'd afforded to Jonathon only a little while earlier seemed suddenly a bad idea too. He was obviously dragging his feet about getting back to her. And now, even her own brother ...

She wished Beth could be there. *She* would have been happy to see her. She'd always been happy to see her. How she missed Beth. She might not show it like Ciaran; she might not even allow herself to feel it like he did. But she missed her so badly. For a moment she pictured Beth in her mind's eye. Beth full of life – laughing and teasing, happy and carefree, the way she'd always been. The best friend anyone could have asked for. But the picture was soon replaced with an image of Beth laid out in the chapel of rest, cold and still. Even now it seemed unreal, and it made Rosie feel sick.

At that moment, Ciaran reached out and took her hand. His grip was weak, and Rosie could feel that his whole body was trembling. She squeezed his fingers gently, a wash of guilt flooding over her. He wasn't ignoring her. He was simply broken. She stayed there for several minutes. Neither of them said a word, but an unspoken understanding seemed to pass between them, and when Rosie left the room a while later, she knew that only time would heal this heartbreak. For all of them.

Later that night as Rosie was on her way to bed, Cassie stopped her on the stairs. "It's your interview tomorrow, isn't it, love?"

Rosie nodded. She was already feeling nervous about it.

"I won't be able to come into town with you, I'm afraid." Cassie's tone was apologetic. "One of the girls in church has been wanting to give me a massage and a bit of a makeover. You know, manicure, pedicure – that kind of thing." She looked slightly embarrassed. "I don't normally go in for that sort of stuff, but Kay seems to feel it'll help me with the grieving process. So I said yes. She has a little salon a couple of villages from here. She booked me in for tomorrow ... before I knew about your interview."

Rosie smiled at her. "I'll be fine, don't worry. You just enjoy your day."

"Ed can drop you off in Northallerton – there's no problem there."

Rosie shook her head. "No, it's okay. I need to learn how to get about on my own, now I'm living up here." Just saying the words felt strange and she grinned.

Cassie smiled too. "I'm so glad you are, Rosie. I felt most unhappy thinking of you down there all by yourself." She reached out to hug her. "I hope you come up with something tomorrow, love. I'll be praying for you while I'm having my nails done."

They said goodnight and Rosie went up to her room. It was almost eleven, but though she was tired, she couldn't shake off the urge to check her e-mails. She quickly logged on and started to get ready for bed. Five minutes later she logged off again, disappointed. Her inbox was empty. Still no reply from Jonathon. She tried to shrug it off as she climbed into bed. Why did it matter anyway? She was up here now, whether he liked it or not. But as she tried to settle down to sleep, she realised it mattered very much.

The woman at the employment agency introduced herself as Paulette Sharp. She was bright and enthusiastic, and confident she would have no trouble finding Rosie the perfect placement.

"How long have you worked with children, Rosie?"

"Five years. Since I left school."

Paulette flicked through Rosie's paperwork. "NVQ Level 3 Early Years Care and Education … . You trained on the job?"

Rosie nodded. "A lot of evening work too."

"Yes, I'm sure." Paulette continued to read. "Your former employer e-mailed me a good reference for you. You've come highly recommended."

Rosie made a mental note to take back all the mean things she'd ever said about her supervisor.

Paulette's face creased into a slight frown for a moment. Then she looked up. "Have you ever worked with older children, Rosie? I mean children older than nursery age?"

It was Rosie's turn to frown. "How old are you meaning?"

"Well – six, seven, eight – that sort of age."

"Yes. Yes, I have. At the nursery we used to run holiday clubs outside of term time – for children up to eight. I've done a few stints in them."

Paulette looked thoughtful. "Do you enjoy working with that age group?"

Rosie admitted that she'd considered the possibility of branching out into that area at some future point.

Paulette nodded. "D'you know, Rosie – I think I might have something that would suit you very well. It's only a temporary vacancy but if you fancied trying it, it would put you on for a few weeks until something else comes up. Non-Teaching Assistant at a primary school in the next village to yours."

"Aylesthwaite?" Rosie ventured.

"No, Miston. It's in the other direction – about the same distance. There are no formal qualifications needed for NTAs other than four GCSEs or equivalent ... and you've easily got that. Plus you've a whole load of other stuff, and lots of experience with children. I think you'd be perfect. Unless you're specifically wanting to work in Northallerton?"

Rosie shook her head. "Not particularly. I quite like the village feel if I'm honest."

Paulette was pleased. "Look, Rosie – I'm going to make a phone call. Why don't you go into the foyer and get yourself a drink while I try and speak to the headteacher. Have you any objections to my passing on your mobile number?"

Rosie said that she hadn't and went off to get a coffee. Several minutes later, Paulette reappeared with good news. The head was very keen to fix up a meeting. How would next day suit? A little surprised at the speed of this response, Rosie said that it would suit her fine.

"Good. I've passed on your number and you can expect a call sometime later today. I think she's eager to get the position filled. Sounds like they're struggling. But she'll fill you in with the details."

Later, as Rosie travelled back to Ridderch Standen, she reflected on the speed of events. Last week, she'd been a nursery nurse in London. Tomorrow, all being well, she was about to be interviewed for a school job in Yorkshire. Her life seemed to be taking off on its own. The only thing she could do was try and go with the flow.

When she arrived back at Oak Lodge, Cassie was nowhere to be seen. Rosie found Ed in his garden studio, sketching out a rough draft for a painting. He looked up and smiled as she walked in. But Rosie could see the sadness in his eyes.

"Cass won't be back for a while," he said gruffly as he flicked his pencil across the canvas. "Kay Jenison has taken her back to her place for a bit o' dinner. She told me to tell you there are plenty of ready meals in the chest freezer and to help yerself. She'll see you later."

"Have *you* eaten yet?" Rosie asked softly.

Ed shook his head. "I'm not bothered at the moment, Rosie. Thanks all the same."

As she walked to the house, Rosie wondered when Ed had last tucked into a meal with any enthusiasm. His large frame seemed wasted these days, his clothes baggy and ill-fitting. In many ways, he bore the same haunted look as Ciaran.

She had something to eat, watched a bit of television and finally went up to her room. A slight headache was beginning to play around her eyes. She lay on the bed to try and relax. However, it wasn't long before her mobile phone began to ring.

"Hello – *Rosie Maconochie?*"

Rosie didn't recognise the voice. "Yes, speaking."

"Hello, I'm Bev Carradine – headteacher at Paddock Hill Primary. Paulette Sharp contacted me earlier with your details."

Rosie sat up quickly and tried to collect herself. *First impressions, girl, first impressions …*

"Did Paulette mention to you the possibility of our meeting together tomorrow at the school? Just an informal chat – to see if you're the kind of person we're looking for."

Rosie confirmed that the suggestion had been made.

"The post is only temporary, Rosie, but it *is* urgent. I'm afraid one of our members of staff has been involved in an accident. I think we're looking at three months minimum before she's able to return to work. We're keen to find someone to fill the position as soon as possible." There was a calm authority in Bev Carradine's voice which Rosie found reassuring.

"What time would you like me to come into school?"

There was a slight pause. "Well, I've been thinking, Rosie. I come through Ridderch Standen every day to get to work. How would you feel about my picking you up outside Saint Edwin's in the morning – say, about ten to eight? It's not out of my way. I just thought it might be easier for you, with your being a newcomer in the area."

At her end of the line, Rosie suppressed a smile. *Sounds fine to me. A little unorthodox from where I'm standing, but maybe that's how they do things up here.*

"Thanks, that'd be great. Do I need to wear a yellow carnation or anything?"

Bev laughed. "No, just look out for my car. Silver BMW. I'll be there about ten to."

They said goodbye and Rosie clicked off her phone. Well, there was one woman who certainly didn't waste time. She lay back on the bed again. Her headache seemed to be getting worse. Glancing at her watch, she saw that it was nearly eight thirty. Perhaps she was overdue an early night; after all, she needed to be in good shape for tomorrow. She scribbled a quick note to Cassie telling her about the day's events and her forthcoming meeting with Bev Carradine. Leaving it on the kitchen table, she took a couple of painkillers and went to bed.

She awoke early next morning and was relieved to find that her head had cleared. She showered and spent the next twenty minutes experimenting with outfits, eventually opting for a skirt suit in soft grey, pinstriped with baby pink. A pale pink blouse complimented it perfectly. She felt quietly confident as she left her room and went downstairs for breakfast.

The kitchen was bathed in soft, golden light. The morning sun had filtered its way through the closed cotton curtains, their pale colour serving to diffuse the rays and give the whole room a brightness which was tinged with optimistic promise. Because of the earliness of the hour, a lovely stillness seemed to brood over the house. The only sound was that of morning birdsong coming from the garden. Rosie suddenly thought of Beth and smiled to herself. The more time she spent at Oak Lodge, the more she understood about her friend. This place had been built into her very being from birth. Its seasons, its moods; its stillness and its happiness. No wonder Beth had been such a together kind of person. No wonder she had come back here to die. This house felt to Rosie like the next best thing to heaven, if such a place existed. As she chomped thoughtfully on her cereal, she couldn't help feeling that it did. And that Beth was there. A sudden ache filled her. How she would love to tell Beth about all this. That she'd moved up to Yorkshire. That she was living in *her* house with *her* family. That she was going for an interview in a school just up the road. She could imagine Beth screaming with laughter at the irony of the whole thing. How Rosie wished they could have shared it together. A single tear trickled down her cheek, but she quickly brushed it away. She could almost hear Beth's voice telling her off. *You've an interview to go to, girl. Don't you go messing up your mascara!*

She shuffled in her chair and took another mouthful of cereal to try and distract herself. But she couldn't stop the thought that rose up from her heart.

Jesus ... if Beth's with you, please tell her about it all. I'd really like her to know. And tell her I'm missing her.

Ed came downstairs at half past seven. Rosie was all ready to leave the house. When he saw her, he smiled admiringly. "You look very smart, Rosie. Very smart. I'm sure they'll be bowled over with you."

Rosie grinned, a slight shyness creeping over her. "Is Cassie awake yet?"

Ed shook his head. "She's fast on, bless her. That massage thing must have done somethin'. She's not been sleepin' right for months. This must be the latest she's stayed in bed for as long as I can remember. She wanted to get up and see you off this morning, but I thought I'd leave her asleep. You don't mind, I hope?"

Rosie smiled. "Not at all. I'll catch up with her later. I'll have more to tell her then."

At quarter to eight, Rosie found herself standing outside Saint Edwin's. Five minutes later, a silver BMW drew up at the side of the road. The driver opened the electric window.

"*Rosie Maconochie?* I'm Bev Carradine – Paddock Hill Primary." The woman looked to be in her early fifties, smartly dressed with short, well-cut dark hair.

Rosie presented her best smile as she opened the passenger door. Suddenly, she felt nervous.

The older woman extended a hand and Rosie shook it. "We can have a little chat as we drive, Rosie," Bev said cheerfully, pulling out onto the road. "Tell me about yourself."

Rosie told her about her work at the nursery and the qualifications she'd obtained whilst working there.

"What made you decide to move up to Yorkshire?"

Rosie could tell from the innocence of Bev's tone that Paulette Sharp had not filled her in with any of the details about Beth. She explained the situation as briefly as she could. "It seemed the best thing to do," she concluded. "To be near my brother while he gets over things. Besides, I was getting ready for a change." She decided not to mention the fact that just before her move she'd felt close to cracking up, and that Cassie's invitation had been something of a lifesaver.

Bev was sympathetic. "I'm sorry to hear that, Rosie. It's very sad with someone so young."

An awkward silence filled the car for a moment or two. Rosie decided to change the subject. "I hope your member of staff's recovering from their accident?"

Bev groaned. "Yes. Yes, she is. But it's going to be a while before she's fit for very much. Parachute jump ... need I say more?"

Rosie winced. "Ouch. She'll make a full recovery, I hope?"

Bev nodded with a smile. "Oh yes. You can't keep a good woman down. Lydia always manages to bounce back."

Rosie suspected this wasn't the first of Lydia's mishaps. "Pity she didn't manage to bounce on this occasion, eh? She'd have saved herself a few broken bones."

Bev threw her head back and laughed. "Good one, Rosie."

The atmosphere was relaxed as they travelled the rest of the way. Bev explained the situation in Helen Walker's class. "It's a Year Three group – a class of twenty-four. Unusual in a village school. Our class sizes are generally smaller. Must have been something in the water the year that little lot came along."

Rosie smiled to herself. She was already warming to Bev Carradine.

"Anyway," Bev continued, "as if that wasn't bad enough, we have a new child in class that needs more or less constant supervision."

"Statemented?" Rosie interjected.

Bev shook her head. "No. Apparently she was fine at her last school. But her parents recently divorced. Six weeks ago the mother moved up here with her new partner and it seems the child has been very unsettled since. Refusing to talk, bouts of crying, a couple of aggressive behaviour incidents – one day she even tried to run away from school. Since that episode, Lydia Vardy hasn't let her out of her sight. Until now of course, with the accident and everything. Poor old Helen Walker's had an awful time of it this week. I've had to move one of our volunteer parent helpers into that class. But she can't be there full time. It's a difficult situation."

Rosie nodded. It certainly sounded it. But it sounded like a challenge too. She'd spent the last few years playworking with preschoolers and caring for little babies. It had been fun, but she was ready for something new. And as Bev pulled into her parking spot at the front of Paddock Hill Primary, Rosie knew she wanted this job very much.

Bev called Helen Walker into her office to meet Rosie. As Bev made coffee for the three of them, Helen and Rosie chatted together, covering much the same ground as had been discussed in the car. At just before half past eight, Rosie noticed the other two women exchange glances as if in a secret understanding. Then Bev leaned forward at her desk. "If you've nothing else arranged, Rosie, how would you like to spend some time in Helen's class this morning? Just sit in and observe for a while. It might give you a better feel of the place – help you get to know the children a bit.

Perhaps let you see what you'd be letting yourself in for if you join us."

Inwardly Rosie glowed. This was looking positive. "Thanks. I'd like that very much."

Bev gave a satisfied smile. "Good. That's settled then. Registration's at eight forty-five. We don't have assembly until after lunch on Thursdays, so Helen will be getting straight into teaching this morning." She checked her watch. "Eight thirty – go to it, ladies!"

Rosie took a seat in a back corner of the classroom. It wasn't long before earlycomers began to drift in. Some of the boys eyed her with slight suspicion, discussing the intruder in low, conspiratorial whispers as they made their way to a small cloakroom which adjoined the front end of the classroom. The girls seemed a little more welcoming. Some of them viewed her with wide, curious eyes, while others smiled at her shyly. Rosie found the experience rather amusing, if slightly disconcerting. These children might only be seven or eight, but they were a whole lot different from the age group she was used to working with. She was glad when Helen called the class to attention.

"Right, Class Three! This morning we have a visitor. She's going to be spending some time with us and watching how well we do our work. So I want you all to try very hard to show her what a lovely class we have here. Now we're going to say good morning to her. Her name is Miss Maconochie." Helen flashed a quick grin at Rosie, then signalled the children to stand to their feet.

"G-o-o-d m-o-r-n-i-n-g, M-i-s-s M-a-c-o-n-o-c-h-i-e!" Their slow, singsong voices made Rosie smile. But she was impressed that they'd actually managed to get their tongues around her name. That had to be a good start. She stood to her feet and greeted them in return.

The day began with Literacy Hour. As Helen taught the first part of the lesson from the front, Rosie discreetly looked round at the children. So far, there was no obvious indication of the problem child. She suspected one or two of the boys might be a handful, but Helen didn't let situations develop. At one point, she stopped teaching and turned to a chubby boy with sandy hair. "Josh – I was hoping we might have a better day than yesterday. Now I won't have you spoiling lessons for everyone else. If I have to tell you off again, I'll send you to Mrs Carradine." There wasn't another murmur from Josh for the rest of the morning.

After Literacy came Science. Helen invited Rosie to walk about the classroom and look at the models the children had been making. It was on her way round that Rosie spotted a small, pale-faced girl who seemed very much cut off from the children around her. Rosie stopped at her table and smiled. "Is this your model? It's very good."

The child stared up at her, and Rosie couldn't help noticing a dark emptiness in her eyes. The chair next to the little girl was vacant so she sat down at her side. Suddenly there was no doubt in her mind that this was the pupil causing much concern in Helen's class right now. But she could see that helping her wasn't going to be an easy task; in the half-hour that followed, not a single word passed the child's lips. The other children on the table came to Rosie's rescue, chattering enthusiastically and showing off their models with pride. By breaktime, Rosie felt as though she'd been accepted. But she was also beginning to recognise the challenge ahead of her. This little girl was going to be a hard nut to crack.

When the bell went, the children filed out of the classroom and disappeared into the playground. All except for one. Helen came over to Rosie. "Well sussed," she said in a low voice. "Thanks for watching her." Then in a louder tone she added, "Miss Maconochie – this is Molly."

Rosie put a hand gently on Molly's shoulder. "Hello, Molly. We've been getting to know each other already, haven't we?"

The little girl flinched slightly. Helen shot Rosie a sympathetic glance. It was then that Bev Carradine appeared in the doorway. "Coming to the staffroom for a drink, Rosie?"

Helen nodded encouragingly. "You go. I'll stay here and keep an eye on her. One of the staff will bring me a drink in a bit."

As they walked along the corridor, Bev enquired as to how the morning had gone. Rosie said it had gone well, but she could understand the problems they were having with Molly.

"So ..." Bev asked as they entered the staffroom, "d'you think you can help us out?"

Rosie felt confident that she could.

"Well, there's one thing, Rosie –" Bev's voice was cheerful as she flicked on the kettle and pulled two mugs from a rack. "We break up tomorrow for Easter. That would give you two weeks' grace before we throw you in."

Rosie grinned. "Sounds good to me."

The staffroom was already half full and buzzing with conversation. There were various nods and smiles in Rosie's direction. It felt like a friendly place. At that moment, the door swung open again and laughing voices made Rosie spin round.

"Oh dear," Bev groaned in mock despair. "Our fragile peace is shattered."

But Rosie was completely shocked. "Jonathon ...!"

The grin on Jonathon's face turned to a look of astonishment. "*Rosie?* What on earth are you doing here?"

Chapter 25

"So … you two know each other then?" Bev didn't try to hide her surprise as she looked from one to the other. Rosie was too taken aback to reply. She felt her face colouring up and wanted to kick herself. Her cheeks burned hot as though in silent admission of some secret guilt. Why did he have this ridiculous effect on her?

Thankfully, Jonathon came to the rescue. "We met just before Christmas. But I've had connections with Rosie's family for years – through church." He smiled at Rosie, his blue eyes filled with an expression she couldn't quite fathom. She rolled his words around in her mind. *Rosie's family* … it sounded strange to her ears. Perhaps this was the first time she'd heard the two words together in the same sentence. She shot him a grateful smile and lowered her head, willing her face to cool down.

"Rosie's come to see if she can help us out in Helen's class." Bev spoke matter-of-factly as she turned back to the task of making coffee.

"Excellent!" Jonathon sounded genuinely pleased at the disclosure. "She'd be ideal for it."

But Rosie suddenly had doubts. Hadn't Jonathon blanked her last two e-mails? Short of some technological explanation, his behaviour didn't make sense. And now here she was, about to take up a job in the same school as him. Uncomfortable seemed an understatement.

At that moment the door opened again and one of the receptionists came over with a message for Bev. Bev turned to Rosie apologetically. "Sorry, Rosie. I'm wanted on the phone by someone from the LEA. Will you be alright for a few minutes?"

Before Rosie had time to respond, Jonathon interjected. "I'll look after her. We've some catching up to do anyway."

Bev threw Rosie a wry smile as she turned to the door. "I can always rely on Mr Kirkbride. One of my most dedicated teachers."

They moved to a corner of the staffroom and sat down. Jonathon leaned forward and spoke in a low voice. "I need to say sorry, Rosie – for not getting back to you."

Rosie shrugged. "No worries." Despite her best efforts to appear cool about it, she felt a sudden awkwardness. "I don't have to take the job. Nothing's been decided yet."

Jonathon frowned. "Why, don't you want it? It's a good school, Rosie. You'd be happy here, I'm sure."

"No, it's not that. It's just that –" She broke off, her face beginning to redden again. "I had no idea you worked here. I'd have probably thought twice about coming today if I'd known."

Jonathon frowned again, a half-smile playing around his mouth. "Am I that bad?"

Inwardly Rosie groaned. This was all coming out wrong. "No ... that's not what I meant." Swallowing her pride, she went straight to the point. "I was beginning to think you weren't talking to me. I wondered if I'd managed to upset you or something." She gave a slight laugh to hide her embarrassment.

Jonathon nodded slowly. "I really am sorry, Rosie. Believe it or not, I was actually going to get in touch with you this evening."

If it had been anyone else, Rosie knew she wouldn't have believed it. But somehow, she found it hard to imagine that Jonathon would lie to her.

"I've had an awful lot on ... and I don't just mean school work." He grinned and rolled his eyes theatrically.

Rosie understood that she was meant to read between the lines. "Not woman trouble, I hope?"

He smiled evasively. "You could say that."

"All sorted now?" She tried to sound bright, but it was strangely difficult.

"Getting there. Lauren's staying up in Durham till Thursday, so I'm going to see her this weekend."

Rosie did her best to ignore the disconcerting feelings of disappointment that were pricking her mind. "Taking her Easter egg, eh?"

Jonathon smiled but said nothing. It was an awkward moment and Rosie was horrified to feel her cheeks beginning to tingle with heat again. Before she could think of anything to change the subject, the door opened and Bev walked back in. She quickly bent her face towards Jonathon. "So you've no objections if I take the job then?"

"Rosie, I'll object very strongly if you don't."

She smiled gratefully and stood to her feet. "I'll see you later."

The rest of the morning passed uneventfully and by the time Bev invited Rosie into her office at lunchtime, both sides knew that she was right for the position.

"Are you okay for this afternoon?" Rosie was ready to offer her services.

Bev nodded. "We've a parent volunteer covering for this afternoon and all of tomorrow, Rosie. But we'll start you straight after the holidays. We should have got your CRB clearance through by then."

Back at Oak Lodge, Cassie was delighted with the news. "That'll put you on nicely for now, love. You never know – if they like you, you might find yourself with something permanent."

And later that night, there was a message from Jonathon.

Hi Rosie –
Welcome to the team! I talked briefly with Bev this afternoon and she was pretty chuffed with you. Needless to say, I dropped in a few good words on your behalf ...! You'll enjoy your time at Paddock Hill – we're like a big family. The kids are great and we have some really decent staff. I'm sure you're gonna fit in well. Bev says you're starting after Easter. You can travel in with me if you'd like to – and home again of course.
Good on you for coming up here, Rosie. It was a brave move, but you've done the right thing (even if it means you get to be pestered by me every day).
Probably won't see you till I get back from Durham, but feel free to e-mail. I promise I'll get back to you.
Luv Jonathon.

Rosie shook her head and smiled sadly to herself. *A brave move? Yeah, right.* She scanned through the e-mail again. There was nothing she particularly needed to reply to, and somehow the word 'Durham' seemed to dry up any inspiration she might otherwise have felt. She shut the laptop down and got ready for bed. Two weeks until she was due to start work. What on earth would she do with herself until then?

The next few days passed slowly. Over the course of the weekend, both of Beth's brothers called at Oak Lodge with their families. Everyone seemed genuinely happy at Rosie's decision to move north. Meg and Tammy made no secret of their approval.

"Does that mean you'll stay here forever, Rosie?" Tammy's eyes were wide with expectancy.

"Course she will, silly," Meg jumped in. "Grandma's adopted her now – haven't you, Grandma?"

Feeling slightly embarrassed, Rosie shot Cassie a glance.

Cassie smiled reassuringly. "Rosie knows she can stay here as long as she wants to, sweetheart. She and Uncle Ciaran are part of the family – this is their home. And we're all glad they're here, aren't we?"

The children nodded enthusiastically in reply, and Rosie felt an enormous sense of relief. *Rosie's family.* Jonathon's words came back to her. *Rosie's family ...* . What a warmth there was in those few, small syllables.

Later on, she thought about her brother shut away in his room, locked in his own devastating grief. Did he realise he'd been 'adopted'? Did he know how much Beth's family cared for him, for both of them? She doubted it. Yet suddenly, she very much wanted him to know. Making her way down the landing to his room, she was surprised to hear the sound of a violin playing. Knocking softly at his door, she half wondered if he would answer and was pleased when he opened it. He motioned her to enter, then closed the door after her. She noticed he had put his violin and bow on the bed.

"Heard you playing, Kitch."

Collapsing into a chair, Ciaran threw back his head and stared at the ceiling. "*Playing?*" He spat the word with frustration. "That wasn't playing. I can hardly get a decent note out of it. Everything's discordant –" His voice tailed off, full of quiet despair.

Rosie eyed him with concern. There was something wild about his appearance these days. His dark, curly hair fell almost to his shoulders now, and there was a haunted agony in his handsome features that worried her. She went over to the bed and picked up the instrument. "Course you can, Kitch. Come on. Play something – anything."

But Ciaran shook his head. "No. It's over, Rosie." He clenched his fists as he spoke. "When she went, the music went with her. I don't care if I never play again."

Rosie swallowed hard. She'd never seen him like this. He looked like a soul in torment. "I know you can't see it right now, Kitch," she said at length, "but one day, you *will* start to get over this. It won't always be as dark as it seems now. Perhaps your music will help in some way."

Ciaran shook his head again, his eyes uncomprehending, almost angry. "How can anything help, Ros? She was everything to me. Everything. Nothing makes any sense without Beth. I might as well have died with her."

Rosie's heart skipped a beat. He didn't mean that, surely? But seeing the expression of desolation on his face, she knew that he was serious – at least for the moment.

"Don't say that. Beth wouldn't want you talking that way. She loved you too, y'know. She'd never have wanted you to give up on everything – your music of all things ..."

Her mind went back to the day Beth had told her about the tune she'd been working on as a gift for Ciaran. *'Chant du Rossignol' – something for him to remember me by,* she'd said. Rosie wondered how far she'd managed to get with it in the end. Her death had come so suddenly, so unexpectedly early, she doubted that Ciaran knew the piece existed. She certainly wasn't going to ask him.

"No," she said softly to herself, "Beth would never have wanted you to give up on your music." She hadn't realised she was thinking aloud until Ciaran rounded on her.

"And what would *you* know about it, Rosie?" His dark eyes flashed hot as he glared at her. "You've never been in this position! You've never loved anyone like I loved Beth! Never! So what makes you think you can stand there dishing out your advice like you know what you're talking about?"

Rosie was stunned. In all their lives he had never addressed her with such aggression. She opened her mouth, but found no words came. Ciaran's eyes were fixed on her, still blazing with emotion but now starting to fill with tears. After a few moments he cursed under his breath, then looked away.

Rosie took a step backwards, her own eyes beginning to sting. "I cared for Beth too, y'know." Her voice bore none of the burning passion of Ciaran's. Instead, it sounded thin and small; a strangled tone that she hardly recognised. "Okay, so I might not have felt the same way about her that you did. But she was the nearest thing to family I ever had, other than you. She was like my sister. She said so herself. And I miss her too, Kitch. Just because I keep it inside doesn't mean I don't." She turned from him and headed towards the door. Closing it behind her, she heard the sound of muffled sobbing. But she knew she couldn't go back to offer any comfort. She just wanted to get to her room before she fell apart.

She saw nothing of Ciaran for the next couple of days. He didn't appear for meals and she didn't notice him leaving the house for his usual walks. Afraid of another angry scene, she was wary about visiting his room again. But it didn't stop the dark unease that she felt about him. On Wednesday, just after noon, Cassie stopped her in the kitchen. "Would you take this tray up to your brother, Rosie love?"

Rosie's heart sank. Reluctant to mention to Cassie anything about Ciaran's vitriolic outburst, she dutifully picked up the tray and began to make her way upstairs. But with every step she took, an increasing fear gripped her. By the time she reached his room, she found herself praying he wouldn't answer the door. Giving a couple of light, token knocks, she set the tray down on the landing. In no time at all she was back downstairs in the kitchen.

Cassie looked surprised. "Is he okay?"

Rosie tried to think quickly. "I – I think so. I just left the tray outside. Thought he might eat more if he's left alone. Didn't want him to feel obliged to talk to me if he's not up to it."

Cassie nodded understandingly. "Ed's a bit the same at the moment. Not eating right. Spending hours in his shed. That's how he deals with things, Ed. Throws himself into his painting. It's as if he has to paint the pain out of himself."

Rosie said nothing. She wished Ciaran would do the same with his music. Surely that would be healthier than sitting all day in his room wanting to die. She realised then that Cassie was looking at her.

"And what about you, Rosie? Are *you* alright? Are you managing to work through things – come to terms with all of it?"

The question caught Rosie off guard. With the memory of Ciaran's tongue-lashing still ringing in her brain, the mere fact that Cassie had even thought to enquire was oddly reassuring. She nodded. "Yeah, guess I'm okay. As okay as I can be anyway. And you?"

A sadness passed over Cassie's face in that moment. She slowly exhaled, then smiled bravely. "I'm finding it tough if I'm honest, love. Really quite tough. There's a silence that never seems to go away. No matter how many people are in the house, or how much noise they make. One voice has gone. Gone forever as far as this world's concerned. And I miss that voice, Rosie ... I'd never have imagined I could miss it so much. The silence of that one little voice seems louder than all the noise in the house combined." Tears began to trickle down Cassie's cheeks as she spoke, but she made no attempt to hide them. "I don't know if you feel the same way, love. I just find myself wishing a hundred times a day that she'd walk in through that door and we'd realise it had all been some horrible dream." She shrugged her shoulders resignedly. "Ah well, Rosie. Now you know how I feel at the moment."

Rosie gave a weak smile. Suddenly she missed Beth more than ever.

Later that night she was surprised to find an e-mail from Jonathon.

Hi Rosie –
Just letting you know I'm home. It rained torrentially most of the time I was up there, so I'm rather happy to be back in Ridderch Standen again. How are things with you? You're settled in now I hope. And how's everyone else – Cassie and Ed – your brother? You've all been on my mind recently. I guess this is the time the loss really starts to hit ... now that the funeral's over and all the well-wishers have gone on their way. You guys are the ones left to live with the situation. Please know you're in my prayers (you gave me permission, remember!) I'll be round to see you soon.
Luv Jonathon

Trust Jonathon to hit the nail on the head. He couldn't have been more accurate if he'd been a fly crawling up and down the walls over these last few miserable days. Yet somehow, Rosie conceded inwardly as she sat poised to reply, just knowing he was back in the area brought a sliver of brightness into the equation.

No. 46 CCS June 16th 1917

Still here, Emily, but hoping to leave within the next twenty-four hours. I've had a bit of bother with my left eye for a few days. It was very bloodshot and my vision was quite blurred, so I reckon something had got in it. Some debris I think; hardly surprising if you could have seen the air after the mines went up. It's a wonder we didn't all choke to death.

Anyway, the MO was concerned about it and decided to keep me in until it cleared up. He said he'd had another similar case in that same day – poor chap ended up losing his eye altogether. I think the doctor was eager to avoid that with me if he could. Well, I have to say there's been a big improvement. I'm more or less returned to full strength, I reckon. All ready to go out and be shot at some more ...!

I was given something rather interesting this morning, Em. After breakfast I was having a little walk around when I came across a Welshman who'd copped for it in the aftermath of one of the

Kruisstraat mines. He was in a bad way, poor fellow. He'd lost both legs and a good part of his face, and I could see he wasn't going to be around for long. I tried to give him a cheery smile as I passed his bed, but he signalled me to come over to him. When I did, he turned his head to me and started to say something. It was hard to understand him at first, Em; his mouth was so twisted and distended with his injury. But I eventually understood that he wanted me to look inside his tunic pocket. When I did so, I found one of the brass Princess Mary tins. You know the ones – sent to all the troops who were out here for Christmas '14. You must have seen one, I'm sure. Well, this fellow motioned me to open it. What should I discover inside but a small New Testament. I could tell from his face that he wanted me to read something from it, so I turned to the portion called the Gospel of Saint John. I only knew what to do because I've seen Boxer do the same thing when we've had a burial. Anyway, I read quite a bit of this out to him and he seemed very settled by it (unlike me, I have to say. I felt rather fraudulent, like some bumbling, unqualified padre.) After a little while I told him I'd have to be on my way as I knew the doctor would be on his rounds at any time. Pressing the Bible into the tin, I made as if to put the thing back in his tunic pocket, but he started to wave his hand as though objecting. It was a few moments before I realised that he wanted me to keep it. I was rather touched by the gesture and thanked him, resolving in my mind to visit him later and perhaps read to him some more. This afternoon I went back to see him, but was surprised to find someone else in his bed. I asked one of the nurses if he'd been moved, and it was then that I discovered that the poor chap had died about an hour after I'd left him.

I keep taking the tin out to have a little look. I must say I feel quite honoured to have it in my possession. I'm sure none of the other lads in my platoon will have one – none of us came out here early enough. I know Albert Bandy has though. He keeps his cigarettes in his.

The following day was dull and overcast. Shortly after lunch, Rosie felt an urge to get out for a walk.

"Going anywhere special?" Cassie enquired as she saw her reaching for her jacket.

"Dunno. Guess I'll just go where my feet take me."

Cassie nodded. "Your brother had a walk earlier. I think he's asleep at the moment. I put my head round the door ten minutes ago to see if he wanted a sandwich, but he was fast on."

Rosie couldn't think of anything to reply. Ciaran felt like a stranger to her at the moment. She was embarrassed at the lack of contact between them and hoped Cassie hadn't noticed it. She realised, however, that Cassie was looking at her sympathetically. "He'll come round, Rosie. Time heals, love. I know it's hard at the moment, but he will come round in the end. You just hang on in there."

Rosie looked down at the floor. She knew she didn't want to crack in front of Cassie. Despite Ciaran's recent harshness towards her, she still felt a strong tie of loyalty to him. They'd always stuck together in the past. Somehow it didn't seem right to go telling the tale just because he'd sounded off at her. Biting her lip, she mumbled something in response then headed for the door. Suddenly she knew exactly where she had to go.

A slight breeze had picked up by the time she entered the churchyard. Cutting across the grass, she stepped over the patch of ground where she'd slipped on the frozen leaves at Christmas. Her eyes moved to the war memorial a couple of yards away, and in particular to the name of Private Philip Matthew Bocking. Strange to see that name now. No longer just a bunch of letters chiselled on a stone, some long-dead hero sleeping on a roll of honour. It was as though she'd known him once.

She soon found herself standing by a small mound. It was curiously colourful, covered for the most part by flowers and messages. The blooms seemed to jostle for space on the low hump of earth, and Rosie could see that they formed a kind of floral visitors' book, each contribution telling its own tale of personal loss. Amongst the flower heads she noticed a small, fluffy chicken

– a soft toy left by Meg and Tammy – along with an Easter greeting for Auntie Beth. There was a basket of polyanthuses from Ben and his family, a beautiful arrangement of spring plants from the people of Saint Edwin's, roses from Ciaran, carnations from Ed and Cassie, and countless bunches of flowers in varying states of health or decay. Some of the accompanying message cards were illegible, having been exposed to the inclemency of the elements for too long, but some were still readable. Rosie scanned a few before looking away. The sight of it all made her feel terribly sad. Situated a couple of yards from the plot, however, in a patch of empty ground, was perhaps the saddest sight of all. The large, white arrangement which had accompanied Beth's coffin at her funeral; the one that read – *'BETHY'*. Most of its flowers had turned brown, the odd white head standing out simply because of its rarity. The name could still be discerned, but now there was a pathos about the display. Though the freshness and beauty were gone, it seemed that no one could pluck up courage to dispose of the thing. Perhaps it was the last warm link to Beth. Rosie wasn't sure, but she found it hard to look at it for very long.

"*Why*, Beth?" She spoke into the air. "Why did you have to go and die on us? We were friends, weren't we? Couldn't you have fought a bit harder – stayed around a bit longer? Everybody was rooting for you ..."

The breeze seemed to swallow up her words. It ruffled her hair and flittered through the petals strewn on Beth's grave. Frustrated, Rosie kicked her foot against the ground. Beth hadn't heard a thing. She was gone. And no amount of flowers would ever bring her back.

For some time she stood there, staring down at the tributes. After a while her mind began to blank, until the flowers became a blur before her eyes and she was barely conscious of her surroundings. How long she was there she had no idea. She hardly cared.

The sudden crack of a twig snapped her back to reality. "Hi, Rosie. Cassie said I might find you here."

Rosie spun round to see Jonathon standing there. She quickly tried to pull herself together. "Hi. Just thought I'd come and see my friend." She forced a smile. "Judging by all the flowers, it seems like I'm the only one in the village who hasn't been visiting."

"Doesn't matter, does it?" Jonathon said softly. "Everyone deals with it differently, Rosie. There are no rules to say what you should or shouldn't do. Some people find it helps to visit a grave ... some people won't go within a mile of one. You have to do what's right for you."

In that moment their eyes met. To her consternation, Rosie felt her heart turn over. Fleetingly, she found herself remembering the day Jonathon had taken her in his arms just before she'd returned to London. Now, as he fixed her with his gaze, everything in her wanted him to do it again. She shuffled uncomfortably. "I'm struggling to get my head round it all. My brother's really not handling it. It seems to be destroying him." Just saying the words brought a lump to her throat. "He's talking like he wants to die too."

Jonathon nodded thoughtfully. "That's understandable."

He said no more, but somehow his comment bothered Rosie. *Understandable?* Was that all he could come up with? What if Ciaran went and did something stupid – would that be understandable too?

A light gust of wind swirled around them and she shivered. The momentary chill seemed to connect with a coldness that went so much deeper; that icy, black fear again, tingling through her veins, setting her whole frame on edge with its menacing taunts. Beginning to panic, she cast her eyes around the place in an attempt to distract her mind from the dark whisperings. The sky had brightened slightly, and though the sun hadn't yet managed to pierce through the blanket of cloud, there was now the faintest hint that before the day was out, it might. But Rosie hardly noticed it.

She looked out across the churchyard, at the crosses and the monuments. Some were large and extravagant, others smaller and more humble. Whatever the size, she knew that every one of them represented a person. A person who had once lived and breathed, laughed and loved. Just like Beth. She lowered her head, gulping back a silent sob. It was all too sickening.

As if he could read her thoughts, Jonathon moved closer to her. "Sometimes there doesn't seem much point to it all from where we're standing, does there?"

Rosie shook her head. "I don't think there is. Not when you look at someone like Beth. She didn't even get a decent shot at it. Twenty-four ... what age is that to die?"

"You're right," Jonathon agreed simply.

There he goes again, she thought irritably. *Is he going to agree with everything today? What if I tell him I've decided to jump under a train? Will he just tell me to go ahead?* She dug her hands into her pockets in frustration.

Jonathon kicked at a clod of earth. "You know, Rosie, none of it makes any sense if you take eternity out of the equation. If this short life is all there is, it's a completely futile waste of everybody's time."

Rosie shivered again. Why did the world seem such a frightening place all of a sudden – even with Jonathon right beside her? Up to now he'd always managed to make things feel better. Yet somehow, everything felt different today.

Jonathon bent down and picked up a flower head that had become separated from its stem. The petals were already limp and brown and a tiny insect was crawling around its inner florets. He extended his palm towards her. "Do you think this flower's ever gonna live again, Rosie?"

Rosie stared down at his hand. Was he trying to be smart or something?

Reading her expression, Jonathon smiled gently. "Okay. Pretty dumb question. But there is a serious point to it." He crumpled up the flower head and dropped it to the ground. "A few weeks ago that flower must have looked beautiful. In some hothouse somewhere, growing to its little heart's content. Until someone came along and ... snip!" He scissored the air with his fingers. "It suddenly became a *cut* flower."

On any other occasion Rosie would have feigned a sorrowful response at this point; a quick burst on an imaginary violin perhaps, or a couple of theatrical sniffs. But right now she simply felt agitated. What exactly was he driving at?

If Jonathon had noticed her irritation, he didn't let it bother him. "At first, you wouldn't notice the difference. I guess the florist would shove it in some water, give it a bit of plant food. I dunno, it's not really my thing – but I've seen my mum fiddling about with flowers sometimes. She could make a bunch of dandelions look good in a vase."

Somehow this revelation softened Rosie a little. She let her face relax slightly.

"One thing's for sure though," Jonathon continued. "That flower's on borrowed time now. It may look the part – still even smell nice. But you and I both know the dying process has begun. Within a week – two weeks max possibly – it's gonna be a shrivelled up, wilted shadow of its former glory. And it'll probably stink a bit."

"Sweet." Rosie shrugged miserably. She still wasn't following his thread.

Jonathon looked down at the crumpled flower head again. "It's a bit like us, Rosie."

Rosie arched an eyebrow. "Brown, stinky flowers?"

Jonathon shook his head, smiling. "Once that flower becomes separated from its source of life, it's just a matter of time before the effects start to show. It might look lovely for a while. But there's only so much you can do with something that's effectively dead in the water – if you'll pardon the pun."

"You're forgiven," said Rosie humourlessly.

Jonathon was quiet for a few moments. "Y'know, Rosie, that's pretty much the situation we humans find ourselves in. We were separated from our source of life even before we were born. From the second we come into this world, we're a bit like cut flowers. Beautiful, but on borrowed time. Oh, we bloom and grow for a while. Give us food and water – it's amazing how long some of us can last. We can even look pretty good for a few years. But we all know it's gotta end some time. We're dead men walking."

His words made Rosie feel sick. She looked down at the ground, determined not to let him see it. "Well then," she said at last, "not much hope for us, is there?"

"Now that's just it, Rosie … ." There was a sudden brightness in Jonathon's voice. "There's every hope. Okay, the scenario I just gave was fairly grim, I admit. But let's face it, the picture *is* grim if you strip the whole life thing down to mere biological existence. Like I said before, if you take eternity out of the equation and this short life is all there is, it's a futile waste of everybody's time. When I talked about our being separated from our source of life, I wasn't talking about *biological* life; I'm talking about *real* life, *eternal* life – something that's on a whole new level. Something that never winds down or gets old. It goes on and on and on. More wonderful, more vibrant than anything we've ever imagined. Yet, until we encounter it, we don't even know it exists." He was looking at her intently now. "God's desire for everyone on this planet is that they encounter *him*. That they become reconnected. *He's* the source of life, Rosie. In fact, he's the whole point of our being here." His blue eyes seemed to burn as he searched her face. "Life down here was never meant to be the way we've made it. Pleasing ourselves, looking out for number one. Stepping on anyone and everyone to get what we want. Money, career, possessions – all the stupid stuff we go after. Just filling in our years till we're too old to enjoy ourselves, then ending up in a place like this. Deep down, Rosie, we know there's got to be more to it than that. This life is supposed to be the place where we find God – where we allow him to find *us*. Where we get plugged back into our life source. That's the most crucial, the most vital thing that can happen to any human being. It's what we were made for. Tragically, Rosie, so many people never get to that point. They settle for so much less … shutting him out, right to the end. And then it's too late." He cast a glance across the churchyard as though surveying the evidence of his words. His face became sober. "He doesn't want people to be separated from him, Rosie. That breaks his heart. Can you believe that almighty God would be broken-hearted for such as us?"

Rosie smiled awkwardly. "You're really into all this stuff, aren't you?"

"You bet. There's no better way to live – and there's definitely no other way to die. You don't need to worry about Beth, Rosie.

She got it before the end. What did she say in her letter? *'I believe – I'm gonna live forever.'* That's why she went out so happy." Jonathon's voice softened. "God's always looking for new children, Rosie. He has a father's heart towards his creation. He longs for that connection to be restored."

Rosie's stomach knotted. *A father's heart …?* Nonchalantly, she tossed back her hair. "I wouldn't know about that. My dad left when I was a little kid. The father stuff's a bit out of my experience."

"That's sad, Rosie." Jonathon looked apologetic. "But, y'know, God's a much better father than any earthly father. Wouldn't you like to start over again – with a new dad?"

Rosie lifted her eyes and looked towards the gate of the churchyard. In her mind's eye she could see her mother teetering towards it in her heels. And Mickey, hobbling heavily along beside her. As she stared at the gate, her thoughts went back to another day. A day many, many years before. The day her mum had broken the exciting news. They were moving, she'd announced. Going to live with a new daddy.

As the memory surfaced in her mind, Rosie's throat tightened. She clenched her fists inside her pockets, desperately hoping that Jonathon wouldn't notice that her whole body had gone rigid.

"Rosie …?"

Had he asked her something? Embarrassed, she tried to pull back into the conversation. "Sorry – missed that. I drifted for a moment. What was it you said?"

Jonathon smiled gently. "I was just asking if you were coming to any of the Easter services here. Don't know if Cassie's already mentioned it to you."

Rosie hung her head for a few seconds. She didn't want to dampen Jonathon's enthusiasm, but right now, Easter services were the last thing on her mind. She couldn't very well admit it to him but, dead men walking aside, the whole 'new dad' deal was about the last straw. She could feel her circuits threatening to blow. "Dunno yet. You've given me a lot to think about. Perhaps I need time to process it all, eh?" It seemed a lame thing to say, but it was the best excuse she could come up with.

Jonathon looked at her, his blue eyes filling with concern. He nodded. "Come on. Let's get you home."

Rosie didn't argue. Jonathon's words were resonating in her head. She felt like a cut flower alright. Much more of this and she'd be ready for the compost heap.

Chapter 26

Carlesands June 21st 1917

Well, Emily, here's a surprise. I was discharged by the MO, only to be told that I was being given four days' home leave. An officer came round, looked at my name, rank and regiment, then simply told me to get off home for a few days – 'while you have the chance', he said. His words sounded rather cryptic at first, but before I left the CCS I was beginning to pick up some talk of a big push coming up very soon; a weighty offensive to follow on the back of Messines. Ah well, suppose I'll know all about it soon enough. I won't find out from anyone over here, that's for sure. Sometimes when we discuss things, I find myself wondering if we're talking about the same war, so ill-informed are the folk at home. I have to say, Mother has been very distressed at the reports in the newspapers of the Gotha air raids over London. I think it would break her heart to know how many times a day in the trenches we come close to being bombed out of existence.

I've visited with your family again. Mother accompanied me and we spent a pleasant time talking with your parents and brother. Jack is much stronger, though he still limps painfully and I fear his hearing's been affected. No doubt you'll be able to use the skills you've acquired on the field to help him when you return home. As we were leaving your house, my attention was caught by the sound of a nightingale singing from one of the bushes. I stood for a moment and listened. The last time I'd heard such a sound was just before the Messines mines went up. I think it was a shock to me to hear such exquisite notes rising from the loveliness of a summer garden. My poor brain could hardly take in such a wealth of pleasure. I found myself almost listening for the next shell. In this last couple of years, Em, I've learned to look for beauty in the midst of darkness and despair. To suddenly have so much for eyes and ears to feast on was, for a moment, quite overwhelming. Is that like heaven, I wonder? I hardly know. It seems to me we have learned to live in hell.

Bailleul June 30th 1917

Here I am, back at last with the boys. Our battalion is currently in reserve, stationed at Bailleul, south-west of Ypres. The mood amongst the men is relaxed at present, though it seems I was right about the coming offensive. We don't know yet exactly when it will be, but it seems there is to be a grand push to break out of the salient once and for all. I can't see it happening myself, if I'm honest. We've been here long enough with little to show for it. But I have to say there's a steady optimism in the air since our boys blew up the Messines Ridge. Perhaps it really has been a turning point. I don't know, Em. All I do know is that we're here to follow orders, and leave the responsibility to those at the top. I hope they know what they're doing. We've lasted this long, but who knows when our luck will run out?

In the midst of all our uncertainties, some things never change. The sun still shines in the sky and the larks still soar overhead. There's a bit of a lull in the firing at the moment and we can actually hear them singing. Boxer seems quite inspired by it all. He keeps breaking into song himself. I have to say, he has rather a fine voice.

We visited the shop where Jimmy clicked with the shopkeeper's daughter last year, but it turns out that she's away at the present time, staying with an aunt in Bordeaux. It was plain to see that Jimmy was disappointed, but we soon managed to buck him up. He's a handsome enough fellow. When we all get home there'll be no shortage of young ladies waiting to hear of his exploits, I'm sure. I think it matters a great deal to Jimmy to find himself a wife. But then, that's easy to understand when he's never had a family to call his own.

Poperinghe July 8th 1917

The sense of imminence is growing. More and more men are daily streaming into the area now. Munitions and supplies too – everything's multiplying around us. Quite what's afoot, one can only imagine. And yet, at least for the moment, we're not required to play too active a part in it. We've set up camp in fields just outside Pop. Boxer, Jimmy and I mean to pay another visit to Toc H as soon as we're able. Not as easy as you'd think, Em. We might be in reserve, but the officers are determined to keep our minds on the job. We seem to find ourselves in endless drills or parades, as if there's anything new we need to learn! But I think they fear we'll mutiny like the French if they don't keep us busy.

We did have a break yesterday afternoon. A few of us found a little café on the outskirts of the town. It turned out there was an old piano in the place. One of the boys remembered that I'd once told him I played a bit, and he asked the proprietor if I could have a go. I was reluctant at first, but they all started on at me so in the end I gave in. I soon got into it; in fact it wasn't long before I was taking requests, can you believe? (If I'd charged for each one I could have retired on the earnings!)

We passed a rather pleasant afternoon. Later, as evening fell, we had a stroll around the area. Though we saw plenty of evidence of long-range shelling, the place seemed sufficiently removed from the heat of battle as to give us a sense of relative safety. We could hear the boom of the heavy guns off towards the front, but the air was still warm and there was plenty of light, and somehow we managed to find distraction in our ramble. We talked about things we'd like to do when the war is over. I said I'd like to train a bit more in music – see where that might take me. I imagine the other two think this afternoon's little piano recital has quite gone to my head! Jimmy is fixed on becoming a master baker. He wants to set up his own shop like Mr Egley, eventually employ a couple of boys to do deliveries. Orphans perhaps – like he was when Mr Egley took him in. I can see his heart is set on it. His face lit up as he spoke. We encouraged him warmly of course. The transformation in Jimmy is quite remarkable. In some strange way, I think this war has been the making of him.

Boxer, of course, remains resolute in his determination to become a minister. I happen to think he'll make a very good one.

Rosie flopped back against the pillow. Everything felt exhausting for her at the moment. She'd been ill in bed for five days and this was the liveliest she'd been since Easter Saturday. Worried, Cassie had sent for the doctor. A virus, he'd pronounced, and prescribed bed rest. Rosie hadn't argued. Now it was Thursday lunchtime, and though she was starting to feel slightly more herself, eating was the last thing she felt like doing. She tapped in a quick message to Jonathon. Not least of all to thank him for the Easter egg he'd sent round with Cassie after church on Sunday. "He said he'd like to visit you when you're up to it," Cassie had ventured as she'd sponged her forehead. But at the time, Rosie had been almost deliriously feverish and had barely managed a grunt in reply. Now as she thought about Jonathon, she wasn't sure whether she could handle a visit. Everything in her wanted to see him; yet at the same time, everything in her did not. Since their conversation the week before, she'd felt strangely ill at ease. Some of the things he'd said had struck uncomfortably close to home. It was hard to know how to pick up where they'd left off. At least being ill had given her an excuse for keeping her distance until she got her head round things.

Later that afternoon she got dressed and went out into the garden. It was the first time she'd been outdoors in five days, and as soon as the fresh air hit her she felt that sense of disorientation that often follows a bout of viral illness. She sat on the bench and pulled her jacket tightly round her. Despite the sunshine, there was still a nip in the air, and she felt it all the more keenly for having been so long indoors. As she sat, she listened. To the whisper of the breeze in the trees. To the symphony of birdsong. To the drone of an aeroplane high in the sky, off, no doubt, to some warmer land far beyond the horizons of her own small world. For a moment she found herself wishing she were on it.

"You okay, Rosie love?" Cassie's voice sounded from the back of the house. Rosie turned to see her coming towards the bench. She moved up to make room for her.

"Yeah. Just making an effort to get back into life." She smiled weakly. "I feel so spaced out. Anybody'd think I'd been on the whisky for the last month."

Cassie looked sympathetic. "You've been really poorly, love. It was a nasty bug, whatever it was. Still, you're on the mend now – that's the main thing." She patted Rosie's hand gently. "Let's hope you're ready to start your new job on Monday. We'll have to take extra special care of you, won't we?"

There was such a look of genuine love in her eyes that Rosie had to turn away. How could this woman, who had just buried her only daughter, treat her with such kindness and affection? She'd nursed her through the last few days as though she'd been her own flesh and blood. Rosie's mind struggled to compute it all. She found herself wondering about Ciaran. "How's my brother? He's not caught it, I hope?" The thought of Cassie having to nurse both of them was almost embarrassing.

Cassie shook her head. "No, he's not ill. Not physically anyway. But I think a virus is far easier to tend than a broken heart. There's no medication can touch one of those, Rosie. Only the Lord can bind up the broken-hearted, but I don't think your brother's ready to hear that yet."

Another aeroplane passed overhead just then, the hum of its engines faint but distinctive against the backdrop of springtime sounds. Rosie looked up at it. "Do you think he can sort anything – God, I mean?"

Cassie's eyes widened slightly. "God ...? Oh yes, Rosie. Anything." There was no hesitation in her reply.

Rosie focused her gaze on a flowering cherry tree at the edge of the garden. Swathes of daffodils encircled its base, their pale yellow heads dancing in the soft wind; clustered in front of them, clumps of blue muscari seemed to catch the colour of the sky and thicken it to violet within their tiny petals. Everything spoke of new life, but Rosie felt empty inside

"He didn't sort it for Beth, did he?"

Cassie looked faintly surprised. "Is that how you see it, love?"

Rosie felt a stab of guilt. *Full marks for insensitivity, girl. Maybe you should put it down to the virus. Maybe it's left you temporarily unhinged.* But before she could stop herself, her mouth started speaking again. "I mean – she died, right? You can't really say he sorted that situation. *Can* you?"

Cassie didn't answer straight away. "I suppose that depends on how you look at things, Rosie." She glanced down the garden, her face pensive. "Y'know, when the children were younger, I always used to tell them that I didn't mind what they did in life as long as they followed the Lord and were happy. Ed was the same. We never tried to push them into doing anything. We just encouraged them to follow their dreams and keep their hearts right before God. That was all that really mattered to us. As far as we were concerned, it was up to God where he took them after that. As the boys grew up, they never lost their faith in him. They chose their paths, got married – they always served the Lord. They were easy kids to raise. Now as for our little Beth ... ." Her face broke into a sad smile. "Somehow she was different. I could tell once she hit a certain age that she was going to have to go away before she could come back, if you understand."

Rosie nodded. "I think I do."

"In her mid-teens, I noticed she was starting to drop off church meetings. Suddenly she wouldn't talk about things in the same way she used to. Sometimes she'd leave the room if the conversation got onto God, as though she was uncomfortable. I never tried to force her back, though my heart ached about it all. Then she got her place at music college. I prayed so hard for her, Rosie. I couldn't bear the thought of my little girl out in the big wide world without the Lord. I prayed and prayed she'd find him again." Cassie shook her head sadly. "Oh, don't get me wrong. I was thrilled with the way her career was moving. We were all so proud of her. I'll never forget that night at the Laureate last October – I must have been the proudest mother on the planet." Her eyes began to well with tears. "But beyond all that, Rosie, the thing that still meant most to me was that she find her way back to God." She pulled a tissue from her sleeve and dabbed at her cheeks. "Perhaps if I'd known how it would come about, I could never have prayed. It's a good thing the future's veiled to us, isn't it?"

"You think God made her sick then – to get her attention? Is that what you're saying?" Rosie was suddenly unnerved by the possibility of such a notion.

Cassie shook her head. "You know, Rosie, I don't believe sickness is ever God's design. When Jesus walked on earth, he went around healing people of their diseases. In fact –" There was a sudden catch in her throat. She tried to collect herself. "In fact, I've found myself wondering what would have happened if Jesus had walked into our home during the last days of Beth's life. I can't help thinking she would have still been with us." Tears ran down Cassie's cheeks now. "I don't know, Rosie. Jesus often challenged his own disciples about their lack of faith. Perhaps that's it. Perhaps we have more faith in the power of sickness to destroy us than we have in the power of God to heal us." She shook her head again. "I just don't know, love. I might be getting on in years, but I still have an awful lot to learn when it comes to spiritual things."

"So you *don't* think God made her sick?" Rosie was anxious to clarify the point.

Cassie thought for a moment. "Like I said, Rosie, I don't believe sickness is ever God's perfect design. But I think there's a difference between what God designs and what God permits. The most important thing in Beth's case was that she made her peace with her Maker. In the light of eternity, a human life – whether it spans five minutes or a hundred years – is nothing but a breath, a fleeting shadow." Cassie gulped back a sob. "Beth will understand that now."

Rosie felt bad as she witnessed Cassie's distress. She wished she'd never brought the subject up. Maybe she was being selfish seeking for answers to questions that were far too big. Feeling awkward, she rubbed her hands together as though to warm them.

"You're getting cold, Rosie." Cassie dabbed her eyes as she spoke, her tone bearing no trace of resentment or irritation at Rosie's indelicate probing.

"No, I'm okay," Rosie answered quietly. "It's nice out here. I've been indoors too long."

Cassie didn't argue. She nodded gently and pointed towards the flowering cherry. A young sparrow had landed on a birdfeeder suspended from one of the tree's branches. It grappled clumsily on the footrest as it tried to peck at the seed. Cassie's face relaxed into a smile. "I love watching the birds, don't you, love? I think they have such a lot to teach us."

They watched as another sparrow came to join the first. For a few moments the two tiny creatures broke into a squabble, pecking at each other and flicking their wings as though in territorial competition. Then, just as suddenly, the argument ended and each bird settled on its own rest and began to feed.

Cassie exhaled slowly. "You know, Rosie, I don't pretend to understand everything. I don't know why Beth got sick. I don't know why she had to die, if indeed she had to die at all. All I do know is –" She pointed once more to the two small birds on the feeder. "God's word says that not one sparrow will fall to the ground apart from the will of the Father." She closed her eyes as though seeing the text in her mind. "*And even the very hairs of your head are all numbered. So don't be afraid; you are worth more than many sparrows.*" She turned to Rosie. "Y'know, love – if it had been up to me, things would have been very different. I would never have chosen this path. But then, I don't see the end from the beginning, and my Heavenly Father does. So I leave it in his hands. I know that one day everything will become clear. Until then I simply trust him."

Rosie was quiet. Even in her grief and confusion Cassie portrayed uncommon serenity. Rosie could see that the trust she spoke of was absolutely genuine. It was attractive, enviable. Yet for Rosie, the words *'trust'* and *'father'* seemed frustratingly incompatible.

Cassie reached out and took her hand. "You asked me if God could sort anything, Rosie. And I still say – yes, he can. As I said, I don't always understand him or the way he works. But even in those dark and difficult times, he lets me know he's there; lets me sense his presence, gives me his peace. And somehow that makes everything alright. He's not like anyone you've ever known before, Rosie. Really. He's not like anyone you've ever known."

Rosie's heart ached. Everything in her was longing to believe Cassie's words. It was clear now that both Cassie and Jonathon were talking about the same person. Yet there were so many things that seemed to stand in the way; things Rosie wished she could tell Cassie ... things she'd never told a living soul.

But she knew she never would. She would never tell anyone. And the thought that God might already know about them was almost too much to handle.

By the time Monday morning came round, Rosie was sufficiently recovered as to be able to start work. She still felt slightly fragile but was determined to give the new job her best shot. She'd arranged for a lift with Jonathon the previous evening. Now as they walked into the school together, he put his hand on her arm. "All the best, Rosie. See you at break hopefully." And then he was gone. Was it her imagination or had he seemed a little quiet on their way here? She tried to put it out of her mind as she made her way to Helen Walker's classroom.

Nothing about Molly Guest's appearance suggested she'd even remotely enjoyed her Easter holiday. The child's face seemed even paler than Rosie remembered, and her mournful eyes were underlined with dark circles. She stood in the doorway of the classroom whimpering softly as her mother attempted to push her inside.

"Come on, Molly. We're going to have fun today," Helen cajoled, skilfully concealing her exasperation as she tried to prise the girl's fingers from her mother's sleeve. Rosie felt sorry for the young mother as she watched the scene. The woman was clearly distressed as she uttered apologies first to Helen and then to the child. Helen signalled to Rosie to come over. "Mrs Guest, this is Rosie Maconochie. She's standing in for Mrs Vardy. She'll be keeping a close eye on your daughter. Don't worry – Molly always settles down once you've left."

Looking barely convinced, the mother nodded gratefully, and with a final gentle pull managed to extricate herself from her daughter's grasp. Once the door was shut, Rosie and Helen exchanged glances.

"Looks like we *are* going to have fun today," Helen muttered under her breath. "Boy, am I glad *you're* here."

The first part of the morning went slowly. Molly remained subdued, refusing to speak or write a word. During Literacy, Helen did a tour of the tables to observe how each child was getting on. When she arrived at Molly's table she shrugged resignedly. "Looks like she's having one of those days, Rosie. She used to do this sometimes with Lydia. I doubt we'll force anything out of her today. No point getting your hair off about it ... just do what you can."

Easier said than done, thought Rosie as she watched Molly scribbling agitatedly on a piece of rough paper.

At breaktime, Rosie offered to stay in the classroom and keep an eye on the girl. It was clear that keeping her out of the playground was going to be the best option for the moment.

Helen frowned. "Are you sure, Rosie? I would have stayed in with her myself."

"No, you're okay. Might give me chance to get to know her a bit, away from all the other kids." *Better show willing,* she thought stoically, *seeing as it's my first day.*

But getting to know Molly was no easy task. Despite Rosie's best efforts to engage her in conversation, the girl sat staring at the table, her only contribution to the exchange being the odd shake or nod of the head. About five minutes before the end of break, the classroom door opened unexpectedly. The sound of it made Rosie jump and she spun round to see who'd come in.

"Hi, Rosie. Brought you a drink –" Jonathon's brightness faded as he frowned and nodded towards Molly. "Is she okay?"

Rosie turned again to see the child hunched over, her face pressed down against the table, her arms wrapped around her head.

Jonathon studied her for a moment. "Perhaps it's best I leave you two alone. Just thought I'd bring you a coffee anyway. Catch up with you later."

When Jonathon had gone, Rosie put her arm around Molly's shoulder. "Come on, Molly. What's wrong?" But even as she spoke, she felt the girl's frame go rigid beneath her touch. She withdrew her hand and sat back, wondering how best to proceed. Moments later Helen arrived.

"Everything alright?" She glanced at Molly and shot Rosie a sympathetic look. "Don't worry, I'll hold the fort at dinnertime. I've some work to do anyway. She'll be able to stay in here with me."

Rosie felt secretly relieved. So far, her first day's efforts with Molly had proved nothing short of unfruitful. Suddenly she looked forward to the prospect of escaping the confines of the classroom.

When dinnertime came, she made her way to the staffroom and took her lunch out of the fridge. She spotted a spare seat next to a young woman with bobbed red hair and striking green eyes. "Okay if I sit here?"

The young woman smiled enthusiastically. "Sure, take a seat. You're the new NTA, aren't you? I'm Chrissie. Chrissie Havers."

Rosie introduced herself and they quickly fell into conversation. When she chanced to glance up at the wall clock, Rosie was surprised to see how much of the dinner hour had already passed. Funny; there'd been no sign of Jonathon at all. She made casual mention of it to Chrissie.

"Oh *Jon* –" Chrissie replied breezily. "He does football club on Mondays. Poor guy, he's out there come rain or shine. One of these days his team's gonna go all the way. Or so he keeps telling us." She broke into a chuckle and Rosie smiled too. But secretly, she couldn't help feeling slightly threatened by the familiar tone in which Chrissie spoke about Jonathon. She found herself recalling her own cyber correspondence with him, and realised that in all the time they'd been e-mailing each other, she'd never yet felt at liberty to call him Jon. Moreover, as that realisation broke upon her mind, she found her thoughts going back to the day she'd first come into the staffroom at Paddock Hill. When she'd been standing by the kettle with Bev. When the door had burst open and Jonathon had come in laughing and joking. Of course. He'd been with Chrissie Havers then. It was the red hair Rosie remembered; perhaps the green eyes too. But it had all happened so quickly, it was hard to be sure. Now as she thought about it, Rosie felt strangely upset. She did her best to hide it as the conversation continued, trying hard to stay in tune with the theme of the thing, making sure her smiles and nods came in all the right places. But while her face endeavoured to engage with Chrissie, her mind was a whirl of half-formed notions. The more Chrissie spoke, the more Rosie noticed the flash of her green eyes and the singsong laughter in her voice. It wasn't just that. This girl was nice too. The sort of person you couldn't help warming to, even if you tried ...

Rosie mentally kicked herself. What was the matter with her? So what if Chrissie and Jonathon *were* close? They were workmates, weren't they? Weren't workmates allowed to be close?

The bell went and Chrissie jumped to her feet. "Well, have to fly. Like to be in class before any of my little darlings get there. Been great getting to know you, Rosie. See you later."

As Chrissie hurried out, Rosie went over to the sink to wash her cup. She was disturbed by the thoughts assailing her mind. But then, most things to do with Jonathon seemed to have a way of disturbing her these days. She was so preoccupied, she didn't realise how hot the water was becoming until it scalded her fingers. It was at that moment that the door opened and Jonathon himself walked in. Still dressed in a navy tracksuit, his hair was damp with sweat and his cheeks flushed from being outside. Despite herself, Rosie felt her heart turn over as she looked at him.

"Good game?"

Jonathon grinned. "I think some of them have been overdoing it on the Easter eggs. It'll take a couple of weeks to knock 'em back into shape, I reckon." He flicked on the kettle and pulled a mug from the cupboard. "I'm gonna have to get a move on – I still need to get changed."

Rosie hesitated. "D'you want me to make your drink and bring it down to your class on my way back?"

"*Would* you, Rosie?" Jonathon was grateful. "Year 6 kids are usually okay on their own for five minutes or so, but I don't like to push it. I'll just nip and get out of this gear. Tea, no sugar."

He disappeared and Rosie quickly set about the task. Minutes later she found her way to his classroom. Jonathon seemed to be going through a register and didn't notice her enter. He was half sitting on his own desk at the front, one foot placed firmly on the floor to balance him, the other swinging slightly in mid-air as he straddled the corner of the wooden table. Back in his office-type clothes, his combed, blond hair still a little damp around the edges, he suddenly had all the appearance of a real teacher. It was the first time Rosie had seen him *in situ*. She fleetingly remembered the scruffy gardener she'd originally met in the churchyard. For a moment she wondered if she really knew Jonathon at all.

He looked up as she approached him. "Oh thanks, Rosie. You're a star." As his eyes locked with hers, she felt a flush of self-consciousness. Mumbling a reply, she excused herself and quickly exited the room, hoping beyond hope that none of Jonathon's astute Year 6 kids would notice the deepening crimson of her cheeks as their teacher thanked her for his cup of tea.

The rest of the afternoon went by surprisingly quickly. Helen began a new geography topic and the children were encouraged to share their experiences of foreign holidays with the rest of the class. It was an enlightening session, full of comic moments and childhood observations. Molly, however, remained resolutely taciturn throughout, her expression barely altering as the afternoon ticked by. She seemed in a world of her own, insulated from the cheerful company of her classmates by invisible walls of silence. By the end of the day Rosie felt she'd achieved little. On the way home Jonathon was sympathetic. "You'll get through to her eventually, Rosie. Though I have to say she seems a poor little thing – you're gonna need some patience by the look of it. Perhaps she's one of those kids that struggle to come back to school after holidays. Feel a bit like that myself sometimes." He laughed to himself then turned to her. "I'm absolutely sure you're the right one for the job." He smiled gently before fixing his attention back on the road, but in that moment she saw in his eyes a look she did not understand. More disturbingly, she struggled to understand the effect it had upon her. When they arrived at Oak Lodge, Jonathon pulled up outside but left the engine running. Rosie thanked him. "Am I still okay for a lift in the morning?"

"Course you are. I said so, didn't I?"

It was the gentlest of rebukes, without the slightest hint of irritation or annoyance. But Rosie understood the meaning of it. Jonathon had given his word, and she should relax in that. He wasn't about to let her down.

As she stepped out onto the path, Jonathon called after her. "Any more news of my Uncle Philip? You won't forget to e-mail just because you're gonna be seeing me every day, will you?"

Before she had time to answer, he pulled away.

That night in her room, Rosie opened the diary and flicked through it until she found her page. Keeping a thumb in her place, she leafed through the rest of the notebook. Still some pages to go, but not all that much left now. One thing was sure; Sam's writing didn't make it through to the back cover. She thought back over the last few months. Strange how this dilapidated old book had become part of her life. And strange how the only one to have really shared it with her had been Jonathon. Beth had died long before she'd reached the end. That seemed to Rosie a both sad and ironic thing as she recalled Beth's uninhibited excitement at her unusual find. Funny. The diary had never managed to make Rosie excited. But, in some peculiar, deep down way, she knew it had become precious to her. Now as she looked at it, she wished it didn't have to end. Somehow, scanning the remaining pages of pencilled scribble, she realised there were few conclusions to be drawn. The blank pages that followed on from them seemed pregnant with mournful inevitability, their yellowed emptiness shouting louder than all the vibrant paragraphs Sam had ever penned. She began to type.

Poperinghe July 14th 1917

The three of us visited Toc H yesterday. How good it was to go back, Emily. It doesn't seem at all changed to me (perhaps a few more holes in its outer walls, but nothing too grave). Inside, the atmosphere was just as I remember; charged with cheerfulness and goodwill – a veritable haven for us weary Tommies!

We spent a little time in the library, then afterwards watched some fellows perform a comic play. We laughed till our sides hurt. In fact, Em, I can't remember laughing like that in a long time. For a brief while, it didn't seem to matter that the German army was just across the way. I think maybe our enemies need to laugh too.

Despite the fun we had, Em, I think perhaps the thing that struck me most about our visit this time was the service in the chapel. Even I'm surprised to find that I've begun to warm to such things. When we sang the hymns, I found myself wishing their words could be true. When the address was given, my heart began to be pierced by a slender hope. But the thing that affected me most was to see a group of men – among them our own pal, Jimmy – standing by the little font waiting to be baptised. I don't know that anything has ever moved me like that. Boxer was as happy as any man I've ever seen, and I found myself remembering the day he told me he'd made up his mind to look out for Jimmy. No one would recognise the fellow now. To be honest, I could wish I were more like him myself. Boxer has done an impressive job.

After the baptisms we had communion, and I myself partook of it. I couldn't help feeling that, for me, there was something missing. I'm not like Boxer and Jimmy; I know that in my heart. But suddenly, I find I would rather like to be. To have that same peace and confidence, no matter what happens. Is it because of what I know is coming? Am I simply wanting to believe because I'm fearful about the next big push? Would God view me as a coward for that? I'm sure I can't be on my own in my anxieties. Who knows for how many of us these first communions will prove to have been our last rites?

Rosie's fingers lingered on the keyboard. Poor Sam. He seemed to have as many questions as she did.

Hi Jon ...

She paused for a moment and looked at the shortened name. But it didn't feel right. Sighing in exasperation, she tapped in the rest of the letters.

A bit of bedtime reading for you. It's a wonder I'm not wearing jam jar specs with the size of this writing. One thing's for certain. There can't have been anything wrong with Sam's eyesight.
See you tomorrow
Rosie

That night she struggled to get to sleep. Every time her mind began to sink into relaxation, a mosaic of images seemed to throw itself up on the screen of her semi-consciousness. At first they were mainly images of Molly. Molly clinging to her mother in the class doorway. Molly burying her head in her hands at the sight of Jonathon. Molly sitting mute through a whole class participation session as if in a complete world of her own. But as the night dragged on, other scenes came into play. Confused, interweaving scenes. Battlefields and football fields. Men in khaki singing hymns, Jonathon in khaki accompanying on piano; whilst all around, young boys kicked soccer balls and Helen Walker got annoyed.

What time she finally dropped off, Rosie had no idea. But somewhere on the journey between consciousness and sleep, as her emotional defences settled quietly for the night and her heart came out of its hiding place, a gentle realisation crystallised some place deep in her mind. In a twilight dream, she pictured Jonathon holding a girl with flame red hair and emerald eyes. A girl whose name was suddenly no longer Chrissie Havers, but Lauren. Rosie was too near sleep to give vent to the pain of it all. Yet tonight, there was one thing she knew before she drifted away. Jonathon might belong to someone else. But she was in love with him.

Chapter 27

For the rest of that week, Rosie tried her best to focus her attention on Molly. As the days went by there were slight signs of progress. To anyone else they would have been barely noticeable. But Rosie was sure she sensed a thawing in the child's reserve. By Thursday, she felt it was time to attempt the playground together. They walked around outside, observing the other children as they engaged in various games and activities. Molly stuck close to Rosie's side, her hands thrust in her jacket pockets, her eyes peeking furtively through her untidy fringe. At one point, they came across a group of girls skipping with a long rope. They stopped to watch. A bustling, ruddy-faced dinner lady came over and smiled at Rosie.

"They go through a bout of this every year, y'know." She pointed as two of the girls ran in and started jumping over the circling rope. "I remember when *we* used to do skipping. Surprised it's not gone out of fashion. Kids today seem to 'ave so much else to occupy them."

Molly seemed entranced as she watched the girls. Glancing sideways at her, Rosie noticed the faintest sparkle in the child's usually mournful eyes. In her enthusiasm, the cheery dinner lady blew it.

"Fancy a go, little love? I'm sure the big girls would give you a turn." She made as if to take Molly's hand, but Molly immediately backed up against Rosie, a look of horror on her face. The magic of the moment was gone. The dinner lady shrugged apologetically. Turning to Rosie, she lowered her voice. "Bit on the shy side, is she?"

Rosie managed to conceal her annoyance. Forcing a smile, she took Molly's hand and said it was time they were getting back inside. For the remaining quarter of an hour of dinner they sat in the classroom and looked at a book. Helen came in just before the bell went.

"Are you okay, Rosie? You've hardly had a break all week. I'm sure one of the lunchtime supervisors would keep a close eye on her if you wanted to take twenty minutes out."

Rosie winced. *Yeah, right. Like Mrs Tactful out there. Thanks but no thanks.* She shook her head. "Really, I'm fine. I feel I'm getting somewhere with her at last. Besides, this is the first time she's been out there since before the holidays. I think we can build up her confidence if I stay with her."

It was mostly true. What Rosie omitted to mention was the fact that she was finding it increasingly difficult these days to be around Jonathon. Stupidly, it hurt her to see him talking with Chrissie in the staffroom. Of course she knew now that Chrissie wasn't the real threat. It had always been Lauren. In all the months she'd known Jonathon, Lauren had been there in the background. But Rosie had never *seen* Lauren. It was hard to imagine what kind of woman had managed to capture Jonathon's heart. Yet watching the easy warmth with which he conversed with Chrissie, and listening to Chrissie's bright, engaging laughter, it wasn't hard to make the substitution.

No, Rosie thought resignedly. *Being around Molly seems a much better use of my time.*

On their way home on Friday, Rosie felt particularly quiet. Jonathon tried to draw her into conversation.

"You okay?"

"Yeah. Just tired I guess."

"How's it going with Molly?"

"Better. I think we're getting somewhere."

"I knew you'd do it, Rosie. I had every confidence in you." A slight pause. "I've missed seeing you in the staffroom."

She quickly glanced at him, but his eyes were fixed on the road ahead. She felt a stab of pain at his words. She'd missed *him* more than he could know, but in every way differently to the way he'd missed her. It hurt like crazy.

"Doing anything nice this weekend?" He pulled up at traffic lights and turned to look at her.

Rosie shrugged. "Nothing planned as yet. You?"

The lights changed and Jonathon pulled out. "I'm away for the weekend. Going off tonight if I can throw some things together."

Rosie's heart sank. She tried to sound bright. "To see Lauren?" *Might as well face facts.*

But Jonathon shook his head. "Lauren's just flown to South Africa for three months – research trip. No; I'm off to see my parents."

Aren't you the lucky one? Rosie nodded but said nothing. She didn't want to come out with anything petulant. It wasn't Jonathon's fault that he seemed to have everything. Parents that actually wanted to see him. A doting girlfriend who just happened to be dead brainy too. *Whereas I,* thought Rosie grimly, *could probably disappear from the planet and be gone a fortnight before anyone noticed.* She knew it was self-pity raising its ugly head, but she'd stopped counting the days since Ciaran had blown up at her. *He* obviously wasn't missing her company. And *he* was about the only family she had.

As Jonathon pulled up outside Oak Lodge, he turned to her. Somehow today he looked tired, and Rosie found herself wishing she could touch his cheek and say something to him. Even tired he looked beautiful.

"Have a good weekend, Rosie. Pick you up Monday."

They said goodbye and he drove off. Rosie walked slowly up the path and went into the house. Ed was just coming out of the kitchen. When he saw her, his face furrowed with concern. "You alright, Rosie? You look a bit peaky. D'you want a cuppa?"

"Please. I'll take it up to my room. Think I need a lie-down. This week's really knocked it out of me – don't think I'm back to full strength yet." It sounded plausible, even to her own ears.

She watched as Ed made the tea. His thick fingers and heavy wrists seemed at odds with the detailed and beautiful paintings his hands produced. And yet, she conceded inwardly, like Cassie's, they were special hands. Rugged and gnarled, yet loving. Father's hands.

A few minutes later, Rosie sat by the window in her room and stared out over the garden. It looked pretty in its springtime adornment, as did the sea of farmland that rolled out beyond it. The whole scene was bright and charged with new colour; life after death, freshness after decay. Everything shouted that summer was just around the corner. But as Rosie gazed at the sight, nature's cheerful statement just added insult to injury. Her life was falling apart again. Her emotions had been so wrung out over the last few months, she hardly knew what to expect next. The Jonathon thing felt like the last straw. She was fast coming to the conclusion that getting the job at Paddock Hill had been a huge mistake. Maybe even coming up to Yorkshire had been too …

A horrible wave of loneliness swept over her. She had no idea where she belonged any more. Here she was, living in the house of a couple who were tacitly pretending to be her parents while she went through a rough patch. Her own brother hadn't spoken a civil word to her in goodness knows how long. Her best friend was dead. And the guy she suddenly realised she loved was already spoken for. She didn't have a home to call her own. Even her job was borrowed from someone who'd been stupid enough to bust herself up doing a parachute jump. What did her life count for any more? Had it ever really counted for anything anyway? A surge of anger rose up in her throat and she glared at the sky.

Oh, God! Don't you see anything that goes on? What am I supposed to do with all this mess?

Her hands trembled with emotion as she stared out. At that moment, even a thunderbolt from heaven would have been better than the silence that enveloped her. But nothing changed. The sky was still seaside blue; small patches of cumulus still drifted across it like picture book clouds. Life looked beautiful – and suddenly Rosie hated it like she never had before.

It was over an hour later when she awoke to hear someone knocking lightly on her door. For a few moments she struggled to come round. She couldn't even remember lying down on the bed.

"Rosie? Am I alright to come in?" It was Cassie.

Rosie tried to sit up. Her head and limbs felt heavy, as though she'd been injected with something. "Yeah, sure."

Cassie put her head round the door. "Just letting you know, love, dinner will be about quarter of an hour."

Rosie straightened. "Oh, I'm sorry … I meant to help you with it. I didn't mean to fall asleep." She rubbed the back of her head in frustration. She felt bad at the idea of Cassie waiting on her hand and foot. It was embarrassing. But Cassie didn't seem in the least put out.

"You must have needed it, Rosie. You've done well to get through a whole week after being so poorly."

Poorly? That's just the half of it, Rosie thought gloomily as Cassie disappeared downstairs. She stood up and went back over to the window. As her head began to clear, everything came flooding back. Gulping down the lump of hopelessness that was threatening to clog her throat again, she knew she had to do something. She did some quick reckoning in her head. Twelve or thirteen weeks until school broke up for summer. Lydia Vardy might or might not be fully recovered by then. But that was immaterial. Come July, her own obligation to Paddock Hill would be over. She would get in touch with her old nursery, see if there were any jobs going down there, try and find a little bedsit. One thing was sure; she couldn't stay in Ridderch Standen much longer. She'd imagined that coming up here would be the answer to everything. A little piece of paradise; an impregnable fortress in a lousy world. But now she knew that even a place like this was no defence against the storms that raged inside her own heart. After all, hadn't even Mickey managed to turn up and sully the place with his presence? Surely that should have been a warning. Nowhere was safe. It had all been a fantasy. Oak Lodge had been no more able to protect her than anywhere else. And now with the torment of seeing Jonathon day in, day out, she realised she had no choice but to leave. In fairness to Bev Carradine, Helen Walker, and especially little Molly Guest, she would give the next three months her best shot. After that she was out.

When she'd tidied her hair and straightened her clothes, she made her way downstairs for dinner. She wouldn't say anything to Cassie just yet; that would seem ungrateful. And besides, she didn't want to run the risk of being talked out of her decision. As her foot touched the bottom step, she remembered something else. The diary. She needed to get that finished and e-mailed. After that, contact with Jonathon must be kept to a bare minimum. Journeys to and from school; the occasional exchange in the staffroom. Anything else was too painful.

As she turned towards the dining room, she almost collided with Ed carrying a tray.

"Just takin' this up to your brother."

Before she had time to think, Rosie reached out and took the tray from him. "I'll take it. You go and get your dinner."

Ed shrugged. "Okay, love." He hesitated for a moment. "You might need to bang a bit. He's not so good right now. Just sits there rockin' half the time. Cass goes up to him a lot, but she can't get him to eat much." He turned back towards the dining room.

Rosie felt guilty as she climbed the stairs. She and Ciaran hadn't spoken in almost three weeks. In fact she'd hardly seen him. Just the odd fleeting glimpse of him around the place, the occasional nod if they'd passed on the landing. But even then he'd seemed in a complete world of his own. She wondered if the brother she'd grown up with really had died with Beth. And she couldn't help feeling bad about Ed and Cassie; going through the tragedy of losing their daughter and having to put up with a pair of dysfunctional wrecks living in their home.

She tapped lightly on Ciaran's door. Feeling suddenly awkward, she was tempted to put the tray on the floor and hurry downstairs before he had chance to answer. But remembering Ed's words, she waited a few moments before knocking again. There was a slight shuffling sound from inside the room, then the door opened. Rosie was shocked at what she saw. Ciaran's face was so thin now, she wondered if he'd eaten at all since they'd last spoken. His dark eyes seemed somehow darker, his wild hair wilder. His whole appearance was that of one wretched with grief. She noticed his hands were shaking as he took the tray from her. The sight of him hurt her so much, she wasn't sure whether to smile or cry. She did neither.

"Try and eat something," she muttered in a low voice before turning to go back downstairs.

"Rosie ...!"

The cry was so faint, she only just heard it. She swung round to see Ciaran still in the doorway of his room. He had put the tray down and was standing with his arms hanging helplessly by his sides. As his eyes met hers, he reached out towards her.

"Sorry, Rosie." His voice was hoarse as he clung to her. "I'm just hurting like hell. I'm so sorry."

"That's okay. I'm sorry too." Rosie could barely hold back the tears. As they held each other, she could feel Ciaran's whole body trembling. She was sorry alright. Sorrier than he could know, about more things than he could possibly understand. Right now, she felt sorry for just being alive. Yet somehow, just saying the word relieved a little of the pain.

After a few moments Ciaran loosened his grip on her. "You'd better go for your dinner, Ros." He wiped his eyes on his sleeve. "Thanks for bringing mine up … and for being there for me."

She nodded. "Just make sure you eat it. I'll be checking on you."

He smiled the faintest of smiles. But to Rosie it was like an unexpected birthday present.

Poperinghe July 18th 1917

At last it begins. Our preliminary bombardment started up a couple of days ago, and what a show, Em. There's hardly been a break in the firing since it began – our boys are sending them over thick and fast. It wasn't long, of course, before the German guns took up the tune. So here we are, a right old fight going on and the real battle hasn't even started yet. I don't suppose the Tommies at the front will be getting much of a night's sleep. As for us, we're still back here for the moment, camped just outside Pop. There's a lot of speculation as to when we'll be on the move, but no one seems to know anything for sure. No news yet as to when the offensive is due to kick off properly, but when it does, you can bet the PBI will take the brunt of it.

Poperinghe July 27th 1917

A week on and still here, Em. There's nothing much to report. Still no news of anything definite, though the rumours are that zero hour could be any time now. The bombardment goes on relentlessly and the ground shudders with the force of it. One wonders how, after three years of this, there's anything left to shell.

I received a parcel from home today. There was an embroidered bookmark, three letters – one each from Father, Mother, and Kitty – and a fruit cake that Mother had baked for my birthday. I was glad to receive it, especially as last year's birthday package never arrived. We were at the Somme then, and I can remember wondering if everyone had forgotten me. It wasn't until I went home on leave that I found out that Mother actually had sent me a cake, though I never did find out what happened to it. Blown to pieces probably or diverted by some hungry Tommy. Well anyway, this year's got here safely, and Boxer, Jimmy and I have been thoroughly enjoying it!

Ypres August 1st 1917

Well, the offensive officially began in the early hours of yesterday morning. We've been on the move most of the day and now find ourselves in Ypres. As we get closer to the action, we begin to have some idea of the scale of the push. Ypres is swarming with troops; men like us on their way to the front, and men who have been there throughout the bombardment, now on their way out. They look completely exhausted, much too weary to celebrate that their stint for the moment is over. I could rather envy them tonight, Em. Tomorrow we will be out there, facing who knows what. I can't help feeling anxious about it all, though I could never tell anyone but you. Perhaps it's because I've just had my birthday. I find myself plagued with thoughts that this will be my last. That next year, Mother will have no boy to bake a cake for. Listen to me, Em! How terribly gloomy I sound. Perhaps it's nothing more than this dismal weather that's dampening my spirits. After a steady drizzle in the early part of yesterday, the rain has suddenly become quite torrential. I can't think it will make for easy traversing when we get going tomorrow.

Hooge August 2nd 1917

Weather abysmal today. Earlier, we left Ypres and came along the Menin Road. What a sight met our eyes! The rain has turned the whole front into a sea of mud and we saw men trying to wade through the stuff, up to their knees or higher. At one bit, we passed a provisions wagon and a couple of mules that had got stuck in a really deep patch. It was most distressing to watch, Em. The creatures were struggling to free themselves, their eyes rolling in utter terror. But there was nothing anyone could do to help them. In the end their driver shot them both. When we looked back a few minutes later, there was barely anything left to see. The whole lot had practically disappeared under the mud.

The noise of the firing was simply terrible. From our position on the road we could see the explosions going off all around; no break, no pause – quite, quite merciless. Tramping along, knowing you're heading straight into something like that, is the strangest feeling. Somehow it doesn't seem real. You have to shut your mind off and let your feet carry you forward. You can't afford to think about it too much. Neither can you get windy or give in to your nerve. That would be disaster. No; each man must do his best, as he expects everyone else to do. Though after the scenes we've witnessed today, Em, I think we all feel exhausted and dispirited already. I can't imagine how we're supposed to win a war in these conditions. Still, I suppose we have the consolation of assuming that the Germans are in the same stew.

August 3rd 1917

We're part of reinforcements moving up towards Glencorse. Rain and more rain. At this rate we'll be swimming the rest of the way.

Sanctuary Wood August 8th 1917

Weather's dry at last, though I think it will take some time before the ground begins to recover. Still pockets of flood water all around, compounding our discomfort. This place has been shelled so many times, it's little more than a quagmire anyway. 'Wood' is far too grand a name for it. It's hard to imagine the green and pleasant sight it must once have presented. Now it's mud and holes, skeletal trunks and ripped off branches. Hardly the place for an afternoon's outing. Still, at least now that the sun's out we're not cold and dripping wet all the time. We're expecting to see some action soon.

Sanctuary Wood August 11th 1917

I spoke too soon. The heavens have opened once more and we're soaked to the skin again. Of course I'm sure that will make little difference to the overall battle plan. After all, the chaps doing the planning are hidden away in their nice, dry headquarters. What would they know about standing up to their thighs in shell holes full of water?

Soon there is to be an attempt to take Glencorse Wood. No mean feat when we hear how stiffly fortified it is. Already today I narrowly escaped being ripped to pieces by a shell fragment which found its way over here. It came whistling down within a yard of me. The fellow behind me wasn't so fortunate. It sliced him in two – right across, just under the shoulder blades. When I looked at his severed head lying in the mud, his face still bore the most awful look of surprise. I confess I felt quite sick for a moment, Em. I begin to think there's little chance of our coming out of this.

Sanctuary Wood August 13th 1917

Emily, I am more sick at heart than I can say. Jimmy is dead. Our own pal, Jimmy. I can hardly bring myself to believe it. It happened on a burial party of all the wretched ironies. We've had a fair number of losses recently with things being so lively in the area. Albert Bandy had sent a few of us out to see to the poor fellows who'd copped for it. It's a rotten job at the best of times, but I have to say, it seems rather pointless in our present situation. What with the mud and the shelling, a body's not in the ground two minutes before it's blown out again. It's quite terrible. Even the mud itself seems to ooze with blood. It's a good thing the folk back home don't see the vile indignity of it all.

Well, this is how it happened. At just after ten o'clock we were right on the edge of Sanctuary Wood, between the wood and Stirling Castle, when we came in for some very heavy shelling. We'd just dug a hole to bury a fellow when there was the most tremendous explosion and I found myself absolutely covered in thick sludge. I was so stunned, I remember thinking, 'Well, no doubt that's ruined all our night's work'. But when the smoke cleared, I could hear Boxer yelling to me. Jimmy had taken a bad hit and was bleeding profusely from a stomach wound. We managed to drag him about a hundred yards or so until we found a little mound to hide behind. There were no stretcher bearers to be seen, and there seemed little point in trying to shout for one because it was obvious Jimmy was slipping away fast. Boxer cradled Jimmy's head in his arms and started to say something to him. I couldn't quite make it out at first because of the din, but when I bent closer I heard him saying these words – "When my father and mother forsake me, then the Lord will take me in". He just kept saying it over and over again. Jimmy lay there staring up at us as the lifeblood spilled from his wound. I'll be honest, Em, I felt like crying. But do you know, as Boxer spoke, I began to see a faint smile on Jimmy's face. When his eyes started to flicker and we knew it was all but over, Boxer bent very close to him and said, "Soon be home now, Jimmy. You'll soon be home." And then he was gone.

We dug a hole behind the mound and buried him there. Boxer did a little service as I've seen him do so many. But this was very different. How could we have known we'd be burying our own mate before the night was out? Both of us were quite heartbroken, and it struck me that this was perhaps the first time that anyone had shed tears for Jimmy. The thought affected me with great sadness.

Somehow we managed to carry on with our dreadful task, though I don't know how. Before we left to go back, I went to check that Jimmy's grave was still intact. It was – but who knows for how long? I can't bear to think of him being shelled out of it. I wondered if we should have buried him further back. Boxer seems to take a rather different view of it all. He tried to reassure me and told me I shouldn't fret; that God had sent his angels to collect Jimmy the moment he closed his eyes. His body, he insisted, was nothing more than a pile of old clothes now.

Of course, I realise that what he says is sound common sense. But Jimmy was like a brother to us, and I think that knowing we're the only family he had, I feel a sense of responsibility towards him.

It's almost three in the morning now and I'm more miserable than I can ever remember. We've a big one coming up soon, and I feel sick with unhappiness. I don't know that I have any fight left in me.

Rosie had no idea how long she'd been there. An hour – maybe two? Her eyes stung from squinting at the tiny writing and her neck was knotted with the effort of her concentration. She stretched for a few seconds then looked back down at the notebook. There was only one more entry. Her eyes strayed across the first few words but then she flipped the book shut. Somehow in that moment, she didn't want to know how it ended. One thing she felt sure about. There would be no happy ending. Nothing ended happily; she knew that now. Jimmy hadn't lived to find himself a wife. Ciaran had found one, only to lose her again within the space of a few years. She tapped in a brief message to Jonathon then closed down her computer. For the rest of the evening she did little more than watch telly.

Jonathon didn't mention the diary as they drove to school on Monday morning. Obviously he hadn't checked his e-mails since getting back from his weekend away. Rosie decided not to mention it either.

"You've had your hair cut," she commented, just for something to say.

Jonathon grinned. "My mum does it for me. She always half scalps me, bless her. It'll be alright in a few days."

Rosie pretended to go along with his self-ribbing. In truth, she thought it made him look more handsome than ever. His blue eyes seemed bluer and the line of his jaw smoother and more defined. Her heart hurt at the sight of him, but she steeled herself not to let it show. "Football club today?"

"Yep. One of these days we're gonna surprise everyone and bring home a cup."

Rosie nodded. *According to Chrissie Havers, so you keep saying.*

When she arrived in the classroom, Molly seemed to be waiting for her. As Rosie approached the table, the child bent forward and slightly moved the empty chair that was next to her.

"Thank you, Molly. That's very kind of you." Rosie sat down, touched by the little girl's gesture.

Lessons during the morning went well, and though Molly didn't participate vocally, she seemed to listen attentively. Rosie was pleased to see that the pieces of work she managed to produce were of a good standard. Towards noon the weather broke and it began to rain. While the rest of the class went off to the dining hall, Rosie and Molly ate their packed lunches in the classroom as usual. But it wasn't long before the other children began to drift back in. It was too wet to go outside. Helen Walker came in looking flustered. "Just what I didn't need today," she growled. "I had some lesson planning I needed to do."

Rosie thought for a moment. "Perhaps we could get them all to draw something ... give them coloured pencils or crayons. Make it like a competition – maybe give a little prize to the child we feel has put in the most thought. I could sit near the front with Molly and supervise everybody. And you could sit in a quiet corner and get on with what you need to do. So long as they behave themselves you don't have to get involved."

Helen smiled gratefully. "Are you sure, Rosie? You do seem to be working above and beyond the call of duty this week."

Rosie grinned. "How hard can it be?"

While Rosie was settling Molly at a table near the front, Helen addressed the class. "Right everybody, Miss Maconochie's going to tell you what you'll be doing. I'll be working at the back, so it would be lovely if everyone could be nice and quiet." She winked at Rosie and Rosie stood to her feet.

"Okay. I'd like you all to draw a picture; it could be a person, or a place, or an object. It could be something that makes you happy, or sad – or scared or excited. Anything that's special or important to you. You can use colours if you like, but you don't have to. Just think about your picture for a few minutes, then see what you can do. We'll collect the pictures in and have a look at them. Tomorrow, the child we think has tried the hardest and put in the most thought will win a bar of chocolate."

If she'd had any doubts about the bargaining power of the potential prize, she needn't have worried. A buzz of excitement ran around the classroom. As she handed out the blank sheets of paper, Rosie couldn't help smiling to herself. Had there ever been a time when the prospect of a bar of chocolate would have affected *her* with the same cutthroat determination to win. Had she ever been so young? If she had, it seemed an awfully long time ago.

Later, when school had finished, she laid the pictures in rows across the class tables and studied them with Helen.

"A lot of effort has gone into these," Helen commented ruefully. "How do we pick a winner?"

Looking at the collection, Rosie was beginning to wish she'd never come up with the idea. Though it was clear that some children were significantly more artistically gifted than others, the prize had been offered for the most thoughtfully produced picture, not necessarily the most aesthetically impressive. And, Rosie had to concede, despite the young age of the artists, almost all the subjects were at least identifiable. This decision wasn't going to be easy. At that moment the door opened. It was Jonathon.

"Hi, Rosie. Just came to see if you were ready."

Helen seized the opportunity. "Jonathon! Just the person we need. Be a love and tell us which one of these you think deserves a prize."

"The one that shows the most thought," corrected Rosie.

Jonathon looked over the pictures for a while. "What's the prize?" he asked at last.

"Chocolate bar."

Jonathon nodded. "D'you know what I'd do? I'd award first prize to this one –" He leaned forward and picked up a brightly coloured picture of a seaside scene. "Because it really is brilliant. But I'd buy a couple of bags of snack-size chocolate bars to share round everyone else. Looking at these, I think they've all tried hard."

Rosie smiled wryly. "Very diplomatic."

"Very expensive," retorted Helen. "You and your bright ideas, Kirkbride. Good job I haven't got a class full of kids with allergies."

Jonathon grinned. "Just telling you what *I'd* do."

Rosie began to collect up the pictures. "Sounds fair enough to me. Don't worry, Helen, I'll buy the extras seeing as it was my idea to do a prize."

Helen pulled a face. "I'll go halves – so long as you promise not to do it again."

That night as she lay in bed, Rosie went back over the day. Her mind teemed with a riot of coloured images; characters and scenes of every description, a collective cornucopia of favourite things. Or not so favourite in some cases. Her thoughts went back to one particular picture. One she hadn't managed to get out of her head. Helen hadn't seemed to notice it. And if Jonathon had, he hadn't said anything.

It had been a simple enough drawing; in many respects typical for the age group. Four people. A man in a turquoise outfit, brown hair, smiley upturned mouth. A woman with huge, blue eyes and yellow hair, flicked up at the bottom. Between them, in a pink dress, a smiling little girl with stick arms and legs. And towards the far edge of the paper, a second man; dressed in black, with black dots for eyes and a straight line for a mouth. In the top corner, in oversized letters, the picture was signed *'Molly Guest.'* But Rosie could have picked it out without its signature. She felt terribly sad for the little girl. Family divided. Uprooted from home. Forced to share a house with a man that wasn't daddy. Poor little kid. She knew how it felt. Maybe she could get Molly to talk about her picture; at least get some of her feelings out in the open. Resolving to try, Rosie soon fell into a fitful sleep.

"Got your snack bars?" Jonathon asked as she got into the car next morning.

Rosie patted her bag knowingly. "Wouldn't dare go without them. Helen's given me the job of announcing the winner."

"Perhaps my suggestion will save your skin then."

It was raining heavily and Jonathon seemed to be concentrating hard as they drove along. They lapsed into silence. For a while, the only sounds to be heard were the drumming of raindrops on the windscreen, the hum of the engine, and the swish of the wipers on full speed. Rosie stared out of the window at the bleary countryside and stifled a sigh. Whenever she was around Jonathon these days, her heart ached. She found herself longing for the end of term.

"Hey, thanks for the e-mail by the way. Didn't open it till last night." They were about five minutes from school and Jonathon was leaning forward as he tried to focus his gaze through the driving rain. "Poor old Jimmy, eh? I was gutted about it."

Rosie breathed out slowly. This seemed as good a time as any to tell him. "There's only one more entry."

Jonathon shot her a split-second glance. "Really?" He didn't attempt to conceal his disappointment.

Rosie tried to pretend she hadn't noticed it. "Don't know if my eyesight will ever be the same again. It's been hard work."

Jonathon didn't reply. He looked thoughtful as they continued their drive. When they pulled into the car park, he switched off the engine and turned to her. "You've done a great job with it, Rosie. Beth would have been proud of you."

There was a gentleness in his eyes which turned her insides over. Why did he have to look at her like that? It hurt so much, it made her want to cry.

He smiled encouragingly. "D'you think your eyesight will hold out for the last bit? I've got my own little folder set up now. I've even been doing a bit of reading up on the history of it all. Been quite a journey, hasn't it?"

Swallowing the ache in her throat, Rosie returned his smile. "Yeah, guess it has. I'll get it to you soon as I can."

Chapter 28

Sanctuary Wood August 14th 1917

In the aftermath of Jimmy's death, I find myself disheartened and depressed. The rain continues, the ground becomes more impassable, and the battle goes on. Soon we'll be getting into position for an attack on Glencorse Wood. All the signs suggest it's to be in the next day or so. Despite the rain, I think there's little chance of it being called off.

I haven't been back to Jimmy's grave. I cannot bear to. Even though it's less than two days since we buried him, I dread to think what I would find. The activity has been so fierce, I fear even the dead will have been dragged back into the fray. I wonder if it's time for me to face what I can only think is the inevitable ...

Sam looked around him. Every man was filthy; caked in mud, uniforms hardly recognisable. It made all the parades of the past seem utterly futile. Pointless, idealistic exercises, a world apart from the true state of things. *This* was the reality of war. Drenched, bespattered men sheltering in trenches that were no more than muddy ditches. Weapons so dreadful, they could dismember a fellow in a split second without even wiping the smile off his face. The wounded drowning without trace in a sea of slime that had the cheek to call itself a battlefield. It had all seemed so glorious once upon a time.

"Sam?"

Sam blinked. He hadn't realised Boxer was talking to him. "Ugh? Sorry. I was miles away."

"So I could see, mate." Boxer smiled. "Listen, I've been thinking. You know we said we should write to Mr and Mrs Egley to tell them about Jimmy? Maybe we should do it today. With the attack coming up, I mean. Y'know, just in case –"

He didn't elaborate but Sam understood perfectly. Just in case they were next. He nodded absently and looked down at the sodden ground. Following the logic through, the whole thing was insane.

Boxer frowned gently. "Cheer up, it was only a suggestion. I'll do it myself if you like."

Sam felt suddenly agitated. "Doesn't it bother you, all this? All this waste. Knowing we're probably gonna cop for it any day now. What point has there been in any of it? How many friends have we seen go down? And for what, Boxer? Just to gain a few miserable yards of swamp. It's enough to send a man out of his mind."

Boxer's face became grave. "I can't make any sense of it either, Sam. Not if I look at it like that. So much of what men do is pointless. Pointless and painful."

Sam felt an ache in his heart. It seemed like his life was ebbing away already. He would probably never hold Emily in his arms now. The odds were stacked so steeply against them; tales of horror from Glencorse were the talk of the place. He might as well stop kidding himself. All he could hope for now was a nice, clean bullet to put an end to this unknowing once and for all.

"Sin has reaped a terrible harvest," Boxer continued quietly as if to himself. "A horrible, terrible harvest. Ever since the garden of Eden."

"Sin?" Sam looked at him blankly. "Garden of Eden? You really believe all that Adam and Eve stuff?" He shook his head incredulously. It certainly wasn't the first time Boxer had talked about such matters. In the past Sam had always listened to his friend's religious ramblings with a mixture of politeness and genuine interest. There had even been times when Boxer's words had caused Sam to search his own soul. In the light of their present dire situation, however, Sam couldn't help feeling irritated. It seemed to him unreasonable that Boxer should use the occasion to bring up fairy stories about apples in gardens.

But there was no hesitation in Boxer's reply. "Course I do. How else do you explain the mess we're in? You don't think God intended the world to be like this, do you? All this suffering and sorrow?"

"Can't really see what it has to do with Adam and Eve." Sam didn't bother to hide his vexation.

Boxer was unperturbed by it. "It has everything to do with them. This thing goes right back to the beginning. When God made Adam, he gave him a command. Just one, Sam. One tree whose fruit he wasn't to eat. God was quite clear when he gave the instruction. He warned Adam exactly what would happen if he disobeyed."

Here we go, thought Sam. *Just what I expected – apples in gardens.* He decided to humour his friend. "Maybe Adam thought God was holding something back from him. I used to feel the same way when my mother baked scones and wouldn't let us touch them till we'd had our dinner. Didn't stop me. If I knew cabbage was going to be on the menu, I'd sneak one upstairs and hide it under my pillow."

Boxer looked at him patiently. "D'you remember when we first became soldiers, Sam? When we were warned never to stick our heads above the parapet when the bullets were flying? There's always that temptation when things suddenly go quiet, isn't there? That curiosity to find out what's happening. Just a quick glimpse over at the enemy lines. Until the sergeant's words echo in our minds and jerk us back to our senses. He's not trying to spoil our fun. He's trying to stop us getting our faces blown off. Just be glad your mother never came up with an exploding scone recipe."

Despite himself, Sam had to smile at that one.

Boxer ran a muddy hand across his forehead. "D'you get the point, Sam? Adam thought he knew better than his maker. When he went against God's command, his rebellion triggered a chain of events he could never have dreamed of. In one swoop, sickness, sorrow and death came into the world. Oh, God had warned him what would happen, but Adam paid no heed. And it wasn't long before his children began to follow in his footsteps. One of his sons had murdered his own brother by the fourth chapter of the Bible." He shook his head sadly. "Look at history, Sam. The thing has got bigger and more destructive down each new century. But did we ever imagine we'd witness anything like we've seen since we've been out here?"

Sam didn't answer. How could anyone have imagined it? It went beyond the mind's ability to grasp.

Boxer closed his eyes for a moment. "Y'know, Sam, the Bible asks us the question – what causes wars and fights among us? And it gives us the answer. It's the selfish desires that rage within us. Mankind has forgotten God. It's every man for himself. That's what sin has done to us. Sin is the most fatal sickness this world has ever known."

Sam was annoyed at himself that he couldn't argue the point. Boxer might have some strange notions, but Sam couldn't come up with a better explanation for the brutal carnage that was all around them. A shell screamed through the air, exploding some two hundred yards from their position. Sam felt numb. Usually when they started dropping close, his heart would begin to pound with nervous adrenaline. But not today. Today his heart felt like a lead weight, like that of a man who had begun to die already. The mud squelched beneath his feet as he turned to face Boxer. "If what you're saying is right, things are never going to get any better. That means this whole war really has been a waste of time."

Boxer looked thoughtful. "There *is* a cure, Sam."

"Cure? How d'you mean, *cure?*"

"When I said sin was the most fatal sickness the world has ever known, I really meant it. Unfortunately every one of us is born with it. It's come down the family line, if you care to put it that way. From our forefather, Adam."

"If you happen to believe in him," interjected Sam, trying hard to hold on to his scepticism.

Boxer shrugged. "Doesn't matter whether you believe in him or not, Sam. You were still born with it. I'll bet you can't even remember the first time you did something wrong. No one ever had to teach you. Selfishness is as natural as breathing, no matter how decent and respectable we think we might be. It's like that for all of us born into this world. All that is except one."

Sam raised his eyebrows.

"I'm talking about Jesus," Boxer said slowly. "A lot of people see him as just a good man. A powerful teacher. But he's so much more than that, Sam. You see, *he* came down from heaven. He wasn't descended from Adam; Jesus *had* no human father. Oh, we know Joseph took Mary as his wife and brought Jesus up as his own son. But in reality, Jesus' father was none other than God himself. That's why he's the only one to have been born without the sin disease. And the only one in a position to reconcile us *back* to God."

"I'll bet he wondered what hit him when he arrived down here," Sam said quietly, scanning their wretched surroundings. He wasn't trying to be irreverent. He didn't even know if he believed a word he was saying. But somehow, he felt too weary to withstand Boxer's reasoning.

Boxer smiled gently. "That's why he came, Sam – to deal with this mess. It's why he died. God couldn't just overlook all the world's sin and pretend it never happened. It's like crime and punishment; you can't have the first without the second. That wouldn't be justice. Even we humans know that. There had to be punishment, Sam. In fact the Bible tells us quite plainly that our sin warrants the death penalty. But in his great love for us, God absorbed the blow himself. He chose to satisfy the demands of his own justice by sending his own son to take our place." Boxer studied Sam's face for a moment. "Let me put it another way, Sam. You and I, and millions of other men, find ourselves out here – or on the Italian or Eastern fronts – wherever you like. We just happen to have been born at a time when the world was getting ready to explode. We didn't know that, did we? We didn't know that by the time we reached our early twenties we'd be out here fighting for king and country. That once we joined up, our lives would no longer be our own. Yet here we are, Sam. And we can't get out of it. We're here – stuck here. Because, though we didn't realise it at the time, you and I were not born free men. Our future was sealed the moment we took our first breath, simply because of the time and place in which we happened to be born. And now, years on, we find ourselves enslaved to something far, far bigger, far more powerful than we could ever have imagined in our worst nightmares. Even though, deep down, our hearts may tell us we were surely made for better things, this was always going to be our destiny, Sam. We were never going to escape it."

"Thanks," Sam said flatly. "That makes me feel a great deal better. The story of a whole generation in one miserable nutshell."

He flicked a louse from the back of his hand and squashed it into the mud with his heel. "No wonder Wilf put a gun to his head."

There was a shadow of a smile on Boxer's face. "Hang on, mate, I haven't finished yet. That first bit was just the bad news. Now, let's look at our present situation. We both know, don't we, that sometime within the next couple of days our company's about to take part in one of its biggest offensives to date? It's anyone's guess as to when it will all kick off, but one thing we *do* know. When that order comes down the line, when those whistles blow, we'll have no choice but to advance. Even though every fibre in us will shrink at the prospect – let's face it, the odds are so against us there's a fair old chance we won't survive – we simply won't get a say in it."

Sam's face contorted at the bluntness of Boxer's words.

"Right," Boxer continued. "Now let's suppose it gets to an hour before jump off. As the rum rations are passed along, the awful reality of the situation dawns on you. So far, despite all the action you've seen, you've managed to get away with no more than a few bumps and scratches. This time, however, your heart begins to sense that this will be your final battle. As the moments tick by, the realisation torments you. You wonder how much longer your legs will hold you upright. A man next to you starts to weep. Less than an hour is all you have left. Less than an hour ... ." Boxer stopped for a moment and looked directly at his friend.

Sam's face was ashen. He wasn't sure where Boxer's story was leading, but it seemed to have a scarily prophetic ring about it.

Boxer took up the tale again. "Suddenly a fellow, a high ranking chap – a Field Marshal, let's say – appears in the trench beside you and makes you an incredible proposition. He offers to take *your* place on the front line. Offers to wear your uniform, eat what's left of your mouldy rations, put *himself* in the line of fire once the whistles blow. He's a Field Marshal, remember. He has the authority to do it. The authority to make the offer, and the authority to cover you completely should you decide to take him up on it. You won't get shot for cowardice or desertion. You can simply swap places, shake hands, and get off home. Spend the rest of the war waiting for that little lady to come back – y'know, the one you once mentioned to me." There was a slight twinkle in his eye and Sam smiled sadly.

"Not much chance of that, is there?"

"Yes," Boxer coaxed, "but if such a fellow were to come along, wouldn't you jump at the chance? Come on, Sam. Any man in his right mind would."

Sam nodded slowly. If it meant he could be there in one piece to welcome Emily home, he'd jump at the chance alright.

"Right!" said Boxer, an intensity building in his voice. "Well, we know Field Marshal Haig isn't likely to stand in for you and send you home. You're out here for the duration like the rest of us. But when it comes to the *eternal* home, Sam, that's exactly what Jesus did do. He saw us stuck fast in our sin and selfishness, drowning in all the awful mess we've created. And he knew we could never get ourselves out of it. Without intervention we were destined for destruction. So he came and took our place, Sam. He took our place so that we had a chance to get home safely."

Another shell whistled through the air and exploded nearby. Sam tried to close his ears to the screams.

Boxer shrugged resignedly. "Let's face it, pal. Neither of us know if we'll come out of this next fight alive. But whether we do or whether we don't, God's desire for us is that we get home safely. Doesn't matter if you end up living to be a hundred, or you get shot in the next twenty-four hours; he wants you in his family, Sam. If you trust Jesus to settle the score between you and God, you'll become one of his children. Your destiny will be changed. Heaven will be waiting for you. Think of it – with God forever, and all the believers who've ever gone on before. Don't you want that, pal? All of this gone, forgotten. Just love, joy, beauty and peace, like the Garden of Eden all over again. And a new body ... not a scrap of shrapnel in sight. You'd even get to see Jimmy again. All you have to do is accept his offer, Sam. Turn from your own ways – admit your need of him. But he won't force you. The choice is entirely yours."

Sam hung his head. Boxer made it all sound so real. If only *he* could have the same assurance. But looking around, it was desperately hard to believe in any place where joy, beauty and peace abounded. Maybe it was wishful thinking. Something Boxer had created in his imagination to stop him going completely mad. Whatever it was, it was powerful. Boxer had been a source of strength to Sam from the day they'd met.

"I – I suppose it's normal for a chap to be scared to die ...?" Sam spoke falteringly, afraid of looking a coward or a fool, but unable to keep the question within his heart any longer. His earlier cynicism had all but melted in the heat of the terrors now threatening him.

"Course it is, Sam." Boxer looked at him kindly. "But it does help if you know where you're going. Look how gently Jimmy passed on – and smiling too. Oh yes. That makes all the difference ..."

I said no more after that, Em. My heart has become so heavy, I can scarcely bear to hope any more. Thinking of all that Boxer has said, I begin to wonder if perhaps it's too late for me. The fight is soon and I cannot clear my head to think properly. I feel I've lost my chance with you, and with God too, if indeed he's there at all. I don't want to die. I've tried so hard to stay alive. I wish some Field Marshal really would swap me places, for a while at least. Just to give me a little more time to think. My doubts and fears seem so many now. Oh that God would give me a sign. That he would break into this dark hell and let me know he is truly there.

Rosie sat up straight in her chair. It was the last entry. It had been even more difficult to read than usual. The pages were blotched and dirty as though they'd been impregnated with liquid filth and allowed to dry. Probably exactly what had happened. Her eyes went over the closing sentence once again. Reading it made her feel terribly depressed. It seemed so desolate, so desperate – and now so final. Though she had done so before, she flicked through the remaining pages of the notebook just to make sure there was nothing she'd missed. All blank. As blank and empty as the silence in the heavens. Sam had cried out. She had cried out. But there had been no answer. It seemed there would never be an answer for people like them.

Jonathon was eager to talk when he picked her up the next morning. "I was pretty gutted when I read your e-mail last night. What a horrible note to go out on." He looked genuinely sad about it.

Rosie shrugged as dismissively as she could. "Well, let's hope he went out quick and clean. That's what he wanted after all."

Jonathon frowned slightly. "Well yeah – I guess. It's just not how I hoped it would end, that's all."

"Not all stories have happy endings." Rosie's jaw tightened. "If you think they do, you've been watching too many films." She turned her head to look out of the window and never saw the flash of hurt that passed across Jonathon's face.

For the rest of the journey he didn't bring the subject up again. It was obvious to him that Rosie didn't want to discuss it any further, but Jonathon was soon deep in thought. From the sudden curtailment of the diary it seemed reasonable to assume that Sam had suffered the same fate as Boxer. Most likely his name would feature on some war memorial somewhere, carved in marble or stone for future generations to look upon. But that wasn't the thing that troubled Jonathon. Sam had come so close. Had he ever taken that final step, made the choice that Boxer had described? Jonathon hoped with all his heart that he had. How tragic to have come so close and missed it right at the last minute. He sighed quietly. It was something he would never know – not in this life anyway.

It was Thursday dinnertime. So far, Molly had been having a difficult day. Rosie decided it might be best for them to stay indoors for the whole break. She went over to one of the classroom cupboards and pulled out a piece of work. "I liked your picture, Molly."

Molly sniffed, unconvinced.

"No, I did. Really. I wondered if you wanted to tell me about it." She placed the picture on the table and Molly stared down at it, her expression inscrutable.

"I guess this is you," Rosie ventured, pointing to the stick girl. There was the slightest flicker of acknowledgement. Rosie felt encouraged to continue. "And *this* – this must be your mum, because it's so like her. I recognised her straightaway."

Molly blinked, her features softening a little.

"Now, this man here ..." Rosie pointed to the figure in the bright turquoise outfit. "I don't think I've met him. Who is he?"

For a moment or two Molly stared hard at the paper. Then her gaze moved to the window. A tiny sound escaped her lips, but Rosie was unable to make out the words. "What was that, Molly? I didn't quite catch it."

Molly repeated the sound only marginally louder. "My daddy."

"Ah right. So that's Daddy, is it?" Rosie was just debating whether to stay with Dad or move on to the figure at the edge of the picture when Molly's eyes suddenly welled with tears. Momentarily, Rosie wondered if she'd done the right thing bringing the picture out of the cupboard.

As the tears spilled over and began to run down her cheeks, the little girl bent forward on her chair. "I don't feel well," she whimpered quietly.

Rosie put an arm around her small shoulders. She was sure it was an emotional reaction but decided to go along with it. "What's wrong, Molly?"

The girl was beginning to sob softly. "My tummy hurts."

Rosie nodded knowingly. She'd come across this countless times at the nursery. Kids who struggled to settle always seemed to be plagued by the same complaint. She suggested a trip to the toilet. Molly complied, sniffing all the way.

"I'll stay outside in the corridor," Rosie smiled encouragingly as she propelled the little girl towards a cubicle. "You give me a shout if you need to."

It was a good ten minutes before Molly reappeared. She looked pale, and barely better than she had before she'd gone in.

Rosie felt sorry for her. The poor kid was obviously taking things hard.

During the rest of the afternoon the situation hardly improved. At home time Rosie waited with Molly on the school steps. Mrs Guest was slightly late and looked flustered as she hurried towards the entrance.

"I'm so sorry. The traffic was shocking." She ran an agitated hand through her bleached hair.

Rosie tried to put her at ease. "That's okay. Molly and I were having a little chat anyway." She looked down at the girl, wishing she would at least attempt to look pleased to see her mother. But there wasn't even the merest flicker of a smile on Molly's face. Rosie decided to go for a different tack. "She hasn't felt very well today."

Mrs Guest frowned. "Oh sweetie, what's the matter?" She moved towards her daughter with obvious concern. Molly looked as though she might cry again.

"She was complaining of tummy ache earlier."

Mrs Guest sighed guiltily. "Hope it's not the takeaway we had last night. Honestly, I've only been in this job a couple of months and they've upped my hours already. I'm not getting chance to cook, clean or anything. We're living on rubbish at the moment."

Rosie shook her head. "No, I'm sure it's not that." She hesitated for a moment. "She's been a bit upset with herself today, that's all." Seeing a fresh wave of guilt flood Mrs Guest's face, she found herself wondering if divorce was worth all the hassle.

The following morning Molly arrived at school extra early. Her mother wanted to speak to Rosie. Mrs Guest seemed as flustered as ever, and the speed of her words suggested she really needed to be elsewhere. "I still don't think she's well, Miss Maconochie. I offered to let her stay home with Colin – he's my partner. He hasn't managed to find a regular job yet, so he's at home a lot of the time. But anyway she didn't want to, so I didn't push her." She bent towards Rosie and lowered her voice. "She hasn't taken to him yet. She's still missing her dad, bless her. She's very quiet with

Col. Not naughty, just quiet. It's a difficult situation." She looked stressed out and Rosie couldn't help feeling sorry for her.

"Don't worry, Mrs Guest. I'll keep a close eye on her. Thanks for filling me in. By the way, call me Rosie."

Mrs Guest smiled gratefully. She started to walk away, but suddenly turned back. "Molly likes you a lot, Rosie. I can tell by the way she talks about you at home. Thank you for taking time to help her."

For Rosie, it was things like that that made the job worthwhile.

As the days went by, Rosie felt a growing bond between herself and Molly. It was a relationship based not so much on verbal communication as on intuitive understanding. As the days turned into weeks, Rosie became expert at reading Molly's mood within minutes of her arrival at school. There were good days and there were bad days. On good days, Rosie was able to leave the child to work at a table with her classmates while she moved around to offer her help elsewhere. On bad days, she had all on to get Molly to do any work at all. During one particularly frustrating morning, Rosie found herself remembering the drawing competition. She hit upon an idea. If she could get Molly to draw a picture of how she was feeling, maybe it would open up an alternative way for them to communicate. On this particular occasion, all the child managed to produce was an angry scribble, but it broke the impasse. After that, Rosie resorted to the technique several times. On those days when words seemed to be getting her nowhere, she found that encouraging Molly to draw her feelings on paper was the key to breaking down the little girl's resistance. Sometimes they drew together just for fun. As the days became warmer, they began to take paper and pencils out onto the school field and sketch away during dinner breaks. Rosie noticed a measure of natural talent in Molly's work; an eye for detail and the beginnings of her own distinctive style. She was sure that, with encouragement, it could be nurtured and developed.

It wasn't long before they began to be joined by other children, and soon Miss Maconochie's 'Art Group' became an established feature of dinnertime breaks. Strangely, Molly didn't seem to mind the intrusion. It was almost as if she enjoyed being able to participate in a group on her own terms. Observing her, Rosie felt a growing sense of satisfaction that her efforts with the child were at last starting to bear fruit.

At least one area of my life is paying off, Rosie tried to reassure herself. Over the last couple of weeks, she'd managed to compartmentalise her head a little. One part of her still ached for Jonathon. That was the part that she kept firmly in check; the part that caused her to rattle off meaningless small talk on their journeys to and from school. To his credit, Jonathon had quickly learned to respect her distance and hadn't tried to force anything deeper from her.

Her favourite part at the moment, however, was the part she played at school. Rosie the professional. Competent, innovative, reliable. And now Molly's friend. Seeing the child's growing trust in her made her life seem suddenly worthwhile. She tried not to think about the looming summer holidays and the end of her contract. She would do her best while she had the opportunity. Make hay while the sun shone. Anyway, Molly's confidence must be growing a little. Surely there would come a day soon when she'd be able to stand on her own two feet.

One afternoon towards the end of May, one of the receptionists came into class with a message for Helen. Helen passed it on to Rosie. "Molly's mother's just rung in. She has to stay over at work. Her partner Colin will be picking Molly up from school."

Rosie frowned. "How will we know it's him? I've no idea what he looks like."

Helen waved dismissively. "Don't worry. I met him once when Molly first started here. I'll take her out onto the front at home time if you like."

"Then I'll come with you," Rosie asserted, "so I'll know him in future."

Colin was nothing like Molly's depiction of him. If Rosie had expected some swarthy, sinister character, she was to be disappointed. Colin was slim and mousy-haired, his pale grey eyes bearing no resemblance to the black dots Rosie had anticipated. As Helen made the cursory introductions, he gave Rosie a brief smile. It was a strange smile and, for a moment, Rosie couldn't help feeling that they'd met before. She dismissed the notion and turned her attention to Molly. She was slightly disconcerted to realise that the girl had managed to slip up the steps behind them and was standing rigid in the entrance doorway. Rosie went towards her. "Come on, Molly. Colin's here because your mum has to work today."

The look in the child's eyes hurt her terribly. It was obvious the poor kid couldn't stand the usurper. Rosie felt like a traitor. Helen wasn't so emotionally attached. She took Molly's hand and led her gently but firmly back down the steps, handing her over to Colin with a sympathetic smile. Rosie saw the little girl stiffen slightly. But the thing that got to her most was the glance Molly shot her as Colin led her out of the playground. In that moment, Rosie felt like the biggest let-down in the world.

"Ever thought of going into teaching?" Jonathon asked out of the blue as they were on their way home from school one day. It was a warm June afternoon and Rosie had been daydreaming as she stared out of the window.

She shrugged. "Teaching? No, not really. Why d'you ask?"

"I think you'd be very good at it. You're certainly very committed. You give a hundred and ten per cent to those kids. I hardly seem to see you these days."

She glanced at him, not sure if the last comment had been a dig. But his face was calm, without the slightest trace of sarcasm or complaint. His comment had been nothing more than an objective observation, and it stung her. How she wished he'd missed her. How she wished her absence had distressed him. She fell into silence. How she wished she had her own car.

Sports day was coming up. As the nice weather continued, a date was fixed for the last week in June. Helen Walker was determined to drum up some enthusiasm. "We're going to have a couple of practices up on the field to make sure we're really good on the day. Our mums and dads will be coming to watch so we want to do our best, don't we?"

As the children chorused in affirmation, Rosie looked over at Molly. She hoped that last remark hadn't upset her. She thought back to her own school sports days. There had never been a dad there to watch *her*. Her mother had even missed on a couple of occasions. Rosie had hated every minute of the things. But Molly didn't appear to have noticed Helen's words. She was staring out of the window, seemingly in a world of her own.

The first practice fell later that week. The children changed into PE kits and filed out onto the school field, buzzing with excitement at the prospect of missing proper lessons. Molly was quiet. She stuck close to Rosie as they followed on behind the rest of the class. Rosie bent down to talk to her. "You okay?"

Molly shook her head. "I don't feel well. I don't want to run." Her voice sounded small and unhappy. Rosie nodded slowly. The stomach aches had started again, and in the last few days Molly had spoken little. Perhaps, Rosie imagined, it was the thought of having to perform in front of so many strangers. As the practice races commenced, she tried to encourage Molly. "Just do your best, that's the main thing. It doesn't matter if you don't win."

It was just as well. As Molly's group stood at the starting line for their race, Rosie couldn't help noticing how thin the child was. Poking out of her baggy blue shorts like two sticks, her legs looked hardly capable of supporting her body. When the whistle went, each child set off from their position with as much effort as they could muster. Molly did too; but in terms of ground coverage, her effort was pitifully unrewarded. Watching Molly race was like watching someone trying to run through treacle. Her skinny arms wheeled in the air as she tried to keep up with her classmates, but it was hopeless. By the time Molly made the finish line, the candidates for the next race were drumming their feet ready to start. Rosie grimaced. Whoever had invented sports day needed a good slap.

Later, as they walked back into school, Rosie noticed that the little girl was hobbling slightly. "Have you hurt your foot?"

Molly shook her head.

"You're walking a bit funny, that's all," Rosie pressed. "I just wondered if you'd twisted your ankle or something."

Molly sniffed. "Tummy ache," she said pathetically before looking away.

Rosie squeezed her shoulder gently. Kids like Molly shouldn't be put through this kind of ordeal.

That afternoon Mrs Guest arrived to pick the child up from school. She bubbled with excitement when she spotted Rosie. "I've just found out I can get sports day off." Turning towards her daughter, she smiled broadly. "That means I'll be able to come and watch you, sweetie."

Rosie hoped she hadn't been banking on a positive response. Molly hardly flinched at the news. She was kicking an invisible pebble around with the toe of her sandal. Her mother might as well have been invisible too.

The day before sports day the weather broke. The forecast for the following day was heavy rain.

"I think we're going to have to cancel," Bev Carradine conceded gloomily. "No point parents taking a day out of work just to sit in the school hall."

Helen Walker managed to shrug off the disappointment pretty quickly. "Between you and me, Rosie, I hate sports day. Always scared stiff one of them might do themselves an injury." She thought for a moment. "We'll have a film afternoon instead."

After dinner she put the proposition to the class, suggesting that one of them might bring in a favourite DVD for the class to watch. She handed out small scraps of paper. "Right. Put your name and the name of your favourite DVD on your piece of paper. We'll put them all in a hat and Miss Maconochie can pick one out.

If we think it's suitable the winning child can bring their DVD into school tomorrow. How does that sound?"

The idea went down well. Later, the rain stopped for a brief spell. While the children were outside for afternoon break, Helen and Rosie quickly went through the submissions.

"You can't be too careful, Rosie," Helen commented knowingly. "You'd be amazed at what some parents will let their children watch." After removing a couple of dubious entries from the pile, she hurriedly threw the scraps of paper into an old dressing up hat and handed the whole lot to Rosie. "Here. You can do the honours."

Five minutes later, when the children had come back into class, Rosie plunged her hand theatrically into the hat. "And the winner is ..."

A hush of excitement fell over the whole room.

"Jake Rawlinson with ... *Monsters, Inc.*!"

The two women exchanged glances and Rosie saw the faintest twinkle in Helen's eye.

"Right, Jake – do you hear that?" Helen fixed the boy with a hard stare. "Your class is counting on you. Don't forget to bring it in or I'll have to show my favourite Numeracy DVD instead. It's over three hours long."

Observing the look of dismay on Jake's face, Rosie doubted he'd forget.

"Well, no sports day," Jonathon commented ruefully on their way home. "Some of my Year 6 lot are gutted. It would have been their last one before they leave. I'll have to find a way of making it up to them."

Rosie shrugged absently. "Show them a film. We're watching *Monsters, Inc.*"

"Monsters w*hat?*"

"*Monsters, Inc.* – it's a kid's film."

Jonathon shook his head. "Never heard of it. What's that about then?"

Rosie rolled her eyes. The film had been out ages. She'd seen it three times at least, but then, that *had* been one of the perks of working at the nursery. “Well, where to start?” She began to run the movie through in her head. “The story’s set in this place called Monstropolis. All the inhabitants are monsters, see. Monsters of every kind. Y’know, hairy, scaly, furry. One-eyed, twenty-eyed – big teeth, false teeth … you get the picture?” She could see that Jonathon was trying his best to imagine it. “Right. Now the whole of Monstropolis is dependent upon one thing for its energy source.” She paused for effect. “Scream power.”

Jonathon raised an eyebrow.

“And the only way they can obtain this power is by harnessing the screams of human children.” Rosie hoped it was making at least a little sense. “That’s where Monsters, Inc. comes in. Monsters Incorporated – that’s the main processing plant. At Monsters, Inc., they’ve figured out a way to get through into the human world. Somehow, they manage to get hold of closet doors from the rooms of kids in the human world and bring them into the Monsters, Inc. factory. Each child is then assigned his or her own monster … tailor-made to scare them most. Are you getting this so far?”

Jonathon nodded tentatively. “I think so.”

“Well, every night, said monster goes through door, magically appears in child’s room, scares kid half to death and comes back out again.” Rosie rattled off the process like a teacher explaining a mathematical equation. “Meanwhile, outside the door, another Monsters, Inc. worker – ’cause these guys work in pairs – he’s collecting the screams and seeing how many canisters of scream power they can produce each shift. There’s a bit of a contest going on at the factory. Which team can break this week’s scare record and all that sorta thing.” She shot him a half-smile. “To be honest, most of the monsters are kinda cute really. The whole scary thing is an act. They’re actually more terrified of human kids than the kids are of them.”

“Is that it?” Jonathon looked less than convinced.

“Well, no – lots of other things happen …” Looking at his expression, she wondered if there was any point in continuing. It wasn’t the easiest film plot to describe and she hardly felt she was doing it justice. “It’s actually very funny and quite clever. And there are some strong positive messages in it. I won't spoil it for you in case you decide to watch it sometime."

"Thanks." Jonathon stifled a smile. "I'll bear that in mind."

As it turned out, Rosie didn't get to watch the film the next day. During the morning sessions there was quite a bit of classroom disruption caused by two of the boys, Josh Bryce and Oliver Packer. As dinnertime approached, Helen Walker was running out of patience. She gave the boys an ultimatum. One more incident and they would both miss the film. The final straw came in the dining hall queue. A provocation, an exchange of sly kicks, and suddenly Josh's tray upturned, spilling his dinner all over the dining hall floor. Helen was furious when she heard the news.

"I warned them, Rosie. They've been building up to this all day. And they're two of our oldest boys too. They ought to be growing out of this." She sighed resignedly. "I'm going to have to follow this through. I can't afford to go soft on them – I taught Olly's brother two years ago. Little *monster* ..."

Rosie gave a wry smile. "Perhaps it's not the best film for them to watch then. Don't want Olly picking up any monstrous ideas, do we?"

It was decided that Rosie would supervise the two boys during their punishment. They sat at a table on a corridor near Bev Carradine's office. Rosie handed them both worksheets then settled down to mark some spelling tests. It wasn't long before she noticed Josh rubbing his eyes.

"I really wanted to watch that film," he said miserably, not even trying to hide his tears.

"So did I, Josh," Rosie replied gently. "I was looking forward to it. But you see what happens when we keep doing what we know is wrong. It doesn't just hurt us, it hurts other people as well. *I* haven't done anything wrong, have I? But I have to sit out here too."

It was a simple lesson in consequences, and just as much for Oliver's benefit as Josh's. *Probably more so,* thought Rosie grimly. In her opinion, it was Oliver who was the real problem. Josh was just a daft kid who was easily led. After a moment's reflection, Josh looked suitably remorseful.

"Sorry, miss." He wiped his eyes and looked down at his worksheet once more. But Oliver sat impenitent, scowling as he stared down the corridor. Rosie didn't care to imagine what he'd be like with a few more years on his back. She swallowed a sigh. It looked like it was going to be a long afternoon.

She was relieved when the ordeal at last came to an end. Two girls from the class arrived to announce that the film was finished, the rain had stopped for the moment, and everyone was going outside for a late break. "And Mrs Walker would like a word as soon as possible, Miss Maconochie ..." added Jess.

Picking up the worksheets, Rosie made her way back to the classroom. On entering, she was surprised to see Helen with an arm around Molly's shoulders. Helen turned and gave her a worried look. "I've sent our lot outside," she said in a low voice. "The rest of school is already out there. Bev says they can stay out half an hour if the rain holds off." She rolled her eyes in Molly's direction. "I think something must have upset her. But I can't get a word out of her. She's so quiet, I didn't realise she was crying till all the other kids started to go outside."

Rosie moved to Molly's side. She couldn't see the child's expression. Her head was bent forward so that her straggly hair fell over most of her face. Rosie exchanged glances with Helen. "D'you want me to see if I can get through to her? It's not like it's the first time we've been here, is it?" She smiled half-heartedly.

Helen nodded and stood to her feet. "You go for it, Rosie."

"So. What's up, Molly?" Rosie asked when they were alone. "Was it the film? Did it frighten you?"

Silence.

Rosie breathed out slowly. "Those monsters aren't real, y'know." She wished she could say that they were just men dressed up in silly costumes. Somehow, computer generated imagery was a difficult concept to explain to an eight-year-old.

Molly rubbed at her eyes. Still she said nothing.

Oh well, thought Rosie, *when all else fails.* "How's about we draw, Molly?" Even though there was no response, Rosie went over to the cupboard and pulled out some paper. She took a pencil and began to doodle, racking her mind for inspiration.

"I know," she announced after a few moments, "I'll draw some things that frighten *me*, shall I? Don't look till I've finished." She quickly sketched a stripy snake with over-large eyes and bared tongue. Then she drew a huge spider with eight furry legs. She pretended not to notice Molly peeping through her fingers. She finished with a picture of a little mouse scurrying up a chair leg. In all honesty, none of them were particular phobias of hers, but in the interests of helping Molly she reasoned it didn't matter too much. She slid the paper along the table. "There. What do you think of that, eh? Bet you're not scared of things like that."

Molly stared down at the images for some time. Nothing in her vacant expression gave anything away. It soon became clear that she wasn't ready for talking yet. Rosie passed her a piece of paper. "Okay. Now what frightens Molly? I'll go over there and tidy the bookshelf while you draw something for me. You can use the colours if you like." She moved across the room, leaving Molly alone with the blank sheet.

For a few minutes Rosie sensed little movement coming from the table area. At one point she stole a surreptitious glance in the child's direction. But Molly was just sitting there, in exactly the same position that Rosie had left her. Rosie pretended to continue her tidying. In truth there was little to tidy. She was about to go back to the table when she suddenly caught movement from the corner of her eye. Molly had picked up a coloured pencil and was moving it slowly and deliberately across the page. Inwardly Rosie breathed a sigh of relief. She moved quietly over to the window and looked out at the other children in the playground. She couldn't help feeling frustrated that she'd not been in class for the film showing. *She* would have noticed Molly's distress. Got her out of the room before the thing got her so wound up …

It was about ten minutes later when she realised that Molly had stopped drawing. She moved over to the table and tried to smile encouragingly. The picture had been turned face down.

"Are you going to let me look at what you've drawn, Molly?"

Molly wouldn't meet her gaze. Rosie gently picked up the sheet and turned it over. On the left side of the paper, in vivid shocking pink, was something that looked like an oversized wardrobe. Below it was an orange bed-shaped object, complete with large white pillow and clumsily drawn duvet cover. Set against the whiteness of the pillow, and sketched with no sense of scale whatsoever, Rosie could see a tiny face and two tiny stick arms. The middle section of the paper was blank, but over towards the right side of the sheet, outlined in purple and covered with pink swirly patterns, was the shape of a door.

But it was the final detail of the picture which made Rosie's blood run cold. Next to the door, a figure. A figure dressed in black, with black dots for eyes and a straight line for a mouth.

For a few moments Rosie couldn't speak. Swallowing hard, she tried to look at Molly, but the girl's face was hidden again by the straggly hair. Only her small white fingers fidgeting nervously on the table top gave any indication of what was going on inside her head. Trying to stop her own hands from shaking, Rosie spoke as gently as she could.

"So ... would you like to tell me about your picture, Molly?"

Chapter 29

At ten past three Helen came back in with the rest of the class. Rosie shot Molly a brief, reassuring smile then hurriedly folded the picture and slipped it inside her own bag. As the children began getting their things ready to go home, Helen sidled over to her. "Everything okay?"

"Yeah, fine," Rosie lied. Her head was reeling. Professionally, she knew what she had to do. Report her suspicions immediately. But that was a difficult course to contemplate when, right now, everything in her just wanted to vomit. Looking at Helen, Rosie felt a stab of guilt. She knew Helen trusted her judgement unreservedly when it came to Molly. It had been that way pretty much from the beginning. Such was the bond now between Rosie and the child that it was easy to forget that Molly was actually one of *Helen's* pupils. Surely the teacher had a right to be informed of the situation straightaway? Surely that would be correct child protection procedure? But for Rosie in that moment, correct procedure was the last thing on her mind. This business had suddenly become overwhelmingly, sickeningly personal. As she tried to chew the matter over in her head, a sudden, irate outburst from the older woman confirmed Rosie in her silence. Oliver Packer had done it again, and now Helen was well and truly fuming. At least it made the decision easy. Rosie liked Helen but she didn't rate her as the world's most sensitive person, even on the best of days. This thing with Molly needed handling with kid gloves. If her superior's livid expression was anything to go by, now was clearly not a good time.

When the final bell went, Rosie quietly escorted Molly to the front of the school. On the way there, the two of them hardly spoke. They didn't need to. The silence between them was loaded with new understanding, and Rosie found the burden almost crushing. Mrs Guest made an uncharacteristically punctual appearance and Rosie felt a mixture of sickness and heart-rending sorrow as she handed the child over. She watched as the pair left the playground. The young mother trying too hard as usual, desperately overcompensating for her own perceived failures; the girl, distant and unresponsive. It was a pitiful scene.

When she got back to the classroom, Rosie was relieved to find Helen in deep discussion with Chrissie Havers. She quickly pulled her things together. "Gotta shoot. In a bit of a rush today –"

"Okay, Rosie." Helen barely glanced up. "Thanks for all your help. See you tomorrow."

She was in the car park before Jonathon. As she stood waiting by his car, the enormity of the thing began to hit her. By the time Jonathon arrived, her stomach was churning and her whole body felt like jelly. As soon as he flicked the remote central locking, she opened the door and almost collapsed into the passenger seat. It didn't escape Jonathon's notice. "You alright, Rosie?"

Trying desperately to hold herself together, she nodded shakily. Frowning, Jonathon fired the engine and pulled slowly out of the car park. As they drove along the first stretch of the journey, neither of them said a word. For his part, Jonathon had learned in recent weeks to back off when Rosie went quiet. Now, as they travelled, he respected her silence and put on some music.

After several minutes Rosie turned to him. *"Jonathon ...?"* Her voice cracked as she tried to speak.

Jonathon instinctively slowed down. "Yeah?"

Rosie closed her eyes for a moment. "Would you park up somewhere? There's something I need to tell you."

Jonathon shot her a sideways glance. "Sure, course. Just give me a couple of minutes – there's a lay-by not too far from here." Moments later he pulled off the road and cut the engine. Unfastening his seatbelt, he switched off the music and turned to face her. "What is it, Rosie?"

She stared at the dashboard. "It's Molly. I know what's wrong with her."

Jonathon's eyes narrowed slightly. "Go on."

Rosie swallowed. For a moment she wanted to rewind, pretend none of it was happening. But this was Molly they were talking about. "She's being abused."

Her words hung in the air, pulsating and raw. Rosie stared through the front window. It was out now. She'd said the words, and it was out.

"You're sure about this, Rosie?" Jonathon faltered. "How do you know?"

Fingers trembling, Rosie pulled Molly's picture from her bag and handed it to him.

He studied it for several moments and frowned. "I can see why you might think that way."

Rosie shook her head. She was angry at herself for not having realised it sooner. She of all people. Leaning forward against the dashboard, she buried her face in her hands. "I know who the guy is too."

"*How* do you know all this, Rosie?" Jonathon spoke quietly, his tone suddenly cautious.

She sat up straight. "Don't you believe me or something?"

"No, it's not that. It's just –"

Rosie's face flushed. "Just what?"

Jonathon ran a hand through his hair. "All I meant was ... well, it's a pretty stiff charge to bring – on the basis of a picture, I mean."

"You don't believe me, do you?" she interrupted. "Of all the people I thought I could trust, you don't believe me! You haven't even heard me out yet." She swore and banged her fist against the dashboard.

"Rosie, I'm sorry. I didn't mean ..." He didn't finish the sentence but reached out to touch her arm.

She pushed his hand away angrily as hot tears pricked her eyes. "What *did* you mean? D'you think I make a habit of going around throwing out smutty accusations? Or is it just that you think nothing like that could ever happen to anyone in *your* neat, perfect little world?" Her eyes flashed with anger and she realised she was shouting. But she was past the point of no return. "Wake up, Jonathon! This sorta thing's going on all the time. Just because you spend half your life in church and never see it doesn't mean it isn't happening! Quit staring through your stained glass windows. Out there things are ugly. Take it from one who knows."

As soon as the words were out of her mouth she wanted to pull them back. She'd never meant to have a go at him. Or swear at him. Poor guy had just walked into the firing line at the wrong moment. Every nerve in her body felt taut, like wire ready to snap. She bit her lip hard and closed her eyes against the tears. It had all come out so wrong. He probably hated her now.

She felt Jonathon take her hand in his. "Rosie, I'm sorry. Guess I was just shocked when you said it. I wasn't expecting anything like that." He squeezed her fingers gently. "I didn't let you finish. I'm so sorry. Please go on."

Rosie sank back against the seat. In her mind's eye she could see Molly's frightened face again. As the image impressed itself upon her, a lump came to her throat. She swallowed it back. For Molly's sake she had to finish this.

"I asked her if she wanted to talk about her picture," she began hesitantly. "For a moment I thought she was going to. Her eyes – if you could have seen her eyes." Her voice broke then, and Jonathon tightened his grip on her hand.

"Did she say anything at all?"

Rosie dropped her head and began to tremble. "Yes. Yes, she did. Not a lot, but enough." She steeled herself. "Her words were: *I can't say nothing. He says it's a secret.* She didn't need to say any more. I knew then. I just knew."

A sob rose in her throat and she buried her face in her hands once more. Jonathon leaned over and put both arms around her. Pulling her towards him, he held her firmly. She let him. She was too unhappy to flinch at the irony of it all. Only yesterday it would have been nothing but a distant dream to imagine herself in his arms, her head against his chest, his fingers smoothing her hair as they did now. To think it had taken something like this to make it happen. Tears streamed down her face, but they were silent tears. Somehow she managed to bite back the real anguish she was feeling. The sobs that threatened to choke her. The waves of nausea that turned her insides over. She tried to ignore the comfort of Jonathon's closeness. Right now she needed all her strength to stay together.

After a while she straightened up and briefly wiped her eyes. Jonathon released his hold and sat back in his own seat.

"I'm gonna need to see Bev tomorrow. And Helen will have to be there too."

Jonathon nodded. "If you want me to come with you, you know where I am. I'll be more than happy to be there."

"I'll see how it goes. It might depend what time she can see me." She looked at him directly. "I guess the thing that matters most is knowing you're with me on this. That you don't think I'm some crazy drama queen."

Jonathon nodded again. "I'm with you, Rosie. I'm with you all the way." Their eyes locked, and he looked at her for just a moment too long. She turned away. It hurt too much.

That night she hardly slept. She felt more tense than she could ever remember. The more she tried to relax, the faster her heart seemed to pound. She tried reading but nothing would go in. The words seemed to swim on the page like unintelligible scribbles. In the end she gave up. Closing her eyes brought no relief either. Jumbled images thrust themselves into her mind, each jostling for her attention, none of them conducive to sleep. A whole procession of faces began to pass before her inner vision. *Molly ... Colin ... Mrs Guest ... her own mother ... Gavin ... Ciaran ... Jonathon.* And Mickey. At one point she had a sudden moment of clarity.

Mickey. *Of course.* That was where she'd seen Colin before. It had been the eyes. So oddly familiar, in a disquieting, unclean kind of way. How could she have missed it? She recalled the strange smile Colin had given her that day outside school. Had he recognised something in her too? The thought of it made her want to throw up.

Eventually she fell into a fitful sleep, but it wasn't long before a bad dream caused her to wake with a start. At quarter to five she conceded defeat and went downstairs for a drink. When at last the clock reached seven, she dragged herself wearily back upstairs for a shower. It was going to be a long day.

Somehow she managed to get through the morning sessions at school. Molly was even quieter than usual, and Rosie desperately wanted to reassure her that she was on the case. But she said nothing. She'd arranged a meeting with Bev and Helen for twelve fifteen. A volunteer parent helper had been asked to keep an eye on the child during the dinner hour. It looked like abandonment; Rosie could only hope that one day Molly would understand.

"So, Rosie, what's all this about then?" Bev was frowning as she posed the question. Rosie wasn't sure if her frown was one of genuine intrigue, or a result of her struggle to open the particularly awkward pot of pasta salad she was holding in her hand. "Drat!" The lid suddenly flipped open and splattered the front of Bev's blouse with dressing. "Hang on. I'll just go clean myself up."

Rosie stifled a sigh as Bev disappeared to the loo. *Take as long as you like. Who said this was important?* She forced herself to make small talk with Helen while Bev was out of the room. The last thing she needed was Helen trying to draw anything out of her. She only wanted to tell this story once. A couple of minutes later Bev returned.

"Right. Fire away, Rosie."

Taking a deep breath, Rosie began. She talked briefly about the picture competition and Molly's original drawing. "I didn't think anything of it at that stage. I just took it at face value. Family breakup. Bad guy who shows up in dad's place. Nothing we didn't know about already."

She then went on to mention the stomach aches and the mood swings, admitting that she hadn't suspected anything untoward in that area either. Finally, there was the second picture. As she began to relate the circumstances leading up to it, Rosie laid the drawing on Bev's desk. "After the film yesterday Molly was very distressed. When Helen took the other kids outside, I stayed in class with her. But I couldn't get a word out of her. Usually when she doesn't want to talk I try and get her to draw. Well, it seemed I was getting nowhere fast so I decided to go for that approach. Now from the way she was acting, I guessed something must have frightened her. I figured if I could just get her to put her fear down on paper, I could maybe talk her through it – y'know, rationalise it, throw a bit of grown-up logic in there and take the sting out of it. So I asked her to draw something she found scary. At this point, you understand, I'm thinking monsters and that kind of thing. Well, it all took a little longer than usual 'cause she was pretty upset with herself. But this is what she came up with in the end." She gestured towards the picture. "Wasn't quite what I was expecting, I can tell you. At that point I did what I normally do when she's refusing to communicate – I asked her if she wanted to talk about her drawing. In the general run of things there are times when she will and times when she won't. It all depends on her mood. Still, on this occasion I figured I'd got nothing to lose, so I went ahead and asked her." Rosie pulled a small notebook from her bag and glanced down at it. "I made notes detailing exactly what was said between us. To be honest, there was very *little* said between us. I simply asked her if she wanted to talk about her picture. Straightaway I could see the struggle in her eyes. Obviously I couldn't help her out. I had to sit there all quiet and calm, like she'd just shown me a picture of her favourite teddy. Then suddenly she spoke. *'I can't say nothing,'* she said. *'He says it's a secret.'* Straight out, just like that. I didn't probe or try fishing for info. It just came out, almost like she was willing me to understand. As soon as she'd said the words she went straight back into herself ... facedown on the desk, not another sound. I guess it had taken every ounce of her courage just to say those two little sentences. By the way, talking of *'he'*, I'm pretty sure I know who the *'he'* is. The two pictures show him practically identical." She took another deep breath and exhaled slowly. "Putting everything together, there's only one conclusion I can draw. Dunno how you two feel about it." She slid the notebook across the table to Bev. "Anyway, here. Everything's in the notes."

There was nothing else to add. Rosie knew she'd done the best she could in reporting her suspicions; it was up to Bev now. For several moments no one spoke. Rosie's heart began to race. She could hear the blood pulsing in her ears as the silence in the room grew louder. Why didn't someone say something? Her mind went back to the previous day and the near bust-up she'd had with poor Jonathon. Despite herself, she could feel the same defensive anger starting to bubble in her guts again. It was scary. She knew it would only take one wrong word. How was she supposed to stay professional with all this lot kicking off inside her?

It was then that Bev pushed aside the half-eaten pasta salad and leaned forward. Her expression was grave. "I think we have to pass this on to somebody, Rosie. Like right away."

Rosie nodded, her eyes suddenly welling with tears. She felt the anger dissipate as quickly as it had come, and now waves of relief turned her limbs to jelly. She realised there was a long road ahead for Molly, a road she herself knew only too well. But at least the horrible secret was out now. It was the first step on the journey to breaking free.

"They'll no doubt want to involve you initially, Rosie," Bev continued. "You've got pretty close to her over the last few weeks."

"Guess there's always the possibility I'm wrong," Rosie ventured. Not for one minute did she believe that to be the case, but it seemed wise to come up with a get-out clause.

Bev dismissed the suggestion out of hand. "I'd rather you be wrong and speak out than be right and keep quiet, Rosie. Put it this way, there's enough in all this to make *me* worried. What do you say, Helen?"

Helen was saying very little. She looked slightly shell-shocked, and Rosie couldn't help wondering if she felt bad for having missed it herself. She smiled at her sadly. *Don't beat yourself up about it, Helen. Some of us have a distinct advantage when it comes to spotting things like this. Can't believe it took me so long.*

Although it was a huge relief to have handed the matter over to Bev, Rosie was exhausted by home time. A combination of shattered emotions and lack of sleep had left her feeling completely spaced out. Jonathon seemed to perceive her condition and didn't press for information. "I take it everything went well," was all he said.

"Yeah," Rosie managed to reply. "Bev's sorting it out from here."

When they arrived at Oak Lodge, Jonathon looked at her gently. "Good work, Rosie. Well done for having the courage of your convictions. And thanks for coming to me first to share your concerns. That makes me feel like a friend." He hesitated for a moment as though he might say more but, seeming to think better of it, he simply smiled. "You look tired. You should get an early night. Sweet dreams for later."

Rosie felt like crying as she got out of the car. *That makes me feel like a friend ...?* If only he knew how much his words tore her up.

Even though she went to bed at just after nine and dropped off almost immediately, her dreams were anything but sweet. If the previous night had been bad, this night was far worse. As soon as sleep hit her, a swathe of memories seemed to surface from the darkest recesses of her subconscious, producing the vilest mix of nightmares she could ever remember. She awoke next morning wishing she'd forced herself to stay up all night. It felt as though she'd done precisely that. She was just thankful it was Saturday.

Some time after lunch she decided to go out for a walk. Her brain needed fresh air and she knew just where she wanted to go. The afternoon sun burned hot as she made her way towards Beth's grave. On arriving there, she looked down at its new collection of flowers. There was a picture in a plastic wallet from Meg and Tammy. *'Missing you, Auntie Beth'*, it read in childish handwriting. It was a sentiment Rosie could echo.

I miss you too, Beth. If ever I needed someone to talk to.

But deep down, Rosie knew she could never have told Beth what was going on in her heart right now. She couldn't tell anyone. For a long while she stood staring down at the flowers, hardly seeing anything.

I hope you're happy where you are, Beth. Some days I could almost wish I was with you. But somehow I don't think your God notices me.

She gave a long, heavy sigh. Everything in her felt like crying, but she was too weary to do even that.

Anyway, just wanted to let you know, I'm gonna be moving on soon. I can't stay here any more. The whole thing's got too complicated. Put in a good word for me up there. I'm gonna need all the help I can get.

Out of the corner of her eye she became aware of a figure walking through the churchyard towards her. Even without looking up, she instinctively knew it was Jonathon.

"We'll have to stop meeting like this," he smiled as he approached her. He looked down at the flowers as if wondering what to say next. "I've been doing a bit of reading up," he began tentatively. "Looks like our boys died in the Third Battle of Ypres – in the build up to the Passchendaele offensive. Guess you've heard of Passchendaele?"

Rosie shrugged. "I think so. Vaguely." But she hardly cared.

Jonathon pointed to a scattering of poppies by the wall at the edge of the churchyard. Their scarlet heads bobbed in the light breeze, nodding on their fragile stems as though in some delicate dance. "In Flanders Fields –" he remarked thoughtfully.

Rosie was only half listening. She frowned. "Sorry?"

"*In Flanders Fields.* It's a poem by a guy called John McCrae. We had to learn it at school once. Apparently he wrote it after seeing one of his mates blown to bits. I seem to remember our teacher telling us it was written during one of the Ypres battles. Dunno which one. None of it meant much to me back then. Guess I understand things a little better now."

He paused for a moment, then began softly and slowly:

In Flanders fields the poppies blow
Between the crosses, row on row,
That mark our place; and in the sky
The larks, still bravely singing, fly
Scarce heard amid the guns below.

We are the Dead. Short days ago
We lived, felt dawn, saw sunset glow,
Loved, and were loved, and now we lie
In Flanders fields.

Observing her face, he stopped. "D'you want me to go on?"

Rosie closed her eyes and shook her head. She didn't want to hurt him. But his words felt like salt in a wound. Somehow the poem struck a painful chord. Short months ago she herself had lived, felt dawn, seen sunset glow, loved and been loved …

She'd been just a regular girl, getting on with life in the way regular girls were supposed to. There'd even been a boyfriend in there somewhere. Before all this had happened. She stared down at Beth's grave again. It seemed to her now that Beth's illness hadn't just killed Beth. It felt like it was killing her too. Slowly, everything around her seemed to be dying. Her relationships, her dreams. Her hope. Soon her life would be dead and buried, just like Beth's, like Jimmy's, like Sam's.

"I've decided to go back to London as soon as my contract runs out," she announced as calmly as she could. "It's been good to have a change, but there's nothing really keeping me here now. And the thing with Molly, well, it's left a bit of a taste in my mouth. I need to put it behind me. Start again."

The look that flashed across Jonathon's face told her that he hadn't been expecting the news. He nodded slowly. "I understand." There was a pause. "But if that's the case, Rosie, I'm going to make a request. We have some special youth meetings this weekend at church. They're for our young people but anyone can go. I sometimes help with youth work so I'll be there." He hesitated for a moment. "Would you come tonight, Rosie? Please … would you come with me?"

Swallowing back a sigh, Rosie looked across the churchyard. She didn't want to go, yet somehow she couldn't find the energy to protest. She shrugged her shoulders and smiled weakly. "Okay. If it means that much to you."

"It does," Jonathon said quietly. "I'll pick you up quarter to seven."

That evening, as she got ready to go out, Rosie wasn't quite sure whether to go for a formal or casual look. Even simple decisions seemed hard these days. In the end she went for jeans and a floaty top. After all, she reasoned, it might be church but it *was* a youth event. How many kids went out dressed like office workers?

"You look lovely, Rosie," Cassie commented when she came downstairs. "Going anywhere nice?"

"Some youth thing with Jonathon," Rosie mumbled resignedly. "He's picking me up in five minutes."

"Oh, bet that'll be fun. They put some marvellous stuff on for the young people." Cassie looked wistful. "Wish they'd had things like that when we were that age." She was thoughtful for a moment. "Go with an open mind, Rosie love. You might really enjoy it."

Rosie managed a half-hearted smile. *I'll do my best.*

Jonathon arrived punctually and Rosie felt suddenly nervous as she made her way to the car. She couldn't help wondering what on earth she was letting herself in for. When they arrived at the church, a steady stream of young people was filtering into the building. She walked slowly with Jonathon to join the end of the queue. *Oh well,* she mused grimly, *bit too late to change my mind now.*

By the time they got inside, the church was already pretty full. Jonathon began moving down the aisle towards some empty seats near the front. Rosie followed with a degree of trepidation. It was a short journey, but fraught with interruptions. She soon lost count of the number of folk who came over to say hello. And they didn't leave it there. Rosie was slightly disconcerted at the way everyone went about greeting each other. As well as their exuberance of speech, there seemed to be a great deal of hugging and flinging of arms around one another. The whole thing struck her as being rather bizarre. Physical demonstrativeness never having been her strong point, she was only glad that the enthusiastic welcomers targeted their hugs at Jonathon and had the decency to tone things down to a handshake when introduced to her. Noticing her unease, Jonathon tried to step up his efforts to get to the front. When at last they made it, they found a couple of free seats and sat down. *Great,* thought Rosie, feeling more uncomfortable than ever. *Ringside view. Just what I wanted. Not.*

She gave herself a couple of minutes to cool down, then did a quick scan of the building. She couldn't help but be impressed at the size of the gathering. "Do all these kids come here normally?"

Jonathon looked around. "Most of them. Some of them have brought friends too by the looks of it. We have a good youth group. They're a brilliant bunch."

Rosie took another surreptitious glance across the church. Any preconceived notions she may have nursed about churchgoing youngsters were quickly dashed. There was a noticeable absence of anyone that remotely resembled her idea of a religious nutcase. And not a geek in sight. In fact there were some very good-looking faces amongst the crowd, and many of them seemed to shine with a clean, bright joy that Rosie had never seen in kids that age. They even wore trendy clothes. Quite what she'd been expecting she wasn't sure, but somehow this lot were a pleasant surprise.

Another surprise came as the event got under way. A man stood up to introduce the evening's guests.

"All the way from the United States of America, will you please welcome ... *'BROKEN BREAD'*!"

The audience went wild as a group of about twenty young people bounced to the front of the church. Immediately, a backing track started to play. Most of the group began singing along with great energy, but a handful of them got straight into a dance routine. The music was upbeat and fast, and Rosie had to concede, at least to herself, that the dancers were good. It felt like a workout just watching them. The first track was followed by a couple of equally energetic hip-hop numbers and then the music faded. A tall, dark-haired boy moved to the front of the group.

"Good evening, everybody!" he cried out in a strong drawl. The kids in the church went crazy again. The boy grinned and waited until the din subsided. "My name's Tony, and we're *'BROKEN BREAD'* from Missouri in the US. We're currently touring the United Kingdom sharing with young people the wonderful things that God has done, and is doing, in our lives ..."

This should be interesting, thought Rosie. She wasn't cynical. These days she felt too tired to be cynical. Maybe if she'd gone along to an event like this a few months ago she would have been. Either that or she might have been angry. But tonight she felt quietly prepared to listen. After all, she had little to lose now.

Tony continued to speak for a few moments, recounting highlights of the tour so far and sharing funny anecdotes about the different members of the team. Then he introduced a young man called Danny. Danny looked about seventeen, with olive skin and wiry black hair. He began by singing a song that he'd written himself. He had a strong, Middle Eastern-sounding accent, and Rosie struggled to pick up on some of his phrases. But she could tell from his face that he meant every word that came from his lips. When he'd finished singing, he went on to tell the audience a dramatic story of how God had saved and changed his life. He spoke slowly and carefully, and this time Rosie didn't miss a thing. It was a moving account of rejection, addiction and despair; a life in ruins, now turned good. Indeed *that* seemed to be the prevailing theme of the whole evening. Interspersed with songs, dances and drama sketches, the audience heard story after story from different members of the group, each one relating their own vivid experience. Their faces shone as they spoke and Rosie could see that, for them at least, it was all very real. Her head began to spin. She found herself thinking about Boxer. Cassie. Beth. Jonathon. Everyone appeared to be saying the same thing. Yet somehow, for her anyway, it all seemed so hopelessly out of reach.

The last person to speak was a young woman called Amy. As she stepped towards the front of the group, Rosie noticed her eyes. They were a limpid blue, far-seeing and full of knowing. Rosie guessed Amy couldn't be much older than herself – a year or two at the most. But those eyes seemed to belong to someone so much older. Amy sang a song and then spoke for a few minutes on something from the Bible. Her voice was clear and strong and became more animated as her message went on. Yet as she continued to speak, Rosie found her own thoughts beginning to drift. She tried to force herself to concentrate, but it was impossible. The strong threads of despair in her mind suddenly seemed to tighten into a rope. It was okay for all these people. It obviously worked for them. So what was wrong with *her?* Was she so messed up as to be beyond all hope – beyond even God's reach? It was an awful thought, but somehow it was hard to draw any other conclusion. The more she heard about God, the further she felt from him. Remote, cut off. Destined, it seemed, to always find herself standing on the outside looking in. Something of a lost cause.

She became aware that someone was closing the meeting with a prayer. There came an announcement that there would be refreshments over at the Youth House.

"Fancy going over?" Jonathon's voice brought her up with a start.

She quickly pulled herself together. "Sure. Why not?"

Rosie had never been inside the Youth House before. The grey stone building was across the lane from the main church. Inside, a combination of background music, vibrant posters, and easy chairs and sofas gave the place a homely, chilled out feel. In a far corner was a snack bar where people were queuing to be served. The two of them lined up.

"Did you enjoy it then?" Jonathon looked at her expectantly.

Rosie felt cornered. *Had* she enjoyed it? Well, leaving aside the fact that she'd come out feeling a complete and hopeless loser, yes, she'd had a whale of a time. She tried to think of an objective answer. For the last couple of hours she'd been taken into the lives of a whole bunch of courageously honest people. Listened to their despairs, heard their struggles; even seen them come through to a place of hope. That had to be good. Even if hope always seemed to elude her. She turned to Jonathon and faked a smile. "Yeah, I did enjoy it. Thanks." She was glad that he just returned the smile and said nothing further.

When they eventually got their drinks, they went and stood in a space by an open wooden staircase. Jonathon seemed a little subdued and Rosie felt obliged to try and strike up conversation. She pointed to the steps. "What's up there then?"

Jonathon shook himself from his preoccupation. "Oh, there are two other rooms. One's a library – we call it '*The Book Den*'. You can borrow books, DVDs, music, stuff like that. The other room's a mini chapel. Both the rooms upstairs are meant to be quiet. If the kids want to make a noise they do it down here. That's the theory anyway."

Rosie nodded. "Sounds a bit like Toc-H. Y'know – Talbot House, Tubby Clayton's place."

Jonathon's face momentarily brightened as the similarity dawned on him. "I never thought of that," he said simply.

As they stood there, a succession of young people came over to say hello. Another string of introductions began and Rosie had to force herself to be friendly. She felt tired now and just wanted to be on her own. She'd never realised church could be quite so exhausting. Suddenly, however, an unexpected accent interrupted her thoughts. It was Amy, the American girl.

"Hey – you guys mind if I join you?" Her voice was soft and unassuming.

Jonathon quickly made the introductions and told Amy how much they'd enjoyed the evening. The two of them chatted for a few moments and Amy gleaned that it was Rosie's first visit to a youth meeting.

"Actually, Rosie, it was *you* I was rather hoping to talk to." Amy looked at her kindly. Then she turned to Jonathon. "I'd appreciate if I could have a little one-on-one time with this lady. Is there anywhere quieter we could go?"

"You could try one of the rooms upstairs," Jonathon suggested. "Can't think there'll be anyone up there at the moment."

"Would that be okay with you, Rosie?" Amy asked.

Without thinking, Rosie found herself nodding. Seconds later her brain went into overdrive. What on earth was she doing? And just what was this whole 'one-on-one' deal? Of all the dumb things she'd ever agreed to, this had to be the dumbest. She shot Jonathon a questioning glance. Surely he'd be joining them?

But Jonathon shook his head gently. "I'll stay here. You girls are probably best on your own."

Rosie felt shaky as she followed Amy up the steps. Everything in her wanted to turn and run. When they reached the chapel they went inside and found a seat. There was a moment's awkward silence before Amy began. "I noticed you when I was speaking up at the front, Rosie. I knew I had to talk with you." She hesitated for a second. "Dunno how long we've got up here before the guys downstairs wanna lock up, so guess I'll just cut to the chase. I believe God spoke to me about you."

Rosie tensed up. *Did she just say ...? Okay, so why am I here and where's the door?*

Amy leaned over and patted her arm. "Hey, don't worry. It's nothing to be scared of. Really."

Rosie wasn't convinced. She made a mental note to thump Jonathon the minute she managed to extricate herself from Amy's clutches.

Amy continued. "Before I came over to the Youth House just now, I spent a few minutes praying back at the church. I believe God gave me a picture to share with you. Well, three pictures in fact." She smiled gently. "Dunno if you're familiar with that kinda thing, but sometimes God does speak through pictures. He seems to talk to me quite a lot that way."

Rosie bit her lip. *Speaking through pictures?* It was a concept she understood all too well; she and Molly had got it off to a fine art. Still, hearing that God did it too was something of a revelation.

Leaning back in her chair, Amy looked at her directly. "Could I tell you about it?"

Suddenly curious, Rosie tried to ignore the ripples of fear that were making her heart pound in her chest. For the second time in ten minutes, against all her finer judgement, she found herself nodding.

Amy closed her eyes as she began. "First of all, I saw a big ol' brick house with a long yard and a wall at the bottom. Standing on the sidewalk in front of that wall I saw a little girl. She was only a tiny little thing – and she was staring down the road as if she was looking for someone. I could see right down the road myself and there wasn' a soul in sight. But this li'l girl, she just stood there looking. Looking down that ol' road." Amy's eyes were sad as she spoke and she waited a moment before continuing. "Then the scene changed. I saw another house, this one smaller and darker somehow. I saw that same li'l girl standing in front of it, and she was holding some kinda bag in her hand. I only saw her there for the briefest time. Then the scene changed again. This time I found myself inside that second house. In a dimly lit room – I sensed we were somewhere upstairs – I could see that same child huddled over in a corner. She was sitting on the floor, all hunched up, holdin' in her arms a little wooden box. She was hugging it to herself like it was some kinda teddy bear, and I guessed there must be something very precious inside of it. Then suddenly I saw a figure come into the room. The little girl's face became real scared. I saw her trying to hug the box even closer to her. But the figure went over to the corner of the room and tore it from her grasp. The li'l girl just sat there staring down at her empty hands. Then the picture ended." She stopped and opened her eyes. "Does this mean anything to you, Rosie?"

Rosie sat perfectly still, too shocked to speak. For a few moments she allowed Amy's words to sink in.

The old brick house in Wicklow. The day her father had left and she'd stood crying out in the street. The day her mother had taken them to live with Mickey. That hated house with its hated rooms. Especially the one that had become her own.

She closed her eyes as she remembered it. She could almost smell it, even now. Swallowing hard, she forced herself to picture the last scene. The day he'd first taken her box. The most precious thing she had. A wave of grief and remembered terror swept over her. As panic rose in her throat, she opened her eyes and tried to steady herself. Did this girl have any idea what she'd just said? It had been like listening to an audio guide of her childhood. She couldn't look at Amy as she responded to the question. "Yes. Yes, it does."

Amy nodded gently, a look of tremendous compassion in her eyes. "Can I tell you about something, Rosie? It's not a subject I talk about too much, but I really feel it's right I share it with you. If you're okay with that?"

Somehow Rosie managed an affirmative response.

Amy folded her hands and sat slowly back in her chair. "A few years ago there was a guy in my school who wanted to date me. He was a strange kinda guy. Good looking, but strange. Most people thought so. I didn't wanna date him and I tried to tell him so, but he started to get kinda heavy – y'know, a little obsessed. He made me nervous. Well, one night I'm cutting through a park on my way home from a friend's house when suddenly this guy comes up behind me, gets a hold of me and tells me he has a knife. He drags me over to some trees, pushes me to the ground and tries to rape me. Well, I kick and scream – I'm scared outta my mind by this time – and then he pulls the knife on me." Her voice trailed off. Lifting her hands, she tucked her long blonde hair behind her ears.

Rosie was shocked. Down the right side of Amy's face, just in front of the ear, a deep, ugly scar ran from her hairline to her jaw and down into her neck.

"Someone heard me scream and came running over with a dog. The guy slashed me as his parting shot before he bolted." Amy gave a little laugh. "I used to have my hair short. Now I wear it like a veil."

Rosie didn't say a word. Amy was so beautiful. It seemed obscene that anyone could do a thing like that.

"I didn't know the Lord back then," Amy began again. "Actually, that ordeal was the thing that threw me onto him. I was in pretty bad shape after the attack. Nerve damage, intense trauma, flashbacks and nightmares. Deep down, I knew I could so easily have been killed. I couldn't talk properly at first. I found it hard to go out. I heard later that they'd arrested the boy. He'd stolen a car and a handgun from an uncle's house and was on his way to another state when they caught up with him. Turned out the poor guy really *was* crazy." She shook her head sadly. "I thought my life was over. Felt like my whole world had fallen in on me, like my future had *died* on me. I can't describe the despair I went through, Rosie. I just couldn't imagine ever being able to function normally again. Then one day a friend took me to a meeting a bit like the one we had tonight. That's when I was introduced to Jesus … ." She stopped. Her blue eyes welled with tears. "I dunno what you've been through, Rosie. I guess *your* wounds are on the inside. But I know you're hurting. I just know it." She was quiet for a moment. "Y'know, sometimes life feels like we've tripped and tumbled down a rocky hillside. We hurt in so many places, we don't know which bit to cry over. We lie there at the bottom, caked in dirt, all grazed and bloodied. We feel no better than last week's trash. But the Father, he wants to scoop us up in his arms and hold us tightly to his chest. That's what he's always wanted – to pick us up and take us home. Clean us up and wash off all the filth. Pick the gravel out of our wounds. Oh, it might take a while, Rosie. When we're hurting all over we cry and yell, just like little kids. But the Father doesn't stop till the job is done. He loves us too much to leave us messed up. And he's gentle. So gentle. D'you know, he sings over us as he works on us. How beautiful is that? There's no safer place for us to be, Rosie. And when he's finished, we can just fall asleep in his lap, all our cuts and grazes shiny pink. They're clean now and the Father knows they'll heal well."

For a few moments Rosie said nothing. Amy's story had troubled her. She didn't want to sound cruel but suddenly there was something she needed to understand. "What about your scar? Surely you can't say *that* healed well?"

Amy smiled a beautiful smile. "D'you know something, Rosie? If some guy came along now and offered me a perfect, flawless face in exchange for the peace that God has put in my heart, I wouldn't give him the time of day. This face is only for a lifetime, honey. But God's peace, that's for ever. I've been able to forgive the boy who did it. I pray for him every time I look at myself in the mirror. I want him to know Jesus too. There's only God could've done that in my heart, Rosie. Give him a chance. Let him help you. I dunno how he'll do it, but I know he wants to. And he never messes up." She picked up her Bible and flicked through it. "There's a story in here about another lady that was hurting. Things had gotten a bit hot at home and she'd run away. One day, as she was alone in the desert, God found her and began to speak to her about her future. D'you know what she did? She gave him a name. *El Roi – You are the God who sees me.*" Amy stopped for a moment. "You see, Rosie, that was when it dawned on her. He'd seen everything. He knew exactly where she was at. He was just waiting to step into her situation. And all she could say was, *'I have now seen the One who sees me'*. He *sees* you, Rosie. He's seen everything that ever happened to you. Even if no one else has."

For a moment their eyes met. Then something inside Rosie broke. The pain, the fear, all the loss and isolation of her past seemed to erupt through the top of her head like a long-imprisoned wailing breaking free. She began to sob uncontrollably, hardly caring that Amy was there. She wept for her parents, for Molly, for her own lost innocence. She wept for Beth and the death of a priceless friendship. She wept for Ciaran and for the sorrow that had driven such a wedge between them. She even wept for Jimmy and for Sam, and for all the dreams that had perished so cruelly in their youthful hearts. Somewhere deep inside her guts there was a pain that was beyond pain. A great, moaning, roaring wound that had to be wept over. And so she wept.

As the tears coursed down her cheeks, she rocked backwards and forwards in her seat, gripping herself against the agony of it all. "Oh God," she whispered in anguish, "I can't do this on my own any more. It hurts too much. If there's anything you can do with this miserable life, please... *please* take over."

The moment the stammering words left her lips, a flood of overwhelming love engulfed her. It was at once both powerful and gentle, surging through her being like waves of liquid fire. Never in her life had she experienced anything like it. She knew it was coming straight from the heart of God.

She had no idea how long she was there. She vaguely recalled coming to her senses at some point to find Amy holding her hands and singing softly. Some time after that she knew she must have thanked Amy and said goodbye. She knew too that she must have travelled back to Oak Lodge with Jonathon. And she always said goodnight to Ed and Cassie before going up to bed, so she must have done that as well. But she had little recollection of any of those things. Her mind was filled with a consuming thought.

He is the God who sees me. And he loves me.

That night, as she lay in the darkness, she knew something had changed. For the first time in as long as she could remember, her mind was at peace. A thick, heavy peace that seemed to hang in the air around her; a peace that flooded her being with every breath. She pulled the covers around her face and sighed. But it was a sigh of the most wonderful contentment.

He knows about everything, and now he's coming to clean up all the mess.

She listened to the silence. It seemed to her the most beautiful sound she had ever heard.

Thank you, Lord, for seeing me. Thank you for loving me enough to come after me, even when I thought you didn't care. I never realised you were there all along. Thank you for not giving up on me ...

Tears dribbled down her cheeks and into her hair. She knew there were many, many things he needed to sort out in her life. But now there was something else she knew too. From this night onward she belonged to God.

As her eyes began to droop and much-needed sleep crept upon her, her mind went back to the little upper room in the Youth House. She knew she would never forget the beautiful American girl who had shared her scars with her.

Chapter 30

Rosie awoke the following morning to the sound of birdsong. As her mind slowly adjusted to the idea of being awake, memories of the previous evening came flooding back. Reaching for one of the curtains, she pulled it back slightly so that a shaft of sunlight streamed into the room. She found herself smiling at the brightness of it.

Thank you, Lord, that you see me this morning. Thank you for everything.

She pictured the crowd at the youth meeting the night before. God had singled her out. From everybody there, he'd singled her out to speak to. Her. *Rosie Maconochie.* She closed her eyes and hugged herself happily. She'd never realised God would take the time to do a thing like that. Even in those days when she'd conceded he might just exist, she'd always thought of him as remote and distant, too busy running the universe to intervene in the affairs of mere mortals. But here he was, reaching down out of heaven to speak to *her.* It was almost too wonderful to be true. And yet she knew it *was* true. Only God could have shown Amy the things she'd described the evening before. And only God could have given Rosie the joy she felt inside her this morning. Even here in this room – away from all the music and excitement of the previous night, away from the comforting presence of Amy – Rosie knew that God was as close to her as her own breath. She felt like a new person.

An hour later she saw Cassie fixing her hair ready for the Sunday morning service. She hesitated. Would it seem pushy to ask if she could go too? To actually volunteer rather than waiting to be invited? It certainly wouldn't be the coolest thing she'd ever done. For a moment the old Rosie stiffened at the thought of it. But today a new voice seemed to vie for her attention. A quieter, more gentle voice. *Go on,* it said. *Don't let pride stop you. You know that's where you need to be.*

"Any chance I could come along, Cassie?" The words were out before she knew it.

Cassie smiled gently. "Course you can, love. We'll be setting off about ten fifteen."

Even Saint Edwin's looked different today. Brighter somehow, sunnier. In a strange way, it felt like coming home. So much had happened since she'd last sat in this place. Could it really have been only half a day ago? She wanted to pinch herself to make sure.

As they waited for the service to begin, Cassie turned to her. "Didn't get chance to ask you last night, love – how did the youth thing go? Did you enjoy it?"

The question was sincerely asked. But as Rosie looked into the gentle grey eyes, she sensed that Cassie already knew the answer. "Let's just say I wouldn't have missed it."

Cassie nodded knowingly and reached for her hand. "What a precious girl you are, Rosie," she said softly. Rosie squeezed her fingers. She felt like crying.

As the service got under way, Rosie was amazed to discover that today everything suddenly made sense. Instead of irritating her, the songs made her happy. And the prayers were no longer in a foreign language; they actually echoed the sentiments of her own heart. She even understood Tim's sermon. She was almost disappointed when the whole thing came to an end. Later, across at the church hall for refreshments, she spotted Jonathon coming towards her. He looked mildly curious.

She smiled sheepishly and shrugged her shoulders. "Okay, you win. He got me too."

Jonathon's face creased into a frown. Then the meaning of her words sunk in. "*Really?* Oh wow, Rosie! That's awesome!" For a moment he stood gazing at her, a look of incredulous joy on his face. Seized by impulse, he leaned over and quickly kissed her cheek. "I'd give you a big hug," he grinned awkwardly, "but I'd probably slop coffee all over you."

Rosie felt herself reddening. Somehow she hadn't been prepared for such an exuberant reaction. Now as her face grew warm, she could feel the tingle of Jonathon's kiss on her skin.

Jonathon leaned closer again. "I wanted to ask you about things last night but you weren't very with it."

This reminder caused Rosie a twinge of embarrassment. She shrugged again and smiled. "I hardly remember you driving me home to be honest. I didn't make a total idiot of myself, did I? It was all a bit mind-blowing, the thing with Amy. I didn't know what'd hit me."

Jonathon looked at her intently. Today his eyes seemed bluer and more piercing than ever. "No, Rosie. You weren't an idiot at all. Sometimes when God does business with us, it *is* mind-blowing. I've been there a few times myself, believe me. But I'd rather have my mind blown by God than anything else. He knows what he's doing, and he knows exactly what we need."

As he spoke, Rosie was struck by the passion she saw in him. She'd seen it before, on those occasions in the past when he'd tried to talk to her about Jesus. None of it had made much sense to her back then. But today, for the first time, she began to understand it. This was what made him tick. Jonathon was a man on fire from the inside.

The next day Rosie was interviewed by two women from Social Services. The following day Molly was not in school. Bev Carradine put Rosie in the picture. "She won't be coming back to us for the rest of this term. Not sure what will happen in September, but they'll inform us."

Rosie felt sad. "I wish there was something more we could do to help her."

Bev shook her head. "I'm afraid our bit's done, Rosie. Molly's safe now, and the police are on the case. Unless they need to speak to us, we can't really get involved any further."

That's not strictly true, thought Rosie as she lay on her bed later that evening. She might not be able to *see* Molly any more, but there was one thing she *could* do for her.

Father, please look after little Molly. Please take care of her. Watch over her and keep her safe. And one day, Lord, please let her come to know you as I've done. Let her know you as the God who sees everything. As the one who loves her enough to die for her. And heal her hurts, Lord. Heal her wounds. Amen.

The journeys to and from school didn't seem quite so painful now. Rosie's heart still turned over every time she set eyes on Jonathon, yet somehow it was easier to bear now that God was in her heart too. Their topics of conversation varied little. Sunday service, Tuesday Bible study, Thursday prayer meeting. All they seemed to talk about these days was God or the latest church event. And Rosie loved it.

One day, as he drove her home from school, Jonathon smiled and shook his head. "I can't believe you're the same girl, Rosie. Listening to you talk, I can hardly believe the change in you."

Rosie tried to look offended. "Not sure how I'm supposed to take that. Was I some kind of hideous reprobate or something?"

Jonathon gave a little laugh and shook his head again. "No, I didn't mean that. I'm just so thrilled to see you like this. So – so *plugged in.*"

He looked genuinely delighted, and suddenly it pained Rosie to see him so happy on her account. If only things could have been different between them. She consoled herself with the thought that soon she would be free to move on. *A new life,* she told herself; and with God looking after her now, surely things would work out this time.

In the last week of term, however, she found herself in a dilemma. Bev Carradine summoned her to the office. "I've just had a call from Lydia Vardy. She won't be coming back to us after all. Seems she got talking to someone from the Children's Department on one of her hospital visits. There was a playworker's post going, so Lydia applied. They've just rung to say she's got the job. She starts in September." Bev hesitated for a moment, then leaned over the desk. "How would you feel about staying on with us, Rosie? We've come to value you a great deal – and the kids love you. How would you like a permanent position at Paddock Hill?"

Rosie was taken aback. This was the last thing she'd been expecting. "I'm not sure what to say. I'd kinda planned on going back to London when I'd finished my stint here ... guess this throws a different light on things."

Bev nodded slowly. "I understand. Well, the offer's there, Rosie. Do you want to think about it for a couple of weeks and let me know? It might be easier for you to make a decision once we break up. Whatever you decide to do, I just want to thank you for your input while you've been here." She gave a knowing smile. "Some of it has been quite literally life-changing – for one little girl at least."

Rosie stood up from her chair. "Thanks, I've loved working here. I'll think about what you've said. Give me a fortnight. I'll get back to you as soon as I've made up my mind."

Her mind was pretty much made up already. In any other circumstances she'd have jumped at the opportunity. Paddock Hill was the ideal place of work. Great staff, great kids, beautiful setting. How could you improve on perfection? But the thought of seeing Jonathon day in, day out on a permanent basis was too much to contemplate. How would she cope on the inevitable day he announced his engagement to Lauren in front of the whole staff room? It didn't bear thinking about. Rosie couldn't bring herself to turn Bev's offer down flat. But deep in her heart, she knew that staying on in Ridderch Standen wasn't really an option any more.

It was a beautiful sunny morning in the second week of the long summer break. Rosie had just made herself a coffee and was on her way upstairs to her room. She'd been thinking about Bev's job offer again. She knew she needed to get back to her, but there seemed something so final about saying no.

Oh Lord, what do I do about this? Couldn't you persuade Jonathon to move to Durham or Cornwall or wherever Lauren is these days? It would make life a whole lot easier for me.

Her prayer was interrupted by the sound of Ciaran calling to her. She turned to see him standing on the landing in front of his room. "Are you busy, Ros?" There was a sigh in his voice as he spoke.

"Not really. Just thinking about some stuff, that's all."

Ciaran nodded absently. "Just wondered if you fancied helping me." He pushed open his bedroom door and pointed. "I've been looking through some of Beth's things – y'know, all the stuff she brought up from London. Thought I'd go through it a bit at a time. See what I should keep ... or if there's anything I should give to other people." He looked overwhelmed just thinking about it, and Rosie's heart went out to him. He sighed again. "Some of this stuff I've never even seen before. Didn't know she'd got it. Wondered if you wanted to help me for half an hour. We don't have to do it for very long, but I guess I have to make a start sometime."

Rosie couldn't bring herself to say no. "Course I will. Lead the way."

Ciaran had already pulled out several boxes from their hiding places, and across the room, through the open doors of a large built-in closet, Rosie could see a further pile of random paraphernalia. It seemed that something had been squeezed into every available crevice. She rolled her eyes. Working in half hour stretches this could take weeks. They decided to make a start on the books first. Sitting cross-legged on the floor, they took a box each and began to separate the books into piles.

"Wonder if Ed and Cassie might like some of these," Ciaran ventured as he flicked through yet another dusty tome. "Can't see me ever reading them, but I want everything to go to a good home, Ros."

Rosie said nothing. Poor Ciaran. She doubted he'd be able to bring himself to throw away even so much as a dirty tissue that had belonged to Beth. Still, if sitting here sifting through stuff made him feel he was doing something, it was a worthwhile exercise. Certainly a step in the right direction.

It was well over half an hour later when Ciaran straightened up. "Well, I think that's my box finished. I've found a couple of things

Ben might be interested in." He stood to his feet and walked over to the closet. Surveying its contents for a couple of moments, he shook his head. "Dunno what I'm gonna do with all this lot." He reached into the closet and pulled out a small, battered suitcase.

Rosie gave a slight gasp. "Hey, wait a minute – I remember her *getting* that case! It's from the bookshop at Applemarket. Remember when the two of us went for the day last October? The old guy gave it to her for nothing. Said she'd been his best customer all week." Her mind was suddenly flooded with memories. It had been a wonderful, perfect day. Beth had been so happy; they both had. Could it really have been less than a year ago?

"Don't know that there's much in it, Ros. I seem to remember having a quick look when we first came up here." Ciaran flicked the catches and opened the lid of the case. "Yeah, like I thought. Just some old music scores." He put his hand inside and lifted out a pile of papers. Tossing them onto the bed, he suddenly frowned. Peeping out from between the sheets of music was a large brown envelope marked *'PRIVATE'*. Curious, he picked it up and opened it. "Wonder what *this* could be."

Rosie had only half heard him. She was still thinking back to her day out with Beth.

"*Chant – du – Rossignol …* " Ciaran began, his pronunciation awkward. "This looks like Bethy's writing."

Rosie looked up. "What did you say?"

Ciaran was holding a wedge of manuscript sheets in his hand. "It's a piece of music – *'Chant du Rossignol'* or something. But it looks like Beth's handwriting to me."

Rosie straightened. "It *is* Beth's handwriting! I wondered where *that* had got to. She was composing it for *you,* Kitch. She told me about it a while back. It was meant to be a surprise for you, but I guess she died before she ever finished it." Rosie looked over at the shabby little case from the bookshop. "Did Beth ever show you the soldier's diary she found – written by a guy in the First World War – Sam his name was? Well, seems he put together this little tune too. *'Chant du Rossignol – Song of the Nightingale'*. He had a bit of a thing about nightingales –

nicknamed them all Rosie, would you believe?" She gave Ciaran a moment to comment on the coincidence but soon realised she probably wasn't making much sense. "Anyway, Beth took a liking to the tune. Felt she could do something with it. Said she was gonna work on it, y'know, fill it out a bit. She wanted to give it to you as something to remember her by." Noticing her brother's face, she broke off. He was staring forlornly down at the manuscript in his hand. She leaned over and touched his shoulder. "Maybe you've done enough for today. Let me tidy this stuff away for now, eh? We can tackle a bit more some other time."

Ciaran nodded, still staring down at the papers in his hand. Pulling together the pile of music sheets from the bed, Rosie went to put them back into the case. Her eyes were momentarily drawn to an old newspaper lining the bottom of it. In a moment of curiosity, she lifted it out to take a look. But the newspaper was instantly forgotten the second she saw the array of objects hidden underneath it. Especially one of them. She gave a low whistle as she reached in and took out an old brass tin. *'Christmas 1914'* read the inscription on its lid. Rosie had never seen it before, yet she recognised it immediately. She hurriedly replaced the music scores and shut the case. After tidying away the other stray items in the room, she made a tentative request. "Mind if I take this tin to have a look at, Kitch?"

At that moment Ciaran was in a world of his own. Then he looked up and gave her a weak smile. "She did this for me, you say? Bless her ... she never mentioned a word of it."

"Like I said," Rosie began softly, "it was supposed to be a surprise. She was intending to give it to you herself, but in the end everything happened so suddenly."

Ciaran got up and walked towards his keyboard. "I'll give it a go on here. But there are quite a few parts to it, Ros. Wonder how she managed to do all this without me twigging."

Rosie held out the tin again. "Before I leave you to practise, could I take this to have a look at?"

But Ciaran was miles away. Without even looking up, he gave an affirmative gesture and started to hum his way through the notes. Clasping the tin gratefully, Rosie left the room.

It was clear the tin had been through hard times. The brass was dull and tarnished but, despite a few dints here and there, Rosie could still make out the embossed words on its lid – and the profile of a woman's face. *Princess Mary no doubt,* she mused as she eased it open. *Now inside here, if I'm not mistaken, there should be ...*

And there it was. A small, black New Testament, inscribed with gold lettering. The one from which Sam had read scriptures to the dying Welshman. She pulled gently at its top cover in an attempt to remove it from the tin. But as she worked it loose from its position, her eyes fell on something else sandwiched beneath it.

Come on – pick up! Rosie drummed her fingers agitatedly on her mobile as it started to ring out. After a few moments Jonathon's voice sounded at the other end.

"Hello ... *Rosie?*"

"Hi, where are you?"

"I've just arrived up at the churchyard. Thought I'd do a spot of tidying up while the weather's good. Are you okay, Rosie? You sound a bit flustered."

"Yeah, yeah, I'm fine. Look – have you started work yet?" She was struggling to contain the urgency she felt.

"No. Like I said, I only just got here."

"Good, then hang on. I'll be up there in a few minutes. You're not gonna believe what I've found ... ."

Without another word, she clicked off her phone. Ten minutes later she arrived at the churchyard to find Jonathon sitting on the bench waiting for her. His head was tilted back and his eyes were closed as he faced towards the sun. Rosie couldn't help noticing how brown his arms looked against the white of his tee shirt, or how his fair hair was now streaked with flashes of pale blond. *Some folk would pay a fortune for highlights like that,* she thought ruefully, trying to ignore the effect he had on her. She coughed to signal her arrival.

"Hi Rosie. So what's all this about then? I've been racking my brains trying to come up with ideas. You sure know how to leave a guy in suspense."

Rosie flopped onto the bench and smiled mysteriously. Putting a hand into her bag, she pulled out the tin and waited for Jonathon's reaction. For a split second nothing registered. Then a look of recognition dawned on his face. He reached out and took it from her. "*Sam's tin …!* Where on earth did you find this?"

"It was in the bottom of the old case the bookshop man gave Beth – d'you remember me telling you about it? That was where Beth first found the diary. She never mentioned the tin though. Guess she can't have realised what it was. She must have brought the case up when she came to Yorkshire. I've just been in Ciaran's room helping him go through some of her stuff, and suddenly there it was – with Sam's tin hidden away at the bottom under an old newspaper." She looked down at the tin lying in Jonathon's hands. "*Someone* was determined to keep it safe. I very nearly missed it."

Jonathon opened the lid. "Hey, the Welshman's New Testament too!"

Rosie smiled. "Yeah. But that's not all. Take a look at this." She reached into her bag again and pulled out a letter. "This was in the bottom of the tin – squashed under the Bible. Talk about a tight fit."

Jonathon took the letter from her. It was not in an envelope and was written on several thin sheets of paper which had been folded in half, then in half again. Both sides of each page had been used, and judging from the severity of the fold marks, it was clear that the document had been compressed in its hiding place for some considerable time. Rosie nudged him. "Go on, read it. I already have."

Carefully smoothing out the pages, Jonathon looked down at the tiny pencilled writing.

Royal United Hospital, Bath, September 14th 1917

My dearest Em, at last my war is over. I find myself here in England, and never has our land looked more beautiful to me. I've been told that I cannot return to the fighting. I've been shot up quite badly, and though I shall recover in time, the doctor tells me that I'll always walk with a slight limp. But I'm not going to complain about such a small thing. I've kept all my limbs, which is more than can be said for so, so many. I can still hardly believe that I'm alive. That I'm here, in our beloved England, surrounded by English sights and sounds, quieted by soothing English voices. Knowing that I'm safe, in one piece ... that I never have to go back to the line again. I can only hope and pray that for the sake of those still out there – for you especially, my dearest, bravest girl – this war will end soon.

There's something I need to tell you, Emily. At the moment I find myself separated from my diary. It's still in my bag, wherever that may be. But I've been heavily impressed to commit to paper an account of something that happened to me a month ago, during the early morning hours of August 17th.

On the night of August 16th, we were preparing to make an attack on Glencorse Wood. I think, if truth were told, most of us were sick with fear at the prospect. The reports we'd heard about recent attempts to capture the place were dismal. Though estimated casualty figures varied, the general story was the same. The Germans had got the place well and truly covered, and it seemed there was little chance that any of us would get out alive.

It's a strange feeling, Em, to be so utterly trapped in a thing. To know you have no choice but to go forward; to know that in going forward you will probably never make it back. In reality that's been the situation all the time we've been out here, but somehow it really came home to me that night. I felt quite depressed about it all. Of course Boxer, being Boxer, noticed my unhappy state. We fell into a little chat and he began to remind me of some of the things he'd told me in the many times we'd talked before. As he spoke, I found myself wishing I could have just a little more time. I knew deep down that I wasn't ready to die, not in the way Jimmy had been. I sensed something wasn't right, and it troubled me. But the night hours marched on with no regard for my disquiet, and I couldn't shake off the feeling that each one that passed was bringing me closer to my end.

As the time for jump off drew closer, I remember suddenly hearing a nightingale begin to sing. It seemed strange to hear one so late in the year. I wondered if perhaps she was singing to comfort us. Did she know our fate even more surely than we did? Was she singing our requiem? I shared my forebodings with Boxer. He made some characteristically calm reply. How I found myself wishing I could be more like him.

At dawn the first wave of infantry went over. We were in the second wave and were due to follow on shortly afterwards. Just before we went, Boxer clapped a hand on my shoulder and said a prayer for me. We left from Jargon Trench (if indeed you could call it a trench) and as soon as I saw the scene ahead, it seemed to me that we were running straight into the jaws of hell. Up in front we could see men dropping down everywhere – just dropping like little birds from the sky. I confess I felt sick with fear, but my legs kept moving, albeit with difficulty. Parts of the ground were so cloggy with mud it was impossible to go at any speed. The noise was absolutely terrible. We were being shelled, bombed, machine-gunned; they were throwing everything they had at us. Though our gunners were hitting back, I for one had all on to keep my nerve as we headed into the carnage. At one point I remember Boxer shouting to me to keep to his left. Not understanding his instruction, I complied without further thought. Shortly afterwards, however, I understood the reason for it. Just ahead of us I saw four men go down, one after the other, and it was then that I realised they'd been shot at from some position towards our right. I knew in that moment that we were the next targets in line and that Boxer was trying to shield me. Despite the deafening noise and the terror of the situation, I suddenly found myself praying. As I remember, it wasn't the most eloquent of prayers, Em. I just cried out to God and begged him to spare us …

The next thing I recall was seeing Boxer fall to the ground. He called out to me, but just as he did, I took a hit myself and then I was on the ground too. As I lay there, I struggled to turn so that I could look over at him. I could see he was trying to tell me something, but when I saw the blood coming out of his mouth I knew he was done for. Then a terrible pain began to grip at my hip and thigh. It grew so intense that I thought I would pass out from the agony of it. But no such relief came. I lay staring across at Boxer, wondering how long it would take for death to claim me too. Boxer was quite still now, his eyes open but vacant, a bright stream of blood oozing from his mouth. 'Oh God,' I found myself saying, 'it's all over. Boxer's dead and I am dying. How I wish you could have been that Field Marshal he spoke of. But it's all over now. It's all over … .'

I have never felt despair like I felt in that moment. A terrible darkness seemed to clutch at my soul and I began to weep. Was this the beginning of death? Or was I slipping half-dead into hell? I hardly knew. But all around me I could hear the whistle of steel and the screams of men, and I knew that hell could not be much different.

How long I lay like that I cannot say. I tried to close my eyes to lessen the pain, but somehow that made the thing more fearful. As the minutes crawled past, my agonies grew worse, and though my heart was terrified to die, I knew I had reached the limits of my endurance. Even as I sensed my own life ebbing away, my ears were filled with the groans of my dying comrades. It was more than I could bear. Feeling totally without hope, I began to pray for God to take me.

Though the daylight had taken hold now, the sky was still thick with smoke from the firing. From my position on the ground I tried to look around me. It was then that I perceived two figures emerging out of the grey haze. They looked like stretcher bearers but had no stretcher with them, and they seemed to proceed across the boggy terrain with little trouble. At first they appeared to be advancing in my direction. But as they got nearer, I realised that they were not coming towards me but towards Boxer. When they reached him, one of the men bent down and picked him up in his arms as though he weighed no more than a feather. Then, without further ado, they began to walk away. A sudden desperation gripped me. Surely if they could rescue Boxer they could rescue me? Perhaps they hadn't noticed me. I cried out after them but my voice seemed to make little impression on the terrible noise all around. My anguish grew. More desperately I cried out again. It was then that the second man turned and looked at me. He was not the man carrying Boxer, you understand, but the other fellow. He looked at me with the most piercing eyes I've ever seen. 'Please …' I begged him, 'please help me.' But he shook his head. 'It is not your time,' he said. And then he reached down and touched my forehead.

Emily, I don't know if I'll ever be able to describe the feeling that went through my body in that moment. A lightning bolt could not have hit me with more force. At once my blood was set on fire. Yet, with each pulsation of my heart, I felt its heat begin to cool my wounds until I could almost forget my pain. Not understanding, I lifted my head to glance at the man once more, but he had turned to leave and did not look at me again. I watched as they began to walk away – the first man carrying Boxer in his arms, the second treading slowly behind him. I did not take my eyes off them until they disappeared from sight, and then I lay there for some time, still staring in that direction, wondering what on earth to make of it all. After a long while I tried to turn my head again. But when I looked towards the spot where Boxer had been lying, I was shocked. His body was still there. Immediately I noticed his eyes. They were closed now and on his face I saw the faintest smile. My own forehead was still burning from the stranger's touch and still the blood in my veins made my limbs tingle.

It was in that moment that I understood. God had sent his angels for Boxer, just as he always told me would happen. But even more incredible than that, I knew that God had spared my life.

Suddenly I was filled with the strangest emotion, Em. A joy – but a weeping too. And just then, I heard the nightingale begin to sing again. I found myself recalling something Boxer had said of her just before the battle. 'Perhaps she's trying to show us that it's possible to sing in the darkness … if we know the One who gives songs in the night.'

That little bird sang for hours, Em, or so it seemed to me as I lay there. She was the sweetest and brightest of companions, and I feel sure she was sent to me. The last I remember of her was when I saw stretcher bearers coming in my direction. I must have slipped into unconsciousness then, because the next thing I recall was waking up in a CCS to see a nurse standing by my bed. 'Thank God', she said when I opened my eyes.

'Thank God indeed,' I thought. 'Thank God indeed.'

And so it is that I've survived, Emily. Plucked from almost certain destruction, given a second chance to live – how can I ever be the same? I have set my heart to go after the God who saved me. He heard my cry and showed me mercy. For that I'll be eternally grateful. I can only pray that you, my sweetest girl, will find him too.

Jonathon stared down at the letter in his hands. For a few moments he was silent.

Rosie shuffled slightly on the bench. "Looks like it's been in the tin forever, doesn't it? Wonder if Emily ever did get to read it."

Still Jonathon said nothing. But when he finally looked up at her, Rosie could see that his eyes were filled with tears. "I don't know what to say, Rosie. I'm blown away, I really am." He carefully folded the pencilled pages and handed them back to her. "Thanks. Thanks so much for showing me this. And the diary. Everything. It means a lot." Taking the New Testament from her knee, he began to leaf through it, pausing at John's Gospel and running his fingers lightly over the text. "Wonder which bit Sam read to the Welshman." There was an almost reverential softness about his voice.

"Probably Chapter 3," offered Rosie. "That's become one of my favourites recently."

Looking up again, Jonathon shot her the gentlest of smiles. "Yeah. I'll bet he read that."

He continued to turn the pages for several moments, but when he got to the last leaf he stopped. Inside the back cover was a newspaper cutting. It was folded down the middle and someone had secured one side of it to the book with sticky tape.

Rosie frowned. "Never noticed that before. I was too busy reading the letter."

Jonathon opened out the cutting. A photograph of an elderly couple smiled up at them. The woman was bright-eyed and beautiful for all her years, her husband, gentle-faced and clearly as much in love with her as ever. Rosie and Jonathon peered closer to read the words printed underneath.

Congratulations to the Reverend
Samuel and Mrs Emily Chetwynd
On the occasion of their Golden Wedding
April 3rd 1970

"*Reverend Samuel and Mrs Emily Chetwynd ...?*" Jonathon repeated the names slowly and shook his head. "This just gets better."

Rosie stared at the photo. So this, at last, was Sam. "Looks like he got his girl after all," she said softly. "Guess your Uncle Boxer would have been chuffed about the Reverend bit."

Jonathon nodded, a faint smile beginning to play on his lips. "Reckon old Sam must be in heaven himself by now. No doubt he's told Boxer and Jimmy all about it. Bet that was some reunion, eh?"

Rosie closed her eyes and tried to picture the scene. After months of reading Sam's diary, it was hard to imagine the three friends wearing anything but filthy khaki uniforms. Yet somehow, she couldn't help feeling that such souvenirs of suffering would be out of place in heaven. She suddenly felt Jonathon reach for her hand.

"Rosie?"

Surprised, she opened her eyes and glanced at him. He was looking at her, his face set in an expression she didn't quite understand.

"Come on." He pulled her to her feet and began to lead her across the grass. When they reached the war memorial, he loosed his hold on her and stepped towards it. Slowly, he ran a finger under Boxer's name. "D'you remember, Rosie, the day after you sent me the last diary entry? When you said that not all stories had happy endings?"

Rosie remembered it all too well. And the hurt she'd felt when she'd said it. So much seemed to have happened since then.

"You were right," he continued quietly, "not all stories *do* have happy endings. But I doubt either of us could have come up with a better ending for Sam's."

Rosie shrugged. There was no arguing with that. She was beginning to realise that nobody could finish a story quite like God could. "Okay," she conceded. "Guess I don't mind being wrong on this occasion."

For a few moments, the only sound was that of the breeze, soft and welcome in the hot noon sunshine. Jonathon dug his hands into his pockets and looked down. "I hear Bev's asked you to stay on at Paddock Hill."

Rosie nodded, slightly taken aback by the sudden change of subject.

"But I hear that you're still considering going back to London."

Rosie nodded again, her heart quickening. *Please don't ask me to explain, Jonathon.*

He looked directly at her. "Is that what you want, Rosie – to go back to London?"

She lowered her head. "I – I don't know. It just seems the best thing to do."

"But is it what you *want* to do?" Jonathon persisted softly. "You seemed so unhappy before you came up here. I can't quite understand why you want to go back."

Swallowing hard, Rosie closed her eyes. She could feel herself filling up. *Please, Jonathon. Please don't even try to understand.*

Suddenly she felt his hands take hers. "Rosie, would you stay if I asked you to? Would – would you stay for me?"

For a moment Rosie wasn't sure if she'd heard properly. She lifted her head and looked at him through her tears. "Stay for *you?* I'm not sure I know what you mean." She felt his grip tighten as he looked at her with an intensity that made her weak. His blue eyes had never seemed more beautiful to her.

"Rosie ... would you stay if I told you that I don't want you to leave. That I can't bear it if you leave." His voice dropped to a whisper. "Would you stay if I told you I was in love with you?"

Rosie stared at him. *In love with me? But that's impossible ... you're supposed to be in love with Lauren –*

As if he could read her thoughts, Jonathon shook his head. "That's over, Rosie. That's been over since Easter. As soon as I heard you were coming to live up here, I knew in my heart what I had to do. I couldn't go on with Lauren knowing I was in love with someone else."

Rosie was struggling to take in what she was hearing. "But you never said anything. Not a word. I never would have guessed for a minute ... ." She stopped, her voice fading to nothing.

Jonathon gently tilted her face towards him. "I felt the Lord tell me to hold back. It was more important that *he* got hold of you before *I* tried to. I was okay with that plan until the day we were over by Beth's grave – that day you told me you were thinking of going back to London. I panicked a bit then, Rosie. My prayer life went into a whole new league."

Rosie looked down again, fresh tears pricking her eyes. "I can't believe it," she muttered. "I just can't believe it."

Jonathon touched her cheek softly. "D'you know when I first started to fall in love with you?"

Rosie's head was reeling. "No. I'm not sure I know anything any more."

Jonathon smiled. "It was the first time I saw you. The day you fell on the leaves over there." He turned and pointed to the spot. "After that I couldn't get your face out of my head. When you agreed to start e-mailing me I was so happy. You don't know the number of times I've thanked God for that diary, Rosie. Every e-mail you sent just made me love you more."

Rosie couldn't hold back the tears now. "Some days," she whispered, "*your* e-mails were the only thing holding me together."

Jonathon pulled her close and held her. "I love you, Rosie. With all that I am, I love you."

As his words began to register, Rosie sank her head against his chest. As she breathed in the fragrance of his skin, she thought back to the last time she'd found herself in Jonathon's arms. How wonderful that had seemed. How frustratingly, painfully wonderful. Now as she listened to the steady pulse of his heart, an overwhelming realisation dawned in her mind. It was beating for her.

Lord Jesus, I don't know what to say. Thank you seems too small. But thank you, thank you, thank you ...

After a few moments Jonathon pulled back and held her at arms length. Wiping away her tears with his finger, he looked into her eyes. "Rosie Maconochie, please can I kiss you? Only God knows how long I've wanted to."

Rosie's heart melted. In all her life she'd never been asked a more beautiful question. Stepping forward, she let him hold her again. It was like coming home. As Jonathon's lips touched hers, she knew with every fibre of her being that she would love this man for the rest of her days.

"You're safe now," he whispered, holding her as though he'd never let her go. But in the safety of his strong arms, Rosie sensed that greater arms were holding both of them. And in that moment, she needed no one to tell her that God writes the most precious stories of all.

Epilogue

Laureate Hall, London, April 21st 2007

As the last faint notes drifted high into the atmosphere, Rosie sat motionless, hardly daring to breathe. She gazed down at the violinist on the stage, her heart bursting with pride. He'd done it. And no sister in the world could have been happier than she felt in that moment.

As the applause broke out and people began to stand to their feet, Rosie thanked God for the miracle she'd just witnessed. The concert had been Ciaran's idea. A concert in Beth's memory, he'd said – all the profits to go for research into cancer. Emmett Mallory had jumped at it, and the rest of the orchestra too. It was clear that Beth still held a unique place in people's hearts.

Of course, the highlight of the evening had been the premier performance of a very special piece of music; '*Chant du Rossignol – Rosie's Song*'. In the programme, Ciaran had made some poignant dedications.

In memory of my beautiful wife, Beth Maconochie. A precious lady, loved by all, and a greater musician than I could ever hope to be. Beth was the joy of my heart. I will never forget my princess. Heaven is richer today.

And with grateful thanks to Samuel Chetwynd for birthing this exquisite melody. He knew what it means to sing in the darkness.

Beth's family – what can I say? I never knew folks like you existed. You saved my life. Thank you. I'm proud to be a part of you.

And finally, my dear sister, Rosie, who wouldn't let the music die in me. You've always been there, Ros. This one's for you.

As she joined the applause for her brother, Rosie's heart was full. All around her, standing to their feet and clapping with great vigour were the Simmons clan; just as eighteen months earlier – Ed and Cassie, Ben, Josh and their wives and children. But this time there was someone else too. Rosie quickly touched the ring on her left hand and smiled to herself. Very soon she would have her own family – her own husband. This ring was Jonathon's promise to her.

She felt Cassie slip an arm around her waist. "Isn't it wonderful, Rosie? Your brother will go from strength to strength now, you watch."

Yes, he will, thought Rosie. Over the last few months she'd watched the tentative changes in Ciaran and been greatly encouraged. He was spending quite a bit of time with the orchestra in London now, but on his trips back to Yorkshire he'd even started coming to church with her. Of course, she knew he still had his bad days. But Rosie also knew that Jesus was in the picture now, and that would make all the difference.

As the clapping subsided and people began to move, Jonathon turned to her. "I've had a brilliant idea where we could go for our honeymoon." There was a twinkle in his eyes. "Some holiday companies do Battlefield Tours. They have one for Ypres. Tour of the trenches, Last Post at the Menin Gate – we could even squeeze in a visit to Toc-H. What d'you think?"

Rosie smiled at him and shook her head. *Who said the age of romance was dead?* She popped a kiss on his cheek. "I think you've been a bachelor far too long, Jon."

But she couldn't help feeling that somewhere up in heaven, Uncle Philip and his mates might find it a very novel idea indeed.